PENGUIN

SELECTED

D. H. L

David Herbert Lawrence was born at Eastwood, Nottinghamshire, in 1885, fourth of the five children of a miner and his middle-class wife. He attended Nottingham High School and Nottingham University College. His first novel, *The White Peacock*, was published in 1911, just a few weeks after the death of his mother to whom he had been abnormally close. At this time he finally ended his relationship with Jessie Chambers (the Miriam of *Sons and Lovers*) and became engaged to Louie Burrows. His career as a schoolteacher was ended in 1911 by the illness which was ultimately diagnosed as tuberculosis.

In 1912 Lawrence eloped to Germany with Frieda Weekley, the German wife of his former modern languages tutor. They were married on their return to England in 1914. Lawrence was now living, precariously, by his writing. His greatest novels, *The Rainbow* and *Women in Love*, were completed in 1915 and 1916. The former was suppressed, and he could not find a publisher for the latter.

After the war Lawrence began his 'savage pilgrimage' in search of a more fulfilling mode of life than industrial Western civilization could offer. This took him to Sicily, Ceylon, Australia and, finally, New Mexico. The Lawrences returned to Europe in 1925. Lawrence's last novel, *Lady Chatterley's Lover*, was banned in 1928, and his paintings confiscated in 1929. He died in Vence in 1930 at the age of 44.

Lawrence spent most of his short life living. Nevertheless he produced an amazing quantity of work – novels, stories, poems, plays, essays, travel books, translations and letters . . . After his death Frieda wrote: 'What he had seen and felt and known he gave in his writing to his fellow men, the splendour of living, the hope of more and more life . . . a heroic and immeasurable gift.'

•

Brian Finney teaches literature in the Department of Extra-Mural Studies at the University of London. The thesis for his doctorate was a study of D. H. Lawrence's short fiction. As well as the present edition, he has edited *St Mawr and Other Stories* for Cambridge University Press. He is also the author of *Since How It Is: A Study of Beckett's Later Fiction* and *Christopher Isherwood: A Critical Biography*.

Miriam Mohan.

Selected Short Stories

D. H. LAWRENCE

EDITED WITH AN
INTRODUCTION AND NOTES
BY BRIAN FINNEY

PENGUIN BOOKS

Penguin Books Ltd, Harmondsworth, Middlesex, England
Viking Penguin Inc., 40 West 23rd Street, New York, New York 10010, U.S.A.
Penguin Books Australia Ltd, Ringwood, Victoria, Australia
Penguin Books Canada Limited, 2801 John Street, Markham, Ontario, Canada L3R 1B4
Penguin Books (N.Z.) Ltd, 182–190 Wairau Road, Auckland 10, New Zealand

This selection first published in the Penguin English Library 1982
Reprinted 1983, 1985
Reprinted in Penguin Classics 1985, 1987

Printed and bound in Great Britain by
Cox & Wyman Ltd, Reading
Filmset in Monophoto Ehrhardt by
Northumberland Press Ltd, Gateshead, Tyne and Wear

Contents

Lawrence's Life and Works: a Chronology

1885	David Herbert Richards Lawrence born in Eastwood, Nottinghamshire, the fourth child of Arthur Lawrence, miner, and Lydia, *née* Beardsall, formerly a schoolmistress.
1891–8 1898–1901	He attends Beauvale Board School and becomes the first boy from that school to win a County Council Scholarship to Nottingham High School, which he attends until 1901.
1901	Begins frequent visits to Chambers family at Haggs Farm, and his relationship with Jessie Chambers (the Miriam of *Sons and Lovers*) which was to develop into an 'unofficial engagement'.
1901–2	Works as a clerk at Haywood's surgical appliances factory. Has to leave after severe attack of pneumonia.
1902–6	Pupil–teacher at British School, Eastwood. Sits the King's Scholarship examination in December 1904 and is placed in the first division of the first class. A few months later he matriculates and qualifies himself to take a two-year teachers' certificate course at Nottingham University College, beginning in September 1906.
1906–8	Writes his first poems and stories and begins his first novel *Laetitia* (later *The White Peacock*). Wins *Nottinghamshire Guardian* Christmas 1907 short story competition with 'A Prelude'. Loses his faith in 'a personal, human God'.
1908–11	Teaches at Davidson Road School, Croydon. Meets Ford Madox Hueffer who begins to publish his poems and stories in the *English Review* and introduces him to the London literary world. In 1910 he writes his second novel, *The Trespasser*, in conjunction with Helen Corke, and begins *Paul Morel* (later *Sons and Lovers*). His relationship with Jessie Chambers comes to an end. He has a brief affair with Alice Dax, wife of an Eastwood chemist, then becomes engaged to Louie Burrows, who had been a fellow-student at college. In December 1910 Mrs Lawrence dies of cancer. In January 1911 *The White Peacock* is published by Heinemann. Edward Garnett becomes Lawrence's mentor. Lawrence becomes seriously ill with pneumonia and has to give up schoolteaching.
1912	In March Lawrence meets Frieda Weekley, wife of his former modern languages tutor, and six weeks later elopes with her to Germany. Lawrence records the vicissitudes of their relationship in '*Look! We Have Come Through!*'. They walk over the Alps into Italy and settle at Gargnano, where Lawrence finishes *Sons and Lovers* and begins *The Insurrection of Miss Houghton* (later to be rewritten as *The Lost Girl*).
1913	Begins *The Sisters*, eventually to be split into *The Rainbow* and *Women in Love*, and *Italian Sketches* (later *Twilight in Italy*). They return to England in June and begin friendship with John Middleton

Murry and Katherine Mansfield. They return to Italy (Lerici) in
1914 September. Lawrence works mainly on *The Sisters* until June, when they return to England to marry (Frieda having at last obtained her divorce) and to find a publisher for *The Rainbow*. The wedding takes place at Kensington Registry Office on 13 July 1914. Lawrence works on revising his short stories for *The Prussian Officer*. The outbreak of war the following month prevents the Lawrences from returning to Italy. At Chesham and Greatham during the next six months, Lawrence rewrites *The Rainbow*. He begins important
1915 friendships with Lady Cynthia Asquith, Lady Ottoline Morrell, Bertrand Russell and E. M. Forster. In August they move to Hampstead. Lawrence develops his idea of an ideal community, Rananim, envisaged, at this stage, in Florida. His plans to form a revolutionary anti-war party with Russell and Murry collapse. *The Rainbow* is published by Methuen and immediately suppressed. This blow, together with the war, ill-health, increasing poverty, the defection of several friends, humiliating examinations for military service, and his inability to get permission to leave the country, brings Lawrence close to despair and misanthropy – his 'nightmare'.

1916 The Lawrences move to Cornwall where Lawrence writes *Women in Love*.

1917 He begins *Studies in Classic American Literature*. The Lawrences are evicted from Cornwall on suspicion of spying. In London Lawrence begins *Aaron's Rod*.

1918 They move to Newbury, in Berkshire, then to Mountain Cottage, Middleton-by-Wirksworth, Derbyshire. Lawrence writes *Movements in European History*.

1919 Lawrence is very ill with influenza. Moves back to Berkshire. In November the Lawrences leave for Italy and settle in Capri.

1920 Moves to Fontana Vecchia, Taormina, Sicily. Visits Maurice Magnus at Monte Cassino.

1920–21 Writes *The Lost Girl*, *Mr Noon*, *Sea and Sardinia* and the two psychoanalysis books; begins *Birds, Beasts and Flowers*; finishes *Aaron's Rod*. Revises stories for *England, My England* and *The Ladybird*.

1922 Translates Verga. Visits the Brewsters in Ceylon on the way to Australia, where he spends the summer at Thirroul, N.S.W., writing *Kangaroo*. Goes to New Mexico in September at the invitation of Mabel Dodge Luhan. In December settles at Del Monte ranch, Questa, near Taos. Finishes *Studies in Classic American Literature*.

1923 Finishes *Birds, Beasts and Flowers*. Spends the summer at Chapala in Mexico where he writes *Quetzalcoatl* (the first version of *The Plumed Serpent*). Rewrites Mollie Skinner's novel *The House of Ellis* as *The Boy in the Bush*. Frieda returns to England in August; Lawrence follows in December.

1924 Dinner at the Café Royal where Lawrence invites his friends to form a community at the ranch in Taos. Only Dorothy Brett accepts and accompanies the Lawrences to New Mexico in March. Frieda acquires Lobo ranch, later renamed Kiowa, from Mabel in exchange for the manuscript of *Sons and Lovers*. That summer at the ranch

Lawrence writes *The Woman Who Rode Away*, *St Mawr*, *The Princess* and the New Mexico sections of *Mornings in Mexico*. Lawrence's father dies. In November the Lawrences move to Oaxaca, Mexico, where Lawrence writes the Mexican sections of *Mornings in Mexico* and rewrites *Quetzalcoatl*.

1925 In February Lawrence almost dies of malaria. In Mexico City a doctor tells Frieda that he is dying of consumption. He puts rouge on his cheeks to get back across the border. Recuperates at the ranch and writes *David* and *Reflections on the Death of a Porcupine*. In September the Lawrences return to Europe and settle at Spotorno in Italy, where Lawrence writes *Sun*.

1926 Writes *The Virgin and the Gipsy*. Quarrels with Frieda and leaves her for several weeks. Has an abortive affair with Dorothy Brett. In May the Lawrences move to the Villa Mirenda, Scandicci, near Florence. In the late summer Lawrence makes his last visit to England. On his return he writes *The First Lady Chatterley*. Takes up painting seriously.

1927 Writes second version of *Lady Chatterley's Lover*. Makes Etruscan pilgrimage with Earl Brewster. Writes *The Escaped Cock* and *Etruscan Places*. Begins final version of *Lady Chatterley's Lover*. Prepares *The Woman Who Rode Away and Other Stories* for publication.

1928 In June the Lawrences move to Switzerland and settle at Gsteig. Lawrence is too weak to work, except on newspaper articles and painting. In October he visits Richard Aldington on Port Cros, then settles in Bandol. Begins *Pansies*. *Lady Chatterley's Lover* published, with consequent furore.

1929 Visits Paris in the spring, then Mallorca. Lawrence's paintings exhibited at the Warren Gallery in London. On the day the show is raided by the police Lawrence collapses at Forte dei Marmi. He goes to Bavaria for treatment, but returns, no better, to Bandol in September. Writes *Nettles* and *Last Poems*. Begins *Apocalypse*.

1930 On Dr Morland's recommendation Lawrence enters Ad Astra sanatorium at Vence in February. After three weeks with no improvement, he is moved by Frieda and Aldous and Maria Huxley to a nearby villa where he dies the following night. He is buried at Vence.

1935 Lawrence's body exhumed, cremated, and the ashes taken to Taos where Frieda's third husband, Angelo Ravagli, has built a small shrine above the ranch.

1956 Frieda dies and is buried outside the shrine.

KEITH SAGAR

Introduction

1907–14: The Formative Years

As a literary form the short story has a long history. But it was not until the late nineteenth century that it acquired the psychological subtlety and open-endedness that helped it to become a major fictional mode of the twentieth century. One of its greatest practitioners was D. H. Lawrence. To follow the development of his stories from the gauche anecdotes of his early twenties to the sophisticated parodies of the genre that he wrote in the last years of his life is like retracing the history of the genre from its pre-Chekhovian social realism and watching it reach forward to the verbal play and self-conscious artifice of post-Modernist writers such as Borges and Beckett.

Like many of his fellow Modernists, Lawrence was self-taught. Ford Madox Ford reckoned that he had 'never known any young man who was so well read in all the dullnesses that spread between Milton and George Eliot'.* The first stories that he wrote in the winter of 1907 for a competition in his local newspaper are sentimental, heavily plotted and psychologically naïve. During the following seven years he patiently wrote, rewrote and revised his stories to force them to accommodate his maturing vision of modern life. Plot becomes subordinated to urgent thematic impulses which require new modes of narrative expression. For instance he completely transformed 'The White Stocking', which he first wrote in 1907 as a fictionalized account of an embarrassing incident that happened to his mother in her youth. Over the next seven years he painfully reshaped it into a subtle psychological portrayal of the dramatic conflict between love and desire, ending in a release of emotion that undercuts the very medium he is using – verbal communication. This oblique focus on the ineffectuality of language, a language which is simultaneously being used to tell the story, is quintessentially Modernist.

What had happened during those seven formative years? In the first place Lawrence was learning to replace literary models from the past with his own voice expressing his own convictions, among them

* E. Nehls, *D. H. Lawrence: A Composite Biography*, 3 vols. (University of Wisconsin Press, 1957–9), Vol. 1, p.116.

the conviction that emotion and sensation are more powerful, if unconscious, psychological forces than reason and intellect. It is man's 'passionate sub-conscious', he wrote later, 'which makes the story,' not 'the mechanical upper half'.* This belief led to a search for a more satisfactory form than the rigid closed structure he had inherited from the Edwardian generation of writers, Bennett, Galsworthy and Wells. Their tight rules of construction reflected the tightly structured society of their England.

But once the power of the unconscious to shape man's destiny is given proper recognition a new form is needed to accommodate its less predictable operations. As Lawrence was to observe in his introduction to a collection of Giovanni Verga's short stories: 'The emotional mind, however apparently muddled, has its own rhythms, its own commas and colons and full-stops.'† What was needed, Lawrence decided, was a looser narrative form altogether: 'We need an apparent formlessness, definite form is mechanical.'‡ For this reason he even turned his back on Henry James, himself a precursor of Modernism, because, as Lawrence saw it, 'subtle conventional design was his aim'.§ In other words James had only modified his predecessors' obsession for artistic form. Whereas for Lawrence 'a great deal of the meaning of life and of art lies in the apparently dull spaces, the pauses, the unimportant passages'.|| During Lawrence's formative period between 1907 and 1914 the gradual subordination of plot to thematic considerations is accompanied by a jettisoning of conventional form for an apparent formlessness that reflects the irrational movements of the unconscious psyche.

Of course it would be wrong to suggest that Lawrence replaced the nineteenth century's reliance on man's mental abilities by a Freudian advocacy of the superiority of the unconscious. Between 1907 and 1914 Lawrence was evolving a dualistic vision of man which recognized the need to balance intellect against emotion, and reason against feeling. Because he became especially aware of the imbalance into which man had been thrown by the Industrial Revolution, he appears to celebrate the life of the passions at the expense of the

* *The Collected Letters of D. H. Lawrence*, 2 vols., ed. H. T. Moore (Heinemann, 1962), pp.841, 852.

† *Phoenix: The Posthumous Papers of D. H. Lawrence*, ed. E. D. McDonald (Heinemann, 1936), p.250.

‡ ibid., p.248.

§ *Collected Letters*, op. cit., p.388.

|| *Phoenix*, op. cit., p.248.

more conscious life of the mind. In fact he is only trying to redress the balance. It is the underlying concern with life's dual nature which informs the shape of his earlier stories – almost all of which were collected in *The Prussian Officer* in 1914. One has only to think of the closing tableaux of the two lovers restored by touch to the source of their true passion in 'The White Stocking', or of the dead bodies of the officer and his orderly laid out side by side in the title story, to see how positive and negative instances of life's essential duality provide both the matter and the shape of these stories.

The first eight stories in this selection all belong to this first phase in Lawrence's life. All were rewritten or drastically revised between 1913 and 1914. Because he forgot about it, 'Love Among the Haystacks', which dates from 1913, shows Lawrence still clinging to some of the pre-Modernist insistence on plot (especially in its over-tidy happy ending) that has been shed in the remaining seven stories – all of which were further revised in 1914 for inclusion in *The Prussian Officer*. Yet already the need to strike an equipoise between the polarized attitudes which each of the brothers in this story displays simultaneously provides it with artistic shape. The first half concentrates on the deathly nature of Geoffrey's morbid self-consciousness. The unconscious self that he has repressed for so long recoils on himself, first nearly killing his brother, then producing his suicidal wish 'not to be'. By way of contrast his brother Maurice is completely at home in the night-time of the senses, ritually immersing himself in the water-trough and pollen of the meadow before spending the night with his sweetheart in the hayrick. In the final sections Lawrence cleverly reverses this situation. Geoffrey is restored to his cut-off feelings by his encounter with Lydia, while Maurice's apparent equipoise is found in the light of morning to be still wanting the reasoning powers which help cement the coming together of Geoffrey and Lydia.

This need to achieve a balance between conscious and unconscious forces in the human psyche lies at the root of all these early stories, and many of the later ones too. Yet the fact remains that Lawrence is still largely unaware of the philosophical basis underpinning the fiction of this period. Each new story is a separate exploration of a unique situation – one, moreover, which is frequently developed from an incident in his own life or in the lives of those close to him. A comparison of the different versions of some of these earlier stories shows among other things how rapidly he acquired the ability to transform the raw material of life into the detached vision of the self-critical artist.

'Odour of Chrysanthemums', for example, offers a corrective to the still somewhat one-sided portrayal of his parents offered in *Sons and Lovers*. Elizabeth Bates, apart from her external appearance, is clearly modelled on Lawrence's mother. But this later fictional rendering of his mother can hardly be said to hand her the laurels of victory, an accusation that Jessie Chambers levelled with some justification at the novel. It is an accusation which can still be made at his dramatic treatment of the same situation in *The Widowing of Mrs Holroyd* (1913) and his earlier, penultimate version of 'Odour of Chrysanthemums'. But the final version of 1914 metes out an even-handed judgement: both husband and wife 'had denied each other in life'. Elizabeth Bates is made to realize how the love she had offered her husband had in reality concealed a deeper self-love that had driven him to drink as a form of self-protection. Simultaneously Lawrence uses almost all the other characters in the story – the children, their grandfather and grandmother – to undermine the mother's egotistical version of who was to blame for the virtual breakdown of the marriage. At the end of the story she resembles the shrivelled chrysanthemums which presage her own demise when they are knocked over and swept away at the arrival of the corpse of her unloved husband.

Artistic criticism and self-criticism inform one another at this period of Lawrence's career. Perhaps the clearest example of this process is the evolution of 'The Shades of Spring' from 'A Modern Lover'. The earlier story, dating from 1909–10, is a barely disguised account of Lawrence's unsuccessful attempt to persuade Jessie Chambers to sleep with him at this time. The narrative viewpoint is indistinguishable from that of the autobiographically-based hero. The heroine's refusal is represented as rank cowardice: 'It was as if she had tipped over the fine vessel that held the wine of his desire', he writes sanctimoniously. By 1914 he has written and then again revised the story, on each occasion allowing the narrative to expose more of his hero's hypocrisy. The heroine of 'The Shades of Spring', unlike Jessie's fictional counterpart in *Sons and Lovers*, is now portrayed as a natural child of the landscape they both once shared. Far from revealing Miriam's fear of the world of nature and of natural sexuality, the heroine reverses roles by leading Paul's counterpart in the story through the countryside and showing him a series of animal matings – the last of which is her own liaison with the gamekeeper. Where Paul accused Miriam of fondling the soul out of daffodils, Hilda turns the same accusation on Syson. Syson's return to the landscape of his past reflects Lawrence's repeated return to this formative love affair in his fiction; in both cases the journey is one of painful self-discovery and self-criticism. By closely attending to the probabilities within his fictive models Lawrence has been brought to realize that his earlier fictional embodiments of Jessie were distortions produced by his need for self-justification. The writing of the successive versions of this story were – even more so than in the case of *Sons and Lovers* – therapeutic acts for the man as much as for the artist.

Further evidence of the rapid advances that Lawrence was making in purely literary terms during this period appears in the growing confidence with which he employs metaphor and symbol. Touch and sight in particular are used by him in a wide variety of situations to represent the battle raging between conscious and unconscious forces within his different characters. Touch connects them to one another's deepest emotional currents, while sight often signifies the penetrating impact of the intellect. It is touch which gives Adams his temporary hold over Elsie in 'The White Stocking'. In particular Lawrence uses the tactile dream-like rhythms of the dance to symbolize the lure of the purely physical enticements of the sexual act – still unmentionable at this time. Whiston's angry blow at the climax of the story is a very different form of touch that restores the flow of feeling between the two lovers. Yet in 'The Prussian Officer' the captain's similar use of brute force is employed as the expression of a perverted sexuality, which ultimately causes his death when the orderly turns the same brute force on him. In such stories Lawrence gives narrative life to his belief that these unconscious forces are powerful enough to kill or nearly kill anyone opposing them.

Sight is used equally skilfully to suggest the presence of the conscious mind. In 'The Prussian Officer' the captain with his penetrating gaze forces his orderly into unwilling consciousness. To restore himself to the dark life of the unconscious senses the orderly has to resort to a tactile counter-measure in the act of murder. By pursuing the logic of his two sets of metaphors Lawrence shows how all that is left to his unthinking orderly is permanent darkness, and it is no accident that he is killed by the sun, the source of light and sight and of the consciousness so fatally lacking in his constitution. If this all sounds too schematic, the reader should turn to the description of the last night which the delirious orderly spends in the forest, where Lawrence uses the lightning to represent the spasmodic and distorted glimpses of the real world left to the orderly. What at first glance appears to be no more than a magnificent description of a storm at night also functions as an interior landscape.

Lawrence's use of complex symbolism has become equally sophisticated during this period. Sometimes he introduces it with the lightest of touches, as is the case with the chrysanthemums in 'Odour of Chrysanthemums' or the distant mountains in 'The Prussian Officer' (where they taunt the orderly with their unattainable detachment so fatally wanting in him). In at least one story, 'Second Best', symbolism is employed as the dominant narrative mode. The mole, blind, burying underground, feeling its way by touch, becomes the natural embodiment of all those unconscious feelings that Frances has been struggling to subdue in herself. Appropriately it revels in its own sensuous existence, 'delighted to ecstasy by the sunlight'. Equally fitting is its ferocity in defending itself. In enacting the killing of the mole, the story prefigures the similar action which Frances takes in killing off her emotional self so successfully that she can offer up her dead love, like the second mole she seeks out and kills, to a man she has no feelings for.

Immediately after Frances has witnessed the death of the mole the glittering landscape loses its magic for her, seeming 'scarcely worth the notice'. But in the next two paragraphs Lawrence takes care to re-affirm the beauty of the surrounding countryside. This use of nature as a norm against which characters can be implicitly judged by the reader without interference from the author occurs repeatedly in the stories of this time. In 'The Thorn in the Flesh' the perverted nature of Bachmann's voluntary subjection to an authority external to himself is subtly exposed by juxtaposing him as he marches in file surrounded by his fellow soldiers against the open spaces of the countryside, with its wild poppies and 'the distant space of sky and fields all free with air and sunshine'. Natural freedom is what both he and his sweetheart have unnaturally sacrificed by embracing servitude. It takes another force of nature, sexuality, to restore them to themselves, after which they can shake off the authority of army and employer without fear for the consequences.

To rely on any form of external prop for one's deepest satisfaction is fatal in Lawrence's view, whether the prop is the armed forces, as is the case with Bachmann and with Alfred in 'Daughters of the Vicar', class, as it is with the Lindleys, or morality as it is with the Lindleys' daughter, Mary, both in the latter story. In Mary's case nature, which she has repressed in overcoming her repulsion at her husband's physical deformities, reasserts itself in the form of her baby for whom she feels all those natural emotions that she had so laboriously subdued. The conflict between these mutually opposed demands tears her apart, leaving her 'purposeless, without real being'. Her sister chooses to override the proprieties of class to fulfil her wholly natural desire for Alfred. But, in a touch of realism, she is made to pay a high price for her social rebellion – exile from her class-ridden native country. Nevertheless nature triumphs in this story. In the firelit scene in which she and Alfred finally overcome external restraints of class and education, their coming together unites all the polarities of human nature which Lawrence has been evoking in these early stories – sight and touch, light and darkness, mind and body, conscious and unconscious being.

1915–22: The War Years and their Aftermath

In late 1914 Lawrence wrote the first crude formulation of his own philosophy of life in what began as a study of Thomas Hardy. Out of this first attempt at what he called a 'pseudo-philosophy' grew the more ambitious exposition of his *Weltanschauung*, 'The Crown', written in 1915. 'The Crown' occupies a similar position in Lawrence's work to that of *A Vision*, published ten years later, in the work of Yeats. Both works attempt to systematize their authors' intuitive responses to life by widening the frame of reference to interpret the nature and history of Western civilization. In 'The Crown' Lawrence extended his dualistic explanation of human nature to embrace life and death, autocracy and democracy, pagan sensuality and Christian spirituality. Like Yeats he was haunted by a sense of apocalypse, confirmed by the outbreak of war. He was convinced that the Christian democratic ideal was finally destroying itself. He saw the First World War as the inevitable outcome of the collective death-wish inherent in individuals such as the two protagonists in 'The Prussian Officer' or the Lindleys, Mary and Massy in 'Daughters of the Vicar'.

This formulation of his metaphysic necessarily affected the nature of the stories he wrote over the next seven years, 1915 to 1922. All eight stories in this selection emanating from this middle period and collected (with one exception) in *England, My England* (1922) show a new awareness of the wider significance of individual characters' actions and behaviour. Most of the stories reflect the destructive spirit finding such monstrous expression on the battlefields of France. But, with the exception of 'England, My England', the stories concentrate on individuals at home warring with themselves and one another.

Lawrence is more interested in analysing individual self-destruction than the mass-destruction it produced.

The earliest of these stories, 'The Mortal Coil', is a perfect example of how two individuals indulge in mutual destruction. Like Bachmann in 'The Thorn in the Flesh', Friedeburg, the hero of this story, has sacrificed his chance of self-fulfilment by placing his life in the hands of the army. Once he has isolated himself from this parental substitute by accumulating impossible gambling debts, he is left with nothing to live for, and tries to fill the vacuum in his life with his sensuous but predatory mistress. She reacts to him rather as Ursula responds to Skrebensky in *The Rainbow*: recoiling against his nullity but tempted to fill it with the egotism of her own will. Lawrence portrays their sado-masochistic relationship with fine artistic subtlety. Her egotism is first suggested by the way in which she repeatedly writes her name on a sheet of paper. Both imitate beasts of prey in their reactions to one another, and both try to rob the other of their flame of life; he prefiguring her death when he tries to stem the candle light, she showing the same fatal flaw when calculating how she might grasp the scarlet blossoms of the cactus. It is artistically appropriate that she is finally asphyxiated by poisonous fumes (what else does his love amount to?) while he is left longing for self-annihilation in a different kind of war in which he too hopes to win 'the prize of death'.

In 'England, My England' Lawrence takes another such mutually destructive relationship. But in this case he employs his new metaphysic to enlarge the significance of the action. The theme underlying this story is Lawrence's conviction that the outbreak of the First World War was the immediate consequence of a death-wish back home, a death-wish inherent in Western civilization at large at that moment of history, suffering as he thought it did from an excessive subscription to Christian ideals of asceticism and universal love. In Egbert and Winifred he posits the polarities of pagan sensuality and Christian spirituality. As husband and wife gradually force each other to adopt extreme positions either of which is fatal in isolation, so, Lawrence implies, modern civilization has reached a similar disintegration into warring opposites. As he wrote to a friend, the 'story is the story of most men and women who are married today – of most men at the War, and wives at home'.* Winifred is as responsible as Egbert for his eventual death, willing as she is 'to serve the soldier, if not the

* *Collected Letters*, op. cit., p.364.

man', in a spirit of Christian 'duty and sacrifice'. In the powerfully imagined death-scene Lawrence, by his avoidance of the first person, imbues Egbert with an archetypal significance – the anonymous representative of the millions of Europeans fulfilling the death-wish inherent in their civilization.

'England, My England' is a marvellous example of the way metaphysic and what Lawrence called 'art-utterance' are held in a momentary state of fruitful tension. The philosophy is at any rate itself the distillation of his earlier fiction. In this middle period its validity is constantly being tested within successive fictive models. 'Art,' as Lawrence wrote, 'must contain the essential criticism of the morality to which it adheres.'* In this sense 'The Horse Dealer's Daughter' provides a corrective to the wholly negative diagnosis of the condition of modern civilization offered in 'England, My England'. The story opens with the portrait of a family in disintegration, set on the path of destruction. Mabel's brothers are all resigned to placing themselves in various forms of animal subjection similar to that in which a soldier like Egbert found himself in the army. Mabel herself prefers to opt for death rather than such a death-in-life. Like Egbert she wills her own extinction. Her last-minute rescue by Dr Fergusson involves both of them experiencing near-death in their ritualistic submersion in the 'foul earthy water' of the 'cold dead pond'. But in this instance death is only a prelude to rebirth. Lawrence makes skilful use of biblical language to draw striking parallels between Christ's death and resurrection, and the near-death and resurrection to a life made meaningful by the love of Mabel and Fergusson. As the war drew on Lawrence came to believe that 'if we have our fill of destruction, then we shall turn again to creation'.† The story prefigures this hope for the future while simultaneously stressing the painful nature of the regenerative process.

The formulation of a metaphysic allowed Lawrence to write about a wide variety of domestic situations in such a way that they reflected the schizophrenic condition of his war-torn society. Isobel in 'The Blind Man', for instance, finds herself split between her husband, blinded in the war, at home in the dark animal world of the senses, and her best friend, all forehead and eyes, intellectually knowing but annihilated by physical contact with another human being. The antinomies of Lawrence's metaphysic extend beyond the two men to the

* *Phoenix*, op. cit., p.476.

† *Phoenix II: Uncollected, Unpublished and Other Prose Works*, ed. W. Roberts and H. T. Moore (Heinemann, 1968), p.404.

two distinct worlds of the farmhouse – the 'animal grossness of the back' in which the husband is 'a tower of darkness', and the wife's bright, civilized living-quarters at the front in which the husband's deficiencies are revealed. The polarization from which both men suffer is given ironic expression at the conclusion of the story, holding all three characters in suspended balance – the husband convinced he has found a blood-brother, the friend annihilated by the contact forced on him, and the wife divided between her twin loyalties, forced to lie by the polarized nature of the two men in her life.

In concentrating on the war at home many of the stories of this period focus on the war between the sexes. Both 'England, My England' and 'The Mortal Coil' establish a causal link between sexual and military warfare. A further three stories represent the hero as the male predator ruthlessly seeking out his mate in defiance of norms of social behaviour. In 'You Touched Me' and 'Samson and Delilah' the heroine initially seeks protection behind the barriers of social taboo, but capitulates in the end, not so much to the man as to her own elemental sexual nature. In 'Tickets, Please' the sexual victims of the promiscuous hero seek to exact their own form of social justice, but at a cost as it turns out.

In 'You Touched Me' Matilda and her sister hide from the natural world outside behind the Pottery House wall, which resembles what Lawrence calls elsewhere 'the little fold of law and order, the little walled city'.* Outside is life in the raw: inside is 'a deserted quiet' in which the two class-conscious sisters pursue a sexless existence. Unable to marry someone of their own class, they find an unconscious outlet for their frustration by adopting an antagonistic attitude to all men, their father included. But they have reckoned without Hadrian, a prototypal outsider – adopted as an orphan, an emigrant to Canada, temporarily returned from the outside world to be greeted by condescension on the part of both sisters. It is only after Matilda has laid her hand on him one night in mistake for her father that he becomes aware of the sexuality which lies buried beneath her antagonistic exterior. After this, class, money, manners are all swept aside as Hadrian ruthlessly pursues Matilda for his mate. Hadrian contrives to confront Matilda with her own sexuality by removing these various external barriers. His unexpected success on the last page of the story is intended to represent a victory for both of them, although the improbability of this outcome suggests that

* *Phoenix*, op. cit., p.419.

this is an instance where the metaphysic has been asserted to the detriment of the 'art-utterance'.

The same could also be claimed of 'Samson and Delilah', where a husband returns without warning to his wife after deserting her and their daughter sixteen years previously. Once again the male hunter arrives from the wild outside to defy the proprieties of social behaviour. Lawrence deliberately provokes a reaction of outrage to Willie's conduct, encouraging the reader to identify with the sergeant's indignant response: 'A dirty action – as isn't allowed by law.' Like Delilah, Alice has Willie bound up in a moment of weakness and delivered to the Philistine soldiers whose false god is the divinity of social law and order. But, like Matilda, Alice ultimately succumbs to her own sexual drive. Willie is meant to emerge as the liberator of both from the inhibitions of society. Yet again Lawrence appears to have allowed theory to override requirements of narrative probability; at least the magazine ending of 1917 describes her submission as accompanied by 'a groan of helpless, desirous resentment'. But in 1921 Lawrence erased even her natural irritation in an attempt to highlight the irrational nature of the sexual drive.

'Tickets, Please' is perhaps a more wholly satisfactory treatment of the same theme. Possibly it owes its success to the way in which Lawrence distances the subject by drawing a loose parallel with Euripides' play, *The Bacchae*. In the course of the play Dionysus punishes Pentheus, king of Thebes, for opposing his cult by driving his mother and the entire female population raving from the city; finally Pentheus is torn limb from limb by his possessed mother and her fellow revellers. In his story Lawrence uses the resemblances to the classical play to focus attention on the impersonal forces underlying the action of his modern dramatis personae. John Thomas, like Pentheus, shows a reckless disregard for the Bacchic conductresses, and is made to suffer a form of death at their hands for his irreligious attitude to the opposite sex. But Annie, like Pentheus' mother, ironically discovers defeat in the midst of victory when it becomes clear that her revenge has destroyed the love which John Thomas secretly harboured for her all along. Like Pentheus' mother she is, in effect, driven into exile for the part she played. Perhaps the metaphysic is also more satisfactorily integrated in this story because John Thomas, unlike the hero of the other two stories of sexual conflict, is more explicitly subject to criticism within the narrative. At the same time one can see how Lawrence's growing assurance in his own philosophy drove him to seek out a less naturalistic literary mode that would offer a more satisfactory narrative outlet for his widening set of beliefs.

This use of a classical parallel in 'Tickets, Please' and of biblical models in 'Samson and Delilah' and 'The Horse Dealer's Daughter' goes hand in hand with a more confident use of comedy. All three stories open on a comic note and normally modulate into a more serious tone towards the end. In 'Fanny and Annie', however, Lawrence makes sustained use of comedy throughout. In one sense it is a comic reworking and reversal of the basic situation in 'Second Best'. Seen in a comic light second best turns out best of all in the end. The butt of Lawrence's humour in this story is the same social disparity (in this case between Fanny and Harry) that he had criticized earlier in stories such as 'Daughters of the Vicar'. But in 'Fanny and Annie' Lawrence chooses to laugh away the absurd barriers of class with which the English seek to control their far deeper passions. Fanny might resent Harry's commonness, but she resents even more the irresistible 'thorn of desire' that he arouses in her. Even his hilarious chapel solos in which 'he handled his aitches so hopelessly' nevertheless contain 'a certain defiant passion which crisped the blood' – of an unwilling Fanny in particular.

Like Louisa and Matilda, Fanny is faced with an internal conflict between class and desire. The principal difference lies in Lawrence's handling of this conflict. His uproarious play with Harry's aspirates neatly undercuts the narrative exponent of his views. But Harry is sexually attractive for all his commonness, and Fanny is forced to choose both or neither. She is presented with a second opportunity to exercise this choice when Harry is denounced in the middle of the harvest festival service by the mother of Annie who is reaping her own harvest after Harry and others have sown their seed in her fertile ground. In the finale, Fanny's comic immersion in the gossiping working-class household of Harry's family ensures that her choice is realistic, not just the outcome demanded by the metaphysic. If anything 'Fanny and Annie' reverses the pattern of the other three stories: opening with a doomladen, potentially tragic heroine who is saved from her fate by the comic hero, Harry, who 'wouldn't think the Queen was any too good for him, if he'd a mind to her'. In this story, at least, Lawrence's skilful manipulation of the comic genre is responsible for the successful narrative embodiment of this obsessive sexual strand to his metaphysic.

1923–8: A Period of Formal Experimentation

Lawrence continued to extend and refine his philosophical system in various essays written between 1917 and 1921. As he grew more assertive about what he called his 'pollyanalytics' he was compelled to search for new narrative forms that lent themselves more readily to the expression of an ever-widening set of associated concepts. The need to link the actions of individuals to larger historical, social, political and religious forces led him to reject the more naturalistic narrative modes of his youth in favour of literary forms traditionally open to symbolic interpretation. In this final period he reaches new heights of formal inventiveness, experimenting with genres like myth, the fairy story and satiric comedy – all of which traditionally present individuals as representatives of universal patterns of behaviour. Or he makes use of conventional literary forms like the ghost story and the murder story only to break their mechanistic rules and reverse the reader's normal expectations.

Two of the stories in this collection show Lawrence turning to primitive myths in which the heroine is confronted with the natural world from which she and her kind have become dangerously alienated. 'The Woman Who Rode Away' offers a negative vision of the fatal consequences of such alienation; 'Sun', on the other hand, offers a positive example of a woman restored to the cosmos and to health. The eponymous heroine of 'The Woman Who Rode Away' is never given a name, as if to emphasize her status as a type rather than an individual. Surrounded by a landscape devastated by her husband's mining operations, she is, like him, completely alienated from the world of nature. A product of American civilization, this representative white woman flees from her personalized society to the impersonal experience of the Chilchuis, a primitive Indian tribe descended from the Aztecs. By partly drawing on Prescott's account of Aztec mythology,* Lawrence transforms her mad journey to this primitive race from the past into an apocalyptic account of the rush towards extinction that he felt Western civilization was pursuing by its perverse exploitation of the natural world. The Chilchuis are nature's savage instruments, by means of which it restores the balance that the heroine and her race have upset by denying the force of nature within and outside themselves. Before she meets her horrific end the

* W. H. Prescott's *The History of the Conquest of Mexico* was read by Lawrence in March 1923.

heroine is granted drug-induced glimpses of what it could be like to be at one with nature, when she feels 'as if all her senses were diffused on the air, that she could distinguish the sound of evening flowers unfolding'. Here the metaphysic finds entirely credible expression within the narrative. Whether Lawrence retains equal control over the savage finale is for the reader to decide. It is intended to show one form of excess leading to its opposite, both equally abhorrent. The Chilchuis are meant to be barbaric agents of a power greater than themselves, furies pursuing vengeance for the hubris of the white race. Suffering from the opposite excess, their mindless, tribal, impersonal experience is equally a way of death – one which modern civilization in the form of the heroine has willed upon itself.

'Oh, what a catastrophe for man when he cut himself off from the rhythm of the year, from his unison with the sun and the earth,'* Lawrence lamented late in his life. In 'Sun' he creates his own myth, although drawing on biblical and classical myths in the process, in which modern man – or rather woman – is reunited with the cosmos. The major protagonist of this story is not the neurotic New York wife and mother, Juliet, but the sun itself to which she is made to submit. Lawrence uses his outstanding descriptive powers to imbue the sun with a magnificence that leaves Juliet, by comparison, in the passive role of a ripening flower responding irresistibly to its impersonal procreative force. The Sicilian garden, in which she bares herself to the sun as to a lover, is a combination of 'the vivid wildness of the old classic places' (the cypress, according to Frazer, being sacred to the healing god's sanctuary) and the Garden of Eden before the Fall where, as Lawrence writes in the story, even 'the snake was part of the place'. As spring turns to summer so her womb, like the plants in her garden, opens, awaiting pollination, wanting 'man-dew only, utterly improvident'. However, Lawrence gives his paradisial fable an ironic ending when the procreative agent turns out to be 'the branded little city man', her husband, rather than the peasant. The process of natural selection is cruelly countermanded by the dictates of a society to which Lawrence was a lifelong opponent.

In his flight from realistic narrative modes, Lawrence made a number of forays into the traditionally escapist genres of the ghost story and the murder story. Yet invariably he turns the conventions of each genre upside down. His ghosts, spirits of the dead, show more life than the living who have themselves become 'ghosts' in Lawrence's

* *Phoenix II*, op. cit., p.504.

redefinition of the term. Similarly murder, Lawrence explained in his essay on Edgar Allan Poe, need not entail physical death for the victim, who can continue to live 'in the post-mortem reality, a living dead'.* Drawing on the tradition of the psychological ghost and murder story established by Henry James, Lawrence forces his readers to abandon the imaginary world of Gothic horror and underground vaults for the reality of 'that which takes place *beneath* the consciousness'.†

In 'The Border Line', first called 'Crossing the Frontier', it rapidly becomes clear that in her journey east Katherine is crossing more than the political frontier between France and Germany. She is also making a psychic journey from her present husband, Philip, with whom Lawrence associates the prevailing ethic of Christian democracy, to her previous husband, Alan, now dead, who is identified with values of a pagan, aristocratic past. Appropriately his spirit returns to her in the border town of Strasbourg, emblematic of post-war Germany, which has reverted to its frozen, barbaric past. Just as the ghostly presence of primitive Germany shows more vitality in the story than the dying spirit of the victorious democratic nations in the West, so the ghostly presence of her previous husband proves more real to Katherine than Philip's frail grasp on life. Philip's death is another of Lawrence's symbolic enactments of the apocalypse awaiting a civilization over-dependent on Christian democratic values. The ending anticipates Lawrence's subsequent use of myth. When Alan, in the form of a pine-tree, repossesses Katherine he (somewhat arbitrarily) becomes identified with the Tree of Life in the Garden of Eden, the wintry equivalent of the summer sun in the Edenic fable of 'Sun'.

Lawrence was well aware of the mechanistic nature of the conventional murder story and criticized Poe for turning his characters into mere automatons. In the same essay he redefined murder in psychological terms as 'a lust to get at the very quick of life itself, and kill it'.‡ Using this radically new definition he is able to restore to the murder story the emotional and psychological interest which the genre traditionally excludes. 'The Lovely Lady' is a parody in this sense. Pauline, the lovely lady herself, has turned first one son, then a second, into substitute lovers, rather as Lawrence's own mother had done. Hers is a parasitical nature which has killed her first son and is slowly draining the life-force out of the other. Her niece is forced to use unnatural means (the rainpipe) to expose Pauline's unnatural act

* *The Symbolic Meaning*, ed. A. Arnold (Centaur Press, 1962), p.107.

† *Studies in Classic American Literature* (Penguin Books, 1971), p.85.

‡ ibid., p.86.

of psychic murder. In a somewhat improbable volte-face, Pauline's external defences collapse, leaving her with nothing vital within herself on which to fall back. The crowning irony of this burlesque murder story is that the murderess finally kills herself.

'The Rocking-Horse Winner', like 'The Lovely Lady', was written to order for an anthology, in this case a collection of stories of the uncanny. Once again Lawrence seizes on the genre as an excuse to upset normal expectations. He gives the contemporary obsession with material success a spectral insubstantiality that ultimately leads to the extinction of the innocent young recipient of these pernicious values. Possibly with Henry James's 'Turn of the Screw' in mind, Lawrence combines the genre of the supernatural with that of the fairy story. He internalizes the supernatural, and borrows from the fairy story its traditional simplification of life's complexities in order to draw attention to the moral of the story: 'lucky in money, unlucky in love'. A neat parable of the acquisitive society's implicit death-wish, Paul's unnatural as well as supernatural means of pursuing wealth finally achieves a fortune for his insatiable mother at the cost of his life. Lawrence makes particularly skilful use of the various traditional attributes of the fairy tale – its simplified vocabulary and repetitive patterns of speech, its convention of giving voices to inanimate objects, and its reliance on symbolism (the wooden horse, for instance, that takes its rider nowhere). Even the reversal of the normal happy ending is integral to Lawrence's parodic purpose.

'The Man Who Loved Islands' echoes 'The Rocking-Horse Winner' when it begins with the traditional opening line of a fairy tale, only omitting the 'Once upon a time'. Cathcart, the protagonist of this story, is at first called 'the Master', then 'the islander', finally simply 'he'. Throughout this moral fable of our time Lawrence maintains a stance of comic detachment. Like the woman who rode away the islander suffers from egotism, at first disguised as idealism, which carries him to ever smaller islands in an insane hubristic attempt to fill them with his personality. This unnatural desire to master nature leads him to desert the 'world' of his first island for the 'refuge' of his second island and finally for the barren rock that constitutes his third island. Rather like Swift's Gulliver, the islander's idealism leads directly to his revulsion from human nature. In the end he is overcome by the elements themselves, the most rudimentary manifestation of the natural forces he has denied all his life. The coloured, peopled first island is successively abandoned for the restricted society of the grey second island, then for the deathly white emptiness of the third island.

Universal love turns to universal hate, not its opposite but its natural consequence. It is a beautifully controlled allegory in which the medium happily accommodates the message.

The other major literary mode which Lawrence explored in these final years is that of satiric comedy, a natural development from his earlier use of pure comedy. At this time he was waging almost incessant war on the shibboleths of Western society, much in the same way as the satirists of pre-Christian times used their formidable magic powers of invective against their society's enemies. The major difference between Lawrence and these originators of the genre is that his enemies were actually the pillars of his society. 'Satire,' Lawrence wrote, 'exists for the very purpose of killing the social being, showing him what an inferior he is and, with all his parade of social honesty, how subtly and corruptly debased.'* Three stories exemplify this vein of satire: 'Jimmy and the Desperate Woman', which pillories the kind of society *littérateur* who owes his success to his dependence on the world of books in place of real feelings; 'Things', an ironic masterpiece that gives comic expression to the paradoxical connection between idealism and materialism; and 'Mother and Daughter', a light-hearted satiric fable about the counter-revolution likely to overtake a society which has overridden what Lawrence believed were inescapable differences between the sexes.

Jimmy, the hero of the first of these stories, is an editor who lives his life straight out of books. His idea of the perfect self-abasing wife (a Gretchen or Ruth) is a literary fantasy. It is wholly in character that he should decide to propose to a poetess whom he knows only by correspondence. Lawrence maintains an ironic distance between Jimmy and the reader in order to expose the discrepancy between Jimmy's cerebral interpretation of events and what the narrative asserts to be actually the case. Thus on his way north to meet his poetess, Jimmy imagines himself 'some modern Ulysses wandering in the realms of Hecate', a version that is immediately undercut by Lawrence's description of the actual dismal scene in which heroism of any kind is out of the question. Again and again there is the ironical juxtaposition of Jimmy's fantasies, such as his picture of 'an unsophisticated, wild-blooded woman', against the reality, 'a tall woman with a face like a mask of passive anger'. This kind of yawning disparity is the source of much of the humour in this story. Of course the principal structural contrast is between the personalities of Jimmy,

* *Phoenix*, op. cit., p.453.

for whom the life of the mind is all, and the poetess's miner-husband, whose powerful physical presence and insistence on the life of the senses annihilates Jimmy. Yet Lawrence preserves his detachment from the miner as well, leaving the irony to work its satiric intent without direct narrative intervention. Even the conclusion is ironic when it becomes clear that Jimmy is destined to be defeated as much by himself as by the couple over whom he is deludedly celebrating his hollow victory.

'Things' represents one of the peaks of Lawrence's achievement in the genre of the short story. A lifelong opponent to material possessions, Lawrence first traced the connection between idealism and materialism when he was working out his metaphysic during the early years of the War. This story gives comic narrative expression to his conviction that, because the idealist artificially represses feelings in favour of ideas (i.e. ideals), he removes himself from contact with those feelings. These repressed feelings subterraneously find a perverted outlet in an acquisitive appetite for objects. If the theory is hard to grasp, this humorous little story makes it readily comprehensible. The two New England idealists begin by fleeing the industrial materialism of America to 'live a full and beautiful life' in Europe on a pittance. The story traces their circular journey back to their materialist roots via Paris, where 'both painted, but not desperately' (true to form, they lack passion), and Italy, where they took up Buddhism which similarly 'let them down'. Even then they still had 'freedom' and 'so much "beauty"'. Lawrence's mimetic style is his chief satiric instrument in this story. The prose repeatedly echoes, in the form of indirect speech, the over-emphatic language the idealists employ to conceal the truth from themselves. When he writes that 'they still *loved* "Indian thought"', or that Erasmus 'did not *want* to earn a living', Lawrence cunningly contrives to deny what the reported speech is affirming. In the same way he reports their acquisitive accumulation of antiques with the ironical rider: 'Of course they did not buy the things for the things' sakes, but for the sake of "beauty".' He also uses the Americans' own jargon to undercut their pretensions, referring for example to their lovely 'things' as 'the chunk of Europe which they had bitten off' in order to draw attention to their sheer *appetite* for possessions. Right up to the last sentence Lawrence humorously maintains an ironic detachment, allowing his idealists to expose themselves, in this wonderfully controlled short story.

'Mother and Daughter' was the last story he wrote in his short lifetime. It shows him at his most self-conscious in a Modernist sense.

He twice evokes Balzac to justify his precision about purely invented statistics. He constantly draws parallels with literary precedents, especially such fantastic ones as *The Arabian Nights*. He even makes fun of his own metaphorical use of language when, for instance, he reports that 'another fool male was mystically knocked on the head'. The story is about two generations of women, the older so domineering that the younger is driven in reaction to revert to 'the harem type'. The Turkish Delight (Lawrence adopts the mother's contemptuous nickname for her daughter's fiancé with mischievous glee) is physically repulsive, self-interested and a comically absurd representative of the male chauvinism of which Lawrence was himself later accused. The story shows how it is the mother's antagonism to men that is responsible for her daughter's capitulation to this ridiculous example of the 'patriarchal and tribal' kind of male that was earlier given more sinister embodiment in the Chilchuis of 'The Woman Who Rode Away'. There are moments when the art falters and the doctrine intrudes, as it does during the proposal scene. But for the most part the irony is sustained and the satirical intention effected by comic means alone.

One is left wondering how Lawrence would have developed had he lived a normal lifespan. Would the didactic element finally have got the better of his artistic instinct? Or would it have pushed him further in his reaction against narrative realism, as it has done his post-Modernist successors? One has only to look back at the astonishing advances he made during the twenty years in which he was writing stories to be certain that he would have continued to experiment and change for as long as he was engaged in the art of fiction.

The twenty-five stories selected for this edition have been chosen to show the wide range of Lawrence's work in this genre at its best. They have been arranged as far as is determinable in chronological order. Brief details of their dates of composition and publication are given in the Notes at the back. In all cases except 'The Border Line' the text chosen is the last version to have been approved by Lawrence during his lifetime (cf. A Note on the Text). This is the first edition to print 'The Border Line' in its longer original version of 1924 as Lawrence wanted it (cf. Notes, p.535).

I would like to thank the following individuals and libraries for their help in obtaining copies of the texts used in this edition: Michael

Black, the British Library, W. E. Forster, Damion Grant, George Lazarus, Keith Sagar, and the University of London Library.

A NOTE ON THE TEXT

The text of the stories in this selection is reproduced from the following publications:

From *Love Among the Haystacks* (Nonesuch Press, 1930)
'Love Among the Haystacks'

From *The Prussian Officer* (Duckworth, 1914)
'The White Stocking'
'Odour of Chrysanthemums'
'Daughters of the Vicar'
'Second Best'
'The Shades of Spring'
'The Prussian Officer'
'The Thorn in the Flesh'

From *Seven Arts* (New York, July 1917)
'The Mortal Coil'

From *England, My England* (Secker, 1924)
'England, My England'
'The Horse Dealer's Daughter'
'Samson and Delilah'
'Tickets, Please'
'The Blind Man'
'Fanny and Annie'
'You Touched Me'

From *The Woman Who Rode Away and Other Stories* (Secker, 1928)
'Jimmy and the Desperate Woman'
'The Woman Who Rode Away'

From *Hutchinson's Magazine* (London, September 1925)
'The Border Line'

From *Sun* (Black Sun Press, Paris, October 1928)
'Sun'

From *The Ghost Book, 16 New Stories of the Uncanny Compiled by Lady C. Asquith* (Hutchinson, 1926)
'The Rocking-Horse Winner'

From *The Woman Who Rode Away and Other Stories* (Knopf, New York, 1928)
'The Man Who Loved Islands'

From *The Black Cap, New Stories of Murder and Mystery Compiled by C. Asquith* (Hutchinson, 1927)
'The Lovely Lady'

From *The Fortnightly Review* (London, October 1928)
'Things'

From *The New Criterion* (London, April 1929)
'Mother and Daughter'

Love Among the Haystacks

I

THE two large fields lay on a hillside facing south. Being newly cleared of hay, they were golden green, and they shone almost blindingly in the sunlight. Across the hill, half-way up, ran a high hedge, that flung its black shadow finely across the molten glow of the sward. The stack was being built just above the hedge. It was of great size, massive, but so silvery and delicately bright in tone that it seemed not to have weight. It rose dishevelled and radiant among the steady, golden-green glare of the field. A little farther back was another, finished stack.

The empty wagon was just passing through the gap in the hedge. From the far-off corner of the bottom field, where the sward was still striped grey with winrows,[1] the loaded wagon launched forward, to climb the hill to the stack. The white dots of the hay-makers showed distinctly among the hay.

The two brothers were having a moment's rest, waiting for the load to come up. They stood wiping their brows with their arms, sighing from the heat and the labour of placing the last load. The stack they rode was high, lifting them up above the hedge-tops, and very broad, a great slightly-hollowed vessel into which the sunlight poured, in which the hot, sweet scent of hay was suffocating. Small and inefficacious the brothers looked, half-submerged in the loose, great trough, lifted high up as if on an altar reared to the sun.

Maurice, the younger brother, was a handsome young fellow of twenty-one, careless and debonair, and full of vigour. His grey eyes, as he taunted his brother, were bright and baffled with a strong emotion. His swarthy face had the same peculiar smile, expectant and glad and nervous, of a young man roused for the first time in passion.

'Tha sees,' he said, as he leaned on the pommel of his fork, 'tha thowt as tha'd done me one, didna ter?' He smiled as he spoke, then fell again into his pleasant torment of musing.

'I thought nowt – tha knows so much,' retorted Geoffrey, with the touch of a sneer. His brother had the better of him. Geoffrey was a very heavy, hulking fellow, a year older than Maurice. His blue eyes were unsteady, they glanced away quickly; his mouth was morbidly sensitive. One felt him wince away, through the whole of his great body. His inflamed self-consciousness was a disease in him.

'Ah but though, I know tha did,' mocked Maurice. 'Tha went slinkin' off' – Geoffrey winced convulsively – 'thinking as that wor the last night as any of us'ud ha'e ter stop here, an' so tha'd leave me to sleep out, though it wor thy turn –'

He smiled to himself, thinking of the result of Geoffrey's ruse.

'I didna go slinkin' off neither,' retorted Geoffrey, in his heavy, clumsy manner, wincing at the phrase. 'Didna my feyther send me to fetch some coal –'

'Oh yes, oh yes – we know all about it. But tha sees what tha missed, my lad.'

Maurice, chuckling, threw himself on his back in the bed of hay. There was absolutely nothing in his world, then, except the shallow ramparts of the stack, and the blazing sky. He clenched his fists tight, threw his arms across his face, and braced his muscles again. He was evidently very much moved, so acutely that it was hardly pleasant, though he still smiled. Geoffrey, standing behind him, could just see his red mouth, with the young moustache like black fur, curling back and showing the teeth in a smile. The elder brother leaned his chin on the pommel of his fork, looking out across the country.

Far away was the faint blue heap of Nottingham. Between, the country lay under a haze of heat, with here and there a flag of colliery smoke waving. But near at hand, at the foot of the hill, across the deep-hedged high road, was only the silence of the old church and the castle farm, among their trees. The large view only made Geoffrey more sick. He looked away, to the wagons crossing the field below him, the empty cart like a big insect moving down hill, the load coming up, rocking like a ship, the brown head of the horse ducking, the brown knees lifted and planted strenuously. Geoffrey wished it would be quick.

'Tha didna think –'

Geoffrey started, coiled within himself, and looked down at the handsome lips moving in speech below the brown arms of his brother.

'Tha didna think 'er'd be thur wi' me – or tha wouldna ha' left me to it,' Maurice said, ending with a little laugh of excited memory. Geoffrey flushed with hate, and had an impulse to set his foot on that moving, taunting mouth, which was there below him. There was silence for a time, then, in a peculiar tone of delight, Maurice's voice came again, spelling out the words, as it were:

'Ich bin klein, mein Herz ist rein,
Ist niemand d'rin als Christ allein.'[2]

Maurice chuckled, then, convulsed at a twinge of recollection, keen as pain, he twisted over, pressed himself into the hay.

'Can thee say thy prayers in German?' came his muffled voice.

'I non want,' growled Geoffrey.

Maurice chuckled. His face was quite hidden, and in the dark he was going over again his last night's experiences.

'What about kissing 'er under th' ear, Sonny,' he said, in a curious, uneasy tone. He writhed, still startled and inflamed by his first contact with love.

Geoffrey's heart swelled within him, and things went dark. He could not see the landscape.

'An' there's just a nice two-handful of her bosom,' came the low, provocative tones of Maurice, who seemed to be talking to himself.

The two brothers were both fiercely shy of women, and until this hay harvest, the whole feminine sex had been represented by their mother and in presence of any other women they were dumb louts. Moreover, brought up by a proud mother, a stranger in the country, they held the common girls as beneath them, because beneath their mother, who spoke pure English, and was very quiet. Loud-mouthed and broad-tongued the common girls were. So these two young men had grown up virgin but tormented.

Now again Maurice had the start of Geoffrey, and the elder brother was deeply mortified. There was a danger of his sinking into a morbid state, from sheer lack of living, lack of interest. The foreign governess at the Vicarage, whose garden lay beside the top field, had talked to the lads through the hedge, and had fascinated them. There was a great elder bush, with its broad creamy flowers crumbling on to the garden path, and into the field. Geoffrey never smelled elder-flower without starting and wincing, thinking of the strange foreign voice that had so startled him as he mowed out with the scythe in the hedge bottom. A baby had run through the gap, and the Fräulein, calling in German, had come brushing down the flowers in pursuit. She had started so on seeing a man standing there in the shade, that for a moment she could not move: and then she had blundered into the rake which was lying by his side. Geoffrey, forgetting she was a woman when he saw her pitch forward, had picked her up carefully, asking: 'Have you hurt you?'

Then she had broken into a laugh, and answered in German, showing him her arms, and knitting her brows. She was nettled rather badly.

'You want a dock leaf,' he said. She frowned in a puzzled fashion.

'A dock leaf?' she repeated. He had rubbed her arms with the green leaf.

And now, she had taken to Maurice. She had seemed to prefer himself at first. Now she had sat with Maurice in the moonlight, and had let him kiss her. Geoffrey sullenly suffered, making no fight.

Unconsciously, he was looking at the Vicarage garden. There she was, in a golden-brown dress. He took off his hat, and held up his right hand in greeting to her. She, a small, golden figure, waved her hand negligently from among the potato rows. He remained, arrested, in the same posture, his hat in his left hand, his right arm upraised, thinking. He could tell by the negligence of her greeting that she was waiting for Maurice. What did she think of himself? Why wouldn't she have him?

Hearing the voice of the wagoner leading the load, Maurice rose. Geoffrey still stood in the same way, but his face was sullen, and his upraised hand was slack with brooding. Maurice faced up-hill. His eyes lit up and he laughed. Geoffrey dropped his own arm, watching.

'Lad!' chuckled Maurice. 'I non knowed 'er wor there.' He waved his hand clumsily. In these matters Geoffrey did better. The elder brother watched the girl. She ran to the end of the path, behind the bushes, so that she was screened from the house. Then she waved her handkerchief wildly. Maurice did not notice the manoeuvre. There was the cry of a child. The girl's figure vanished, reappeared holding up a white childish bundle, and came down the path. There she put down her charge, sped up-hill to a great ash-tree, climbed quickly to a large horizontal bar that formed the fence there, and, standing poised, blew kisses with both her hands, in a foreign fashion that excited the brothers. Maurice laughed aloud, as he waved his red handkerchief.

'Well, what's the danger?' shouted a mocking voice from below. Maurice collapsed, blushing furiously.

'Nowt!' he called.

There was a hearty laugh from below.

The load rode up, sheered with a hiss against the stack, then sank back again upon the scotches.[3] The brothers ploughed across the mass of hay, taking the forks. Presently a big, burly man, red and glistening, climbed to the top of the load. Then he turned round, scrutinized the hillside from under his shaggy brows. He caught sight of the girl under the ash-tree.

'Oh, that's who it is,' he laughed. 'I thought it was some such bird, but I couldn't see her.'

The father laughed in a hearty, chaffing way, then began to teem the load. Geoffrey, on the stack above, received his great forkfuls, and swung them over to Maurice, who took them, placed them, building the stack. In the intense sunlight, the three worked in silence, knit together in a brief passion of work. The father stirred slowly for a moment, getting the hay from under his feet. Geoffrey waited, the blue tines of his fork glittering in expectation: the mass rose, his fork swung beneath it, there was a light clash of blades, then the hay was swept on to the stack, caught by Maurice, who placed it judiciously. One after another, the shoulders of the three men bowed and braced themselves. All wore light blue, bleached shirts, that stuck close to their backs. The father moved mechanically, his thick, rounded shoulders bending and lifting dully: he worked monotonously. Geoffrey flung away his strength. His massive shoulders swept and flung the hay extravagantly.

'Dost want to knock me ower?' asked Maurice angrily. He had to brace himself against the impact. The three men worked intensely, as if some will urged them. Maurice was light and swift at the work, but he had to use his judgement. Also, when he had to place the hay along the far ends, he had some distance to carry it. So he was too slow for Geoffrey. Ordinarily, the elder would have placed the hay as far as possible where his brother wanted it. Now, however, he pitched his forkfuls into the middle of the stack. Maurice strode swiftly and handsomely across the bed, but the work was too much for him. The other two men, clenched in their receive and deliver, kept up a high pitch of labour. Geoffrey still flung the hay at random. Maurice was perspiring heavily with heat and exertion, and was getting worried. Now and again, Geoffrey wiped his arm across his brow, mechanically, like an animal. Then he glanced with satisfaction at Maurice's moiled condition, and caught the next forkful.

'Wheer dost think thou'rt hollin' it, fool!' panted Maurice, as his brother flung a forkful out of reach.

'Wheer I've a mind,' answered Geoffrey.

Maurice toiled on, now very angry. He felt the sweat trickling down his body: drops fell into his long black lashes, blinding him, so that he had to stop and angrily dash his eyes clear. The veins stood out in his swarthy neck. He felt he would burst, or drop, if the work did not soon slacken off. He heard his father's fork dully scrape the cart bottom.

'There, the last,' the father panted. Geoffrey tossed the last light lot at random, took off his hat, and, steaming in the sunshine as he wiped himself, stood complacently watching Maurice struggle with clearing the bed.

'Don't you think you've got your bottom corner a bit far out?' came the father's voice from below. 'You'd better be drawing in now, hadn't you?'

'I thought you said next load,' Maurice called, sulkily.

'Aye! All right. But isn't this bottom corner – ?'

Maurice, impatient, took no notice.

Geoffrey strode over the stack, and stuck his fork in the offending corner. 'What – here?' he bawled in his great voice.

'Aye – isn't it a bit loose?' came the irritating voice.

Geoffrey pushed his fork in the jutting corner, and, leaning his weight on the handle, shoved. He thought it shook. He thrust again with all his power. The mass swayed.

'What art up to, tha fool!' cried Maurice, in a high voice.

'Mind who tha'rt callin' a fool,' said Geoffrey, and he prepared to push again. Maurice sprang across, and elbowed his brother aside. On the yielding, swaying bed of hay, Geoffrey lost his foothold, and fell grovelling. Maurice tried the corner.

'It's solid enough,' he shouted angrily.

'Aye – all right,' came the conciliatory voice of the father; 'you do get a bit of rest now there's such a long way to cart it,' he added reflectively.

Geoffrey had got to his feet.

'Tha'll mind who tha'rt nudging, I can tell thee,' he threatened heavily; adding, as Maurice continued to work, 'an' tha non ca's him a fool again, dost hear?'

'Not till next time,' sneered Maurice.

As he worked silently round the stack, he neared where his brother stood like a sullen statue, leaning on his fork-handle, looking out over the countryside. Maurice's heart quickened in its beat. He worked forward, until a point of his fork caught in the leather of Geoffrey's boot, and the metal rang sharply.

'Are ter going ta shift thysen?' asked Maurice threateningly. There was no reply from the great block. Maurice lifted his upper lip like a dog. Then he put out his elbow, and tried to push his brother into the stack, clear of his way.

'Who are ter shovin'?' came the deep, dangerous voice.

'Thaïgh,' replied Maurice, with a sneer, and straightway the two brothers set themselves against each other, like opposing bulls, Maurice trying his hardest to shift Geoffrey from his footing, Geoffrey leaning all his weight in resistance. Maurice, insecure in his footing, staggered a little, and Geoffrey's weight followed him. He went slithering over the edge of the stack.

Geoffrey turned white to the lips, and remained standing, listening. He heard the fall. Then a flush of darkness came over him, and he remained standing only because he was planted. He had not strength to move. He could hear no sound from below, was only faintly aware of a sharp shriek from a long way off. He listened again. Then he filled with sudden panic.

'Feyther!' he roared, in his tremendous voice: 'Feyther! Feyther!'

The valley re-echoed with the sound. Small cattle on the hill-side looked up. Men's figures came running from the bottom field, and much nearer a woman's figure was racing across the upper field. Geoffrey waited in terrible suspense.

'Ah-h!' he heard the strange, wild voice of the girl cry out. 'Ah-h!' – and then some foreign wailing speech. Then: 'Ah-h! Are you dea-ed!'

He stood sullenly erect on the stack, not daring to go down, longing to hide in the hay, but too sullen to stoop out of sight. He heard his eldest brother come up, panting:

'Whatever's amiss!' and then the labourer, and then his father.

'Whatever have you been doing?' he heard his father ask, while yet he had not come round the corner of the stack. And then, in a low, bitter tone:

'Eh, he's done for! I'd no business to ha' put it all on that stack.'

There was a moment or two of silence, then the voice of Henry, the eldest brother, said crisply:

'He's not dead – he's coming round.'

Geoffrey heard, but was not glad. He had as lief[4] Maurice were dead. At least that would be final: better than meeting his brother's charges, and of seeing his mother pass to the sick-room. If Maurice was killed, he himself would not explain, no, not a word, and they could hang him if they liked. If Maurice were only hurt, then everybody would know, and Geoffrey could never lift his face again. What added torture, to pass along, everybody knowing. He wanted something that he could stand back to, something definite, if it were only the knowledge that he had killed his brother. He *must* have something firm to back up to, or he would go mad. He was so lonely, he who above all needed the support of sympathy.

'No, he's commin' to; I tell you he is,' said the labourer.

'He's not dea-ed, he's not dea-ed,' came the passionate, strange sing-song of the foreign girl. 'He's not dead – no-o.'

'He wants some brandy – look at the colour of his lips,' said the crisp, cold voice of Henry. 'Can you fetch some?'

'Wha-at? Fetch?' Fraülein did not understand.

'Brandy,' said Henry, very distinct.

'Brrandy!' she re-echoed.

'You go, Bill,' groaned the father.

'Aye, I'll go,' replied Bill, and he ran across the field.

Maurice was not dead, nor going to die. This Geoffrey now realized. He was glad after all that the extreme penalty was revoked. But he hated to think of himself going on. He would always shrink now. He had hoped and hoped for the time when he would be careless, bold as Maurice, when he would not wince and shrink. Now he would always be the same, coiling up in himself like a tortoise with no shell.

'Ah-h! He's getting better!' came the wild voice of the Fräulein, and she began to cry, a strange sound, that startled the men, made the animal bristle within them. Geoffrey shuddered as he heard, between her sobbing, the impatient moaning of his brother as the breath came back.

The labourer returned at a run, followed by the Vicar. After the brandy, Maurice made more moaning, hiccuping noise. Geoffrey listened in torture. He heard the Vicar asking for explanations. All the united, anxious voices replied in brief phrases.

'It was that other,' cried the Fräulein. 'He knocked him over – Ha!'

She was shrill and vindictive.

'I don't think so,' said the father to the Vicar, in a quite audible but private tone, speaking as if the Fräulein did not understand his English.

The Vicar addressed his children's governess in bad German. She replied in a torrent which he would not confess was too much for him. Maurice was making little moaning, sighing noises.

'Where's your pain, boy, eh?' the father asked, pathetically.

'Leave him alone a bit,' came the cool voice of Henry. 'He's winded, if no more.'

'You'd better see that no bones are broken,' said the anxious Vicar.

'It wor a blessing as he should a dropped on that heap of hay just there,' said the labourer. 'If he'd happened to ha' catched hisself on this nog o' wood 'e wouldna ha' stood much chance.'

Geoffrey wondered when he would have courage to venture down. He had wild notions of pitching himself head foremost from the stack: if he could only extinguish himself, he would be safe. Quite frantically, he longed not to be. The idea of going through life thus coiled up within himself in morbid self-consciousness, always lonely, surly, and a misery, was enough to make him cry out. What would they all think when they knew he had knocked Maurice off that high stack?

They were talking to Maurice down below. The lad had recovered in great measure, and was able to answer faintly.

'Whatever was you doin'?' the father asked gently. 'Was you playing about with our Geoffrey? – Aye, and where is he?'

Geoffrey's heart stood still.

'I dunno,' said Henry, in a curious, ironic tone.

'Go an' have a look,' pleaded the father, infinitely relieved over one son, anxious now concerning the other. Geoffrey could not bear that his eldest brother should climb up and question him in his high-pitched drawl of curiosity. The culprit doggedly set his feet on the ladder. His nailed boots slipped a rung.

'Mind yourself,' shouted the overwrought father.

Geoffrey stood like a criminal at the foot of the ladder, glancing furtively at the group. Maurice was lying, pale and slightly convulsed, upon a heap of hay. The Fräulein was kneeling beside his head. The Vicar had the lad's shirt full open down the breast, and was feeling for broken ribs. The father kneeled on the other side, the labourer and Henry stood aside.

'I can't find anything broken,' said the Vicar, and he sounded slightly disappointed.

'There's nowt broken to find,' murmured Maurice, smiling.

The father started. 'Eh?' he said. 'Eh?' and he bent over the invalid.

'I say it's not hurt me,' repeated Maurice.

'What were you doing?' asked the cold, ironic voice of Henry. Geoffrey turned his head away: he had not yet raised his face.

'Nowt as I know on,' he muttered in a surly tone.

'Why!' cried Fräulein in a reproachful tone. 'I see him – knock him over!' She made a fierce gesture with her elbow. Henry curled his long moustache sardonically.

'Nay lass, niver,' smiled the wan Maurice. 'He was fur enough away from me when I slipped.'

'Oh, ah!' cried the Fräulein, not understanding.

'Yi,' smiled Maurice indulgently.

'I think you're mistaken,' said the father, rather pathetically, smiling at the girl as if she were 'wanting'.

'Oh no,' she cried. 'I *see* him.'

'Nay, lass,' smiled Maurice quietly.

She was a Pole, named Paula Jablonowsky: young, only twenty years old, swift and light as a wild cat, with a strange, wild-cat way of grinning. Her hair was blonde and full of life, all crisped into many tendrils with vitality, shaking round her face. Her fine blue eyes were peculiarly lidded, and she seemed to look piercingly, then languorously, like a wild cat. She had somewhat Slavonic cheekbones, and was very much freckled. It was evident that the Vicar, a pale, rather cold man, hated her.

Maurice lay pale and smiling in her lap, whilst she cleaved to him like a mate. One felt instinctively that they were mated. She was ready at any minute to fight with ferocity in his defence, now he was hurt. Her looks at Geoffrey were full of fierceness. She bowed over Maurice and caressed him with her foreign-sounding English.

'You say what you lai-ike,' she laughed, giving him lordship over her.

'Hadn't you better be going and looking what has become of Margery?' asked the Vicar in tones of reprimand.

'She is with her mother – I heared her. I will go in a whai-ile,' smiled the girl, coolly.

'Do you feel as if you could stand?' asked the father, still anxiously.

'Aye, in a bit,' smiled Maurice.

'You want to get up?' caressed the girl, bowing over him, till her face was not far from his.

'I'm in no hurry,' he replied, smiling brilliantly.

This accident had given him quite a strange new ease, an authority. He felt extraordinarily glad. New power had come to him all at once.

'You in no hurry,' she repeated, gathering his meaning. She smiled tenderly: she was in his service.

'She leaves us in another month – Mrs Inwood could stand no more of her,' apologized the Vicar quietly to the father.

'Why, is she – ?'

'Like a wild thing – disobedient, and insolent.'

'Ha!'

The father sounded abstract.

'No more foreign governesses for me.'

Maurice stirred, and looked up at the girl.

'You stand up?' she asked brightly. 'You well?'

He laughed again, showing his teeth winsomely. She lifted his head, sprung to her feet, her hands still holding his head, then she took him under the armpits and had him on his feet before anyone could help. He was much taller than she. He grasped her strong shoulders heavily, leaned against her, and, feeling her round, firm breast doubled up against his side, he smiled, catching his breath.

'You see I'm all right,' he gasped. 'I was only winded.'

'You all raïght?' she cried, in great glee.

'Yes, I am.'

He walked a few steps after a moment.

'There's nowt ails me, Father,' he laughed.

'Quite well, you?' she cried in a pleading tone. He laughed outright, looked down at her, touching her cheek with his fingers.

'That's it – if tha likes.'

'If I lai-ike!' she repeated, radiant.

'She's going at the end of three weeks,' said the Vicar consolingly to the farmer.

II

While they were talking, they heard the far-off hooting of a pit.

'There goes th' loose a',' [5] said Henry, coldly. 'We're *not* going to get that corner up to-day.'

The father looked round anxiously.

'Now, Maurice, are you sure you're all right?' he asked.

'Yes, I'm all right. Haven't I told you?'

'Then you sit down there, and in a bit you can be getting dinner out. Henry, you go on the stack. Wheer's Jim? Oh, he's minding the hosses. Bill, and you, Geoffrey, you can pick while Jim loads.'

Maurice sat down under the wych elm to recover. The Fräulein had fled back. He made up his mind to ask her to marry him. He had got fifty pounds of his own, and his mother would help him. For a long time he sat musing, thinking what he would do. Then, from the float he fetched a big basket covered with a cloth, and spread the dinner. There was an immense rabbit pie, a dish of cold potatoes, much bread, a great piece of cheese, and a solid rice pudding.

These two fields were four miles from the home farm. But they had been in the hands of the Wookeys for several generations, therefore the father kept them on, and everyone looked forward to the hay harvest at Greasley: it was a kind of picnic. They brought dinner and tea in the milk-float, which the father drove over in the morning. The lads and the labourers cycled. Off and on, the harvest lasted a fortnight. As the high road from Alfreton to Nottingham ran at the foot of the fields, someone usually slept in the hay under the shed to guard the tools. The sons took it in turns. They did not care for it much, and were for that reason anxious to finish the harvest on this day. But work went slack and disjointed after Maurice's accident.

When the load was teemed, they gathered round the white cloth, which was spread under a tree between the hedge and the stack, and, sitting on the ground, ate their meal. Mrs Wookey sent always a clean cloth, and knives and forks and plates for everybody. Mr Wookey was always rather proud of this spread: everything was so proper.

'There now,' he said, sitting down jovially. 'Doesn't this look nice now – eh?'

They all sat round the white spread, in the shadow of the tree and the stack, and looked out up the fields as they ate. From their shady coolness, the gold sward seemed liquid, molten with heat. The horse with the empty wagon wandered a few yards, then stood feeding. Everything was still as a trance. Now and again, the horse between the shafts of the load that stood propped beside the stack, jingled his loose bit as he ate. The men ate and drank in silence, the father reading the newspaper, Maurice leaning back on a saddle, Henry reading the *Nation*, the others eating busily.

Presently 'Helloa! 'Er's 'ere again!' exclaimed Bill. All looked up. Paula was coming across the field carrying a plate.

'She's bringing something to tempt your appetite, Maurice,' said the eldest brother ironically. Maurice was midway through a large wedge of rabbit pie, and some cold potatoes.

'Aye, bless me if she's not,' laughed the father. 'Put that away, Maurice, it's a shame to disappoint her.'

Maurice looked round very shamefaced, not knowing what to do with his plate.

'Give it over here,' said Bill. 'I'll polish him off.'

'Bringing something for the invalid?' laughed the father to the Fräulein. 'He's looking up nicely.'

'I bring him some chicken, him!' She nodded her head at Maurice childishly. He flushed and smiled.

'Tha doesna mean ter bust 'im,' said Bill.

Everybody laughed aloud. The girl did not understand, so she laughed also. Maurice ate his portion very sheepishly.

The father pitied his son's shyness.

'Come here and sit by me,' he said. 'Eh, Fräulein! Is that what they call you?'

'I sit by you, Father,' she said innocently.

Henry threw his head back and laughed long and noiselessly.

She settled near to the big, handsome man.

'My name,' she said, 'is Paula Jablonowsky.'

'Is what?' said the father, and the other men went into roars of laughter.

'Tell me again,' said the father. 'Your name – ?'

'Paula.'

'Paula? Oh – well, it's a rum sort of name, eh? His name –' he nodded at his son.

'Maurice – I know.' She pronounced it sweetly, then laughed into the father's eyes. Maurice blushed to the roots of his hair.

They questioned her concerning her history, and made out that she came from Hanover, that her father was a shop-keeper, and that she had run away from home because she did not like her father. She had gone to Paris.

'Oh,' said the father, now dubious. 'And what did you do there?'

'In school – in a young ladies' school.'

'Did you like it?'

'Oh no – no laïfe – no life!'

'What?'

'When we go out – two and two – all together – no more. Ah, no life, no life.'

'Well, that's a winder!' exclaimed the father. 'No life in Paris! And have you found much life in England?'

'No – ah no. I don't like it.' She made a grimace at the Vicarage.

'How long have you been in England?'

'Chreestmas – so.'

'And what will you do?'

'I will go to London, or to Paris. Ah, Paris! – Or get married!' She laughed into the father's eyes.

The father laughed heartily.

'Get married, eh? And who to?'

'I don't know. I am going away.'

'The country's too quiet for you?' asked the father.

'Too quiet – hm!' she nodded in assent.

'You wouldn't care for making butter and cheese?'

'Making butter – hm!' She turned to him with a glad, bright gesture. 'I like it.'

'Oh,' laughed the father. 'You would, would you?'

She nodded vehemently, with glowing eyes.

'She'd like anything in the shape of a change,' said Henry judicially.

'I think she would,' agreed the father. It did not occur to them that she fully understood what they said. She looked at them closely, then thought with bowed head.

'Hullo!' exclaimed Henry, the alert. A tramp was slouching towards them through the gap. He was a very seedy, slinking fellow, with a tang of horsey braggadocio about him. Small, thin, and ferrety, with a week's red beard bristling on his pointed chin, he came slouching forward.

'Have yer got a bit of a job goin'?' he asked.

'A bit of a job,' repeated the father. 'Why, can't you see as we've a'most done?'

'Aye – but I noticed you was a hand short, an' I thowt as 'appen you'd gie me half a day.'

'What, are *you* any good in a hay close?' asked Henry, with a sneer.

The man stood slouching against the haystack. All the others were seated on the floor. He had an advantage.

'I could work aside any on yer,' he bragged.

'Tha looks it,' laughed Bill.

'And what's your regular trade?' asked the father.

'I'm a jockey by rights. But I did a bit o' dirty work for a boss o' mine, an' I was landed. *'E* got the benefit, *I* got kicked out. *'E* axed me – an' then 'e looked as if 'e'd never seed me.'

'Did he, though!' exclaimed the father sympathetically.

' 'E did that!' asserted the man.

'But we've got nothing for you,' said Henry coldly.

'What does the boss say?' asked the man, impudent.

'No, we've no work you can do,' said the father. 'You can have a bit o' something to eat, if you like.'

'I should be glad of it,' said the man.

He was given the chunk of rabbit pie that remained. This he ate greedily. There was something debased, parasitic, about him, which disgusted Henry. The others regarded him as a curiosity.

'That was nice and tasty,' said the tramp, with gusto.

'Do you want a piece of bread 'n' cheese?' asked the father.

'It'll help to fill up,' was the reply.

The man ate this more slowly. The company was embarrassed by his presence, and could not talk. All the men lit their pipes, the meal over.

'So you dunna want any help?' said the tramp at last.

'No – we can manage what bit there is to do.'

'You don't happen to have a fill of bacca to spare, do you?'

The father gave him a good pinch.

'You're all right here,' he said, looking round. They resented this familiarity. However, he filled his clay pipe and smoked with the rest.

As they were sitting silent, another figure came through the gap in the hedge, and noiselessly approached. It was a woman. She was rather small and finely made. Her face was small, very ruddy, and comely, save for the look of bitterness and aloofness that it wore. Her hair was drawn tightly back under a sailor hat. She gave an impression of cleanness, of precision and directness.

'Have you got some work?' she asked of her man. She ignored the rest. He tucked his tail between his legs.

'No, they haven't got no work for me. They've just gave me a draw of bacca.'

He was a mean crawl of a man.

'An' am I goin' to wait for you out there on the lane all day?'

'You needn't if you don't like. You could go on.'

'Well, are you coming?' she asked contemptuously. He rose to his feet in a rickety fashion.

'You needn't be in such a mighty hurry,' he said. 'If you'd wait a bit you might get summat.'

She glanced for the first time over the men. She was quite young, and would have been pretty, were she not so hard and callous-looking.

'Have you had your dinner?' asked the father.

She looked at him with a kind of anger, and turned away. Her face was so childish in its contours, contrasting strangely with her expression.

'Are you coming?' she said to the man.

'He's had his tuck-in. Have a bit, if you want it,' coaxed the father.

'What have you had?' she flashed to the man.

'He's had all what was left o' th' rabbit pie,' said Geoffrey, in an indignant, mocking tone, 'and a great hunk o' bread an' cheese.'

'Well, it was gave me,' said the man.

The young woman looked at Geoffrey, and he at her. There was a sort of kinship between them. Both were at odds with the world. Geoffrey smiled satirically. She was too grave, too deeply incensed even to smile.

'There's a cake here, though – you can have a bit o' that,' said Maurice blithely.

She eyed him with scorn.

Again she looked at Geoffrey. He seemed to understand her. She turned, and in silence departed. The man remained obstinately sucking at his pipe. Everybody looked at him with hostility.

'We'll be getting to work,' said Henry, rising, pulling off his coat. Paula got to her feet. She was a little bit confused by the presence of the tramp.

'I go,' she said, smiling brilliantly. Maurice rose and followed her sheepishly.

'A good grind, eh?' said the tramp, nodding after the Fräulein. The men only half-understood him, but they hated him.

'Hadn't you better be getting off?' said Henry.

The man rose obediently. He was all slouching, parasitic insolence. Geoffrey loathed him, longed to exterminate him. He was exactly the worst foe of the hyper-sensitive: insolence without sensibility, preying on sensibility.

'Aren't you goin' to give me summat for her? It's nowt she's had all day, to my knowin'. She'll 'appen eat it if I take it 'er – though she gets more than I've any knowledge of' – this with a lewd wink of jealous spite. 'And then tries to keep a tight hand on me,' he sneered, taking the bread and cheese, and stuffing it in his pocket.

III

Geoffrey worked sullenly all the afternoon, and Maurice did the horse-raking. It was exceedingly hot. So the day wore on, the atmosphere thickened, and the sunlight grew blurred. Geoffrey was picking with Bill – helping to load the wagons from the winrows. He was sulky, though extraordinarily relieved: Maurice would not tell. Since the quarrel neither brother had spoken to the other. But their silence was entirely amicable, almost affectionate. They had both been deeply moved, so much so that their ordinary intercourse was interrupted: but underneath, each felt a strong regard for the other. Maurice was peculiarly happy, his feeling of affection swimming over everything. But Geoffrey was still sullenly hostile to the most part of the world. He felt isolated. The free and easy intercommunication between the other workers left him distinctly alone. And he was a man who could not bear to stand alone, he was too much afraid of the vast confusion of life surrounding him, in which he was helpless. Geoffrey mistrusted himself with everybody.

The work went on slowly. It was unbearably hot, and everyone was disheartened.

'We s'll have getting-on-for another day of it,' said the father at tea-time, as they sat under the tree.

'Quite a day,' said Henry.

'Somebody'll have to stop, then,' said Geoffrey. 'It 'ud better be me.'

'Nay, lad, I'll stop,' said Maurice, and he hid his head in confusion.

'Stop again to-night!' exclaimed the father. 'I'd rather you went home.'

'Nay, I'm stoppin',' protested Maurice.

'He wants to do his courting,' Henry enlightened them.

The father thought seriously about it.

'I don't know . . .' he mused, rather perturbed.

But Maurice stayed. Towards eight o'clock, after sundown, the men mounted their bicycles, the father put the horse in the float, and all departed. Maurice stood in the gap of the hedge and watched them go, the cart rolling and swinging downhill, over the grass stubble, the cyclists dipping swiftly like shadows in front. All passed through the gate, there was a quick clatter of hoofs on the roadway under the lime trees, and they were gone. The young man was very much excited, almost afraid, at finding himself alone.

Darkness was rising from the valley. Already, up the steep hill the cart-lamps crept indecisively, and the cottage windows were lit. Everything looked strange to Maurice, as if he had not seen it before. Down the hedge a large lime-tree teemed with scent that seemed almost like a voice speaking. It startled him. He caught a breath of the over-sweet fragrance, then stood still, listening expectantly.

Up hill, a horse whinneyed. It was the young mare. The heavy horses went thundering across to the far hedge.

Maurice wondered what to do. He wandered round the deserted stacks restlessly. Heat came in wafts, in thick strands. The evening was a long time cooling. He thought he would go and wash himself. There was a trough of pure water in the hedge bottom. It was filled by a tiny spring that filtered over the brim of the trough down the lush hedge bottom of the lower field. All round the trough, in the upper field, the land was marshy, and there the meadow-sweet stood like clots of mist, very sickly-smelling in the twilight. The night did not darken, for the moon was in the sky, so that as the tawny colour drew off the heavens they remained pallid with a dimmed moon. The purple bell-flowers in the hedge went black, the ragged robin turned its pink to a faded white, the meadow-sweet gathered light as if it were phosphorescent, and it made the air ache with scent.

Maurice kneeled on the slab of stone bathing his hands and arms, then his face. The water was deliciously cool. He had still an hour before Paula would come: she was not due till nine. So he decided to take his bath at night instead of waiting till morning. Was he not sticky, and was not Paula coming to talk to him? He was delighted the thought had occurred to him. As he soused his head in the trough, he wondered what the little creatures that lived in the velvety silt at the bottom would think of the taste of soap. Laughing to himself, he squeezed his cloth into the water. He washed himself from head to foot, standing in the fresh, forsaken corner of the field, where no one could see him by daylight, so that now, in the veiled grey tinge of moonlight, he was no more noticeable than the crowded flowers. The night had on a new look: he never remembered to have seen the lustrous grey sheen of it before, nor to have noticed how vital the lights looked, like live folk inhabiting the silvery spaces. And the tall trees, wrapped obscurely in their mantles, would not have surprised him had they begun to move in converse. As he dried himself, he discovered little wanderings in the air, felt on his sides soft touches and caresses that were peculiarly delicious: sometimes they startled him, and he laughed as if he were not alone. The flowers, the meadow-sweet particularly, haunted him. He reached to put his hand over their fleeciness. They touched his thighs. Laughing, he gathered them and dusted himself all over with their cream dust and fragrance. For a moment he hesitated in wonder at himself: but the subtle glow in the hoary and black night reassured him. Things never had looked so personal and full of beauty, he had never known the wonder in himself before.

At nine o'clock he was waiting under the elder-bush, in a state of high trepidation, but feeling that he was worthy, having a sense of his own wonder. She was late. At a quarter-past nine she came, flitting swiftly, in her own eager way.

'No, she would *not* go to sleep,' said Paula, with a world of wrath in her tone. He laughed bashfully. They wandered out into the dim, hillside field.

'I have sat – in that bedroom – for an hour, for hours,' she cried indignantly. She took a deep breath: 'Ah, breathe!' she smiled.

She was very intense, and full of energy.

'I want' – she was clumsy with the language – 'I want – I should laike – to run – there!' She pointed across the field.

'Let's run, then,' he said, curiously.

'Yes!'

And in an instant she was gone. He raced after her. For all he was so young and limber, he had difficulty in catching her. At first he could scarcely see her, though he could hear the rustle of her dress. She sped with astonishing fleetness. He overtook her, caught her by the arm, and they stood panting, facing one another with laughter.

'I could win,' she asserted blithely.

'Tha couldna,' he replied, with a peculiar, excited laugh. They walked on, rather breathless. In front of them suddenly appeared the dark shapes of the three feeding horses.

'We ride a horse?' she said.

'What, bareback?' he asked.

'You say?' She did not understand.

'With no saddle?'

'No saddle – yes – no saddle.'

'Coop, lass!' he said to the mare, and in a minute he had her by the forelock, and was leading her down to the stacks, where he put a halter on her. She was a big, strong mare. Maurice seated the Fräulein, clambered himself in front of the girl, using the wheel of the wagon as a mount, and together they trotted uphill, she holding lightly round his waist. From the crest of the hill they looked round.

The sky was darkening with an awning of cloud. On the left the hill rose black and wooded, made cosy by a few lights from cottages along the highway. The hill spread to the right, and tufts of trees shut round. But in front was a great vista of night, a sprinkle of cottage candles, a twinkling cluster of lights, like an elfish fair in full swing, at the colliery, an encampment of light at a village, a red flare on the sky far off, above an iron-foundry, and in the farthest distance the dim breathing of town lights. As they watched the night stretch far out, her arms tightened round his waist, and he pressed his elbows to his side, pressing her arms closer still. The horse moved restlessly. They clung to each other.

'Tha doesna want to go right away?' he asked the girl behind him.

'I stay with you,' she answered softly, and he felt her crouching close against him. He laughed curiously. He was afraid to kiss her, though he was urged to do so. They remained still, on the restless horse, watching the small lights lead deep into the night, an infinite distance.

'I don't want to go,' he said, in a tone half pleading.

She did not answer. The horse stirred restlessly.

'Let him run,' cried Paula, 'fast!'

She broke the spell, startled him into a little fury. He kicked the mare, hit her, and away she plunged downhill. The girl clung tightly to the young man. They were riding bareback down a rough, steep hill. Maurice clung hard with hands and knees. Paula held him fast round the waist, leaning her head on his shoulders, and thrilling with excitement.

'We shall be off, we shall be off,' he cried, laughing with excitement; but she only crouched behind and pressed tight to him. The mare tore across the field. Maurice expected every moment to be flung on to the grass. He gripped with all the strength of his knees. Paula tucked herself behind him, and often wrenched him almost from his hold. Man and girl were taut with effort.

At last the mare came to a standstill, blowing. Paula slid off, and in an instant Maurice was beside her. They were both highly excited. Before he knew what he was doing, he had her in his arms, fast, and was kissing her, and laughing. They did not move for some time. Then, in silence, they walked towards the stacks.

It had grown quite dark, the night was thick with cloud. He walked with his arm round Paula's waist, she with her arm round him. They were near the stacks when Maurice felt a spot of rain.

'It's going to rain,' he said.

'Rain!' she echoed, as if it were trivial.

'I s'll have to put the stack-cloth on,' he said gravely. She did not understand.

When they got to the stacks, he went round to the shed, to return staggering in the darkness under the burden of the immense and heavy cloth. It had not been used once during the hay harvest.

'What are you going to do?' asked Paula, coming close to him in the darkness.

'Cover the top of the stack with it,' he replied. 'Put it over the stack, to keep the rain out.'

'Ah!' she cried, 'up there!' He dropped his burden. 'Yes,' he answered.

Fumblingly he reared the long ladder up the side of the stack. He could not see the top.

'I hope it's solid,' he said, softly.

A few smart drops of rain sounded drumming on the cloth. They seemed like another presence. It was very dark indeed between the great buildings of hay. She looked up the black wall, and shrank to him.

'You carry it up there?' she asked.

'Yes,' he answered.

'I help you?' she said.

And she did. They opened the cloth. He clambered first up the steep ladder, bearing the upper part, she followed closely, carrying her full share. They mounted the shaky ladder in silence, stealthily.

IV

As they climbed the stacks a light stopped at the gate on the high road. It was Geoffrey, come to help his brother with the cloth. Afraid of his own intrusion, he wheeled his bicycle silently towards the shed. This was a corrugated iron erection, on the opposite side of the hedge from the stacks. Geoffrey let his light go in front of him, but there was no sign from the lovers. He thought he saw a shadow slinking away. The light of the bicycle lamp sheered yellowly across the dark, catching a glint of raindrops, a mist of darkness, shadow of leaves and strokes of long grass. Geoffrey entered the shed – no one was there. He walked slowly and doggedly round to the stacks. He had passed the wagon, when he heard something sheering down upon him. Starting back under the wall of hay, he saw the long ladder slither across the side of the stack, and fall with a bruising ring.

'What wor that?' he heard Maurice, aloft, ask cautiously.

'Something fall,' came the curious, almost pleased voice of the Fräulein.

'It wor niver th' ladder,' said Maurice. He peered over the side of the stack. He lay down, looking.

'It is an' a'!' he exclaimed. 'We knocked it down with the cloth, dragging it over.'

'We fast up here?' she exclaimed with a thrill.

'We are that – without I shout and make 'em hear at the Vicarage.'

'Oh no,' she said quickly.

'I don't want to,' he replied, with a short laugh. There came a swift clatter of raindrops on the cloth. Geoffrey crouched under the wall of the other stack.

'Mind where you tread – here, let me straighten this end,' said Maurice, with a peculiar intimate tone – a command and an embrace. 'We s'll have to sit under it. At any rate, we shan't get wet.'

'Not get wet!' echoed the girl, pleased, but agitated.

Geoffrey heard the slide and rustle of the cloth over the top of the stack, heard Maurice telling her to 'Mind!'

'Mind!' she repeated. 'Mind! you say "Mind!"'

'Well, what if I do?' he laughed. 'I don't want you to fall over th' side, do I?' His tone was masterful, but he was not quite sure of himself.

There was silence a moment or two.

'Maurice!' she said, plaintively.

'I'm here,' he answered, tenderly, his voice shaky with excitement that was near to distress. 'There, I've done. Now should we – we'll sit under this corner.'

'Maurice!' she was rather pitiful.

'What? You'll be all right,' he remonstrated, tenderly indignant.

'I be all raïght,' she repeated, 'I be all raïght, Maurice?'

'Tha knows tha will – I canna ca' thee Powla. Should I ca' thee Minnie?'

It was the name of a dead sister.

'Minnie?' she exclaimed in surprise.

'Aye, should I?'

She answered in full-throated German. He laughed shakily.

'Come on – come on under. But do yer wish you was safe in th' Vicarage? Should I shout for somebody?' he asked.

'I don't wish, no!' She was vehement.

'Art sure?' he insisted, almost indignantly.

'Sure – I quite sure.' She laughed.

Geoffrey turned away at the last words. Then the rain beat heavily. The lonely brother slouched miserably to the hut, where the rain played a mad tattoo. He felt very miserable, and jealous of Maurice.

His bicycle lamp, downcast, shone a yellow light on the stark floor of the shed or hut with one wall open. It lit up the trodden earth, the shafts of tools lying piled under the beam, beside the dreary grey metal of the building. He took off the lamp, shone it round the hut. There were piles of harness, tools, a big sugar box, a deep bed of hay – then the beams across the corrugated iron, all very dreary and stark. He shone the lamp into the night: nothing but the furtive glitter of rain-drops through the mist of darkness, and black shapes hovering round.

Geoffrey blew out the light and flung himself on to the hay. He would put the ladder up for them in a while, when they would be wanting it. Meanwhile he sat and gloated over Maurice's felicity. He was imaginative, and now he had something concrete to work upon. Nothing in the whole of life stirred him so profoundly, and so utterly, as the thought of this woman. For Paula was strange, foreign, different from the ordinary girls: the rousing, feminine quality seemed in her concentrated, brighter, more fascinating than in anyone he had known, so that he felt most like a moth near a candle. He would have loved her wildly – but Maurice had got her. His thoughts beat the same course, round and round. What was it like when you kissed her, when she held you tight round the waist, how did she feel towards Maurice, did she love to touch him, was he fine and attractive to her; what did she think of himself – she merely disregarded him, as she would disregard a horse in a field; why should she do so, why couldn't he make her regard himself, instead of Maurice: he would never command a woman's regard like that, he always gave in to her too soon; if only some woman would come and take him for what he was worth, though he was such a stumbler and showed to such disadvantage, ah, what a grand thing it would be; how he would kiss her. Then round he went again in the same course, brooding almost like a madman. Meanwhile the rain drummed deep on the shed, then grew lighter and softer. There came the drip, drip of the drops falling outside.

Geoffrey's heart leaped up his chest, and he clenched himself, as a black shape crept round the post of the shed and, bowing, entered silently. The young man's heart beat so heavily in plunges, he could not get his breath to speak. It was shock, rather than fear. The form felt towards him. He sprang up, gripped it with his great hands, panting 'Now, then!'

There was no resistance, only a little whimper of despair.

'Let me go,' said a woman's voice.

'What are you after?' he asked, in deep, gruff tones.

'I thought 'e was 'ere,' she wept despairingly, with little, stubborn sobs.

'An' you've found what you didn't expect, have you?'

At the sound of his bullying she tried to get away from him.

'Let me go,' she said.

'Who did you expect to find here?' he asked, but more his natural self.

'I expected my husband – him as you saw at dinner. Let me go.'

'Why, is it you?' exclaimed Geoffrey. 'Has he left you?'

'Let me go,' said the woman sullenly, trying to draw away. He realized that her sleeve was very wet, her arm slender under his grasp. Suddenly he grew ashamed of himself: he had no doubt hurt her, gripping her so hard. He relaxed, but did not let her go.

'An' are you searching round after that snipe as was here at dinner?' he asked. She did not answer.

'Where did he leave you?'

'I left him – here. I've seen nothing of him since.'

'I s'd think it's good riddance,' he said. She did not answer. He gave a short laugh, saying:

'I should ha' thought you wouldn't ha' wanted to clap eyes on him again.'

'He's my husband – an' he's not goin' to run off if I can stop him.'

Geoffrey was silent, not knowing what to say.

'Have you got a jacket on?' he asked at last.

'What do you think? You've got hold of it.'

'You're wet through, aren't you?'

'I shouldn't be dry, comin' through that teemin' rain. But 'e's not here, so I'll go.'

'I mean,' he said humbly, 'are you wet through?'

She did not answer. He felt her shiver.

'Are you cold?' he asked, in surprise and concern.

She did not answer. He did not know what to say.

'Stop a minute,' he said, and he fumbled in his pocket for his matches. He struck a light, holding it in the hollow of his large, hard palm. He was a big man, and he looked anxious. Shedding the light on her, he saw she was rather pale, and very weary looking. Her old sailor hat was sodden and drooping with rain. She wore a fawn-coloured jacket of smooth cloth. This jacket was black-wet where the rain had beaten, her skirt hung sodden, and dripped on to her boots. The match went out.

'Why, you're wet through!' he said.

She did not answer.

'Shall you stop in here while it gives over?' he asked. She did not answer.

' 'Cause if you will, you'd better take your things off, an' have th' rug. There's a horse-rug in the box.'

He waited, but she would not answer. So he lit his bicycle lamp, and rummaged in the box, pulling out a large brown blanket, striped with scarlet and yellow. She stood stock still. He shone the light on her. She was very pale, and trembling fitfully.

'Are you that cold?' he asked in concern. 'Take your jacket off, and your hat, and put this right over you.'

Mechanically, she undid the enormous fawn-coloured buttons, and unpinned her hat. With her black hair drawn back from her low, honest brow, she looked little more than a girl, like a girl driven hard with womanhood by stress of life. She was small, and natty, with neat little features. But she shivered convulsively.

'Is something a-matter with you?' he asked.

'I've walked to Bulwell and back,' she quivered, 'looking for him – an' I've not touched a thing since this morning.' She did not weep – she was too dreary-hardened to cry. He looked at her in dismay, his mouth half open: 'Gormin', as Maurice would have said.

' 'Aven't you had nothing to eat?' he said.

Then he turned aside to the box. There, the bread remaining was kept, and the great piece of cheese, and such things as sugar and salt, with all table utensils: there was some butter.

She sat down drearily on the bed of hay. He cut her a piece of bread and butter, and a piece of cheese. This she took, but ate listlessly.

'I want a drink,' she said.

'We 'aven't got no beer,' he answered. 'My father doesn't have it.'

'I want water,' she said.

He took a can and plunged through the wet darkness, under the great black hedge, down to the trough. As he came back he saw her in the half-lit little cave sitting bunched together. The soaked grass wet his feet – he thought of her. When he gave her a cup of water, her hand touched his and he felt her fingers hot and glossy. She trembled so she spilled the water.

'Do you feel badly?' he asked.

'I can't keep myself still – but it's only with being tired and having nothing to eat.'

He scratched his head contemplatively, waited while she ate her piece of bread and butter. Then he offered her another piece.

'I don't want it just now,' she said.

'You'll have to eat summat,' he said.

'I couldn't eat any more just now.'

He put the piece down undecidedly on the box. Then there was another long pause. He stood up with bent head. The bicycle, like a restful animal, glittered behind him, turning towards the wall. The woman sat hunched on the hay, shivering.

'Can't you get warm?' he asked.

'I shall by an' by – don't you bother. I'm taking your seat – are you stopping here all night?'

'Yes.'

'I'll be goin' in a bit,' she said.

'Nay, I non want you to go. I'm thinkin' how you could get warm.'

'Don't you bother about me,' she remonstrated, almost irritably.

'I just want to see as the stacks is all right. You take your shoes an' stockin's an' all your wet things off: you can easy wrap yourself all over in that rug, there's not so much of you.'

'It's raining – I s'll be all right – I s'll be going in a minute.'

'I've got to see as the stacks is safe. Take your wet things off.'

'Are you coming back?' she asked.

'I mightn't, not till morning.'

'Well, I s'll be gone in ten minutes, then. I've no rights to be here, an' I s'll not let anybody be turned out for me.'

'You won't be turning me out.'

'Whether or no, I shan't stop.'

'Well, shall you if I come back?' he asked. She did not answer.

He went. In a few moments, she blew the light out. The rain was falling steadily, and the night was a black gulf. All was intensely still. Geoffrey listened everywhere: no sound save the rain. He stood between the stacks, but only heard the trickle of water, and the light swish of rain. Everything was lost in blackness. He imagined death was like that, many things dissolved in silence and darkness, blotted out, but existing. In the dense blackness he felt himself almost extinguished. He was afraid he might not find things the same. Almost frantically, he stumbled, feeling his way, till his hand touched the wet metal. He had been looking for a gleam of light.

'Did you blow the lamp out?' he asked, fearful lest the silence should answer him.

'Yes,' she answered humbly. He was glad to hear her voice. Groping into the pitch-dark shed, he knocked against the box, part of whose cover served as table. There was a clatter and a fall.

'That's the lamp, an' the knife, an' the cup,' he said. He struck a match.

'Th' cup's not broke.' He put it into the box.

'But th' oil's spilled out o' th' lamp. It always was a rotten old thing.' He hastily blew out his match, which was burning his fingers. Then he struck another light.

'You don't want a lamp, you know you don't, and I s'll be going directly, so you come an' lie down an' get your night's rest. I'm not taking any of your place.'

He looked at her by the light of another match. She was a queer little bundle, all brown, with gaudy border folding in and out, and her little face peering at him. As the match went out she saw him beginning to smile.

'I can sit right at this end,' she said. 'You lie down.'

He came and sat on the hay, at some distance from her. After a spell of silence:

'Is he really your husband?' he asked.

'He is!' she answered grimly.

'Hm!' Then there was silence again.

After a while: 'Are you warm now?'

'Why do you bother yourself?'

'I don't bother myself – do you follow him because you like him?' He put it very timidly. He wanted to know.

'I don't – I wish he was dead,' this with bitter contempt. Then doggedly: 'But he's my husband.'

He gave a short laugh.

'By Gad!' he said.

Again, after a while: 'Have you been married long?'

'Four years.'

'Four years – why, how old are you?'

'Twenty-three.'

'Are you turned twenty-three?'

'Last May.'

'Then you're four month older than me.' He mused over it. They were only two voices in the pitch-black night. It was eerie silence again.

'And do you just tramp about?' he asked.

'He reckons he's looking for a job. But he doesn't like work in any shape or form. He was a stableman when I married him, at Greenhalgh's, the horse-dealers, at Chesterfield, where I was housemaid. He left that job when the baby was only two month, and I've been badgered about from pillar to post ever sin'. They say a rolling stone gathers no moss . . .'

'An' where's the baby?'

'It died when it was ten month old.'

Now the silence was clinched between them. It was quite a long time before Geoffrey ventured to say sympathetically: 'You haven't much to look forward to.'

'I've wished many a score time when I've started shiverin' an' shakin' at nights, as I was taken bad for death. But we're not that handy at dying.'

He was silent. 'But what ever shall you do?' he faltered.

'I s'll find him, if I drop by th' road.'

'Why?' he asked, wondering, looking her way, though he saw nothing but solid darkness.

'Because I shall. He's not going to have it all his own road.'

'But why don't you leave him?'

'Because he's *not goin' to have it all his own road.*'

She sounded very determined, even vindictive. He sat in wonder, feeling uneasy, and vaguely miserable on her behalf. She sat extraordinarily still. She seemed like a voice only, a presence.

'Are you warm now?' he asked, half afraid.

'A bit warmer – but my feet!' She sounded pitiful.

'Let me warm them with my hands,' he asked her. 'I'm hot enough.'

'No, thank you,' she said, coldly.

Then, in the darkness, she felt she had wounded him. He was writhing under her rebuff, for his offer had been pure kindness.

'They're 'appen dirty,' she said, half mocking.

'Well – mine is – an' I have a bath a'most every day,' he answered.

'I don't know when they'll get warm,' she moaned to herself.

'Well, then, put them in my hands.'

She heard him faintly rattling the match-box, and then a phosphorescent glare began to fume in his direction. Presently he was holding two smoking, blue-green blotches of light towards her feet. She was afraid. But her feet ached so, and the impulse drove her on, so she placed her soles lightly on the two blotches of smoke. His large hands clasped over her instep, warm and hard.

'They're like ice!' he said, in deep concern.

He warmed her feet as best he could, putting them close against him. Now and again convulsive tremors ran over her. She felt his warm breath on the balls of her toes, that were bunched up in his hands. Leaning forward, she touched his hair delicately with her fingers. He thrilled. She fell to gently stroking his hair, with timid, pleading finger-tips.

'Do they feel any better?' he asked, in a low voice, suddenly lifting his face to her. This sent her hand sliding softly over his face, and her finger-tips caught on his mouth. She drew quickly away. He put his hand out to find hers, in his other palm holding both her feet. His wandering hand met her face. He touched it curiously. It was wet. He put his big fingers cautiously on her eyes, into two little pools of tears.

'What's a matter?' he asked, in a low, choked voice.

She leaned down to him, and gripped him tightly round the neck, pressing him to her bosom in a little frenzy of pain. Her bitter disillusionment with life, her unalleviated shame and degradation during the last four years, had driven her into loneliness, and hardened her till a large part of her nature was caked and sterile. Now she softened again, and her spring might be beautiful. She had been in a fair way to make an ugly old woman.

She clasped the head of Geoffrey to her breast, which heaved and fell, and heaved again. He was bewildered, full of wonder. He allowed the woman to do as she would with him. Her tears fell on his hair, as she wept noiselessly; and he breathed deep as she did. At last she let go her clasp. He put his arms round her.

'Come and let me warm you,' he said, folding her up on his knee, and lapping her with his heavy arms against himself. She was small and *câline*.[6] He held her very warm and close. Presently she stole her arms round him.

'You *are* big,' she whispered.

He gripped her hard, started, put his mouth down wanderingly, seeking her out. His lips met her temple. She slowly, deliberately turned her mouth to his, and with opened lips, met him in a kiss, his first love kiss.

V

It was breaking cold dawn when Geoffrey woke. The woman was still sleeping in his arms. Her face in sleep moved all his tenderness: the tight shutting of her mouth, as if in resolution to bear what was very hard to bear, contrasted so pitifully with the small mould of her features. Geoffrey pressed her to his bosom: having her, he felt he could bruise the lips of the scornful, and pass on erect, unabateable. With her to complete him, to form the core of him, he was firm and whole. Needing her so much, he loved her fervently.

Meanwhile the dawn came like death, one of those slow, livid mornings that seem to come in a cold sweat. Slowly, and painfully, the air began to whiten. Geoffrey saw it was not raining. As he was watching the ghastly transformation outside, he felt aware of something. He glanced down: she was open-eyed, watching him; she had golden-brown, calm eyes, that immediately smiled into his. He also smiled, bowed softly down and kissed her. They did not speak for some time. Then:

'What's thy name?' he asked curiously.

'Lydia,' she said.

'Lydia!' he repeated, wonderingly. He felt rather shy.

'Mine's Geoffrey Wookey,' he said.

She merely smiled at him.

They were silent for a considerable time. By morning light, things look small. The huge trees of the evening were dwindling to hoary, small, uncertain things, trespassing in the sick pallor of the atmosphere.

There was a dense mist, so that the light could scarcely breathe. Everything seemed to quiver with cold and sickliness.

'Have you often slept out?' he asked her.

'Not so very,' she answered.

'You won't go after *him*?' he asked.

'I s'll have to,' she replied, but she nestled in to Geoffrey. He felt a sudden panic.

'You musn't,' he exclaimed, and she saw he was afraid for himself. She let it be, was silent.

'We couldn't get married?' he asked, thoughtfully.

'No.'

He brooded deeply over this. At length:

'Would you go to Canada with me?'

'We'll see what you think in two months' time,' she replied quietly, without bitterness.

'I s'll think the same,' he protested, hurt.

She did not answer, only watched him steadily. She was there for him to do as he liked with; but she would not injure his fortunes; no, not to save his soul.

'Haven't you got no relations?' he asked.

'A married sister at Crick.'

'On a farm?'

'No – married a farm labourer – but she's very comfortable. I'll go there, if you want me to, just till I can get another place in service.'

He considered this.

'Could you get on a farm?' he asked wistfully.

'Greenhalgh's was a farm.'

He saw the future brighten: she would be a help to him. She agreed to go to her sister, and to get a place of service – until Spring, he said, when they would sail for Canada. He waited for her assent.

'You will come with me, then?' he asked.

'When the time comes,' she said.

Her want of faith made him bow his head: she had reason for it.

'Shall you walk to Crick, or go from Langley Mill to Ambergate? But it's only ten mile to walk. So we can go together up Hunt's Hill – you'd have to go past our lane-end, then I could easy nip down an' fetch you some money,' he said, humbly.

'I've got half a sovereign by me – it's more than I s'll want.'

'Let's see it,' he said.

After a while, fumbling under the blanket, she brought out the piece of money. He felt she was independent of him. Brooding rather bitterly, he told himself she'd forsake him. His anger gave him courage to ask:

'Shall you go in service in your maiden name?'

'No.'

He was bitterly wrathful with her – full of resentment.

'I bet I s'll niver see you again,' he said, with a short, hard laugh. She put her arms round him, pressed him to her bosom, while the tears rose to her eyes. He was reassured, but not satisfied.

'Shall you write to me to-night?'

'Yes, I will.'

'And can I write to you – who shall I write to?'

'Mrs Bredon.'

' "Bredon"!' he repeated bitterly.

He was exceedingly uneasy.

The dawn had grown quite wan. He saw the hedges drooping wet down the grey mist. Then he told her about Maurice.

'Oh, you *shouldn't*!' she said. 'You should ha' put the ladder up for them, you *should*.'

'Well – I don't care.'

'Go and do it now – and I'll go.'

'No, don't you. Stop an' see our Maurice, go on, stop an' see him – then I s'll be able to tell him.'

She consented in silence. He had her promise she would not go before he returned. She adjusted her dress, found her way to the trough, where she performed her toilet.

Geoffrey wandered round to the upper field. The stacks looked wet in the mist, the hedge was drenched. Mist rose like steam from the grass, and the near hills were veiled almost to a shadow. In the valley, some peaks of black poplar showed fairly definite, jutting up. He shivered with chill.

There was no sound from the stacks, and he could see nothing. After all, he wondered, were they up there. But he reared the ladder to the place whence it had been swept, then went down the hedge to gather dry sticks. He was breaking off thin dead twigs under a holly tree when he heard, on the perfectly still air: 'Well I'm dashed!'

He listened intently. Maurice was awake.

'Sithee here!' the lad's voice exclaimed. Then, after a while, the foreign sound of the girl:

'What – oh, thair!'

'Aye, th' ladder's there, right enough.'

'You said it had fall down.'

'Well, I heard it drop – an' I couldna feel it nor see it.'

'You said it had fall down – you lie, you liar.'

'Nay, as true as I'm here –'

'You tell me lies – make me stay here – you tell me lies –' She was passionately indignant.

'As true as I'm standing here –' he began.

'Lies! – lies! – lies!' she cried. 'I don't believe you, never. You *mean*, you *mean*, *mean*, *mean*!'

'A' raïght, then!' he was now incensed, in his turn.

'You are bad, mean, mean, mean.'

'Are yer commin' down?' asked Maurice, coldly.

'No – I will not come with you – mean, to tell me lies.'

'Are ter commin' down?'

'No, I don't want you.'

'A' raïght, then!'

Geoffrey, peering through the holly tree, saw Maurice negotiating the ladder. The top rung was below the brim of the stack, and rested on the cloth, so it was dangerous to approach. The Fräulein watched him from the end of the stack, where the cloth thrown back showed the light, dry hay. He slipped slightly, she screamed. When he had got on to the ladder, he pulled the cloth away, throwing it back, making it easy for her to descend.

'Now are ter comin'?' he asked.

'No!' she shook her head violently, in a pet.

Geoffrey felt slightly contemptuous of her. But Maurice waited.

'Are ter comin'?' he called again.

'No,' she flashed, like a wild cat.

'All right, then I'm going.'

He descended. At the bottom, he stood holding the ladder.

'Come on, while I hold it steady,' he said.

There was no reply. For some minutes he stood patiently with his foot on the bottom rung of the ladder. He was pale, rather washed-out in his appearance, and he drew himself together with cold.

'Are ter commin', or aren't ter?' he asked at length. Still there was no reply.

'Then stop up till tha'rt ready,' he muttered, and he went away. Round the other side of the stacks he met Geoffrey.

'What, are thaïgh here?' he exclaimed.

'Bin here a' naïght,' replied Geoffrey. 'I come to help thee wi' th' cloth, but I found it on, an' th' ladder down, so I thowt tha'd gone.'

'Did ter put th' ladder up?'

'I did a bit sin.'

Maurice brooded over this, Geoffrey struggled with himself to get out his own news. At last he blurted:

'Tha knows that woman as wor here yis'day dinner – 'er come back, an' stopped i' th' shed a' night, out o' th' rain.'

'Oh – ah!' said Maurice, his eye kindling, and a smile crossing his pallor.

'An' I s'll gi'e her some breakfast.'

'Oh – ah!' repeated Maurice.

'It's th' man as is good-for-nowt, not her,' protested Geoffrey. Maurice did not feel in a position to cast stones.

'Tha pleases thysen,' he said, 'what ter does.' He was very quiet, unlike himself. He seemed bothered and anxious, as Geoffrey had not seen him before.

'What's up wi' thee?' asked the elder brother, who in his own heart was glad, and relieved.

'Nowt,' was the reply.

They went together to the hut. The woman was folding the blanket. She was fresh from washing, and looked very pretty. Her hair, instead of being screwed tightly back, was coiled in a knot low down, partly covering her ears. Before, she had deliberately made herself plain-looking: now she was neat and pretty, with a sweet, womanly gravity.

'Hello. I didn't think to find you here,' said Maurice, very awkwardly, smiling. She watched him gravely without reply. 'But it was better in shelter than outside, last night,' he added.

'Yes,' she replied.

'Shall you get a few more sticks?' Geoffrey asked him. It was a new thing for Geoffrey to be leader. Maurice obeyed. He wandered forth into the damp, raw morning. He did not go to the stack, as he shrank from meeting Paula.

At the mouth of the hut, Geoffrey was making the fire. The woman got out coffee from the box: Geoffrey set the tin to boil. They were arranging breakfast when Paula appeared. She was hatless. Bits of hay stuck in her hair, and she was white-faced – altogether, she did not show to advantage.

'Ah – you!' she exclaimed, seeing Geoffrey.

'Hello!' he answered. 'You're out early.'

'Where's Maurice?'

'I dunno, he should be back directly.'

Paula was silent.

'When have you come?' she asked.

'I come last night, but I could see nobody about. I got up half an hour sin', an' put th' ladder up ready to take the stack-cloth up.'

Paula understood, and was silent. When Maurice returned with the faggots, she was crouched warming her hands. She looked up at him, but he kept his eyes averted from her. Geoffrey met the eyes of Lydia, and smiled. Maurice put his hands to the fire.

'You cold?' asked Paula tenderly.

'A bit,' he answered, quite friendly, but reserved. And all the while the four sat round the fire, drinking their smoked coffee, eating each a small piece of toasted bacon, Paula watched eagerly for the eyes of Maurice, and he avoided her. He was gentle, but would not give his eyes to her looks. And Geoffrey smiled constantly to Lydia, who watched gravely.

The German girl succeeded in getting safely into the Vicarage, her escapade unknown to anyone save the housemaid. Before a week was out, she was openly engaged to Maurice, and when her month's notice expired, she went to live at the farm.

Geoffrey and Lydia kept faith one with the other.

The White Stocking

I

'I'M getting up, Teddilinks,' said Mrs Whiston, and she sprang out of bed briskly.

'What the Hanover's[1] got you?' asked Whiston.

'Nothing. Can't I get up?' she replied animatedly.

It was about seven o'clock, scarcely light yet in the cold bedroom. Whiston lay still and looked at his wife. She was a pretty little thing, with her fleecy, short black hair all tousled ... He watched her as she dressed quickly, flicking her small, delightful limbs, throwing her clothes about her. Her slovenliness and untidiness did not trouble him. When she picked up the edge of her petticoat, ripped off a torn string of white lace, and flung it on the dressing-table, her careless abandon made his spirit glow. She stood before the mirror and roughly scrambled together her profuse little mane of hair. He watched the quickness and softness of her young shoulders, calmly, like a husband, and appreciatively.

'Rise up,' she cried, turning to him with a quick wave of her arm – 'and shine forth.'

They had been married two years. But still, when she had gone out of the room, he felt as if all his light and warmth were taken away, he became aware of the raw, cold morning. So he rose himself, wondering casually what had roused her so early. Usually she lay in bed as late as she could.

Whiston fastened a belt round his loins and went downstairs in shirt and trousers. He heard her singing in her snatchy fashion. The stairs creaked under his weight. He passed down the narrow little passage, which she called a hall, of the seven and sixpenny house which was his first home.

He was a shapely young fellow of about twenty-eight, sleepy now and easy with well-being. He heard the water drumming into the kettle, and she began to whistle. He loved the quick way she dodged the supper cups under the tap to wash them for breakfast. She looked an untidy minx, but she was quick and handy enough.

'Teddilinks,' she cried.

'What?'

'Light a fire, quick.'

She wore an old, sack-like dressing-jacket of black silk pinned across her breast. But one of the sleeves, coming unfastened, showed some delightful pink upper-arm.

'Why don't you sew your sleeve up?' he said, suffering from the sight of the exposed soft flesh.

'Where?' she cried, peering round. 'Nuisance,' she said, seeing the gap, then with light fingers went on drying the cups.

The kitchen was of fair size, but gloomy. Whiston poked out the dead ashes.

Suddenly a thud was heard at the door down the passage.

'I'll go,' cried Mrs Whiston, and she was gone down the hall.

The postman was a ruddy-faced man who had been a soldier. He smiled broadly, handing her some packages.

'They've not forgot you,' he said impudently.

'No – lucky for them,' she said, with a toss of the head. But she was interested only in her envelopes this morning. The postman waited inquisitively, smiling in an ingratiating fashion. She slowly, abstractedly, as if she did not know anyone was there, closed the door in his face, continuing to look at the addresses on her letters.

She tore open the thin envelope. There was a long, hideous, cartoon valentine. She smiled briefly and dropped it on the floor. Struggling with the string of a packet, she opened a white cardboard box, and there lay a white silk handkerchief packed neatly under the paper lace of the box, and her initial, worked in heliotrope, fully displayed. She smiled pleasantly, and gently put the box aside. The third envelope contained another white packet – apparently a cotton handkerchief neatly folded. She shook it out. It was a long white stocking, but there was a little weight in the toe. Quickly, she thrust down her arm, wriggling her fingers into the toe of the stocking, and brought out a small box. She peeped inside the box, then hastily opened a door on her left hand, and went into the little, cold sitting-room. She had her lower lip caught earnestly between her teeth.

With a little flash of triumph, she lifted a pair of pearl ear-rings from the small box, and she went to the mirror. There, earnestly, she began to hook them through her ears, looking at herself sideways in the glass. Curiously concentrated and intent she seemed as she fingered the lobes of her ears, her head bent on one side.

Then the pearl ear-rings dangled under her rosy, small ears. She shook her head sharply, to see the swing of the drops. They went chill against her neck, in little, sharp touches. Then she stood still to look at herself, bridling her head in the dignified fashion. Then she simpered at herself. Catching her own eye, she could not help winking at herself and laughing.

She turned to look at the box. There was a scrap of paper with this posy:

'Pearls may be fair, but thou art fairer.
Wear these for me, and I'll love the wearer.'

She made a grimace and a grin. But she was drawn to the mirror again, to look at her ear-rings.

Whiston had made the fire burn, so he came to look for her. When she heard him, she started round quickly, guiltily. She was watching him with intent blue eyes when he appeared.

He did not see much, in his morning-drowsy warmth. He gave her, as ever, a feeling of warmth and slowness. His eyes were very blue, very kind, his manner simple.

'What ha' you got?' he asked.

'Valentines,' she said briskly, ostentatiously turning to show him the silk handkerchief. She thrust it under his nose. 'Smell how good,' she said.

'Who's that from?' he replied, without smelling.

'It's a valentine,' she cried. 'How do I know who it's from?'

'I'll bet you know,' he said.

'Ted! – I don't!' she cried, beginning to shake her head, then stopping because of the ear-rings.

He stood still a moment, displeased.

'They've no right to send you valentines, now,' he said.

'Ted! – Why not? You're not jealous, are you? I haven't the least idea who it's from. Look – there's my initial' – she pointed with an emphatic finger at the heliotrope embroidery –

'E for Elsie,
Nice little gelsie,'

she sang.

'Get out,' he said. 'You know who it's from.'

'Truth, I don't,' she cried.

He looked round, and saw the white stocking lying on a chair.

'Is this another?' he said.

'No, that's a sample,' she said. 'There's only a comic.' And she fetched in the long cartoon.

He stretched it out and looked at it solemnly.

'Fools!' he said, and went out of the room.

She flew upstairs and took off the ear-rings. When she returned, he was crouched before the fire blowing the coals. The skin of his face was flushed, and slightly pitted, as if he had had small-pox. But his neck was white and smooth and goodly. She hung her arms round his neck as he crouched there, and clung to him. He balanced on his toes.

'This fire's a slow-coach,' he said.

'And who else is a slow-coach?' she said.

'One of us two, I know,' he said, and he rose carefully. She remained clinging round his neck, so that she was lifted off her feet.

'Ha! – swing me,' she cried.

He lowered his head, and she hung in the air, swinging from his neck, laughing. Then she slipped off.

'The kettle is singing,' she sang, flying for the teapot. He bent down again to blow the fire. The veins in his neck stood out, his shirt collar seemed too tight.

'Doctor Wyer,
Blow the fire,
Puff! puff! puff!'

she sang, laughing.

He smiled at her.

She was so glad because of her pearl ear-rings.

Over the breakfast she grew serious. He did not notice. She became portentous in her gravity. Almost it penetrated through his steady good-humour to irritate him.

'Teddy!' she said at last.

'What?' he asked.

'I told you a lie,' she said, humbly tragic.

His soul stirred uneasily.

'Oh aye?' he said casually.

She was not satisfied. He ought to be more moved.

'Yes,' she said.

He cut a piece of bread.

'Was it a good one?' he asked.

She was piqued. Then she considered – *was* it a good one? Then she laughed.

'No,' she said, 'it wasn't up to much.'

'Ah!' he said easily, but with a steady strength of fondness for her in his tone. 'Get it out then.'

It became a little more difficult.

'You know that white stocking,' she said earnestly. 'I told you a lie. It wasn't a sample. It was a valentine.'

A little frown came on his brow.

'Then what did you invent it as a sample for?' he said. But he knew this weakness of hers. The touch of anger in his voice frightened her.

'I was afraid you'd be cross,' she said pathetically.

'I'll bet you were vastly afraid,' he said.

'I *was*, Teddy.'

There was a pause. He was resolving one or two things in his mind.

'And who sent it?' he asked.

'I can guess,' she said, 'though there wasn't a word with it – except –'

She ran to the sitting-room and returned with a slip of paper.

> 'Pearls may be fair, but thou art fairer.
> Wear these for me, and I'll love the wearer.'

He read it twice, then a dull red flush came on his face.

'And *who* do you guess it is?' he asked, with a ringing of anger in his voice.

'I suspect it's Sam Adams,' she said, with a little virtuous indignation.

Whiston was silent for a moment.

'Fool!' he said. 'An' what's it got to do with pearls? – and how can he say "wear these for me" when there's only one? He hasn't got the brain to invent a proper verse.'

He screwed the slip of paper into a ball and flung it into the fire.

'I suppose he thinks it'll make a pair with the one last year,' she said.

'Why, did he send one then?'

'Yes. I thought you'd be wild if you knew.'

His jaw set rather sullenly.

Presently he rose, and went to wash himself, rolling back his sleeves and pulling open his shirt at the breast. It was as if his fine, clear-cut temples and steady eyes were degraded by the lower, rather brutal part of his face. But she loved it. As she whisked about, clearing the table, she loved the way in which he stood washing himself. He was such a man. She liked to see his neck glistening with water as he swilled it. It amused her and pleased her and thrilled her. He was so sure, so permanent, he had her so utterly in his power. It gave her a delightful, mischievous sense of liberty. Within his grasp, she could dart about excitingly.

He turned round to her, his face red from the cold water, his eyes fresh and very blue.

'You haven't been seeing anything of him, have you?' he asked roughly.

'Yes,' she answered, after a moment, as if caught guilty. 'He got into the tram with me, and he asked me to drink a coffee and a Benedictine in the Royal.'

'You've got it off fine and glib,' he said sullenly. 'And did you?'

'Yes,' she replied, with the air of a traitor before the rack.

The blood came up into his neck and face, he stood motionless, dangerous.

'It was cold, and it was such fun to go into the Royal,' she said.

'You'd go off with a nigger for a packet of chocolate,' he said, in anger and contempt, and some bitterness. Queer how he drew away from her, cut her off from him.

'Ted – how beastly!' she cried. 'You know quite well –' She caught her lip, flushed, and the tears came to her eyes.

He turned away, to put on his necktie. She went about her work, making a queer pathetic little mouth, down which occasionally dripped a tear.

He was ready to go. With his hat jammed down on his head, and his overcoat buttoned up to his chin, he came to kiss her. He would be miserable all the day if he went without. She allowed herself to be kissed. Her cheek was wet under his lips, and his heart burned. She hurt him so deeply. And she felt aggrieved, and did not quite forgive him.

In a moment she went upstairs to her ear-rings. Sweet they looked nestling in the little drawer – sweet! She examined them with voluptuous pleasure, she threaded them in her ears, she looked at herself, she posed and postured and smiled, and looked sad and tragic and winning and appealing, all in turn before the mirror. And she was happy, and very pretty.

She wore her ear-rings all morning, in the house. She was self-conscious, and quite brilliantly winsome, when the baker came, wondering if he would notice. All the tradesmen left her door with a glow in them, feeling elated, and unconsciously favouring the delightful little creature, though there had been nothing to notice in her behaviour.

She was stimulated all the day. She did not think about her husband. He was the permanent basis from which she took these giddy little flights into nowhere. At night, like chickens and curses, she would come home to him, to roost.[2]

Meanwhile Whiston, a traveller and confidential support of a small firm, hastened about his work, his heart all the while anxious for her, yearning for surety, and kept tense by not getting it.

II

She had been a warehouse girl in Adams's lace factory before she was married. Sam Adams was her employer. He was a bachelor of forty, growing stout, a man well dressed and florid, with a large brown moustache and thin hair. From the rest of his well-groomed, showy appearance, it was evident his baldness was a chagrin to him. He had a good presence, and some Irish blood in his veins.

His fondness for the girls, or the fondness of the girls for him, was notorious. And Elsie, quick, pretty, almost witty little thing – she *seemed* witty, although, when her sayings were repeated, they were entirely trivial – she had a great attraction for him. He would come into the warehouse dressed in a rather sporting reefer coat, of fawn colour, and trousers of fine black-and-white check, a cap with a big peak and a scarlet carnation in his button-hole, to impress her. She was only half impressed. He was too loud for her good taste. Instinctively perceiving this, he sobered down to navy blue. Then a well-built man, florid, with large brown whiskers, smart navy blue suit, fashionable boots, and manly hat, he was the irreproachable. Elsie was impressed.

But meanwhile Whiston was courting her, and she made splendid little gestures, before her bedroom mirror, of the constant-and-true sort.

'True, true till death –'

That was her song. Whiston was made that way, so there was no need to take thought for him.

Every Christmas Sam Adams gave a party at his house, to which he invited his superior work-people – not factory hands and labourers, but those above. He was a generous man in his way, with a real warm feeling for giving pleasure.

Two years ago Elsie had attended this Christmas-party for the last time. Whiston had accompanied her. At that time he worked for Sam Adams.

She had been very proud of herself, in her close-fitting, full-skirted dress of blue silk. Whiston called for her. Then she tripped beside him, holding her large cashmere shawl across her breast. He strode with long strides, his trousers handsomely strapped under his boots, and her silk shoes bulging the pockets of his full-skirted overcoat.

They passed through the park gates, and her spirits rose. Above them the Castle Rock looked grandly in the night, the naked trees stood still and dark in the frost, along the boulevard.

They were rather late. Agitated with anticipation, in the cloak-room she gave up her shawl, donned her silk shoes, and looked at herself in the mirror. The loose bunches of curls on either side her face danced prettily, her mouth smiled.

She hung a moment in the door of the brilliantly lighted room. Many people were moving within the blaze of lamps, under the crystal chandeliers, the full skirts of the women balancing and floating, the side-whiskers and white cravats of the men bowing above. Then she entered the light.

In an instant Sam Adams was coming forward, lifting both his arms in boisterous welcome. There was a constant red laugh on his face.

'Come late, would you,' he shouted, 'like royalty.'

He seized her hands and led her forward. He opened his mouth wide when he spoke, and the effect of the warm, dark opening behind the brown whiskers was disturbing. But she was floating into the throng on his arm. He was very gallant.

'Now then,' he said, taking her card to write down the dances, 'I've got carte blanche, haven't I?'

'Mr Whiston doesn't dance,' she said.

'I am a lucky man!' he said, scribbling his initials. 'I was born with an *amourette*[3] in my mouth.'

He wrote on, quietly. She blushed and laughed, not knowing what it meant.

'Why, what is that?' she said.

'It's you, even littler than you are, dressed in little wings,' he said.

'I should have to be pretty small to get in your mouth,' she said.

'You think you're too big, do you!' he said easily.

He handed her her card, with a bow.

'Now I'm set up, my darling, for this evening,' he said.

Then, quick, always at his ease, he looked over the room. She waited in front of him. He was ready. Catching the eye of the band, he nodded. In a moment, the music began. He seemed to relax, giving himself up.

'Now then, Elsie,' he said, with a curious caress in his voice that seemed to lap the outside of her body in a warm glow, delicious. She gave herself to it. She liked it.

He was an excellent dancer. He seemed to draw her close in to him by some male warmth of attraction, so that she became all soft and pliant to him, flowing to his form, whilst he united her with him and they lapsed along in one movement. She was just carried in a kind of strong, warm flood, her feet moved of themselves, and only the music threw her away from him, threw her back to him, to his clasp, in his strong form moving against her, rhythmically, deliciously.

When it was over, he was pleased and his eyes had a curious gleam which thrilled her and yet had nothing to do with her. Yet it held her. He did not speak to her. He only looked straight into her eyes with a curious, gleaming look that disturbed her fearfully and deliciously. But also there was in his look some of the automatic irony of the *roué*. It left her partly cold. She was not carried away.

She went, driven by an opposite, heavier impulse, to Whiston. He stood looking gloomy, trying to admit that she had a perfect right to enjoy herself apart from him. He received her with rather grudging kindliness.

'Aren't you going to play whist?' she asked.

'Aye,' he said. 'Directly.'

'I do wish you could dance.'

'Well, I can't,' he said. 'So you enjoy yourself.'

'But I should enjoy it better if I could dance with you.'

'Nay, you're all right,' he said. 'I'm not made that way.'

'Then you ought to be!' she cried.

'Well, it's my fault, not yours. You enjoy yourself,' he bade her. Which she proceeded to do, a little bit irked.

She went with anticipation to the arms of Sam Adams, when the time came to dance with him. It *was* so gratifying, irrespective of the man. And she felt a little grudge against Whiston, soon forgotten when her host was holding her near to him, in a delicious embrace. And she watched his eyes, to meet the gleam in them, which gratified her.

She was getting warmed right through, the glow was penetrating into her, driving away everything else. Only in her heart was a little tightness, like conscience.

When she got a chance, she escaped from the dancing-room to the card-room. There, in a cloud of smoke, she found Whiston playing cribbage. Radiant, roused, animated, she came up to him and greeted him. She was too strong, too vibrant a note in the quiet room. He lifted his head, and a frown knitted his gloomy forehead.

'Are you playing cribbage? Is it exciting? How are you getting on?' she chattered.

He looked at her. None of these questions needed answering, and he did not feel in touch with her. She turned to the cribbage-board.

'Are you white or red?' she asked.

'He's red,' replied the partner.

'Then you're losing,' she said, still to Whiston. And she lifted the red peg from the board. 'One – two – three – four – five – six – seven – eight – Right up there you ought to jump –'

'Now put it back in its right place,' said Whiston.

'Where was it?' she asked gaily, knowing her transgression. He took the little red peg away from her and stuck it in its hole.

The cards were shuffled.

'What a shame you're losing!' said Elsie.

'You'd better cut for him,' said the partner.

She did so, hastily. The cards were dealt. She put her hand on his shoulder, looking at his cards.

'It's good,' she cried, 'isn't it?'

He did not answer, but threw down two cards. It moved him more strongly than was comfortable, to have her hand on his shoulder, her curls dangling and touching his ears, whilst she was roused to another man. It made the blood flame over him.

At that moment Sam Adams appeared, florid and boisterous, intoxicated more with himself, with the dancing, than with wine. In his eyes the curious, impersonal light gleamed.

'I thought I should find you here, Elsie,' he cried boisterously, a disturbing, high note in his voice.

'What made you think so?' she replied, the mischief rousing in her.

The florid, well-built man narrowed his eyes to a smile.

'I should never look for you among the ladies,' he said, with a kind of intimate, animal call to her. He laughed, bowed, and offered her his arm.

'Madam, the music waits.'

She went almost helplessly, carried along with him, unwilling, yet delighted.

That dance was an intoxication to her. After the first few steps, she felt herself slipping away from herself. She almost knew she was going, she did not even want to go. Yet she must have chosen to go. She lay in the arm of the steady, close man with whom she was dancing, and she seemed to swim away out of contact with the room, into him. She had passed into another, denser element of him, an essential privacy. The room was all vague around her, like an atmosphere, like under sea, with a flow of ghostly, dumb movements. But she herself was held real against her partner, and it seemed she was connected with him, as if the movements of his body and limbs were her own movements, yet not her own movements – and oh, delicious! He also was given up, oblivious, concentrated, into the dance. His eye was unseeing. Only his large, voluptuous body gave off a subtle activity. His fingers seemed to search into her flesh. Every moment, and every moment, she felt she would give way utterly, and sink molten: the fusion point was coming when she would fuse down into perfect unconsciousness at his feet and knees. But he bore her round the room in the dance, and he seemed to sustain all her body with his limbs, his body, and his warmth seemed to come closer into her, nearer, till it would fuse right through her, and she would be as liquid to him, as an intoxication only.

It was exquisite. When it was over, she was dazed, and was scarcely breathing. She stood with him in the middle of the room as if she were alone in a remote place. He bent over her. She expected his lips on her bare shoulder, and waited. Yet they were not alone, they were not alone. It was cruel.

''Twas good, wasn't it, my darling?' he said to her, low and delighted. There was a strange impersonality about his low, exultant call that appealed to her irresistibly. Yet why was she aware of some part shut off in her? She pressed his arm, and he led her towards the door.

She was not aware of what she was doing, only a little grain of resistant trouble was in her. The man, possessed, yet with a superficial presence of mind, made way to the dining-room, as if to give her refreshment, cunningly working to his own escape with her. He was molten hot, filmed over with presence of mind, and bottomed with cold disbelief.

In the dining-room was Whiston, carrying coffee to the plain, neglected ladies. Elsie saw him, but felt as if he could not see her. She was beyond his reach and ken. A sort of fusion existed between her and the large man at her side. She ate her custard, but an incomplete fusion all the while sustained and contained her within the being of her employer.

But she was growing cooler. Whiston came up. She looked at him, and saw him with different eyes. She saw his slim, young man's figure real and enduring before her. That was he. But she was in the spell with the other man, fused with him, and she could not be taken away.

'Have you finished your cribbage?' she asked, with hasty evasion of him.

'Yes,' he replied. 'Aren't you getting tired of dancing?'

'Not a bit,' she said.

'Not she,' said Adams heartily. 'No girl with any spirit gets tired of dancing. – Have something else, Elsie. Come – sherry. Have a glass of sherry with us, Whiston.'

Whilst they sipped the wine, Adams watched Whiston almost cunningly, to find his advantage.

'We'd better be getting back – there's the music,' he said. 'See the women get something to eat, Whiston, will you, there's a good chap.'

And he began to draw away. Elsie was drifting helplessly with him. But Whiston put himself beside them, and went along with them. In silence they passed through to the dancing-room. There Adams hesitated, and looked round the room. It was as if he could not see.

A man came hurrying forward, claiming Elsie, and Adams went to his other partner. Whiston stood watching during the dance. She was conscious of him standing there observant of her, like a ghost, or a judgment, or a guardian angel. She was also conscious, much more intimately and impersonally, of the body of the other man moving somewhere in the room. She still belonged to him, but a feeling of distraction possessed her, and helplessness. Adams danced on, adhering to Elsie, waiting his time, with the persistence of cynicism.

The dance was over. Adams was detained. Elsie found herself beside Whiston. There was something shapely about him as he sat, about his knees and his distinct figure, that she clung to. It was as if he had enduring form. She put her hand on his knee.

'Are you enjoying yourself?' he asked.

'*Ever* so,' she replied, with a fervent, yet detached tone.

'It's going on for one o'clock,' he said.

'Is it?' she answered. It meant nothing to her.

'Should we be going?' he said.

She was silent. For the first time for an hour or more an inkling of her normal consciousness returned. She resented it.

'What for?' she said.

'I thought you might have had enough,' he said.

A slight soberness came over her, an irritation at being frustrated of her illusion.

'Why?' she said.

'We've been here since nine,' he said.

That was no answer, no reason. It conveyed nothing to her. She sat detached from him. Across the room Sam Adams glanced at her. She sat there exposed for him.

'You don't want to be too free with Sam Adams,' said Whiston cautiously, suffering. 'You know what he is.'

'How, free?' she asked.

'Why – you don't want to have too much to do with him.'

She sat silent. He was forcing her into consciousness of her position. But he could not get hold of her feelings, to change them. She had a curious, perverse desire that he should not.

'I like him,' she said.

'What do you find to like in him?' he said, with a hot heart.

'I don't know – but I like him,' she said.

She was immutable. He sat feeling heavy and dulled with rage. He was not clear as to what he felt. He sat there unliving whilst she danced. And she, distracted, lost to herself between the opposing forces of the two men, drifted. Between the dances, Whiston kept near to her. She was scarcely conscious. She glanced repeatedly at her card, to see when she would dance again with Adams, half in desire, half in dread. Sometimes she met his steady, glaucous eye as she passed him in the dance. Sometimes she saw the steadiness of his flank as he danced. And it was always as if she rested on his arm, were borne along, upborne by him, away from herself. And always there was present the other's antagonism. She was divided.

The time came for her to dance with Adams. Oh, the delicious closing of contact with him, of his limbs touching her limbs, his arm supporting her. She seemed to resolve. Whiston had not made himself real to her. He was only a heavy place in her consciousness.

But she breathed heavily, beginning to suffer from the closeness of strain. She was nervous. Adams also was constrained. A tightness, a tension was coming over them all. And he was exasperated, feeling something counteracting physical magnetism, feeling a will stronger with her than his own, intervening in what was becoming a vital necessity to him.

Elsie was almost lost to her own control. As she went forward with him to take her place at the dance, she stooped for her pocket-handkerchief. The music sounded for quadrilles. Everybody was ready. Adams stood with his body near her, exerting his attraction over her. He was tense and fighting. She stooped for her pocket-handkerchief, and shook it as she rose. It shook out and fell from her hand. With agony, she saw she had taken a white stocking instead of a handkerchief. For a second it lay on the floor, a twist of white stocking. Then, in an instant, Adams picked it up, with a little, surprised laugh of triumph.

'That'll do for me,' he whispered – seeming to take possession of her. And he stuffed the stocking in his trousers pocket, and quickly offered her his handkerchief.

The dance began. She felt weak and faint, as if her will were turned to water. A heavy sense of loss came over her. She could not help herself anymore. But it was peace.

When the dance was over, Adams yielded her up. Whiston came to her.

'What was it as you dropped?' Whiston asked.

'I thought it was my handkerchief – I'd taken a stocking by mistake,' she said, detached and muted.

'And he's got it?'

'Yes.'

'What does he mean by that?'

She lifted her shoulders.

'Are you going to let him keep it?' he asked.

'I don't let him.'

There was a long pause.

'Am I to go and have it out with him?' he asked, his face flushed, his blue eyes going hard with opposition.

'No,' she said, pale.

'Why?'

'No – I don't want to say anything about it.'

He sat exasperated and nonplussed.

'You'll let him keep it, then?' he asked.

She sat silent and made no form of answer.

'What do you mean by it?' he said, dark with fury. And he started up.

'No!' she cried. 'Ted!' And she caught hold of him, sharply detaining him.

It made him black with rage.

'Why?' he said.

Then something about her mouth was pitiful to him. He did not understand, but he felt she must have her reasons.

'Then I'm not stopping here,' he said. 'Are you coming with me?'

She rose mutely, and they went out of the room. Adams had not noticed.

In a few moments they were in the street.

'What the hell do you mean?' he said, in a black fury.

She went at his side, in silence, neutral.

'That great hog, an' all,' he added.

Then they went a long time in silence through the frozen, deserted darkness of the town. She felt she could not go indoors. They were drawing near her house.

'I don't want to go home,' she suddenly cried in distress and anguish. 'I don't want to go home.'

He looked at her.

'Why don't you?' he said.

'I don't want to go home,' was all she could sob.

He heard somebody coming.

'Well, we can walk a bit further,' he said.

She was silent again. They passed out of the town into the fields. He held her by the arm – they could not speak.

'What's a-matter?' he asked at length, puzzled.

She began to cry again.

At last he took her in his arms, to soothe her. She sobbed by herself, almost unaware of him.

'Tell me what's a-matter, Elsie,' he said. 'Tell me what's a-matter – my dear – tell me, then –'

He kissed her wet face, and caressed her. She made no response. He was puzzled and tender and miserable.

At length she became quiet. Then he kissed her, and she put her arms round him, and clung to him very tight, as if for fear and anguish. He held her in his arms, wondering.

'Ted!' she whispered, frantic. 'Ted!'

'What, my love?' he answered, becoming also afraid.

'Be good to me,' she cried. 'Don't be cruel to me.'

'No, my pet,' he said, amazed and grieved. 'Why?'

'Oh, be good to me,' she sobbed.

And he held her very safe, and his heart was white-hot with love for her. His mind was amazed. He could only hold her against his chest that was white-hot with love and belief in her. So she was restored at last.

III

She refused to go to her work at Adams's any more. Her father had to submit and she sent in her notice – she was not well. Sam Adams was ironical. But he had a curious patience. He did not fight.

In a few weeks, she and Whiston were married. She loved him with passion and worship, a fierce little abandon of love that moved him to the depths of his being, and gave him a permanent surety and sense of realness in himself. He did not trouble about himself any more: he felt he was fulfilled and now he had only the many things in the world to busy himself about. Whatever troubled him, at the bottom was surety. He had found himself in this love.

They spoke once or twice of the white stocking.

'Ah!' Whiston exclaimed. 'What does it matter?'

He was impatient and angry, and could not bear to consider the matter. So it was left unresolved.

She was quite happy at first, carried away by her adoration of her husband. Then gradually she got used to him. He always was the ground of her happiness, but she got used to him, as to the air she breathed. He never got used to her in the same way.

Inside of marriage she found her liberty. She was rid of the responsibility of herself. Her husband must look after that. She was free to get what she could out of her time.

So that, when, after some months, she met Sam Adams, she was not quite as unkind to him as she might have been. With a young wife's new and exciting knowledge of men, she perceived he was in love with her, she knew he had always kept an unsatisfied desire for her. And, sportive, she could not help playing a little with this, though she cared not one jot for the man himself.

When Valentine's day came, which was near the first anniversary of her wedding day, there arrived a white stocking with a little amethyst brooch. Luckily Whiston did not see it, so she said nothing of it to him. She had not the faintest intention of having anything to do with Sam Adams, but once a little brooch was in her possession, it was hers, and she did not trouble her head for a moment how she had come by it. She kept it.

Now she had the pearl ear-rings. They were a more valuable and a more conspicuous present. She would have to ask her mother to give them to her, to explain their presence. She made a little plan in her head. And she was extraordinarily pleased. As for Sam Adams, even if he saw her wearing them, he would not give her away. What fun, if he saw her wearing his ear-rings! She would pretend she had inherited them from her grandmother, her mother's mother. She laughed to herself as she went down town in the afternoon, the pretty drops dangling in front of her curls. But she saw no one of importance.

Whiston came home tired and depressed. All day the male in him had been uneasy, and this had fatigued him. She was curiously against him, inclined, as she sometimes was nowadays, to make mock of him and jeer at him and cut him off. He did not understand this, and it angered him deeply. She was uneasy before him.

She knew he was in a state of suppressed irritation. The veins stood out on the backs of his hands, his brow was drawn stiffly. Yet she could not help goading him.

'What did you do wi' that white stocking?' he asked, out of a gloomy silence, his voice strong and brutal.

'I put it in a drawer – why?' she replied flippantly.

'Why didn't you put it on the fire back?' he said harshly. 'What are you hoarding it up for?'

'I'm not hoarding it up,' she said. 'I've got a pair.'

He relapsed into gloomy silence. She, unable to move him, ran away upstairs, leaving him smoking by the fire. Again she tried on the ear-rings. Then another little inspiration came to her. She drew on the white stockings, both of them.

Presently she came down in them. Her husband still sat immovable and glowering by the fire.

'Look!' she said. 'They'll do beautifully.'

And she picked up her skirts to her knees, and twisted round, looking at her pretty legs in the neat stockings.

He filled with unreasonable rage, and took the pipe from his mouth.

'Don't they look nice?' she said. 'One from last year and one from this, they just do. Save you buying a pair.'

And she looked over her shoulders at her pretty calves, and the dangling frills of her knickers.

'Put your skirts down and don't make a fool of yourself,' he said.

'Why a fool of myself?' she asked.

And she began to dance slowly round the room, kicking up her feet half reckless, half jeering, in a ballet-dancer's fashion. Almost fearfully, yet in defiance, she kicked up her legs at him, singing as she did so. She resented him.

'You little fool, ha' done with it,' he said. 'And you'll backfire them stockings, I'm telling you.' He was angry. His face flushed dark, he kept his head bent. She ceased to dance.

'I shan't,' she said. 'They'll come in very useful.'

He lifted his head and watched her, with lighted, dangerous eyes.

'You'll put 'em on the fire back, I tell you,' he said.

It was a war now. She bent forward, in a ballet-dancer's fashion, and put her tongue between her teeth.

'I shan't backfire them stockings,' she sang, repeating his words, 'I shan't, I shan't, I shan't.'

And she danced round the room doing a high kick to the tune of her words. There was a real biting indifference in her behaviour.

'We'll see whether you will or not,' he said, 'trollops! You'd like Sam Adams to know you was wearing 'em, wouldn't you? That's what would please you.'

'Yes, I'd like him to see how nicely they fit me, he might give me some more then.'

And she locked down at her pretty legs.

He knew somehow that she *would* like Sam Adams to see how pretty her legs looked in the white stockings. It made his anger go deep, almost to hatred.

'Yer nasty trolley,' he cried. 'Put yer petticoats down, and stop being so foul-minded.'

'I'm not foul-minded,' she said. 'My legs are my own. And why shouldn't Sam Adams think they're nice?'

There was a pause. He watched her with eyes glittering to a point.

'Have you been havin' owt to do with him?' he asked.

'I've just spoken to him when I've seen him,' she said. 'He's not as bad as you would make out.'

'Isn't he?' he cried, a certain wakefulness in his voice. 'Them who has anything to do wi' him is too bad for me, I tell you.'

'Why, what are you frightened of him for?' she mocked.

She was rousing all his uncontrollable anger. He sat glowering. Every one of her sentences stirred him up like a red-hot iron. Soon it would be too much. And she was afraid herself; but she was neither conquered nor convinced.

A curious little grin of hate came on his face. He had a long score against her.

'What am I frightened of him for?' he repeated automatically. 'What am I frightened of him for? Why, for you, you stray-running little bitch.'

She flushed. The insult went deep into her, right home.

'Well, if you're so dull –' she said, lowering her eyelids, and speaking coldly, haughtily.

'If I'm so dull I'll break your neck the first word you speak to him,' he said, tense.

'Pf!' she sneered. 'Do you think I'm frightened of you?' She spoke coldly, detached.

She was frightened, for all that, white round the mouth.

His heart was getting hotter.

'You *will* be frightened of me, the next time you have anything to do with him,' he said.

'Do you think *you'd* ever be told – ha!'

Her jeering scorn made him go white-hot, molten. He knew he was incoherent, scarcely responsible for what he might do. Slowly, unseeing, he rose and went out of doors, stifled, moved to kill her.

He stood leaning against the garden fence, unable either to see or hear. Below him, far off, fumed the lights of the town. He stood still, unconscious with a black storm of rage, his face lifted to the night.

Presently, still unconscious of what he was doing, he went indoors again. She stood, a small stubborn figure with tight-pressed lips and big, sullen, childish eyes, watching him, white with fear. He went heavily across the floor and dropped into his chair.

There was a silence.

'*You're* not going to tell me everything I shall do, and everything I shan't,' she broke out at last.

He lifted his head.

'I tell you *this*,' he said, low and intense. 'Have anything to do with Sam Adams, and I'll break your neck.'

She laughed, shrill and false.

'How I hate your word "break your neck",' she said, with a grimace of the mouth. 'It sounds so common and beastly. Can't you say something else –'

There was a dead silence.

'And besides,' she said, with a queer chirrup of mocking laughter, 'what do you know about anything? He sent me an amethyst brooch and a pair of pearl ear-rings.'

'He what?' said Whiston, in a suddenly normal voice. His eyes were fixed on her.

'Sent me a pair of pearl ear-rings, and an amethyst brooch,' she repeated, mechanically, pale to the lips.

And her big, black, childish eyes watched him, fascinated, held in her spell.

He seemed to thrust his face and his eyes forward at her, as he rose slowly and came to her. She watched transfixed in terror. Her throat made a small sound, as she tried to scream.

Then, quick as lightning, the back of his hand struck her with a crash across the mouth, and she was flung back blinded against the wall. The shock shook a queer sound out of her. And then she saw him still coming on, his eyes holding her, his fist drawn back, advancing slowly. At any instant the blow might crash into her.

Mad with terror, she raised her hands with a queer clawing movement to cover her eyes and her temples, opening her mouth in a dumb shriek. There was no sound. But the sight of her slowly arrested him. He hung before her, looking at her fixedly, as she stood crouched against the wall with open, bleeding mouth, and wide-staring eyes, and two hands clawing over her temples. And his lust to see her bleed, to break her and destroy her, rose from an old source against her. It carried him. He wanted satisfaction.

But he had seen her standing there, a piteous, horrified thing, and he turned his face aside in shame and nausea. He went and sat heavily in his chair, and a curious ease, almost like sleep, came over his brain.

She walked away from the wall towards the fire, dizzy, white to the lips, mechanically wiping her small, bleeding mouth. He sat motionless. Then, gradually, her breath began to hiss, she shook, and was sobbing silently, in grief for herself. Without looking, he saw. It made his mad desire to destroy her come back.

At length he lifted his head. His eyes were glowing again, fixed on her.

'And what did he give them you for?' he asked, in a steady, unyielding voice.

Her crying dried up in a second. She also was tense.

'They came as valentines,' she replied, still not subjugated, even if beaten.

'When, to-day?'

'The pearl ear-rings to-day – the amethyst brooch last year.'

'You've had it a year?'

'Yes.'

She felt that now nothing would prevent him if he rose to kill her. She could not prevent him any more. She was yielded up to him. They both trembled in the balance, unconscious.

'What have you had to do with him?' he asked, in a barren voice.

'I've not had anything to do with him,' she quavered.

'You just kept 'em because they were jewellery?' he said.

A weariness came over him. What was the worth of speaking any more of it? He did not care any more. He was dreary and sick.

She began to cry again, but he took no notice. She kept wiping her mouth on her handkerchief. He could see it, the blood-mark. It made him only more sick and tired of the responsibility of it, the violence, the shame.

When she began to move about again, he raised his head once more from his dead, motionless position.

'Where are the things?' he said.

'They are upstairs,' she quavered. She knew the passion had gone down in him.

'Bring them down,' he said.

'I won't,' she wept, with rage. 'You're not going to bully me and hit me like that on the mouth.'

And she sobbed again. He looked at her in contempt and compassion and in rising anger.

'Where are they?' he said.

'They're in the little drawer under the looking-glass,' she sobbed.

He went slowly upstairs, struck a match, and found the trinkets. He brought them downstairs in his hand.

'These?' he said, looking at them as they lay in his palm.

She looked at them without answering. She was not interested in them any more.

He looked at the little jewels. They were pretty.

'It's none of their fault,' he said to himself.

And he searched round slowly, persistently, for a box. He tied the things up and addressed them to Sam Adams. Then he went out in his slippers to post the little package.

When he came back she was still sitting crying.

'You'd better go to bed,' he said.

She paid no attention. He sat by the fire. She still cried.

'I'm sleeping down here,' he said. 'Go you to bed.'

In a few moments she lifted her tear-stained, swollen face and looked at him with eyes all forlorn and pathetic. A great flash of anguish went over his body. He went over, slowly, and very gently took her in his hands. She let herself be taken. Then as she lay against his shoulder, she sobbed aloud:

'I never meant –'

'My love – my little love –' he cried, in anguish of spirit, holding her in his arms.

Odour of Chrysanthemums

I

THE small locomotive engine, Number 4, came clanking, stumbling down from Selston with seven full waggons. It appeared round the corner with loud threats of speed, but the colt that it startled from among the gorse, which still flickered indistinctly in the raw afternoon, outdistanced it at a canter. A woman, walking up the railway line to Underwood, drew back into the hedge, held her basket aside, and watched the footplate of the engine advancing. The trucks thumped heavily past, one by one, with slow inevitable movement, as she stood insignificantly trapped between the jolting black waggons and the hedge; then they curved away towards the coppice where the withered oak leaves dropped noiselessly, while the birds, pulling at the scarlet hips beside the track, made off into the dusk that had already crept into the spinney. In the open, the smoke from the engine sank and cleaved to the rough grass. The fields were dreary and forsaken, and in the marshy strip that led to the whimsey, a reedy pit-pond, the fowls had already abandoned their run among the alders, to roost in the tarred fowl-house. The pit-bank loomed up beyond the pond, flames like red sores licking its ashy sides, in the afternoon's stagnant light. Just beyond rose the tapering chimneys and the clumsy black head-stocks of Brinsley Colliery. The two wheels were spinning fast up against the sky, and the winding-engine rapped out its little spasms. The miners were being turned up.

The engine whistled as it came into the wide bay of railway lines beside the colliery, where rows of trucks stood in harbour.

Miners, single, trailing and in groups, passed like shadows diverging home. At the edge of the ribbed level of sidings squat a low cottage, three steps down from the cinder track. A large bony vine clutched at the house, as if to claw down the tiled roof. Round the bricked yard grew a few wintry primroses. Beyond, the long garden sloped down to a bush-covered brook course. There were some twiggy apple trees, winter-crack trees, and ragged cabbages. Beside the path hung dishevelled pink chrysanthemums, like pink cloths hung on bushes. A woman came stooping out of the felt-covered fowl-house, half-way down the garden. She closed and padlocked the door, then drew herself erect, having brushed some bits from her white apron.

She was a tall woman of imperious mien, handsome, with definite black eyebrows. Her smooth black hair was parted exactly. For a few moments she stood steadily watching the miners as they passed along the railway: then she turned towards the brook course. Her face was calm and set, her mouth was closed with disillusionment. After a moment she called:

'John!' There was no answer. She waited, and then said distinctly:

'Where are you?'

'Here!' replied a child's sulky voice from among the bushes. The woman looked piercingly through the dusk.

'Are you at that brook?' she asked sternly.

For answer the child showed himself before the raspberry-canes that rose like whips. He was a small, sturdy boy of five. He stood quite still, defiantly.

'Oh!' said the mother, conciliated. 'I thought you were down at that wet brook – and you remember what I told you –'

The boy did not move or answer.

'Come, come on in,' she said more gently, 'it's getting dark. There's your grandfather's engine coming down the line!'

The lad advanced slowly, with resentful, taciturn movement. He was dressed in trousers and waistcoat of cloth that was too thick and hard for the size of the garments. They were evidently cut down from a man's clothes.

As they went slowly towards the house he tore at the ragged wisps of chrysanthemums and dropped the petals in handfuls along the path.

'Don't do that – it does look nasty,' said his mother. He refrained, and she, suddenly pitiful, broke off a twig with three or four wan flowers and held them against her face. When mother and son reached the yard her hand hesitated, and instead of laying the flower aside, she pushed it in her apron-band. The mother and son stood at the foot of the three steps looking across the bay of lines at the passing home of the miners. The trundle of the small train was imminent. Suddenly the engine loomed past the house and came to a stop opposite the gate.

The engine-driver, a short man with round grey beard, leaned out of the cab high above the woman.

'Have you got a cup of tea?' he said in a cheery, hearty fashion.

It was her father. She went in, saying she would mash. Directly, she returned.

'I didn't come to see you on Sunday,' began the little grey-bearded man.

'I didn't expect you,' said his daughter.

The engine-driver winced; then, reassuming his cheery, airy manner, he said:

'Oh, have you heard then? Well, and what do you think –?'

'I think it is soon enough,' she replied.

At her brief censure the little man made an impatient gesture, and said coaxingly, yet with dangerous coldness:

'Well, what's a man to do? It's no sort of life for a man of my years, to sit at my own hearth like a stranger. And if I'm going to marry again it may as well be soon as late – what does it matter to anybody?'

The woman did not reply, but turned and went into the house. The man in the engine-cab stood assertive, till she returned with a cup of tea and a piece of bread and butter on a plate. She went up the steps and stood near the footplate of the hissing engine.

'You needn't 'a' brought me bread an' butter,' said her father. 'But a cup of tea' – he sipped appreciatively – 'it's very nice.' He sipped for a moment or two, then: 'I hear as Walter's got another bout on,' he said.

'When hasn't he?' said the woman bitterly.

'I heered tell of him in the "Lord Nelson" braggin' as he was going to spend that b— afore he went: half a sovereign that was.'

'When?' asked the woman.

'A' Sat'day night – I know that's true.'

'Very likely,' she laughed bitterly. 'He gives me twenty-three shillings.'

'Aye, it's a nice thing, when a man can do nothing with his money but make a beast of himself!' said the grey-whiskered man. The woman turned her head away. Her father swallowed the last of his tea and handed her the cup.

'Aye,' he sighed, wiping his mouth. 'It's a settler, it is –'

He put his hand on the lever. The little engine strained and groaned, and the train rumbled towards the crossing. The woman again looked across the metals. Darkness was settling over the spaces of the railway and trucks: the miners, in grey sombre groups, were still passing home. The winding-engine pulsed hurriedly, with brief pauses. Elizabeth Bates looked at the dreary flow of men, then she went indoors. Her husband did not come.

The kitchen was small and full of firelight; red coals piled glowing up the chimney mouth. All the life of the room seemed in the white, warm hearth and the steel fender reflecting the red fire. The cloth was laid for tea; cups glinted in the shadows. At the back, where the lowest stairs protruded into the room, the boy sat struggling with a knife and a piece of whitewood. He was almost hidden in the shadow. It was half-past four. They had but to await the father's coming to begin tea. As the mother watched her son's sullen little struggle with the wood, she saw herself in his silence and pertinacity; she saw the father in her child's indifference to all but himself. She seemed to be occupied by her husband. He had probably gone past his home, slunk past his own door, to drink before he came in, while his dinner spoiled and wasted in waiting. She glanced at the clock, then took the potatoes to strain them in the yard. The garden and fields beyond the brook were closed in uncertain darkness. When she rose with the saucepan, leaving the drain steaming into the night behind her, she saw the yellow lamps were lit along the high road that went up the hill away beyond the space of the railway lines and the field.

Then again she watched the men trooping home, fewer now and fewer.

Indoors the fire was sinking and the room was dark red. The woman put her saucepan on the hob, and set a batter pudding near the mouth of the oven. Then she stood unmoving. Directly, gratefully, came quick young steps to the door. Someone hung on the latch a moment, then a little girl entered and began pulling off her outdoor things, dragging a mass of curls, just ripening from gold to brown, over her eyes with her hat.

Her mother chid her for coming late from school, and said she would have to keep her at home the dark winter days.

'Why, mother, it's hardly a bit dark yet. The lamp's not lighted, and my father's not home.'

'No, he isn't. But it's a quarter to five! Did you see anything of him?'

The child became serious. She looked at her mother with large, wistful blue eyes.

'No, mother, I've never seen him. Why? Has he come up an' gone past, to Old Brinsley? He hasn't, mother, 'cos I never saw him.'

'He'd watch that,' said the mother bitterly, 'he'd take care as you didn't see him. But you may depend upon it, he's seated in the "Prince o' Wales". He wouldn't be this late.'

The girl looked at her mother piteously.

'Let's have our teas, mother, should we?' said she.

The mother called John to table. She opened the door once more and looked out across the darkness of the lines. All was deserted: she could not hear the winding-engines.

'Perhaps,' she said to herself, 'he's stopped to get some ripping[1] done.'

They sat down to tea. John, at the end of the table near the door, was almost lost in the darkness. Their faces were hidden from each other. The girl crouched against the fender slowly moving a thick piece of bread before the fire. The lad, his face a dusky mark on the shadow, sat watching her who was transfigured in the red glow.

'I do think it's beautiful to look in the fire,' said the child.

'Do you?' said her mother. 'Why?'

'It's so red, and full of little caves – and it feels so nice, and you can fair smell it.'

'It'll want mending directly,' replied her mother, 'and then if your father comes he'll carry on and say there never is a fire when a man comes home sweating from the pit. – A public-house is always warm enough.'

There was silence till the boy said complainingly: 'Make haste, our Annie.'

'Well, I am doing! I can't make the fire do it no faster, can I?'

'She keeps wafflin' it about so's to make 'er slow,' grumbled the boy.

'Don't have such an evil imagination, child,' replied the mother.

Soon the room was busy in the darkness with the crisp sound of crunching. The mother ate very little. She drank her tea determinedly, and sat thinking. When she rose her anger was evident in the stern unbending of her head. She looked at the pudding in the fender, and broke out:

'It is a scandalous thing as a man can't even come home to his dinner! If it's crozzled up to a cinder I don't see why I should care. Past his very door he goes to get to a public-house, and here I sit with his dinner waiting for him –'

She went out. As she dropped piece after piece of coal on the red fire, the shadows fell on the walls, till the room was almost in total darkness.

'I canna see,' grumbled the invisible John. In spite of herself, the mother laughed.

'You know the way to your mouth,' she said. She set the dustpan outside the door. When she came again like a shadow on the hearth, the lad repeated, complaining sulkily:

'I canna see.'

'Good gracious!' cried the mother irritably, 'you're as bad as your father if it's a bit dusk!'

Nevertheless she took a paper spill from a sheaf on the mantelpiece and proceeded to light the lamp that hung from the ceiling in the middle of the room. As she reached up, her figure displayed itself just rounding with maternity.

'Oh, mother – !' exclaimed the girl.

'What?' said the woman, suspended in the act of putting the lamp glass over the flame. The copper reflector shone handsomely on her, as she stood with uplifted arm, turning to face her daughter.

'You've got a flower in your apron!' said the child, in a little rapture at this unusual event.

'Goodness me!' exclaimed the woman, relieved. 'One would think the house was afire.' She replaced the glass and waited a moment before turning up the wick. A pale shadow was seen floating vaguely on the floor.

'Let me smell!' said the child, still rapturously, coming forward and putting her face to her mother's waist.

'Go along, silly!' said the mother, turning up the lamp. The light revealed their suspense so that the woman felt it almost unbearable. Annie was still bending at her waist. Irritably, the mother took the flowers out from her apron-band.

'Oh, mother – don't take them out!' Annie cried, catching her hand and trying to replace the sprig.

'Such nonsense!' said the mother, turning away. The child put the pale chrysanthemums to her lips, murmuring:

'Don't they smell beautiful!'

Her mother gave a short laugh.

'No,' she said, 'not to me. It was chrysanthemums when I married him, and chrysanthemums when you were born, and the first time they ever brought him home drunk, he'd got brown chrysanthemums in his button-hole.'

She looked at the children. Their eyes and their parted lips were wondering. The mother sat rocking in silence for some time. Then she looked at the clock.

'Twenty minutes to six!' In a tone of fine bitter carelessness she continued: 'Eh, he'll not come now till they bring him. There he'll stick! But he needn't come rolling in here in his pit-dirt, for *I* won't wash him. He can lie on the floor – Eh, what a fool I've been, what a fool! And this is what I came here for, to this dirty hole, rats and all, for him to slink past his very door. Twice last week – he's begun now –'

She silenced herself, and rose to clear the table.

While for an hour or more the children played, subduedly intent, fertile of imagination, united in fear of the mother's wrath, and in dread of their father's home-coming, Mrs Bates sat in her rocking-chair making a 'singlet' of thick cream-coloured flannel, which gave a dull wounded sound as she tore off the grey edge. She worked at her sewing with energy, listening to the children, and her anger wearied itself, lay down to rest, opening its eyes from time to time and steadily watching, its ears raised to listen. Sometimes even her anger quailed and shrank, and the mother suspended her sewing, tracing the footsteps that thudded along the sleepers outside; she would lift her head sharply to bid the children 'hush', but she recovered herself in time, and the footsteps went past the gate, and the children were not flung out of their playing world.

But at last Annie sighed, and gave in. She glanced at her waggon of slippers, and loathed the game. She turned plaintively to her mother.

'Mother!' – but she was inarticulate.

John crept out like a frog from under the sofa. His mother glanced up.

'Yes,' she said, 'just look at those shirt-sleeves!'

The boy held them out to survey them, saying nothing. Then somebody called in a hoarse voice away down the line, and suspense bristled in the room, till two people had gone by outside, talking.

'It is time for bed,' said the mother.

'My father hasn't come,' wailed Annie plaintively. But her mother was primed with courage.

'Never mind. They'll bring him when he does come – like a log.' She meant there would be no scene. 'And he may sleep on the floor till he wakes himself. I know he'll not go to work tomorrow after this!'

The children had their hands and faces wiped with a flannel. They were very quiet. When they had put on their nightdresses, they said their prayers, the boy mumbling. The mother looked down at them, at the brown silken bush of intertwining curls in the nape of the girl's neck, at the little black head of the lad, and her heart burst with anger at their father who caused all three such distress. The children hid their faces in her skirts for comfort.

When Mrs Bates came down, the room was strangely empty, with a tension of expectancy. She took up her sewing and stitched for some time without raising her head. Meantime her anger was tinged with fear.

II

The clock struck eight and she rose suddenly, dropping her sewing on her chair. She went to the stairfoot door, opened it, listening. Then she went out, locking the door behind her.

Something scuffled in the yard, and she started, though she knew it was only the rats with which the place was overrun. The night was very dark. In the great bay of railway lines, bulked with trucks, there was no trace of light, only away back she could see a few yellow lamps at the pit-top, and the red smear of the burning pit-bank on the night. She hurried along the edge of the track, then, crossing the converging lines, came to the stile by the white gates, whence she emerged on the road. Then the fear which had led her shrank. People were walking up to New Brinsley; she saw the lights in the houses; twenty yards further on were the broad windows of the 'Prince of Wales', very warm and bright, and the loud voices of men could be heard distinctly. What a fool she had been to imagine that anything had happened to him! He was merely drinking over there at the 'Prince of Wales'. She faltered. She had never yet been to fetch him, and she never would go. So she continued her walk towards the long straggling line of houses, standing blank on the highway. She entered a passage between the dwellings.

'Mr Rigley? – Yes! Did you want him? No, he's not in at this minute.'

The raw-boned woman leaned forward from her dark scullery and peered at the other, upon whom fell a dim light through the blind of the kitchen window.

'Is it Mrs Bates?' she asked in a tone tinged with respect.

'Yes. I wondered if your Master was at home. Mine hasn't come yet.'

''Asn't 'e! Oh, Jack's been 'ome an 'ad 'is dinner an' gone out. E's just gone for 'alf an hour afore bedtime. Did you call at the "Prince of Wales"?'

'No –'

'No, you didn't like – ! It's not very nice.' The other woman was indulgent. There was an awkward pause. 'Jack never said nothink about – about your Mester,' she said.

'No! – I expect he's stuck in there!'

Elizabeth Bates said this bitterly, and with recklessness. She knew that the woman across the yard was standing at her door listening, but she did not care. As she turned:

'Stop a minute! I'll just go an' ask Jack if e' knows anythink,' said Mrs Rigley.

'Oh, no – I wouldn't like to put – !'

'Yes, I will, if you'll just step inside an' see as th' childer doesn't come downstairs and set theirselves afire.'

Elizabeth Bates, murmuring a remonstrance, stepped inside. The other woman apologized for the state of the room.

The kitchen needed apology. There were little frocks and trousers and childish undergarments on the squab and on the floor, and a litter of playthings everywhere. On the black American cloth of the table were pieces of bread and cake, crusts, slops, and a teapot with cold tea.

'Eh, ours is just as bad,' said Elizabeth Bates, looking at the woman, not at the house. Mrs Rigley put a shawl over her head and hurried out, saying:

'I shanna be a minute.'

The other sat, noting with faint disapproval the general untidiness of the room. Then she fell to counting the shoes of various sizes scattered over the floor. There were twelve. She sighed and said to herself, 'No wonder!' – glancing at the litter. There came the scratching of two pairs of feet on the yard, and the Rigleys entered. Elizabeth Bates rose. Rigley was a big man, with very large bones. His head looked particularly bony. Across his temple was a blue scar, caused by a wound got in the pit, a wound in which the coal-dust remained blue like tattooing.

''Asna 'e come whoam yit?' asked the man, without any form of greeting, but with deference and sympathy. 'I couldna say wheer he is – 'e's non ower theer!' – he jerked his head to signify the 'Prince of Wales'.

''E's 'appen gone up to th' "Yew",' said Mrs Rigley.

There was another pause. Rigley had evidently something to get off his mind:

'Ah left 'im finishin' a stint,' he began. 'Loose-all[2] 'ad bin gone about ten minutes when we com'n away, an' I shouted, "Are ter comin', Walt?" an' 'e said, "Go on, Ah shanna be but a'ef a minnit," so we com'n ter th' bottom, me an' Bowers, thinkin' as 'e wor just behint, an' 'ud come up i' th' next bantle[3] –'

He stood perplexed, as if answering a charge of deserting his mate. Elizabeth Bates, now again certain of disaster, hastened to reassure him:

'I expect 'e's gone up to th' "Yew Tree", as you say. It's not the first time. I've fretted myself into a fever before now. He'll come home when they carry him.'

'Ay, isn't it too bad!' deplored the other woman.

'I'll just step up to Dick's an' see if 'e *is* theer,' offered the man, afraid of appearing alarmed, afraid of taking liberties.

'Oh, I wouldn't think of bothering you that far,' said Elizabeth Bates, with emphasis, but he knew she was glad of his offer.

As they stumbled up the entry, Elizabeth Bates heard Rigley's wife run across the yard and open her neighbour's door. At this, suddenly all the blood in her body seemed to switch away from her heart.

'Mind!' warned Rigley. 'Ah've said many a time as Ah'd fill up them ruts in this entry, sumb'dy 'll be breakin' their legs yit.'

She recovered herself and walked quickly along with the miner.

'I don't like leaving the children in bed, and nobody in the house,' she said.

'No, you dunna!' he replied courteously. They were soon at the gate of the cottage.

'Well, I shanna be many minnits. Dunna you be frettin' now, 'e'll be all right,' said the butty.

'Thank you very much, Mr Rigley,' she replied.

'You're welcome!' he stammered, moving away. 'I shanna be many minnits.'

The house was quiet. Elizabeth Bates took off her hat and shawl, and rolled back the rug. When she had finished, she sat down. It was a few minutes past nine. She was startled by the rapid chuff of the winding-engine at the pit, and the sharp whirr of the brakes on the rope as it descended. Again she felt the painful sweep of her blood, and she put her hand to her side, saying aloud, 'Good gracious! – it's only the nine o'clock deputy going down,' rebuking herself.

She sat still, listening. Half an hour of this, and she was wearied out.

'What am I working myself up like this for?' she said pitiably to herself, 'I s'll only be doing myself some damage.'

She took out her sewing again.

At a quarter to ten there were footsteps. One person! She watched for the door to open. It was an elderly woman, in a black bonnet and a black woollen shawl – his mother. She was about sixty years old, pale, with blue eyes, and her face all wrinkled and lamentable. She shut the door and turned to her daughter-in-law peevishly.

'Eh, Lizzie, whatever shall we do, whatever shall we do!' she cried.

Elizabeth drew back a little, sharply.

'What is it, mother?' she said.

The elder woman seated herself on the sofa.

'I don't know, child, I can't tell you!' – she shook her head slowly. Elizabeth sat watching her, anxious and vexed.

'I don't know,' replied the grandmother, sighing very deeply. 'There's no end to my troubles, there isn't. The things I've gone through, I'm sure it's enough – !' She wept without wiping her eyes, the tears running.

'But, mother,' interrupted Elizabeth, 'what do you mean? What is it?'

The grandmother slowly wiped her eyes. The fountains of her tears were stopped by Elizabeth's directness. She wiped her eyes slowly.

'Poor child! Eh, you poor thing!' she moaned. 'I don't know what we're going to do, I don't – and you as you are – it's a thing, it is indeed!'

Elizabeth waited.

'Is he dead?' she asked, and at the words her heart swung violently, though she felt a slight flush of shame at the ultimate extravagance of the question. Her words sufficiently frightened the old lady, almost brought her to herself.

'Don't say so, Elizabeth! We'll hope it's not as bad as that; no, may the Lord spare us that, Elizabeth. Jack Rigley came just as I was sittin' down to a glass afore going to bed, an' 'e said, " 'Appen you'll go down th' line, Mrs Bates. Walt's had an accident. 'Appen you'll go an' sit wi' 'er till we can get him home." I hadn't time to ask him a word afore he was gone. An' I put my bonnet on an' come straight down, Lizzie. I thought to myself, "Eh, that poor blessed child, if anybody should come an' tell her of a sudden, there's no knowin' what'll 'appen to 'er." You mustn't let it upset you, Lizzie – or you know what to expect. How long is it, six months – or is it five, Lizzie? Ay!' – the old woman shook her head – 'time slips on, it slips on! Ay!'

Elizabeth's thoughts were busy elsewhere. If he was killed – would she be able to manage on the little pension and what she could earn? – she counted up rapidly. If he was hurt – they wouldn't take him to the hospital – how tiresome he would be to nurse! – but perhaps she'd be able to get him away from the drink and his hateful ways. She would – while he was ill. The tears offered to come to her eyes at the picture. But what sentimental luxury was this she was beginning? – She turned to consider the children. At any rate she was absolutely necessary for them. They were her business.

'Ay!' repeated the old woman, 'it seems but a week or two since he brought me his first wages. Ay – he was a good lad, Elizabeth, he was, in his way. I don't know why he got to be such a trouble, I don't. He was a happy lad at home, only full of spirits. But there's no mistake he's been a handful of trouble, he has! I hope the Lord'll spare him to mend his ways. I hope so, I hope so. You've had a sight o' trouble with him, Elizabeth, you have indeed. But he was a jolly enough lad wi' me, he was, I can assure you. I don't know how it is ...'

The old woman continued to muse aloud, a monotonous irritating sound, while Elizabeth thought concentratedly, startled once, when she heard the winding-engine chuff quickly, and the brakes skirr with a shriek. Then she heard the engine more slowly, and the brakes made no sound. The old woman did not notice. Elizabeth waited in suspense. The mother-in-law talked, with lapses into silence.

'But he wasn't your son, Lizzie, an' it makes a difference. Whatever he was, I remember him when he was little, an' I learned to understand him and to make allowances. You've got to make allowances for them –'

It was half-past ten, and the old woman was saying: 'But it's trouble from beginning to end; you're never too old for trouble, never too old for that –' when the gate banged back, and there were heavy feet on the steps.

'I'll go, Lizzie, let me go,' cried the old woman, rising. But Elizabeth was at the door. It was a man in pit-clothes.

'They're bringin' 'im, Missis,' he said. Elizabeth's heart halted a moment. Then it surged on again, almost suffocating her.

'Is he – is it bad?' she asked.

The man turned away, looking at the darkness:

'The doctor says 'e'd been dead hours. 'E saw 'im i' th' lamp-cabin.'

The old woman, who stood just behind Elizabeth, dropped into a chair, and folded her hands, crying: 'Oh, my boy, my boy!'

'Hush!' said Elizabeth, with a sharp twitch of a frown. 'Be still, mother, don't waken th' children: I wouldn't have them down for anything!'

The old woman moaned softly, rocking herself. The man was drawing away. Elizabeth took a step forward.

'How was it?' she asked.

'Well, I couldn't say for sure,' the man replied, very ill at ease. ''E wor finishin' a stint an' th' butties 'ad gone, an' a lot o' stuff come down atop 'n 'im.'

'And crushed him?' cried the widow, with a shudder.

'No,' said the man, 'it fell at th' back of 'im. 'E wor under th' face, an' it niver touched 'im. It shut 'im in. It seems 'e wor smothered.'

Elizabeth shrank back. She heard the old woman behind her cry:

'What? – what did 'e say it was?'

The man replied, more loudly: ' 'E wor smothered!'

Then the old woman wailed aloud, and this relieved Elizabeth.

'Oh, mother,' she said, putting her hand on the old woman, 'don't waken th' children, don't waken th' children.'

She wept a little, unknowing, while the old mother rocked herself and moaned. Elizabeth remembered that they were bringing him home, and she must be ready. 'They'll lay him in the parlour,' she said to herself, standing a moment pale and perplexed.

Then she lighted a candle and went into the tiny room. The air was cold and damp, but she could not make a fire, there was no fire-place. She set down the candle and looked round. The candle-light glittered on the lustre-glasses, on the two vases that held some of the pink chrysanthemums, and on the dark mahogany. There was a cold, deathly smell of chrysanthemums in the room. Elizabeth stood looking at the flowers. She turned away, and calculated whether there would be room to lay him on the floor, between the couch and the chiffonier. She pushed the chairs aside. There would be room to lay him down and to step round him. Then she fetched the old red table-cloth, and another old cloth, spreading them down to save her bit of carpet. She shivered on leaving the parlour; so, from the dresser-drawer she took a clean shirt and put it at the fire to air. All the time her mother-in-law was rocking herself in the chair and moaning.

'You'll have to move from there, mother,' said Elizabeth. 'They'll be bringing him in. Come in the rocker.'

The old mother rose mechanically, and seated herself by the fire, continuing to lament. Elizabeth went into the pantry for another candle, and there, in the little penthouse under the naked tiles, she heard them coming. She stood still in the pantry doorway, listening. She heard them pass the end of the house, and come awkwardly down the three steps, a jumble of shuffling footsteps and muttering voices. The old woman was silent. The men were in the yard.

Then Elizabeth heard Matthews, the manager of the pit, say: 'You go in first, Jim. Mind!'

The door came open, and the two women saw a collier backing into the room, holding one end of a stretcher, on which they could see the nailed pit-boots of the dead man. The two carriers halted, the man at the head stooping to the lintel of the door.

'Wheer will you have him?' asked the manager, a short, white-bearded man.

Elizabeth roused herself and came from the pantry carrying the unlighted candle.

'In the parlour,' she said.

'In there, Jim!' pointed the manager, and the carriers backed round into the tiny room. The coat with which they had covered the body fell off as they awkwardly turned through the two doorways, and the women saw their man, naked to the waist, lying stripped for work. The old woman began to moan in a low voice of horror.

'Lay th' stretcher at th' side,' snapped the manager, 'an' put 'im on th' cloths. Mind now, mind! Look you now – !'

One of the men had knocked off a vase of chrysanthemums. He stared awkwardly, then they set down the stretcher. Elizabeth did not look at her husband. As soon as she could get in the room, she went and picked up the broken vase and the flowers.

'Wait a minute!' she said.

The three men waited in silence while she mopped up the water with a duster.

'Eh, what a job, what a job, to be sure!' the manager was saying, rubbing his brow with trouble and perplexity. 'Never knew such a thing in my life, never! He'd no business to ha' been left. I never knew such a thing in my life! Fell over him clean as a whistle, an' shut him in. Not four foot of space, there wasn't – yet it scarce bruised him.'

He looked down at the dead man, lying prone, half naked, all grimed with coal-dust.

'"'Sphyxiated," the doctor said. It *is* the most terrible job I've ever known. Seems as if it was done o' purpose. Clean over him, an' shut 'im in, like a mouse-trap' – he made a sharp, descending gesture with his hand.

The colliers standing by jerked aside their heads in hopeless comment.

The horror of the thing bristled upon them all.

Then they heard the girl's voice upstairs calling shrilly: 'Mother, mother – who is it? Mother, who is it?'

Elizabeth hurried to the foot of the stairs and opened the door:

'Go to sleep!' she commanded sharply. 'What are you shouting about? Go to sleep at once – there's nothing –'

Then she began to mount the stairs. They could hear her on the boards, and on the plaster floor of the little bedroom. They could hear her distinctly:

'What's the matter now? – what's the matter with you, silly thing?' – her voice was much agitated, with an unreal gentleness.

'I thought it was some men come,' said the plaintive voice of the child. 'Has he come?'

'Yes, they've brought him. There's nothing to make a fuss about. Go to sleep now, like a good child.'

They could hear her voice in the bedroom, they waited whilst she covered the children under the bedclothes.

'Is he drunk?' asked the girl, timidly, faintly.

'No! No – he's not! He – he's asleep.'

'Is he asleep downstairs?'

'Yes – and don't make a noise.'

There was silence for a moment, then the men heard the frightened child again:

'What's that noise?'

'It's nothing, I tell you, what are you bothering for?'

The noise was the grandmother moaning. She was oblivious of everything, sitting on her chair rocking and moaning. The manager put his hand on her arm and bade her 'Sh – sh!!'

The old woman opened her eyes and looked at him. She was shocked by this interruption, and seemed to wonder.

'What time is it?' – the plaintive thin voice of the child, sinking back unhappily into sleep, asked this last question.

'Ten o'clock,' answered the mother more softly. Then she must have bent down and kissed the children.

Matthews beckoned to the men to come away. They put on their caps and took up the stretcher. Stepping over the body, they tiptoed out of the house. None of them spoke till they were far from the wakeful children.

When Elizabeth came down she found her mother alone on the parlour floor, leaning over the dead man, the tears dropping on him.

'We must lay him out,' the wife said. She put on the kettle, then returning knelt at the feet, and began to unfasten the knotted leather laces. The room was clammy and dim with only one candle, so that she had to bend her face almost to the floor. At last she got off the heavy boots and put them away.

'You must help me now,' she whispered to the old woman. Together they stripped the man.

When they arose, saw him lying in the naïve dignity of death, the women stood arrested in fear and respect. For a few moments they remained still, looking down, the old mother whimpering. Elizabeth felt countermanded. She saw him, how utterly inviolable he lay in himself. She had nothing to do with him. She could not accept it. Stooping, she laid her hand on him, in claim. He was still warm, for the mine was hot where he had died. His mother had his face between her hands, and was murmuring incoherently. The old tears fell in succession as drops from wet leaves; the mother was not weeping, merely her tears flowed. Elizabeth embraced the body of her husband, with cheek and lips. She seemed to be listening, inquiring, trying to get some connection. But she could not. She was driven away. He was impregnable.

She rose, went into the kitchen, where she poured warm water into a bowl, brought soap and flannel and a soft towel.

'I must wash him,' she said.

Then the old mother rose stiffly, and watched Elizabeth as she carefully washed his face, carefully brushing the big blond moustache from his mouth with the flannel. She was afraid with a bottomless fear, so she ministered to him. The old woman, jealous, said:

'Let me wipe him!' – and she kneeled on the other side drying slowly as Elizabeth washed, her big black bonnet sometimes brushing the dark head of her daughter. They worked thus in silence for a long time. They never forgot it was death, and the touch of the man's dead body gave them strange emotions, different in each of the women; a great dread possessed them both, the mother felt the lie was given to her womb, she was denied; the wife felt the utter isolation of the human soul, the child within her was a weight apart from her.

At last it was finished. He was a man of handsome body, and his face showed no traces of drink. He was blonde, full-fleshed, with fine limbs. But he was dead.

'Bless him,' whispered his mother, looking always at his face, and speaking out of sheer terror. 'Dear lad – bless him!' She spoke in a faint, sibilant ecstasy of fear and mother love.

Elizabeth sank down again to the floor, and put her face against his neck, and trembled and shuddered. But she had to draw away again. He was dead, and her living flesh had no place against his. A great dread and weariness held her: she was so unavailing. Her life was gone like this.

'White as milk he is, clear as a twelve-month baby, bless him, the darling!' the old mother murmured to herself. 'Not a mark on him, clear and clean and white, beautiful as ever a child was made,' she murmured with pride. Elizabeth kept her face hidden.

'He went peaceful, Lizzie – peaceful as sleep. Isn't he beautiful, the lamb? Ay – he must ha' made his peace, Lizzie. 'Appen he made it all right, Lizzie, shut in there. He'd have time. He wouldn't look like this if he hadn't made his peace. The lamb, the dear lamb. Eh, but he had a hearty laugh. I loved to hear it. He had the heartiest laugh, Lizzie, as a lad –'

Elizabeth looked up. The man's mouth was fallen back, slightly open under the cover of the moustache. The eyes, half shut, did not show glazed in the obscurity. Life with its smoky burning gone from him, had left him apart and utterly alien to her. And she knew what a stranger he was to her. In her womb was ice of fear, because of this separate stranger with whom she had been living as one flesh. Was this what it all meant – utter, intact separateness, obscured by heat of living? In dread she turned her face away. The fact was too deadly. There had been nothing between them, and yet they had come together, exchanging their nakedness repeatedly. Each time he had taken her, they had been two isolated beings, far apart as now. He was no more responsible than she. The child was like ice in her womb. For as she looked at the dead man, her mind, cold and detached, said clearly: 'Who am I? What have I been doing? I have been fighting a husband who did not exist. *He* existed all the time. What wrong have I done? What was that I have been living with? There lies the reality, this man.' – And her soul died in her for fear: she knew she had never seen him, he had never seen her, they had met in the dark and had fought in the dark, not knowing whom they met nor whom they fought. And now she saw, and turned silent in seeing. For she had been wrong. She had said he was something he was not; she had felt familiar with him. Whereas he was apart all the while, living as she never lived, feeling as she never felt.

In fear and shame she looked at his naked body, that she had known falsely. And he was the father of her children. Her soul was torn from her body and stood apart. She looked at his naked body and was ashamed, as if she had denied it. After all, it was itself. It seemed awful to her. She looked at his face, and she turned her own face to the wall. For his look was other than hers, his way was not her way. She had denied him what he was – she saw it now. She had refused him as himself. – And this had been her life, and his life. – She was grateful to death, which restored the truth. And she knew she was not dead.

And all the while her heart was bursting with grief and pity for him. What had he suffered? What stretch of horror for this helpless man! She was rigid with agony. She had not been able to help him. He had been cruelly injured, this naked man, this other being, and she could make no reparation. There were the children – but the children belonged to life. This dead man had nothing to do with them. He and she were only channels through which life had flowed to issue in the children. She was a mother – but how awful she knew it now to have been a wife. And he, dead now, how awful he must have felt it to be a husband. She felt that in the next world he would be a stranger to her. If they met there, in the beyond, they would only be ashamed of what had been before. The children had come, for some mysterious reason, out of both of them. But the children did not unite them. Now he was dead, she knew how eternally he was apart from her, how eternally he had nothing more to do with her. She saw this episode of her life closed. They had denied each other in life. Now he had withdrawn. An anguish came over her. It was finished then: it had become hopeless between them long before he died. Yet he had been her husband. But how little!

'Have you got his shirt, 'Lizabeth?'

Elizabeth turned without answering, though she strove to weep and behave as her mother-in-law expected. But she could not, she was silenced. She went into the kitchen and returned with the garment.

'It is aired,' she said, grasping the cotton shirt here and there to try. She was almost ashamed to handle him; what right had she or anyone to lay hands on him; but her touch was humble on his body. It was hard work to clothe him. He was so heavy and inert. A terrible dread gripped her all the while: that he could be so heavy and utterly inert, unresponsive, apart. The horror of the distance between them was almost too much for her – it was so infinite a gap she must look across.

At last it was finished. They covered him with a sheet and left him lying, with his face bound. And she fastened the door of the little parlour, lest the children should see what was lying there. Then, with peace sunk heavy on her heart, she went about making tidy the kitchen. She knew she submitted to life, which was her immediate master. But from death, her ultimate master, she winced with fear and shame.[4]

Daughters of the Vicar

I

MR LINDLEY was first vicar of Aldecross. The cottages of this tiny hamlet had nestled in peace since their beginning, and the country folk had crossed the lanes and farm-lands, two or three miles, to the parish church at Greymeed, on the bright Sunday mornings.

But when the pits were sunk, blank rows of dwellings started up beside the high roads, and a new population, skimmed from the floating scum of workmen, was filled in, the cottages and the country people almost obliterated.

To suit the convenience of these new collier-inhabitants, a church must be built at Aldecross. There was not too much money. And so the little building crouched like a humped stone-and-mortar mouse, with two little turrets at the west corners for ears, in the fields near the cottages and the apple trees, as far as possible from the dwellings down the high road. It had an uncertain, timid look about it. And so they planted big-leaved ivy, to hide its shrinking newness. So that now the little church stands buried in its greenery, stranded and sleeping among the fields, while the brick houses elbow nearer and nearer, threatening to crush it down. It is already obsolete.

The Reverend Ernest Lindley, aged twenty-seven, and newly married, came from his curacy in Suffolk to take charge of his church. He was just an ordinary young man, who had been to Cambridge and taken orders. His wife was a self-assured young woman, daughter of a Cambridgeshire rector. Her father had spent the whole of his thousand a year, so that Mrs Lindley had nothing of her own. Thus the young married people came to Aldecross to live on a stipend of about a hundred and twenty pounds, and to keep up a superior position.

They were not very well received by the new, raw, disaffected population of colliers. Being accustomed to farm labourers, Mr Lindley had considered himself as belonging indisputably to the upper or ordering classes. He had to be humble to the county families, but still, he was of their kind, whilst the common people were something different. He had no doubts of himself.

He found, however, that the collier population refused to accept this arrangement. They had no use for him in their lives, and they told him so, callously. The women merely said, 'they were throng,'[1] or else, 'Oh, it's no good you coming here, we're Chapel.' The men were quite good-humoured so long as he did not touch them too nigh, they were cheerfully contemptuous of him, with a preconceived contempt he was powerless against.

At last, passing from indignation to silent resentment, even, if he dared have acknowledged it, to conscious hatred of the majority of his flock, and unconscious hatred of himself, he confined his activities to a narrow round of cottages, and he had to submit. He had no particular character, having always depended on his position in society to give him position among men. Now he was so poor, he had no social standing even among the common vulgar tradespeople of the district, and he had not the nature nor the wish to make his society agreeable to them, nor the strength to impose himself where he would have liked to be recognized. He dragged on, pale and miserable and neutral.

At first his wife raged with mortification. She took on airs and used a high hand. But her income was too small, the wrestling with tradesmen's bills was too pitiful, she only met with general, callous ridicule when she tried to be impressive.

Wounded to the quick of her pride, she found herself isolated in an indifferent, callous population. She raged indoors and out. But soon she learned that she must pay too heavily for her outdoor rages, and then she only raged within the walls of the rectory. There her feeling was so strong, that she frightened herself. She saw herself hating her husband, and she knew that, unless she were careful, she would smash her form of life and bring catastrophe upon him and upon herself. So in very fear, she went quiet. She hid, bitter and beaten by fear, behind the only shelter she had in the world, her gloomy, poor parsonage.

Children were born one every year; almost mechanically, she continued to perform her maternal duty, which was forced upon her. Gradually, broken by the suppressing of her violent anger and misery and disgust, she became an invalid and took to her couch.

The children grew up healthy, but unwarmed and rather rigid. Their father and mother educated them at home, made them very proud and very genteel, put them definitely and cruelly in the upper classes, apart from the vulgar around them. So they lived quite isolated. They were good-looking, and had that curiously clean, semi-transparent look of the genteel, isolated poor.

Gradually Mr and Mrs Lindley lost all hold on life, and spent their hours, weeks and years merely haggling to make ends meet, and bitterly repressing and pruning their children into gentility, urging them to ambition, weighting them with duty. On Sunday morning the whole family, except the mother, went down the lane to church, the long-legged girls in skimpy frocks, the boys in black coats and long, grey, unfitting trousers. They passed by their father's parishioners with mute, clear faces, childish mouths closed in pride that was like a doom to them, and childish eyes already unseeing. Miss Mary, the eldest, was the leader. She was a long, slim thing with a fine profile and a proud, pure look of submission to a high fate. Miss Louisa, the second, was short and plump and obstinate-looking. She had more enemies than ideals. She looked after the lesser children, Miss Mary after the elder. The collier children watched this pale, distinguished procession of the vicar's family pass mutely by, and they were impressed by the air of gentility and distance, they made mock of the trousers of the small sons, they felt inferior in themselves, and hate stirred their hearts.

In her time, Miss Mary received as governess a few little daughters of tradesmen; Miss Louisa managed the house and went among her father's church-goers, giving lessons on the piano to the colliers' daughters at thirteen shillings for twenty-six lessons.

II

One winter morning, when his daughter Mary was about twenty years old, Mr Lindley, a thin, unobtrusive figure in his black overcoat and his wideawake,[2] went down into Aldecross with a packet of white papers under his arm. He was delivering the parish almanacs.

A rather pale, neutral man of middle age, he waited while the train thumped over the level-crossing, going up to the pit which rattled busily just along the line. A wooden-legged man hobbled to open the gate, Mr Lindley passed on. Just at his left hand, below the road and the railway, was the red roof of a cottage, showing through the bare twigs of apple trees. Mr Lindley passed round the low wall, and descended the worn steps that led from the highway down to the cottage which crouched darkly and quietly away below the rumble of passing trains and the clank of coal-carts in a quiet little under-world of its own. Snowdrops with tight-shut buds were hanging very still under the bare currant bushes.

The clergyman was just going to knock when he heard a clinking noise, and turning saw through the open door of a black shed just behind him an elderly woman in a black lace cap stooping among reddish big cans, pouring a very bright liquid into a tundish.[3] There was a smell of paraffin. The woman put down her can, took the tundish and laid it on a shelf, then rose with a tin bottle. Her eyes met those of the clergyman.

'Oh, is it you, Mr Lin'ley!' she said, in a complaining tone. 'Go in.'

The minister entered the house. In the hot kitchen sat a big, elderly man with a great grey beard, taking snuff. He grunted in a deep, muttering voice, telling the minister to sit down, and then took no more notice of him, but stared vacantly into the fire. Mr Lindley waited.

The woman came in, the ribbons of her black lace cap, or bonnet, hanging on her shawl. She was of medium stature, everything about her was tidy. She went up a step out of the kitchen, carrying the paraffin tin. Feet were heard entering the room up the step. It was a little haberdashery shop, with parcels on the shelves of the walls, a big, old-fashioned sewing machine with tailor's work lying round it, in the open space. The woman went behind the counter, gave the child who had entered the paraffin bottle, and took from her a jug.

'My mother says shall yer put it down,' said the child, and she was gone. The woman wrote in a book, then came into the kitchen with her jug. The husband, a very large man, rose and brought more coal to the already hot fire. He moved slowly and sluggishly. Already he was going dead; being a tailor, his large form had become an encumbrance to him. In his youth he had been a great dancer and boxer. Now he was taciturn, and inert. The minister had nothing to say, so he sought for his phrases. But John Durant took no notice, existing silent and dull.

Mrs Durant spread the cloth. Her husband poured himself beer into a mug, and began to smoke and drink.

'Shall you have some?' he growled through his beard at the clergyman, looking slowly from the man to the jug, capable of this one idea.

'No, thank you,' replied Mr Lindley, though he would have liked some beer. He must set the example in a drinking parish.

'We need a drop to keep us going,' said Mrs Durant.

She had rather a complaining manner. The clergyman sat on uncomfortably while she laid the table for the half-past ten lunch. Her husband drew up to eat. She remained in her little round arm-chair by the fire.

She was a woman who would have liked to be easy in her life, but to whose lot had fallen a rough and turbulent family, and a slothful husband who did not care what became of himself or anybody. So, her rather good-looking square face was peevish, she had that air of having been compelled all her life to serve unwillingly, and to control where she did not want to control. There was about her, too, that masterful *aplcmb* of a woman who has brought up and ruled her sons: but even them she had ruled unwillingly. She had enjoyed managing her little haberdashery-shop, riding in the carrier's cart to Nottingham, going through the big warehouses to buy her goods. But the fret of managing her sons she did not like. Only she loved her youngest boy, because he was her last, and she saw herself free.

This was one of the houses the clergyman visited occasionally. Mrs Durant, as part of her regulation, had brought up all her sons in the Church. Not that she had any religion. Only, it was what she was used to. Mr Durant was without religion. He read the fervently evangelical 'Life of John Wesley' with a curious pleasure, getting from it a satisfaction as from the warmth of the fire, or a glass of brandy. But he cared no more about John Wesley, in fact, than about John Milton, of whom he had never heard.

Mrs Durant took her chair to the table.

'I don't feel like eating,' she sighed.

'Why – aren't you well?' asked the clergyman, patronizing.

'It isn't that,' she sighed. She sat with shut, straight mouth. 'I don't know what's going to become of us.'

But the clergyman had ground himself down so long, that he could not easily sympathize.

'Have you any trouble?' he asked.

'Ay, have I any trouble!' cried the elderly woman. 'I shall end my days in the workhouse.'

The minister waited unmoved. What could she know of poverty, in her little house of plenty!

'I hope not,' he said.

'And the one lad as I wanted to keep by me –' she lamented.

The minister listened without sympathy, quite neutral.

'And the lad as would have been a support to my old age! What is going to become of us?' she said.

The clergyman, justly, did not believe in the cry of poverty, but wondered what had become of the son.

'Has anything happened to Alfred?' he asked.

'We've got word he's gone for a Queen's sailor,' she said sharply.

'He has joined the Navy!' exclaimed Mr Lindley. 'I think he could scarcely have done better – to serve his Queen and country on the sea . . .'

'He is wanted to serve *me*,' she cried. 'And I wanted my lad at home.'

Alfred was her baby, her last, whom she had allowed herself the luxury of spoiling.

'You will miss him,' said Mr Lindley, 'that is certain. But this is no regrettable step for him to have taken – on the contrary.'

'That's easy for you to say, Mr Lindley,' she replied tartly. 'Do you think I want my lad climbing ropes at another man's bidding, like a monkey – ?'

'There is no *dishonour*, surely, in serving in the Navy?'

'Dishonour this dishonour that,' cried the angry old woman. 'He goes and makes a slave of himself, and he'll rue it.'

Her angry, scornful impatience nettled the clergyman and silenced him for some moments.

'I do not see,' he retorted at last, white at the gills and inadequate, 'that the Queen's service is any more to be called slavery than working in a mine.'

'At home he was at home, and his own master. *I* know he'll find a difference.'

'It may be the making of him,' said the clergyman. 'It will take him away from bad companionship and drink.'

Some of the Durants' sons were notorious drinkers, and Alfred was not quite steady.

'And why indeed shouldn't he have his glass?' cried the mother. 'He picks no man's pocket to pay for it!'

The clergyman stiffened at what he thought was an allusion to his own profession, and his unpaid bills.

'With all due consideration, I am glad to hear he has joined the Navy,' he said.

'Me with my old age coming on, and his father working very little! I'd thank you to be glad about something else besides that, Mr Lindley.'

The woman began to cry. Her husband, quite impassive, finished his lunch of meat-pie, and drank some beer. Then he turned to the fire, as if there were no one in the room but himself.

'I shall respect all men who serve God and their country on the sea, Mrs Durant,' said the clergyman stubbornly.

'That is very well, when they're not your sons who are doing the dirty work. – It makes a difference,' she replied tartly.

'I should be proud if one of my sons were to enter the Navy.'

'Ay – well – we're not all of us made alike –'

The minister rose. He put down a large folded paper.

'I've brought the almanac,' he said.

Mrs Durant unfolded it.

'I do like a bit of colour in things,' she said, petulantly.

The clergyman did not reply.

'There's that envelope for the organist's fund –' said the old woman, and rising, she took the thing from the mantelpiece, went into the shop, and returned sealing it up.

'Which is all I can afford,' she said.

Mr Lindley took his departure, in his pocket the envelope containing Mrs Durant's offering for Miss Louisa's services. He went from door to door delivering the almanacs, in dull routine. Jaded with the monotony of the business, and with the repeated effort of greeting half-known people, he felt barren and rather irritable. At last he returned home.

In the dining-room was a small fire. Mrs Lindley, growing very stout, lay on her couch. The vicar carved the cold mutton; Miss Louisa, short and plump and rather flushed, came in from the kitchen; Miss Mary, dark, with a beautiful white brow and grey eyes, served the vegetables; the children chattered a little, but not exuberantly. The very air seemed starved.

'I went to the Durants,' said the vicar, as he served out small portions of mutton; 'it appears Alfred has run away to join the Navy.'

'Do him good,' came the rough voice of the invalid.

Miss Louisa, attending to the youngest child, looked up in protest.

'Why has he done that?' asked Mary's low, musical voice.

'He wanted some excitement, I suppose,' said the vicar. 'Shall we say grace?'

The children were arranged, all bent their heads, grace was pronounced, at the last word every face was being raised to go on with the interesting subject.

'He's just done the right thing, for once,' came the rather deep voice of the mother; 'save him from becoming a drunken sot, like the rest of them.'

'They're not *all* drunken, mama,' said Miss Louisa, stubbornly.

'It's no fault of their upbringing if they're not. Walter Durant is a standing disgrace.'

'As I told Mrs Durant,' said the vicar, eating hungrily, 'it is the best thing he could have done. It will take him away from temptation during the most dangerous years of his life – how old is he – nineteen?'

'Twenty,' said Miss Louisa.

'Twenty!' repeated the vicar. 'It will give him wholesome discipline and set before him some sort of standard of duty and honour – nothing could have been better for him. But –'

'We shall miss him from the choir,' said Miss Louisa, as if taking opposite sides to her parents.

'That is as it may be,' said the vicar. 'I prefer to know he is safe in the Navy, than running the risk of getting into bad ways here.'

'Was he getting into bad ways?' asked the stubborn Miss Louisa.

'You know, Louisa, he wasn't quite what he used to be,' said Miss Mary gently and steadily. Miss Louisa shut her rather heavy jaw sulkily. She wanted to deny it, but she knew it was true.

For her he had been a laughing, warm lad, with something kindly and something rich about him. He had made her feel warm. It seemed the days would be colder since he had gone.

'Quite the best thing he could do,' said the mother with emphasis.

'I think so,' said the vicar. 'But his mother was almost abusive because I suggested it.'

He spoke in an injured tone.

'What does she care for her children's welfare?' said the invalid. 'Their wages is all her concern.'

'I suppose she wanted him at home with her,' said Miss Louisa.

'Yes, she did – at the expense of his learning to be a drunkard like the rest of them,' retorted her mother.

'George Durant doesn't drink,' defended her daughter.

'Because he got burned so badly when he was nineteen – in the pit – and that frightened him. The Navy is a better remedy than that, at least.'

'Certainly,' said the vicar. 'Certainly.'

And to this Miss Louisa agreed. Yet she could not but feel angry that he had gone away for so many years. She herself was only nineteen.

III

It happened when Miss Mary was twenty-three years old, that Mr Lindley was very ill. The family was exceedingly poor at the time, such a lot of money was needed, so little was forthcoming. Neither Miss Mary nor Miss Louisa had suitors. What chance had they? They met no eligible young men in Aldecross. And what they earned was a mere drop in a void. The girls' hearts were chilled and hardened with fear of this perpetual, cold penury, this narrow struggle, this horrible nothingness of their lives.

A clergyman had to be found for the church work. It so happened the son of an old friend of Mr Lindley's was waiting three months before taking up his duties. He would come and officiate, for nothing. The young clergyman was keenly expected. He was not more than twenty-seven, a Master of Arts of Oxford, had written his thesis on Roman Law. He came of an old Cambridgeshire family, had some private means, was going to take a church in Northamptonshire with a good stipend, and was not married. Mrs Lindley incurred new debts, and scarcely regretted her husband's illness.

But when Mr Massy came, there was a shock of disappointment in the house. They had expected a young man with a pipe and a deep voice, but with better manners than Sidney, the eldest of the Lindleys. There arrived instead a small, chétif[4] man, scarcely larger than a boy of twelve, spectacled, timid in the extreme, without a word to utter at first; yet with a certain inhuman self-sureness.

'What a little abortion!' was Mrs Lindley's exclamation to herself on first seeing him, in his buttoned-up clerical coat. And for the first time for many days, she was profoundly thankful to God that all her children were decent specimens.

He had not normal powers of perception. They soon saw that he lacked the full range of human feelings, but had rather a strong, philosophical mind, from which he lived. His body was almost unthinkable, in intellect he was something definite. The conversation at once took a balanced, abstract tone when he participated. There was no spontaneous exclamation, no violent assertion or expression of personal conviction, but all cold, reasonable assertion. This was very hard on Mrs Lindley. The little man would look at her, after one of her pronouncements, and then give, in his thin voice, his own calculated version, so that she felt as if she were tumbling into thin air through a hole in the flimsy floor on which their conversation stood. It was she who felt a fool. Soon she was reduced to a hardy silence.

Still, at the back of her mind, she remembered that he was an unattached gentleman, who would shortly have an income altogether of six or seven hundred a year. What did the man matter, if there were pecuniary ease! The man was a trifle thrown in. After twenty-two years her sentimentality was ground away, and only the millstone of poverty mattered to her. So she supported the little man as a representative of a decent income.

His most irritating habit was that of a sneering little giggle, all on his own, which came when he perceived or related some illogical absurdity on the part of another person. It was the only form of humour he had. Stupidity in thinking seemed to him exquisitely funny. But any novel was unintelligibly meaningless and dull, and to an Irish sort of humour he listened curiously, examining it like mathematics, or else simply not hearing. In normal human relationship he was not there. Quite unable to take part in simple everyday talk, he padded silently round the house, or sat in the dining-room looking nervously from side to side, always apart in a cold, rarefied little world of his own. Sometimes he made an ironic remark, that did not seem humanly relevant, or he gave his little laugh, like a sneer. He had to defend himself and his own insufficiency. And he answered questions grudgingly, with a yes or no, because he did not see their import and was nervous. It seemed to Miss Louisa he scarcely distinguished one person from another, but that he liked to be near her, or to Miss Mary, for some sort of contact which stimulated him unknown.

Apart from all this, he was the most admirable workman. He was unremittingly shy, but perfect in his sense of duty: as far as he could conceive Christianity, he was a perfect Christian. Nothing that he realized he could do for anyone did he leave undone, although he was so incapable of coming into contact with another being, that he could not proffer help. Now he attended assiduously to the sick man, investigated all the affairs of the parish or the church which Mr Lindley had in control, straightened out accounts, made lists of the sick and needy, padded round with help and to see what he could do. He heard of Mrs Lindley's anxiety about her sons, and began to investigate means of sending them to Cambridge. His kindness almost frightened Miss Mary. She honoured it so, and yet she shrank from it. For, in it all Mr Massy seemed to have no sense of any person, any human being whom he was helping: he only realized a kind of mathematical working out, solving of given situations, a calculated well-doing. And it was as if he had accepted the Christian tenets as axioms. His religion consisted in what his scrupulous, abstract mind approved of.

Seeing his acts, Miss Mary must respect and honour him. In consequence she must serve him. To this she had to force herself, shuddering and yet desirous, but he did not perceive it. She accompanied him on his visiting in the parish, and whilst she was cold with admiration for him, often she was touched with pity for the little padding figure with bent shoulders, buttoned up to the chin in his overcoat. She was a handsome, calm girl, tall, with a beautiful repose. Her clothes were poor, and she wore a black silk scarf, having no furs. But she was a lady. As the people saw her walking down Aldecross beside Mr Massy, they said:

'My word, Miss Mary's got a catch. Did ever you see such a sickly little shrimp!'

She knew they were talking so, and it made her heart grow hot against them, and she drew herself as it were protectively towards the little man beside her. At any rate, she could see and give honour to his genuine goodness.

He could not walk fast, or far.

'You have not been well?' she asked, in her dignified way.

'I have an internal trouble.'

He was not aware of her slight shudder. There was silence, whilst she bowed to recover her composure, to resume her gentle manner towards him.

He was fond of Miss Mary. She had made it a rule of hospitality that he should always be escorted by herself or by her sister on his visits in the parish, which were not many. But some mornings she was engaged. Then Miss Louisa took her place. It was no good Miss Louisa's trying to adopt to Mr Massy an attitude of queenly service. She was unable to regard him save with aversion. When she saw him from behind, thin and bent-shouldered, looking like a sickly lad of thirteen, she disliked him exceedingly, and felt a desire to put him out of existence. And yet a deeper justice in Mary made Louisa humble before her sister.

They were going to see Mr Durant, who was paralysed and not expected to live. Miss Louisa was crudely ashamed at being admitted to the cottage in company with the little clergyman.

Mrs Durant was, however, much quieter in the face of her real trouble.

'How is Mr Durant?' asked Louisa.

'He is no different – and we don't expect him to be,' was the reply. The little clergyman stood looking on.

They went upstairs. The three stood for some time looking at the bed, at the grey head of the old man on the pillow, the grey beard over the sheet. Miss Louisa was shocked and afraid.

'It is so dreadful,' she said, with a shudder.

'It is how I always thought it would be,' replied Mrs Durant.

Then Miss Louisa was afraid of her. The two women were uneasy, waiting for Mr Massy to say something. He stood, small and bent, too nervous to speak.

'Has he any understanding?' he asked at length.

'Maybe,' said Mrs Durant. 'Can you hear, John?' she asked loudly. The dull blue eye of the inert man looked at her feebly.

'Yes, he understands,' said Mrs Durant to Mr Massy. Except for the dull look in his eyes, the sick man lay as if dead. The three stood in silence. Miss Louisa was obstinate but heavy-hearted under the load of unlivingness. It was Mr Massy who kept her there in discipline. His non-human will dominated them all.

Then they heard a sound below, a man's footsteps, and a man's voice called subduedly:

'Are you upstairs, mother?'

Mrs Durant started and moved to the door. But already a quick, firm step was running up the stairs.

'I'm a bit early, mother,' a troubled voice said, and on the landing they saw the form of the sailor. His mother came and clung to him. She was suddenly aware that she needed something to hold on to. He put his arms round her, and bent over her, kissing her.

'He's not gone, mother?' he asked anxiously, struggling to control his voice.

Miss Louisa looked away from the mother and son who stood together in the gloom on the landing. She could not bear it that she and Mr Massy should be there. The latter stood nervously, as if ill at ease before the emotion that was running. He was a witness, nervous, unwilling, but dispassionate. To Miss Louisa's hot heart it seemed all, all wrong that they should be there.

Mrs Durant entered the bedroom, her face wet.

'There's Miss Louisa and the vicar,' she said, out of voice and quavering.

Her son, red-faced and slender, drew himself up to salute. But Miss Louisa held out her hand. Then she saw his hazel eyes recognize her for a moment, and his small white teeth showed in a glimpse of the greeting she used to love. She was covered with confusion. He went round to the bed; his boots clicked on the plaster floor, he bowed his head with dignity.

'How are you, dad?' he said, laying his hand on the sheet, faltering. But the old man stared fixedly and unseeing. The son stood perfectly still for a few minutes, then slowly recoiled. Miss Louisa saw the fine outline of his breast, under the sailor's blue blouse, as his chest began to heave.

'He doesn't know me,' he said, turning to his mother. He gradually went white.

'No, my boy!' cried the mother, pitiful, lifting her face. And suddenly she put her face against his shoulder, he was stooping down to her, holding her against him, and she cried aloud for a moment or two. Miss Louisa saw his sides heaving, and heard the sharp hiss of his breath. She turned away, tears streaming down her face. The father lay inert upon the white bed, Mr Massy looked queer and obliterated, so little now that the sailor with his sunburned skin was in the room. He stood waiting. Miss Louisa wanted to die, she wanted to have done. She dared not turn round again to look.

'Shall I offer a prayer?' came the frail voice of the clergyman, and all kneeled down.

Miss Louisa was frightened of the inert man upon the bed. Then she felt a flash of fear of Mr Massy, hearing his thin, detached voice. And then, calmed, she looked up. On the far side of the bed were the heads of the mother and son, the one in the black lace cap, with the small white nape of the neck beneath, the other, with brown, sun-scorched hair too close and wiry to allow of a parting, and neck tanned firm, bowed as if unwillingly. The great grey beard of the old man did not move, the prayer continued. Mr Massy prayed with a pure lucidity, that they all might conform to the higher Will. He was like something that dominated the bowed heads, something dispassionate that governed them inexorably. Miss Louisa was afraid of him. And she was bound, during the course of the prayer, to have a little reverence for him. It was like a foretaste of inexorable, cold death, a taste of pure justice.

That evening she talked to Mary of the visit. Her heart, her veins were possessed by the thought of Alfred Durant as he held his mother in his arms; then the break in his voice, as she remembered it again and again, was like a flame through her; and she wanted to see his face more distinctly in her mind, ruddy with the sun, and his golden-brown eyes, kind and careless, strained now with a natural fear, the fine nose tanned hard by the sun, the mouth that could not help smiling at her. And it went through her with pride, to think of his figure, a straight, fine jet of life.

'He is a handsome lad,' said she to Miss Mary, as if he had not been a year older than herself. Underneath was the deeper dread, almost hatred, of the inhuman being of Mr Massy. She felt she must protect herself and Alfred from him.

'When I felt Mr Massy there,' she said, 'I almost hated him. What right had he to be there!'

'Surely he has all right,' said Miss Mary after a pause. 'He is *really* a Christian.'

'He seems to me nearly an imbecile,' said Miss Louisa.

Miss Mary, quiet and beautiful, was silent for a moment:

'Oh, no,' she said. 'Not *imbecile* –'

'Well then – he reminds me of a six months' child – or a five months' child – as if he didn't have time to get developed enough before he was born.'

'Yes,' said Miss Mary, slowly. 'There is something lacking. But there is something wonderful in him: and he is really *good* –'

'Yes,' said Miss Louisa, 'it doesn't seem right that he should be. What right has *that* to be called goodness!'

'But it *is* goodness,' persisted Mary. Then she added, with a laugh: 'And come, you wouldn't deny that as well.'

There was a doggedness in her voice. She went about very quietly. In her soul, she knew what was going to happen. She knew that Mr Massy was stronger than she, and that she must submit to what he was. Her physical self was prouder, stronger than he, her physical self disliked and despised him. But she was in the grip of his moral, mental being. And she felt the days allotted out to her. And her family watched.

IV

A few days after, old Mr Durant died. Miss Louisa saw Alfred once more, but he was stiff before her now, treating her not like a person, but as if she were some sort of will in command and he a separate, distinct will waiting in front of her. She had never felt such utter steel-plate separation from anyone. It puzzled her and frightened her. What had become of him? And she hated the military discipline – she was antagonistic to it. Now he was not himself. He was the will which obeys set over against the will which commands. She hesitated over accepting this. He had put himself out of her range. He had ranked himself inferior, subordinate to her. And that was how he would get away from her, that was how he would avoid all connection with her: by fronting her impersonally from the opposite camp, by taking up the abstract position of an inferior.

She went brooding steadily and sullenly over this, brooding and brooding. Her fierce, obstinate heart could not give way. It clung to its own rights. Sometimes she dismissed him. Why should he, inferior, trouble her?

Then she relapsed to him, and almost hated him. It was his way of getting out of it. She felt the cowardice of it, his calmly placing her in a superior class, and placing himself inaccessibly apart, in an inferior, as if she, the sensient woman who was fond of him, did not count. But she was not going to submit. Dogged in her heart she held on to him.

V

In six months' time Miss Mary had married Mr Massy. There had been no love-making, nobody had made any remark. But everybody was tense and callous with expectation. When one day Mr Massy asked for Mary's hand, Mr Lindley started and trembled from the thin, abstract voice of the little man. Mr Massy was very nervous, but so curiously absolute.

'I shall be very glad,' said the vicar, 'but of course the decision lies with Mary herself.' And his still feeble hand shook as he moved a Bible on his desk.

The small man, keeping fixedly to his idea, padded out of the room to find Miss Mary. He sat a long time by her, while she made some conversation, before he had readiness to speak. She was afraid of what was coming, and sat stiff in apprehension. She felt as if her body would rise and fling him aside. But her spirit quivered and waited. Almost in expectation she waited, almost wanting him. And then she knew he would speak.

'I have already asked Mr Lindley,' said the clergyman, while suddenly she looked with aversion at his little knees, 'if he would consent to my proposal.' He was aware of his own disadvantage, but his will was set.

She went cold as she sat, and impervious, almost as if she had become stone. He waited a moment nervously. He would not persuade her. He himself never even heard persuasion, but pursued his own course. He looked at her, sure of himself, unsure of her, and said:

'Will you become my wife, Mary?'

Still her heart was hard and cold. She sat proudly.

'I should like to speak to mama first,' she said.

'Very well,' replied Mr Massy. And in a moment he padded away.

Mary went to her mother. She was cold and reserved.

'Mr Massy has asked me to marry him, mama,' she said. Mrs Lindley went on staring at her book. She was cramped in her feeling.

'Well, and what did you say?'

They were both keeping calm and cold.

'I said I would speak to you before answering him.'

This was equivalent to a question. Mrs Lindley did not want to reply to it. She shifted her heavy form irritably on the couch. Miss Mary sat calm and straight, with closed mouth.

'Your father thinks it would not be a bad match,' said the mother, as if casually.

Nothing more was said. Everybody remained cold and shut-off. Miss Mary did not speak to Miss Louisa, the Reverend Ernest Lindley kept out of sight.

At evening Miss Mary accepted Mr Massy.

'Yes, I will marry you,' she said, with even a little movement of tenderness towards him. He was embarrassed, but satisfied. She could see him making some movement towards her, could feel the male in him, something cold and triumphant, asserting itself. She sat rigid, and waited.

When Miss Louisa knew, she was silent with bitter anger against everybody, even against Mary. She felt her faith wounded. Did the real things to her not matter after all? She wanted to get away. She thought of Mr Massy. He had some curious power, some unanswerable right. He was a will that they could not controvert. – Suddenly a flush started in her. If he had come to her she would have flipped him out of the room. He was never going to touch *her*. And she was glad. She was glad that her blood would rise and exterminate the little man, if he came too near to her, no matter how her judgment was paralysed by him, no matter how he moved in abstract goodness. She thought she was perverse to be glad, but glad she was. 'I would just flip him out of the room,' she said, and she derived great satisfaction from the open statement. Nevertheless, perhaps she ought still to feel that Mary, on her plane, was a higher being than herself. But then Mary was Mary, and she was Louisa, and that also was inalterable.

Mary, in marrying him, tried to become a pure reason such as he was, without feeling or impulse. She shut herself up, she shut herself rigid against the agonies of shame and the terror of violation which came at first. She *would* not feel, and she *would* not feel. She was a pure will acquiescing to him. She elected a certain kind of fate. She would be good and purely just, she would live in a higher freedom than she had ever known, she would be free of mundane care, she was a pure will towards right. She had sold herself, but she had a new freedom. She had got rid of her body. She had sold a lower thing, her body, for a higher thing, her freedom from material things. She considered that she paid for all she got from her husband. So, in a kind of independence, she moved proud and free. She had paid with her body: that was henceforward out of consideration. She was glad to be rid of it. She had bought her position in the world – that henceforth was taken for granted. There remained only the direction of her activity towards charity and high-minded living.

She could scarcely bear other people to be present with her and her husband. Her private life was her shame. But then, she could keep it hidden. She lived almost isolated in the rectory of the tiny village miles from the railway. She suffered as if it were an insult to her own flesh, seeing the repulsion which some people felt for her husband, or the special manner they had of treating him, as if he were a 'case'. But most people were uneasy before him, which restored her pride.

If she had let herself, she would have hated him, hated his padding round the house, his thin voice devoid of human understanding, his bent little shoulders and rather incomplete face that reminded her of an abortion. But rigorously she kept to her position. She took care of him and was just to him. There was also a deep craven fear of him, something slave-like.

There was not much fault to be found with his behaviour. He was scrupulously just and kind according to his lights. But the male in him was cold and self-complete, and utterly domineering. Weak, insufficient little thing as he was, she had not expected this of him. It was something in the bargain she had not understood. It made her hold her head, to keep still. She knew, vaguely, that she was murdering herself. After all, her body was not quite so easy to get rid of. And this manner of disposing of it – ah, sometimes she felt she must rise and bring about death, lift her hand for utter denial of everything, by a general destruction.

He was almost unaware of the conditions about him. He did not fuss in the domestic way, she did as she liked in the house. Indeed, she was a great deal free of him. He would sit obliterated for hours. He was kind, and almost anxiously considerate. But when he considered he was right, his will was just blindly male, like a cold machine. And on most points he was logically right, or he had with him the right of the creed they both accepted. It was so. There was nothing for her to go against.

Then she found herself with child, and felt for the first time horror, afraid before God and man. This also she had to go through – it was the right. When the child arrived, it was a bonny, healthy lad. Her heart hurt in her body, as she took the baby between her hands. The flesh that was trampled and silent in her must speak again in the boy. After all, she had to live – it was not so simple after all. Nothing was finished completely. She looked and looked at the baby, and almost hated it, and suffered an anguish of love for it. She hated it because it made her live again in the flesh, when she *could* not live in the flesh, she could not. She wanted to trample her flesh down, down, extinct, to live in the mind. And now there was this child. It was too cruel, too racking. For she must love the child. Her purpose was broken in two again. She had to become amorphous, purposeless, without real being. As a mother, she was a fragmentary, ignoble thing.

Mr Massy, blind to everything else in the way of human feeling, became obsessed by the idea of his child. When it arrived, suddenly it filled the whole world of feeling for him. It was his obsession, his terror was for its safety and well-being. It was something new, as if he himself had been born a naked infant, conscious of his own exposure, and full of apprehension. He who had never been aware of anyone else, all his life, now was aware of nothing but the child. Not that he ever played with it, or kissed it, or tended it. He did nothing for it. But it dominated him, it filled, and at the same time emptied his mind. The world was all baby for him.

This his wife must also bear, his question: 'What is the reason that he cries?' – his reminder, at the first sound: 'Mary, that is the child,' – his restlessness if the feeding-time were five minutes past. She had bargained for this – now she must stand by her bargain.

VI

Miss Louisa, at home in the dingy vicarage, had suffered a great deal over her sister's wedding. Having once begun to cry out against it, during the engagement, she had been silenced by Mary's quiet: 'I don't agree with you about him, Louisa, I *want* to marry him.' Then Miss Louisa had been angry deep in her heart, and therefore silent. This dangerous state started the change in her. Her own revulsion made her recoil from the hitherto undoubted Mary.

'I'd beg the streets barefoot first,' said Miss Louisa, thinking of Mr Massy.

But evidently Mary could perform a different heroism. So she, Louisa the practical, suddenly felt that Mary, her ideal, was questionable after all. How could she be pure – one cannot be dirty in act and spiritual in being. Louisa distrusted Mary's high spirituality. It was no longer genuine for her. And if Mary were spiritual and misguided, why did not her father protect her? Because of the money. He disliked the whole affair, but he backed away, because of the money. And the mother frankly did not care: her daughters could do as they liked. Her mother's pronouncement:

'Whatever happens to *him*, Mary is safe for life,' – so evidently and shallowly a calculation, incensed Louisa.

'I'd rather be safe in the workhouse,' she cried.

'Your father will see to that,' replied her mother brutally. This speech, in its indirectness, so injured Miss Louisa that she hated her mother deep, deep in her heart, and almost hated herself. It was a long time resolving itself out, this hate. But it worked and worked, and at last the young woman said:

'They are wrong – they are all wrong. They have ground out their souls for what isn't worth anything, and there isn't a grain of love in them anywhere. And I *will* have love. They want us to deny it. They've never found it, so they want to say it doesn't exist. But I *will* have it. I *will* love – it is my birthright. I will love the man I marry – that is all I care about.'

So Miss Louisa stood isolated from everybody. She and Mary had parted over Mr Massy. In Louisa's eyes, Mary was degraded, married to Mr Massy. She could not bear to think of her lofty, spiritual sister degraded in the body like this. Mary was wrong, wrong, wrong: she was not superior, she was flawed, incomplete. The two sisters stood apart. They still loved each other, they would love each other as long as they lived. But they had parted ways. A new solitariness came over the obstinate Louisa, and her heavy jaw set stubbornly. She was going on her own way. But which way? She was quite alone, with a blank world before her. How could she be said to have any way? Yet she had her fixed will to love, to have the man she loved.

VII

When her boy was three years old, Mary had another baby, a girl. The three years had gone by monotonously. They might have been an eternity, they might have been brief as a sleep. She did not know. Only, there was always a weight on top of her, something that pressed down her life. The only thing that had happened was that Mr Massy had had an operation. He was always exceedingly fragile. His wife had soon learned to attend to him mechanically, as part of her duty.

But this third year, after the baby girl had been born, Mary felt oppressed and depressed. Christmas drew near: the gloomy, unleavened Christmas of the rectory, where all the days were of the same dark fabric. And Mary was afraid. It was as if the darkness were coming upon her.

'Edward, I should like to go home for Christmas,' she said, and a certain terror filled her as she spoke.

'But you can't leave baby,' said her husband, blinking.

'We can all go.'

He thought, and stared in his collective fashion.

'Why do you wish to go?' he asked.

'Because I need a change. A change would do me good, and it would be good for the milk.'

He heard the will in his wife's voice, and was at a loss. Her language was unintelligible to him. And while she was breeding, either about to have a child, or nursing, he regarded her as a special sort of being.

'Wouldn't it hurt baby to take her by the train?' he said.

'No,' replied the mother, 'why should it?'

They went. When they were in the train, it began to snow. From the window of his first-class carriage the little clergyman watched the big flakes sweep by, like a blind drawn across the country. He was obsessed by thought of the baby, and afraid of the draughts of the carriage.

'Sit right in the corner,' he said to his wife, 'and hold baby close back.'

She moved at his bidding, and stared out of the window. His eternal presence was like an iron weight on her brain. But she was going partially to escape for a few days.

'Sit on the other side, Jack,' said the father. 'It is less draughty. Come to this window.'

He watched the boy in anxiety. But his children were the only beings in the world who took not the slightest notice of him.

'Look, mother, look!' cried the boy. 'They fly right in my face' – he meant the snowflakes.

'Come into this corner,' repeated his father, out of another world.

'He's jumped on this one's back, mother, an' they're riding to the bottom!' cried the boy, jumping with glee.

'Tell him to come on this side,' the little man bade his wife.

'Jack, kneel on this cushion,' said the mother, putting her white hand on the place.

The boy slid over in silence to the place she indicated, waited still for a moment, then almost deliberately, stridently cried:

'Look at all those in the corner, mother, making a heap,' and he pointed to the cluster of snowflakes with finger pressed dramatically on the pane, and he turned to his mother a bit ostentatiously.

'All in a heap!' she said.

He had seen her face, and had her response, and he was somewhat assured. Vaguely uneasy, he was reassured if he could win her attention.

They arrived at the vicarage at half-past two, not having had lunch.

'How are you, Edward?' said Mr Lindley, trying on his side to be fatherly. But he was always in a false position with his son-in-law, frustrated before him, therefore, as much as possible, he shut his eyes and ears to him. The vicar was looking thin and pale and ill-nourished. He had gone quite grey. He was, however, still haughty; but, since the growing-up of his children, it was a brittle haughtiness, that might break at any moment and leave the vicar only an impoverished, pitiable figure. Mrs Lindley took all the notice of her daughter, and of the children. She ignored her son-in-law. Miss Louisa was clucking and laughing and rejoicing over the baby. Mr Massy stood aside, a bent, persistent little figure.

'Oh a pretty! – a little pretty! oh a cold little pretty come in a railway-train!' Miss Louisa was cooing to the infant, crouching on the hearthrug opening the white woollen wraps and exposing the child to the fireglow.

'Mary,' said the little clergyman, 'I think it would be better to give baby a warm bath; she may take a cold.'

'I think it is not necessary,' said the mother, coming and closing her hand judiciously over the rosy feet and hands of the mite. 'She is not chilly.'

'Not a bit,' cried Miss Louisa. 'She's not caught cold.'

'I'll go and bring her flannels,' said Mr Massy, with one idea.

'I can bath her in the kitchen then,' said Mary, in an altered, cold tone.

'You can't, the girl is scrubbing there,' said Miss Louisa. 'Besides, she doesn't want a bath at this time of day.'

'She'd better have one,' said Mary, quietly, out of submission. Miss Louisa's gorge rose, and she was silent. When the little man padded down with the flannels on his arm, Mrs Lindley asked:

'Hadn't *you* better take a hot bath, Edward?'

But the sarcasm was lost on the little clergyman. He was absorbed in the preparations round the baby.

The room was dull and threadbare, and the snow outside seemed fairy-like by comparison, so white on the lawn and tufted on the bushes. Indoors the heavy pictures hung obscurely on the walls, everything was dingy with gloom.

Except in the fireglow, where they had laid the bath on the hearth. Mrs Massy, her black hair always smoothly coiled and queenly, kneeled by the bath, wearing a rubber apron, and holding the kicking child. Her husband stood holding the towels and the flannels to warm. Louisa, too cross to share in the joy of the baby's bath, was laying the table. The boy was hanging on the door-knob, wrestling with it to get out. His father looked round.

'Come away from the door, Jack,' he said, ineffectually. Jack tugged harder at the knob as if he did not hear. Mr Massy blinked at him.

'He must come away from the door, Mary,' he said. 'There will be a draught if it is opened.'

'Jack, come away from the door, dear,' said the mother, dexterously turning the shiny wet baby on to her towelled knee, then glancing round: 'Go and tell Auntie Louisa about the train.'

Louisa, also afraid to open the door, was watching the scene on the hearth. Mr Massy stood holding the baby's flannel, as if assisting at some ceremonial. If everybody had not been subduedly angry, it would have been ridiculous.

'I want to see out of the window,' Jack said. His father turned hastily.

'Do *you* mind lifting him on to a chair, Louisa,' said Mary hastily. The father was too delicate.

When the baby was flannelled, Mr Massy went upstairs and returned with four pillows, which he set in the fender to warm. Then he stood watching the mother feed her child, obsessed by the idea of his infant.

Louisa went on with her preparations for the meal. She could not have told why she was so sullenly angry. Mrs Lindley, as usual, lay silently watching.

Mary carried her child upstairs, followed by her husband with the pillows. After a while he came down again.

'What is Mary doing? Why doesn't she come down to eat?' asked Mrs Lindley.

'She is staying with baby. The room is rather cold. I will ask the girl to put in a fire.' He was going absorbedly to the door.

'But Mary has had nothing to eat. It is *she* who will catch cold,' said the mother, exasperated.

Mr Massy seemed as if he did not hear. Yet he looked at his mother-in-law, and answered:

'I will take her something.'

He went out. Mrs Lindley shifted on her couch with anger. Miss Louisa glowered. But no one said anything, because of the money that came to the vicarage from Mr Massy.

Louisa went upstairs. Her sister was sitting by the bed, reading a scrap of paper.

'Won't you come down and eat?' the younger asked.

'In a moment or two,' Mary replied, in a quiet, reserved voice, that forbade anyone to approach her.

It was this that made Miss Louisa most furious. She went downstairs, and announced to her mother:

'I am going out. I may not be home to tea.'

VIII

No one remarked on her exit. She put on her fur hat, that the village people knew so well, and the old Norfolk jacket. Louisa was short and plump and plain. She had her mother's heavy jaw, her father's proud brow, and her own grey, brooding eyes that were very beautiful when she smiled. It was true, as the people said, that she looked sulky. Her chief attraction was her glistening, heavy, deep-blond hair, which shone and gleamed with a richness that was not entirely foreign to her.

'Where am I going?' she said to herself, when she got outside in the snow. She did not hesitate, however, but by mechanical walking found herself descending the hill towards Old Aldecross. In the valley that was black with trees, the colliery breathed in stertorous pants, sending out high conical columns of steam that remained upright, whiter than the snow on the hills, yet shadowy, in the dead air. Louisa would not acknowledge to herself whither she was making her way, till she came to the railway crossing. Then the bunches of snow in the twigs of the apple tree that leaned towards the fence told her she must go and see Mrs Durant. The tree was in Mrs Durant's garden.

Alfred was now at home again, living with his mother in the cottage below the road. From the highway hedge, by the railway crossing, the snowy garden sheered down steeply, like the side of a hole, then dropped straight in a wall. In this depth the house was snug, its chimney just level with the road. Miss Louisa descended the stone stairs, and stood below in the little backyard, in the dimness and the semi-secrecy. A big tree leaned overhead, above the paraffin hut. Louisa felt secure from all the world down there. She knocked at the open door, then looked round. The tongue of garden narrowing in from the quarry bed was white with snow: she thought of the thick fringes of snowdrops it would show beneath the currant bushes in a month's time. The ragged fringe of pinks hanging over the garden brim behind her was whitened now with snow-flakes, that in summer held white blossom to Louisa's face. It was pleasant, she thought, to gather flowers that stooped to one's face from above.

She knocked again. Peeping in, she saw the scarlet glow of the kitchen, red firelight falling on the brick floor and on the bright chintz cushions. It was alive and bright as a peep-show. She crossed the scullery, where still an almanac hung. There was no one about. 'Mrs Durant,' called Louisa softly, 'Mrs Durant.'

She went up the brick step into the front room, that still had its little shop counter and its bundles of goods, and she called from the stair-foot. Then she knew Mrs Durant was out.

She went into the yard to follow the old woman's footsteps up the garden path.

She emerged from the bushes and raspberry canes. There was the whole quarry bed, a wide garden white and dimmed, brindled with dark bushes, lying half submerged. On the left, overhead, the little colliery train rumbled by. Right away at the back was a mass of trees.

Louisa followed the open path, looking from right to left, and then she gave a cry of concern. The old woman was sitting rocking slightly among the ragged snowy cabbages. Louisa ran to her, found her whimpering with little, involuntary cries.

'Whatever have you done?' cried Louisa, kneeling in the snow.

'I've – I've – I was pulling a brussel-sprout stalk – and – oh-h! – something tore inside me. I've had a pain,' the old woman wept from shock and suffering, gasping between her whimpers, – 'I've had a pain there – a long time – and now – oh – oh!' She panted, pressed her hand on her side, leaned as if she would faint, looking yellow against the snow. Louisa supported her.

'Do you think you could walk now?' she asked.

'Yes,' gasped the old woman.

Louisa helped her to her feet.

'Get the cabbage – I want it for Alfred's dinner,' panted Mrs Durant. Louisa picked up the stalk of brussel-sprouts, and with difficulty got the old woman indoors. She gave her brandy, laid her on the couch, saying:

'I'm going to send for a doctor – wait just a minute.'

The young woman ran up the steps to the public-house a few yards away. The landlady was astonished to see Miss Louisa.

'Will you send for a doctor at once to Mrs Durant,' she said, with some of her father in her commanding tone.

'Is something the matter?' fluttered the landlady in concern.

Louisa, glancing out up the road, saw the grocer's cart driving to Eastwood. She ran and stopped the man, and told him.

Mrs Durant lay on the sofa, her face turned away, when the young woman came back.

'Let me put you to bed,' Louisa said. Mrs Durant did not resist.

Louisa knew the ways of the working people. In the bottom drawer of the dresser she found dusters and flannels. With the old pit-flannel she snatched out the oven shelves, wrapped them up, and put them in the bed. From the son's bed she took a blanket, and, running down, set it before the fire. Having undressed the little old woman, Louisa carried her upstairs.

'You'll drop me, you'll drop me!' cried Mrs Durant.

Louisa did not answer, but bore her burden quickly. She could not light a fire, because there was no fire-place in the bedroom. And the floor was plaster. So she fetched the lamp, and stood it lighted in one corner.

'It will air the room,' she said.

'Yes,' moaned the old woman.

Louisa ran with more hot flannels, replacing those from the oven shelves. Then she made a bran-bag and laid it on the woman's side. There was a big lump on the side of the abdomen.

'I've felt it coming a long time,' moaned the old lady, when the pain was easier, 'but I've not said anything; I didn't want to upset our Alfred.'

Louisa did not see why 'our Alfred' should be spared.

'What time is it?' came the plaintive voice.

'A quarter to four.'

'Oh!' wailed the old lady, 'he'll be here in half an hour, and no dinner ready for him.'

'Let me do it?' said Louisa, gently.

'There's that cabbage – and you'll find the meat in the pantry – and there's an apple pie you can hot up. But *don't you* do it – !'

'Who will, then?' asked Louisa.

'I don't know,' moaned the sick woman, unable to consider.

Louisa did it. The doctor came and gave serious examination. He looked very grave.

'What is it, doctor?' asked the old lady, looking up at him with old, pathetic eyes in which already hope was dead.

'I think you've torn the skin in which a tumour hangs,' he replied.

'Ay!' she murmured, and she turned away.

'You see, she may die any minute – and it *may* be swaled away,'[5] said the old doctor to Louisa.

The young woman went upstairs again.

'He says the lump may be swaled away, and you may get quite well again,' she said.

'Ay!' murmured the old lady. It did not deceive her. Presently she asked:

'Is there a good fire?'

'I think so,' answered Louisa.

'He'll want a good fire,' the mother said. Louisa attended to it.

Since the death of Durant, the widow had come to church occasionally, and Louisa had been friendly to her. In the girl's heart the purpose was fixed. No man had affected her as Alfred Durant had done, and to that she kept. In her heart, she adhered to him. A natural sympathy existed between her and his rather hard, materialistic mother.

Alfred was the most lovable of the old woman's sons. He had grown up like the rest, however, headstrong and blind to everything but his own will. Like the other boys, he had insisted on going into the pit as soon as he left school, because that was the only way speedily to become a man, level with all the other men. This was a great chagrin to his mother, who would have liked to have this last of her sons a gentleman.

But still he remained constant to her. His feeling for her was deep and unexpressed. He noticed when she was tired, or when she had a new cap. And he bought little things for her occasionally. She was not wise enough to see how much he lived by her.

At the bottom he did not satisfy her, he did not seem manly enough. He liked to read books occasionally, and better still he liked to play the piccolo. It amused her to see his head nod over the instrument as he made an effort to get the right note. It made her fond of him, with tenderness, almost pity, but not with respect. She wanted a man to be fixed, going his own way without knowledge of women. Whereas she knew Alfred depended on her. He sang in the choir because he liked singing. In the summer he worked in the garden, attended to the fowls and pigs. He kept pigeons. He played on Saturday in the cricket or football team. But to her he did not seem the man, the independent man her other boys had been. He was her baby – and whilst she loved him for it, she was a little bit contemptuous of him.

There grew up a little hostility between them. Then he began to drink, as the others had done; but not in their blind, oblivious way. He was a little self-conscious over it. She saw this, and she pitied it in him. She loved him most, but she was not satisfied with him because he was not free of her. He could not quite go his own way.

Then at twenty he ran away and served his time in the Navy. This made a man of him. He had hated it bitterly, the service, the subordination. For years he fought with himself under the military discipline, for his own self-respect, struggling through blind anger and shame and a cramping sense of inferiority. Out of humiliation and self-hatred, he rose into a sort of inner freedom. And his love for his mother, whom he idealised, remained the fact of hope and of belief.

He came home again, nearly thirty years old, but naïve and inexperienced as a boy, only with a silence about him that was new: a sort of dumb humility before life, a fear of living. He was almost quite chaste. A strong sensitiveness had kept him from women. Sexual talk was all very well among men, but somehow it had no application to living women. There were two things for him, the *idea* of women, with which he sometimes debauched himself, and real women, before whom he felt a deep uneasiness, and a need to draw away. He shrank and defended himself from the approach of any woman. And then he felt ashamed. In his innermost soul he felt he was not a man, he was less than the normal man. In Genoa he went with an under officer to a drinking house where the cheaper sort of girl came in to look for lovers. He sat there with his glass, the girls looked at him, but they never came to him. He knew that if they did come he could only pay for food and drink for them, because he felt a pity for them, and was anxious lest they lacked good necessities. He could not have gone with one of them: he knew it, and was ashamed, looking with curious envy at the swaggering, easy-passionate Italian whose body went to a woman by instinctive impersonal attraction. They were men, he was not a man. He sat feeling short, feeling like a leper. And he went away imagining sexual scenes between himself and a woman, walking wrapt in this indulgence. But when the ready woman presented herself, the very fact that she was a palpable woman made it impossible for him to touch her. And this incapacity was like a core of rottenness in him.

So several times he went, drunk, with his companions, to the licensed prostitute houses abroad. But the sordid insignificance of the experience appalled him. It had not been anything really: it meant nothing. He felt as if he were, not physically, but spiritually impotent: not actually impotent, but intrinsically so.

He came home with this secret, never changing burden of his unknown, unbestowed self torturing him. His navy training left him in perfect physical condition. He was sensible of, and proud of his body. He bathed and used dumb-bells, and kept himself fit. He played cricket and football. He read books and began to hold fixed ideas which he got from the Fabians.[6] He played his piccolo, and was considered an expert. But at the bottom of his soul was always this canker of shame and incompleteness: he was miserable beneath all his healthy cheerfulness, he was uneasy and felt despicable among all his confidence and superiority of ideas. He would have changed with any mere brute, just to be free of himself, to be free of this shame of self-consciousness. He saw some collier lurching straight forward without misgiving, pursuing his own satisfactions, and he envied him. Anything, he would have given anything for this spontaneity and this blind stupidity which went to its own satisfaction direct.

IX

He was not unhappy in the pit. He was admired by the men, and well enough liked. It was only he himself who felt the difference between himself and the others. He seemed to hide his own stigma. But he was never sure that the others did not really despise him for a ninny, as being less a man than they were. Only he pretended to be more manly, and was surprised by the ease with which they were deceived. And, being naturally cheerful, he was happy at his work. He was sure of himself there. Naked to the waist, hot and grimy with labour, they squatted on their heels for a few minutes and talked, seeing each other dimly by the light of the safety lamps, while the black coal rose jutting round them, and the props of wood stood like little pillars in the low, black, very dark temple. Then the pony came and the gang-lad with a message from Number 7, or with a bottle of water from the horse-trough or some news of the world above. The day passed pleasantly enough. There was an ease, a go-as-you-please about the day underground, a delightful camaraderie of men shut off alone from the rest of the world, in a dangerous place, and a variety of labour, holing, loading, timbering, and a glamour of mystery and adventure in the atmosphere, that made the pit not unattractive to him when he had again got over his anguish of desire for the open air and the sea.

This day there was much to do and Durant was not in humour to talk. He went on working in silence through the afternoon.

'Loose-all' came, and they tramped to the bottom. The whitewashed underground office shone brightly. Men were putting out their lamps. They sat in dozens round the bottom of the shaft, down which black, heavy drops of water fell continuously into the sump. The electric lights shone away down the main underground road.

'Is it raining?' asked Durant.

'Snowing,' said an old man, and the younger was pleased. He liked to go up when it was snowing.

'It'll just come right for Christmas,' said the old man.

'Ay,' replied Durant.

'A green Christmas, a fat churchyard,' said the other sententiously.

Durant laughed, showing his small, rather pointed teeth.

The cage came down, a dozen men lined on. Durant noticed tufts of snow on the perforated, arched roof of the chain, and he was pleased.

He wondered how it liked its excursion underground. But already it was getting soppy with black water.

He liked things about him. There was a little smile on his face. But underlying it was the curious consciousness he felt in himself.

The upper world came almost with a flash, because of the glimmer of snow. Hurrying along the bank, giving up his lamp at the office, he smiled to feel the open about him again, all glimmering round him with snow. The hills on either side were pale blue in the dusk, and the hedges looked savage and dark. The snow was trampled between the railway lines. But far ahead, beyond the black figures of miners moving home, it became smooth again, spreading right up to the dark wall of the coppice.

To the west there was a pinkness, and a big star hovered half revealed. Below, the lights of the pit came out crisp and yellow among the darkness of the buildings, and the lights of Old Aldecross twinkled in rows down the bluish twilight.

Durant walked glad with life among the miners, who were all talking animatedly because of the snow. He liked their company, he liked the white dusky world. It gave him a little thrill to stop at the garden gate and see the light of home down below, shining on the silent blue snow.

X

By the big gate of the railway, in the fence, was a little gate, that he kept locked. As he unfastened it, he watched the kitchen light that shone on to the bushes and the snow outside. It was a candle burning till night set in, he thought to himself. He slid down the steep path to the level below. He liked making the first marks in the smooth snow. Then he came through the bushes to the house. The two women heard his heavy boots ring outside on the scraper, and his voice as he opened the door:

'How much worth of oil do you reckon to save by that candle, mother?' He liked a good light from the lamp.

He had just put down his bottle and snap-bag and was hanging his coat behind the scullery door, when Miss Louisa came upon him. He was startled, but he smiled.

His eyes began to laugh – then his face went suddenly straight, and he was afraid.

'Your mother's had an accident,' she said.

'How?' he exclaimed.

'In the garden,' she answered. He hesitated with his coat in his hands. Then he hung it up and turned to the kitchen.

'Is she in bed?' he asked.

'Yes,' said Miss Louisa, who found it hard to deceive him. He was silent. He went into the kitchen, sat down heavily in his father's old chair, and began to pull off his boots. His head was small, rather finely shapen. His brown hair, close and crisp, would look jolly whatever happened. He wore heavy moleskin trousers that gave off the stale, exhausted scent of the pit. Having put on his slippers, he carried his boots into the scullery.

'What is it?' he asked, afraid.

'Something internal,' she replied.

He went upstairs. His mother kept herself calm for his coming. Louisa felt his tread shake the plaster floor of the bedroom above.

'What have you done?' he asked.

'It's nothing, my lad,' said the old woman, rather hard. 'It's nothing. You needn't fret, my boy, it's nothing more the matter with me than I had yesterday, or last week. The doctor said I'd done nothing serious.'

'What were you doing?' asked her son.

'I was pulling up a cabbage, and I suppose I pulled too hard; for, oh – there was such a pain –'

Her son looked at her quickly. She hardened herself.

'But who doesn't have a sudden pain sometimes, my boy. We all do.'

'And what's it done?'

'I don't know,' she said, 'but I don't suppose it's anything.'

The big lamp in the corner was screened with a dark green, so that he could scarcely see her face. He was strung tight with apprehension and many emotions. Then his brow knitted.

'What did you go pulling your inside out at cabbages for,' he asked, 'and the ground frozen? You'd go on dragging and dragging, if you killed yourself.'

'Somebody's got to get them,' she said.

'You needn't do yourself harm.'

But they had reached futility.

Miss Louisa could hear plainly downstairs. Her heart sank. It seemed so hopeless between them.

'Are you sure it's nothing much, mother?' he asked, appealing, after a little silence.

'Ay, it's nothing,' said the old woman, rather bitter.

'I don't want you to – to – to be badly – you know.'

'Go an' get your dinner,' she said. She knew she was going to die: moreover, the pain was torture just then. 'They're only cosseting me up a bit because I'm an old woman. Miss Louisa's *very* good – and she'll have got your dinner ready, so you'd better go and eat it.'

He felt stupid and ashamed. His mother put him off. He had to turn away. The pain burned in his bowels. He went downstairs. The mother was glad he was gone, so that she could moan with pain.

He had resumed the old habit of eating before he washed himself. Miss Louisa served his dinner. It was strange and exciting to her. She was strung up tense, trying to understand him and his mother. She watched him as he sat. He was turned away from his food, looking in the fire. Her soul watched him, trying to see what he was. His black face and arms were uncouth, he was foreign. His face was masked black with coal-dust. She could not see him, she could not even know him. The brown eyebrows, the steady eyes, the coarse, small moustache above the closed mouth – these were the only familiar indications. What was he, as he sat there in his pit-dirt? She could not see him, and it hurt her.

She ran upstairs, presently coming down with the flannels and the bran-bag, to heat them, because the pain was on again.

He was half-way through his dinner. He put down the fork, suddenly nauseated.

'They will soothe the wrench,' she said. He watched, useless and left out.

'Is she bad?' he asked.

'I think she is,' she answered.

It was useless for him to stir or comment. Louisa was busy. She went upstairs. The poor old woman was in a white, cold sweat of pain. Louisa's face was sullen with suffering as she went about to relieve her. Then she sat and waited. The pain passed gradually, the old woman sank into a state of coma. Louisa still sat silent by the bed. She heard the sound of water downstairs. Then came the voice of the old mother, faint but unrelaxing:

'Alfred's washing himself – he'll want his back washing –'

Louisa listened anxiously, wondering what the sick woman wanted.

'He can't bear if his back isn't washed –' the old woman persisted, in a cruel attention to his needs. Louisa rose and wiped the sweat from the yellowish brow.

'I will go down,' she said soothingly.

'If you would,' murmured the sick woman.

Louisa waited a moment. Mrs Durant closed her eyes, having discharged her duty. The young woman went downstairs. Herself, or the man, what did they matter? Only the suffering woman must be considered.

Alfred was kneeling on the hearthrug, stripped to the waist, washing himself in a large panchion of earthenware. He did so every evening, when he had eaten his dinner; his brothers had done so before him. But Miss Louisa was strange in the house.

He was mechanically rubbing the white lather on his head, with a repeated, unconscious movement, his hand every now and then passing over his neck. Louisa watched. She had to brace herself to this also. He bent his head into the water, washed it free of soap, and pressed the water out of his eyes.

'Your mother said you would want your back washing,' she said.

Curious how it hurt her to take part in their fixed routine of life! Louisa felt the almost repulsive intimacy being forced upon her. It was all so common, so like herding. She lost her own distinctness.

He ducked his face round, looking up at her in what was a very comical way. She had to harden herself.

'How funny he looks with his face upside down,' she thought. After all, there was a difference between her and the common people. The water in which his arms were plunged was quite black, the soap-froth was darkish. She could scarcely conceive him as human. Mechanically, under the influence of habit, he groped in the black water, fished out soap and flannel, and handed them backward to Louisa. Then he remained rigid and submissive, his two arms thrust straight in the panchion, supporting the weight of his shoulders. His skin was beautifully white and unblemished, of an opaque, solid whiteness. Gradually Louisa saw it: this also was what he was. It fascinated her. Her feeling of separateness passed away: she ceased to draw back from contact with him and his mother. There was this living centre. Her heart ran hot. She had reached some goal in this beautiful, clear, male body. She loved him in a white, impersonal heat. But the sun-burnt, reddish neck and ears: they were more personal, more curious. A tenderness rose in her, she loved even his queer ears. A person – an intimate being he was to her. She put down the towel and went upstairs again, troubled in her heart. She had only seen one human being in her life – and that was Mary. All the rest were strangers. Now her soul was going to open, she was going to see another. She felt strange and pregnant.

'He'll be more comfortable,' murmured the sick woman abstractedly, as Louisa entered the room. The latter did not answer. Her own heart was heavy with its own responsibility. Mrs Durant lay silent awhile, then she murmured plaintively:

'You mustn't mind, Miss Louisa.'

'Why should I?' replied Louisa, deeply moved.

'It's what we're used to,' said the old woman.

And Louisa felt herself excluded again from their life. She sat in pain, with the tears of disappointment distilling her heart. Was that all?

Alfred came upstairs. He was clean, and in his shirt-sleeves. He looked a workman now. Louisa felt that she and he were foreigners, moving in different lives. It dulled her again. Oh, if she could only find some fixed relations, something sure and abiding.

'How do you feel?' he said to his mother.

'It's a bit better,' she replied wearily, impersonally. This strange putting herself aside, this abstracting herself and answering him only what she thought good for him to hear, made the relations between mother and son poignant and cramping to Miss Louisa. It made the man so ineffectual, so nothing. Louisa groped as if she had lost him. The mother was real and positive – he was not very actual. It puzzled and chilled the young woman.

'I'd better fetch Mrs Harrison?' he said, waiting for his mother to decide.

'I suppose we shall have to have somebody,' she replied.

Miss Louisa stood by, afraid to interfere in their business. They did not include her in their lives, they felt she had nothing to do with them, except as a help from outside. She was quite external to them. She felt hurt and powerless against this unconscious difference. But something patient and unyielding in her made her say:

'I will stay and do the nursing: you can't be left.'

The other two were shy, and at a loss for an answer.

'Wes'll manage to get somebody,' said the old woman wearily. She did not care very much what happened, now.

'I will stay until to-morrow, in any case,' said Louisa. 'Then we can see.'

'I'm sure you've no right to trouble yourself,' moaned the old woman. But she must leave herself in any hands.

Miss Louisa felt glad that she was admitted, even in an official capacity. She wanted to share their lives. At home they would need her, now Mary had come. But they must manage without her.

'I must write a note to the vicarage,' she said.

Alfred Durant looked at her inquiringly, for her service. He had always that intelligent readiness to serve, since he had been in the Navy. But there was a simple independence in his willingness, which she loved. She felt nevertheless it was hard to get at him. He was so deferential, quick to take the slightest suggestion of an order from her, implicitly, that she could not get at the man in him.

He looked at her very keenly. She noticed his eyes were golden brown, with a very small pupil, the kind of eyes that can see a long way off. He stood alert, at military attention. His face was still rather weather-reddened.

'Do you want pen and paper?' he asked, with deferential suggestion to a superior, which was more difficult for her than reserve.

'Yes, please,' she said.

He turned and went downstairs. He seemed to her so self-contained, so utterly sure in his movement. How was she to approach him? For he would take not one step towards her. He would only put himself entirely and impersonally at her service, glad to serve her, but keeping himself quite removed from her. She could see he felt real joy in doing anything for her, but any recognition would confuse him and hurt him. Strange it was to her, to have a man going about the house in his shirt-sleeves, his waistcoat unbuttoned, his throat bare, waiting on her. He moved well, as if he had plenty of life to spare. She was attracted by his completeness. And yet, when all was ready, and there was nothing more for him to do, she quivered, meeting his questioning look.

As she sat writing, he placed another candle near her. The rather dense light fell in two places on the overfoldings of her hair till it glistened heavy and bright, like a dense golden plumage folded up. Then the nape of her neck was very white, with fine down and pointed wisps of gold. He watched it as it were a vision, losing himself. She was all that was beyond him, of revelation and exquisiteness. All that was ideal and beyond him, she was that – and he was lost to himself in looking at her. She had no connection with him. He did not approach her. She was there like a wonderful distance. But it was a treat, having her in the house. Even with this anguish for his mother tightening about him, he was sensible of the wonder of living this evening. The candles glistened on her hair, and seemed to fascinate him. He felt a little awe of her, and a sense of uplifting, that he and she and his mother should be together for a time, in the strange, unknown atmosphere. And, when he got out of the house, he was afraid. He saw the stars above ringing with fine brightness, the snow beneath just visible, and a new night was gathering round him. He was afraid almost with obliteration. What was this new night ringing about him, and what was he? He could not recognize himself nor any of his surroundings. He was afraid to think of his mother. And yet his chest was conscious of her, and of what was happening to her. He could not escape from her, she carried him with her into an unformed, unknown chaos.

XI

He went up the road in an agony, not knowing what it was all about, but feeling as if a red-hot iron were gripped round his chest. Without thinking, he shook two or three tears on to the snow. Yet in his mind he did not believe his mother would die. He was in the grip of some greater consciousness. As he sat in the hall of the vicarage, waiting whilst Mary put things for Louisa into a bag, he wondered why he had been so upset. He felt abashed and humbled by the big house, he felt again as if he were one of the rank and file. When Miss Mary spoke to him, he almost saluted.

'An honest man,' thought Mary. And the patronage was applied as salve to her own sickness. She had station, so she could patronize: it was almost all that was left to her. But she could not have lived without having a certain position. She could never have trusted herself outside a definite place, nor respected herself except as a woman of superior class.

As Alfred came to the latch-gate, he felt the grief at his heart again, and saw the new heavens. He stood a moment looking northward to the Plough climbing up the night, and at the far glimmer of snow in distant fields. Then his grief came on like physical pain. He held tight to the gate, biting his mouth, whispering 'Mother!' It was a fierce, cutting, physical pain of grief, that came on in bouts, as his mother's pain came on in bouts, and was so acute he could scarcely keep erect. He did not know where it came from, the pain, nor why. It had nothing to do with his thoughts. Almost it had nothing to do with him. Only it gripped him and he must submit. The whole tide of his soul, gathering in its unknown towards this expansion into death, carried him with it helplessly, all the fritter of his thought and consciousness caught up as nothing, the heave passing on towards its breaking, taking him further than he had ever been. When the young man had regained himself, he went indoors, and there he was almost gay. It seemed to excite him. He felt in high spirits: he made whimsical fun of things. He sat on one side of his mother's bed, Louisa on the other, and a certain gaiety seized them all. But the night and the dread was coming on.

Alfred kissed his mother and went to bed. When he was half undressed the knowledge of his mother came upon him, and the suffering seized him in its grip like two hands, in agony. He lay on the bed screwed up tight. It lasted so long, and exhausted him so much, that he fell asleep, without having the energy to get up and finish undressing. He awoke after midnight to find himself stone cold. He undressed and got into bed, and was soon asleep again.

At a quarter to six he woke, and instantly remembered. Having pulled on his trousers and lighted a candle, he went into his mother's room. He put his hand before the candle flame so that no light fell on the bed.

'Mother!' he whispered.

'Yes,' was the reply.

There was a hesitation.

'Should I go to work?'

He waited, his heart was beating heavily.

'I think I'd go, my lad.'

His heart went down in a kind of despair.

'You want me to?'

He let his hand down from the candle flame. The light fell on the bed. There he saw Louisa lying looking up at him. Her eyes were upon him. She quickly shut her eyes and half buried her face in the pillow, her back turned to him. He saw the rough hair like bright vapour about her round head, and the two plaits flung coiled among the bedclothes. It gave him a shock. He stood almost himself, determined. Louisa cowered down. He looked, and met his mother's eyes. Then he gave way again, and ceased to be sure, ceased to be himself.

'Yes, go to work, my boy,' said the mother.

'All right,' replied he, kissing her. His heart was down at despair, and bitter. He went away.

'Alfred!' cried his mother faintly.

He came back with beating heart.

'What, mother?'

'You'll always do what's right, Alfred?' the mother asked, beside herself in terror now he was leaving her. He was too terrified and bewildered to know what she meant.

'Yes,' he said.

She turned her cheek to him. He kissed her, then went away, in bitter despair. He went to work.

XII

By midday his mother was dead. The word met him at the pit-mouth. As he had known, inwardly, it was not a shock to him, and yet he trembled. He went home quite calmly, feeling only heavy in his breathing.

Miss Louisa was still at the house. She had seen to everything possible. Very succinctly, she informed him of what he needed to know. But there was one point of anxiety for her.

'You *did* half expect it – it's not come as a blow to you?' she asked, looking up at him. Her eyes were dark and calm and searching. She too felt lost. He was so dark and inchoate.

'I suppose – yes,' he said stupidly. He looked aside, unable to endure her eyes on him.

'I could not bear to think you might not have guessed,' she said.

He did not answer.

He felt it a great strain to have her near him at this time. He wanted to be alone. As soon as the relatives began to arrive, Louisa departed and came no more. While everything was arranging, and a crowd was in the house, whilst he had business to settle, he went well enough, with only those uncontrollable paroxysms of grief. For the rest, he was superficial. By himself, he endured the fierce, almost insane bursts of grief which passed again and left him calm, almost clear, just wondering. He had not known before that everything could break down, that he himself could break down, and all be a great chaos, very vast and wonderful. It seemed as if life in him had burst its bounds, and he was lost in a great, bewildering flood, immense and unpeopled. He himself was broken and spilled out amid it all. He could only breathe panting in silence. Then the anguish came on again.

When all the people had gone from the Quarry Cottage, leaving the young man alone with an elderly housekeeper, then the long trial began. The snow had thawed and frozen, a fresh fall had whitened the grey, this then began to thaw. The world was a place of loose grey slosh. Alfred had nothing to do in the evenings. He was a man whose life had been filled up with small activities. Without knowing it, he had been centralized, polarized in his mother. It was she who had kept him. Even now, when the old housekeeper had left him, he might still have gone on in his old way. But the force and balance of his life was lacking. He sat pretending to read, all the time holding his fists clenched, and holding himself in, enduring he did not know what. He walked the black and sodden miles of field-paths, till he was tired out: but all this was only running away from whence he must return. At work he was all right. If it had been summer he might have escaped by working in the garden till bedtime. But now, there was no escape, no relief, no help. He, perhaps, was made for action rather than for understanding; for doing than for being. He was shocked out of his activities, like a swimmer who forgets to swim.

For a week, he had the force to endure this suffocation and struggle, then he began to get exhausted, and knew it must come out. The instinct of self-preservation became strongest. But there was the question: Where was he to go? The public-house really meant nothing to him, it was no good going there. He began to think of emigration. In another country he would be all right. He wrote to the emigration offices.

On the Sunday after the funeral, when all the Durant people had attended church, Alfred had seen Miss Louisa, impassive and reserved, sitting with Miss Mary, who was proud and very distant, and with the other Lindleys, who were people removed. Alfred saw them as people remote. He did not think about it. They had nothing to do with his life. After service Louisa had come to him and shaken hands.

'My sister would like you to come to supper one evening, if you would be so good.'

He looked at Miss Mary, who bowed. Out of kindness, Mary had proposed this to Louisa, disapproving of herself even as she did so. But she did not examine herself closely.

'Yes,' said Durant awkwardly, 'I'll come if you want me.' But he vaguely felt that it was misplaced.

'You'll come to-morrow evening, then, about half-past six.'

He went. Miss Louisa was very kind to him. There could be no music, because of the babies. He sat with his fists clenched on his thighs, very quiet and unmoved, lapsing, among all those people, into a kind of muse or daze. There was nothing between him and them. They knew it as well as he. But he remained very steady in himself, and the evening passed slowly. Mrs Lindley called him 'young man'.

'Will you sit here, young man?'

He sat there. One name was as good as another. What had they to do with him?

Mr Lindley kept a special tone for him, kind, indulgent, but patronizing. Durant took it all without criticism or offence, just submitting. But he did not want to eat – that troubled him, to have to eat in their presence. He knew he was out of place. But it was his duty to stay yet awhile. He answered precisely, in monosyllables.

When he left he winced with confusion. He was glad it was finished. He got away as quickly as possible. And he wanted still more intensely to go right away, to Canada.

Miss Louisa suffered in her soul, indignant with all of them, with him too, but quite unable to say why she was indignant.

XIII

Two evenings after, Louisa tapped at the door of the Quarry Cottage, at half-past six. He had finished dinner, the woman had washed up and gone away, but still he sat in his pit dirt. He was going later to the New Inn. He had begun to go there because he must go somewhere. The mere contact with other men was necessary to him, the noise, the warmth, the forgetful flight of the hours. But still he did not move. He sat alone in the empty house till it began to grow on him like something unnatural.

He was in his pit dirt when he opened the door.

'I have been wanting to call – I thought I would,' she said, and she went to the sofa. He wondered why she wouldn't use his mother's round armchair. Yet something stirred in him, like anger, when the housekeeper placed herself in it.

'I ought to have been washed by now,' he said, glancing at the clock, which was adorned with butterflies and cherries, and the name of 'T. Brooks, Mansfield.' He laid his black hands along his mottled dirty arms. Louisa looked at him. There was the reserve, and the simple neutrality towards her, which she dreaded in him. It made it impossible for her to approach him.

'I am afraid,' she said, 'that I wasn't kind in asking you to supper.'

'I'm not used to it,' he said, smiling with his mouth, showing the interspaced white teeth. His eyes, however, were steady and unseeing.

'It's not *that*,' she said hastily. Her repose was exquisite and her dark grey eyes rich with understanding. He felt afraid of her as she sat there, as he began to grow conscious of her.

'How do you get on alone?' she asked.

He glanced away to the fire.

'Oh –' he answered, shifting uneasily, not finishing his answer.

Her face settled heavily.

'How close it is in this room. You have such immense fires. I will take off my coat,' she said.

He watched her take off her hat and coat. She wore a cream cashmir blouse embroidered with gold silk. It seemed to him a very fine garment, fitting her throat and wrists close. It gave him a feeling of pleasure and cleanness and relief from himself.

'What were you thinking about, that you didn't get washed?' she asked, half intimately. He laughed, turning aside his head. The whites of his eyes showed very distinct in his black face.

'Oh,' he said, 'I couldn't tell you.'

There was a pause.

'Are you going to keep this house on?' she asked.

He stirred in his chair, under the question.

'I hardly know,' he said. 'I'm very likely going to Canada.'

Her spirit became very quiet and attentive.

'What for?' she asked.

Again he shifted restlessly on his seat.

'Well' – he said slowly – 'to try the life.'

'But which life?'

'There's various things – farming or lumbering or mining. I don't mind much what it is.'

'And is that what you want?'

He did not think in these times, so he could not answer.

'I don't know,' he said, 'till I've tried.'

She saw him drawing away from her for ever.

'Aren't you sorry to leave this house and garden?' she asked.

'I don't know,' he answered reluctantly. 'I suppose our Fred would come in – that's what he's wanting.'

'You don't want to settle down?' she asked.

He was leaning forward on the arms of his chair. He turned to her. Her face was pale and set. It looked heavy and impassive, her hair shone richer as she grew white. She was to him something steady and immovable and eternal presented to him. His heart was hot in an anguish of suspense. Sharp twitches of fear and pain were in his limbs. He turned his whole body away from her. The silence was unendurable. He could not bear her to sit there any more. It made his heart go hot and stifled in his breast.

'Were you going out to-night?' she asked.

'Only to the New Inn,' he said.

Again there was silence.

She reached for her hat. Nothing else was suggested to her. She *had* to go. He sat waiting for her to be gone, for relief. And she knew that if she went out of that house as she was, she went out a failure.

Yet she continued to pin on her hat; in a moment she would have to go. Something was carrying her.

Then suddenly a sharp pang, like lightning, seared her from head to foot, and she was beyond herself.

'Do you want me to go?' she asked, controlled, yet speaking out of a fiery anguish, as if the words were spoken from her without her intervention.

He went white under his dirt.

'Why?' he asked, turning to her in fear, compelled.

'Do you want me to go?' she repeated.

'Why?' he asked again.

'Because I wanted to stay with you,' she said, suffocated, with her lungs full of fire.

His face worked, he hung forward a little, suspended, staring straight into her eyes, in torment, in an agony of chaos, unable to collect himself. And as if turned to stone, she looked back into his eyes. Their souls were exposed bare for a few moments. It was agony. They could not bear it. He dropped his head, whilst his body jerked with little sharp twitchings.

She turned away for her coat. Her soul had gone dead in her. Her hands trembled, but she could not feel any more. She drew on her coat. There was a cruel suspense in the room. The moment had come for her to go. He lifted his head. His eyes were like agate, expressionless, save for the black points of torture. They held her, she had no will, no life any more. She felt broken.

'Don't you want me?' she said helplessly.

A spasm of torture crossed his eyes, which held her fixed.

'I – I –' he began, but he could not speak. Something drew him from his chair to her. She stood motionless, spellbound, like a creature given up as prey. He put his hand tentatively, uncertainly, on her arm. The expression of his face was strange and inhuman. She stood utterly motionless. Then clumsily he put his arms round her, and took her, cruelly, blindly, straining her till she nearly lost consciousness, till he himself had almost fallen.

Then, gradually, as he held her gripped, and his brain reeled round, and he felt himself falling, falling from himself, and whilst she, yielded up, swooned to a kind of death of herself, a moment of utter darkness came over him, and they began to wake up again as if from a long sleep. He was himself.

After a while his arms slackened, she loosened herself a little, and put her arms round him, as he held her. So they held each other close, and hid each against the other for assurance, helpless in speech. And it was ever her hands that trembled more closely upon him, drawing him nearer into her, with love.

And at last she drew back her face and looked up at him, her eyes wet, and shining with light. His heart, which saw, was silent with fear. He was with her. She saw his face all sombre and inscrutable, and he seemed eternal to her. And all the echo of pain came back into the rarity of bliss, and all her tears came up.

'I love you,' she said, her lips drawn and sobbing. He put down his head against her, unable to hear her, unable to bear the sudden coming of the peace and passion that almost broke his heart. They stood together in silence whilst the thing moved away a little.

At last she wanted to see him. She looked up. His eyes were strange and glowing, with a tiny black pupil. Strange, they were, and powerful over her. And his mouth came to hers, and slowly her eyelids closed, as his mouth sought hers closer and closer, and took possession of her.

They were silent for a long time, too much mixed up with passion and grief and death to do anything but hold each other in pain and kiss with long, hurting kisses wherein fear was transfused into desire. At last she disengaged herself. He felt as if his heart were hurt, but glad, and he scarcely dared look at her.

'I'm glad,' she said also.

He held her hands in passionate gratitude and desire. He had not yet the presence of mind to say anything. He was dazed with relief.

'I ought to go,' she said.

He looked at her. He could not grasp the thought of her going, he knew he could never be separated from her any more. Yet he dared not assert himself. He held her hands tight.

'Your face is black,' she said.

He laughed.

'Yours is a bit smudged,' he said.

They were afraid of each other, afraid to talk. He could only keep her near to him. After a while she wanted to wash her face. He brought her some warm water, standing by and watching her. There was something he wanted to say, that he dared not. He watched her wiping her face, and making tidy her hair.

'They'll see your blouse is dirty,' he said.

She looked at her sleeves and laughed for joy.

He was sharp with pride.

'What shall you do?' he asked.

'How?' she said.

He was awkward at a reply.

'About me,' he said.

'What do you want me to do?' she laughed.

He put his hand out slowly to her. What did it matter!

'But make yourself clean,' she said.

XIV

As they went up the hill, the night seemed dense with the unknown. They kept close together, feeling as if the darkness were alive and full of knowledge, all around them. In silence they walked up the hill. At first the street lamps went their way. Several people passed them. He was more shy than she, and would have let her go had she loosened in the least. But she held firm.

Then they came into the true darkness, between the fields. They did not want to speak, feeling closer together in silence. So they arrived at the Vicarage gate. They stood under the naked horse-chestnut tree.

'I wish you didn't have to go,' he said.

She laughed a quick little laugh.

'Come to-morrow,' she said, in a low tone, 'and ask father.'

She felt his hand close on hers.

She gave the same sorrowful little laugh of sympathy. Then she kissed him, sending him home.

At home, the old grief came on in another paroxysm, obliterating Louisa, obliterating even his mother for whom the stress was raging like a burst of fever in a wound. But something was sound in his heart.

XV

The next evening he dressed to go to the vicarage, feeling it was to be done, not imagining what it would be like. He would not take this seriously. He was sure of Louisa, and this marriage was like fate to him. It filled him also with a blessed feeling of fatality. He was not responsible, neither had her people anything really to do with it.

They ushered him into the little study, which was fireless. By and by the vicar came in. His voice was cold and hostile as he said:

'What can I do for you, young man?'

He knew already, without asking.

Durant looked up at him, again like a sailor before a superior. He had the subordinate manner. Yet his spirit was clear.

'I wanted, Mr Lindley –' he began respectfully, then all the colour suddenly left his face. It seemed now a violation to say what he had to say. What was he doing there? But he stood on, because it had to be done. He held firmly to his own independence and self-respect. He must not be indecisive. He must put himself aside: the matter was bigger than just his personal self. He must not feel. This was his highest duty.

'You wanted –' said the vicar.

Durant's mouth was dry, but he answered with steadiness:

'Miss Louisa – Louisa – promised to marry me –'

'You asked Miss Louisa if she would marry you – yes –' corrected the vicar. Durant reflected he had not asked her this:

'If she would marry me, sir. I hope you – don't mind.'

He smiled. He was a good-looking man, and the vicar could not help seeing it.

'And my daughter was willing to marry you?' said Mr Lindley.

'Yes,' said Durant seriously. It was pain to him, nevertheless. He felt the natural hostility between himself and the elder man.

'Will you come this way?' said the vicar. He led into the dining-room, where were Mary, Louisa, and Mrs Lindley. Mr Massy sat in a corner with a lamp.

'This young man has come on your account, Louisa?' said Mr Lindley.

'Yes,' said Louisa, her eyes on Durant, who stood erect, in discipline. He dared not look at her, but he was aware of her.

'You don't want to marry a collier, you little fool,' cried Mrs Lindley harshly. She lay obese and helpless upon the couch, swathed in a loose, dove-grey gown.

'Oh, hush, mother,' cried Mary, with quiet intensity and pride.

'What means have you to support a wife?' demanded the vicar's wife roughly.

'I!' Durant replied, starting. 'I think I can earn enough.'

'Well, and how much?' came the rough voice.

'Seven and six a day,' replied the young man.

'And will it get to be any more?'

'I hope so.'

'And are you going to live in that poky little house?'

'I think so,' said Durant, 'if it's all right.'

He took small offence, only was upset, because they would not think him good enough. He knew that, in their sense, he was not.

'Then she's a fool, I tell you, if she marries you,' cried the mother roughly, casting her decision.

'After all, mama, it is Louisa's affair,' said Mary distinctly, 'and we must remember –'

'As she makes her bed, she must lie – but she'll repent it,' interrupted Mrs Lindley.

'And after all,' said Mr Lindley, 'Louisa cannot quite hold herself free to act entirely without consideration for her family.'

'What do you want, papa?' asked Louisa sharply.

'I mean that if you marry this man, it will make my position very difficult for me, particularly if you stay in this parish. If you were moving quite away, it would be simpler. But living here in a collier's cottage, under my nose, as it were – it would be almost unseemly. I have my position to maintain, and a position which may not be taken lightly.'

'Come over here, young man,' cried the mother, in her rough voice, 'and let us look at you.'

Durant, flushing, went over and stood – not quite at attention, so that he did not know what to do with his hands. Miss Louisa was angry to see him standing there, obedient and acquiescent. He ought to show himself a man.

'Can't you take her away and live out of sight?' said the mother. 'You'd both of you be better off.'

'Yes, we can go away,' he said.

'Do you want to?' asked Miss Mary clearly.

He faced round. Mary looked very stately and impressive. He flushed.

'I do if it's going to be a trouble to anybody,' he said.

'For yourself, you would rather stay?' said Mary.

'It's my home,' he said, 'and that's the house I was born in.'

'Then' – Mary turned clearly to her parents, 'I really don't see how you can make the conditions, papa. He has his own rights, and if Louisa wants to marry him –'

'Louisa, Louisa!' cried the father impatiently. 'I cannot understand why Louisa should not behave in the normal way. I cannot see why she should only think of herself, and leave her family out of count. The thing is enough in itself, and she ought to try to ameliorate it as much as possible. And if –'

'But I love the man, papa,' said Louisa.

'And I hope you love your parents, and I hope you want to spare them as much of the – the loss of prestige, as possible.'

'We *can* go away to live,' said Louisa, her face breaking to tears. At last she was really hurt.

'Oh, yes, easily,' Durant replied hastily, pale, distressed.

There was dead silence in the room.

'I think it would really be better,' murmured the vicar, mollified.

'Very likely it would,' said the rough-voiced invalid.

'Though I think we ought to apologize for asking such a thing,' said Mary haughtily.

'No,' said Durant. 'It will be best all round.' He was glad there was no more bother.

'And shall we put up the banns here or go to the registrar?' he asked clearly, like a challenge.

'We will go to the registrar,' replied Louisa decidedly.

Again there was a dead silence in the room.

'Well, if you will have your own way, you must go your own way,' said the mother emphatically.

All the time Mr Massy had sat obscure and unnoticed in a corner of the room. At this juncture he got up, saying:

'There is baby, Mary.'

Mary rose and went out of the room, stately; her little husband padded after her. Durant watched the fragile, small man go, wondering.

'And where,' asked the vicar, almost genial, 'do you think you will go when you are married?'

Durant started.

'I was thinking of emigrating,' he said.

'To Canada? or where?'

'I think to Canada.'

'Yes, that would be very good.'

Again there was a pause.

'We shan't see much of you then, as a son-in-law,' said the mother, roughly but amicably.

'Not much,' he said.

Then he took his leave. Louisa went with him to the gate. She stood before him in distress.

'You won't mind them, will you?' she said humbly.

'I don't mind them, if they don't mind me!' he said. Then he stooped and kissed her.

'Let us be married soon,' she murmured, in tears.

'All right,' he said. 'I'll go to-morrow to Barford.'

Second Best

'OH, I'm tired!' Frances exclaimed petulantly, and in the same instant she dropped down on the turf, near the hedge-bottom. Anne stood a moment surprised, then, accustomed to the vagaries of her beloved Frances, said:

'Well, and aren't you always likely to be tired, after travelling that blessed long way from Liverpool yesterday?' and she plumped down beside her sister. Anne was a wise young body of fourteen, very buxom, brimming with common sense. Frances was much older, about twenty-three, and whimsical, spasmodic. She was the beauty and the clever child of the family. She plucked the goose-grass buttons from her dress in a nervous, desperate fashion. Her beautiful profile, looped above with black hair, warm with the dusky-and-scarlet complexion of a pear, was calm as a mask, her thin brown hand plucked nervously.

'It's not the journey,' she said, objecting to Anne's obtuseness. Anne looked inquiringly at her darling. The young girl, in her self-confident, practical way, proceeded to reckon up this whimsical creature. But suddenly she found herself full in the eyes of Frances; felt two dark, hectic eyes flaring challenge at her, and she shrank away. Frances was peculiar for these great, exposed looks, which disconcerted people by their violence and their suddenness.

'What's a matter, poor old duck?' asked Anne, as she folded the slight, wilful form of her sister in her arms. Frances laughed shakily, and nestled down for comfort on the budding breasts of the strong girl.

'Oh, I'm only a bit tired,' she murmured, on the point of tears.

'Well, of course you are, what do you expect?' soothed Anne. It was a joke to Frances that Anne should play elder, almost mother to her. But then, Anne was in her unvexed teens; men were like big dogs to her: while Frances, at twenty-three, suffered a good deal.

The country was intensely morning-still. On the common everything shone beside its shadow, and the hillside gave off heat in silence. The brown turf seemed in a low state of combustion, the leaves of the oaks were scorched brown. Among the blackish foliage in the distance shone the small red and orange of the village.

The willows in the brook-course at the foot of the common suddenly shook with a dazzling effect like diamonds. It was a puff of wind. Anne resumed her normal position. She spread her knees, and put in her lap a handful of hazel nuts, whity-green leafy things, whose one cheek was tanned between brown and pink. These she began to crack and eat. Frances, with bowed head, mused bitterly.

'Eh, you know Tom Smedley?' began the young girl, as she pulled a tight kernel out of its shell.

'I suppose so,' replied Frances sarcastically.

'Well, he gave me a wild rabbit what he'd caught, to keep with my tame one – and it's living.'

'That's a good thing,' said Frances, very detached and ironic.

'Well, it *is*! He reckoned he'd take me to Ollerton Feast,[1] but he never did. Look here, he took a servant from the rectory; I saw him.'

'So he ought,' said Frances.

'No, he oughtn't! and I told him so. And I told him I should tell you – an' I have done.'

Click and snap went a nut between her teeth. She sorted out the kernel, and chewed complacently.

'It doesn't make much difference,' said Frances.

'Well, 'appen it doesn't; but I was mad with him all the same.'

'Why?'

'Because I was; he's no right to go with a servant.'

'He's a perfect right,' persisted Frances, very just and cold.

'No, he hasn't, when he'd said he'd take me.'

Frances burst into a laugh of amusement and relief.

'Oh, no; I'd forgot that,' she said, adding, 'And what did he say when you promised to tell me?'

'He laughed and said, "She won't fret her fat[2] over that."'

'And she won't,' sniffed Frances.

There was silence. The common, with its sere, blonde-headed thistles, its heaps of silent bramble, its brown-husked gorse in the glare of sunshine, seemed visionary. Across the brook began the immense pattern of agriculture, white chequering of barley stubble, brown squares of wheat, khaki patches of pasture, red stripes of fallow, with the woodland and the tiny village dark like ornaments, leading away to the distance, right to the hills, where the check-pattern grew smaller and smaller, till, in the blackish haze of heat, far off, only the tiny white squares of barley stubble showed distinct.

'Eh, I say, here's a rabbit hole!' cried Anne suddenly. 'Should we watch if one comes out? You won't have to fidget, you know.'

The two girls sat perfectly still. Frances watched certain objects in her surroundings: they had a peculiar, unfriendly look about them: the weight of greenish elderberries on their purpling stalks; the twinkling of the yellowing crab-apples that clustered high up in the hedge, against the sky: the exhausted, limp leaves of the primroses lying flat in the hedge-bottom: all looked strange to her. Then her eyes caught a movement. A mole was moving silently over the warm, red soil, nosing, shuffling hither and thither, flat, and dark as a shadow, shifting about, and as suddenly brisk, and as silent, like a very ghost of *joie de vivre*. Frances started, from habit was about to call on Anne to kill the little pest. But, to-day, her lethargy of unhappiness was too much for her. She watched the little brute paddling, snuffing, touching things to discover them, running in blindness, delighted to ecstasy by the sunlight and the hot, strange things that caressed its belly and its nose. She felt a keen pity for the little creature.

'Eh, our Fran, look there! It's a mole.'

Anne was on her feet, standing watching the dark, unconscious beast. Frances frowned with anxiety.

'It doesn't run off, does it?' said the young girl softly. Then she stealthily approached the creature. The mole paddled fumblingly away. In an instant Anne put her foot upon it, not too heavily. Frances could see the struggling, swimming movement of the little pink hands of the brute, the twisting and twitching of its pointed nose, as it wrestled under the sole of the boot.

'It *does* wriggle!' said the bonny girl, knitting her brows in a frown at the eerie sensation. Then she bent down to look at her trap. Frances could now see, beyond the edge of the boot-sole, the heaving of the velvet shoulders, the pitiful turning of the sightless face, the frantic rowing of the flat, pink hands.

'Kill the thing,' she said, turning away her face.

'Oh – I'm not,' laughed Anne, shrinking. 'You can, if you like.'

'I *don't* like,' said Frances, with quiet intensity.

After several dabbling attempts, Anne succeeded in picking up the little animal by the scruff of its neck. It threw back its head, flung its long blind snout from side to side, the mouth open in a peculiar oblong, with tiny pinkish teeth at the edge. The blind, frantic mouth gaped and writhed. The body, heavy and clumsy, hung scarcely moving.

'Isn't it a snappy little thing,' observed Anne twisting to avoid the teeth.

'What are you going to do with it?' asked Frances sharply.

'It's got to be killed – look at the damage they do. I s'll take it home and let dadda or somebody kill it. I'm not going to let it go.'

She swaddled the creature clumsily in her pocket-handkerchief and sat down beside her sister. There was an interval of silence, during which Anne combated the efforts of the mole.

'You've not had much to say about Jimmy this time. Did you see him often in Liverpool?' Anne asked suddenly.

'Once or twice,' replied Frances, giving no sign of how the question troubled her.

'And aren't you sweet on him any more, then?'

'I should think I'm not, seeing that he's engaged.'

'Engaged? Jimmy Barrass! Well, of all things! I never thought *he'd* get engaged.'

'Why not, he's as much right as anybody else?' snapped Frances.

Anne was fumbling with the mole.

''Appen so,' she said at length; 'but I never thought Jimmy would, though.'

'Why not?' snapped Frances.

'*I* don't know – this blessed mole, it'll not keep still! – who's he got engaged to?'

'How should I know?'

'I thought you'd ask him; you've known him long enough. I s'd think he thought he'd get engaged now he's a Doctor of Chemistry.'

Frances laughed in spite of herself.

'What's that got to do with it?' she asked.

'I'm sure it's got a lot. He'll want to feel *somebody* now, so he's got engaged. Hey, stop it; go in!'

But at this juncture the mole almost succeeded in wriggling clear. It wrestled and twisted frantically, waved its pointed blind head, its mouth standing open like a little shaft, its big, wrinkled hands spread out.

'Go in with you!' urged Anne, poking the little creature with her forefinger, trying to get it back into the handkerchief. Suddenly the mouth turned like a spark on her finger.

'Oh!' she cried, 'he's bit me.'

She dropped him to the floor. Dazed, the blind creature fumbled round. Frances felt like shrieking. She expected him to dart away in a flash, like a mouse, and there he remained groping; she wanted to cry to him to be gone. Anne, in a sudden decision of wrath, caught up her sister's walking-cane. With one blow the mole was dead. Frances was startled and shocked. One moment the little wretch was fussing in the heat, and the next it lay like a little bag, inert and black – not a struggle, scarce a quiver.

'It is dead!' Frances said breathlessly. Anne took her finger from her mouth, looked at the tiny pinpricks, and said:

'Yes, he is, and I'm glad. They're vicious little nuisances, moles are.'

With which her wrath vanished. She picked up the dead animal.

'Hasn't it got a beautiful skin,' she mused, stroking the fur with her forefinger, then with her cheek.

'Mind,' said Frances sharply. 'You'll have the blood on your skirt!'

One ruby drop of blood hung on the small snout, ready to fall. Anne shook it off on to some harebells. Frances suddenly became calm; in that moment, grown-up.

'I suppose they have to be killed,' she said, and a certain rather dreary indifference succeeded to her grief. The twinkling crab-apples, the glitter of brilliant willows now seemed to her trifling, scarcely worth the notice. Something had died in her, so that things lost their poignancy. She was calm, indifference overlying her quiet sadness. Rising, she walked down to the brook course.

'Here, wait for me,' cried Anne, coming tumbling after.

Frances stood on the bridge, looking at the red mud trodden into pockets by the feet of cattle. There was not a drain of water left, but everything smelled green, succulent. Why did she care so little for Anne, who was so fond of her? she asked herself. Why did she care so little for anyone? She did not know, but she felt a rather stubborn pride in her isolation and indifference.

They entered a field where stooks of barley stood in rows, the straight, blonde tresses of the corn streaming on to the ground. The stubble was bleached by the intense summer, so that the expanse glared white. The next field was sweet and soft with a second crop of seeds; thin, straggling clover whose little pink knobs rested prettily in the dark green. The scent was faint and sickly. The girls came up in single file, Frances leading.

Near the gate a young man was mowing with the scythe some fodder for the afternoon feed of the cattle. As he saw the girls he left off working and waited in an aimless kind of way. Frances was dressed in white muslin, and she walked with dignity, detached and forgetful. Her lack of agitation, her simple, unheeding advance made him nervous. She had loved the far-off Jimmy for five years, having had in return his half-measures. This man only affected her slightly.

Tom was of medium stature, energetic in build. His smooth, fair-skinned face was burned red, not brown, by the sun, and this ruddiness enhanced his appearance of good humour and easiness. Being a year older than Frances, he would have courted her long ago had she been so inclined. As it was, he had gone his uneventful way amiably, chatting with many a girl, but remaining unattached, free of trouble for the most part. Only he knew he wanted a woman. He hitched his trousers just a trifle self-consciously as the girls approached. Frances was a rare, delicate kind of being, whom he realized with a queer and delicious stimulation in his veins. She gave him a slight sense of suffocation. Somehow, this morning, she affected him more than usual. She was dressed in white. He, however, being matter-of-fact in his mind, did not realize. His feeling had never become conscious, purposive.

Frances knew what she was about. Tom was ready to love her as soon as she would show him. Now that she could not have Jimmy, she did not poignantly care. Still, she would have something. If she could not have the best – Jimmy, whom she knew to be something of a snob – she would have the second best, Tom. She advanced rather indifferently.

'You are back, then!' said Tom. She marked the touch of uncertainty in his voice.

'No,' she laughed, 'I'm still in Liverpool,' and the undertone of intimacy made him burn.

'This isn't you, then?' he asked.

Her heart leapt up in approval. She looked in his eyes, and for a second was with him.

'Why, what do you think?' she laughed.

He lifted his hat from his head with a distracted little gesture. She liked him, his quaint ways, his humour, his ignorance, and his slow masculinity.

'Here, look here, Tom Smedley,' broke in Anne.

'A moudiwarp! Did you find it dead?' he asked.

'No, it bit me,' said Anne.

'Oh, aye! An' that got your rag out, did it?'

'No, it didn't!' Anne scolded sharply. 'Such language!'

'Oh, what's up wi' it?'

'I can't bear you to talk broad.'

'Can't you?'

He glanced at Frances.

'It isn't nice,' Frances said. She did not care, really. The vulgar speech jarred on her as a rule; Jimmy was a gentleman. But Tom's manner of speech did not matter to her.

'I like you to talk *nicely*,' she added.

'Do you,' he replied, tilting his hat, stirred.

'And generally you *do*, you know,' she smiled.

'I s'll have to have a try,' he said, rather tensely gallant.

'What?' she asked brightly.

'To talk nice to you,' he said. Frances coloured furiously, bent her head for a moment, then laughed gaily, as if she liked this clumsy hint.

'Eh now, you mind what you're saying,' cried Anne, giving the young man an admonitory pat.

'You wouldn't have to give yon mole many knocks like that,' he teased, relieved to get on safe ground, rubbing his arm.

'No indeed, it died in one blow,' said Frances, with a flippancy that was hateful to her.

'You're not so good at knockin' 'em?' he said, turning to her.

'I don't know, if I'm cross,' she said decisively.

'No?' he replied, with alert attentiveness.

'I could,' she added, harder, 'if it was necessary.'

He was slow to feel her difference.

'And don't you consider it *is* necessary?' he asked, with misgiving.

'W – ell – is it?' she said, looking at him steadily, coldly.

'I reckon it is,' he replied, looking away, but standing stubborn.

She laughed quickly.

'But it isn't necessary for *me*,' she said, with slight contempt.

'Yes, that's quite true,' he answered.

She laughed in a shaky fashion.

'*I know it is*,' she said; and there was an awkward pause.

'Why, would you *like* me to kill moles then?' she asked tentatively, after a while.

'They do us a lot of damage,' he said, standing firm on his own ground, angered.

'Well, I'll see the next time I come across one,' she promised, defiantly. Their eyes met, and she sank before him, her pride troubled. He felt uneasy and triumphant and baffled, as if fate had gripped him. She smiled as she departed.

'Well,' said Anne, as the sisters went through the wheat stubble; 'I don't know what you two's been jawing about, I'm sure.'

'Don't you?' laughed Frances significantly.

'No, I don't. But, at any rate, Tom Smedley's a good deal better to my thinking than Jimmy, so there – and nicer.'

'Perhaps he is,' said Frances coldly.

And the next day, after a secret, persistent hunt, she found another mole playing in the heat. She killed it, and in the evening, when Tom came to the gate to smoke his pipe after supper, she took him the dead creature.

'Here you are then!' she said.

'Did you catch it?' he replied, taking the velvet corpse into his fingers and examining it minutely. This was to hide his trepidation.

'Did you think I couldn't?' she asked, her face very near his.

'Nay, I didn't know.'

She laughed in his face, a strange little laugh that caught her breath, all agitation, and tears, and recklessness of desire. He looked frightened and upset. She put her hand to his arm.

'Shall you go out wi' me?' he asked, in a difficult, troubled tone.

She turned her face away, with a shaky laugh. The blood came up in him, strong, overmastering. He resisted it. But it drove him down, and he was carried away. Seeing the winsome, frail nape of her neck, fierce love came upon him for her, and tenderness.

'We s'll 'ave to tell your mother,' he said. And he stood, suffering, resisting his passion for her.

'Yes,' she replied, in a dead voice. But there was a thrill of pleasure in this death.

The Shades of Spring

I

It was a mile nearer through the wood. Mechanically, Syson turned up by the forge and lifted the field-gate. The blacksmith and his mate stood still, watching the trespasser. But Syson looked too much a gentleman to be accosted. They let him go in silence across the small field to the wood.

There was not the least difference between this morning and those of the bright springs, six or eight years back. White and sandy-gold fowls still scratched round the gate, littering the earth and the field with feathers and scratched-up rubbish. Between the two thick holly bushes in the wood-hedge was the hidden gap, whose fence one climbed to get into the wood; the bars were scored just the same by the keeper's boots. He was back in the eternal.

Syson was extraordinarily glad. Like an uneasy spirit he had returned to the country of his past, and he found it waiting for him, unaltered. The hazel still spread glad little hands downwards, the bluebells here were still wan and few, among the lush grass and in shade of the bushes.

The path through the wood, on the very brow of a slope, ran winding easily for a time. All around were twiggy oaks, just issuing their gold, and floor spaces diapered with woodruff, with patches of dog-mercury and tufts of hyacinth. Two fallen trees still lay across the track. Syson jolted down a steep, rough slope, and came again upon the open land, this time looking north as through a great window in the wood. He stayed to gaze over the level fields of the hill-top, at the village which strewed the bare upland as if it had tumbled off the passing waggons of industry, and been forsaken. There was a stiff, modern, grey little church, and blocks and rows of red dwellings lying at random; at the back, the twinkling headstocks of the pit, and the looming pit-hill. All was naked and out-of-doors, not a tree! It was quite unaltered.

Syson turned, satisfied, to follow the path that sheered downhill into the wood. He was curiously elated, feeling himself back in an enduring vision. He started. A keeper was standing a few yards in front, barring the way.

'Where might you be going this road, sir?' asked the man. The tone of his question had a challenging twang. Syson looked at the fellow with an impersonal, observant gaze. It was a young man of four or five and twenty, ruddy and well favoured. His dark blue eyes now stared aggressively at the intruder. His black moustache, very thick, was cropped short over a small, rather soft mouth. In every other respect the fellow was manly and good-looking. He stood just above middle height; the strong forward thrust of his chest, and the perfect ease of his erect, self-sufficient body, gave one the feeling that he was taut with animal life, like the thick jet of a fountain balanced in itself. He stood with the butt of his gun on the ground, looking uncertainly and questioningly at Syson. The dark, restless eyes of the trespasser, examining the man and penetrating into him without heeding his office, troubled the keeper and made him flush.

'Where is Naylor? Have you got his job?' Syson asked.

'You're not from the House, are you?' inquired the keeper. It could not be, since everyone was away.

'No, I'm not from the House,' the other replied. It seemed to amuse him.

'Then might I ask where you were making for?' said the keeper, nettled.

'Where I am making for?' Syson repeated. 'I am going to Willey-Water Farm.'

'This isn't the road.'

'I think so. Down this path, past the well, and out by the white gate.'

'But that's not the public road.'

'I suppose not. I used to come so often, in Naylor's time, I had forgotten. Where is he, by the way?'

'Crippled with rheumatism,' the keeper answered reluctantly.

'Is he?' Syson exclaimed in pain.

'And who might you be?' asked the keeper, with a new intonation.

'John Adderley Syson; I used to live in Cordy Lane.'

'Used to court Hilda Millership?'

Syson's eyes opened with a pained smile. He nodded. There was an awkward silence.

'And you – who are you?' asked Syson.

'Arthur Pilbeam – Naylor's my uncle,' said the other.

'You live here in Nuttall?'

'I'm lodgin' at my uncle's – at Naylor's.'

'I see!'

'Did you say you was goin' down to Willey-Water?' asked the keeper.

'Yes.'

There was a pause of some moments, before the keeper blurted: '*I'm* courtin' Hilda Millership.'

The young fellow looked at the intruder with a stubborn defiance, almost pathetic. Syson opened new eyes.

'Are you?' he said, astonished. The keeper flushed dark.

'She and me are keeping company,' he said.

'I didn't know!' said Syson. The other man waited uncomfortably.

'What, is the thing settled?' asked the intruder.

'How, settled?' retorted the other sulkily.

'Are you going to get married soon, and all that?'

The keeper stared in silence for some moments, impotent.

'I suppose so,' he said, full of resentment.

'Ah!' Syson watched closely.

'I'm married myself,' he added, after a time.

'You are?' said the other incredulously.

Syson laughed in his brilliant, unhappy way.

'This last fifteen months,' he said.

The keeper gazed at him with wide, wondering eyes, apparently thinking back, and trying to make things out.

'Why, didn't you know?' asked Syson.

'No, I didn't,' said the other sulkily.

There was silence for a moment.

'Ah well!' said Syson, 'I will go on. I suppose I may.' The keeper stood in silent opposition. The two men hesitated in the open, grassy space, set around with small sheaves of sturdy bluebells; a little open platform on the brow of the hill. Syson took a few indecisive steps forward, then stopped.

'I say, how beautiful!' he cried.

He had come in full view of the downslope. The wide path ran from his feet like a river, and it was full of bluebells, save for a green winding thread down the centre, where the keeper walked. Like a stream the path opened into azure shallows at the levels, and there were pools of bluebells, with still the green thread winding through, like a thin current of ice-water through blue lakes. And from under the twig-purple of the bushes swam the shadowed blue, as if the flowers lay in flood water over the woodland.

'Ah, isn't it lovely!' Syson exclaimed; this was his past, the country he had abandoned, and it hurt him to see it so beautiful. Woodpigeons cooed overhead, and the air was full of the brightness of birds singing.

'If you're married, what do you keep writing to her for, and sending her poetry books and things?' asked the keeper. Syson stared at him, taken aback and humiliated. Then he began to smile.

'Well,' he said, 'I did not know about you . . .'

Again the keeper flushed darkly.

'But if you are married –' he charged.

'I am,' answered the other cynically.

Then, looking down the blue, beautiful path, Syson felt his own humiliation. 'What right *have* I to hang on to her?' he thought, bitterly self-contemptuous.

'She knows I'm married and all that,' he said.

'But you keep sending her books,' challenged the keeper.

Syson, silenced, looked at the other man quizzically, half pitying. Then he turned.

'Good day,' he said, and was gone. Now, everything irritated him: the two sallows, one all gold and perfume and murmur, one silver-green and bristly, reminded him, that here he had taught her about pollination. What a fool he was! What god-forsaken folly it all was!

'Ah well,' he said to himself; 'the poor devil seems to have a grudge against me. I'll do my best for him.' He grinned to himself, in a very bad temper.

II

The farm was less than a hundred yards from the wood's edge. The wall of trees formed the fourth side to the open quadrangle. The house faced the wood. With tangled emotions, Syson noted the plum blossom falling on the profuse, coloured primroses, which he himself had brought here and set. How they had increased! There were thick tufts of scarlet, and pink, and pale purple primroses under the plum trees. He saw somebody glance at him through the kitchen window, heard men's voices.

The door opened suddenly: very womanly she had grown! He felt himself going pale.

'You? – Addy!' she exclaimed, and stood motionless.

'Who?' called the farmer's voice. Men's low voices answered. Those low voices, curious and almost jeering, roused the tormented spirit in the visitor. Smiling brilliantly at her, he waited.

'Myself – why not?' he said.

The flush burned very deep on her cheek and throat.

'We are just finishing dinner,' she said.

'Then I will stay outside.' He made a motion to show that he would sit on the red earthenware pipkin that stood near the door among the daffodils, and contained the drinking water.

'Oh no, come in,' she said hurriedly. He followed her. In the doorway, he glanced swiftly over the family, and bowed. Everyone was confused. The farmer, his wife, and the four sons sat at the coarsely laid dinner-table, the men with arms bare to the elbows.

'I am sorry I come at lunch-time,' said Syson.

'Hello, Addy!' said the farmer, assuming the old form of address, but his tone cold. 'How are you?'

And he shook hands.

'Shall you have a bit?' he invited the young visitor, but taking for granted the offer would be refused. He assumed that Syson was become too refined to eat so roughly. The young man winced at the imputation.

'Have you had any dinner?' asked the daughter.

'No,' replied Syson. 'It is too early. I shall be back at half-past one.'

'You call it lunch, don't you?' asked the eldest son, almost ironical. He had once been an intimate friend of this young man.

'We'll give Addy something when we've finished,' said the mother, an invalid, deprecating.

'No – don't trouble. I don't want to give you any trouble,' said Syson.

'You could allus live on fresh air an' scenery,' laughed the youngest son, a lad of nineteen.

Syson went round the buildings, and into the orchard at the back of the house, where daffodils all along the hedgerow swung like yellow, ruffled birds on their perches. He loved the place extraordinarily, the hills ranging round, with bear-skin woods covering their giant shoulders, and small red farms like brooches clasping their garments; the blue streak of water in the valley, the bareness of the home pasture, the sound of myriad-threaded bird-singing, which went mostly unheard. To his last day, he would dream of this place, when he felt the sun on his face, or saw the small handfuls of snow between the winter twigs, or smelt the coming of spring.

Hilda was very womanly. In her presence he felt constrained. She was twenty-nine, as he was, but she seemed to him much older. He felt foolish, almost unreal, beside her. She was so static. As he was fingering some shed plum blossom on a low bough, she came to the back door to shake the table-cloth. Fowls raced from the stackyard, birds rustled from the trees. Her dark hair was gathered up in a coil like a crown on her head. She was very straight, distant in her bearing. As she folded the cloth, she looked away over the hills.

Presently Syson returned indoors. She had prepared eggs and curd cheese, stewed gooseberries and cream.

'Since you will dine to-night,' she said, 'I have only given you a light lunch.'

'It is awfully nice,' he said. 'You keep a real idyllic atmosphere – your belt of straw and ivy buds.'

Still they hurt each other.

He was uneasy before her. Her brief, sure speech, her distant bearing, were unfamiliar to him. He admired again her grey-black eyebrows, and her lashes. Their eyes met. He saw, in the beautiful grey and black of her glance, tears and a strange light, and at the back of all, calm acceptance of herself, and triumph over him.

He felt himself shrinking. With an effort he kept up the ironic manner.

She sent him into the parlour while she washed the dishes. The long low room was refurnished from the Abbey sale, with chairs upholstered in claret-coloured rep, many years old, and an oval table of polished walnut, and another piano, handsome, though still antique. In spite of the strangeness, he was pleased. Opening a high cupboard let into the thickness of the wall, he found it full of his books, his old lesson-books, and volumes of verse he had sent her, English and German. The daffodils in the white window-bottoms shone across the room, he could almost feel their rays. The old glamour caught him again. His youthful water-colours on the wall no longer made him grin; he remembered how fervently he had tried to paint for her, twelve years before.

She entered, wiping a dish, and he saw again the bright, kernel-white beauty of her arms.

'You are quite splendid here,' he said, and their eyes met.

'Do you like it?' she asked. It was the old, low, husky tone of intimacy. He felt a quick change beginning in his blood. It was the old, delicious sublimation, the thinning, almost the vaporizing of himself, as if his spirit were to be liberated.

'Aye,' he nodded, smiling at her like a boy again. She bowed her head.

'This was the countess's chair,' she said in low tones. 'I found her scissors down here between the padding.'

'Did you? Where are they?'

Quickly, with a lilt in her movement, she fetched her work-basket, and together they examined the long-shanked old scissors.

'What a ballad of dead ladies!'[1] he said, laughing, as he fitted his fingers into the round loops of the countess's scissors.

'I knew you could use them,' she said, with certainty. He looked at his fingers, and at the scissors. She meant his fingers were fine enough for the small-looped scissors.

'That is something to be said for me,' he laughed, putting the scissors aside. She turned to the window. He noticed the fine, fair down on her cheek and her upper lip, and her soft, white neck, like the throat of a nettle flower, and her fore-arms, bright as newly blanched kernels. He was looking at her with new eyes, and she was a different person to him. He did not know her. But he could regard her objectively now.

'Shall we go out awhile?' she asked.

'Yes!' he answered. But the predominant emotion, that troubled the excitement and perplexity of his heart, was fear, fear of that which he saw. There was about her the same manner, the same intonation in her voice, now as then, but she was not what he had known her to be. He knew quite well what she had been for him. And gradually he was realizing that she was something quite other, and always had been.

She put no covering on her head, merely took off her apron, saying, 'We will go by the larches.' As they passed the old orchard, she called him in to show him a blue-tit's nest in one of the apple trees, and a sycock's in the hedge. He rather wondered at her surety, at a certain hardness like arrogance hidden under her humility.

'Look at the apple buds,' she said, and he then perceived myriads of little scarlet balls among the drooping boughs. Watching his face, her eyes went hard. She saw the scales were fallen from him, and at last he was going to see her as she was. It was the thing she had most dreaded in the past, and most needed, for her soul's sake. Now he was going to see her as she was. He would not love her, and he would know he never could have loved her. The old illusion gone, they were strangers, crude and entire. But he would give her her due – she would have her due from him.

She was brilliant as he had not known her. She showed him nests: a jenny wren's in a low bush.

'See this jinty's!' she exclaimed.

He was surprised to hear her use the local name. She reached carefully through the thorns, and put her fingers in the nest's round door.

'Five!' she said. 'Tiny little things.'

She showed him nests of robins, and chaffinches, and linnets, and buntings; of a wagtail beside the water.

'And if we go down, nearer the lake, I will show you a kingfisher's . . .'

'Among the young fir trees,' she said, 'there's a throstle's or a blackie's on nearly every bough, every ledge. The first day, when I had seen them all, I felt as if I mustn't go in the wood. It seemed a city of birds: and in the morning, hearing them all, I thought of the noisy early markets. I was afraid to go in my own wood.'

She was using the language they had both of them invented. Now it was all her own. He had done with it. She did not mind his silence, but was always dominant, letting him see her wood. As they came along a marshy path where forget-me-nots were opening in a rich blue drift: 'We know all the birds, but there are many flowers we can't find out,' she said. It was half an appeal to him, who had known the names of things.

She looked dreamily across to the open fields that slept in the sun.

'I have a lover as well, you know,' she said, with assurance, yet dropping again almost into the intimate tone.

This woke in him the spirit to fight her.

'I think I met him. He is good-looking – also in Arcady.'[2]

Without answering, she turned into a dark path that led up-hill, where the trees and undergrowth were very thick.

'They did well,' she said at length, 'to have various altars to various gods, in old days.'

'Ah yes!' he agreed. 'To whom is the new one?'

'There are no old ones,' she said. 'I was always looking for this.'

'And whose is it?' he asked.

'I don't know,' she said, looking full at him.

'I'm very glad, for your sake,' he said, 'that you are satisfied.'

'Aye – but the man doesn't matter so much,' she said. There was a pause.

'No!' he exclaimed, astonished, yet recognizing her as her real self.

'It is one's self that matters,' she said. 'Whether one is being one's own self and serving one's own God.'

There was silence, during which he pondered. The path was almost flowerless, gloomy. At the side, his heels sank into soft clay.

III

'I,' she said, very slowly, 'I was married the same night as you.'

He looked at her.

'Not legally, of course,' she replied. 'But – actually.'

'To the keeper?' he said, not knowing what else to say.

She turned to him.

'You thought I could not?' she said. But the flush was deep in her cheek and throat, for all her assurance.

Still he would not say anything.

'You see' – she was making an effort to explain – '*I* had to understand also.'

'And what does it amount to, this *understanding*?' he asked.

'A very great deal – does it not to you?' she replied. 'One is free.'

'And you are not disappointed?'

'Far from it!' Her tone was deep and sincere.

'You love him?'

'Yes, I love him.'

'Good!' he said.

This silenced her for a while.

'Here, among his things, I love him,' she said.

His conceit would not let him be silent.

'It needs this setting?' he asked.

'It does,' she cried. 'You were always making me to be not myself.'

He laughed shortly.

'But is it a matter of surroundings?' he said. He had considered her all spirit.

'I am like a plant,' she replied. 'I can only grow in my own soil.'

They came to a place where the undergrowth shrank away, leaving a bare, brown space, pillared with the brick-red and purplish trunks of pine trees. On the fringe, hung the sombre green of elder trees, with flat flowers in bud, and below were bright, unfurling pennons of fern. In the midst of the bare space stood a keeper's log hut. Pheasant-coops were lying about, some occupied by a clucking hen, some empty.

Hilda walked over the brown pine-needles to the hut, took a key from among the eaves, and opened the door. It was a bare wooden place with a carpenter's bench and form, carpenter's tools, an axe, snares, straps, some skins pegged down, everything in order. Hilda closed the door. Syson examined the weird flat coats of wild animals, that were pegged down to be cured. She turned some knotch in the side wall, and disclosed a second, small apartment.

'How romantic!' said Syson.

'Yes. He is very curious – he has some of a wild animal's cunning – in a nice sense – and he is inventive, and thoughtful – but not beyond a certain point.'

She pulled back a dark green curtain. The apartment was occupied almost entirely by a large couch of heather and bracken, on which was spread an ample rabbit-skin rug. On the floor were patchwork rugs of cat-skin, and a red calf-skin, while hanging from the wall were other furs. Hilda took down one, which she put on. It was a cloak of rabbit-skin and of white fur, with a hood, apparently of the skins of stoats. She laughed at Syson from out of this barbaric mantle, saying:

'What do you think of it?'

'Ah –! I congratulate you on your man,' he replied.

'And look!' she said.

In a little jar on a shelf were some sprays, frail and white, of the first honeysuckle.

'They will scent the place at night,' she said.

He looked round curiously.

'Where does he come short, then?' he asked. She gazed at him for a few moments. Then, turning aside:

'The stars aren't the same with him,' she said. 'You could make them flash and quiver, and the forget-me-nots come up at me like phosphorescence. You could make things *wonderful*. I have found it out – it is true. But I have them all for myself, now.'

He laughed, saying:

'After all, stars and forget-me-nots are only luxuries. You ought to make poetry.'

'Aye,' she assented. 'But I have them all now.'

Again he laughed bitterly at her.

She turned swiftly. He was leaning against the small window of the tiny, obscure room, and was watching her, who stood in the doorway, still cloaked in her mantle. His cap was removed, so she saw his face and head distinctly in the dim room. His black, straight, glossy hair was brushed clean back from his brow. His black eyes were watching her, and his face, that was clear and cream, and perfectly smooth, was flickering.

'We are very different,' she said bitterly.

Again he laughed.

'I see you disapprove of me,' he said.

'I disapprove of what you have become,' she said.

'You think we might' – he glanced at the hut – 'have been like this – you and I?'

She shook her head.

'You! no; never! You plucked a thing and looked at it till you had found out all you wanted to know about it, then you threw it away,' she said.

'Did I?' he asked. 'And could your way never have been my way? I suppose not.'

'Why should it?' she said. 'I am a separate being.'

'But surely two people sometimes go the same way,' he said.

'You took me away from myself,' she said.

He knew he had mistaken her, had taken her for something she was not. That was his fault, not hers.

'And did you always know?' he asked.

'No – you never let me know. You bullied me. I couldn't help myself. I was glad when you left me, really.'

'I know you were,' he said. But his face went paler, almost deathly luminous.

'Yet,' he said, 'it was you who sent me the way I have gone.'

'I!' she exclaimed, in pride.

'You *would* have me take the Grammar School scholarship – and you would have me foster poor little Botell's fervent attachment to me, till he couldn't live without me – and because Botell was rich and influential. You triumphed in the wine-merchant's offer to send me to Cambridge, to befriend his only child. You wanted me to rise in the world. And all the time you were sending me away from you – every new success of mine put a separation between us, and more for you than for me. You never wanted to come with me: you wanted just to send me to see what it was like. I believe you even wanted me to marry a lady. You wanted to triumph over society in me.'

'And I am responsible,' she said, with sarcasm.

'I distinguished myself to satisfy you,' he replied.

'Ah!' she cried, 'you always wanted change, change, like a child.'

'Very well! And I am a success, and I know it, and I do some good work. But – I thought you were different. What right have you to a man?'

'What do you want?' she said, looking at him with wide, fearful eyes.

He looked back at her, his eyes pointed, like weapons.

'Why, nothing,' he laughed shortly.

There was a rattling at the outer latch, and the keeper entered. The woman glanced round, but remained standing, fur-cloaked, in the inner doorway. Syson did not move.

The other man entered, saw, and turned away without speaking. The two also were silent.

Pilbeam attended to his skins.

'I must go,' said Syson.

'Yes,' she replied.

'Then I give you "To our vast and varying fortunes."' He lifted his hand in pledge.

'"To our vast and varying fortunes,"' she answered gravely, and speaking in cold tones.

'Arthur!' she said.

The keeper pretended not to hear. Syson, watching keenly, began to smile. The woman drew herself up.

'Arthur!' she said again, with a curious upward inflection, which warned the two men that her soul was trembling on a dangerous crisis.

The keeper slowly put down his tool and came to her.

'Yes,' he said.

'I wanted to introduce you,' she said, trembling.

'I've met him a'ready,' said the keeper.

'Have you? It is Addy, Mr Syson, whom you know about. – This is Arthur, Mr Pilbeam,' she added, turning to Syson. The latter held out his hand to the keeper, and they shook hands in silence.

'I'm glad to have met you,' said Syson. 'We drop our correspondence, Hilda?'

'Why need we?' she asked.

The two men stood at a loss.

'*Is* there no need?' said Syson.

Still she was silent.

'It is as you will,' she said.

They went all three together down the gloomy path.

'"Qu'il était bleu, le ciel, et grand l'espoir,"'[3] quoted Syson, not knowing what to say.

'What do you mean?' she said. 'Besides, *we* can't walk in *our* wild oats – we never sowed any.'

Syson looked at her. He was startled to see his young love, his nun, his Botticelli angel, so revealed. It was he who had been the fool. He and she were more separate than any two strangers could be. She only wanted to keep up a correspondence with him – and he, of course, wanted it kept up, so that he could write to her, like Dante to some Beatrice who had never existed save in the man's own brain.[4]

At the bottom of the path she left him. He went along with the keeper, towards the open, towards the gate that closed on the wood. The two men walked almost like friends. They did not broach the subject of their thoughts.

Instead of going straight to the high-road gate, Syson went along the wood's edge, where the brook spread out in a little bog, and under the alder trees, among the reeds, great yellow stools and bosses of marigolds shone. Threads of brown water trickled by, touched with gold from the flowers. Suddenly there was a blue flash in the air, as a kingfisher passed.

Syson was extraordinarily moved. He climbed the bank to the gorse bushes, whose sparks of blossom had not yet gathered into a flame. Lying on the dry brown turf, he discovered sprigs of tiny purple milkwort and pink spots of lousewort. What a wonderful world it was – marvellous, for ever new. He felt as if it were underground, like the fields of monotone hell, notwithstanding. Inside his breast was a pain like a wound. He remembered the poem of William Morris, where in the Chapel of Lyonesse a knight lay wounded, with the truncheon of a spear deep in his breast, lying always as dead, yet did not die, while day after day the coloured sunlight dipped from the painted window across the chancel, and passed away.[5] He knew now it never had been true, that which was between him and her, not for a moment. The truth had stood apart all the time.

Syson turned over. The air was full of the sound of larks, as if the sunshine above were condensing and falling in a shower. Amid this bright sound, voices sounded small and distinct.

'But if he's married, an' quite willing to drop it off, what has ter against it?' said the man's voice.

'I don't want to talk about it now. I want to be alone.'

Syson looked through the bushes. Hilda was standing in the wood, near the gate. The man was in the field, loitering by the hedge, and playing with the bees as they settled on the white bramble flowers.

There was silence for a while, in which Syson imagined her will among the brightness of the larks. Suddenly the keeper exclaimed 'Ah!' and swore. He was gripping at the sleeve of his coat, near the shoulder. Then he pulled off his jacket, threw it on the ground, and absorbedly rolled up his shirt sleeve right to the shoulder.

'Ah!' he said vindictively, as he picked out the bee and flung it away. He twisted his fine, bright arm, peering awkwardly over his shoulder.

'What is it?' asked Hilda.

'A bee – crawled up my sleeve,' he answered.

'Come here to me,' she said.

The keeper went to her, like a sulky boy. She took his arm in her hands.

'Here it is – and the sting left in – poor bee!'

She picked out the sting, put her mouth to his arm, and sucked away the drop of poison. As she looked at the red mark her mouth had made, and at his arm, she said, laughing:

'That is the reddest kiss you will ever have.'

When Syson next looked up, at the sound of voices, he saw in the shadow the keeper with his mouth on the throat of his beloved, whose head was thrown back, and whose hair had fallen, so that one rough rope of dark brown hair hung across his bare arm.

'No,' the woman answered. 'I am not upset because he's gone. You won't understand . . .'

Syson could not distinguish what the man said. Hilda replied, clear and distinct:

'You know I love you. He has gone quite out of my life – don't trouble about him . . .' He kissed her, murmuring. She laughed hollowly.

'Yes,' she said, indulgent. 'We will be married, we will be married. But not just yet.' He spoke to her again. Syson heard nothing for a time. Then she said:

'You must go home, now, dear – you will get no sleep.'

Again was heard the murmur of the keeper's voice, troubled by fear and passion.

'But why should we be married at once?' she said. 'What more would you have, by being married? It is most beautiful as it is.'

At last he pulled on his coat and departed. She stood at the gate, not watching him, but looking over the sunny country.

When at last she had gone, Syson also departed, going back to town.

The Prussian Officer

I

THEY had marched more than thirty kilometres since dawn, along the white, hot road where occasional thickets of trees threw a moment of shade, then out into the glare again. On either hand, the valley, wide and shallow, glittered with heat; dark green patches of rye, pale young corn, fallow and meadow and black pine woods spread in a dull, hot diagram under a glistening sky. But right in front the mountains ranged across, pale blue and very still, snow gleaming gently out of the deep atmosphere. And towards the mountains, on and on, the regiment marched between the rye fields and the meadows, between the scraggy fruit trees set regularly on either side the high road. The burnished, dark green rye threw off a suffocating heat, the mountains drew gradually nearer and more distinct. While the feet of the soldiers grew hotter, sweat ran through their hair under their helmets, and their knapsacks could burn no more in contact with their shoulders, but seemed instead to give off a cold, prickly sensation.

He walked on and on in silence, staring at the mountains ahead, that rose sheer out of the land, and stood fold behind fold, half earth, half heaven, the heaven, the barrier with slits of soft snow, in the pale, bluish peaks.

He could now walk almost without pain. At the start, he had determined not to limp. It had made him sick to take the first steps, and during the first mile or so, he had compressed his breath, and the cold drops of sweat had stood on his forehead. But he had walked it off. What were they after all but bruises! He had looked at them, as he was getting up: deep bruises on the backs of his thighs. And since he had made his first step in the morning, he had been conscious of them, till now he had a tight, hot place in his chest, with suppressing the pain, and holding himself in. There seemed no air when he breathed. But he walked almost lightly.

The Captain's hand had trembled at taking his coffee at dawn: his orderly saw it again. And he saw the fine figure of the Captain wheeling on horseback at the farm-house ahead, a handsome figure in pale blue uniform with facings of scarlet, and the metal gleaming on the black helmet and the sword-scabbard, and dark streaks of sweat coming on the silky bay horse. The orderly felt he was connected with that figure moving so suddenly on horseback: he followed it like a shadow, mute and inevitable and damned by it. And the officer was always aware of the tramp of the company behind, the march of his orderly among the men.

The Captain was a tall man of about forty, grey at the temples. He had a handsome, finely knit figure, and was one of the best horsemen in the West. His orderly, having to rub him down, admired the amazing riding-muscles of his loins.

For the rest, the orderly scarcely noticed the officer any more than he noticed himself. It was rarely he saw his master's face: he did not look at it. The Captain had reddish-brown, stiff hair, that he wore short upon his skull. His moustache was also cut short and bristly over a full, brutal mouth. His face was rather rugged, the cheeks thin. Perhaps the man was the more handsome for the deep lines in his face, the irritable tension of his brow, which gave him the look of a man who fights with life. His fair eyebrows stood bushy over light blue eyes that were always flashing with cold fire.

He was a Prussian aristocrat, haughty and overbearing. But his mother had been a Polish Countess. Having made too many gambling debts when he was young, he had ruined his prospects in the Army, and remained an infantry captain. He had never married: his position did not allow of it, and no woman had ever moved him to it. His time he spent riding – occasionally he rode one of his own horses at the races – and at the officers' club. Now and then he took himself a mistress. But after such an event, he returned to duty with his brow still more tense, his eyes still more hostile and irritable. With the men, however, he was merely impersonal, though a devil when roused; so that, on the whole, they feared him, but had no great aversion from him. They accepted him as the inevitable.

To his orderly he was at first cold and just and indifferent: he did not fuss over trifles. So that his servant knew practically nothing about him, except just what orders he would give, and how he wanted them obeyed. That was quite simple. Then the change gradually came.

The orderly was a youth of about twenty-two, of medium height, and well built. He had strong, heavy limbs, was swarthy, with a soft, black, young moustache. There was something altogether warm and young about him. He had firmly marked eyebrows over dark, expressionless eyes, that seemed never to have thought, only to have received life direct through his senses, and acted straight from instinct.

Gradually the officer had become aware of his servant's young, vigorous, unconscious presence about him. He could not get away from the sense of the youth's person, while he was in attendance. It was like a warm flame upon the older man's tense, rigid body, that had become almost unliving, fixed. There was something so free and self-contained about him, and something in the young fellow's movement, that made the officer aware of him. And this irritated the Prussian. He did not choose to be touched into life by his servant. He might easily have changed his man, but he did not. He now very rarely looked direct at his orderly, but kept his face averted, as if to avoid seeing him. And yet as the young soldier moved unthinking about the apartment, the elder watched him, and would notice the movement of his strong young shoulders under the blue cloth, the bend of his neck. And it irritated him. To see the soldier's young, brown, shapely peasant's hand grasp the loaf or the wine-bottle sent a flash of hate or of anger through the elder man's blood. It was not that the youth was clumsy: it was rather the blind, instinctive sureness of movement of an unhampered young animal that irritated the officer to such a degree.

Once, when a bottle of wine had gone over, and the red gushed out on to the tablecloth, the officer had started up with an oath, and his eyes, bluey like fire, had held those of the confused youth for a moment. It was a shock for the young soldier. He felt something sink deeper, deeper into his soul, where nothing had ever gone before. It left him rather blank and wondering. Some of his natural completeness in himself was gone, a little uneasiness took its place. And from that time an undiscovered feeling had held between the two men.

Henceforward the orderly was afraid of really meeting his master. His subconsciousness remembered those steely blue eyes and the harsh brows, and did not intend to meet them again. So he always stared past his master, and avoided him. Also, in a little anxiety, he waited for the three months to have gone, when his time would be up. He began to feel a constraint in the Captain's presence, and the soldier even more than the officer wanted to be left alone, in his neutrality as servant.

He had served the Captain for more than a year, and knew his duty. This he performed easily, as if it were natural to him. The officer and his commands he took for granted, as he took the sun and the rain, and he served as a matter of course. It did not implicate him personally.

But now if he were going to be forced into a personal interchange with his master he would be like a wild thing caught, he felt he must get away.

But the influence of the young soldier's being had penetrated through the officer's stiffened discipline, and perturbed the man in him. He, however, was a gentleman, with long, fine hands and cultivated movements, and was not going to allow such a thing as the stirring of his innate self. He was a man of passionate temper, who had always kept himself suppressed. Occasionally there had been a duel, an outburst before the soldiers. He knew himself to be always on the point of breaking out. But he kept himself hard to the idea of the Service. Whereas the young soldier seemed to live out his warm, full nature, to give it off in his very movements, which had a certain zest, such as wild animals have in free movement. And this irritated the officer more and more.

In spite of himself, the Captain could not regain his neutrality of feeling towards his orderly. Nor could he leave the man alone. In spite of himself, he watched him, gave him sharp orders, tried to take up as much of his time as possible. Sometimes he flew into a rage with the young soldier, and bullied him. Then the orderly shut himself off, as it were out of earshot, and waited, with sullen, flushed face, for the end of the noise. The words never pierced to his intelligence, he made himself, protectively, impervious to the feelings of his master.

He had a scar on his left thumb, a deep seam going across the knuckle. The officer had long suffered from it, and wanted to do something to it. Still it was there, ugly and brutal on the young, brown hand. At last the Captain's reserve gave way. One day, as the orderly was smoothing out the tablecloth, the officer pinned down his thumb with a pencil, asking:

'How did you come by that?'

The young man winced and drew back at attention.

'A wood axe, Herr Hauptmann,' he answered.

The officer waited for further explanation. None came. The orderly went about his duties. The elder man was sullenly angry. His servant avoided him. And the next day he had to use all his will-power to avoid seeing the scarred thumb. He wanted to get hold of it and – A hot flame ran in his blood.

He knew his servant would soon be free, and would be glad. As yet, the soldier had held himself off from the elder man. The Captain grew madly irritable. He could not rest when the soldier was away, and when he was present, he glared at him with tormented eyes. He hated those fine, black brows over the unmeaning, dark eyes, he was infuriated by the free movement of the handsome limbs, which no military discipline could make stiff. And he became harsh and cruelly bullying, using contempt and satire. The young soldier only grew more mute and expressionless.

'What cattle were you bred by, that you can't keep straight eyes? Look me in the eyes when I speak to you.'

And the soldier turned his dark eyes to the other's face, but there was no sight in them: he stared with the slightest possible cast, holding back his sight, perceiving the blue of his master's eyes, but receiving no look from them. And the elder man went pale, and his reddish eyebrows twitched. He gave his order, barrenly.

Once he flung a heavy military glove into the young soldier's face. Then he had the satisfaction of seeing the black eyes flare up into his own, like a blaze when straw is thrown on a fire. And he had laughed with a little tremor and a sneer.

But there were only two months more. The youth instinctively tried to keep himself intact: he tried to serve the officer as if the latter were an abstract authority and not a man. All his instinct was to avoid personal contact, even definite hate. But in spite of himself the hate grew, responsive to the officer's passion. However, he put it in the background. When he had left the Army he could dare acknowledge it. By nature he was active, and had many friends. He thought what amazing good fellows they were. But, without knowing it, he was alone. Now this solitariness was intensified. It would carry him through his term. But the officer seemed to be going irritably insane, and the youth was deeply frightened.

The soldier had a sweetheart, a girl from the mountains, independent and primitive. The two walked together, rather silently. He went with her, not to talk, but to have his arm round her, and for the physical contact. This eased him, made it easier for him to ignore the Captain; for he could rest with her held fast against his chest. And she, in some unspoken fashion, was there for him. They loved each other.

The Captain perceived it, and was mad with irritation. He kept the young man engaged all the evenings long, and took pleasure in the dark look that came on his face. Occasionally, the eyes of the two men met, those of the younger sullen and dark, doggedly unalterable, those of the elder sneering with restless contempt.

The officer tried hard not to admit the passion that had got hold of him. He would not know that his feeling for his orderly was anything but that of a man incensed by his stupid, perverse servant. So, keeping quite justified and conventional in his consciousness, he let the other thing run on. His nerves, however, were suffering. At last he slung the end of a belt in his servant's face. When he saw the youth start back, the pain-tears in his eyes and the blood on his mouth, he had felt at once a thrill of deep pleasure and of shame.

But this, he acknowledged to himself, was a thing he had never done before. The fellow was too exasperating. His own nerves must be going to pieces. He went away for some days with a woman.

It was a mockery of pleasure. He simply did not want the woman. But he stayed on for his time. At the end of it, he came back in an agony of irritation, torment, and misery. He rode all the evening, then came straight in to supper. His orderly was out. The officer sat with his long, fine hands lying on the table, perfectly still, and all his blood seemed to be corroding.

At last his servant entered. He watched the strong, easy young figure, the fine eyebrows, the thick black hair. In a week's time the youth had got back his old well-being. The hands of the officer twitched and seemed to be full of mad flame. The young man stood at attention, unmoving, shut off.

The meal went in silence. But the orderly seemed eager. He made a clatter with the dishes.

'Are you in a hurry?' asked the officer, watching the intent, warm face of his servant. The other did not reply.

'Will you answer my question?' said the Captain.

'Yes, sir,' replied the orderly, standing with his pile of deep Army plates. The Captain waited, looked at him, then asked again:

'Are you in a hurry?'

'Yes, sir,' came the answer, that sent a flash through the listener.

'For what?'

'I was going out, sir.'

'I want you this evening.'

There was a moment's hesitation. The officer had a curious stiffness of countenance.

'Yes, sir,' replied the servant, in his throat.

'I want you to-morrow evening also – in fact, you may consider your evenings occupied, unless I give you leave.'

The mouth with the young moustache set close.

'Yes, sir,' answered the orderly, loosening his lips for a moment.

He again turned to the door.

'And why have you a piece of pencil in your ear?'

The orderly hesitated, then continued on his way without answering. He set the plates in a pile outside the door, took the stump of pencil from his ear, and put it in his pocket. He had been copying a verse for his sweetheart's birthday card. He returned to finish clearing the table. The officer's eyes were dancing, he had a little, eager smile.

'Why have you a piece of pencil in your ear?' he asked.

The orderly took his hands full of dishes. His master was standing near the great green stove, a little smile on his face, his chin thrust forward. When the young soldier saw him his heart suddenly ran hot. He felt blind. Instead of answering, he turned dazedly to the door. As he was crouching to set down the dishes, he was pitched forward by a kick from behind. The pots went in a stream down the stairs, he clung to the pillar of the banisters. And as he was rising he was kicked heavily again, and again, so that he clung sickly to the post for some moments. His master had gone swiftly into the room and closed the door. The maid-servant downstairs looked up the staircase and made a mocking face at the crockery disaster.

The officer's heart was plunging. He poured himself a glass of wine, part of which he spilled on the floor, and gulped the remainder, leaning against the cool, green stove. He heard his man collecting the dishes from the stairs. Pale, as if intoxicated, he waited. The servant entered again. The Captain's heart gave a pang, as of pleasure, seeing the young fellow bewildered and uncertain on his feet, with pain.

'Schöner!' he said.

The soldier was a little slower in coming to attention.

'Yes, sir!'

The youth stood before him, with pathetic young moustache, and fine eyebrows very distinct on his forehead of dark marble.

'I asked you a question.'

'Yes, sir.'

The officer's tone bit like acid.

'Why had you a pencil in your ear?'

Again the servant's heart ran hot, and he could not breathe. With dark, strained eyes, he looked at the officer, as if fascinated. And he stood there sturdily planted, unconscious. The withering smile came into the Captain's eyes, and he lifted his foot.

'I – I forgot it – sir,' panted the soldier, his dark eyes fixed on the other man's dancing blue ones.

'What was it doing there?'

He saw the young man's breast heaving as he made an effort for words.

'I had been writing.'

'Writing what?'

Again the soldier looked up and down. The officer could hear him panting. The smile came into the blue eyes. The soldier worked his dry throat, but could not speak. Suddenly the smile lit like a flame on the officer's face, and a kick came heavily against the orderly's thigh. The youth moved a pace sideways. His face went dead, with two black, staring eyes.

'Well?' said the officer.

The orderly's mouth had gone dry, and his tongue rubbed in it as on dry brown-paper. He worked his throat. The officer raised his foot. The servant went stiff.

'Some poetry, sir,' came the crackling, unrecognizable sound of his voice.

'Poetry, what poetry?' asked the Captain, with a sickly smile.

Again there was the working in the throat. The Captain's heart had suddenly gone down heavily, and he stood sick and tired.

'For my girl, sir,' he heard the dry, inhuman sound.

'Oh!' he said, turning away. 'Clear the table.'

'Click!' went the soldier's throat; then again, 'click!' and then the half-articulate:

'Yes, sir.'

The young soldier was gone, looking old, and walking heavily.

The officer, left alone, held himself rigid, to prevent himself from thinking. His instinct warned him that he must not think. Deep inside him was the intense gratification of his passion, still working powerfully. Then there was a counter-action, a horrible breaking down of something inside him, a whole agony of reaction. He stood there for an hour motionless, a chaos of sensations, but rigid with a will to keep blank his consciousness, to prevent his mind grasping. And he held himself so until the worst of the stress had passed, when he began to drink, drank himself to an intoxication, till he slept obliterated. When he woke in the morning he was shaken to the base of his nature. But he had fought off the realization of what he had done. He had prevented his mind from taking it in, had suppressed it along with his instincts, and the conscious man had nothing to do with it. He felt only as after a bout of intoxication, weak, but the affair itself all dim and not to be recovered. Of the drunkenness of his passion he successfully refused remembrance. And when his orderly appeared with coffee, the officer assumed the same self he had had the morning before. He refused the event of the past night – denied it had ever been – and was successful in his denial. He had not done any such thing – not he himself. Whatever there might be lay at the door of a stupid, insubordinate servant.

The orderly had gone about in a stupor all the evening. He drank some beer because he was parched, but not much, the alcohol made his feeling come back, and he could not bear it. He was dulled, as if nine-tenths of the ordinary man in him were inert. He crawled about disfigured. Still, when he thought of the kicks, he went sick, and when he thought of the threat of more kicking, in the room afterwards, his heart went hot and faint, and he panted, remembering the one that had come. He had been forced to say, 'For my girl.' He was much too done even to want to cry. His mouth hung slightly open, like an idiot's. He felt vacant, and wasted. So, he wandered at his work, painfully, and very slowly and clumsily, fumbling blindly with the brushes, and finding it difficult, when he sat down, to summon the energy to move again. His limbs, his jaw, were slack and nerveless. But he was very tired. He got to bed at last, and slept inert, relaxed, in a sleep that was rather stupor than slumber, a dead night of stupefaction shot through with gleams of anguish.

In the morning were the manoeuvres. But he woke even before the bugle sounded. The painful ache in his chest, the dryness of his throat, the awful steady feeling of misery made his eyes come awake and dreary at once. He knew, without thinking, what had happened. And he knew that the day had come again, when he must go on with his round. The last bit of darkness was being pushed out of the room. He would have to move his inert body and go on. He was so young, and had known so little trouble, that he was bewildered. He only wished it would stay night, so that he could lie still, covered up by the darkness. And yet nothing would prevent the day from coming, nothing would save him from having to get up and saddle the Captain's horse, and make the Captain's coffee. It was there, inevitable. And then, he thought, it was impossible. Yet they would not leave him free. He must go and take the coffee to the Captain. He was too stunned to understand it. He only knew it was inevitable – inevitable, however long he lay inert.

At last, after heaving at himself, for he seemed to be a mass of inertia, he got up. But he had to force every one of his movements from behind, with his will. He felt lost, and dazed, and helpless. Then he clutched hold of the bed, the pain was so keen. And looking at his thighs, he saw the darker bruises on his swarthy flesh and he knew that, if he pressed one of his fingers on one of the bruises, he should faint. But he did not want to faint – he did not want anybody to know. No one should ever know. It was between him and the Captain. There were only the two people in the world now – himself and the Captain.

Slowly, economically, he got dressed and forced himself to walk. Everything was obscure, except just what he had his hands on. But he managed to get through his work. The very pain revived his dull senses. The worst remained yet. He took the tray and went up to the Captain's room. The officer, pale and heavy, sat at the table. The orderly, as he saluted, felt himself put out of existence. He stood still for a moment submitting to his own nullification – then he gathered himself, seemed to regain himself, and then the Captain began to grow vague, unreal, and the younger soldier's heart beat up. He clung to this situation – that the Captain did not exist – so that he himself might live. But when he saw his officer's hand tremble as he took the coffee, he felt everything falling shattered. And he went away, feeling as if he himself were coming to pieces, disintegrated. And when the Captain was there on horseback, giving orders, while he himself stood, with rifle and knapsack, sick with pain, he felt as if he must shut his eyes – as if he must shut his eyes on everything. It was only the long agony of marching with a parched throat that filled him with one single, sleep-heavy intention: to save himself.

II

He was getting used even to his parched throat. That the snowy peaks were radiant among the sky, that the whity-green glacier-river twisted through its pale shoals, in the valley below, seemed almost supernatural. But he was going mad with fever and thirst. He plodded on uncomplaining. He did not want to speak, not to anybody. There were two gulls, like flakes of water and snow, over the river. The scent of green rye soaked in sunshine came like a sickness. And the march continued, monotonously, almost like a bad sleep.

At the next farm-house, which stood low and broad near the high road, tubs of water had been put out. The soldiers clustered round to drink. They took off their helmets, and the steam mounted from their wet hair. The Captain sat on horseback, watching. He needed to see his orderly. His helmet threw a dark shadow over his light, fierce eyes, but his moustache and mouth and chin were distinct in the sunshine. The orderly must move under the presence of the figure of the horseman. It was not that he was afraid, or cowed. It was as if he was disembowelled, made empty, like an empty shell. He felt himself as nothing, a shadow creeping under the sunshine. And, thirsty as he was, he could scarcely drink, feeling the Captain near him. He would not take off his helmet to wipe his wet hair. He wanted to stay in shadow, not to be forced into consciousness. Starting, he saw the light heel of the officer prick the belly of the horse; the Captain cantered away, and he himself could relapse into vacancy.

Nothing, however, could give him back his living place in the hot, bright morning. He felt like a gap among it all. Whereas the Captain was prouder, overriding. A hot flash went through the young servant's body. The Captain was firmer and prouder with life, he himself was empty as a shadow. Again the flash went through him, dazing him out. But his heart ran a little firmer.

The company turned up the hill, to make a loop for the return. Below, from among the trees, the farm-bell clanged. He saw the labourers, mowing barefoot at the thick grass, leave off their work and go downhill, their scythes hanging over their shoulders, like long, bright claws curving down behind them. They seemed like dream-people, as if they had no relation to himself. He felt as in a blackish dream: as if all the other things were there and had form, but he himself was only a consciousness, a gap that could think and perceive.

The soldiers were tramping silently up the glaring hillside. Gradually his head began to revolve, slowly, rhythmically. Sometimes it was dark before his eyes, as if he saw this world through a smoked glass, frail shadows and unreal. It gave him a pain in his head to walk.

The air was too scented, it gave no breath. All the lush green-stuff seemed to be issuing its sap, till the air was deathly, sickly with the smell of greenness. There was the perfume of clover, like pure honey and bees. Then there grew a faint acrid tang – they were near the beeches; and then a queer clattering noise, and a suffocating, hideous smell; they were passing a flock of sheep, a shepherd in a black smock, holding his crook. Why should the sheep huddle together under this fierce sun? He felt that the shepherd would not see him, though he could see the shepherd.

At last there was the halt. They stacked rifles in a conical stack, put down their kit in a scattered circle around it, and dispersed a little, sitting on a small knoll high on the hillside. The chatter began. The soldiers were steaming with heat, but were lively. He sat still, seeing the blue mountains rising upon the land, twenty kilometres away. There was a blue fold in the ranges, then out of that, at the foot, the broad, pale bed of the river, stretches of whity-green water between pinkish-grey shoals among the dark pine woods. There it was, spread out a long way off. And it seemed to come downhill, the river. There was a raft being steered, a mile away. It was a strange country. Nearer, a red-roofed, broad farm with white base and square dots of windows crouched beside the wall of beech foliage on the wood's edge. There were long strips of rye and clover and pale green corn. And just at his feet, below the knoll, was a darkish bog, where globe flowers stood breathless still on their slim stalks. And some of the pale gold bubbles were burst, and a broken fragment hung in the air. He thought he was going to sleep.

Suddenly something moved into this coloured mirage before his eyes. The Captain, a small, light-blue and scarlet figure, was trotting evenly between the strips of corn, along the level brow of the hill. And the man making flag-signals was coming on. Proud and sure moved the horseman's figure, the quick, bright thing, in which was concentrated all the light of this morning, which for the rest lay a fragile, shining shadow. Submissive, apathetic, the young soldier sat and stared. But as the horse slowed to a walk, coming up the last steep path, the great flash flared over the body and soul of the orderly. He sat waiting. The back of his head felt as if it were weighted with a heavy piece of fire. He did not want to eat. His hands trembled slightly as he moved them. Meanwhile the officer on horseback was approaching slowly and proudly. The tension grew in the orderly's soul. Then again, seeing the Captain ease himself on the saddle, the flash blazed through him.

The Captain looked at the patch of light blue and scarlet, and dark heads, scattered closely on the hillside. It pleased him. The command pleased him. And he was feeling proud. His orderly was among them in common subjection. The officer rose a little on his stirrups to look. The young soldier sat with averted, dumb face. The Captain relaxed on his seat. His slim-legged, beautiful horse, brown as a beech nut, walked proudly uphill. The Captain passed into the zone of the company's atmosphere: a hot smell of men, of sweat, of leather. He knew it very well. After a word with the lieutenant, he went a few paces higher, and sat there, a dominant figure, his sweat-marked horse swishing its tail, while he looked down on his men, on his orderly, a nonentity among the crowd.

The young soldier's heart was like fire in his chest, and he breathed with difficulty. The officer, looking downhill, saw three of the young soldiers, two pails of water between them, staggering across a sunny green field. A table had been set up under a tree, and there the slim lieutenant stood, importantly busy. Then the Captain summoned himself to an act of courage. He called his orderly.

The flame leapt into the young soldier's throat as he heard the command, and he rose blindly, stifled. He saluted, standing below the officer. He did not look up. But there was the flicker in the Captain's voice.

'Go to the inn and fetch me ...' the officer gave his commands. 'Quick!' he added.

At the last word, the heart of the servant leapt with a flash, and he felt the strength come over his body. But he turned in mechanical obedience, and set off at a heavy run downhill, looking almost like a bear, his trousers bagging over his military boots. And the officer watched this blind, plunging run all the way.

But it was only the outside of the orderly's body that was obeying so humbly and mechanically. Inside had gradually accumulated a core into which all the energy of that young life was compact and concentrated. He executed his commission, and plodded quickly back uphill. There was a pain in his head, as he walked, that made him twist his features unknowingly. But hard there in the centre of his chest was himself, himself, firm, and not to be plucked to pieces.

The Captain had gone up into the wood. The orderly plodded through the hot, powerfully smelling zone of the company's atmosphere. He had a curious mass of energy inside him now. The Captain was less real than himself. He approached the green entrance to the wood. There, in the half-shade, he saw the horse standing, the sunshine and the flickering shadow of leaves dancing over his brown body. There was a clearing where timber had lately been felled. Here, in the gold-green shade beside the brilliant cup of sunshine, stood two figures, blue and pink, the bits of pink showing out plainly. The Captain was talking to his lieutenant.

The orderly stood on the edge of the bright clearing, where great trunks of trees, stripped and glistening, lay stretched like naked, brown-skinned bodies. Chips of wood littered the trampled floor, like splashed light, and the bases of the felled trees stood here and there, with their raw, level tops. Beyond was the brilliant, sunlit green of a beech.

'Then I will ride forward,' the orderly heard his Captain say. The lieutenant saluted and strode away. He himself went forward. A hot flash passed through his belly, as he tramped towards his officer.

The Captain watched the rather heavy figure of the young soldier stumble forward, and his veins, too, ran hot. This was to be man to man between them. He yielded before the solid, stumbling figure with bent head. The orderly stooped and put the food on a level-sawn tree-base. The Captain watched the glistening, sun-inflamed, naked hands. He wanted to speak to the young soldier, but could not. The servant propped a bottle against his thigh, pressed open the cork, and poured out the beer into the mug. He kept his head bent. The Captain accepted the mug.

'Hot!' he said, as if amiably.

The flame sprang out of the orderly's heart, nearly suffocating him.

'Yes, sir,' he replied, between shut teeth.

And he heard the sound of the Captain's drinking, and he clenched his fists, such a strong torment came into his wrists. Then came the faint clang of the closing pot-lid. He looked up. The Captain was watching him. He glanced swiftly away. Then he saw the officer stoop and take a piece of bread from the tree-base. Again the flash of flame went through the young soldier, seeing the stiff body stoop beneath him, and his hands jerked. He looked away. He could feel the officer was nervous. The bread fell as it was being broken. The officer ate the other piece. The two men stood tense and still, the master laboriously chewing his bread, the servant staring with averted face, his fist clenched.

Then the young soldier started. The officer had pressed open the lid of the mug again. The orderly watched the lid of the mug, and the white hand that clenched the handle, as if he were fascinated. It was raised. The youth followed it with his eyes. And then he saw the thin, strong throat of the elder man moving up and down as he drank, the strong jaw working. And the instinct which had been jerking at the young man's wrists suddenly jerked free. He jumped, feeling as if it were rent in two by a strong flame.

The spur of the officer caught in a tree-root, he went down backwards with a crash, the middle of his back thudding sickeningly against a sharp-edged tree-base, the pot flying away. And in a second the orderly, with serious, earnest young face, and underlip between his teeth, had got his knee in the officer's chest and was pressing the chin backward over the farther edge of the tree-stump, pressing, with all his heart behind in a passion of relief, the tension of his wrists exquisite with relief. And with the base of his palms he shoved at the chin, with all his might. And it was pleasant, too, to have that chin, that hard jaw already slightly rough with beard, in his hands. He did not relax one hair's breadth, but, all the force of all his blood exulting in his thrust, he shoved back the head of the other man, till there was a little 'cluck' and a crunching sensation. Then he felt as if his head went to vapour. Heavy convulsions shook the body of the officer, frightening and horrifying the young soldier. Yet it pleased him, too, to repress them. It pleased him to keep his hands pressing back the chin, to feel the chest of the other man yield in expiration to the weight of his strong, young knees, to feel the hard twitchings of the prostrate body jerking his own whole frame, which was pressed down on it.

But it went still. He could look into the nostrils of the other man, the eyes he could scarcely see. How curiously the mouth was pushed out, exaggerating the full lips, and the moustache bristling up from them. Then, with a start, he noticed the nostrils gradually filled with blood. The red brimmed, hesitated, ran over, and went in a thin trickle down the face to the eyes.

It shocked and distressed him. Slowly, he got up. The body twitched and sprawled there, inert. He stood and looked at it in silence. It was a pity *it* was broken. It represented more than the thing which had kicked and bullied him. He was afraid to look at the eyes. They were hideous now, only the whites showing, and the blood running to them. The face of the orderly was drawn with horror at the sight. Well, it was so. In his heart he was satisfied. He had hated the face of the Captain. It was extinguished now. There was a heavy relief in the orderly's soul. That was as it should be. But he could not bear to see the long, military body lying broken over the tree-base, the fine fingers crisped. He wanted to hide it away.

Quickly, busily, he gathered it up and pushed it under the felled tree-trunks, which rested their beautiful, smooth length either end on logs. The face was horrible with blood. He covered it with the helmet. Then he pushed the limbs straight and decent, and brushed the dead leaves off the fine cloth of the uniform. So, it lay quite still in the shadow under there. A little strip of sunshine ran along the breast, from a chink between the logs. The orderly sat by it for a few moments. Here his own life also ended.

Then, through his daze, he heard the lieutenant, in a loud voice, explaining to the men outside the wood, that they were to suppose the bridge on the river below was held by the enemy. Now they were to march to the attack in such and such a manner. The lieutenant had no gift of expression. The orderly, listening from habit, got muddled. And when the lieutenant began it all again he ceased to hear.

He knew he must go. He stood up. It surprised him that the leaves were glittering in the sun, and the chips of wood reflecting white from the ground. For him a change had come over the world. But for the rest it had not – all seemed the same. Only he had left it. And he could not go back. It was his duty to return with the beer-pot and the bottle. He could not. He had left all that. The lieutenant was still hoarsely explaining. He must go, or they would overtake him. And he could not bear contact with anyone now.

He drew his fingers over his eyes, trying to find out where he was. Then he turned away. He saw the horse standing in the path. He went up to it and mounted. It hurt him to sit in the saddle. The pain of keeping his seat occupied him as they cantered through the wood. He would not have minded anything, but he could not get away from the sense of being divided from the others. The path led out of the trees. On the edge of the wood he pulled up and stood watching. There in the spacious sunshine of the valley soldiers were moving in a little swarm. Every now and then, a man harrowing on a strip of fallow shouted to his oxen, at the turn. The village and the white-towered church was small in the sunshine. And he no longer belonged to it – he sat there, beyond, like a man outside in the dark. He had gone out from everyday life into the unknown, and he could not, he even did not want to go back.

Turning from the sun-blazing valley, he rode deep into the wood. Tree-trunks, like people standing grey and still, took no notice as he went. A doe, herself a moving bit of sunshine and shadow, went running through the flecked shade. There were bright green rents in the foliage. Then it was all pine wood, dark and cool. And he was sick with pain, he had an intolerable great pulse in his head, and he was sick. He had never been ill in his life. He felt lost, quite dazed with all this.

Trying to get down from the horse, he fell, astonished at the pain and his lack of balance. The horse shifted uneasily. He jerked its bridle and sent it cantering jerkily away. It was his last connection with the rest of things.

But he only wanted to lie down and not be disturbed. Stumbling through the trees, he came on a quiet place where beeches and pine trees grew on a slope. Immediately he had lain down and closed his eyes, his consciousness went racing on without him. A big pulse of sickness beat in him as if it throbbed through the whole earth. He was burning with dry heat. But he was too busy, too tearingly active in the incoherent race of delirium to observe.

III

He came to with a start. His mouth was dry and hard, his heart beat heavily, but he had not the energy to get up. His heart beat heavily. Where was he? – the barracks – at home? There was something knocking. And, making an effort, he looked round – trees, and litter of greenery, and reddish, bright, still pieces of sunshine on the floor. He did not believe he was himself, he did not believe what he saw. Something was knocking. He made a struggle towards consciousness, but relapsed. Then he struggled again. And gradually his surroundings fell into relationship with himself. He knew, and a great pang of fear went through his heart. Somebody was knocking. He could see the heavy, black rags of a fir tree overhead. Then everything went black. Yet he did not believe he had closed his eyes. He had not. Out of the blackness sight slowly emerged again. And someone was knocking. Quickly, he saw the blood-disfigured face of his Captain, which he hated. And he held himself still with horror. Yet, deep inside him, he knew that it was so, the Captain should be dead. But the physical delirium got hold of him. Someone was knocking. He lay perfectly still, as if dead, with fear. And he went unconscious.

When he opened his eyes again, he started, seeing something creeping swiftly up a tree-trunk. It was a little bird. And the bird was whistling overhead. Tap-tap-tap – it was the small, quick bird rapping the tree-trunk with its beak, as if its head were a little round hammer. He watched it curiously. It shifted sharply, in its creeping fashion. Then, like a mouse, it slid down the bare trunk. Its swift creeping sent a flash of revulsion through him. He raised his head. It felt a great weight. Then, the little bird ran out of the shadow across a still patch of sunshine, its little head bobbing swiftly, its white legs twinkling brightly for a moment. How neat it was in its build, so compact, with pieces of white on its wings. There were several of them. They were so pretty – but they crept like swift, erratic mice, running here and there among the beech-mast.

He lay down again exhausted, and his consciousness lapsed. He had a horror of the little creeping birds. All his blood seemed to be darting and creeping in his head. And yet he could not move.

He came to with a further ache of exhaustion. There was the pain in his head, and the horrible sickness, and his inability to move. He had never been ill in his life. He did not know where he was or what he was. Probably he had got sunstroke. Or what else? – he had silenced the Captain for ever – some time ago – oh, a long time ago.

There had been blood on his face, and his eyes had turned upwards. It was all right, somehow. It was peace. But now he had got beyond himself. He had never been here before. Was it life, or not life? He was by himself. They were in a big, bright place, those others, and he was outside. The town, all the country, a big bright place of light: and he was outside, here, in the darkened open beyond, where each thing existed alone. But they would all have to come out there sometime, those others. Little, and left behind him, they all were. There had been father and mother and sweetheart. What did they all matter? This was the open land.

He sat up. Something scuffled. It was a little, brown squirrel running in lovely, undulating bounds over the floor, its red tail completing the undulation of its body – and then, as it sat up, furling and unfurling. He watched it, pleased. It ran on again, friskily, enjoying itself. It flew wildly at another squirrel, and they were chasing each other, and making little scolding, chattering noises. The soldier wanted to speak to them. But only a hoarse sound came out of his throat. The squirrels burst away – they flew up the trees. And then he saw the one peeping round at him, half-way up a tree-trunk. A start of fear went through him, though, in so far as he was conscious, he was amused. It still stayed, its little, keen face staring at him half-way up the tree-trunk, its little ears pricked up, its clawey little hands clinging to the bark, its white breast reared. He started from it in panic.

Struggling to his feet, he lurched away. He went on walking, walking, looking for something – for a drink. His brain felt hot and inflamed for want of water. He stumbled on. Then he did not know anything. He went unconscious as he walked. Yet he stumbled on, his mouth open.

When, to his dumb wonder, he opened his eyes on the world again, he no longer tried to remember what it was. There was thick, golden light behind golden-green glitterings, and tall, grey-purple shafts, and darknesses further off, surrounding him, growing deeper. He was conscious of a sense of arrival. He was amid the reality, on the real, dark bottom. But there was the thirst burning in his brain. He felt lighter, not so heavy. He supposed it was newness. The air was muttering with thunder. He thought he was walking wonderfully swiftly and was coming straight to relief – or was it to water?

Suddenly he stood still with fear. There was a tremendous flare of gold, immense – just a few dark trunks like bars between him and it. All the young level wheat was burnished gold glaring on its silky green. A woman, full-skirted, a black cloth on her head for head-dress, was passing like a block of shadow through the glistening, green corn, into the full glare. There was a farm, too, pale blue in shadow, and the timber black. And there was a church spire, nearly fused away in the gold. The woman moved on, away from him. He had no language with which to speak to her. She was the bright, solid unreality. She would make a noise of words that would confuse him, and her eyes would look at him without seeing him. She was crossing there to the other side. He stood against a tree.

When at last he turned, looking down the long, bare grove whose flat bed was already filling dark, he saw the mountains in a wonder-light, not far away, and radiant. Behind the soft, grey ridge of the nearest range the further mountains stood golden and pale grey, the snow all radiant like pure, soft gold. So still, gleaming in the sky, fashioned pure out of the ore of the sky, they shone in their silence. He stood and looked at them, his face illuminated. And like the golden, lustrous gleaming of the snow he felt his own thirst bright in him. He stood and gazed, leaning against a tree. And then everything slid away into space.

During the night the lightning fluttered perpetually, making the whole sky white. He must have walked again. The world hung livid round him for moments, fields a level sheen of grey-green light, trees in dark bulk, and the range of clouds black across a white sky. Then the darkness fell like a shutter, and the night was whole. A faint flutter of a half-revealed world, that could not quite leap out of the darkness! – Then there again stood a sweep of pallor for the land, dark shapes looming, a range of clouds hanging overhead. The world was a ghostly shadow, thrown for a moment upon the pure darkness, which returned ever whole and complete.

And the mere delirium of sickness and fever went on inside him – his brain opening and shutting like the night – then sometimes convulsions of terror from something with great eyes that stared round a tree – then the long agony of the march, and the sun decomposing his blood – then the pang of hate for the Captain, followed by a pang of tenderness and ease. But everything was distorted, born of an ache and resolving into an ache.

In the morning he came definitely awake. Then his brain flamed with the sole horror of thirstiness! The sun was on his face, the dew was steaming from his wet clothes. Like one possessed, he got up. There, straight in front of him, blue and cool and tender, the mountains ranged across the pale edge of the morning sky. He wanted them – he wanted them alone – he wanted to leave himself and be identified with them. They did not move, they were still soft, with white, gentle markings of snow. He stood still, mad with suffering, his hands crisping and clutching. Then he was twisting in a paroxysm on the grass.

He lay still, in a kind of dream of anguish. His thirst seemed to have separated itself from him, and to stand apart, a single demand. Then the pain he felt was another single self. Then there was the clog of his body, another separate thing. He was divided among all kinds of separate beings. There was some strange, agonized connection between them, but they were drawing further apart. Then they would all split. The sun, drilling down on him, was drilling through the bond. Then they would all fall, fall through the everlasting lapse of space. Then again, his consciousness reasserted itself. He roused on to his elbow and stared at the gleaming mountains. There they ranked, all still and wonderful between earth and heaven. He stared till his eyes went black, and the mountains, as they stood in their beauty, so clean and cool, seemed to have it, that which was lost in him.

IV

When the soldiers found him, three hours later, he was lying with his face over his arm, his black hair giving off heat under the sun. But he was still alive. Seeing the open, black mouth the young soldiers dropped him in horror.

He died in the hospital at night, without having seen again.

The doctors saw the bruises on his legs, behind, and were silent.

The bodies of the two men lay together, side by side, in the mortuary, the one white and slender, but laid rigidly at rest, the other looking as if every moment it must rouse into life again, so young and unused, from a slumber.

The Thorn in the Flesh

I

A WIND was running, so that occasionally the poplars whitened as if a flame flew up them. The sky was broken and blue among moving clouds. Patches of sunshine lay on the level fields, and shadows on the rye and the vineyards. In the distance, very blue, the cathedral bristled against the sky, and the houses of the city of Metz clustered vaguely below, like a hill.

Among the fields by the lime trees stood the barracks, upon bare, dry ground, a collection of round-roofed huts of corrugated iron, where the soldiers' nasturtiums climbed brilliantly. There was a tract of vegetable garden at the side, with the soldiers' yellowish lettuces in rows, and at the back the big, hard drilling-yard surrounded by a wire fence.

At this time in the afternoon, the huts were deserted, all the beds pushed up, the soldiers were lounging about under the lime trees waiting for the call to drill. Bachmann sat on a bench in the shade that smelled sickly with blossom. Pale green, wrecked lime flowers were scattered on the ground. He was writing his weekly post card to his mother. He was a fair, long, limber youth, good looking. He sat very still indeed, trying to write his post card. His blue uniform, sagging on him as he sat bent over the card, disfigured his youthful shape. His sunburnt hand waited motionless for the words to come. 'Dear mother' – was all he had written. Then he scribbled mechanically: 'Many thanks for your letter with what you sent. Everything is all right with me. We are just off to drill on the fortifications –' Here he broke off and sat suspended, oblivious of everything, held in some definite suspense. He looked again at the card. But he could write no more. Out of the knot of his consciousness no word would come. He signed himself, and looked up, as a man looks to see if anyone has noticed him in his privacy.

There was a self-conscious strain in his blue eyes, and a pallor about his mouth, where the young, fair moustache glistened. He was almost girlish in his good looks and his grace. But he had something of military consciousness, as if he believed in the discipline for himself, and found satisfaction in delivering himself to his duty. There was also a trace of youthful swagger and dare-devilry about his mouth and his limber body, but this was in suppression now.

He put the post card in the pocket of his tunic, and went to join a group of his comrades who were lounging in the shade, laughing and talking grossly. To-day he was out of it. He only stood near to them for the warmth of the association. In his own consciousness something held him down.

Presently they were summoned to ranks. The sergeant came out to take command. He was a strongly built, rather heavy man of forty. His head was thrust forward, sunk a little between his powerful shoulders, and the strong jaw was pushed out aggressively. But the eyes were smouldering, the face hung slack and sodden with drink.

He gave his orders in brutal, barking shouts, and the little company moved forward, out of the wire-fenced yard to the open road, marching rhythmically, raising the dust. Bachmann, one of the inner file of four deep, marched in the airless ranks, half suffocated with heat and dust and enclosure. Through the moving of his comrades' bodies, he could see the small vines dusty by the roadside, the poppies among the tares fluttering and blown to pieces, the distant spaces of sky and fields all free with air and sunshine. But he was bound in a very dark enclosure of anxiety within himself.

He marched with his usual ease, being healthy and well adjusted. But his body went on by itself. His spirit was clenched apart. And ever the few soldiers drew nearer and nearer to the town, ever the consciousness of the youth became more gripped and separate, his body worked by a kind of mechanical intelligence, a mere presence of mind.

They diverged from the high road and passed in single file down a path among trees. All was silent and green and mysterious, with shadow of foliage and long, green, undisturbed grass. Then they came out in the sunshine on a moat of water, which wound silently between the long, flowery grass, at the foot of the earthworks, that rose in front in terraces walled smooth on the face, but all soft with long grass at the top. Marguerite daisies and lady's-slipper glimmered white and gold in the lush grass, preserved here in the intense peace of the fortifications. Thickets of trees stood round about. Occasionally a puff of mysterious wind made the flowers and the long grass that crested the earthworks above bow and shake as with signals of on-coming alarm.

The group of soldiers stood at the end of the moat, in their light blue and scarlet uniforms, very bright. The sergeant was giving them instructions, and his shout came sharp and alarming in the intense, untouched stillness of the place. They listened, finding it difficult to make the effort of understanding.

Then it was over, and the men were moving to make preparations. On the other side of the moat the ramparts rose smooth and clear in the sun, sloping slightly back. Along the summit grass grew and tall daisies stood ledged high, like magic, against the dark green of the tree-tops behind. The noise of the town, the running of tram-cars, was heard distinctly, but it seemed not to penetrate this still place.

The water of the moat was motionless. In silence the practice began. One of the soldiers took a scaling ladder, and passing along the narrow ledge at the foot of the earthworks, with the water of the moat just behind him, tried to get a fixture on the slightly sloping wall-face. There he stood, small and isolated, at the foot of the wall, trying to get his ladder settled. At last it held, and the clumsy, groping figure in the baggy blue uniform began to clamber up. The rest of the soldiers stood and watched. Occasionally the sergeant barked a command. Slowly the clumsy blue figure clambered higher up the wall-face. Bachmann stood with his bowels turned to water. The figure of the climbing soldier scrambled out on to the terrace up above, and moved, blue and distinct, among the bright green grass. The officer shouted from below. The soldier tramped along, fixed the ladder in another spot, and carefully lowered himself on to the rungs. Bachmann watched the blind foot groping in space for the ladder, and he felt the world fall away beneath him. The figure of the soldier clung cringing against the face of the wall, cleaving, groping downwards like some unsure insect working its way lower and lower, fearing every movement. At last, sweating and with a strained face, the figure had landed safely and turned to the group of soldiers. But still it had a stiffness and a blank, mechanical look, was something less than human.

Bachmann stood there heavy and condemned, waiting for his own turn and betrayal. Some of the men went up easily enough, and without fear. That only showed it could be done lightly, and made Bachmann's case more bitter. If only he could do it lightly, like that.

His turn came. He knew intuitively that nobody knew his condition. The officer just saw him as a mechanical thing. He tried to keep it up, to carry it through on the face of things. His inside gripped tight, as yet under control, he took the ladder and went along under the wall. He placed his ladder with quick success, and wild, quivering hope possessed him. Then blindly he began to climb. But the ladder was not very firm, and at every hitch a great, sick, melting feeling took hold of him. He clung on fast. If only he could keep that grip on himself, he would get through. He knew this, in agony. What he could not understand was the blind gush of white-hot fear, that came with great force whenever the ladder swerved, and which almost melted his belly and all his joints, and left him powerless. If once it melted all his joints and his belly, he was done. He clung desperately to himself. He knew the fear, he knew what it did when it came, he knew he had only to keep a firm hold. He knew all this. Yet, when the ladder swerved, and his foot missed, there was the great blast of fear blowing on his heart and bowels, and he was melting weaker and weaker, in a horror of fear and lack of control, melting to fall.

Yet he groped slowly higher and higher, always staring upwards with desperate face, and always conscious of the space below. But all of him, body and soul, was growing hot to fusion point. He would have to let go for very relief's sake. Suddenly his heart began to lurch. It gave a great, sickly swoop, rose, and again plunged in a swoop of horror. He lay against the wall inert as if dead, inert, at peace, save for one deep core of anxiety, which knew that it was *not* all over, that he was still high in space against the wall. But the chief effort of will was gone.

There came into his consciousness a small, foreign sensation. He woke up a little. What was it? Then slowly it penetrated him. His water had run down his leg. He lay there, clinging, still with shame, half conscious of the echo of the sergeant's voice thundering from below. He waited, in depths of shame beginning to recover himself. He had been shamed so deeply. Then he could go on, for his fear for himself was conquered. His shame was known and published. He must go on.

Slowly he began to grope for the rung above, when a great shock shook through him. His wrists were grasped from above, he was being hauled out of himself up, up to the safe ground. Like a sack he was dragged over the edge of the earthworks by the large hands, and landed there on his knees, grovelling in the grass to recover command of himself, to rise up on his feet.

Shame, blind, deep shame and ignominy overthrew his spirit and left it writhing. He stood there shrunk over himself, trying to obliterate himself.

Then the presence of the officer who had hauled him up made itself felt upon him. He heard the panting of the elder man, and then the voice came down on his veins like a fierce whip. He shrank in tension of shame.

'Put up your head – eyes front,' shouted the enraged sergeant, and mechanically the soldier obeyed the command, forced to look into the eyes of the sergeant. The brutal, hanging face of the officer violated the youth. He hardened himself with all his might from seeing it. The tearing noise of the sergeant's voice continued to lacerate his body.

Suddenly he set back his head, rigid, and his heart leapt to burst. The face had suddenly thrust itself close, all distorted and showing the teeth, the eyes smouldering into him. The breath of the barking words was on his nose and mouth. He stepped aside in revulsion. With a scream the face was upon him again. He raised his arm, involuntarily, in self-defence. A shock of horror went through him, as he felt his forearm hit the face of the officer a brutal blow. The latter staggered, swerved back, and with a curious cry, reeled backwards over the ramparts, his hands clutching the air. There was a second of silence, then a crash to water.

Bachmann, rigid, looked out of his inner silence upon the scene. Soldiers were running.

'You'd better clear,' said one young, excited voice to him. And with immediate instinctive decision he started to walk away from the spot. He went down the tree-hidden path to the high road where the trams ran to and from the town. In his heart was a sense of vindication, of escape. He was leaving it all, the military world, the shame. He was walking away from it.

Officers on horseback rode sauntering down the street, soldiers passed along the pavement. Coming to the bridge, Bachmann crossed over to the town that heaped before him, rising from the flat, picturesque French houses down below at the water's edge, up a jumble of roofs and chasms of streets, to the lovely dark cathedral with its myriad pinnacles making points at the sky.

He felt for the moment quite at peace, relieved from a great strain. So he turned along by the river to the public gardens. Beautiful were the heaped, purple lilac trees upon the green grass, and wonderful the walls of the horse-chestnut trees, lighted like an altar with white flowers on every ledge. Officers went by, elegant and all coloured, women and girls sauntered in the chequered shade. Beautiful it was, he walked in a vision, free.

II

But where was he going? He began to come out of his trance of delight and liberty. Deep within him he felt the steady burning of shame in the flesh. As yet he could not bear to think of it. But there it was, submerged beneath his attention, the raw, steady-burning shame.

It behoved him to be intelligent. As yet he dared not remember what he had done. He only knew the need to get away, away from everything he had been in contact with.

But how? A great pang of fear went through him. He could not bear his shamed flesh to be put again between the hands of authority. Already the hands had been laid upon him, brutally upon his nakedness, ripping open his shame and making him maimed, crippled in his own control.

Fear became an anguish. Almost blindly he was turning in the direction of the barracks. He could not take the responsibility of himself. He must give himself up to someone. Then his heart, obstinate in hope, became obsessed with the idea of his sweetheart. He would make himself her responsibility.

Blenching as he took courage, he mounted the small, quick-hurrying tram that ran out of the town in the direction of the barracks. He sat motionless and composed, static.

He got out at the terminus and went down the road. A wind was still running. He could hear the faint whisper of the rye, and the stronger swish as a sudden gust was upon it. No one was about. Feeling detached and impersonal, he went down a field-path between the low vines. Many little vine trees rose up in spires, holding out tender pink shoots, waving their tendrils. He saw them distinctly and wondered over them. In a field a little way off, men and women were taking up the hay. The bullock-waggon stood by on the path, the men in their blue shirts, the women with white cloths over their heads carried hay in their arms to the cart, all brilliant and distinct upon the shorn, glowing green acres. He felt himself looking out of darkness on to the glamorous, brilliant beauty of the world around him, outside him.

The Baron's house, where Emilie was maidservant, stood square and mellow among trees and garden and fields. It was an old French grange. The barracks was quite near. Bachmann walked, drawn by a single purpose, towards the courtyard. He entered the spacious, shadowy, sun-swept place. The dog, seeing a soldier, only jumped and whined for greeting. The pump stood peacefully in a corner, under a lime tree, in the shade.

The kitchen door was open. He hesitated, then walked in, speaking shyly and smiling involuntarily. The two women started, but with pleasure. Emilie was preparing the tray for afternoon coffee. She stood beyond the table, drawn up, startled, and challenging, and glad. She had the proud, timid eyes of some wild animal, some proud animal. Her black hair was closely banded, her grey eyes watched steadily. She wore a peasant dress of blue cotton sprigged with little red roses, that buttoned tight over her strong maiden breasts.

At the table sat another young woman, the nursery governess, who was picking cherries from a huge heap, and dropping them into a bowl. She was young, pretty, freckled.

'Good day!' she said pleasantly. 'The unexpected.'

Emilie did not speak. The flush came in her dark cheek. She still stood watching, between fear and a desire to escape, and on the other hand joy that kept her in his presence.

'Yes,' he said, bashful and strained, while the eyes of the two women were upon him. 'I've got myself in a mess this time.'

'What?' asked the nursery governess, dropping her hands in her lap. Emilie stood rigid.

Bachmann could not raise his head. He looked sideways at the glistening, ruddy cherries. He could not recover the normal world.

'I knocked Sergeant Huber over the fortifications down into the moat,' he said. 'It was an accident – but –'

And he grasped at the cherries, and began to eat them, unknowing, hearing only Emilie's little exclamation.

'You knocked him over the fortifications!' echoed Fräulein Hesse in horror. 'How?'

Spitting the cherry-stones into his hand, mechanically, absorbedly, he told them.

'Ach!' exclaimed Emilie sharply.

'And how did you get here?' asked Fräulein Hesse.

'I ran off,' he said.

There was a dead silence. He stood, putting himself at the mercy of the women. There came a hissing from the stove, and a stronger smell of coffee. Emilie turned swiftly away. He saw her flat, straight back and her strong loins, as she bent over the stove.

'But what are you going to do?' said Fräulein Hesse, aghast.

'I don't know,' he said, grasping at more cherries. He had come to an end.

'You'd better go to the barracks,' she said. 'We'll get the Herr Baron to come and see about it.'

Emilie was swiftly and quietly preparing the tray. She picked it up, and stood with the glittering china and silver before her, impassive, waiting for his reply. Bachmann remained with his head dropped, pale and obstinate. He could not bear to go back.

'I'm going to try to get into France,' he said.

'Yes, but they'll catch you,' said Fräulein Hesse.

Emilie watched with steady, watchful grey eyes.

'I can have a try, if I could hide till to-night,' he said.

Both women knew what he wanted. And they all knew it was no good. Emilie picked up the tray, and went out. Bachmann stood with his head dropped. Within himself he felt the dross of shame and incapacity.

'You'd never get away,' said the governess.

'I can try,' he said.

To-day he could not put himself between the hands of the military. Let them do as they liked with him to-morrow, if he escaped to-day.

They were silent. He ate cherries. The colour flushed bright into the cheek of the young governess.

Emilie returned to prepare another tray.

'He could hide in your room,' the governess said to her.

The girl drew herself away. She could not bear the intrusion.

'That is all I can think of that is safe from the children,' said Fräulein Hesse.

Emilie gave no answer. Bachmann stood waiting for the two women. Emilie did not want the close contact with him.

'You could sleep with me,' Fräulein Hesse said to her.

Emilie lifted her eyes and looked at the young man, direct, clear, reserving herself.

'Do you want that?' she asked, her strong virginity proof against him.

'Yes – yes –' he said uncertainly, destroyed by shame.

She put back her head.

'Yes,' she murmured to herself.

Quickly she filled the tray, and went out.

'But you can't walk over the frontier in a night,' said Fräulein Hesse.

'I can cycle,' he said.

Emilie returned, a restraint, a neutrality, in her bearing.

'I'll see if it's all right,' said the governess.

In a moment or two Bachmann was following Emilie through the square hall, where hung large maps on the walls. He noticed a child's blue coat with brass buttons on the peg, and it reminded him of Emilie walking holding the hand of the youngest child, whilst he watched, sitting under the lime tree. Already this was a long way off. That was a sort of freedom he had lost, changed for a new, immediate anxiety.

They went quickly, fearfully up the stairs and down a long corridor. Emilie opened her door, and he entered, ashamed, into her room.

'I must go down,' she murmured, and she departed, closing the door softly.

It was a small, bare, neat room. There was a little dish for holy-water, a picture of the Sacred Heart,[1] a crucifix, and a *prie-Dieu*.[2] The small bed lay white and untouched, the wash-hand bowl of red earth stood on a bare table, there was a little mirror and a small chest of drawers. That was all.

Feeling safe, in sanctuary, he went to the window, looking over the courtyard at the shimmering, afternoon country. He was going to leave this land, this life. Already he was in the unknown.

He drew away into the room. The curious simplicity and severity of the little Roman Catholic bedroom was foreign but restoring to him. He looked at the crucifix. It was a long, lean, peasant Christ carved by a peasant in the Black Forest. For the first time in his life, Bachmann saw the figure as a human thing. It represented a man hanging there in helpless torture. He stared at it, closely, as if for new knowledge.

Within his own flesh burned and smouldered the restless shame. He could not gather himself together. There was a gap in his soul. The shame within him seemed to displace his strength and his manhood.

He sat down on his chair. The shame, the roused feeling of exposure acted on his brain, made him heavy, unutterably heavy.

Mechanically, his wits all gone, he took off his boots, his belt, his tunic, put them aside, and lay down, heavy, and fell into a kind of drugged sleep.

Emilie came in a little while, and looked at him. But he was sunk in sleep. She saw him lying there inert, and terribly still, and she was afraid. His shirt was unfastened at the throat. She saw his pure white flesh, very clean and beautiful. And he slept inert. His legs, in the blue uniform trousers, his feet in the coarse stockings, lay foreign on her bed. She went away.

III

She was uneasy, perturbed to her last fibre. She wanted to remain clear, with no touch on her. A wild instinct made her shrink away from any hands which might be laid on her.

She was a foundling, probably of some gipsy race, brought up in a

Roman Catholic Rescue Home. A naïve, paganly religious being, she was attached to the Baroness, with whom she had served for seven years, since she was fourteen.

She came into contact with no one, unless it were with Ida Hesse, the governess. Ida was a calculating, good-natured, not very straightforward flirt. She was the daughter of a poor country doctor. Having gradually come into connection with Emilie, more an alliance than an attachment, she put no distinction of grade between the two of them. They worked together, sang together, walked together, and went together to the rooms of Franz Brand, Ida's sweetheart. There the three talked and laughed together, or the women listened to Franz, who was a forester, playing on his violin.

In all this alliance there was no personal intimacy between the young women. Emilie was naturally secluded in herself, of a reserved, native race. Ida used her as a kind of weight to balance her own flighty movement. But the quick, shifty governess, occupied always in her dealings with admirers, did all she could to move the violent nature of Emilie towards some connection with men.

But the dark girl, primitive yet sensitive to a high degree, was fiercely virgin. Her blood flamed with rage when the common soldiers made the long, sucking, kissing noise behind her as she passed. She hated them for their almost jeering offers. She was well protected by the Baroness.

And her contempt of the common men in general was ineffable. But she loved the Baroness, and she revered the Baron, and she was at her ease when she was doing something for the service of a gentleman. Her whole nature was at peace in the service of real masters or mistresses. For her, a gentleman had some mystic quality that left her free and proud in service. The common soldiers were brutes, merely nothing. Her desire was to serve.

She held herself aloof. When, on Sunday afternoon, she had looked through the windows of the Reichshalle[3] in passing, and had seen the soldiers dancing with the common girls, a cold revulsion and anger had possessed her. She could not bear to see the soldiers taking off their belts and pulling open their tunics, dancing with their shirts showing through the open, sagging tunic, their movements gross, their faces transfigured and sweaty, their coarse hands holding their coarse girls under the arm-pits, drawing the female up to their breasts. She hated to see them clutched breast to breast, the legs of the men moving grossly in the dance.

At evening, when she had been in the garden, and heard on the other side of the hedge the sexual inarticulate cries of the girls in the embraces of the soldiers, her anger had been too much for her, and she had cried, loud and cold:

'What are you doing there, in the hedge?'

She would have had them whipped.

But Bachmann was not quite a common soldier. Fräulein Hesse had found out about him, and had drawn him and Emilie together. For he was a handsome, blond youth, erect and walking with a kind of pride, unconscious yet clear. Moreover, he came of a rich farming stock, rich for many generations. His father was dead, his mother controlled the moneys for the time being. But if Bachmann wanted a hundred pounds at any moment, he could have them. By trade he, with one of his brothers, was a waggon-builder. The family had the farming, smithy, and waggon-building of their village. They worked because that was the form of life they knew. If they had chosen, they could have lived independent upon their means.

In this way, he was a gentleman in sensibility, though his intellect was not developed. He could afford to pay freely for things. He had, moreover, his native, fine breeding. Emilie wavered uncertainly before him. So he became her sweetheart, and she hungered after him. But she was virgin, and shy, and needed to be in subjection, because she was primitive and had no grasp on civilized forms of living, nor on civilized purposes.

IV

At six o'clock came the inquiry of the soldiers: Had anything been seen of Bachmann? Fräulein Hesse answered, pleased to be playing a rôle:

'No, I've not seen him since Sunday – have you, Emilie?'

'No, I haven't seen him,' said Emilie, and her awkwardness was construed as bashfulness. Ida Hesse, stimulated, asked questions, and played her part.

'But it hasn't killed Sergeant Huber?' she cried in consternation.

'No. He fell into the water. But it gave him a bad shock, and smashed his foot on the side of the moat. He's in hospital. It's a bad look-out for Bachmann.'

Emilie, implicated and captive, stood looking on. She was no longer free, working with all this regulated system which she could not understand and which was almost god-like to her. She was put out of her place. Bachmann was in her room, she was no longer the faithful in service serving with religious surety.

Her situation was intolerable to her. All evening long the burden was upon her, she could not live. The children must be fed and put to sleep. The Baron and Baroness were going out, she must give them light refreshment. The man-servant was coming in to supper after returning with the carriage. And all the while she had the insupportable feeling of being out of the order, self-responsible, bewildered. The control of her life should come from those above her, and she should move within that control. But now she was out of it, uncontrolled and troubled. More than that, the man, the lover, Bachmann, who was he, what was he? He alone of all men contained for her the unknown quantity which terrified her beyond her service. Oh, she had wanted him as a distant sweetheart, not close, like this, casting her out of her world.

When the Baron and Baroness had departed, and the young man-servant had gone out to enjoy himself, she went upstairs to Bachmann. He had wakened up, and sat dimly in the room. Out in the open he heard the soldiers, his comrades, singing the sentimental songs of the nightfall, the drone of the concertina rising in accompaniment.

'Wenn ich zu mei . . . nem Kinde geh′. . .
In seinem Au . . . g die Mutter seh′. . . .'[4]

But he himself was removed from it now. Only the sentimental cry of young, unsatisfied desire in the soldiers' singing penetrated his blood and stirred him subtly. He let his head hang; he had become gradually roused: and he waited in concentration, in another world.

The moment she entered the room where the man sat alone, waiting intensely, the thrill passed through her, she died in terror, and after the death, a great flame gushed up, obliterating her. He sat in trousers and shirt on the side of the bed. He looked up as she came in, and she shrank from his face. She could not bear it. Yet she entered near to him.

'Do you want anything to eat?' she said.

'Yes,' he answered, and as she stood in the twilight of the room with him, he could only hear his heart beat heavily. He saw her apron just level with his face. She stood silent, a little distance off, as if she would be there for ever. He suffered.

As if in a spell she waited, standing motionless and looming there, he sat rather crouching on the side of the bed. A second will in him was powerful and dominating. She drew gradually nearer to him, coming up slowly, as if unconscious. His heart beat up swiftly. He was going to move.

As she came quite close, almost invisibly he lifted his arms and put them round her waist, drawing her with his will and desire. He buried his face into her apron, into the terrible softness of her belly. And he was a flame of passion intense about her. He had forgotten. Shame and memory were gone in a whole, furious flame of passion.

She was quite helpless. Her hands leapt, fluttered, and closed over his head, pressing it deeper into her belly, vibrating as she did so. And his arms tightened on her, his hands spread over her loins, warm as flame on her loveliness. It was intense anguish of bliss for her, and she lost consciousness.

When she recovered, she lay translated in the peace of satisfaction.

It was what she had had no inkling of, never known could be. She was strong with eternal gratitude. And he was there with her. Instinctively with an instinct of reverence and gratitude, her arms tightened in a little embrace upon him who held her thoroughly embraced.

And he was restored and completed, close to her. That little, twitching, momentary clasp of acknowledgment that she gave him in her satisfaction, roused his pride unconquerable. They loved each other, and all was whole. She loved him, he had taken her, she was given to him. It was right. He was given to her, and they were one, complete.

Warm, with a glow in their hearts and faces, they rose again, modest, but transfigured with happiness.

'I will get you something to eat,' she said, and in joy and security of service again, she left him, making a curious little homage of departure. He sat on the side of the bed, escaped, liberated, wondering, and happy.

V

Soon she came again with the tray, followed by Fräulein Hesse. The two women watched him eat, watched the pride and wonder of his being, as he sat there blond and naïf again. Emilie felt rich and complete. Ida was a lesser thing than herself.

'And what are you going to do?' asked Fräulein Hesse, jealous.

'I must get away,' he said.

But words had no meaning for him. What did it matter? He had the inner satisfaction and liberty.

'But you'll want a bicycle,' said Ida Hesse.

'Yes,' he said.

Emilie sat silent, removed and yet with him, connected with him in passion. She looked from this talk of bicycles and escape.

They discussed plans. But in two of them was the one will, that Bachmann should stay with Emilie. Ida Hesse was an outsider.

It was arranged, however, that Ida's lover should put out his bicycle, leave it at the hut where he sometimes watched. Bachmann should fetch it in the night, and ride into France. The hearts of all three beat hot in suspense, driven to thought. They sat in a fire of agitation.

Then Bachmann would get away to America, and Emilie would come and join him. They would be in a fine land then. The tale burned up again.

Emilie and Ida had to go round to Franz Brand's lodging. They departed with slight leave-taking. Bachmann sat in the dark, hearing the bugle for retreat sound out of the night. Then he remembered his post card to his mother. He slipped out after Emilie, gave it her to post. His manner was careless and victorious, hers shining and trustful. He slipped back to shelter.

There he sat on the side of the bed, thinking. Again he went over the events of the afternoon, remembering his own anguish of apprehension because he had known he could not climb the wall without fainting with fear. Still, a flush of shame came alight in him at the memory. But he said to himself: 'What does it matter? – I can't help it, well then I can't. If I go up a height, I get absolutely weak, and can't help myself.' Again memory came over him, and a gush of shame, like fire. But he sat and endured it. It had to be endured, admitted, and accepted. 'I'm not a coward, for all that,' he continued. 'I'm not afraid of danger. If I'm made that way, that heights melt me and make me let go my water' – it was torture for him to pluck at this truth – 'if I'm made like that, I shall have to abide by it, that's all. It isn't all of me.' He thought of Emilie, and was satisfied. 'What I am, I am; and let it be enough,' he thought.

Having accepted his own defect, he sat thinking, waiting for Emilie, to tell her. She came at length, saying that Franz could not arrange about his bicycle this night. It was broken. Bachmann would have to stay over another day.

They were both happy. Emilie, confused before Ida, who was excited and prurient, came again to the young man. She was stiff and dignified with an agony of unusedness. But he took her between his hands, and uncovered her, and enjoyed almost like madness her helpless, virgin body that suffered so strongly, and that took its joy so deeply. While the moisture of torment and modesty was still in her eyes, she clasped him closer, and closer, to the victory and the deep satisfaction of both of them. And they slept together, he in repose still satisfied and peaceful, and she lying close in her static reality.

VI

In the morning, when the bugle sounded from the barracks they rose and looked out of the window. She loved his body that was proud and blond and able to take command. And he loved her body that was soft and eternal. They looked at the faint grey vapour of summer steaming off from the greenness and ripeness of the fields. There was no town anywhere, their look ended in the haze of the summer morning. Their bodies rested together, their minds tranquil. Then a little anxiety stirred in both of them from the sound of the bugle. She was called back to her old position, to realize the world of authority she did not understand but had wanted to serve. But this call died away again from her. She had all.

She went downstairs to her work, curiously changed. She was in a new world of her own, that she had never even imagined, and which was the land of promise for all that. In this she moved and had her being. And she extended it to her duties. She was curiously happy and absorbed. She had not to strive out of herself to do her work. The doing came from within her without call or command. It was a delicious outflow, like sunshine, the activity that flowed from her and put her tasks to rights.

Bachmann sat busily thinking. He would have to get all his plans ready. He must write to his mother, and she must send him money to Paris. He would go to Paris, and from thence, quickly, to America. It had to be done. He must make all preparations. The dangerous part was the getting into France. He thrilled in anticipation. During the day he would need a time-table of the trains going to Paris – he would need to think. It gave him delicious pleasure, using all his wits. It seemed such an adventure.

This one day, and he would escape then into freedom. What an agony of need he had for absolute, imperious freedom. He had won to his own being, in himself and Emilie, he had drawn the stigma from his shame, he was beginning to be himself. And now he wanted madly to be free to go on. A home, his work, and absolute freedom to move and to be, in her, with her, this was his passionate desire. He thought in a kind of ecstasy, living an hour of painful intensity.

Suddenly he heard voices, and a tramping of feet. His heart gave a great leap, then went still. He was taken. He had known all along. A complete silence filled his body and soul, a silence like death, a suspension of life and sound. He stood motionless in the bedrom, in perfect suspension.

Emilie was busy passing swiftly about the kitchen preparing the children's breakfasts when she heard the tramp of feet and the voice of the Baron. The latter had come in from the garden, and was wearing an old green linen suit. He was a man of middle stature, quick, finely made, and of whimsical charm. His right hand had been shot in the Franco-Prussian war, and now, as always when he was much agitated, he shook it down at his side, as if it hurt. He was talking rapidly to a young, stiff Ober-leutnant. Two private soldiers stood bearishly in the doorway.

Emilie, shocked out of herself, stood pale and erect, recoiling.

'Yes, if you think so, we can look,' the Baron was hastily and irascibly saying.

'Emilie,' he said, turning to the girl, 'did you put a post card to the mother of this Bachmann in the box last evening?'

Emilie stood erect and did not answer.

'Yes?' said the Baron sharply.

'Yes, Herr Baron,' replied Emilie, neutral.

The Baron's wounded hand shook rapidly in exasperation. The lieutenant drew himself up still more stiffly. He was right.

'And do you know anything of the fellow?' asked the Baron, looking at her with his blazing, greyish-golden eyes. The girl looked back at him steadily, dumb, but her whole soul naked before him. For two seconds he looked at her in silence. Then in silence, ashamed and furious, he turned away.

'Go up!' he said, with his fierce, peremptory command, to the young officer.

The lieutenant gave his order, in military cold confidence, to the soldiers. They all tramped across the hall. Emilie stood motionless, her life suspended.

The Baron marched swiftly upstairs and down the corridor, the lieutenant and the common soldiers followed. The Baron flung open the door of Emilie's room and looked at Bachmann, who stood watching, standing in shirt and trousers beside the bed, fronting the door. He was perfectly still. His eyes met the furious, blazing look of the Baron. The latter shook his wounded hand, and then went still. He looked into the eyes of the soldier, steadily. He saw the same naked soul exposed, as if he looked really into the *man*. And the man was helpless, the more helpless for his singular nakedness.

'Ha!' he exclaimed impatiently, turning to the approaching lieutenant.

The latter appeared in the doorway. Quickly his eyes travelled over the bare-footed youth. He recognized him as his object. He gave the brief command to dress.

Bachmann turned round for his clothes. He was very still, silent in himself. He was in an abstract, motionless world. That the two gentlemen and the two soldiers stood watching him, he scarcely realized. They could not see him.

Soon he was ready. He stood at attention. But only the shell of his body was at attention. A curious silence, a blankness, like something eternal, possessed him. He remained true to himself.

The lieutenant gave the order to march. The little procession went down the stairs with careful, respectful tread, and passed through the hall to the kitchen. There Emilie stood with her face uplifted, motionless and expressionless. Bachmann did not look at her. They knew each other. They were themselves. Then the little file of men passed out into the courtyard.

The Baron stood in the doorway watching the four figures in uniform pass through the chequered shadow under the lime trees. Bachmann was walking neutralized, as if he were not there. The lieutenant went brittle and long, the two soldiers lumbered beside. They passed out into the sunny morning, growing smaller, going towards the barracks.

The Baron turned into the kitchen. Emilie was cutting bread.

'So he stayed the night here?' he said.

The girl looked at him, scarcely seeing. She was too much herself. The Baron saw the dark, naked soul of her body in her unseeing eyes.

'What were you going to do?' he asked.

'He was going to America,' she replied, in a still voice.

'Pah! You should have sent him straight back,' fired the Baron.

Emilie stood at his bidding, untouched.

'He's done for now,' he said.

But he could not bear the dark, deep nakedness of her eyes, that scarcely changed under this suffering.

'Nothing but a fool,' he repeated, going away in agitation, and preparing himself for what he could do.

The Mortal Coil

I

SHE stood motionless in the middle of the room, something tense in her reckless bearing. Her gown of reddish stuff fell silkily about her feet; she looked tall and splendid in the candlelight. Her dark-blond hair was gathered loosely in a fold on top of her head, her young, blossom-fresh face was lifted. From her throat to her feet she was clothed in the elegantly-made dress of silky red stuff, the colour of red earth. She looked complete and lovely, only love could make her such a strange, complete blossom. Her cloak and hat were thrown across a table just in front of her.

Quite alone, abstracted, she stood there arrested in a conflict of emotions. Her hand, down against her skirt, worked irritably, the ball of the thumb rubbing, rubbing across the tips of the fingers. There was a slight tension between her lifted brows.

About her the room glowed softly, reflecting the candlelight from its whitewashed walls, and from the great, bowed, whitewashed ceiling. It was a large attic, with two windows, and the ceiling curving down on either side, so that both the far walls were low. Against one, on one side, was a single bed, opened for the night, the white over-bolster piled back. Not far from this was the iron stove. Near the window closest to the bed was a table with writing materials, and a handsome cactus-plant with clear scarlet blossoms threw its bizarre shadow on the wall. There was another table near the second window, and opposite was the door on which hung a military cloak. Along the far wall, were guns and fishing-tackle, and some clothes too, hung on pegs – all men's clothes, all military. It was evidently the room of a man, probably a young lieutenant.

The girl, in her pure red dress that fell about her feet, so that she looked a woman, not a girl, at last broke from her abstraction and went aimlessly to the writing-table. Her mouth was closed down stubbornly, perhaps in anger, perhaps in pain. She picked up a large seal made of agate, looked at the ingraven coat of arms, then stood rubbing her finger across the cut-out stone, time after time. At last she put the seal down, and looked at the other things – a beautiful old beer-mug used as a tobacco-jar, a silver box like an urn, old and of exquisite shape, a bowl of sealing wax. She fingered the pieces of wax. This, the dark-green, had sealed her last letter. Ah, well! She carelessly turned over the blotting book, which again had his arms stamped on the cover. Then she went away to the window. There, in the window-recess, she stood and looked out. She opened the casement and took a deep breath of the cold night air. Ah, it was good! Far below was the street, a vague golden milky way beneath her, its tiny black figures moving and crossing and re-crossing with marionette, insect-like intentness. A small horse-car rumbled along the lines, so belittled, it was an absurdity. So much for the world! . . . he did not come.

She looked overhead. The stars were white and flashing, they looked nearer than the street, more kin to her, more real. She stood pressing her breast on her arms, her face lifted to the stars, in the long, anguished suspense of waiting. Noises came up small from the street, as from some insect-world. But the great stars overhead struck white and invincible, infallible. Her heart felt cold like the stars.

At last she started. There was a noisy knocking at the door, and a female voice calling:

'Anybody there?'

'Come in,' replied the girl.

She turned round, shrinking from this intrusion, unable to bear it, after the flashing stars.

There entered a thin, handsome dark girl dressed in an extravagantly-made gown of dark purple silk and dark blue velvet. She was followed by a small swarthy, inconspicuous lieutenant in pale-blue uniform.

'Ah *you*! . . . alone?' cried Teresa, the newcomer, advancing into the room. 'Where's the Fritz, then?'

The girl in red raised her shoulders in a shrug, and turned her face aside, but did not speak.

'Not here! You don't know where he is? Ach, the dummy, the lout!' Teresa swung round on her companion.

'Where is he?' she demanded.

He also lifted his shoulders in a shrug.

'He said he was coming in half an hour,' the young lieutenant replied.

'Ha! – half an hour! Looks like it! How long is that ago – two hours?'

Again the young man only shrugged. He had beautiful black eye-lashes, and steady eyes. He stood rather deprecatingly, whilst his girl, golden like a young panther, hung over him.

'One knows where he is,' said Teresa, going and sitting on the opened bed. A dangerous contraction came between the brows of Marta, the girl in red, at this act.

'Wine, Women and Cards!' said Teresa, in her loud voice. 'But they prefer the women on the cards.

"My love he has four Queenies,
Four Queenies has my lo-o-ove." '

she sang. Then she broke off, and turned to Podewils. 'Was he winning when you left him, Karl?'

Again the young baron raised his shoulders.

'Tant pis que mal,'[1] he replied, cryptically.

'Ah, *you*!' cried Teresa, 'with your *tant pis que mal*! Are *you* tant pis que mal?' She laughed her deep, strange laugh. 'Well,' she added, 'he'll be coming in with a fortune for you, Marta –'

There was a vague, unhappy silence.

'I know his fortunes,' said Marta.

'Yes,' said Teresa, in sudden sober irony, 'he's a horse-shoe round your neck, is that young jockey. – But what are you going to do, Matzen dearest? You're not going to wait for him any longer? – Don't dream of it! The idea, waiting for that young gentleman as if you were married to him! – Put your hat on, dearest, and come along with us . . . Where are we going, Karl, you pillar of salt? – Eh? – Geier's? – To Geier's, Marta, my dear. Come, quick, up – you've been martyred enough, Marta, my martyr – haw! – haw!! – put your hat on. Up – away!'

Teresa sprang up like an explosion, anxious to be off.

'No, I'll wait for him,' said Marta, sullenly.

'Don't be such a fool!' cried Teresa, in her deep voice. 'Wait for him! *I'd* give him wait for him. Catch this little bird waiting.' She lifted her hand and blew a little puff across the fingers. 'Choo-fly!' she sang, as if a bird had just flown.

The young lieutenant stood silent with smiling dark eyes. Teresa was quick, and golden as a panther.

'No, but really, Marta, you're not going to wait any more – really! It's stupid for you to play Gretchen[2] – your eyes are much too green. Put your hat on, there's a darling.'

'No,' said Marta, her flower-like face strangely stubborn. 'I'll wait for him. He'll have to come some time.'

There was a moment's uneasy pause.

'Well,' said Teresa, holding her long shoulders for her cloak, 'so long as you don't wait as long as Lenora-fuhr-ums-Morgenrot – ![3] Adieu, my dear, God be with you.'

The young lieutenant bowed a solicitous bow, and the two went out, leaving the girl in red once more alone.

She went to the writing table, and on a sheet of paper began writing her name in stiff Gothic characters, time after time:

Marta Hohenest
Marta Hohenest
Marta Hohenest.

The vague sounds from the street below continued. The wind was cold. She rose and shut the window. Then she sat down again.

At last the door opened, and a young officer entered. He was buttoned up in a dark-blue great-coat, with large silver buttons going down on either side of the breast. He entered quickly, glancing over the room, at Marta, as she sat with her back to him. She was marking with a pencil on paper. He closed the door. Then with fine beautiful movements he divested himself of his coat and went to hang it up. How well Marta knew the sound of his movements, the quick light step! But she continued mechanically making crosses on the paper, her head bent forward between the candles, so that her hair made fine threads and mist of light, very beautiful. He saw this, and it touched him. But he could not afford to be touched any further.

'You have been waiting?' he said formally. The insulting futile question! She made no sign, as if she had not heard. He was absorbed in the tragedy of himself, and hardly heeded her.

He was a slim, good-looking youth, clear-cut and delicate in mould. His features now were pale, there was something evasive in his dilated, vibrating eyes. He was barely conscious of the girl, intoxicated with his own desperation, that held him mindless and distant.

To her, the atmosphere of the room was almost unbreathable, since he had come in. She felt terribly bound, walled up. She rose with a sudden movement that tore his nerves. She looked to him tall and bright and dangerous, as she faced round on him.

'Have you come back with a fortune?' she cried, in mockery, her eyes full of dangerous light.

He was unfastening his belt, to change his tunic. She watched him up and down, all the time. He could not answer, his lips seemed dumb. Besides, silence was his strength.

'Have you come back with a fortune?' she repeated, in her strong, clear voice of mockery.

'No,' he said, suddenly turning. 'Let it please you that – that I've come back at all.'

He spoke desperately, and tailed off into silence. He was a man doomed. She looked at him: he was insignificant in his doom. She turned in ridicule. And yet she was afraid; she loved him.

He had stood long enough exposed, in his helplessness. With difficulty he took a few steps, went and sat down at the writing-table. He looked to her like a dog with its tail between its legs.

He saw the paper, where her name was repeatedly written. She must find great satisfaction in her own name, he thought vaguely. Then he picked up the seal and kept twisting it round in his fingers, doing some little trick. And continually the seal fell on to the table with a sudden rattle that made Marta stiffen cruelly. He was quite oblivious of her.

She stood watching as he sat bent forward in his stupefaction. The fine cloth of his uniform showed the moulding of his back. And something tortured her as she saw him, till she could hardly bear it: the desire of his finely-shaped body, the stupefaction and the abjectness of him now, his immersion in the tragedy of himself, his being unaware of her. All her will seemed to grip him, to bruise some manly nonchalance and attention out of him.

'I suppose you're in a fury with me, for being late?' he said, with impotent irony in his voice. Her fury over trifles, when he was lost in calamity! How great was his real misery, how trivial her small offendedness!

Something in his tone burned her, and made her soul go cold.

'I'm not exactly pleased,' she said coldly, turning away to a window.

Still he sat bent over the table, twisting something with his fingers. She glanced round on him. How nervy he was! He had beautiful hands, and the big topaz signet-ring on his finger made yellow lights. Ah, if only his hands were really dare-devil and reckless! They always seemed so guilty, so cowardly.

'I'm done for now,' he said suddenly, as if to himself, tilting back his chair a little. In all his physical movement he was so fine and poised, so sensitive! Oh, and it attracted her so much!

'Why?' she said, carelessly.

An anger burned in him. She was so flippant. If he were going to be shot, she would not be moved more than about half a pound of sweets.

'Why!' he repeated laconically. 'The same unimportant reason as ever.'

'Debts?' she cried, in contempt.

'Exactly.'

Her soul burned in anger.

'What have you done now? – lost more money?'

'Three thousand marks.'

She was silent in deep wrath.

'More fool you!' she said. Then, in her anger, she was silent for some minutes. 'And so you're done for, for three thousand marks?' she exclaimed, jeering at him. 'You go pretty cheap.'

'Three thousand – and the rest,' he said, keeping up a manly *sang froid*.[4]

'And the rest!' she repeated in contempt. 'And for three thousand – and the rest, your life is over!'

'My career,' he corrected her.

'Oh,' she mocked, 'only your career! I thought it was a matter of life and death. Only your career? Oh, only that!'

His eyes grew furious under her mockery.

'My career *is* my life,' he said.

'Oh, is it! – You're not a *man* then, you are only a career?'

'I am a gentleman.'

'Oh, are you! How amusing! How very amusing, to be a gentleman, and not a man! – I suppose that's what it means, to be a gentleman, to have no guts outside your career?'

'Outside my honour – none.'

'And might I ask what *is* your honour?' She spoke in extreme irony.

'Yes, you may ask,' he replied coolly. 'But if you don't know without being told, I'm afraid I could never explain it.'

'Oh, you couldn't! No, I believe you – you are incapable of explaining it, it wouldn't bear explaining.' There was a long, tense pause. 'So you've made too many debts, and you're afraid they'll kick you out of the army, therefore your honour is gone, is it? – And what then – what after that?'

She spoke in extreme irony. He winced again at her phrase 'kick you out of the army'. But he tilted his chair back with assumed nonchalance.

'I've made too many debts, and I *know* they'll kick me out of the army,' he repeated, thrusting the thorn right home to the quick. 'After that – I can shoot myself. Or I might even be a waiter in a restaurant – or possibly a clerk, with twenty-five shillings a week.'

'Really! – All those alternatives! – Well, why not, why not be a waiter in the Germania? It might be awfully jolly.'

'Why not?' he repeated ironically. 'Because it wouldn't become me.'

She looked at him, at his aristocratic fineness of physique, his extreme physical sensitiveness. And all her German worship for his old, proud family rose up in her. No, he could not be a waiter in the Germania: she could not bear it. He was too refined and beautiful a thing.

'Ha!' she cried suddenly. 'It wouldn't come to that, either. If they kick you out of the army, you'll find somebody to get round – you're like a cat, you'll land on your feet.'

But this was just what he was not. He was not like a cat. His self-mistrust was too deep. Ultimately he had no belief in himself, as a separate isolated being. He knew he was sufficiently clever, an aristocrat, good-looking, the sensitive superior of most men. The trouble was, that apart from the social fabric he belonged to, he felt himself nothing, a cipher. He bitterly envied the common working-men for a certain manly aplomb, a grounded, almost stupid self-confidence he saw in them. Himself – he could lead such men through the gates of hell – for what did he care about danger or hurt to himself, whilst he was leading? But – cut him off from all this, and what was he? A palpitating rag of meaningless human life.

But she, coming from the people, could not fully understand. And it was best to leave her in the dark. The free indomitable self-sufficient being which a man must be in his relation to a woman who loves him – this he could pretend. But he knew he was not it. He knew that the world of man from which he took his value was his mistress beyond any woman. He wished, secretly, cravingly, almost cravenly, in his heart, it was not so. But so it was.

Therefore, he heard her phrase 'you're like a cat,' with some bitter envy.

'Whom shall I get round? – some woman, who will marry me?' he said.

This was a way out. And it was almost the inevitable thing, for him. But he felt it the last ruin of his manhood, even he.

The speech hurt her mortally, worse than death. She would rather he died, because then her own love would not turn to ash.

'Get married, then, if you want to,' she said, in a small broken voice.

'Naturally,' he said.

There was a long silence, a foretaste of barren hopelessness.

'Why is it so terrible to you,' she asked at length, 'to come out of the army and trust to your own resources? Other men are strong enough.'

'Other men are not me,' he said.

Why would she torture him? She seemed to enjoy torturing him. The thought of his expulsion from the army was an agony to him, really worse than death. He saw himself in the despicable civilian clothes, engaged in some menial occupation. And he could not bear it. It was too heavy a cross.

Who was she to talk? She was herself, an actress, daughter of a tradesman. He was himself. How should one of them speak for the other? It was impossible. He loved her. He loved her far better than men usually loved their mistresses. He really cared. – And he was strangely proud of his love for her, as if it were a distinction to him ... But there was a limit to her understanding. There was a point beyond which she had nothing to do with him, and she had better leave him alone. Here in this crisis, which was *his* crisis, his downfall, she should not presume to talk, because she did not understand. – But she loved to torture him, that was the truth.

'Why should it hurt you to work?' she reiterated.

He lifted his face, white and tortured, his grey eyes flaring with fear and hate.

'Work!' he cried. 'What do you think I am worth? – Twenty-five shillings a week, if I am lucky.'

His evident anguish penetrated her. She sat dumbfounded, looking at him with wide eyes. He was white with misery and fear; his hand, that lay loose on the table, was abandoned in nervous ignominy. Her mind filled with wonder, and with deep, cold dread. Did he really care so much? But did it *really* matter so much to him? When he said he was worth twenty-five shillings a week, he was like a man whose soul is pierced. He sat there, annihilated. She looked for him, and he was nothing then. She looked for the man, the free being that loved her. And he was not, he was gone, this blank figure remained. Something with a blanched face sat there in the chair, staring at nothing.

His amazement deepened with intolerable dread. It was as if the world had fallen away into chaos. Nothing remained. She seemed to grasp the air for foothold.

He sat staring in front of him, a dull numbness settled on his brain. He was watching the flame of the candle. And, in his detachment, he realized the flame was a swiftly travelling flood, flowing swiftly from the source of the wick through a white surge and on into the darkness above. It was like a fountain suddenly foaming out, then running on dark and smooth. Could one dam the flood? He took a piece of paper, and cut off the flame for a second.

The girl in red started at the pulse of the light. She seemed to come to, from some trance. She saw his face, clear now, attentive, abstract, absolved. He was quite absolved from his temporal self.

'It isn't true,' she said, 'is it? It's not so tragic, really? – It's only your pride is hurt, your silly little pride?' She was rather pleading.

He looked at her with clear steady eyes.

'My pride!' he said. 'And isn't my pride *me*? What am I without my pride?'

'You are *yourself*,' she said. 'If they take your uniform off you, and turn you naked into the street, you are still *yourself*.'

His eyes grew hot. Then he cried:

'What does it mean, *myself*! It means I put on ready-made civilian clothes and do some dirty drudging elsewhere: that is what *myself* amounts to.'

She knitted her brows.

'But what you are *to me* – that naked self which you are to me – that is something, isn't it? – everything,' she said.

'What is it, if it means nothing?' he said: 'What is it, more than a pound of chocolate *dragées*?[5] – It stands for nothing – unless as you say, a petty clerkship, at twenty-five shillings a week.'

These were all wounds to her, very deep. She looked in wonder for a few moments.

'And what does it stand for now?' she said. 'A magnificent second-lieutenant!'

He made a gesture of dismissal with his hand.

She looked at him from under lowered brows.

'And our love!' she said. 'It means nothing to you, nothing at all?'

'To me as a menial clerk, what does it mean? What does love mean! Does it mean that a man shall be no more than a dirty rag in the world? – What worth do you think I have in love, if in life I am a wretched inky subordinate clerk?'

'What does it matter?'

'It matters everything.'

There was silence for a time, then the anger flashed up in her.

'It doesn't matter to you what *I* feel, whether *I* care or not,' she cried, her voice rising. 'They'll take his little uniform with buttons off him, and he'll have to be a common little civilian, so all he can do is to shoot himself! – It doesn't matter that I'm there –'

He sat stubborn and silent. He thought her vulgar. And her raving did not alter the situation in the least.

'Don't you see what value you put on *me*, you clever little man?' she cried in fury. 'I've loved you, loved you with all my soul, for two years – and you've lied, and said you loved me. And now, what do I get? He'll shoot himself, because his tuppenny vanity is wounded. – Ah, *fool* –!'

He lifted his head and looked at her. His face was fixed and superior.

'All of which,' he said, 'leaves the facts of the case quite untouched!'

She hated his cool little speeches.

'Then shoot yourself,' she cried, 'and you'll be worth *less* than twenty-five shillings a week!'

There was a fatal silence.

'*Then* there'll be no question of worth,' he said.

'Ha!' she ejaculated in scorn.

She had finished. She had no more to say. At length, after they had both sat motionless and silent, separate, for some time, she rose and went across to her hat and cloak. He shrank in apprehension. Now, he could not bear her to go. He shrank as if he were being whipped. She put her hat on, roughly, then swung her warm plaid cloak over her shoulders. Her hat was of black glossy silk, with a sheeny heap of cocks-feathers, her plaid cloak was dark green and blue, it swung open above her clear harsh-red dress. How beautiful she was, like a fiery Madonna!

'Good-bye,' she said, in her voice of mockery. 'I'm going now.'

He sat motionless, as if loaded with fetters. She hesitated, then moved towards the door.

Suddenly, with a spring like a cat, he was confronting her, his back to the door. His eyes were full and dilated, like a cat's, his face seemed to gleam at her. She quivered, as some subtle fluid ran through her nerves.

'Let me go,' she said dumbly. 'I've had enough.' His eyes, with a wide, dark electric pupil, like a cat's, only watched her objectively. And again a wave of female submissiveness went over her.

'I want to go,' she pleaded. 'You know it's no good. – You know this is no good.'

She stood humbly before him. A flexible little grin quivered round his mouth.

'You know you don't want me,' she persisted. 'You know you don't really want me. – You only do this to show your power over me – which is a mean trick.'

But he did not answer, only his eyes narrowed in a sensual, cruel smile. She shrank, afraid, and yet she was fascinated.

'You won't go yet,' he said.

She tried in vain to rouse her real opposition.

'I shall call out,' she threatened. 'I shall shame you before people.'

His eyes narrowed again in the smile of vindictive, mocking indifference.

'Call then,' he said.

And at the sound of his still, cat-like voice, an intoxication ran over her veins.

'I *will*,' she said, looking defiantly into his eyes. But the smile in the dark, full, dilated pupils made her waver into submission again.

'Won't you let me go?' she pleaded sullenly.

Now the smile went openly over his face.

'Take your hat off,' he said.

And with quick, light fingers he reached up and drew out the pins of her hat, unfastened the clasp of her cloak, and laid her things aside.

She sat down in a chair. Then she rose again, and went to the window. In the street below, the tiny figures were moving just the same. She opened the window, and leaned out, and wept.

He looked round at her in irritation as she stood in her long, clear-red dress in the window-recess, leaning out. She was exasperating.

'You will be cold,' he said.

She paid no heed. He guessed, by some tension in her attitude, that she was crying. It irritated him exceedingly, like a madness. After a few minutes of suspense, he went across to her, and took her by the arm. His hand was subtle, soft in its touch, and yet rather cruel than gentle.

'Come away,' he said. 'Don't stand there in the air – come away.'

He drew her slowly away to the bed, she sat down, and he beside her.

'What are you crying for?' he said in his strange, penetrating voice, that had a vibration of exultancy in it. But her tears only ran faster.

He kissed her face, that was soft, and fresh, and yet warm, wet with tears. He kissed her again, and again, in pleasure of the soft, wet saltness of her. She turned aside and wiped her face with her handkerchief, and blew her nose. He was disappointed – yet the way she blew her nose pleased him.

Suddenly she slid away to the floor, and hid her face in the side of the bed, weeping and crying loudly:

'You don't love me – Oh, you don't love me – I thought you did, and you let me go on thinking it – but you don't, no, you don't, and I can't bear it. – Oh, I can't bear it.'

He sat and listened to the strange, animal sound of her crying. His eyes flickered with exultancy, his body seemed full and surcharged with power. But his brows were knitted in tension. He laid his hand softly on her head, softly touched her face, which was buried against the bed.

She suddenly rubbed her face against the sheets, and looked up once more.

'You've deceived me,' she said, as she sat beside him.

'Have I? Then I've deceived myself.' His body felt so charged with male vigour, he was almost laughing in his strength.

'Yes,' she said enigmatically, fatally. She seemed absorbed in her thoughts. Then her face quivered again.

'And I loved you so much,' she faltered, the tears rising. There was a clangour of delight in his heart.

'I love *you*,' he said softly, softly touching her, softly kissing her, in a sort of subtle, restrained ecstasy.

She shook her head stubbornly. She tried to draw away. Then she did break away, and turned to look at him, in fear and doubt. The little, fascinating, fiendish lights were hovering in his eyes like laughter.

'Don't hurt me so much,' she faltered, in a last protest.

A faint smile came on his face. He took her face between his hands and covered it with soft, blinding kisses, like a soft, narcotic rain. He felt himself such an unbreakable fountain-head of powerful blood. He was trembling finely in all his limbs, with mastery.

When she lifted her face and opened her eyes, her face was wet, and her greenish-golden eyes were shining, it was like sudden sunshine in wet foliage. She smiled at him like a child of knowledge, through the tears, and softly, infinitely softly he dried her tears with his mouth and his soft young moustache.

'You'd never shoot yourself, because you're mine, aren't you!' she said, knowing the fine quivering of his body, in mastery.

'Yes,' he said.

'Quite mine?' she said, her voice rising in ecstasy.

'Yes.'

'Nobody else but mine – nothing at all –?'

'Nothing at all,' he re-echoed.

'But me?' came her last words of ecstasy.

'Yes.'

And she seemed to be released free into the infinite of ecstasy.

II

They slept in fulfilment through the long night. But then strange dreams began to fill them both, strange dreams that were neither waking nor sleeping; – only, in curious weariness, through her dreams, she heard at last a continual low rapping. She awoke with difficulty. The rapping began again – she started violently. It was at the door – it would be the orderly rapping for Friedeburg. Everything seemed wild and unearthly. She put her hand on the shoulder of the sleeping man, and pulled him roughly, waited a moment, then pushed him, almost violently, to awake him. He woke with a sense of resentment at her violent handling. Then he heard the knocking of the orderly. He gathered his senses.

'Yes, Heinrich!' he said.

Strange, the sound of a voice! It seemed a far-off tearing sound. Then came the muffled voice of the servant.

'Half past four, Sir.'

'Right!' said Friedeburg, and automatically he got up and made a light. She was suddenly as wide awake as if it were daylight. But it was a strange, false day, like a delirium. She saw him put down the match, she saw him moving about, rapidly dressing. And the movement in the room was a trouble to her. He himself was vague and unreal, a thing seen but not comprehended. She watched all the acts of his toilet, saw all the motions, but never saw him. There was only a disturbance about her, which fretted her, she was not aware of any presence. Her mind, in its strange, hectic clarity, wanted to consider things in absolute detachment. For instance, she wanted to consider the cactus plant. It was a curious object with pure scarlet blossoms. Now, how did these scarlet blossoms come to pass, upon that earthly-looking unliving creature? Scarlet blossoms! How wonderful they were! What were they, then, how could one lay hold on their being? Her mind turned to him. Him, too, how could one lay hold on him, to have him? Where was he, what was he? She seemed to grasp at the air.

He was dipping his face in the cold water – the slight shock was good for him. He felt as if someone had stolen away his being in the night, he was moving about a light, quick shell, with all his meaning absent. His body was quick and active, but all his deep understanding, his soul was gone. He tried to rub it back into his face. He was quite dim, as if his spirit had left his body.

'Come and kiss me,' sounded the voice from the bed. He went over to her automatically. She put her arms around him and looked into his face with her clear brilliant, grey-green eyes, as if she too were looking for his soul.

'How are you?' came her meaningless words.

'All right.'

'Kiss me.'

He bent down and kissed her.

And still her clear, rather frightening eyes seemed to be searching for him inside himself. He was like a bird transfixed by her pellucid, grey-green, wonderful eyes. She put her hands into his soft, thick, fine hair, and gripped her hands full of his hair. He wondered with fear at her sudden painful clutching.

'I shall be late,' he said.

'Yes,' she answered. And she let him go.

As he fastened his tunic he glanced out of the window. It was still night: a night that must have lasted since eternity. There was a moon in the sky. In the streets below the yellow street-lamps burned small at intervals. This was the night of eternity.

There came a knock at the door, and the orderly's voice.

'Coffee, Sir.'

'Leave it there.'

They heard the faint jingle of the tray as it was set down outside.

Friedeburg sat down to put on his boots. Then, with a man's solid tread, he went and took in the tray. He felt properly heavy and secure now in his accoutrement. But he was always aware of her two wonderful, clear, unfolded eyes, looking on his heart, out of her uncanny silence.

There was a strong smell of coffee in the room.

'Have some coffee?' His eyes could not meet hers.

'No, thank you.'

'Just a drop?'

'No, thank you.'

Her voice sounded quite gay. She watched him dipping his bread in the coffee and eating quickly, absently. He did not know what he was doing, and yet the dipped bread and hot coffee gave him pleasure. He gulped down the remainder of his drink, and rose to his feet.

'I must go,' he said.

There was a curious, poignant smile in her eyes. Her eyes drew him to her. How beautiful she was, and dazzling, and frightening, with this look of brilliant tenderness seeming to glitter from her face. She drew his head down to her bosom, and held it fast prisoner there, murmuring with tender, triumphant delight: 'Dear! Dear!'

At last she let him lift his head, and he looked into her eyes, that seemed to concentrate in a dancing, golden point of vision in which he felt himself perish.

'Dear!' she murmured. 'You love me, don't you?'

'Yes,' he said mechanically.

The golden point of vision seemed to leap to him from her eyes, demanding something. He sat slackly, as if spellbound. Her hand pushed him a little.

'Mustn't you go?' she said.

He rose. She watched him fastening the belt round his body, that seemed soft under the fine clothes. He pulled on his great-coat, and put on his peaked cap. He was again a young officer.

But he had forgotten his watch. It lay on the table near the bed. She watched him slinging it on his chain. He looked down at her. How beautiful she was, with her luminous face and her fine, stray hair! But he felt far away.

'Anything I can do for you?' he asked.

'No, thank you – I'll sleep,' she replied, smiling. And the strange golden spark danced on her eyes again, again he felt as if his heart were gone, destroyed out of him. There was a fine pathos too in her vivid, dangerous face.

He kissed her for the last time, saying:

'I'll blow the candles out, then?'

'Yes, my love – and I'll sleep.'

'Yes – sleep as long as you like.'

The golden spark of her eyes seemed to dance on him like a destruction, she was beautiful, and pathetic. He touched her tenderly with his finger-tips, then suddenly blew out the candles, and walked across in the faint moonlight to the door.

He was gone. She heard his boots click on the stone stairs – she heard the far below tread of his feet on the pavement. Then he was gone. She lay quite still, in a swoon of deathly peace. She never wanted to move any more. It was finished. She lay quite still, utterly, utterly abandoned.

But again she was disturbed. There was a little tap at the door, then Teresa's voice saying, with a shuddering sound because of the cold:

'Ugh! – I'm coming to you, Marta my dear. I can't stand being left alone.'

'I'll make a light,' said Marta, sitting up and reaching for the candle. 'Lock the door, will you, Resie, and then nobody can bother us.'

She saw Teresa, loosely wrapped in her cloak, two thick ropes of hair hanging untidily. Teresa looked voluptuously sleepy and easy, like a cat running home to the warmth.

'Ugh!' she said, 'it's cold!'

And she ran to the stove. Marta heard the chink of the little shovel, a stirring of coals, then a clink of the iron door. Then Teresa came running to the bed, with a shuddering little run, she puffed out the light and slid in beside her friend.

'So cold!' she said, with a delicious shudder at the warmth. Marta made place for her, and they settled down.

'Aren't you glad you're not them?' said Resie, with a little shudder at the thought. 'Ugh! – poor devils!'

'I am,' said Marta.

'Ah, sleep – sleep, how lovely!' said Teresa, with deep content. 'Ah, it's so good!'

'Yes,' said Marta.

'Good morning, good night, my dear,' said Teresa, already sleepily.

'Good night,' responded Marta.

Her mind flickered a little. Then she sank unconsciously to sleep. The room was silent.

Outside, the setting moon made peaked shadows of the high-roofed houses; from twin towers that stood like two dark, companion giants in the sky, the hour trembled out over the sleeping town. But the footsteps of hastening officers and cowering soldiers rang on the frozen pavements. Then a lantern appeared in the distance, accompanied by the rattle of a bullock wagon. By the light of the lantern on the wagon-pole could be seen the delicately moving feet and the pale, swinging dewlaps of the oxen. They drew slowly on, with a rattle of heavy wheels, the banded heads of the slow beasts swung rhythmically.

Ah, this was life! How sweet, sweet each tiny incident was! How sweet to Friedeburg, to give his orders ringingly on the frosty air, to see his men like bears shambling and shuffling into their places, with little dancing movements of uncouth playfulness and resentment, because of the pure cold.

Sweet, sweet it was to be marching beside his men, sweet to hear the great thresh-thresh of their heavy boots in the unblemished silence, sweet to feel the immense mass of living bodies co-ordinated into oneness near him, to catch the hot waft of their closeness, their breathing.

Friedeburg was like a man condemned to die, catching at every impression as at an inestimable treasure.

Sweet it was to pass through the gates of the town, the scanty, loose suburb, into the open darkness and space of the country. This was almost best of all. It was like emerging in the open plains of eternal freedom.

They saw a dark figure hobbling along under the dark side of a shed. As they passed, through the open door of the shed, in the golden light were seen the low rafters, the pale, silken sides of the cows, evanescent. And a woman with a red kerchief bound round her head lifted her face from the flank of the beast she was milking, to look at the soldiers threshing like multitudes of heavy ghosts down the darkness. Some of the men called to her, cheerfully, impudently. Ah, the miraculous beauty and sweetness of the merest trifles like these!

They tramped on down a frozen, rutty road, under lines of bare trees. Beautiful trees! Beautiful frozen ruts in the road! Ah, even, in one of the ruts there was a silver of ice and of moon-glimpse. He heard ice tinkle as a passing soldier purposely put his toe in it. What a sweet noise!

But there was a vague uneasiness. He heard the men arguing as to whether dawn were coming. There was the silver moon, still riding on the high seas of the sky. A lovely thing she was, a jewel! But was there any blemish of day? He shrank a little from the rawness of the day to come. This night of morning was so rare and free.

Yes, he was sure. He saw a colourless paleness on the horizon. The earth began to look hard, like a great, concrete shadow. He shrank into himself. Glancing at the ranks of his men, he could see them like a company of rhythmic ghosts. The pallor was actually reflected on their livid faces. This was the coming day. It frightened him.

The dawn came. He saw the rosiness of it hang trembling with light, above the east. Then a strange glamour of scarlet passed over the land. At his feet, glints of ice flashed scarlet, even the hands of the men were red as they swung, sinister, heavy, reddened.

The sun surged up, her rim appeared, swimming with fire, hesitating, surging up. Suddenly there were shadows from trees and ruts, and grass was hoar and ice was gold against the ebony shadow. The faces of the men were alight, kindled with life. Ah, it was magical, it was all too marvellous! If only it were always like this!

When they stopped at the inn for breakfast, at nine o'clock, the smell of the inn went raw and ugly to his heart: beer and yesterday's tobacco!

He went to the door to look at the men biting huge bites from their hunks of grey bread, or cutting off pieces with their clasp-knives. This made him still happy. Women were going to the fountain for water, the soldiers were chaffing them coarsely. He liked all this.

But the magic was going, inevitably, the crystal delight was thawing to desolation in his heart, his heart was cold, cold mud. Ah, it was awful. His face contracted, he almost wept with cold, stark despair.

Still he had the work, the day's hard activity with the men. Whilst this lasted, he could live. But when this was over, and he had to face the horror of his own cold-thawing mud of despair: ah, it was not to be thought of. Still, he was happy at work with the men: the wild desolate place, the hard activity of mock warfare. Would to God it were real: war, with the prize of death!

By afternoon the sky had gone one dead, livid level of grey. It seemed low down, and oppressive. He was tired, the men were tired, and this let the heavy cold soak in to them like despair. Life could not keep it out.

And now, when his heart was so heavy it could sink no more, he must glance at his own situation again. He must remember what a fool he was, his new debts like half thawed mud in his heart. He knew, with the cold misery of hopelessness, that he would be turned out of the army. What then? – what then but death? After all, death was the solution for him. Let it be so.

They marched on and on, stumbling with fatigue under a great leaden sky, over a frozen dead country. The men were silent with weariness, the heavy motion of their marching was like an oppression. Friedeburg was tired too, and deadened, as his face was deadened by the cold air. He did not think any more; the misery of his soul was like a frost inside him.

He heard someone say it was going to snow. But the words had no meaning for him. He marched as a clock ticks, with the same monotony, everything numb and cold-soddened.

They were drawing near to the town. In the gloom of the afternoon he felt it ahead, as unbearable oppression on him. Ah the hideous suburb! What was his life, how did it come to pass that life was lived in a formless, hideous grey structure of hell! What did it all mean? Pale, sulphur-yellow lights spotted the livid air, and people, like soddened shadows, passed in front of the shops that were lit up ghastly in the early twilight. Out of the colourless space, crumbs of snow came and bounced animatedly off the breast of his coat.

At length he turned away home, to his room, to change and get warm and renewed, for he felt as cold-soddened as the grey, cold, heavy bread which felt hostile in the mouths of the soldiers. His life was to him like this dead, cold bread in his mouth.

As he neared his own house, the snow was peppering thinly down. He became aware of some unusual stir about the house-door. He looked – a strange, closed-in wagon, people, police. The sword of Damocles[6] that had hung over his heart, fell. O God, a new shame, some new shame, some new torture! His body moved on. So it would move on through misery upon misery, as is our fate. There was no emergence, only this progress through misery unto misery, till the end. Strange, that human life was so tenacious! Strange, that men had made of life a long, slow process of torture to the soul. Strange, that it was no other than this! Strange, that but for man, this misery would not exist. For it was not God's misery, but the misery of the world of man.

He saw two officials push something white and heavy into the cart, shut the doors behind with a bang, turn the silver handle, and run round to the front of the wagon. It moved off. But still most of the people lingered. Friedeburg drifted near in that inevitable motion which carries us through all our shame and torture. He knew the people talked about him. He went up the steps and into the square hall.

There stood a police-officer, with a note-book in his hand, talking to Herr Kapell, the housemaster. As Friedeburg entered through the swing door, the housemaster, whose brow was wrinkled in anxiety and perturbation, made a gesture with his hand, as if to point out a criminal.

'Ah! – the Herr Baron von Friedeburg!' he said, in self-exculpation.

The police officer turned, saluted politely, and said, with the polite, intolerable *suffisance*[7] of officialdom:

'Good evening! Trouble here!'

'Yes?' said Friedeburg.

He was so frightened, his sensitive constitution was so lacerated, that something broke in him, he was a subservient, murmuring ruin.

'Two young ladies found dead in your room,' said the police-official, making an official statement. But under his cold impartiality of officialdom, what obscene unction! Ah, what obscene exposures now!

'Dead!' ejaculated Friedeburg, with the wide eyes of a child. He became quite child-like, the official had him completely in his power. He could torture him as much as he liked.

'Yes.' He referred to his note-book. 'Asphyxiated by fumes from the stove.'

Friedeburg could only stand wide-eyed and meaningless.

'Please – will you go upstairs?'

The police-official marshalled Friedburg in front of himself. The youth slowly mounted the stairs, feeling as if transfixed through the base of the spine, as if he would lose the use of his legs. The official followed close on his heels.

They reached the bedroom. The policeman unlocked the door. The housekeeper followed with a lamp. Then the official examination began.

'A young lady slept here last night?'

'Yes.'

'Name, please?'

'Marta Hohenest.'

'H-o-h-e-n-e-s-t,' spelled the official. '– And address?'

Friedeburg continued to answer. This was the end of him. The quick of him was pierced and killed. The living dead answered the living dead in obscene antiphony. Question and answer continued, the note-book worked as the hand of the old dead wrote in it the replies of the young who was dead.

The room was unchanged from the night before. There was her heap of clothing, the lustrous, pure-red dress lying soft where she had carelessly dropped it. Even, on the edge of the chair-back, her crimson silk garters hung looped.

But do not look, do not see. It is the business of the dead to bury their dead. Let the young dead bury their own dead, as the old dead have buried theirs. How can the dead remember, they being dead? Only the living can remember, and are at peace with their living who have passed away.

England, My England

HE was working on the edge of the common, beyond the small brook that ran in the dip at the bottom of the garden, carrying the garden path in continuation from the plank bridge on to the common. He had cut the rough turf and bracken, leaving the grey, dryish soil bare. But he was worried because he could not get the path straight, there was a pleat between his brows. He had set up his sticks, and taken the sights between the big pine trees, but for some reason everything seemed wrong. He looked again, straining his keen blue eyes, that had a touch of the Viking in them, through the shadowy pine trees as through a doorway, at the green-grassed garden-path rising from the shadow of alders by the log bridge up to the sunlit flowers. Tall white and purple columbines, and the butt-end of the old Hampshire cottage that crouched near the earth amid flowers, blossoming in the bit of shaggy wildness round about.

There was a sound of children's voices calling and talking: high, childish, girlish voices, slightly didactic and tinged with domineering: 'If you don't come quick, nurse, I shall run out there to where there are snakes.' And nobody had the *sang-froid* to reply: 'Run then, little fool.' It was always, 'No, darling. Very well, darling. In a moment, darling. Darling, you *must* be patient.'

His heart was hard with disillusion: a continual gnawing and resistance. But he worked on. What was there to do but submit!

The sunlight blazed down upon the earth, there was a vividness of flamy vegetation, of fierce seclusion amid the savage peace of the commons. Strange how the savage England lingers in patches: as here, amid these shaggy gorse commons, and marshy, snake-infested places near the foot of the south downs. The spirit of place lingering on primeval, as when the Saxons came, so long ago.

Ah, how he had loved it! The green garden path, the tufts of flowers, purple and white columbines, and great oriental red poppies with their black chaps and mulleins tall and yellow: this flamy garden which had been a garden for a thousand years, scooped out in the little hollow among the snake-infested commons. He had made it flame with flowers, in a sun cup under its hedges and trees. So old, so old a place! And yet he had re-created it.

The timbered cottage with its sloping, cloak-like roof was old and forgotten. It belonged to the old England of hamlets and yeomen. Lost all alone on the edge of the common, at the end of a wide, grassy, briar-entangled lane shaded with oak, it had never known the world of to-day. Not till Egbert came with his bride. And he had come to fill it with flowers.

The house was ancient and very uncomfortable. But he did not want to alter it. Ah, marvellous to sit there in the wide, black, time-old chimney, at night when the wind roared overhead, and the wood which he had chopped himself sputtered on the hearth! Himself on one side the angle, and Winifred on the other.

Ah, how he had wanted her: Winifred! She was young and beautiful and strong with life, like a flame in sunshine. She moved with a slow grace of energy like a blossoming, red-flowered bush in motion. She, too, seemed to come out of the old England, ruddy, strong, with a certain crude, passionate quiescence and a hawthorn robustness. And he, he was tall and slim and agile, like an English archer with his long supple legs and fine movements. Her hair was nut-brown and all in energic curls and tendrils. Her eyes were nut-brown, too, like a robin's for brightness. And he was white-skinned with fine, silky hair that had darkened from fair, and a slightly arched nose of an old country family. They were a beautiful couple.

The house was Winifred's. Her father was a man of energy, too. He had come from the north poor. Now he was moderately rich. He had bought this fair stretch of inexpensive land, down in Hampshire. Not far from the tiny church of the almost extinct hamlet stood his own house, a commodious old farm-house standing back from the road across a bare grassed yard. On one side of this quadrangle was the long, long barn or shed which he had made into a cottage for his youngest daughter Priscilla. One saw little blue-and-white check curtains at the long windows, and inside, overhead, the grand old timbers of the high-pitched shed. This was Prissy's house. Fifty yards away was the pretty little new cottage which he had built for his daughter Magdalen, with the vegetable garden stretching away to the oak copse. And then away beyond the lawns and rose-trees of the house-garden went the track across a shaggy, wild grass space, towards the ridge of tall black pines that grew on a dyke-bank, through the pines and above the sloping little bog, under the wide, desolate oak trees, till there was Winifred's cottage crouching unexpectedly in front, so much alone, and so primitive.

It was Winifred's own house, and the gardens and the bit of common and the boggy slope were hers: her tiny domain. She had married just at the time when her father had bought the estate, about ten years before the war, so she had been able to come to Egbert with this for a marriage portion. And who was more delighted, he or she, it would be hard to say. She was only twenty at the time, and he was only twenty-one. He had about a hundred and fifty pounds a year of his own – and nothing else but his very considerable personal attractions. He had no profession: he earned nothing. But he talked of literature and music, he had a passion for old folk-music, collecting folk-songs and folk-dances, studying the Morris-dance and the old customs. Of course in time he would make money in these ways.

Meanwhile youth and health and passion and promise. Winifred's father was always generous: but still, he was a man from the north with a hard head and a hard skin too, having received a good many knocks. At home he kept the hard head out of sight, and played at poetry and romance with his literary wife and his sturdy, passionate girls. He was a man of courage, not given to complaining, bearing his burdens by himself. No, he did not let the world intrude far into his home. He had a delicate, sensitive wife whose poetry won some fame in the narrow world of letters. He himself, with his tough old barbarian fighting spirit, had an almost child-like delight in verse, in sweet poetry, and in the delightful game of a cultured home. His blood was strong even to coarseness. But that only made the home more vigorous, more robust and Christmassy. There was always a touch of Christmas about him, now he was well off. If there was poetry after dinner, there were also chocolates, and nuts, and good little out-of-the-way things to be munching.

Well then, into this family came Egbert. He was made of quite a different paste. The girls and the father were strong-limbed, thick-blooded people, true English, as holly-trees and hawthorn are English. Their culture was grafted on to them, as one might perhaps graft a common pink rose on to a thorn-stem. It flowered oddly enough, but it did not alter their blood.

And Egbert was a born rose. The age-long breeding had left him with a delightful spontaneous passion. He was not clever, nor even 'literary'. No, but the intonation of his voice, and the movement of his supple, handsome body, and the fine texture of his flesh and his hair, the slight arch of his nose, the quickness of his blue eyes would easily take the place of poetry. Winifred loved him, loved him, this southerner, as a higher being. A *higher* being, mind you. Not a deeper. And as for him, he loved her in passion with every fibre of him. She was the very warm stuff of life to him.

Wonderful then, those days at Crockham Cottage, the first days, all alone save for the woman who came to work in the mornings. Marvellous days, when she had all his tall, supple, fine-fleshed youth to herself, for herself, and he had her like a ruddy fire into which he could cast himself for rejuvenation. Ah, that it might never end, this passion, this marriage! The flame of their two bodies burnt again into that old cottage, that was haunted already by so much by-gone, physical desire. You could not be in the dark room for an hour without the influences coming over you. The hot blood-desire of by-gone yeomen, there in this old den where they had lusted and bred for so many generations. The silent house, dark, with thick, timbered walls and the big black chimney-place, and the sense of secrecy. Dark, with low, little windows, sunk into the earth. Dark, like a lair where strong beasts had lurked and mated, lonely at night and lonely by day, left to themselves and their own intensity for so many generations. It seemed to cast a spell on the two young people. They became different. There was a curious secret glow about them, a certain slumbering flame hard to understand, that enveloped them both. They too felt that they did not belong to the London world any more. Crockham had changed their blood: the sense of the snakes that lived and slept even in their own garden, in the sun, so that he, going forward with the spade, would see a curious coiled brownish pile on the black soil, which suddenly would start up, hiss, and dazzle rapidly away, hissing. One day Winifred heard the strangest scream from the flower-bed under the low window of the living room: ah, the strangest scream, like the very soul of the dark past crying aloud. She ran out, and saw a long brown snake on the flower-bed, and in its flat mouth the one hind leg of a frog was striving to escape, and screaming its strange, tiny, bellowing scream. She looked at the snake, and from its sullen flat head it looked at her, obstinately. She gave a cry, and it released the frog and slid angrily away.

That was Crockham. The spear of modern invention had not passed through it, and it lay there secret, primitive, savage as when the Saxons first came. And Egbert and she were caught there, caught out of the world.

He was not idle, nor was she. There were plenty of things to be done, the house to be put into final repair after the workmen had gone, cushions and curtains to sew, the paths to make, the water to fetch and attend to, and then the slope of the deep-soiled, neglected garden to level, to terrace with little terraces and paths, and to fill with flowers. He worked away, in his shirt-sleeves, worked all day intermittently doing this thing and the other. And she, quiet and rich in herself, seeing him stooping and labouring away by himself, would come to help him, to be near him. He of course was an amateur – a born amateur. He worked so hard, and did so little, and nothing he ever did would hold together for long. If he terraced the garden, he held up the earth with a couple of long narrow planks that soon began to bend with the pressure from behind, and would not need many years to rot through and break and let the soil slither all down again in a heap towards the stream-bed. But there you are. He had not been brought up to come to grips with anything, and he thought it would do. Nay, he did not think there was anything else except little temporary contrivances possible, he who had such a passion for his old enduring cottage, and for the old enduring things of the by-gone England. Curious that the sense of permanency in the past had such a hold over him, whilst in the present he was all amateurish and sketchy.

Winifred could not criticise him. Town-bred, everything seemed to her splendid, and the very digging and shovelling itself seemed romantic. But neither Egbert nor she yet realised the difference between work and romance.

Godfrey Marshall, her father, was at first perfectly pleased with the ménage down at Crockham Cottage. He thought Egbert was wonderful, the many things he had accomplished, and he was gratified by the glow of physical passion between the two young people. To the man who in London still worked hard to keep steady his modest fortune, the thought of this young couple digging away and loving one another down at Crockham Cottage, buried deep among the commons and marshes, near the pale-showing bulk of the downs, was like a chapter of living romance. And they drew the sustenance for their fire of passion from him, from the old man. It was he who fed their flame. He triumphed secretly in the thought. And it was to her father that Winifred still turned, as the one source of all surety and life and support. She loved Egbert with passion. But behind her was the power of her father. It was the power of her father she referred to, whenever she needed to refer. It never occurred to her to refer to Egbert, if she were in difficulty or doubt. No, in all the *serious* matters she depended on her father.

For Egbert had no intention of coming to grips with life. He had no ambition whatsoever. He came from a decent family, from a pleasant country home, from delightful surroundings. He should, of course, have had a profession. He should have studied law or entered business in some way. But no – that fatal three pounds a week would keep him from starving as long as he lived, and he did not want to give himself into bondage. It was not that he was idle. He was always doing something, in his amateurish way. But he had no desire to give himself to the world, and still less had he any desire to fight his way in the world. No, no, the world wasn't worth it. He wanted to ignore it, to go his own way apart, like a casual pilgrim down the forsaken side-tracks. He loved his wife, his cottage and garden. He would make his life there, as a sort of epicurean hermit. He loved the past, the old music and dances and customs of old England. He would try and live in the spirit of these, not in the spirit of the world of business.

But often Winifred's father called her to London: for he loved to have his children round him. So Egbert and she must have a tiny flat in town, and the young couple must transfer themselves from time to time from the country to the city. In town Egbert had plenty of friends, of the same ineffectual sort as himself, tampering with the arts, literature, painting, sculpture, music. He was not bored.

Three pounds a week, however, would not pay for all this. Winifred's father paid. He liked paying. He made her only a very small allowance, but he often gave her ten pounds—or gave Egbert ten pounds. So they both looked on the old man as the mainstay. Egbert didn't mind being patronised and paid for. Only when he felt the family was a little *too* condescending, on account of money, he began to get huffy.

Then of course little children came: a lovely little blonde daughter with a head of thistle-down. Everybody adored the child. It was the first exquisite blonde thing that had come into the family, a little mite with the white, slim, beautiful limbs of its father, and as it grew up the dancing, dainty movement of a wild little daisy-spirit. No wonder the Marshalls all loved the child: they called her Joyce. They themselves had their own grace, but it was slow, rather heavy. They had everyone of them strong, heavy limbs and darkish skins, and they were short in stature. And now they had for one of their own this light little cowslip child. She was like a little poem in herself.

But nevertheless, she brought a new difficulty. Winifred must have a nurse for her. Yes, yes, there must be a nurse. It was the family decree. Who was to pay for the nurse? The grandfather – seeing the father himself earned no money. Yes, the grandfather would pay, as he had paid all the lying-in expenses. There came a slight sense of money-strain. Egbert was living on his father-in-law.

After the child was born, it was never quite the same between him and Winifred. The difference was at first hardly perceptible. But it was there. In the first place Winifred had a new centre of interest. She was not going to adore her child. But she had what the modern mother so often has in the place of spontaneous love: a profound sense of duty towards her child. Winifred appreciated her darling little girl, and felt a deep sense of duty towards her. Strange, that this sense of duty should go deeper than the love for her husband. But so it was. And so it often is. The responsibility of motherhood was the prime responsibility in Winifred's heart: the responsibility of wifehood came a long way second.

Her child seemed to link her up again in a circuit with her own family. Her father and mother, herself, and her child, that was the human trinity for her. Her husband –? Yes, she loved him still. But that was like play. She had an almost barbaric sense of duty and of family. Till she married, her first human duty had been towards her father: he was the pillar, the source of life, the everlasting support. Now another link was added to the chain of duty: her father, herself, and her child.

Egbert was out of it. Without anything happening, he was gradually, unconsciously excluded from the circle. His wife still loved him, physically. But, but – he was *almost* the unnecessary party in the affair. He could not complain of Winifred. She still did her duty towards him. She still had a physical passion for him, that physical passion on which he had put all his life and soul. But – but –

It was for a long while an ever-recurring *but*. And then, after the second child, another blonde, winsome touching little thing, not so proud and flame-like as Joyce – after Annabel came, then Egbert began truly to realise how it was. His wife still loved him. But – and now the but had grown enormous – her physical love for him was of secondary importance to her. It became ever less important. After all, she had had it, this physical passion, for two years now. It was not this that one lived from. No, no – something sterner, realer.

She began to resent her own passion for Egbert – just a little she began to despise it. For after all there he was, he was charming, he was lovable, he was terribly desirable. But – but – oh, the awful looming cloud of that *but*! – he did not stand firm in the landscape of her life like a tower of strength, like a great pillar of significance. No, he was like a cat one has about the house, which will one day disappear and leave no trace. He was like a flower in the garden, trembling in the wind of life, and then gone, leaving nothing to show.

As an adjunct, as an accessory, he was perfect. Many a woman would have adored to have him about her all her life, the most beautiful and desirable of all her possessions. But Winifred belonged to another school.

The years went by, and instead of coming more to grips with life, he relaxed more. He was of a subtle, sensitive, passionate nature. But he simply *would* not give himself to what Winifred called life, *Work*. No, he would not go into the world and work for money. No, he just would not. If Winifred liked to live beyond their small income – well, it was her look-out.

And Winifred did not really want him to go out into the world to work for money. Money became, alas, a word like a firebrand between them, setting them both aflame with anger. But that is because we must talk in symbols. Winifred did not really care about money. She did not care whether he earned or did not earn anything. Only she knew she was dependent on her father for three-fourths of the money spent for herself and her children, that she let that be the *casus belli*,[1] the drawn weapon between herself and Egbert.

What did she want – what did she want? Her mother once said to her, with that characteristic touch of irony: 'Well, dear, if it is your fate to consider the lilies, that toil not, neither do they spin,[2] that is one destiny among many others, and perhaps not so unpleasant as most. Why do you take it amiss, my child?'

The mother was subtler than her children, they very rarely knew how to answer her. So Winifred was only more confused. It was not a question of lilies. At least, if it were a question of lilies, then her children were the little blossoms. They at least *grew*. Doesn't Jesus say: 'Consider the lilies *how they grow*.' Good then, she had her growing babies. But as for that other tall, handsome flower of a father of theirs, he was full grown already, so she did not want to spend her life considering him in the flower of his days.

No, it was not that he didn't earn money. It was not that he was idle. He was *not* idle. He was always doing something, always working away, down at Crockham, doing little jobs. But, oh dear, the little jobs – the garden paths – the gorgeous flowers – the chairs to mend, old chairs to mend!

It was that he stood for nothing. If he had done something unsuccessfully, and *lost* what money they had! If he had but striven with something. Nay, even if he had been wicked, a waster, she would have been more free. She would have had something to resist, at least. A waster stands for something, really. He says: 'No, I will not aid and abet society in this business of increase and hanging together, I will upset the apple-cart as much as I can, in my small way.' Or else he says: 'No, I will *not* bother about others. If I have lusts, they are my own, and I prefer them to other people's virtues.' So, a waster, a scamp, takes a sort of stand. He exposes himself to opposition and final castigation: at any rate in story-books.

But Egbert! What are you to do with a man like Egbert? He had no vices. He was really kind, nay generous. And he was not weak. If he had been weak Winifred could have been kind to him. But he did not even give her that consolation. He was not weak, and he did not want her consolation or her kindness. No, thank you. He was of a fine passionate temper, and of a rarer steel than she. He knew it, and she knew it. Hence she was only the more baffled and maddened, poor thing. He, the higher, the finer, in his way the stronger, played with his garden, and his old folk-songs and Morris-dances, just played, and let her support the pillars of the future on her own heart.

And he began to get bitter, and a wicked look began to come on his face. He did not give in to her; not he. There were seven devils inside his long, slim, white body. He was healthy, full of restrained life. Yes, even he himself had to lock up his own vivid life inside himself, now she would not take it from him. Or rather, now that she only took it occasionally. For she had to yield at times. She loved him so, she desired him so, he was so exquisite to her, the fine creature that he was, finer than herself. Yes, with a groan she had to give in to her own unquenched passion for him. And he came to her then – ah, terrible, ah, wonderful, sometimes she wondered how either of them could live after the terror of the passion that swept between them. It was to her as if pure lightning, flash after flash, went through every fibre of her, till extinction came.

But it is the fate of human beings to live on. And it is the fate of clouds that seem nothing but bits of vapour slowly to pile up, to pile up and fill the heavens and blacken the sun entirely.

So it was. The love came back, the lightning of passion flashed tremendously between them. And there was blue sky and gorgeousness for a little while. And then, as inevitably, as inevitably, slowly the clouds began to edge up again above the horizon, slowly, slowly to lurk about the heavens, throwing an occasional cold and hateful shadow: slowly, slowly to congregate, to fill the empyrean space.

And as the years passed, the lightning cleared the sky more and more rarely, less and less the blue showed. Gradually the grey lid sank down upon them, as if it would be permanent.

Why didn't Egbert do something, then? Why didn't he come to grips with life? Why wasn't he like Winifred's father, a pillar of society, even if a slender, exquisite column? Why didn't he go into harness of some sort? Why didn't he take *some* direction?

Well, you can bring an ass to the water, but you cannot make him drink. The world was the water and Egbert was the ass. And he wasn't having any. He couldn't: he just couldn't. Since necessity did not force him to work for his bread and butter, he would not work for work's sake. You can't make the columbine flowers nod in January, nor make the cuckoo sing in England at Christmas. Why? It isn't his season. He doesn't want to. Nay, he *can't* want to.

And there it was with Egbert. He couldn't link up with the world's work, because the basic desire was absent from him. Nay, at the bottom of him he had an even stronger desire: to hold aloof. To hold aloof. To do nobody any damage. But to hold aloof. It was not his season.

Perhaps he should not have married and had children. But you can't stop the waters flowing.

Which held true for Winifred, too. She was not made to endure aloof. Her family tree was a robust vegetation that had to be stirring and believing. In one direction or another her life *had* to go. In her own home she had known nothing of this diffidence which she found in Egbert, and which she could not understand, and which threw her into such dismay. What was she to do, what was she to do, in face of this terrible diffidence?

It was all so different in her own home. Her father may have had his own misgivings, but he kept them to himself. Perhaps he had no very profound belief in this world of ours, this society which we have elaborated with so much effort, only to find ourselves elaborated to death at last. But Godfrey Marshall was of tough, rough fibre, not without a vein of healthy cunning through it all. It was for him a question of winning through, and leaving the rest to heaven. Without having many illusions to grace him, he still *did* believe in heaven. In a dark and unquestioning way, he had a sort of faith: an acrid faith like the sap of some not-to-be-exterminated tree. Just a blind acrid faith as sap is blind and acrid, and yet pushes on in growth and in faith. Perhaps he was unscrupulous, but only as a striving tree is unscrupulous, pushing its single way in a jungle of others.

In the end, it is only this robust, sap-like faith which keeps man going. He may live on for many generations inside the shelter of the social establishment which he has erected for himself, as pear-trees and currant bushes would go on bearing fruit for many seasons, inside a walled garden, even if the race of man were suddenly exterminated. But bit by bit the wall-fruit-trees would gradually pull down the very walls that sustained them. Bit by bit every establishment collapses, unless it is renewed or restored by living hands, all the while.

Egbert could not bring himself to any more of this restoring or renewing business. He was not aware of the fact: but awareness doesn't help much, anyhow. He just couldn't. He had the stoic and epicurean quality of his old, fine breeding. His father-in-law, however, though he was not one bit more of a fool then Egbert, realised that since we are here we may as well live. And so he applied himself to his own tiny section of the social work, and to doing the best for his family, and to leaving the rest to the ultimate will of heaven. A certain robustness of blood made him able to go on. But sometimes even from him spurted a sudden gall of bitterness against the world and its make-up. And yet – he had his own will-to-succeed, and this carried him through. He refused to ask himself what the success would amount to. It amounted to the estate down in Hampshire, and his children lacking for nothing, and himself of some importance in the world: and *basta*! – Basta! Basta![3]

Nevertheless do not let us imagine that he was a common pusher. He was not. He knew as well as Egbert what disillusion meant. Perhaps in his soul he had the same estimation of success. But he had a certain acrid courage, and a certain will-to-power. In his own small circle he would emanate power, the single power of his own blind self. With all his spoiling of his children, he was still the father of the old English type. He was too wise to make laws and to domineer in the abstract. But he had kept, and all honour to him, a certain primitive dominion over the souls of his children, the old, almost magic prestige of paternity. There it was, still burning in him, the old smoky torch of paternal godhead.

And in the sacred glare of this torch his children had been brought up. He had given the girls every liberty, at last. But he had never really let them go beyond his power. And they, venturing out into the hard white light of our fatherless world, learned to see with the eyes of the world. They learned to criticise their father, even, from some effulgence of worldly white light, to see him as inferior. But this was all very well in the head. The moment they forgot their tricks of criticism, the old red glow of his authority came over them again. He was not to be quenched.

Let the psycho-analyst talk about father complex. It is just a word invented. Here was a man who had kept alive the old red flame of fatherhood, fatherhood that had even the right to sacrifice the child to God, like Isaac. Fatherhood that had life-and-death authority over the children: a great natural power. And till his children could be brought under some other great authority as girls; or could arrive at manhood and become themselves centres of the same power, continuing the same male mystery as men; until such time, willy-nilly, Godfrey Marshall would keep his children.

It had seemed as if he might lose Winifred. Winifred had *adored* her husband, and looked up to him as to something wonderful. Perhaps she had expected in him another great authority, a male authority greater, finer than her father's. For having once known the glow of male power, she would not easily turn to the cold white light of feminine independence. She would hunger, hunger all her life for the warmth and shelter of true male strength.

And hunger she might, for Egbert's power lay in the abnegation of power. He was himself the living negative of power. Even of responsibility. For the negation of power at last means the negation of responsibility. As far as these things went, he would confine himself to himself. He would try to confine his own *influence* even to himself. He would try, as far as possible, to abstain from influencing his children by assuming any responsibility for them. 'A little child shall lead them –'[4] His child should lead, then. He would try not to make it go in any direction whatever. He would abstain from influencing it. Liberty! –

Poor Winifred was like a fish out of water in this liberty, gasping for the denser element which should contain her. Till her child came. And then she knew that she must be responsible for it, that she must have authority over it.

But here Egbert silently and negatively stepped in. Silently, negatively, but fatally he neutralised her authority over her children.

There was a third little girl born. And after this Winifred wanted no more children. Her soul was turning to salt.[5]

So she had charge of the children, they were her responsibility. The money for them had come from her father. She would do her very best for them, and have command over their life and death. But no! Egbert would not take the responsibility. He would not even provide the money. But he would not let her have her way. Her dark, silent, passionate authority he would not allow. It was a battle between them, the battle between liberty and the old blood-power. And of course he won. The little girls loved him and adored him. 'Daddy! Daddy!' They could do as they liked with him. Their mother would have ruled them.

She would have ruled them passionately, with indulgence, with the old dark magic of parental authority, something looming and unquestioned and, after all, divine: if we believe in divine authority. The Marshalls did, being Catholic.

And Egbert, he turned her old dark, Catholic blood-authority into a sort of tyranny. He would not leave her her children. He stole them from her, and yet without assuming responsibility for them. He stole them from her, in emotion and spirit, and left her only to command their behaviour. A thankless lot for a mother. And her children adored him, adored him, little knowing the empty bitterness they were preparing for themselves when they grew up to have husbands: husbands such as Egbert, adorable and null.

Joyce, the eldest, was still his favourite. She was now a quicksilver little thing of six years old. Barbara, the youngest, was a toddler of two years. They spent most of their time down at Crockham, because he wanted to be there. And even Winifred loved the place really. But now, in her frustrated and blinded state, it was full of menace for her children. The adders, the poison-berries, the brook, the marsh, the water that might not be pure – one thing and another. From mother and nurse it was a guerilla gunfire of commands, and blithe, quicksilver disobedience from the three blonde, never-still little girls. Behind the girls was the father, against mother and nurse. And so it was.

'If you don't come quick, nurse, I shall run out there to where there are snakes.'

'Joyce, you *must* be patient. I'm just changing Annabel.'

There you are. There it was: always the same. Working away on the common across the brook he heard it. And he worked on, just the same.

Suddenly he heard a shriek, and he flung the spade from him and started for the bridge, looking up like a startled deer. Ah, there was Winifred – Joyce had hurt herself. He went on up the garden.

'What is it?'

The child was still screaming – now it was – 'Daddy! Daddy! Oh – oh, Daddy!' And the mother was saying:

'Don't be frightened, darling. Let mother look.'

But the child only cried:

'Oh, Daddy, Daddy, Daddy!'

She was terrified by the sight of the blood running from her own knee. Winifred crouched down, with her child of six in her lap, to examine the knee. Egbert bent over also.

'Don't make such a noise, Joyce,' he said irritably. 'How did she do it?'

'She fell on that sickle thing which you left lying about after cutting the grass,' said Winifred, looking into his face with bitter accusation as he bent near.

He had taken his handkerchief and tied it round the knee. Then he lifted the still sobbing child in his arms, and carried her into the house and upstairs to her bed. In his arms she became quiet. But his heart was burning with pain and with guilt. He had left the sickle there lying on the edge of the grass, and so his first-born child whom he loved so dearly had come to hurt. But then it was an accident – it was an accident. Why should he feel guilty? It would probably be nothing, better in two or three days. Why take it to heart, why worry? He put it aside.

The child lay on the bed in her little summer frock, her face very white now after the shock. Nurse had come carrying the youngest child: and little Annabel stood holding her skirt. Winifred, terribly serious and wooden-seeming, was bending over the knee, from which she had taken his blood-soaked handkerchief. Egbert bent forward, too, keeping more *sang froid* in his face than in his heart. Winifred went all of a lump of seriousness, so he had to keep some reserve. The child moaned and whimpered.

The knee was still bleeding profusely – it was a deep cut right in the joint.

'You'd better go for the doctor, Egbert,' said Winifred bitterly.

'Oh, no! Oh, no!' cried Joyce in a panic.

'Joyce, my darling, don't cry!' said Winifred, suddenly catching the little girl to her breast in a strange tragic anguish, the *Mater Dolorata*.[6] Even the child was frightened into silence. Egbert looked at the tragic figure of his wife with the child at her breast, and turned away. Only Annabel started suddenly to cry: 'Joycey, Joycey, don't have your leg bleeding!'

Egbert rode four miles to the village for the doctor. He could not help feeling that Winifred was laying it on rather. Surely the knee itself wasn't hurt! Surely not. It was only a surface cut.

The doctor was out. Egbert left the message and came cycling swiftly home, his heart pinched with anxiety. He dropped sweating off his bicycle and went into the house, looking rather small, like a man who is at fault. Winifred was upstairs sitting by Joyce, who was looking pale and important in bed, and was eating some tapioca pudding. The pale, small, scared face of his child went to Egbert's heart.

'Doctor Wing was out. He'll be here about half-past two,' said Egbert.

'I don't want him to come,' whimpered Joyce.

'Joyce, dear, you must be patient and quiet,' said Winifred. 'He won't hurt you. But he will tell us what to do to make your knee better quickly. That is why he must come.'

Winifred always explained carefully to her little girls: and it always took the words off their lips for the moment.

'Does it bleed yet?' said Egbert.

Winifred moved the bedclothes carefully aside.

'I think not,' she said.

Egbert stooped also to look.

'No, it doesn't,' he said. Then he stood up with a relieved look on his face. He turned to the child.

'Eat your pudding, Joyce,' he said. 'It won't be anything. You've only got to keep still for a few days.'

'You haven't had your dinner, have you, Daddy?'

'Not yet.'

'Nurse will give it to you,' said Winifred.

'You'll be all right, Joyce,' he said, smiling to the child and pushing the blonde hair aside off her brow. She smiled back winsomely into his face.

He went downstairs and ate his meal alone. Nurse served him. She liked waiting on him. All women liked him and liked to do things for him.

The doctor came – a fat country practitioner, pleasant and kind.

'What, little girl, been tumbling down, have you? There's a thing to be doing, for a smart little lady like you! What! And cutting your knee! Tut-tut-tut! That *wasn't* clever of you, now was it? Never mind, never mind, soon be better. Let us look at it. Won't hurt you. Not the least in life. Bring a bowl with a little warm water, nurse. Soon have it all right again, soon have it all right.'

Joyce smiled at him with a pale smile of faint superiority. This was *not* the way in which she was used to being talked to.

He bent down, carefully looking at the little, thin, wounded knee of the child. Egbert bent over him.

'Oh, dear, oh, dear! Quite a deep little cut. Nasty little cut. Nasty little cut. But, never mind. Never mind, little lady. We'll soon have it better. Soon have it better, little lady. What's your name?'

'My name is Joyce,' said the child distinctly.

'Oh, really!' he replied. 'Oh, really! Well, that's a fine name too, in my opinion. Joyce, eh? – And how old might Miss Joyce be? Can she tell me that?'

'I'm six,' said the child, slightly amused and very condescending.

'Six! There now. Add up and count as far as six, can you? Well, that's a clever little girl, a clever little girl. And if she has to drink a spoonful of medicine, she won't make a murmur, I'll be bound. Not like *some* little girls. What? Eh?'

'I take it if mother wishes me to,' said Joyce.

'Ah, there now! That's the style! That's what I like to hear from a little lady in bed because she's cut her knee. That's the style –'

The comfortable and prolix doctor dressed and bandaged the knee and recommended bed and a light diet for the little lady. He thought a week or a fortnight would put it right. No bones or ligatures damaged – fortunately. Only a flesh cut. He would come again in a day or two.

So Joyce was reassured and stayed in bed and had all her toys up. Her father often played with her. The doctor came the third day. He was fairly pleased with the knee. It was healing. It was healing – yes – yes. Let the child continue in bed. He came again after a day or two. Winifred was a trifle uneasy. The wound seemed to be healing on the top, but it hurt the child too much. It didn't look quite right. She said so to Egbert.

'Egbert, I'm sure Joyce's knee isn't healing properly.'

'I think it is,' he said. 'I think it's all right.'

'I'd rather Doctor Wing came again – I don't feel satisfied.'

'Aren't you trying to imagine it worse than it really is?'

'You would say so, of course. But I shall write a post-card to Doctor Wing now.'

The doctor came next day. He examined the knee. Yes, there was inflammation. Yes, there *might* be a little septic poisoning – there might. There might. Was the child feverish?

So a fortnight passed by, and the child *was* feverish, and the knee was more inflamed and grew worse and was painful, painful. She cried in the night, and her mother had to sit up with her. Egbert still insisted it was nothing, really – it would pass. But in his heart he was anxious.

Winifred wrote again to her father. On Saturday the elderly man appeared. And no sooner did Winifred see the thick, rather short figure in its grey suit than a great yearning came over her.

'Father, I'm not satisfied with Joyce. I'm not satisfied with Doctor Wing.'

'Well, Winnie, dear, if you're not satisfied we must have further advice, that is all.'

The sturdy, powerful, elderly man went upstairs, his voice sounding rather grating through the house, as if it cut upon the tense atmosphere.

'How are you, Joyce, darling?' he said to the child. 'Does your knee hurt you? Does it hurt you, dear?'

'It does sometimes.' The child was shy of him, cold towards him.

'Well, dear, I'm sorry for that. I hope you try to bear it, and not trouble mother too much.'

There was no answer. He looked at the knee. It was red and stiff.

'Of course,' he said, 'I think we must have another doctor's opinion. And if we're going to have it, we had better have it at once. Egbert, do you think you might cycle in to Bingham for Doctor Wayne? I found him *very* satisfactory for Winnie's mother.'

'I can go if you think it necessary,' said Egbert.

'Certainly I think it necessary. Even if there *is* nothing, we can have peace of mind. Certainly I think it necessary. I should like Doctor Wayne to come this evening if possible.'

So Egbert set off on his bicycle through the wind, like a boy sent on an errand, leaving his father-in-law a pillar of assurance, with Winifred.

Doctor Wayne came, and looked grave. Yes, the knee was certainly taking the wrong way. The child might be lame for life.

Up went the fire of fear and anger in every heart. Doctor Wayne came again the next day for a proper examination. And, yes, the knee had really taken bad ways. It should be X-rayed. It was very important.

Godfrey Marshall walked up and down the lane with the doctor, beside the standing motor-car: up and down, up and down in one of those consultations of which he had had so many in his life.

As a result he came indoors to Winifred.

'Well, Winnie, dear, the best thing to do is to take Joyce up to London, to a nursing home where she can have proper treatment. Of course this knee has been allowed to go wrong. And apparently there is a risk that the child may even lose her leg. What do you think, dear? You agree to our taking her up to town and putting her under the best care?'

'Oh, father, you *know* I would do anything on earth for her.'

'I know you would, Winnie darling. The pity is that there has been this unfortunate delay already. I can't think what Doctor Wing was doing. Apparently the child is in danger of losing her leg. Well then, if you will have everything ready, we will take her up to town tomorrow. I will order the large car from Denley's to be here at ten.

Egbert, will you take a telegram at once to Doctor Jackson? It is a small nursing home for children and for surgical cases, not far from Baker Street. I'm sure Joyce will be all right there.'

'Oh, father, can't I nurse her myself!'

'Well, darling, if she is to have proper treatment, she had best be in a home. The X-ray treatment, and the electric treatment, and whatever is necessary.'

'It will cost a great deal –' said Winifred.

'We can't think of cost, if the child's leg is in danger – or even her life. No use speaking of cost,' said the elder man impatiently.

And so it was. Poor Joyce, stretched out on a bed in the big closed motor-car – the mother sitting by her head, the grandfather in his short grey beard and a bowler hat, sitting by her feet, thick, and implacable in his responsibility, – they rolled slowly away from Crockham, and from Egbert who stood there bareheaded and a little ignominious, left behind. He was to shut up the house and bring the rest of the family back to town, by train, the next day.

Followed a dark and bitter time. The poor child. The poor, poor child, how she suffered, an agony and a long crucifixion in that nursing home. It was a bitter six weeks which changed the soul of Winifred for ever. As she sat by the bed of her poor, tortured little child, tortured with the agony of the knee, and the still worse agony of these diabolic, but perhaps necessary modern treatments, she felt her heart killed and going cold in her breast. Her little Joyce, her frail, brave, wonderful, little Joyce, frail and small and pale as a white flower! Ah, how had she, Winifred, dared to be so wicked, so wicked, so careless, so sensual.

'Let my heart die! Let my woman's heart of flesh die! Saviour, let my heart die. And save my child. Let my heart die from the world and from the flesh. Oh, destroy my heart that is so wayward. Let my heart of pride die. Let my heart die.'

So she prayed beside the bed of her child. And like the Mother with the seven swords in her breast,[7] slowly her heart of pride and passion died in her breast, bleeding away. Slowly it died, bleeding away, and she turned to the Church for comfort, to Jesus, to the Mother of God, but most of all, to that great and enduring institution, the Roman Catholic Church. She withdrew into the shadow of the Church. She was a mother with three children. But in her soul she died, her heart of pride and passion and desire bled to death, her soul belonged to her church, her body belonged to her duty as a mother.

Her duty as a wife did not enter. As a wife she had no sense of duty:

only a certain bitterness towards the man with whom she had known such sensuality and distraction. She was purely the *Mater Dolorata*. To the man she was closed as a tomb.

Egbert came to see his child. But Winifred seemed to be always seated there, like the tomb of his manhood and his fatherhood. Poor Winifred: she was still young, still strong and ruddy and beautiful like a ruddy hard flower of the field. Strange – her ruddy, healthy face, so sombre, and her strong, heavy, full-blooded body, so still. She, a nun! Never. And yet the gates of her heart and soul had shut in his face with a slow, resonant clang, shutting him out for ever. There was no need for her to go into a convent. Her will had done it.

And between this young mother and this young father lay the child, like a bit of pale silk floss on the pillow, and a little white pain-quenched face. He could not bear it. He just could not bear it. He turned aside. There was nothing to do but to turn aside. He turned aside, and went hither and thither, desultory. He was still attractive and desirable. But there was a little frown between his brow as if he had been cleft there with a hatchet: cleft right in, for ever, and that was the stigma.

The child's leg was saved: but the knee was locked stiff. The fear now was lest the lower leg should wither, or cease to grow. There must be long-continued massage and treatment, daily treatment, even when the child left the nursing home. And the whole of the expense was borne by the grandfather.

Egbert now had no real home. Winifred with the children and nurse was tied to the little flat in London. He could not live there: he could not contain himself. The cottage was shut-up – or lent to friends. He went down sometimes to work in his garden and keep the place in order. Then with the empty house around him at night, all the empty rooms, he felt his heart go wicked. The sense of frustration and futility, like some slow, torpid snake, slowly bit right through his heart. Futility, futility, futility: the horrible marsh-poison went through his veins and killed him.

As he worked in the garden in the silence of day he would listen for a sound. No sound. No sound of Winifred from the dark inside of the cottage: no sound of children's voices from the air, from the common, from the near distance. No sound, nothing but the old dark marsh-venomous atmosphere of the place. So he worked spasmodically through the day, and at night made a fire and cooked some food alone.

He was alone. He himself cleaned the cottage and made his bed. But his mending he did not do. His shirts were slit on the shoulders, when he had been working, and the white flesh showed through. He would feel the air and the spots of rain on his exposed flesh. And he would look again across the common, where the dark, tufted gorse was dying to seed, and the bits of cat-heather were coming pink in tufts, like a sprinkling of sacrificial blood.

His heart went back to the savage old spirit of the place: the desire for old gods, old, lost passions, the passion of the cold-blooded, darting snakes that hissed and shot away from him, the mystery of blood-sacrifices, all the lost, intense sensations of the primeval people of the place, whose passions seethed in the air still, from those long days before the Romans came. The seethe of a lost, dark passion in the air. The presence of unseen snakes.

A queer, baffled, half-wicked look came on his face. He could not stay long at the cottage. Suddenly he must swing on to his bicycle and go – anywhere. Anywhere, away from this place. He would stay a few days with his mother in the old home. His mother adored him and grieved as a mother would. But the little, baffled, half-wicked smile curled on his face, and he swung away from his mother's solicitude as from everything else.

Always moving on – from place to place, friend to friend: and always swinging away from sympathy. As soon as sympathy, like a soft hand, was reached out to touch him, away he swerved, instinctively, as a harmless snake swerves and swerves and swerves away from an outstretched hand. Away he must go. And periodically he went back to Winifred.

He was terrible to her now, like a temptation. She had devoted herself to her children and her church. Joyce was once more on her feet; but, alas! lame, with iron supports to her leg, and a little crutch. It was strange how she had grown into a long, pallid, wild little thing. Strange that the pain had not made her soft and docile, but had brought out a wild, almost mænad temper in the child. She was seven, and long and white and thin, but by no means subdued. Her blonde hair was darkening. She still had long sufferings to face, and, in her own childish consciousness, the stigma of her lameness to bear.

And she bore it. An almost mænad courage seemed to possess her, as if she were a long, thin, young weapon of life. She acknowledged all her mother's care. She would stand by her mother for ever. But some of her father's fine-tempered desperation flashed in her.

When Egbert saw his little girl limping horribly – not only limping but lurching horribly in crippled, childish way, his heart again hardened with chagrin, like steel that is tempered again. There was a tacit understanding between him and his little girl: not what we would call love, but a weapon-like kinship. There was a tiny touch of irony in his manner towards her, contrasting sharply with Winifred's heavy, unleavened solicitude and care. The child flickered back to him with an answering little smile of irony and recklessness: an odd flippancy which made Winifred only the more sombre and earnest.

The Marshalls took endless thought and trouble for the child, searching out every means to save her limb and her active freedom. They spared no effort and no money, they spared no strength of will. With all their slow, heavy power of will they willed that Joyce should save her liberty of movement, should win back her wild, free grace. Even if it took a long time to recover, it should be recovered.

So the situation stood. And Joyce submitted, week after week, month after month, to the tyranny and pain of the treatment. She acknowledged the honourable effort on her behalf. But her flamy reckless spirit was her father's. It was he who had all the glamour for her. He and she were like members of some forbidden secret society who know one another but may not recognize one another. Knowledge they had in common, the same secret of life, the father and the child. But the child stayed in the camp of her mother, honourably, and the father wandered outside like Ishmael,[8] only coming sometimes to sit in the home for an hour or two, an evening or two beside the camp fire, like Ishmael, in a curious silence and tension, with the mocking answer of the desert speaking out of his silence, and annulling the whole convention of the domestic home.

His presence was almost an anguish to Winifred. She prayed against it. That little cleft between his brow, that flickering, wicked, little smile that seemed to haunt his face, and above all, the triumphant loneliness, the Ishmael quality. And then the erectness of his supple body, like a symbol. The very way he stood, so quiet, so insidious, like an erect, supple symbol of life, the living body, confronting her downcast soul, was torture to her. He was like a supple living idol moving before her eyes, and she felt if she watched him she was damned.

And he came and made himself at home in her little home. When he was there, moving in his own quiet way, she felt as if the whole great law of sacrifice, by which she had elected to live, were annulled. He annulled by his very presence the laws of her life. And what did he substitute? Ah, against that question she hardened herself in recoil.

It was awful to her to have to have him about – moving about in his shirt-sleeves, speaking in his tenor, throaty voice to the children.

Annabel simply adored him, and he teased the little girl. The baby, Barbara, was not sure of him. She had been born a stranger to him. But even the nurse, when she saw his white shoulder of flesh through the slits of his torn shirt, thought it a shame.

Winifred felt it was only another weapon of his against her.

'You have other shirts – why do you wear that old one that is all torn, Egbert?' she said.

'I may as well wear it out,' he said subtly.

He knew she would not offer to mend it for him. She *could* not. And no, she would not. Had she not her own gods to honour? And could she betray them, submitting to his Baal and Ashtaroth?[9] And it was terrible to her, his unsheathed presence, that seemed to annul her and her faith, like another revelation. Like a gleaming idol evoked against her, a vivid life-idol that might triumph.

He came and he went – and she persisted. And then the great war broke out. He was a man who could not go to the dogs. He could not dissipate himself. He was pure-bred in his Englishness, and even when he would have liked to be vicious, he could not.

So when the war broke out his whole instinct was against it: against war. He had not the faintest desire to overcome any foreigners or to help in their death. He had no conception of Imperial England, and Rule Britannia was just a joke to him. He was a pure-blooded Englishman, perfect in his race, and when he was truly himself he could no more have been aggressive on the score of his Englishness than a rose can be aggressive on the score of its rosiness.

No, he had no desire to defy Germany and to exalt England. The distinction between German and English was not for him the distinction between good and bad. It was the distinction between blue water-flowers and red or white bush-blossoms: just difference. The difference between the wild boar and the wild bear. And a man was good or bad according to his nature, not according to his nationality.

Egbert was well-bred, and this was part of his natural understanding. It was merely unnatural to him to hate a nation *en bloc*. Certain individuals he disliked, and others he liked, and the mass he knew nothing about. Certain deeds he disliked, certain deeds seemed natural to him, and about most deeds he had no particular feeling.

He had, however, the one deepest pure-bred instinct. He recoiled inevitably from having his feelings dictated to him by the mass feeling. His feelings were his own, his understanding was his own, and he would never go back on either, willingly. Shall a man become inferior to his own true knowledge and self, just because the mob expects it of him?

What Egbert felt subtly and without question, his father-in-law felt also in a rough, more combative way. Different as the two men were, they were two real Englishmen, and their instincts were almost the same.

And Godfrey Marshall had the world to reckon with. There was German military aggression, and the English non-military idea of liberty and the 'conquests of peace' – meaning industrialism. Even if the choice between militarism and industrialism were a choice of evils, the elderly man asserted his choice of the latter, perforce. He whose soul was quick with the instinct of power.

Egbert just refused to reckon with the world. He just refused to decide between German militarism and British industrialism. He chose neither. As for atrocities, he despised the people who committed them, as inferior criminal types. There was nothing national about crime.

And yet, war! War! Just war! Not right or wrong, but just war itself. Should he join? Should he give himself over to war? The question was in his mind for some weeks. Not because he thought England was right and Germany wrong. Probably Germany was wrong, but he refused to make a choice. Not because he felt inspired. No. But just – war.

The deterrent was, the giving himself over into the power of other men, and into the power of the mob-spirit of a democratic army. Should he give himself over? Should he make over his own life and body to the control of something which he *knew* was inferior, in spirit, to his own self? Should he commit himself into the power of an inferior control? Should he? Should he betray himself?

He was going to put himself into the power of his inferiors, and he knew it. He was going to subjugate himself. He was going to be ordered about by petty *canaille*[10] of non-commissioned officers – and even commissioned officers. He who was born and bred free. Should he do it?

He went to his wife, to speak to her.

'Shall I join up, Winifred?'

She was silent. Her instinct also was dead against it. And yet a certain profound resentment made her answer:

'You have three children dependent on you. I don't know whether you have thought of that.'

It was still only the third month of the war, and the old pre-war ideas were still alive.

'Of course. But it won't make much difference to them. I shall be earning a shilling a day, at least.'

'You'd better speak to father, I think,' she replied heavily.

Egbert went to his father-in-law. The elderly man's heart was full of resentment.

'I should say,' he said rather sourly, 'it is the best thing you could do.'

Egbert went and joined up immediately, as a private soldier. He was drafted into the light artillery.

Winifred now had a new duty towards him: the duty of a wife towards a husband who is himself performing his duty towards the world. She loved him still. She would always love him, as far as earthly love went. But it was duty she now lived by. When he came back to her in khaki, a soldier, she submitted to him as a wife. It was her duty. But to his passion she could never again fully submit. Something prevented her, for ever: even her own deepest choice.

He went back again to camp. It did not suit him to be a modern soldier. In the thick, gritty, hideous khaki his subtle physique was extinguished as if he had been killed. In the ugly intimacy of the camp his thoroughbred sensibilities were just degraded. But he had chosen, so he accepted. An ugly little look came on to his face, of a man who has accepted his own degradation.

In the early spring Winifred went down to Crockham to be there when primroses were out, and the tassels hanging on the hazel-bushes. She felt something like a reconciliation towards Egbert, now he was a prisoner in camp most of his days. Joyce was wild with delight at seeing the garden and the common again, after the eight or nine months of London and misery. She was still lame. She still had the irons up her leg. But she lurched about with a wild, crippled agility.

Egbert came for a week-end, in his gritty, thick, sandpaper khaki and puttees and the hideous cap. Nay, he looked terrible. And on his face a slightly impure look, a little sore on his lip, as if he had eaten too much or drunk too much or let his blood become a little unclean. He was almost uglily healthy, with the camp life. It did not suit him.

Winifred waited for him in a little passion of duty and sacrifice, willing to serve the soldier, if not the man. It only made him feel a little more ugly inside. The week-end was torment to him: the memory of the camp, the knowledge of the life he led there; even the sight of his own legs in that abhorrent khaki. He felt as if the hideous cloth went into his blood and made it gritty and dirty. Then Winifred so ready to serve the *soldier*, when she repudiated the man. And the children running around playing and calling in the rather mincing fashion of children who have nurses and governesses and literature in the family. And Joyce so lame! It had all become unreal to him, after the camp. It only set his soul on edge. He left at dawn on the Monday morning, glad to get back to the realness and vulgarity of the camp.

Winifred would never meet him again at the cottage – only in London, where the world was with them. But sometimes he came alone to Crockham, perhaps when friends were staying there. And then he would work awhile in his garden. This summer still it would flame with blue anchusas and big red poppies, the mulleins would sway their soft, downy erections in the air: he loved mulleins: and the honeysuckle would stream out scent like memory, when the owl was whooing. Then he sat by the fire with the friends and with Winifred's sisters, and they sang the folk-songs. He put on thin civilian clothes and his charm and his beauty and the supple dominancy of his body glowed out again. But Winifred was not there.

At the end of the summer he went to Flanders, into action. He seemed already to have gone out of life, beyond the pale of life. He hardly remembered his life any more, being like a man who is going to take a jump from a height, and is only looking to where he must land.

He was twice slightly wounded, in two months. But not enough to put him off duty for more than a day or two. They were retiring again, holding the enemy back. He was in the rear – three machine-guns. The country was all pleasant, war had not yet trampled it. Only the air seemed shattered, and the land awaiting death. It was a small, unimportant action in which he was engaged.

The guns were stationed on a little bushy hillock just outside a village. But occasionally, it was difficult to say from which direction came the sharp crackle of rifle-fire, and beyond, the far-off thud of cannon. The afternoon was wintry and cold.

A lieutenant stood on a little iron platform at the top of the ladders, taking the sights and giving the aim, calling in a high, tense, mechanical voice. Out of the sky came the sharp cry of the directions, then the warning numbers, then 'Fire!' The shot went, the piston of the gun sprang back, there was a sharp explosion, and a very faint film of smoke in the air. Then the other two guns fired, and there was a lull. The officer was uncertain of the enemy's position. The thick clump of horse-chestnut trees below was without change. Only in the far distance the sound of heavy firing continued, so far off as to give a sense of peace.

The gorse bushes on either hand were dark, but a few sparks of flowers showed yellow. He noticed them almost unconsciously as he waited, in the lull. He was in his shirt-sleeves, and the air came chill on his arms. Again his shirt was slit on the shoulders, and the flesh showed through. He was dirty and unkempt. But his face was quiet. So many things go out of consciousness before we come to the end of consciousness.

Before him, below, was the highroad, running between high banks of grass and gorse. He saw the whitish, muddy tracks and deep scores in the road, where the part of the regiment had retired. Now all was still. Sounds that came, came from the outside. The place where he stood was still silent, chill, serene: the white church among the trees beyond seemed like a thought only.

He moved into a lightning-like mechanical response at the sharp cry from the officer overhead. Mechanism, the pure mechanical action of obedience at the guns. Pure mechanical action at the guns. It left the soul unburdened, brooding in dark nakedness. In the end, the soul is alone, brooding on the face of the uncreated flux, as a bird on a dark sea.

Nothing could be seen but the road, and a crucifix knocked slanting and the dark, autumnal fields and woods. There appeared three horsemen on a little eminence, very small, on the crest of a ploughed field. They were our own men. Of the enemy, nothing.

The lull continued. Then suddenly came sharp orders, and a new direction of the guns, and an intense, exciting activity. Yet at the centre the soul remained dark and aloof, alone.

But even so, it was the soul that heard the new sound: the new, deep 'papp!' of a gun that seemed to touch right upon the soul. He kept up the rapid activity at the machine-gun, sweating. But in his soul was the echo of the new, deep sound, deeper than life.

And in confirmation came the awful faint whistling of a shell, advancing almost suddenly into a piercing, tearing shriek that would tear through the membrane of life. He heard it in his ears, but he heard it also in his soul, in tension. There was relief when the thing had swung by and struck, away beyond. He heard the hoarseness of its explosion, and the voice of the soldier calling to the horses. But he did not turn round to look. He only noticed a twig of holly with red berries fall like a gift on to the road below.

Not this time, not this time. Whither thou goest I will go.[11] Did he say it to the shell, or to whom? Whither thou goest I will go. Then, the faint whistling of another shell dawned, and his blood became small and still to receive it. It drew nearer, like some horrible blast of wind; his blood lost consciousness. But in the second of suspension he saw the heavy shell swoop to earth, into the rocky bushes on the right, and earth and stones poured up into the sky. It was as if he heard no sound. The earth and stones and fragments of bush fell to earth again, and there was the same unchanging peace. The Germans had got the aim.

Would they move now? Would they retire? Yes. The officer was giving the last lightning-rapid orders to fire before withdrawing. A shell passed unnoticed in the rapidity of action. And then, into the silence, into the suspense where the soul brooded, finally crashed a noise and a darkness and a moment's flaming agony and horror. Ah, he had seen the dark bird flying towards him, flying home this time. In one instant life and eternity went up in a conflagration of agony, then there was a weight of darkness.

When faintly something began to struggle in the darkness, a consciousness of himself, he was aware of a great load and a clanging sound. To have known the moment of death! And to be forced, before dying, to review it. So, fate, even in death.

There was a resounding of pain. It seemed to sound from the outside of his consciousness: like a loud bell clanging very near. Yet he knew it was himself. He must associate himself with it. After a lapse and a new effort, he identified a pain in his head, a large pain that clanged and resounded. So far he could identify himself with himself. Then there was a lapse.

After a time he seemed to wake up again, and waking, to know that he was at the front, and that he was killed. He did not open his eyes. Light was not yet his. The clanging pain in his head rang out the rest of his consciousness. So he lapsed away from consciousness, in unutterable sick abandon of life.

Bit by bit, like a doom, came the necessity to know. He was hit in the head. It was only a vague surmise at first. But in the swinging of the pendulum of pain, swinging ever nearer and nearer, to touch him into an agony of consciousness and a consciousness of agony, gradually the knowledge emerged – he must be hit in the head – hit on the left brow; if so, there would be blood – was there blood? – could he feel blood in his left eye? Then the clanging seemed to burst the membrane of his brain, like death-madness.

Was there blood on his face? Was hot blood flowing? Or was it dry blood congealing down his cheek? It took him hours even to ask the question: time being no more than an agony in darkness, without measurement.

A long time after he had opened his eyes he realised he was seeing something – something, something, but the effort to recall what was too great. No, no; no recall!

Were they the stars in the dark sky? Was it possible it was stars in the dark sky? Stars? The world? Ah, no, he could not know it! Stars and the world were gone for him, he closed his eyes. No stars, no sky, no world. No. No! The thick darkness of blood alone. It should be one great lapse into the thick darkness of blood in agony.

Death, oh, death! The world all blood, and the blood all writhing with death. The soul like the tiniest little light out on a dark sea, the sea of blood. And the light guttering, beating, pulsing in a windless storm, wishing it could go out, yet unable.

There had been life. There had been Winifred and his children. But the frail death-agony effort to catch at straws of memory, straws of life from the past, brought on too great a nausea. No, no! No Winifred, no children. No world, no people. Better the agony of dissolution ahead than the nausea of the effort backwards. Better the terrible work should go forward, the dissolving into the black sea of death, in the extremity of dissolution, than that there should be any reaching back towards life. To forget! To forget! Utterly, utterly to forget, in the great forgetting of death. To break the core and the unit of life, and to lapse out on the great darkness. Only that. To break the clue, and mingle and commingle with the one darkness, without afterwards or forwards. Let the black sea of death itself solve the problem of futurity. Let the will of man break and give up.

What was that? A light! A terrible light! Was it figures? Was it legs of a horse colossal – colossal above him: huge, huge?

The Germans heard a slight noise, and started. Then, in the glare of a light-bomb, by the side of the heap of earth thrown up by the shell, they saw the dead face.

The Horse Dealer's Daughter

'WELL, Mabel, and what are you going to do with yourself?' asked Joe, with foolish flippancy. He felt quite safe himself. Without listening for an answer, he turned aside, worked a grain of tobacco to the tip of his tongue, and spat it out. He did not care about anything, since he felt safe himself.

The three brothers and the sister sat round the desolate breakfast table, attempting some sort of desultory consultation. The morning's post had given the final tap to the family fortunes, and all was over. The dreary dining-room itself, with its heavy mahogany furniture, looked as if it were waiting to be done away with.

But the consultation amounted to nothing. There was a strange air of ineffectuality about the three men, as they sprawled at table, smoking and reflecting vaguely on their own condition. The girl was alone, a rather short, sullen-looking young woman of twenty-seven. She did not share the same life as her brothers. She would have been good-looking, save for the impassive fixity of her face, 'bull-dog', as her brothers called it.

There was a confused tramping of horses' feet outside. The three men all sprawled round in their chairs to watch. Beyond the dark holly-bushes that separated the strip of lawn from the highroad, they could see a cavalcade of shire horses swinging out of their own yard, being taken for exercise. This was the last time. These were the last horses that would go through their hands. The young men watched with critical, callous look. They were all frightened at the collapse of their lives, and the sense of disaster in which they were involved left them no inner freedom.

Yet they were three fine, well-set fellows enough. Joe, the eldest, was a man of thirty-three, broad and handsome in a hot, flushed way. His face was red, he twisted his black moustache over a thick finger, his eyes were shallow and restless. He had a sensual way of uncovering his teeth when he laughed, and his bearing was stupid. Now he watched the horses with a glazed look of helplessness in his eyes, a certain stupor of downfall.

The great draught-horses swung past. They were tied head to tail, four of them, and they heaved along to where a lane branched off from the highroad, planting their great hoofs floutingly in the fine black mud, swinging their great rounded haunches sumptuously, and trotting a few sudden steps as they were led into the lane, round the corner. Every movement showed a massive, slumbrous strength, and a stupidity which held them in subjection. The groom at the head looked back, jerking the leading rope. And the cavalcade moved out of sight up the lane, the tail of the last horse, bobbed up tight and stiff, held out taut from the swinging great haunches as they rocked behind the hedges in a motion-like sleep.

Joe watched with glazed hopeless eyes. The horses were almost like his own body to him. He felt he was done for now. Luckily he was engaged to a woman as old as himself, and therefore her father, who was steward of a neighbouring estate, would provide him with a job. He would marry and go into harness. His life was over, he would be a subject animal now.

He turned uneasily aside, the retreating steps of the horses echoing in his ears. Then, with foolish restlessness, he reached for the scraps of bacon-rind from the plates, and making a faint whistling sound, flung them to the terrier that lay against the fender. He watched the dog swallow them, and waited till the creature looked into his eyes. Then a faint grin came on his face, and in a high, foolish voice he said:

'You won't get much more bacon, shall you, you little b—?'

The dog faintly and dismally wagged its tail, then lowered its haunches, circled round, and lay down again.

There was another helpless silence at the table. Joe sprawled uneasily in his seat, not willing to go till the family conclave was dissolved. Fred Henry, the second brother, was erect, clean-limbed, alert. He had watched the passing of the horses with more *sang-froid*.[1] If he was an animal, like Joe, he was an animal which controls, not one which is controlled. He was master of any horse, and he carried himself with a well-tempered air of mastery. But he was not master of the situations of life. He pushed his coarse brown moustache upwards, off his lip, and glanced irritably at his sister, who sat impassive and inscrutable.

'You'll go and stop with Lucy for a bit, shan't you?' he asked. The girl did not answer.

'I don't see what else you can do,' persisted Fred Henry.

'Go as a skivvy,' Joe interpolated laconically.

The girl did not move a muscle.

'If I was her, I should go in for training for a nurse,' said Malcolm, the youngest of them all. He was the baby of the family, a young man of twenty-two, with a fresh, jaunty *museau.*[2]

But Mabel did not take any notice of him. They had talked at her and round her for so many years, that she hardly heard them at all.

The marble clock on the mantel-piece softly chimed the half-hour, the dog rose uneasily from the hearthrug and looked at the party at the breakfast table. But still they sat on in ineffectual conclave.

'Oh, all right,' said Joe suddenly, *à propos* of nothing. 'I'll get a move on.'

He pushed back his chair, straddled his knees with a downward jerk, to get them free, in horsey fashion, and went to the fire. Still he did not go out of the room; he was curious to know what the others would do or say. He began to charge his pipe, looking down at the dog and saying, in a high, affected voice:

'Going wi' me? Going wi' me are ter? Tha'rt goin' further than tha counts on just now, dost hear?'

The dog faintly wagged its tail, the man stuck out his jaw and covered his pipe with his hands, and puffed intently, losing himself in the tobacco, looking down all the while at the dog with an absent brown eye. The dog looked up at him in mournful distrust. Joe stood with his knees stuck out, in real horsey fashion.

'Have you had a letter from Lucy?' Fred Henry asked of his sister.

'Last week,' came the neutral reply.

'And what does she say?'

There was no answer.

'Does she *ask* you to go and stop there?' persisted Fred Henry.

'She says I can if I like.'

'Well, then, you'd better. Tell her you'll come on Monday.'

This was received in silence.

'That's what you'll do then, is it?' said Fred Henry, in some exasperation.

But she made no answer. There was a silence of futility and irritation in the room. Malcolm grinned fatuously.

'You'll have to make up your mind between now and next Wednesday,' said Joe loudly, 'or else find yourself lodgings on the kerbstone.'

The face of the young woman darkened, but she sat on immutable.

'Here's Jack Fergusson!' exclaimed Malcolm, who was looking aimlessly out of the window.

'Where?' exclaimed Joe, loudly.

'Just gone past.'

'Coming in?'

Malcolm craned his neck to see the gate.

'Yes,' he said.

There was a silence. Mabel sat on like one condemned, at the head of the table. Then a whistle was heard from the kitchen. The dog got up and barked sharply. Joe opened the door and shouted:

'Come on.'

After a moment a young man entered. He was muffled up in overcoat and a purple woollen scarf, and his tweed cap, which he did not remove, was pulled down on his head. He was of medium height, his face was rather long and pale, his eyes looked tired.

'Hello, Jack! Well, Jack!' exclaimed Malcolm and Joe. Fred Henry merely said, 'Jack.'

'What's doing?' asked the newcomer, evidently addressing Fred Henry.

'Same. We've got to be out by Wednesday. – Got a cold?'

'I have – got it bad, too.'

'Why don't you stop in?'

'*Me* stop in? When I can't stand on my legs, perhaps I shall have a chance.' The young man spoke huskily. He had a slight Scotch accent.

'It's a knock-out, isn't it,' said Joe, boisterously, 'if a doctor goes round croaking with a cold. Looks bad for the patients, doesn't it?'

The young doctor looked at him slowly.

'Anything the matter with *you*, then?' he asked sarcastically.

'Not as I know of. Damn your eyes, I hope not. Why?'

'I thought you were very concerned about the patients, wondered if you might be one yourself.'

'Damn it, no, I've never been patient to no flaming doctor, and hope I never shall be,' returned Joe.

At this point Mabel rose from the table, and they all seemed to become aware of her existence. She began putting the dishes together. The young doctor looked at her, but did not address her. He had not greeted her. She went out of the room with the tray, her face impassive and unchanged.

'When are you off then, all of you?' asked the doctor.

'I'm catching the eleven-forty,' replied Malcolm. 'Are you goin' down wi' th' trap, Joe?'

'Yes, I've told you I'm going down wi' th' trap, haven't I?'

'We'd better be getting her in then. – So long, Jack, if I don't see you before I go,' said Malcolm, shaking hands.

He went out, followed by Joe, who seemed to have his tail between his legs.

'Well, this is the devil's own,' exclaimed the doctor, when he was left alone with Fred Henry. 'Going before Wednesday, are you?'

'That's the orders,' replied the other.

'Where, to Northampton?'

'That's it.'

'The devil!' exclaimed Fergusson, with quiet chagrin.

And there was silence between the two.

'All settled up, are you?' asked Fergusson.

'About.'

There was another pause.

'Well, I shall miss yer, Freddy, boy,' said the young doctor.

'And I shall miss thee, Jack,' returned the other.

'Miss you like hell,' mused the doctor.

Fred Henry turned aside. There was nothing to say. Mabel came in again, to finish clearing the table.

'What are *you* going to do, then, Miss Pervin?' asked Fergusson. 'Going to your sister's, are you?'

Mabel looked at him with her steady, dangerous eyes, that always made him uncomfortable, unsettling his superficial ease.

'No,' she said.

'Well, what in the name of fortune *are* you going to do? Say what you mean to do,' cried Fred Henry, with futile intensity.

But she only averted her head, and continued her work. She folded the white table-cloth, and put on the chenille cloth.

'The sulkiest bitch that ever trod!' muttered her brother.

But she finished her task with perfectly impassive face, the young doctor watching her interestedly all the while. Then she went out.

Fred Henry stared after her, clenching his lips, his blue eyes fixing in sharp antagonism, as he made a grimace of sour exasperation.

'You could bray her into bits, and that's all you'd get out of her,' he said, in a small, narrowed tone.

The doctor smiled faintly.

'What's she *going* to do, then?' he asked.

'Strike me if *I* know!' returned the other.

There was a pause. Then the doctor stirred.

'I'll be seeing you to-night, shall I?' he said to his friend.

'Ay – where's it to be? Are we going over to Jessdale?'

'I don't know. I've got such a cold on me. I'll come round to the Moon and Stars, anyway.'

'Let Lizzie and May miss their night for once, eh?'

'That's it – if I feel as I do now.'

'All's one –'

The two young men went through the passage and down to the back door together. The house was large, but it was servantless now, and desolate. At the back was a small bricked house-yard, and beyond that a big square, gravelled fine and red, and having stables on two sides. Sloping, dank, winter-dark fields stretched away on the open sides.

But the stables were empty. Joseph Pervin, the father of the family, had been a man of no education, who had become a fairly large horse dealer. The stables had been full of horses, there was a great turmoil and come-and-go of horses and of dealers and grooms. Then the kitchen was full of servants. But of late things had declined. The old man had married a second time, to retrieve his fortunes. Now he was dead and everything was gone to the dogs, there was nothing but debt and threatening.

For months, Mabel had been servantless in the big house, keeping the home together in penury for her ineffectual brothers. She had kept house for ten years. But previously, it was with unstinted means. Then, however brutal and coarse everything was, the sense of money had kept her proud, confident. The men might be foul-mouthed, the women in the kitchen might have bad reputations, her brothers might have illegitimate children. But so long as there was money, the girl felt herself established, and brutally proud, reserved.

No company came to the house, save dealers and coarse men. Mabel had no associates of her own sex, after her sister went away. But she did not mind. She went regularly to church, she attended to her father. And she lived in the memory of her mother, who had died when she was fourteen, and whom she had loved. She had loved her father, too, in a different way, depending upon him, and feeling secure in him, until at the age of fifty-four he married again. And then she had set hard against him. Now he had died and left them all hopelessly in debt.

She had suffered badly during the period of poverty. Nothing, however, could shake the curious sullen, animal pride that dominated each member of the family. Now, for Mabel, the end had come. Still she would not cast about her. She would follow her own way just the same. She would always hold the keys of her own situation. Mindless and persistent, she endured from day to day. Why should she think? Why should she answer anybody? It was enough that this was the end, and there was no way out. She need not pass any more darkly along the main street of the small town, avoiding every eye. She need not demean herself any more, going into the shops and buying the cheapest food. This was at an end. She thought of nobody, not even of herself. Mindless and persistent, she seemed in a sort of ecstasy to be coming nearer to her fulfilment, her own glorification, approaching her dead mother, who was glorified.

In the afternoon she took a little bag, with shears and sponge and a small scrubbing brush, and went out. It was a grey, wintry day, with saddened, dark-green fields and an atmosphere blackened by the smoke of foundries not far off. She went quickly, darkly along the causeway, heeding nobody, through the town to the churchyard.

There she always felt secure, as if no one could see her, although as a matter of fact she was exposed to the stare of everyone who passed along under the churchyard wall. Nevertheless, once under the shadow of the great looming church, among the graves, she felt immune from the world, reserved within the thick churchyard wall as in another country.

Carefully she clipped the grass from the grave, and arranged the pinky-white, small chrysanthemums in the tin cross. When this was done, she took an empty jar from a neighbouring grave, brought water, and carefully, most scrupulously sponged the marble headstone and the coping-stone.

It gave her sincere satisfaction to do this. She felt in immediate contact with the world of her mother. She took minute pains, went through the park in a state bordering on pure happiness, as if in performing this task she came into a subtle, intimate connection with her mother. For the life she followed here in the world was far less real than the world of death she inherited from her mother.

The doctor's house was just by the church. Fergusson, being a mere hired assistant, was slave to the countryside. As he hurried now to attend to the outpatients in the surgery, glancing across the graveyard with his quick eye, he saw the girl at her task at the grave. She seemed so intent and remote, it was like looking into another world. Some mystical element was touched in him. He slowed down as he walked, watching her as if spell-bound.

She lifted her eyes, feeling him looking. Their eyes met. And each looked again at once, each feeling, in some way, found out by the other. He lifted his cap and passed on down the road. There remained distinct in his consciousness, like a vision, the memory of her face, lifted from the tombstone in the churchyard, and looking at him with slow, large, portentous eyes. It *was* portentous, her face. It seemed to mesmerise him. There was a heavy power in her eyes which laid hold of his whole being, as if he had drunk some powerful drug. He had been feeling weak and done before. Now the life came back into him, he felt delivered from his own fretted, daily self.

He finished his duties at the surgery as quickly as might be, hastily filling up the bottles of the waiting people with cheap drugs. Then, in perpetual haste, he set off again to visit several cases in another part of his round, before teatime. At all times he preferred to walk, if he could, but particularly when he was not well. He fancied the motion restored him.

The afternoon was falling. It was grey, deadened, and wintry, with a slow, moist, heavy coldness sinking in and deadening all the faculties. But why should he think or notice? He hastily climbed the hill and turned across the dark-green fields, following the black cinder-track. In the distance, across a shallow dip in the country, the small town was clustered like smouldering ash, a tower, a spire, a heap of low, raw, extinct houses. And on the nearest fringe of the town, sloping into the dip, was Oldmeadow, the Pervins' house. He could see the stables and the outbuildings distinctly, as they lay towards him on the slope. Well, he would not go there many more times! Another resource would be lost to him, another place gone: the only company he cared for in the alien, ugly little town he was losing. Nothing but work, drudgery, constant hastening from dwelling to dwelling among the colliers and the iron-workers. It wore him out, but at the same time he had a craving for it. It was a stimulant to him to be in the homes of the working people, moving as it were through the innermost body of their life. His nerves were excited and gratified. He could come so near, into the very lives of the rough, inarticulate, powerfully emotional men and women. He grumbled, he said he hated the hellish hole. But as a matter of fact it excited him, the contact with the rough, strongly-feeling people was a stimulant applied direct to his nerves.

Below Oldmeadow, in the green, shallow, soddened hollow of fields, lay a square, deep pond. Roving across the landscape, the doctor's quick eye detected a figure in black passing through the gate of the field, down towards the pond. He looked again. It would be Mabel Pervin. His mind suddenly became alive and attentive.

Why was she going down there? He pulled up on the path on the slope above, and stood staring. He could just make sure of the small black figure moving in the hollow of the failing day. He seemed to see her in the midst of such obscurity, that he was like a clairvoyant, seeing rather with the mind's eye than with ordinary sight. Yet he could see her positively enough, whilst he kept his eye attentive. He felt, if he looked away from her, in the thick, ugly falling dusk, he would lose her altogether.

He followed her minutely as she moved, direct and intent, like something transmitted rather than stirring in voluntary activity, straight down the field towards the pond. There she stood on the bank for a moment. She never raised her head. Then she waded slowly into the water.

He stood motionless as the small black figure walked slowly and deliberately towards the centre of the pond, very slowly, gradually moving deeper into the motionless water, and still moving forward as the water got up to her breast. Then he could see her no more in the dusk of the dead afternoon.

'There!' he exclaimed. 'Would you believe it?'

And he hastened straight down, running over the wet, soddened fields, pushing through the hedges, down into the depression of callous wintry obscurity. It took him several minutes to come to the pond. He stood on the bank, breathing heavily. He could see nothing. His eyes seemed to penetrate the dead water. Yes, perhaps that was the dark shadow of her black clothing beneath the surface of the water.

He slowly ventured into the pond. The bottom was deep, soft clay, he sank in, and the water clasped dead cold round his legs. As he stirred he could smell the cold, rotten clay that fouled up into the water. It was objectionable in his lungs. Still, repelled and yet not heeding, he moved deeper into the pond. The cold water rose over his thighs, over his loins, upon his abdomen. The lower part of his body was all sunk in the hideous cold element. And the bottom was so deeply soft and uncertain, he was afraid of pitching with his mouth underneath. He could not swim, and was afraid.

He crouched a little, spreading his hands under the water and moving them round, trying to feel for her. The dead cold pond swayed upon his chest. He moved again, a little deeper, and again, with his hands underneath, he felt all around under the water. And he touched her clothing. But it evaded his fingers. He made a desperate effort to grasp it.

And so doing he lost his balance and went under, horribly, suffocating in the foul earthy water, struggling madly for a few moments. At last, after what seemed an eternity, he got his footing, rose again into the air and looked around. He gasped, and knew he was in the world. Then he looked at the water. She had risen near him. He grasped her clothing, and drawing her nearer, turned to take his way to land again.

He went very slowly, carefully, absorbed in the slow progress. He rose higher, climbing out of the pond. The water was now only about his legs; he was thankful, full of relief to be out of the clutches of the pond. He lifted her and staggered on to the bank, out of the horror of wet, grey clay.

He laid her down on the bank. She was quite unconscious and running with water. He made the water come from her mouth, he worked to restore her. He did not have to work very long before he could feel the breathing begin again in her; she was breathing naturally. He worked a little longer. He could feel her live beneath his hands; she was coming back. He wiped her face, wrapped her in his overcoat, looked round into the dim, dark-grey world, then lifted her and staggered down the bank and across the fields.

It seemed an unthinkably long way, and his burden so heavy he felt he would never get to the house. But at last he was in the stable-yard, and then in the house-yard. He opened the door and went into the house. In the kitchen he laid her down on the hearthrug, and called. The house was empty. But the fire was burning in the grate.

Then again he kneeled to attend to her. She was breathing regularly, her eyes were wide open and as if conscious, but there seemed something missing in her look. She was conscious in herself, but unconscious of her surroundings.

He ran upstairs, took blankets from a bed, and put them before the fire to warm. Then he removed her saturated, earthy-smelling clothing, rubbed her dry with a towel, and wrapped her naked in the blankets. Then he went into the dining room, to look for spirits. There was a little whiskey. He drank a gulp himself, and put some into her mouth.

The effect was instantaneous. She looked full into his face, as if she had been seeing him for some time, and yet had only just become conscious of him.

'Dr Fergusson?' she said.

'What?' he answered.

He was divesting himself of his coat, intending to find some dry clothing upstairs. He could not bear the smell of the dead, clayey water, and he was mortally afraid for his own health.

'What did I do?' she asked.

'Walked into the pond,' he replied. He had begun to shudder like one sick, and could hardly attend to her. Her eyes remained full on him, he seemed to be going dark in his mind, looking back at her helplessly. The shuddering became quieter in him, his life came back in him, dark and unknowing, but strong again.

'Was I out of my mind?' she asked, while her eyes were fixed on him all the time.

'Maybe, for the moment,' he replied. He felt quiet, because his strength had come back. The strange fretful strain had left him.

'Am I out of my mind now?' she asked.

'Are you?' he reflected a moment. 'No,' he answered truthfully, 'I don't see that you are.' He turned his face aside. He was afraid now, because he felt dazed, and felt dimly that her power was stronger than his, in this issue. And she continued to look at him fixedly all the time. 'Can you tell me where I shall find some dry things to put on?' he asked.

'Did you dive into the pond for me?' she asked.

'No,' he answered. 'I walked in. But I went in overhead as well.'

There was silence for a moment. He hesitated. He very much wanted to go upstairs to get into dry clothing. But there was another desire in him. And she seemed to hold him. His will seemed to have gone to sleep, and left him, standing there slack before her. But he felt warm inside himself. He did not shudder at all, though his clothes were sodden on him.

'Why did you?' she asked.

'Because I didn't want you to do such a foolish thing,' he said.

'It wasn't foolish,' she said, still gazing at him as she lay on the floor, with a sofa cushion under her head. 'It was the right thing to do. *I* knew best, then.'

'I'll go and shift these wet things,' he said. But still he had not the power to move out of her presence, until she sent him. It was as if she had the life of his body in her hands, and he could not extricate himself. Or perhaps he did not want to.

Suddenly she sat up. Then she became aware of her own immediate condition. She felt the blankets about her, she knew her own limbs. For a moment it seemed as if her reason were going. She looked round, with wild eye, as if seeking something. He stood still with fear. She saw her clothing lying scattered.

'Who undressed me?' she asked, her eyes resting full and inevitable on his face.

'I did,' he replied, 'to bring you round.'

For some moments she sat and gazed at him awfully, her lips parted.

'Do you love me then?' she asked.

He only stood and stared at her, fascinated. His soul seemed to melt.

She shuffled forward on her knees, and put her arms round him, round his legs, as he stood there, pressing her breasts against his knees and thighs, clutching him with strange, convulsive certainty, pressing his thighs against her, drawing him to her face, her throat, as she looked up at him with flaring, humble eyes of transfiguration, triumphant in first possession.

'You love me,' she murmured, in strange transport, yearning and triumphant and confident. 'You love me. I know you love me, I know.'

And she was passionately kissing his knees, through the wet clothing, passionately and indiscriminately kissing his knees, his legs, as if unaware of everything.

He looked down at the tangled wet hair, the wild, bare, animal shoulders. He was amazed, bewildered, and afraid. He had never thought of loving her. He had never wanted to love her. When he rescued her and restored her, he was a doctor, and she was a patient. He had had no single personal thought of her. Nay, this introduction of the personal element was very distasteful to him, a violation of his professional honour. It was horrible to have her there embracing his knees. It was horrible. He revolted from it, violently. And yet – and yet – he had not the power to break away.

She looked at him again, with the same supplication of powerful love, and that same transcendent, frightening light of triumph. In view of the delicate flame which seemed to come from her face like a light, he was powerless. And yet he had never intended to love her. He had never intended. And something stubborn in him could not give way.

'You love me,' she repeated, in a murmur of deep, rhapsodic assurance. 'You love me.'

Her hands were drawing him, drawing him down to her. He was afraid, even a little horrified. For he had, really, no intention of loving her. Yet her hands were drawing him towards her. He put out his hand quickly to steady himself, and grasped her bare shoulder. A flame seemed to burn the hand that grasped her soft shoulder. He had no intention of loving her: his whole will was against his yielding. It was horrible. And yet wonderful was the touch of her shoulders, beautiful the shining of her face. Was she perhaps mad? He had a horror of yielding to her. Yet something in him ached also.

He had been staring away at the door, away from her. But his hand remained on her shoulder. She had gone suddenly very still. He looked down at her. Her eyes were now wide with fear, with doubt, the light was dying from her face, a shadow of terrible greyness was returning. He could not bear the touch of her eyes' question upon him, and the look of death behind the question.

With an inward groan he gave way, and let his heart yield towards her. A sudden gentle smile came on his face. And her eyes, which never left his face, slowly, slowly filled with tears. He watched the strange water rise in her eyes, like some slow fountain coming up. And his heart seemed to burn and melt away in his breast.

He could not bear to look at her any more. He dropped on his knees and caught her head with his arms and pressed her face against his throat. She was very still. His heart, which seemed to have broken, was burning with a kind of agony in his breast. And he felt her slow, hot tears wetting his throat. But he could not move.

He felt the hot tears wet his neck and the hollows of his neck, and he remained motionless, suspended through one of man's eternities. Only now it had become indispensable to him to have her face pressed close to him; he could never let her go again. He could never let her head go away from the close clutch of his arm. He wanted to remain like that for ever, with his heart hurting him in a pain that was also life to him. Without knowing, he was looking down on her damp, soft brown hair.

Then, as it were suddenly, he smelt the horrid stagnant smell of that water. And at the same moment she drew away from him and looked at him. Her eyes were wistful and unfathomable. He was afraid of them, and he fell to kissing her, not knowing what he was doing. He wanted her eyes not to have that terrible, wistful, unfathomable look.

When she turned her face to him again, a faint delicate flush was glowing, and there was again dawning that terrible shining of joy in her eyes, which really terrified him, and yet which he now wanted to see, because he feared the look of doubt still more.

'You love me?' she said, rather faltering.

'Yes.' The word cost him a painful effort. Not because it wasn't true. But because it was too newly true, the *saying* seemed to tear open again his newly-torn heart. And he hardly wanted it to be true, even now.

She lifted her face to him, and he bent forward and kissed her on the mouth, gently, with the one kiss that is an eternal pledge. And as he kissed her his heart strained again in his breast. He never intended to love her. But now it was over. He had crossed over the gulf to her, and all that he had left behind had shrivelled and become void.

After the kiss, her eyes again slowly filled with tears. She sat still, away from him, with her face drooped aside, and her hands folded in her lap. The tears fell very slowly. There was complete silence. He too sat there motionless and silent on the hearthrug. The strange pain of his heart that was broken seemed to consume him. That he should love her? That this was love! That he should be ripped open in this way! – Him, a doctor! – How they would all jeer if they knew! – It was agony to him to think they might know.

In the curious naked pain of the thought he looked again to her. She was sitting there drooped into a muse. He saw a tear fall, and his heart flared hot. He saw for the first time that one of her shoulders was quite uncovered, one arm bare, he could see one of her small breasts; dimly, because it had become almost dark in the room.

'Why are you crying?' he asked, in an altered voice.

She looked up at him, and behind her tears the consciousness of her situation for the first time brought a dark look of shame to her eyes.

'I'm not crying, really,' she said, watching him half frightened.

He reached his hand, and softly closed it on her bare arm.

'I love you! I love you!' he said in a soft, low vibrating voice, unlike himself.

She shrank, and dropped her head. The soft, penetrating grip of his hand on her arm distressed her. She looked up at him.

'I want to go,' she said. 'I want to go and get you some dry things.'

'Why?' he said. 'I'm all right.'

'But I want to go,' she said. 'And I want you to change your things.'

He released her arm, and she wrapped herself in the blanket, looking at him rather frightened. And still she did not rise.

'Kiss me,' she said wistfully.

He kissed her, but briefly, half in anger.

Then, after a second, she rose nervously, all mixed up in the blanket. He watched her in her confusion, as she tried to extricate herself and wrap herself up so that she could walk. He watched her relentlessly, as she knew. And as she went, the blanket trailing, and as he saw a glimpse of her feet and her white leg, he tried to remember her as she was when he had wrapped her in the blanket. But then he didn't want to remember, because she had been nothing to him then, and his nature revolted from remembering her as she was when she was nothing to him.

A tumbling, muffled noise from within the dark house startled him. Then he heard her voice: – 'There are clothes.' He rose and went to the foot of the stairs, and gathered up the garments she had thrown down. Then he came back to the fire, to rub himself down and dress. He grinned at his own appearance when he had finished.

The fire was sinking, so he put on coal. The house was now quite dark, save for the light of a street-lamp that shone in faintly from beyond the holly trees. He lit the gas with matches he found on the mantel-piece. Then he emptied the pockets of his own clothes, and threw all his wet things in a heap into the scullery. After which he gathered up her sodden clothes, gently, and put them in a separate heap on the copper-top in the scullery.

It was six o'clock on the clock. His own watch had stopped. He ought to go back to the surgery. He waited, and still she did not come down. So he went to the foot of the stairs and called:

'I shall have to go.'

Almost immediately he heard her coming down. She had on her best dress of black voile, and her hair was tidy, but still damp. She looked at him – and in spite of herself, smiled.

'I don't like you in those clothes,' she said.

'Do I look a sight?' he answered.

They were shy of one another.

'I'll make you some tea,' she said.

'No, I must go.'

'Must you?' And she looked at him again with the wide, strained, doubtful eyes. And again, from the pain of his breast, he knew how he loved her. He went and bent to kiss her, gently, passionately, with his heart's painful kiss.

'And my hair smells so horrible,' she murmured in distraction. 'And I'm so awful, I'm so awful! Oh, no, I'm too awful.' And she broke into bitter, heart-broken sobbing. 'You can't want to love me, I'm horrible.'

'Don't be silly, don't be silly,' he said, trying to comfort her, kissing her, holding her in his arms. 'I want you, I want to marry you, we're going to be married, quickly, quickly – to-morrow if I can.'

But she only sobbed terribly, and cried:

'I feel awful. I feel awful. I feel I'm horrible to you.'

'No, I want you, I want you,' was all he answered, blindly, with that terrible intonation which frightened her almost more than her horror lest he should *not* want her.

Samson and Delilah

A MAN got down from the motor-omnibus that runs from Penzance to St Just-in-Penwith, and turned northwards, uphill towards the Polestar. It was only half-past six, but already the stars were out, a cold little wind was blowing from the sea, and the crystalline, three-pulse flash of the lighthouse below the cliffs beat rhythmically in the first darkness.

The man was alone. He went his way unhesitating, but looked from side to side with cautious curiosity. Tall, ruined power-houses of tin-mines loomed in the darkness from time to time, like remnants of some by-gone civilisation. The lights of many miners' cottages scattered on the hilly darkness twinkled desolate in their disorder, yet twinkled with the lonely homeliness of the Celtic night.

He tramped steadily on, always watchful with curiosity. He was a tall, well-built man, apparently in the prime of life. His shoulders were square and rather stiff, he leaned forwards a little as he went, from the hips, like a man who must stoop to lower his height. But he did not stoop his shoulders: he bent his straight back from the hips.

Now and again short, stump, thick-legged figures of Cornish miners passed him, and he invariably gave them good-night, as if to insist that he was on his own ground. He spoke with the west-Cornish intonation. And as he went along the dreary road, looking now at the lights of the dwellings on land, now at the lights away to sea, vessels veering round in sight of the Longships Lighthouse, the whole of the Atlantic Ocean in darkness and space between him and America, he seemed a little excited and pleased with himself, watchful, thrilled, veering along in a sense of mastery and of power in conflict.

The houses began to close on the road, he was entering the straggling, formless, desolate mining village, that he knew of old. On the left was a little space set back from the road, and cosy lights of an inn. There it was. He peered up at the sign: 'The Tinners' Rest'. But he could not make out the name of the proprietor. He listened. There was excited talking and laughing, a woman's voice laughing shrilly among the men's.

Stooping a little, he entered the warmly-lit bar. The lamp was burning, a buxom woman rose from the white-scrubbed deal table where the black and white and red cards were scattered, and several men, miners, lifted their faces from the game.

The stranger went to the counter, averting his face. His cap was pulled down over his brow.

'Good-evening!' said the landlady, in her rather ingratiating voice.

'Good-evening. A glass of ale.'

'A glass of ale,' repeated the landlady suavely. 'Cold night – but bright.'

'Yes,' the man assented, laconically. Then he added, when nobody expected him to say any more: 'Seasonable weather.'

'Quite seasonable, quite,' said the landlady. 'Thank you.'

The man lifted his glass straight to his lips, and emptied it. He put it down again on the zinc counter with a click.

'Let's have another,' he said.

The woman drew the beer, and the man went away with his glass to the second table, near the fire. The woman, after a moment's hesitation, took her seat again at the table with the card-players. She had noticed the man: a big fine fellow, well dressed, a stranger.

But he spoke with that Cornish-Yankee accent she accepted as the natural twang among the miners.

The stranger put his foot on the fender and looked into the fire. He was handsome, well coloured, with well-drawn Cornish eyebrows, and the usual dark, bright, mindless Cornish eyes. He seemed abstracted in thought. Then he watched the card-party.

The woman was buxom and healthy, with dark hair and small, quick brown eyes. She was bursting with life and vigour, the energy she threw into the game of cards excited all the men, they shouted, and laughed, and the woman held her breast, shrieking with laughter.

'Oh, my, it'll be the death o' me,' she panted. 'Now, come on, Mr Trevorrow, play fair. Play fair, I say, or I s'll put the cards down.'

'Play fair! Why who's played unfair?' ejaculated Mr Trevorrow. 'Do you mean t'accuse me, as I haven't played fair, Mrs Nankervis?'

'I do. I say it, and I mean it. Haven't you got the queen of spades? Now, come on, no dodging round me. *I* know you've got that queen, as well as I know my name's Alice.'

'Well – if your name's Alice, you'll have to have it –'

'Ay, now – what did I say? Did ever you see such a man? My word, but your missus must be easy took in, by the looks of things.'

And off she went into peals of laughter. She was interrupted by the entrance of four men in khaki, a short, stumpy sergeant of middle age, a young corporal, and two young privates. The woman leaned back in her chair.

'Oh, my!' she cried. 'If there isn't the boys back: looking perished, I believe –'

'Perished, Ma!' exclaimed the sergeant. 'Not yet.'

'Near enough,' said a young private, uncouthly.

The woman got up.

'I'm sure you are, my dears. You'll be wanting your suppers, I'll be bound.'

'We could do with 'em.'

'Let's have a wet first,' said the sergeant.

The woman bustled about getting the drinks. The soldiers moved to the fire, spreading out their hands.

'Have your suppers in here, will you?' she said. 'Or in the kitchen?'

'Let's have it here,' said the sergeant. 'More cosier – *if* you don't mind.'

'You shall have it where you like, boys, where you like.'

She disappeared. In a minute a girl of about sixteen came in. She was tall and fresh, with dark, young, expressionless eyes, and well-drawn brows, and the immature softness and mindlessness of the sensuous Celtic type.

'Ho, Maryann! Evenin', Maryann! How's Maryann, now?' came the multiple greeting.

She replied to everybody in a soft voice, a strange, soft *aplomb* that was very attractive. And she moved round with rather mechanical, attractive movements, as if her thoughts were elsewhere. But she had always this dim far-awayness in her bearing: a sort of modesty. The strange man by the fire watched her curiously. There was an alert, inquisitive, mindless curiosity on his well-coloured face.

'I'll have a bit of supper with you, if I might,' he said.

She looked at him, with her clear, unreasoning eyes, just like the eyes of some non-human creature.

'I'll ask mother,' she said. Her voice was soft-breathing, gently sing-song.

When she came in again:

'Yes,' she said, almost whispering. 'What will you have?'

'What have you got?' he said, looking up into her face.

'There's cold meat –'

'That's for me, then.'

The stranger sat at the end of the table, and ate with the tired, quiet soldiers. Now, the landlady was interested in him. Her brow was knit rather tense, there was a look of panic in her large, healthy face, but her small brown eyes were fixed most dangerously. She was a big woman, but her eyes were small and tense. She drew near the stranger. She wore a rather loud-patterned flannelette blouse, and a dark skirt.

'What will you have to drink with your supper?' she asked, and there was a new, dangerous note in her voice.

He moved uneasily.

'Oh, I'll go on with ale.'

She drew him another glass. Then she sat down on the bench at the table with him and the soldiers, and fixed him with her attention.

'You've come from St Just, have you?' she said.

He looked at her with those clear, dark, inscrutable Cornish eyes, and answered at length:

'No, from Penzance.'

'Penzance! – but you're not thinking of going back there to-night?'

'No – no.'

He still looked at her with those wide, clear eyes that seemed like very bright agate. Her anger began to rise. It was seen on her brow. Yet her voice was still suave and deprecating.

'I *thought* not – but you're not living in these parts, are you?'

'No – no, I'm not living here.' He was always slow in answering, as if something intervened between him and any outside question.

'Oh, I see,' she said. 'You've got relations down here.'

Again he looked straight into her eyes, as if looking her into silence.

'Yes,' he said.

He did not say any more. She rose with a flounce. The anger was tight on her brow. There was no more laughing and card-playing that evening, though she kept up her motherly, suave, good-humoured way with the men. But they knew her, they were all afraid of her.

The supper was finished, the table cleared, the stranger did not go. Two of the young soldiers went off to bed, with their cheery:

'Good-night, Ma. Good-night, Maryann.'

The stranger talked a little to the sergeant about the war, which was in its first year, about the new army, a fragment of which was quartered in this district, about America.

The landlady darted looks at him from her small eyes, minute by minute the electric storm welled in her bosom, as still he did not go. She was quivering with suppressed, violent passion, something frightening and abnormal. She could not sit still for a moment. Her heavy form seemed to flash with sudden, involuntary movements as the minutes passed by, and still he sat there, and the tension on her heart grew unbearable. She watched the hands of the clock move on. Three of the soldiers had gone to bed, only the crop-headed, terrier-like old sergeant remained.

The landlady sat behind the bar fidgeting spasmodically with the newspaper. She looked again at the clock. At last it was five minutes to ten.

'Gentlemen – the enemy!' she said, in her diminished, furious voice. 'Time, please. Time, my dears. And good-night all!'

The men began to drop out, with a brief good-night. It was a minute to ten. The landlady rose.

'Come,' she said. 'I'm shutting the door.'

The last of the miners passed out. She stood, stout and menacing, holding the door. Still the stranger sat on by the fire, his black over-coat opened, smoking.

'We're closed now, sir,' came the perilous, narrowed voice of the landlady.

The little, dog-like, hard-headed sergeant touched the arm of the stranger.

'Closing time,' he said.

The stranger turned round in his seat, and his quick-moving, dark, jewel-like eyes went from the sergeant to the landlady.

'I'm stopping here to-night,' he said, in his laconic Cornish-Yankee accent.

The landlady seemed to tower. Her eyes lifted strangely, frightening.

'Oh! indeed!' she cried. 'Oh, indeed! And whose orders are those, may I ask?'

He looked at her again.

'My orders,' he said.

Involuntarily she shut the door, and advanced like a great, dangerous bird. Her voice rose, there was a touch of hoarseness in it.

'And what might *your* orders be, if you please?' she cried. 'Who might *you* be, to give orders, in the house?'

He sat still, watching her.

'You know who I am,' he said. 'At least, I know who you are.'

'Oh, do you? Oh, do you? And who am *I* then, if you'll be so good as to tell me?'

He stared at her with his bright, dark eyes.

'You're my Missis, you are,' he said. 'And you know it, as well as I do.'

She started as if something had exploded in her.

Her eyes lifted and flared madly.

'*Do* I know it, indeed!' she cried. 'I know no such thing! I know no such thing! Do you think a man's going to walk into this bar, and tell me off-hand I'm his Missis, and I'm going to believe him? – I say to you, whoever you may be, you're mistaken. I know myself for no Missis of yours, and I'll thank you to go out of this house, this minute, before I get those that will put you out.'

The man rose to his feet, stretching his head towards her a little. He was a handsomely built Cornishman in the prime of life.

'What you say, eh? You don't know me?' he said, in his sing-song voice, emotionless, but rather smothered and pressing: it reminded one of the girl's. 'I should know you anywhere, you see. I should! I shouldn't have to look twice to know you, you see. You see, now, don't you?'

The woman was baffled.

'So you may say,' she replied, staccato. 'So you may say. That's easy enough. My name's known, and respected, by most people for ten miles round. But I don't know *you*.'

Her voice ran to sarcasm. 'I can't say I know *you*. You're a *perfect* stranger to me, and I don't believe I've ever set eyes on you before to-night.'

Her voice was very flexible and sarcastic.

'Yes, you have,' replied the man, in his reasonable way. 'Yes, you have. Your name's my name, and that girl Maryann is my girl; she's my daughter. You're my Missis right enough. As sure as I'm Willie Nankervis.'

He spoke as if it were an accepted fact. His face was handsome, with a strange, watchful alertness and a fundamental fixity of intention that maddened her.

'You villain!' she cried. 'You villain, to come to this house and dare to speak to me. You villain, you down-right rascal!'

He looked at her.

'Ay,' he said, unmoved. 'All that.' He was uneasy before her. Only he was not afraid of her. There was something impenetrable about him, like his eyes, which were as bright as agate.

She towered, and drew near to him menacingly.

'You're going out of this house, aren't you?' – She stamped her foot in sudden madness. '*This minute!*'

He watched her. He knew she wanted to strike him.

'No,' he said, with suppressed emphasis. 'I've told you, I'm stopping here.'

He was afraid of her personality, but it did not alter him. She wavered. Her small, tawny-brown eyes concentrated in a point of vivid, sightless fury, like a tiger's. The man was wincing, but he stood his ground. Then she bethought herself. She would gather her forces.

'We'll see whether you're stopping here,' she said. And she turned, with a curious, frightening lifting of her eyes, and surged out of the room. The man, listening, heard her go upstairs, heard her tapping at a bedroom door, heard her saying: 'Do you mind coming down a minute, boys? I want you. I'm in trouble.'

The man in the bar took off his cap and his black overcoat, and threw them on the seat behind him. His black hair was short and touched with grey at the temples. He wore a well-cut, well-fitting suit of dark grey, American in style, and a turn-down collar. He looked well-to-do, a fine, solid figure of a man. The rather rigid look of the shoulders came from his having had his collar-bone twice broken in the mines.

The little terrier of a sergeant, in dirty khaki, looked at him furtively.

'She's your Missis?' he asked, jerking his head in the direction of the departed woman.

'Yes, she is,' barked the man. 'She's that, sure enough.'

'Not seen her for a long time, haven't ye?'

'Sixteen years come March month.'

'Hm!'

And the sergeant laconically resumed his smoking.

The landlady was coming back, followed by the three young soldiers, who entered rather sheepishly, in trousers and shirt and stocking-feet. The woman stood histrionically at the end of the bar, and exclaimed:

'That man refuses to leave the house, claims he's stopping the night here. You know very well I have no bed, don't you? And this house doesn't accommodate travellers. Yet he's going to stop in spite of all! But not while I've a drop of blood in my body, that I declare with my dying breath. And not if you men are worth the name of men, and will help a woman as has no one to help her.'

Her eyes sparkled, her face was flushed pink. She was drawn up like an Amazon.

The young soldiers did not quite know what to do. They looked at the man, they looked at the sergeant, one of them looked down and fastened his braces on the second button.

'What say, sergeant?' asked one whose face twinkled for a little devilment.

'Man says he's husband to Mrs Nankervis,' said the sergeant.

'He's no husband of mine. I declare I never set eyes on him before this night. It's a dirty trick, nothing else, it's a dirty trick.'

'Why, you're a liar, saying you never set eyes on me before,' barked the man near the hearth. 'You're married to me, and that girl Maryann you had by me – well enough you know it.'

The young soldier looked on in delight, the sergeant smoked imperturbed.

'Yes,' sang the landlady, slowly shaking her head in supreme sarcasm, 'it sounds very pretty, doesn't it? But you see we don't believe a word of it, and *how* are you going to prove it?' She smiled nastily.

The man watched in silence for a moment, then he said:

'It wants no proof.'

'Oh, yes, but it does! Oh, yes, but it does, sir, it wants a lot of proving!' sang the lady's sarcasm. 'We're not such gulls as all that, to swallow your words whole.'

But he stood unmoved near the fire. She stood with one hand resting on the zinc-covered bar, the sergeant sat with legs crossed, smoking, on the seat halfway between them, the three young soldiers in their shirts and braces stood wavering in the gloom behind the bar. There was silence.

'Do you know anything of the whereabouts of your husband, Mrs Nankervis? Is he still living?' asked the sergeant, in his judicious fashion.

Suddenly the landlady began to cry, great scalding tears, that left the young men aghast.

'I know nothing of him,' she sobbed, feeling for her pocket handkerchief. 'He left me when Maryann was a baby, went mining to America, and after about six months never wrote a line nor sent me a penny bit. I can't say whether he's alive or dead, the villain. All I've heard of him's to the bad – and I've heard nothing for years an' all, now.' She sobbed violently.

The golden-skinned, handsome man near the fire watched her as she wept. He was frightened, he was troubled, he was bewildered, but none of his emotions altered him underneath.

There was no sound in the room but the violent sobbing of the landlady. The men, one and all, were overcome.

'Don't you think as you'd better go, for to-night?' said the sergeant to the man, with sweet reasonableness. 'You'd better leave it a bit, and arrange something between you. You can't have much claim on a woman, I should imagine, if it's how she says. And you've come down on her a bit too sudden-like.'

The landlady sobbed heart-brokenly. The man watched her large breasts shaken. They seemed to cast a spell over his mind.

'How I've treated her, that's no matter,' he replied. 'I've come back, and I'm going to stop in my own home, – for a bit, anyhow. There you've got it.'

'A dirty action,' said the sergeant, his face flushing dark. 'A dirty action, to come, after deserting a woman for that number of years, and want to force yourself on her! A dirty action – as isn't allowed by the law.'

The landlady wiped her eyes.

'Never you mind about law nor nothing,' cried the man, in a strange, strong voice. 'I'm not moving out of this public to-night.'

The woman turned to the soldiers behind her, and said in a wheedling, sarcastic tone:

'Are we going to stand it, boys? – Are we going to be done like this, Sergeant Thomas, by a scoundrel and a bully as has led a life beyond *mention*, in those American mining-camps, and then wants to come back and make havoc of a poor woman's life and savings, after having left her with a baby in arms to struggle as best she might? It's a crying shame if nobody will stand up for me – a crying shame –!'

The soldiers and the little sergeant were bristling. The woman stooped and rummaged under the counter for a minute. Then, unseen to the man away near the fire, she threw out a plaited grass rope, such as is used for binding bales, and left it lying near the feet of the young soldiers, in the gloom at the back of the bar.

Then she rose and fronted the situation.

'Come now,' she said to the man, in a reasonable, coldly-coaxing tone, 'put your coat on and leave us alone. Be a man, and not worse than a brute of a German. You can get a bed easy enough in St Just, and if you've nothing to pay for it sergeant would lend you a couple of shillings, I'm sure he would.'

All eyes were fixed on the man. He was looking down at the woman like a creature spell-bound or possessed by some devil's own intention.

'I've got money of my own,' he said. 'Don't you be frightened for your money, I've plenty of that, for the time.'

'Well, then,' she coaxed, in a cold, almost sneering propitiation, 'put your coat on and go where you're wanted – be a *man*, not a brute of a German.'

She had drawn quite near to him, in her challenging coaxing intentions. He looked down at her with his bewitched face.

'No, I shan't,' he said. 'I shan't do no such thing. *You'll* put me up for to-night.'

'Shall I?' she cried. And suddenly she flung her arms round him, hung on to him with all her powerful weight, calling to the soldiers: 'Get the rope, boys, and fasten him up. Alfred – John, quick now –'

The man reared, looked round with maddened eyes, and heaved his powerful body. But the woman was powerful also, and very heavy, and was clenched with the determination of death. Her face, with its exulting, horribly vindictive look, was turned up to him from his own breast; he reached back his head frantically, to get away from it. Meanwhile the young soldiers, after having watched this frightful Laocoon[1] swaying for a moment, stirred, and the malicious one darted swiftly with the rope. It was tangled a little.

'Give me the end here,' cried the sergeant.

Meanwhile the big man heaved and struggled, swung the woman round against the seat and the table, in his convulsive effort to get free. But she pinned down his arms like a cuttlefish wreathed heavily upon him. And he heaved and swayed, and they crashed about the room, the soldiers hopping, the furniture bumping.

The young soldier had got the rope once round, the brisk sergeant helping him. The woman sank heavily lower, they got the rope round several times. In the struggle the victim fell over against the table. The ropes tightened till they cut his arms. The woman clung to his knees. Another soldier ran in a flash of genius, and fastened the strange man's feet with the pair of braces. Seats had crashed over, the table was thrown against the wall, but the man was bound, his arms pinned against his sides, his feet tied. He lay half fallen, sunk against the table, still for a moment.

The woman rose, and sank, faint, on to the seat against the wall. Her breast heaved, she could not speak, she thought she was going to die. The bound man lay against the overturned table, his coat all twisted and pulled up beneath the ropes, leaving the loins exposed. The soldiers stood around, a little dazed, but excited with the row.

The man began to struggle again, heaving instinctively against the ropes, taking great, deep breaths. His face, with its golden skin, flushed dark and surcharged, he heaved again. The great veins in his neck stood out. But it was no good, he went relaxed. Then again, suddenly, he jerked his feet.

'Another pair of braces, William,' cried the excited soldier. He threw himself on the legs of the bound man, and managed to fasten the knees. Then again there was stillness. They could hear the clock tick.

The woman looked at the prostrate figure, the strong, straight limbs, the strong back bound in subjection, the wide-eyed face that reminded her of a calf tied in a sack in a cart, only its head stretched dumbly backwards. And she triumphed.

The bound-up body began to struggle again. She watched fascinated the muscles working, the shoulders, the hips, the large, clean thighs. Even now he might break the ropes. She was afraid. But the lively young soldier sat on the shoulders of the bound man, and after a few perilous moments, there was stillness again.

'Now,' said the judicious sergeant to the bound man, 'if we untie you, will you promise to go off and make no more trouble.'

'You'll not untie him in here,' cried the woman. 'I wouldn't trust him as far as I could blow him.'

There was silence.

'We might carry him outside, and undo him there,' said the soldier. 'Then we could get a policeman, if he made any more bother.'

'Yes,' said the sergeant. 'We could do that.' Then again, in an altered, almost severe tone, to the prisoner. 'If we undo you outside, will you take your coat and go without creating any more disturbance?'

But the prisoner would not answer, he only lay with wide, dark, bright eyes, like a bound animal. There was a space of perplexed silence.

'Well, then, do as you say,' said the woman irritably. 'Carry him out amongst you, and let us shut up the house.'

They did so. Picking up the bound man, the four soldiers staggered clumsily into the silent square in front of the inn, the woman following with the cap and the overcoat. The young soldiers quickly unfastened the braces from the prisoner's legs, and they hopped indoors. They were in their stocking-feet, and outside the stars flashed cold. They stood in the doorway watching. The man lay quite still on the cold ground.

'Now,' said the sergeant, in a subdued voice, 'I'll loosen the knot, and he can work himself free, if you go in, Missis.'

She gave a last look at the dishevelled, bound man, as he sat on the ground. Then she went indoors, followed quickly by the sergeant. Then they were heard locking and barring the door.

The man seated on the ground worked and strained at the rope. But it was not so easy to undo himself even now. So, with hands bound, making an effort, he got on his feet, and went and worked the cord against the rough edge of an old wall. The rope, being of a kind of plaited grass, soon frayed and broke, and he freed himself. He had various contusions. His arms were hurt and bruised from the bonds. He rubbed them slowly. Then he pulled his clothes straight, stooped, put on his cap, struggled into his overcoat, and walked away.

The stars were very brilliant. Clear as crystal, the beam from the lighthouse under the cliffs struck rhythmically on the night. Dazed, the man walked along the road past the church-yard. Then he stood leaning up against a wall, for a long time.

He was roused because his feet were so cold. So he pulled himself together, and turned again in the silent night, back towards the inn.

The bar was in darkness. But there was a light in the kitchen. He hesitated. Then very quietly he tried the door.

He was surprised to find it open. He entered, and quietly closed it behind him. Then he went down the step past the bar-counter, and through to the lighted doorway of the kitchen. There sat his wife, planted in front of the range, where a furze fire was burning. She sat in a chair full in front of the range, her knees wide apart on the fender. She looked over her shoulder at him as he entered, but she did not speak. Then she stared in the fire again.

It was a small, narrow kitchen. He dropped his cap on the table that was covered with yellowish American cloth, and took a seat with his back to the wall, near the oven. His wife still sat with her knees apart, her feet on the steel fender and stared into the fire, motionless. Her skin was smooth and rosy in the firelight. Everything in the house was very clean and bright. The man sat silent, too, his head dropped. And thus they remained.

It was a question who would speak first. The woman leaned forward and poked the ends of the sticks in between the bars of the range. He lifted his head and looked at her.

'Others gone to bed, have they?' he asked.

But she remained closed in silence.

' 'S a cold night, out,' he said, as if to himself.

And he laid his large, yet well-shapen workman's hand on the top of the stove, that was polished black and smooth as velvet. She would not look at him, yet she glanced out of the corners of her eyes.

His eyes were fixed brightly on her, the pupils large and electric like those of a cat.

'I should have picked you out among thousands,' he said. 'Though you're bigger than I'd have believed. Fine flesh you've made.'

She was silent for some time. Then she turned in her chair upon him.

'What do you think of yourself,' she said, 'coming back on me like this after over fifteen year? You don't think I've not heard of you, neither, in Butte City and elsewhere?'

He was watching her with his clear, translucent, unchallenged eyes.

'Yes,' he said. 'Chaps comes an' goes – I've heard tell of you from time to time.'

She drew herself up.

'And what lies have you heard about *me*?' she demanded superbly.

'I dunno as I've heard any lies at all – 'cept as you was getting on very well, like.'

His voice ran warily and detached. Her anger stirred again in her violently. But she subdued it, because of the danger there was in him, and more, perhaps, because of the beauty of his head and his level-drawn brows, which she could not bear to forfeit.

'That's more than I can say of *you*,' she said. 'I've heard more harm than good about *you*.'

'Ay, I dessay,' he said, looking in the fire. It was a long time since he had seen the furze burning, he said to himself. There was a silence, during which she watched his face.

'Do you call yourself a *man*?' she said, more in contemptuous reproach than in anger. 'Leave a woman as you've left me, you don't care to what! – and then to turn up in *this* fashion, without a word to say for yourself.'

He stirred in his chair, planted his feet apart, and resting his arms on his knees, looked steadily into the fire, without answering. So near to her was his head, and the close black hair, she could scarcely refrain from starting away, as if it would bite her.

'Do you call that the action of a *man*?' she repeated.

'No,' he said, reaching and poking the bits of wood into the fire with his fingers. 'I didn't call it anything, as I know of. It's no good calling things by any names whatsoever, as I know of.'

She watched him in his actions. There was a longer and longer pause between each speech, though neither knew it.

'I *wonder* what you think of yourself!' she exclaimed, with vexed emphasis. 'I *wonder* what sort of a fellow you take yourself to be!' She was really perplexed as well as angry.

'Well,' he said, lifting his head to look at her, 'I guess I'll answer for my own faults, if everybody else'll answer for theirs.'

Her heart beat fiery hot as he lifted his face to her. She breathed heavily, averting her face, almost losing her self-control.

'And what do you take *me* to be?' she cried, in real helplessness.

His face was lifted watching her, watching her soft, averted face, and the softly heaving mass of her breasts.

'I take you,' he said, with that laconic truthfulness which exercised such power over her, 'to be the deuce of a fine woman – darn me if you're not as fine a built woman as I've seen, handsome with it as well. I shouldn't have expected you to put on such handsome flesh: 'struth I shouldn't.'

Her heart beat fiery hot, as he watched her with those bright agate eyes, fixedly.

'Been very handsome to *you*, for fifteen years, my sakes!' she replied.

He made no answer to this, but sat with his bright, quick eyes upon her.

Then he rose. She started involuntarily. But he only said, in his laconic, measured way:

'It's warm in here now.'

And he pulled off his overcoat, throwing it on the table. She sat as if slightly cowed, whilst he did so.

'Them ropes has given my arms something, by Ga-ard,' he drawled, feeling his arms with his hands.

Still she sat in her chair before him, slightly cowed.

'You was sharp, wasn't you, to catch me like that, eh?' he smiled slowly. 'By Ga-ard, you had me fixed proper, proper you had. Darn me, you fixed me up proper – proper, you did.'

He leaned forwards in his chair towards her.

'I don't think no worse of you for it, no, darned if I do. Fine pluck in a woman's what I admire. That I do, indeed.'

She only gazed into the fire.

'We fet from the start, we did. And, my word, you begin again quick the minute you see me, you did. Darn me, you was too sharp for me. A darn fine woman, puts up a darn good fight. Darn me if I could find a woman in all the darn States as could get me down like that. Wonderful fine woman you be, truth to say, at this minute.'

She only sat glowering into the fire.

'As grand a pluck as a man could wish to find in a woman, true as I'm here,' he said, reaching forward his hand and tentatively touching her between her full, warm breasts, quietly.

She started, and seemed to shudder. But his hand insinuated itself between her breasts, as she continued to gaze in the fire.

'And don't you think I've come back here a-begging,' he said. 'I've more than *one* thousand pounds to my name, I have. And a bit of a fight for a how-de-do pleases me, that it do. But that doesn't mean as you're going to deny as you're my Missis . . .'

Tickets, Please

THERE is in the Midlands a single-line tramway system which boldly leaves the county town[1] and plunges off into the black, industrial countryside, up hill and down dale, through the long ugly villages of workmen's houses, over canals and railways, past churches perched high and nobly over the smoke and shadows, through stark, grimy cold little market-places, tilting away in a rush past cinemas and shops down to the hollow where the collieries are, then up again, past a little rural church, under the ash trees, on in a rush to the terminus, the last little ugly place of industry, the cold little town that shivers on the edge of the wild, gloomy country beyond. There the green and creamy coloured tram-car seems to pause and purr with curious satisfaction. But in a few minutes – the clock on the turret of the Cooperative Wholesale Society's Shops gives the time – away it starts once more on the adventure. Again there are the reckless swoops downhill, bouncing the loops: again the chilly wait in the hill-top market-place: again the breathless slithering round the precipitous drop under the church: again the patient halts at the loops, waiting for the outcoming car: so on and on, for two long hours, till at last the city looms beyond the fat gas-works, the narrow factories draw near, we are in the sordid streets of the great town, once more we sidle to a standstill at our terminus, abashed by the great crimson and cream-coloured city cars, but still perky, jaunty, somewhat dare-devil, green as a jaunty sprig of parsley out of a black colliery garden.

To ride on these cars is always an adventure. Since we are in war-time, the drivers are men unfit for active service: cripples and hunchbacks. So they have the spirit of the devil in them. The ride becomes a steeplechase. Hurray! we have leapt in a clear jump over the canal bridges – now for the four-lane corner. With a shriek and a trail of sparks we are clear again. To be sure, a tram often leaps the rails – but what matter! It sits in a ditch till other trams come to haul it out. It is quite common for a car, packed with one solid mass of living people, to come to a dead halt in the midst of unbroken blackness, the heart of nowhere on a dark night, and for the driver and the girl conductor to call, 'All get off – car's on fire!' Instead, however, of rushing out in a panic, the passengers stolidly reply: 'Get on – get on! We're not coming out. We're stopping where we are. Push on, George.' So till flames actually appear.

The reason for this reluctance to dismount is that the nights are howlingly cold, black, and windswept, and a car is a haven of refuge. From village to village the miners travel, for a change of cinema, of girl, of pub. The trams are desperately packed. Who is going to risk himself in the black gulf outside, to wait perhaps an hour for another tram, then to see the forlorn notice 'Depot Only', because there is something wrong! Or to greet a unit of three bright cars all so tight with people that they sail past with a howl of derision. Trams that pass in the night.

This, the most dangerous tram-service in England, as the authorities themselves declare, with pride, is entirely conducted by girls, and driven by rash young men, a little crippled, or by delicate young men, who creep forward in terror. The girls are fearless young hussies. In their ugly blue uniform, skirts up to their knees, shapeless old peaked caps on their heads, they have all the *sang-froid*[2] of an old non-commissioned officer. With a tram packed with howling colliers, roaring hymns downstairs and a sort of antiphony of obscenities upstairs, the lasses are perfectly at their ease. They pounce on the youths who try to evade their ticket-machine. They push off the men at the end of their distance. They are not going to be done in the eye – not they. They fear nobody – and everybody fears them.

'Hello, Annie!'

'Hello, Ted!'

'Oh, mind my corn, Miss Stone. It's my belief you've got a heart of stone, for you've trod on it again.'

'You should keep it in your pocket,' replies Miss Stone, and she goes sturdily upstairs in her high boots.

'Tickets, please.'

She is peremptory, suspicious, and ready to hit first. She can hold her own against ten thousand. The step of that tram-car is her Thermopylae.[3]

Therefore, there is a certain wild romance aboard these cars – and in the sturdy bosom of Annie herself. The time for soft romance is in the morning, between ten o'clock and one, when things are rather slack: that is, except market-day and Saturday. Thus Annie has time to look about her. Then she often hops off her car and into a shop where she has spied something, while the driver chats in the main road. There is very good feeling between the girls and the drivers. Are they not companions in peril, shipmates aboard this careering vessel of a tram-car, for ever rocking on the waves of a stormy land.

Then, also, during the easy hours, the inspectors are most in evidence. For some reason, everybody employed in this tram-service is young: there are no grey heads. It would not do. Therefore the inspectors are of the right age, and one, the chief, is also good-looking. See him stand on a wet, gloomy morning, in his long oil-skin, his peaked cap well down over his eyes, waiting to board a car. His face is ruddy, his small brown moustache is weathered, he has a faint impudent smile. Fairly tall and agile, even in his waterproof, he springs aboard a car and greets Annie.

'Hello, Annie! Keeping the wet out?'

'Trying to.'

There are only two people in the car. Inspecting is soon over. Then for a long and impudent chat on the foot-board, a good, easy, twelve-mile chat.

The inspector's name is John Thomas Raynor – always called John Thomas, except sometimes, in malice, Coddy.[4] His face sets in fury when he is addressed, from a distance, with this abbreviation. There is considerable scandal about John Thomas in half a dozen villages. He flirts with the girl conductors in the morning, and walks out with them in the dark night, when they leave their tram-car at the depot. Of course, the girls quit the service frequently. Then he flirts and walks out with the newcomer: always providing she is sufficiently attractive, and that she will consent to walk. It is remarkable, however, that most of the girls are quite comely, they are all young, and this roving life aboard the car gives them a sailor's dash and recklessness. What matter how they behave when the ship is in port. Tomorrow they will be aboard again.

Annie, however, was something of a Tartar,[5] and her sharp tongue had kept John Thomas at arm's length for many months. Perhaps, therefore, she liked him all the more: for he always came up smiling, with impudence. She watched him vanquish one girl, then another. She could tell by the movement of his mouth and eyes, when he flirted with her in the morning, that he had been walking out with this lass, or the other, the night before. A fine cock-of-the-walk he was. She could sum him up pretty well.

In this subtle antagonism they knew each other like old friends, they were as shrewd with one another almost as man and wife. But Annie had always kept him sufficiently at arm's length. Besides, she had a boy of her own.

The Statutes fair,[6] however, came in November, at Bestwood. It happened that Annie had the Monday night off. It was a drizzling ugly night, yet she dressed herself up and went to the fair ground. She was alone, but she expected soon to find a pal of some sort.

The roundabouts were veering round and grinding out their music, the side shows were making as much commotion as possible. In the cocoanut shies there were no cocoanuts, but artificial war-time substitutes, which the lads declared were fastened into the irons. There was a sad decline in brilliance and luxury. None the less, the ground was muddy as ever, there was the same crush, the press of faces lighted up by the flares and the electric lights, the same smell of naphtha and a few fried potatoes, and of electricity.

Who should be the first to greet Miss Annie on the show-ground but John Thomas. He had a black overcoat buttoned up to his chin, and a tweed cap pulled down over his brows, his face between was ruddy and smiling and handy as ever. She knew so well the way his mouth moved.

She was very glad to have a 'boy'. To be at the Statutes without a fellow was no fun. Instantly, like the gallant he was, he took her on the Dragons, grim-toothed, round-about switchbacks. It was not nearly so exciting as a tram-car actually. But, then, to be seated in a shaking, green dragon, uplifted above the sea of bubble faces, careering in a rickety fashion in the lower heavens, whilst John Thomas leaned over her, his cigarette in his mouth, was after all the right style. She was a plump, quick, alive little creature. So she was quite excited and happy.

John Thomas made her stay on for the next round. And therefore she could hardly for shame repulse him when he put his arm round her and drew her a little nearer to him, in a very warm and cuddly manner. Besides, he was fairly discreet, he kept his movement as hidden as possible. She looked down, and saw that his red, clean hand was out of sight of the crowd. And they knew each other so well. So they warmed up to the fair.

After the dragons they went on the horses. John Thomas paid each time, so she could but be complaisant. He, of course, sat astride on the outer horse – named 'Black Bess' – and she sat sideways, towards him, on the inner horse – named 'Wildfire'. But of course John Thomas was not going to sit discreetly on 'Black Bess', holding the brass bar. Round they spun and heaved, in the light. And round he swung on his wooden steed, flinging one leg across her mount, and perilously tipping up and down, across the space, half lying back, laughing at her. He was perfectly happy; she was afraid her hat was on one side, but she was excited.

He threw quoits on a table, and won for her two large, pale-blue hat-pins. And then, hearing the noise of the cinemas, announcing another performance, they climbed the boards and went in.

Of course, during these performances pitch darkness falls from time to time, when the machine goes wrong. Then there is a wild whooping, and a loud smacking of simulated kisses. In these moments John Thomas drew Annie towards him. After all, he had a wonderfully warm, cosy way of holding a girl with his arm, he seemed to make such a nice fit. And, after all, it was pleasant to be so held: so very comforting and cosy and nice. He leaned over her and she felt his breath on her hair; she knew he wanted to kiss her on the lips. And, after all, he was so warm and she fitted in to him so softly. After all, she wanted him to touch her lips.

But the light sprang up; she also started electrically, and put her hat straight. He left his arm lying nonchalantly behind her. Well, it was fun, it was exciting to be at the Statutes with John Thomas.

When the cinema was over they went for a walk across the dark, damp fields. He had all the arts of love-making. He was especially good at holding a girl, when he sat with her on a stile in the black, drizzling darkness. He seemed to be holding her in space, against his own warmth and gratification. And his kisses were soft and slow and searching.

So Annie walked out with John Thomas, though she kept her own boy dangling in the distance. Some of the tram-girls chose to be huffy. But there, you must take things as you find them, in this life.

There was no mistake about it, Annie liked John Thomas a good deal. She felt so rich and warm in herself whenever he was near. And John Thomas really liked Annie, more than usual. The soft, melting way in which she could flow into a fellow, as if she melted into his very bones, was something rare and good. He fully appreciated this.

But with a developing acquaintance there began a developing intimacy. Annie wanted to consider him a person, a man; she wanted to take an intelligent interest in him, and to have an intelligent response. She did not want a mere nocturnal presence, which was what he was so far. And she prided herself that he could not leave her.

Here she made a mistake. John Thomas intended to remain a nocturnal presence; he had no idea of becoming an all-round individual to her. When she started to take an intelligent interest in him and his life and his character, he sheered off. He hated intelligent interest. And he knew that the only way to stop it was to avoid it. The possessive female was aroused in Annie. So he left her.

It is no use saying she was not surprised. She was at first startled, thrown out of her count. For she had been so *very* sure of holding him. For a while she was staggered, and everything became uncertain to her. Then she wept with fury, indignation, desolation, and misery. Then she had a spasm of despair. And then, when he came, still impudently, on to her car, still familiar, but letting her see by the movement of his head that he had gone away to somebody else for the time being, and was enjoying pastures new, then she determined to have her own back.

She had a very shrewd idea what girls John Thomas had taken out. She went to Nora Purdy. Nora was a tall, rather pale, but well-built girl, with beautiful yellow hair. She was rather secretive.

'Hey!' said Annie, accosting her; then softly, 'Who's John Thomas on with now?'

'I don't know,' said Nora.

'Why tha does,' said Annie, ironically lapsing into dialect. 'Tha knows as well as I do.'

'Well, I do then,' said Nora. 'It isn't me, so don't bother.'

'It's Cissy Meakin, isn't it?'

'It is, for all I know.'

'Hasn't he got a face on him!' said Annie. 'I don't half like his cheek. I could knock him off the foot-board when he comes round at me.'

'He'll get dropped-on one of these days,' said Nora.

'Ay, he will, when somebody makes up their mind to drop it on him. I should like to see him taken down a peg or two, shouldn't you?'

'I shouldn't mind,' said Nora.

'You've got quite as much cause to as I have,' said Annie. 'But we'll drop on him one of these days, my girl. What? Don't you want to?'

'I don't mind,' said Nora.

But as a matter of fact, Nora was much more vindictive than Annie.

One by one Annie went the round of the old flames. It so happened that Cissy Meakin left the tramway service in quite a short time. Her mother made her leave. Then John Thomas was on the *qui-vive*.[7] He cast his eyes over his old flock. And his eyes lighted on Annie. He thought she would be safe now. Besides, he liked her.

She arranged to walk home with him on Sunday night. It so happened that her car would be in the depôt at half-past nine: the last car would come in at 10.15. So John Thomas was to wait for her there.

At the depôt the girls had a little waiting-room of their own. It was quite rough, but cosy, with a fire and an oven and a mirror, and table and wooden chairs. The half dozen girls who knew John Thomas only too well had arranged to take service this Sunday afternoon. So, as the cars began to come in, early, the girls dropped into the waiting-room. And instead of hurrying off home, they sat around the fire and had a cup of tea. Outside was the darkness and lawlessness of war-time.

John Thomas came on the car after Annie, at about a quarter to ten. He poked his head easily into the girls' waiting-room.

'Prayer-meeting?' he asked.

'Ay,' said Laura Sharp. 'Ladies only.'

'That's me!' said John Thomas. It was one of his favourite exclamations.

'Shut the door, boy,' said Muriel Baggaley.

'On which side of me?' said John Thomas.

'Which tha likes,' said Polly Birkin.

He had come in and closed the door behind him. The girls moved in their circle, to make a place for him near the fire. He took off his great-coat and pushed back his hat.

'Who handles the teapot?' he said.

Nora Purdy silently poured him out a cup of tea.

'Want a bit o' my bread and drippin'?' said Muriel Baggaley to him.

'Ay, give us a bit.'

And he began to eat his piece of bread.

'There's no place like home, girls,' he said.

They all looked at him as he uttered this piece of impudence. He seemed to be sunning himself in the presence of so many damsels.

'Especially if you're not afraid to go home in the dark,' said Laura Sharp.

'Me! By myself I am.'

They sat till they heard the last tram come in. In a few minutes Emma Houselay entered.

'Come on, my old duck!' cried Polly Birkin.

'It *is* perishing,' said Emma, holding her fingers to the fire.

'But – I'm afraid to, go home in, the dark,' sang Laura Sharp, the tune having got into her mind.

'Who're you going with to-night, John Thomas?' asked Muriel Baggaley, coolly.

'To-night?' said John Thomas. 'Oh, I'm going home by myself to-night – all on my lonely-O.'

'That's me!' said Nora Purdy, using his own ejaculation.

The girls laughed shrilly.

'Me as well, Nora,' said John Thomas.

'Don't know what you mean,' said Laura.

'Yes, I'm toddling,' said he, rising and reaching for his overcoat.

'Nay,' said Polly. 'We're all here waiting for you.'

'We've got to be up in good time in the morning,' he said, in the benevolent official manner.

They all laughed.

'Nay,' said Muriel. 'Don't leave us all lonely, John Thomas. Take one!'

'I'll take the lot, if you like,' he responded gallantly.

'That you won't, either,' said Muriel. 'Two's company; seven's too much of a good thing.'

'Nay – take one,' said Laura. 'Fair and square, all above board, and say which.'

'Ay,' cried Annie, speaking for the first time. 'Pick, John Thomas; let's hear thee.'

'Nay,' he said. 'I'm going home quiet to-night. Feeling good, for once.'

'Whereabouts?' said Annie. 'Take a good 'un, then. But tha's got to take one of us!'

'Nay, how can I take one,' he said, laughing uneasily. 'I don't want to make enemies.'

'You'd only make *one*,' said Annie.

'The chosen *one*,' added Laura.

'Oh, my! Who said girls!' exclaimed John Thomas, again turning, as if to escape. 'Well – good-night.'

'Nay, you've got to make your pick,' said Muriel. 'Turn your face to the wall, and say which one touches you. Go on – we shall only just touch your back – one of us. Go on – turn your face to the wall, and don't look, and say which one touches you.'

He was uneasy, mistrusting them. Yet he had not the courage to break away. They pushed him to a wall and stood him there with his face to it. Behind his back they all grimaced, tittering. He looked so comical. He looked around uneasily.

'Go on!' he cried.

'You're looking – you're looking!' they shouted.

He turned his head away. And suddenly, with a movement like a swift cat, Annie went forward and fetched him a box on the side of the head that sent his cap flying and himself staggering. He started round.

But at Annie's signal they all flew at him, slapping him, pinching him, pulling his hair, though more in fun than in spite or anger. He, however, saw red. His blue eyes flamed with strange fear as well as fury, and he butted through the girls to the door. It was locked. He wrenched at it. Roused, alert, the girls stood round and looked at him. He faced them, at bay. At that moment they were rather horrifying to him, as they stood in their short uniforms. He was distinctly afraid.

'Come on, John Thomas! Come on! Choose!' said Annie.

'What are you after? Open the door,' he said.

'We shan't – not till you've chosen!' said Muriel.

'Chosen what?' he said.

'Chosen the one you're going to marry,' she replied.

He hesitated a moment.

'Open the blasted door,' he said, 'and get back to your senses.' He spoke with official authority.

'You've got to choose!' cried the girls.

'Come on!' cried Annie, looking him in the eye. 'Come on! Come on!'

He went forward, rather vaguely. She had taken off her belt, and swinging it, she fetched him a sharp blow over the head with the buckle end. He sprang and seized her. But immediately the other girls rushed upon him, pulling and tearing and beating him. Their blood was now thoroughly up. He was their sport now. They were going to have their own back, out of him. Strange, wild creatures, they hung on him and rushed at him to bear him down. His tunic was torn right up the back, Nora had hold at the back of his collar, and was actually strangling him. Luckily the button burst. He struggled in a wild frenzy of fury and terror, almost mad terror. His tunic was simply torn off his back, his shirt-sleeves were torn away, his arms were naked. The girls rushed at him, clenched their hands on him and pulled at him: or they rushed at him and pushed him, butted him with all their might: or they struck him wild blows. He ducked and cringed and struck sideways. They became more intense.

At last he was down. They rushed on him, kneeling on him. He had neither breath nor strength to move. His face was bleeding with a long scratch, his brow was bruised.

Annie knelt on him, the other girls knelt and hung on to him. Their faces were flushed, their hair wild, their eyes glittering strangely. He lay at last quite still, with face averted, as an animal lies when it is defeated and at the mercy of the captor. Sometimes his eye glanced back at the wild faces of the girls. His breast rose heavily, his wrists were torn.

'Now, then, my fellow!' gasped Annie at length. 'Now then – now –'

At the sound of her terrifying, cold triumph, he suddenly started to struggle as an animal might, but the girls threw themselves upon him with unnatural strength and power, forcing him down.

'Yes – now, then!' gasped Annie at length.

And there was a dead silence, in which the thud of heart-beating was to be heard. It was a suspense of pure silence in every soul.

'Now you know where you are,' said Annie.

The sight of his white, bare arm maddened the girls. He lay in a kind of trance of fear and antagonism. They felt themselves filled with supernatural strength.

Suddenly Polly started to laugh – to giggle wildly – helplessly – and Emma and Muriel joined in. But Annie and Nora and Laura remained the same, tense, watchful, with gleaming eyes. He winced away from these eyes.

'Yes,' said Annie, in a curious low tone, secret and deadly. 'Yes! You've got it now! You know what you've done, don't you? You know what you've done.'

He made no sound nor sign, but lay with bright, averted eyes, and averted, bleeding face.

'You ought to be *killed*, that's what you ought,' said Annie, tensely. 'You ought to be *killed*.' And there was a terrifying lust in her voice.

Polly was ceasing to laugh, and giving long-drawn Oh-h-hs and sighs as she came to herself.

'He's got to choose,' she said vaguely.

'Oh, yes, he has,' said Laura, with vindictive decision.

'Do you hear – do you hear?' said Annie. And with a sharp movement, that made him wince, she turned his face to her.

'Do you hear?' she repeated, shaking him.

But he was quite dumb. She fetched him a sharp slap on the face. He started, and his eyes widened. Then his face darkened with defiance, after all.

'Do you hear?' she repeated.

He only looked at her with hostile eyes.

'Speak!' she said, putting her face devilishly near his.

'What?' he said, almost overcome.

'You've got to *choose*!' she cried, as if it were some terrible menace, and as if it hurt her that she could not exact more.

'What?' he said, in fear.

'Choose your girl, Coddy. You've got to choose her now. And you'll get your neck broken if you play any more of your tricks, my boy. You're settled now.'

There was a pause. Again he averted his face. He was cunning in his overthrow. He did not give in to them really – no, not if they tore him to bits.

'All right, then,' he said, 'I choose Annie.' His voice was strange and full of malice. Annie let go of him as if he had been a hot coal.

'He's chosen Annie!' said the girls in chorus.

'Me!' cried Annie. She was still kneeling, but away from him. He was still lying prostrate, with averted face. The girls grouped uneasily around.

'Me!' repeated Annie, with a terrible bitter accent.

Then she got up, drawing away from him with strange disgust and bitterness.

'I wouldn't touch him,' she said.

But her face quivered with a kind of agony, she seemed as if she would fall. The other girls turned aside. He remained lying on the floor, with his torn clothes and bleeding, averted face.

'Oh, if he's chosen –' said Polly.

'I don't want him – he can choose again,' said Annie, with the same rather bitter hopelessness.

'Get up,' said Polly, lifting his shoulder. 'Get up.'

He rose slowly, a strange, ragged, dazed creature. The girls eyed him from a distance, curiously, furtively, dangerously.

'Who wants him?' cried Laura, roughly.

'Nobody,' they answered, with contempt. Yet each one of them waited for him to look at her, hoped he would look at her. All except Annie, and something was broken in her.

He, however, kept his face closed and averted from them all. There was a silence of the end. He picked up the torn pieces of his tunic, without knowing what to do with them. The girls stood about uneasily, flushed, panting, tidying their hair and their dress unconsciously, and watching him. He looked at none of them. He espied his cap in a corner, and went and picked it up. He put it on his head, and one of the girls burst into a shrill, hysteric laugh at the sight he presented. He, however, took no heed, but went straight to where his overcoat hung on a peg. The girls moved away from contact with him as if he had been an electric wire. He put on his coat and buttoned it down. Then he rolled his tunic-rags into a bundle, and stood before the locked door, dumbly.

'Open the door, somebody,' said Laura.

'Annie's got the key,' said one.

Annie silently offered the key to the girls. Nora unlocked the door.

'Tit for tat, old man,' she said. 'Show yourself a man, and don't bear a grudge.'

But without a word or sign he had opened the door and gone, his face closed, his head dropped.

'That'll learn him,' said Laura.

'Coddy!' said Nora.

'Shut up, for God's sake!' cried Annie fiercely, as if in torture.

'Well, I'm about ready to go, Polly. Look sharp!' said Muriel.

The girls were all anxious to be off. They were tidying themselves hurriedly, with mute, stupified faces.

The Blind Man

Isabel Pervin was listening for two sounds – for the sound of wheels on the drive outside and for the noise of her husband's footsteps in the hall. Her dearest and oldest friend, a man who seemed almost indispensable to her living, would drive up in the rainy dusk of the closing November day. The trap had gone to fetch him from the station. And her husband, who had been blinded in Flanders, and who had a disfiguring mark on his brow, would be coming in from the out-houses.

He had been home for a year now. He was totally blind. Yet they had been very happy. The Grange was Maurice's own place. The back was a farmstead, and the Wernhams, who occupied the rear premises, acted as farmers. Isabel lived with her husband in the handsome rooms in front. She and he had been almost entirely alone together since he was wounded. They talked and sang and read together in a wonderful and unspeakable intimacy. Then she reviewed books for a Scottish newspaper, carrying on her old interest, and he occupied himself a good deal with the farm. Sightless, he could still discuss everything with Wernham, and he could also do a good deal of work about the place – menial work, it is true, but it gave him satisfaction. He milked the cows, carried in the pails, turned the separator, attended to the pigs and horses. Life was still very full and strangely serene for the blind man, peaceful with the almost incomprehensible peace of immediate contact in darkness. With his wife he had a whole world, rich and real and invisible.

They were newly and remotely happy. He did not even regret the loss of his sight in these times of dark, palpable joy. A certain exultance swelled his soul.

But as time wore on, sometimes the rich glamour would leave them. Sometimes, after months of this intensity, a sense of burden overcame Isabel, a weariness, a terrible *ennui*, in that silent house approached between a colonnade of tall-shafted pines. Then she felt she would go mad, for she could not bear it. And sometimes he had devastating fits of depression, which seemed to lay waste his whole being. It was worse than depression – a black misery, when his own life was a torture to him, and when his presence was unbearable to his wife. The dread went down to the roots of her soul as these black days recurred. In a kind of panic she tried to wrap herself up still further in her husband. She forced the old spontaneous cheerfulness and joy to continue. But the effort it cost her was almost too much. She knew she could not keep it up. She felt she would scream with the strain, and would give anything, anything, to escape. She longed to possess her husband utterly; it gave her inordinate joy to have him entirely to herself. And yet, when again he was gone in a black and massive misery, she could not bear him, she could not bear herself; she wished she could be snatched away off the earth altogether, anything rather than live at this cost.

Dazed, she schemed for a way out. She invited friends, she tried to give him some further connection with the outer world. But it was no good. After all their joy and suffering, after their dark, great year of blindness and solitude and unspeakable nearness, other people seemed to them both shallow, prattling, rather impertinent. Shallow prattle seemed presumptuous. He became impatient and irritated, she was wearied. And so they lapsed into their solitude again. For they preferred it.

But now, in a few weeks' time, her second baby would be born. The first had died, an infant, when her husband first went out to France. She looked with joy and relief to the coming of the second. It would be her salvation. But also she felt some anxiety. She was thirty years old, her husband was a year younger. They both wanted a child very much. Yet she could not help feeling afraid. She had her husband on her hands, a terrible joy to her, and a terrifying burden. The child would occupy her love and attention. And then, what of Maurice? What would he do? If only she could feel that he, too, would be at peace and happy when the child came! She did so want to luxuriate in a rich, physical satisfaction of maternity. But the man, what would he do? How could she provide for him, how avert those shattering black moods of his, which destroyed them both?

She sighed with fear. But at this time Bertie Reid wrote to Isabel. He was her old friend, a second or third cousin, a Scotchman, as she was a Scotchwoman. They had been brought up near to one another, and all her life he had been her friend, like a brother, but better than her own brothers. She loved him – though not in the marrying sense. There was a sort of kinship between them, an affinity. They understood one another instinctively. But Isabel would never have thought of marrying Bertie. It would have seemed like marrying in her own family.

Bertie was a barrister and a man of letters, a Scotchman of the intellectual type, quick, ironical, sentimental, and on his knees before the woman he adored but did not want to marry. Maurice Pervin was different. He came of a good old country family – the Grange was not a very great distance from Oxford. He was passionate, sensitive, perhaps over-sensitive, wincing – a big fellow with heavy limbs and a forehead that flushed painfully. For his mind was slow, as if drugged by the strong provincial blood that beat in his veins. He was very sensitive to his own mental slowness, his feelings being quick and acute. So that he was just the opposite to Bertie, whose mind was much quicker than his emotions, which were not so very fine.

From the first the two men did not like each other. Isabel felt that they *ought* to get on together. But they did not. She felt that if only each could have the clue to the other there would be such a rare understanding between them. It did not come off, however. Bertie adopted a slightly ironical attitude, very offensive to Maurice, who returned the Scotch irony with English resentment, a resentment which deepened sometimes into stupid hatred.

This was a little puzzling to Isabel. However, she accepted it in the course of things. Men were made freakish and unreasonable. Therefore, when Maurice was going out to France for the second time, she felt that, for her husband's sake, she must discontinue her friendship with Bertie. She wrote to the barrister to this effect. Bertram Reid simply replied that in this, as in all other matters, he must obey her wishes, if these were indeed her wishes.

For nearly two years nothing had passed between the two friends. Isabel rather gloried in the fact; she had no compunction. She had one great article of faith, which was, that husband and wife should be so important to one another, that the rest of the world simply did not count. She and Maurice were husband and wife. They loved one another. They would have children. Then let everybody and everything else fade into insignificance outside this connubial felicity. She professed herself qute happy and ready to receive Maurice's friends. She was happy and ready: the happy wife, the ready woman in possession. Without knowing why, the friends retired abashed, and came no more. Maurice, of course, took as much satisfaction in this connubial absorption as Isabel did.

He shared in Isabel's literary activities, she cultivated a real interest in agriculture and cattle-raising. For she, being at heart perhaps an emotional enthusiast, always cultivated the practical side of life, and prided herself on her mastery of practical affairs. Thus the husband

and wife had spent the five years of their married life. The last had been one of blindness and unspeakable intimacy. And now Isabel felt a great indifference coming over her, a sort of lethargy. She wanted to be allowed to bear her child in peace, to nod by the fire and drift vaguely, physically, from day to day. Maurice was like an ominous thunder-cloud. She had to keep waking up to remember him.

When a little note came from Bertie, asking if he were to put up a tombstone to their dead friendship, and speaking of the real pain he felt on account of her husband's loss of sight, she felt a pang, a fluttering agitation of re-awakening. And she read the letter to Maurice.

'Ask him to come down,' he said.

'Ask Bertie to come here!' she re-echoed.

'Yes – if he wants to.'

Isabel paused for a few moments.

'I know he wants to – he'd only be too glad,' she replied. 'But what about you, Maurice? How would you like it?'

'I should like it.'

'Well – in that case – But I thought you didn't care for him –'

'Oh, I don't know. I might think differently of him now,' the blind man replied. It was rather abstruse to Isabel.

'Well, dear,' she said, 'if you're quite sure –'

'I'm sure enough. Let him come,' said Maurice.

So Bertie was coming, coming this evening, in the November rain and darkness. Isabel was agitated, racked with her old restlessness and indecision. She had always suffered from this pain of doubt, just an agonising sense of uncertainty. It had begun to pass off, in the lethargy of maternity. Now it returned, and she resented it. She struggled as usual to maintain her calm, composed, friendly bearing, a sort of mask she wore over all her body.

A woman had lighted a tall lamp beside the table, and spread the cloth. The long dining-room was dim, with its elegant but rather severe pieces of old furniture. Only the round table glowed softly under the light. It had a rich, beautiful effect. The white cloth glistened and dropped its heavy, pointed lace corners almost to the carpet, the china was old and handsome, creamy-yellow, with a blotched pattern of harsh red and deep blue, the cups large and bell-shaped, the teapot gallant. Isabel looked at it with superficial appreciation.

Her nerves were hurting her. She looked automatically again at the high, uncurtained windows. In the last dusk she could just perceive outside a huge fir-tree swaying its boughs: it was as if she thought it rather than saw it. The rain came flying on the window panes. Ah, why had she no peace? These two men, why did they tear at her? Why did they not come – why was there this suspense?

She sat in a lassitude that was really suspense and irritation. Maurice, at least, might come in – there was nothing to keep him out. She rose to her feet. Catching sight of her reflection in a mirror, she glanced at herself with a slight smile of recognition, as if she were an old friend to herself. Her face was oval and calm, her nose a little arched. Her neck made a beautiful line down to her shoulder. With hair knotted loosely behind, she had something of a warm, maternal look. Thinking this of herself, she arched her eyebrows and her rather heavy eyelids, with a little flicker of a smile, and for a moment her grey eyes looked amused and wicked, a little sardonic, out of her transfigured Madonna face.

Then, resuming her air of womanly patience – she was really fatally self-determined – she went with a little jerk towards the door. Her eyes were slightly reddened.

She passed down the wide hall, and through a door at the end. Then she was in the farm premises. The scent of dairy, and of farm-kitchen, and of farm-yard and of leather almost overcame her: but particularly the scent of dairy. They had been scalding out the pans. The flagged passage in front of her was dark, puddled and wet. Light came out from the open kitchen door. She went forward and stood in the doorway. The farm-people were at tea, seated at a little distance from her, round a long, narrow table, in the centre of which stood a white lamp. Ruddy faces, ruddy hands holding food, red mouths working, heads bent over the tea-cups: men, land-girls, boys: it was tea-time, feeding-time. Some faces caught sight of her. Mrs Wernham, going round behind the chairs with a large black teapot, halting slightly in her walk, was not aware of her for a moment. Then she turned suddenly.

'Oh, is it Madam!' she exclaimed. 'Come in, then, come in! We're at tea.' And she dragged forward a chair.

'No, I won't come in,' said Isabel. 'I'm afraid I interrupt your meal.'

'No – no – not likely, Madam, not likely.'

'Hasn't Mr Pervin come in, do you know?'

'I'm sure I couldn't say! Missed him, have you, Madam?'

'No, I only wanted him to come in,' laughed Isabel, as if shyly.

'Wanted him, did ye? Get up, boy – get up, now –'

Mrs Wernham knocked one of the boys on the shoulder. He began to scrape to his feet, chewing largely.

'I believe he's in top stable,' said another face from the table.

'Ah! No, don't get up. I'm going myself,' said Isabel.

'Don't you go out of a dirty night like this. Let the lad go. Get along wi' ye, boy,' said Mrs Wernham.

'No, no,' said Isabel, with a decision that was always obeyed. 'Go on with your tea, Tom. I'd like to go across to the stable, Mrs Wernham.'

'Did you ever hear tell!' exclaimed the woman.

'Isn't the trap late?' asked Isabel.

'Why, no,' said Mrs Wernham, peering into the distance at the tall, dim clock. 'No, Madam – we can give it another quarter or twenty minutes yet, good – yes, every bit of a quarter.'

'Ah! It seems late when darkness falls so early,' said Isabel.

'It do, that it do. Bother the days, that they draw in so,' answered Mrs Wernham. 'Proper miserable!'

'They are,' said Isabel, withdrawing.

She pulled on her overshoes, wrapped a large tartan shawl around her, put on a man's felt hat, and ventured out along the causeways of the first yard. It was very dark. The wind was roaring in the great elms behind the outhouses. When she came to the second yard the darkness seemed deeper. She was unsure of her footing. She wished she had brought a lantern. Rain blew against her. Half she liked it, half she felt unwilling to battle.

She reached at last the just visible door of the stable. There was no sign of a light anywhere. Opening the upper half, she looked in: into a simple well of darkness. The smell of horses, and ammonia, and of warmth was startling to her, in that full night. She listened with all her ears, but could hear nothing save the night, and the stirring of a horse.

'Maurice!' she called, softly and musically, though she was afraid. 'Maurice – are you there?'

Nothing came from the darkness. She knew the rain and wind blew in upon the horses, the hot animal life. Feeling it wrong, she entered the stable, and drew the lower half of the door shut, holding the upper part close. She did not stir, because she was aware of the presence of the dark hind-quarters of the horses, though she could not see them, and she was afraid. Something wild stirred in her heart.

She listened intensely. Then she heard a small noise in the distance – far away, it seemed – the chink of a pan, and a man's voice speaking a brief word. It would be Maurice, in the other part of the stable. She stood motionless, waiting for him to come through the partition door. The horses were so terrifyingly near to her, in the invisible.

The loud jarring of the inner door-latch made her start; the door was opened. She could hear and feel her husband entering and invisibly passing among the horses near to her, in darkness as they were, actively intermingled. The rather low sound of his voice as he spoke to the horses came velvety to her nerves. How near he was, and how invisible! The darkness seemed to be in a strange swirl of violent life, just upon her. She turned giddy.

Her presence of mind made her call, quietly and musically:

'Maurice! Maurice – dea-ar!'

'Yes,' he answered. 'Isabel?'

She saw nothing, and the sound of his voice seemed to touch her.

'Hello!' she answered cheerfully, straining her eyes to see him. He was still busy, attending to the horses near her, but she saw only darkness. It made her almost desperate.

'Won't you come in, dear?' she said.

'Yes, I'm coming. Just half a minute. *Stand over – now!* Trap's not come, has it?'

'Not yet,' said Isabel.

His voice was pleasant and ordinary, but it had a slight suggestion of the stable to her. She wished he would come away. Whilst he was so utterly invisible she was afraid of him.

'How's the time?' he asked.

'Not yet six,' she replied. She disliked to answer into the dark. Presently he came very near to her, and she retreated out of doors.

'The weather blows in here,' he said, coming steadily forward, feeling for the doors. She shrank away. At last she could dimly see him.

'Bertie won't have much of a drive,' he said, as he closed the doors.

'He won't indeed!' said Isabel calmly, watching the dark shape at the door.

'Give me your arm, dear,' she said.

She pressed his arm close to her, as she went. But she longed to see him, to look at him. She was nervous. He walked erect, with face rather lifted, but with a curious tentative movement of his powerful, muscular legs. She could feel the clever, careful, strong contact of his feet with the earth, as she balanced against him. For a moment he was a tower of darkness to her, as if he rose out of the earth.

In the house-passage he wavered, and went cautiously, with a curious look of silence about him as he felt for the bench. Then he sat down heavily. He was a man with rather sloping shoulders, but with heavy limbs, powerful legs that seemed to know the earth. His head was small, usually carried high and light. As he bent down to unfasten his gaiters and boots he did not look blind. His hair was brown and crisp, his hands were large, reddish, intelligent, the veins stood out in the wrists; and his thighs and knees seemed massive. When he stood up his face and neck were surcharged with blood, the veins stood out on his temples. She did not look at his blindness.

Isabel was always glad when they had passed through the dividing door into their own regions of repose and beauty. She was a little afraid of him, out there in the animal grossness of the back. His bearing also changed, as he smelt the familiar, indefinable odour that pervaded his wife's surroundings, a delicate, refined scent, very faintly spicy. Perhaps it came from the pot-pourri bowls.

He stood at the foot of the stairs, arrested, listening. She watched him, and her heart sickened. He seemed to be listening to fate.

'He's not here yet,' he said. 'I'll go up and change.'

'Maurice,' she said, 'you're not wishing he wouldn't come, are you?'

'I couldn't quite say,' he answered. 'I feel myself rather on the *qui vive*.'[1]

'I can see you are,' she answered. And she reached up and kissed his cheek. She saw his mouth relax into a slow smile.

'What are you laughing at?' she said roguishly.

'You consoling me,' he answered.

'Nay,' she answered. 'Why should I console you? You know we love each other – you know *how* married we are! What does anything else matter?'

'Nothing at all, my dear.'

He felt for her face, and touched it, smiling.

'*You're* all right, aren't you?' he asked, anxiously.

'I'm wonderfully all right, love,' she answered. 'It's you I am a little troubled about, at times.'

'Why me?' he said, touching her cheeks delicately with the tips of his fingers. The touch had an almost hypnotising effect on her.

He went away upstairs. She saw him mount into darkness, unseeing and unchanging. He did not know that the lamps on the upper corridor were unlighted. He went on into the darkness with unchanging step. She heard him in the bath-room.

Pervin moved about almost unconsciously in his familiar surroundings, dark though everything was. He seemed to know the presence of objects before he touched them. It was a pleasure to him to rock thus through a world of things, carried on the flood in a sort of blood-prescience. He did not think much or trouble much. So long as he kept this sheer immediacy of blood-contact with the substantial world he was happy, he wanted no intervention of visual consciousness. In this state there was a certain rich positivity, bordering sometimes on rapture. Life seemed to move in him like a tide lapping, lapping, and advancing, enveloping all things darkly. It was a pleasure to stretch forth the hand and meet the unseen object, clasp it, and possess it in pure contact. He did not try to remember, to visualise. He did not want to. The new way of consciousness substituted itself in him.

The rich suffusion of this state generally kept him happy, reaching its culmination in the consuming passion for his wife. But at times the flow would seem to be checked and thrown back. Then it would beat inside him like a tangled sea, and he was tortured in the shattered chaos of his own blood. He grew to dread this arrest, this throw-back, this chaos inside himself, when he seemed merely at the mercy of his own powerful and conflicting elements. How to get some measure of control or surety, this was the question. And when the question rose maddening in him, he would clench his fists as if he would *compel* the whole universe to submit to him. But it was in vain. He could not even compel himself.

To-night, however, he was still serene, though little tremors of unreasonable exasperation ran through him. He had to handle the razor very carefully, as he shaved, for it was not at one with him, he was afraid of it. His hearing also was too much sharpened. He heard the woman lighting the lamps on the corridor, and attending to the fire in the visitor's room. And then, as he went to his room he heard the trap arrive. Then came Isabel's voice, lifted and calling, like a bell ringing:

'Is it you, Bertie? Have you come?'

And a man's voice answered out of the wind:

'Hello, Isabel! There you are.'

'Have you had a miserable drive? I'm so sorry we couldn't send a closed carriage. I can't see you at all, you know.'

'I'm coming. No, I liked the drive – it was like Perthshire. Well, how are you? You're looking fit as ever, as far as I can see.'

'Oh, yes,' said Isabel. 'I'm wonderfully well. How are you? Rather thin, I think –'

'Worked to death – everybody's old cry. But I'm all right, Ciss. How's Pervin? – isn't he here?'

'Oh, yes, he's upstairs changing. Yes, he's awfully well. Take off your wet things; I'll send them to be dried.'

'And how are you both, in spirits? He doesn't fret?'

'No – no, not at all. No, on the contrary, really. We've been wonderfully happy, incredibly. It's more than I can understand – so wonderful: the nearness, and the peace –'

'Ah! Well, that's awfully good news –'

They moved away. Pervin heard no more. But a childish sense of desolation had come over him, as he heard their brisk voices. He seemed shut out – like a child that is left out. He was aimless and excluded, he did not know what to do with himself. The helpless desolation came over him. He fumbled nervously as he dressed himself, in a state almost of childishness. He disliked the Scotch accent in Bertie's speech, and the slight response it found on Isabel's tongue. He disliked the slight purr of complacency in the Scottish speech. He disliked intensely the glib way in which Isabel spoke of their happiness and nearness. It made him recoil. He was fretful and beside himself like a child, he had almost a childish nostalgia to be included in the life circle. And at the same time he was a man, dark and powerful and infuriated by his own weakness. By some fatal flaw, he could not be by himself, he had to depend on the support of another. And this very dependence enraged him. He hated Bertie Reid, and at the same time he knew the hatred was nonsense, he knew it was the outcome of his own weakness.

He went downstairs. Isabel was alone in the dining-room. She watched him enter, head erect, his feet tentative. He looked so strong-blooded and healthy, and, at the same time, cancelled. Cancelled – that was the word that flew across her mind. Perhaps it was his scars suggested it.

'You heard Bertie come, Maurice?' she said.

'Yes – isn't he here?'

'He's in his room. He looks very thin and worn.'

'I suppose he works himself to death.'

A woman came in with a tray – and after a few minutes Bertie came down. He was a little dark man, with a very big forehead, thin, wispy hair, and sad, large eyes. His expression was inordinately sad – almost funny. He had odd, short legs.

Isabel watched him hesitate under the door, and glance nervously at her husband. Pervin heard him and turned.

'Here you are, now,' said Isabel. 'Come, let us eat.'

Bertie went across to Maurice.

'How are you, Pervin,' he said, as he advanced.

The blind man stuck his hand out into space, and Bertie took it.

'Very fit. Glad you've come,' said Maurice.

Isabel glanced at them, and glanced away, as if she could not bear to see them.

'Come,' she said. 'Come to table. Aren't you both awfully hungry? I am, tremendously.'

'I'm afraid you waited for me,' said Bertie, as they sat down.

Maurice had a curious monolithic way of sitting in a chair, erect and distant. Isabel's heart always beat when she caught sight of him thus.

'No,' she replied to Bertie. 'We're very little later than usual. We're having a sort of high tea, not dinner. Do you mind? It gives us such a nice long evening, uninterrupted.'

'I like it,' said Bertie.

Maurice was feeling, with curious little movements, almost like a cat kneading her bed, for his place, his knife and fork, his napkin. He was getting the whole geography of his cover into consciousness. He sat erect and inscrutable, remote-seeming. Bertie watched the static figure of the blind man, the delicate tactile discernment of the large, ruddy hands, and the curious mindless silence of the brow, above the scar. With difficulty he looked away, and without knowing what he did, picked up a little crystal bowl of violets from the table, and held them to his nose.

'They are sweet-scented,' he said. 'Where do they come from?'

'From the garden – under the windows,' said Isabel.

'So late in the year – and so fragrant! Do you remember the violets under Aunt Bell's south wall?'

The two friends looked at each other and exchanged a smile, Isabel's eyes lighting up.

'Don't I?' she replied. '*Wasn't* she queer!'

'A curious old girl,' laughed Bertie. 'There's a streak of freakishness in the family, Isabel.'

'Ah – but not in you and me, Bertie,' said Isabel. 'Give them to Maurice, will you?' she added, as Bertie was putting down the flowers. 'Have you smelled the violets, dear? Do! – they are so scented.'

Maurice held out his hand, and Bertie placed the tiny bowl against his large, warm-looking fingers. Maurice's hand closed over the thin white fingers of the barrister. Bertie carefully extricated himself. Then the two watched the blind man smelling the violets. He bent his head and seemed to be thinking. Isabel waited.

'Aren't they sweet, Maurice?' she said at last, anxiously.

'Very,' he said. And he held out the bowl. Bertie took it. Both he and Isabel were a little afraid, and deeply disturbed.

The meal continued. Isabel and Bertie chatted spasmodically. The blind man was silent. He touched his food repeatedly, with quick, delicate touches of his knife-point, then cut irregular bits. He could not bear to be helped. Both Isabel and Bertie suffered: Isabel wondered why. She did not suffer when she was alone with Maurice. Bertie made her conscious of a strangeness.

After the meal the three drew their chairs to the fire, and sat down to talk. The decanters were put on a table near at hand. Isabel knocked the logs on the fire, and clouds of brilliant sparks went up the chimney. Bertie noticed a slight weariness in her bearing.

'You will be glad when your child comes now, Isabel?' he said.

She looked up to him with a quick wan smile.

'Yes. I shall be glad,' she answered. 'It begins to seem long. Yes, I shall be very glad. So will you Maurice, won't you?' she added.

'Yes, I shall,' replied her husband.

'We are both looking forward so much to having it,' she said.

'Yes, of course,' said Bertie.

He was a bachelor, three or four years older than Isabel. He lived in beautiful rooms overlooking the river, guarded by a faithful Scottish man-servant. And he had his friends among the fair sex – not lovers, friends. So long as he could avoid any danger of courtship or marriage, he adored a few women with constant and unfailing homage, and he was chivalrously fond of quite a number. But if they seemed to encroach on him, he withdrew and detested them.

Isabel knew him very well, knew his beautiful constancy, and kindness, also his incurable weakness, which made him unable ever to enter into close contact of any sort. He was ashamed of himself, because he could not marry, could not approach women physically. He wanted to do so. But he could not. At the centre of him he was afraid, helplessly and even brutally afraid. He had given up hope, had ceased to expect any more that he could escape his own weakness. Hence he was a brilliant and successful barrister, also *littérateur* of high repute, a rich man, and a great social success. At the centre he felt himself neuter, nothing.

Isabel knew him well. She despised him even while she admired him. She looked at his sad face, his little short legs, and felt contempt of him. She looked at his dark grey eyes, with their uncanny, almost childlike intuition, and she loved him. He understood amazingly – but she had no fear of his understanding. As a man she patronised him.

And she turned to the impassive, silent figure of her husband. He sat leaning back, with folded arms, and face a little uptilted. His knees were straight and massive. She sighed, picked up the poker, and again began to prod the fire, to rouse the clouds of soft, brilliant sparks.

'Isabel tells me,' Bertie began suddenly, 'that you have not suffered unbearably from the loss of sight.'

Maurice straightened himself to attend, but kept his arms folded.

'No,' he said, 'not unbearably. Now and again one struggles against it, you know. But there are compensations.'

'They say it is much worse to be stone deaf,' said Isabel.

'I believe it is,' said Bertie. 'Are there compensations?' he added, to Maurice.

'Yes. You cease to bother about a great many things.' Again Maurice stretched his figure, stretched the strong muscles of his back, and leaned backwards, with uplifted face.

'And that is a relief,' said Bertie. 'But what is there in place of the bothering? What replaces the activity?'

There was a pause. At length the blind man replied, as out of a negligent, unattentive thinking:

'Oh, I don't know. There's a good deal when you're not active.'

'Is there?' said Bertie. 'What, exactly? It always seems to me that when there is no thought and no action, there is nothing.'

Again Maurice was slow in replying.

'There is something,' he replied. 'I couldn't tell you what it is.'

And the talk lapsed once more, Isabel and Bertie chatting gossip and reminiscence, the blind man silent.

At length Maurice rose restlessly, a big, obtrusive figure. He felt tight and hampered. He wanted to go away.

'Do you mind,' he said, 'if I go and speak to Wernham?'

'No – go along, dear,' said Isabel.

And he went out. A silence came over the two friends. At length Bertie said:

'Nevertheless, it is a great deprivation, Cissie.'

'It is, Bertie. I know it is.'

'Something lacking all the time,' said Bertie.

'Yes, I know. And yet – and yet – Maurice is right. There is something else, something *there*, which you never knew was there, and which you can't express.'

'What is there?' asked Bertie.

'I don't know – it's awfully hard to define it – but something strong and immediate. There's something strange in Maurice's presence – indefinable – but I couldn't do without it. I agree that it seems to put one's mind to sleep. But when we're alone I miss nothing; it seems awfully rich, almost splendid, you know.'

'I'm afraid I don't follow,' said Bertie.

They talked desultorily. The wind blew loudly outside, rain chattered on the window-panes, making a sharp, drum-sound, because of the closed, mellow-golden shutters inside. The logs burned slowly, with hot, almost invisible small flames. Bertie seemed uneasy, there were dark circles round his eyes. Isabel, rich with her approaching maternity, leaned looking into the fire. Her hair curled in odd, loose strands, very pleasing to the man. But she had a curious feeling of old woe in her heart, old, timeless night-woe.

'I suppose we're all deficient somewhere,' said Bertie.

'I suppose so,' said Isabel wearily.

'Damned, sooner or later.'

'I don't know,' she said, rousing herself. 'I feel quite all right, you know. The child coming seems to make me indifferent to everything, just placid. I can't feel that there's anything to trouble about, you know.'

'A good thing, I should say,' he replied slowly.

'Well, there it is. I suppose it's just Nature. If only I felt I needn't trouble about Maurice, I should be perfectly content –'

'But you feel you must trouble about him?'

'Well – I don't know –' She even resented this much effort.

The evening passed slowly. Isabel looked at the clock. 'I say,' she said. 'It's nearly ten o'clock. Where can Maurice be? I'm sure they're all in bed at the back. Excuse me a moment.'

She went out, returning almost immediately.

'It's all shut up and in darkness,' she said. 'I wonder where he is. He must have gone out to the farm –'

Bertie looked at her.

'I suppose he'll come in,' he said.

'I suppose so,' she said. 'But it's unusual for him to be out now.'

'Would you like me to go out and see?'

'Well – if you wouldn't mind. I'd go, but –' She did not want to make the physical effort.

Bertie put on an old overcoat and took a lantern. He went out from the side door. He shrank from the wet and roaring night. Such weather had a nervous effect on him: too much moisture everywhere made him feel almost imbecile. Unwilling, he went through it all. A dog barked violently at him. He peered in all the buildings. At last, as he opened the upper door of a sort of intermediate barn, he heard a grinding noise, and looking in, holding up his lantern, saw Maurice, in his shirt-sleeves, standing listening, holding the handle of a turnip-pulper. He had been pulping sweet roots, a pile of which lay dimly heaped in a corner behind him.

'That you, Wernham?' said Maurice, listening.

'No, it's me,' said Bertie.

A large, half-wild grey cat was rubbing at Maurice's leg. The blind man stooped to rub its sides. Bertie watched the scene, then unconsciously entered and shut the door behind him. He was in a high sort of barn-place, from which, right and left, ran off the corridors in front of the stalled cattle. He watched the slow, stooping motion of the other man, as he caressed the great cat.

Maurice straightened himself.

'You came to look for me?' he said.

'Isabel was a little uneasy,' said Bertie.

'I'll come in. I like messing about doing these jobs.'

The cat had reared her sinister, feline length against his leg, clawing at his thigh affectionately. He lifted her claws out of his flesh.

'I hope I'm not in your way at all at the Grange here,' said Bertie, rather shy and stiff.

'My way? No, not a bit. I'm glad Isabel has somebody to talk to. I'm afraid it's I who am in the way. I know I'm not very lively company. Isabel's all right, don't you think? She's not unhappy, is she?'

'I don't think so.'

'What does she say?'

'She says she's very content – only a little troubled about you.'

'Why me?'

'Perhaps afraid that you might brood,' said Bertie, cautiously.

'She needn't be afraid of that.' He continued to caress the flattened grey head of the cat with his fingers. 'What I am a bit afraid of,' he resumed, 'is that she'll find me a dead weight, always alone with me down here.'

'I don't think you need think that,' said Bertie, though this was what he feared himself.

'I don't know,' said Maurice. 'Sometimes I feel it isn't fair that she's saddled with me.' Then he dropped his voice curiously. 'I say,' he asked, secretly struggling, 'is my face much disfigured? Do you mind telling me?'

'There is a scar,' said Bertie, wondering. 'Yes, it is a disfigurement. But more pitiable than shocking.'

'A pretty bad scar, though,' said Maurice.

'Oh, yes.'

There was a pause.

'Sometimes I feel I am horrible,' said Maurice, in a low voice, talking as if to himself. And Bertie actually felt a quiver of horror.

'That's nonsense,' he said.

Maurice again straightened himself, leaving the cat.

'There's no telling,' he said. Then again, in an odd tone, he added: 'I don't really know you, do I?'

'Probably not,' said Bertie.

'Do you mind if I touch you?'

The lawyer shrank away instinctively. And yet, out of very philanthropy, he said, in a small voice: 'Not at all.'

But he suffered as the blind man stretched out a strong, naked hand to him. Maurice accidentally knocked off Bertie's hat.

'I thought you were taller,' he said, starting. Then he laid his hand on Bertie Reid's head, closing the dome of the skull in a soft, firm grasp, gathering it, as it were; then, shifting his grasp and softly closing again, with a fine, close pressure, till he had covered the skull and the face of the smaller man, tracing the brows, and touching the full, closed eyes, touching the small nose and the nostrils, the rough, short moustache, the mouth, the rather strong chin. The hand of the blind man grasped the shoulder, the arm, the hand of the other man. He seemed to take him, in the soft, travelling grasp.

'You seem young,' he said quietly, at last.

The lawyer stood almost annihilated, unable to answer.

'Your head seems tender, as if you were young,' Maurice repeated. 'So do your hands. Touch my eyes, will you? – touch my scar.'

Now Bertie quivered with revulsion. Yet he was under the power of the blind man, as if hypnotised. He lifted his hand, and laid the fingers on the scar, on the scarred eyes. Maurice suddenly covered them with his own hand, pressed the fingers of the other man upon his disfigured eye-sockets, trembling in every fibre, and rocking slightly, slowly, from side to side. He remained thus for a minute or more, whilst Bertie stood as if in a swoon, unconscious, imprisoned.

Then suddenly Maurice removed the hand of the other man from his brow, and stood holding it in his own.

'Oh, my God,' he said, 'we shall know each other now, shan't we? We shall know each other now.'

Bertie could not answer. He gazed mute and terror-struck, overcome by his own weakness. He knew he could not answer. He had an unreasonable fear, lest the other man should suddenly destroy him.

Whereas Maurice was actually filled with hot, poignant love, the passion of friendship. Perhaps it was this very passion of friendship which Bertie shrank from most.

'We're all right together now, aren't we?' said Maurice. 'It's all right now, as long as we live, so far as we're concerned?'

'Yes,' said Bertie, trying by any means to escape.

Maurice stood with head lifted, as if listening. The new delicate fulfilment of mortal friendship had come as a revelation and surprise to him, something exquisite and unhoped-for. He seemed to be listening to hear if it were real.

Then he turned for his coat.

'Come,' he said, 'we'll go to Isabel.'

Bertie took the lantern and opened the door. The cat disappeared. The two men went in silence along the causeways. Isabel, as they came, thought their footsteps sounded strange. She looked up pathetically and anxiously for their entrance. There seemed a curious elation about Maurice. Bertie was haggard, with sunken eyes.

'What is it?' she asked.

'We've become friends,' said Maurice, standing with his feet apart, like a strange colossus.[2]

'Friends!' re-echoed Isabel. And she looked again at Bertie. He met her eyes with a furtive, haggard look; his eyes were as if glazed with misery.

'I'm so glad,' she said, in sheer perplexity.

'Yes,' said Maurice.

He was indeed so glad. Isabel took his hand with both hers, and held it fast.

'You'll be happier now, dear,' she said.

But she was watching Bertie. She knew that he had one desire – to escape from this intimacy, this friendship, which had been thrust upon him. He could not bear it that he had been touched by the blind man, his insane reserve broken in. He was like a mollusc whose shell is broken.

Fanny and Annie

FLAME-LURID his face as he turned among the throng of flame-lit and dark faces upon the platform. In the light of the furnace she caught sight of his drifting countenance, like a piece of floating fire. And the nostalgia, the doom of home-coming went through her veins like a drug. His eternal face, flame-lit now! The pulse and darkness of red fire from the furnace towers in the sky, lighting the desultory, industrial crowd on the wayside station, lit him and went out.

Of course he did not see her. Flame-lit and unseeing! Always the same, with his meeting eyebrows, his common cap, and his red-and-black scarf knotted round his throat. Not even a collar to meet her! The flames had sunk, there was shadow.

She opened the door of her grimy, branch-line carriage, and began to get down her bags. The porter was nowhere, of course, but there was Harry, obscure, on the outer edge of the little crowd, missing her, of course.

'Here! Harry!' she called, waving her umbrella in the twilight. He hurried forward.

'Tha's come, has ter?' he said, in a sort of cheerful welcome. She got down, rather flustered, and gave him a peck of a kiss.

'Two suit-cases!' she said.

Her soul groaned within her, as he clambered into the carriage after her bags. Up shot the fire in the twilight sky, from the great furnace behind the station. She felt the red flame go across her face. She had come back, she had come back for good. And her spirit groaned dismally. She doubted if she could bear it.

There, on the sordid little station under the furnaces, she stood, tall and distinguished, in her well-made coat and skirt and her broad grey velour hat. She held her umbrella, her bead chatelaine, and a little leather case in her grey-gloved hands, while Harry staggered out of the ugly little train with her bags.

'There's a trunk at the back,' she said in her bright voice. But she was not feeling bright. The twin black cones of the iron foundry blasted their sky-high fires into the night. The whole scene was lurid. The train waited cheerfully. It would wait another ten minutes. She knew it. It was all so deadly familiar.

Let us confess it at once. She was a lady's maid, thirty years old, come back to marry her first-love, a foundry worker: after having kept him dangling, off and on, for a dozen years. Why had she come back? Did she love him? No. She didn't pretend to. She had loved her brilliant and ambitious cousin, who had jilted her, and who had died. She had had other affairs which had come to nothing. So here she was, come back suddenly to marry her first-love, who had waited – or remained single – all these years.

'Won't a porter carry those?' she said, as Harry strode with his workman's stride down the platform towards the guard's van.

'I can manage,' he said.

And with her umbrella, her chatelaine, and her little leather case, she followed him.

The trunk was there.

'We'll get Heather's greengrocer's cart to fetch it up,' he said.

'Isn't there a cab?' said Fanny, knowing dismally enough that there wasn't.

'I'll just put it aside o' the penny-in-the-slot, and Heather's greengrocers'll fetch it about half-past eight,' he said.

He seized the box by its two handles and staggered with it across the level-crossing, bumping his legs against it as he waddled. Then he dropped it by the red sweet-meats machine.

'Will it be safe there?' she said.

'Ay – safe as houses,' he answered. He returned for the two bags. Thus laden, they started to plod up the hill, under the great long black building of the foundry. She walked beside him – workman of workmen he was, trudging with that luggage. The red lights flared over the deepening darkness. From the foundry came the horrible, slow clang, clang, clang of iron, a great noise, with an interval just long enough to make it unendurable.

Compare this with the arrival at Gloucester: the carriage for her mistress, the dog-cart for herself with the luggage; the drive out past the river, the pleasant trees of the carriage-approach; and herself sitting beside Arthur, everybody so polite to her.

She had come home – for good! Her heart nearly stopped beating as she trudged up that hideous and interminable hill, beside the laden figure. What a come-down! What a come-down! She could not take it with her usual bright cheerfulness. She knew it all too well. It is easy to bear up against the unusual, but the deadly familiarity of an old stale past!

He dumped the bags down under a lamp-post, for a rest. There they stood, the two of them, in the lamp-light. Passers-by stared at her, and gave good-night to Harry. Her they hardly knew, she had become a stranger.

'They're too heavy for you, let me carry one,' she said.

'They begin to weigh a bit by the time you've gone a mile,' he answered.

'Let me carry the little one,' she insisted.

'Tha can ha'e it for a minute, if ter's a mind,' he said, handing over the valise.

And thus they arrived in the streets of shops of the little ugly town on top of the hill. How everybody stared at her; my word, how they stared! And the cinema was just going in, and the queues were tailing down the road to the corner. And everybody took full stock of her. 'Night, Harry!' shouted the fellows, in an interested voice.

However, they arrived at her aunt's – a little sweet-shop in a side street. They 'pinged' the door-bell, and her aunt came running forward out of the kitchen.

'There you are, child! Dying for a cup of tea, I'm sure. How are you?'

Fanny's aunt kissed her, and it was all Fanny could do to refrain from bursting into tears, she felt so low. Perhaps it was her tea she wanted.

'You've had a drag with that luggage,' said Fanny's aunt to Harry.

'Ay – I'm not sorry to put it down,' he said, looking at his hand which was crushed and cramped by the bag handle.

Then he departed to see about Heather's green-grocery cart.

When Fanny sat at tea, her aunt, a grey-haired, fair-faced little woman, looked at her with an admiring heart, feeling bitterly sore for her. For Fanny was beautiful: tall, erect, finely coloured, with her delicately arched nose, her rich brown hair, her large lustrous grey eyes. A passionate woman – a woman to be afraid of. So proud, so inwardly violent! She came of a violent race.

It needed a woman to sympathise with her. Men had not the courage. Poor Fanny! She was such a lady, and so straight and magnificent. And yet everything seemed to do her down. Every time she seemed to be doomed to humiliation and disappointment, this handsome, brilliantly sensitive woman, with her nervous, over-wrought laugh.

'So you've really come back, child?' said her aunt.

'I really have, Aunt,' said Fanny.

'Poor Harry! I'm not sure, you know, Fanny, that you're not taking a bit of an advantage of him.'

'Oh, Aunt, he's waited so long, he may as well have what he's waited for.' Fanny laughed grimly.

'Yes, child, he's waited so long, that I'm not sure it isn't a bit hard on him. You know, I *like* him, Fanny – though as you know quite well, I don't think he's good enough for you. And I think he thinks so himself, poor fellow.'

'Don't you be so sure of that, Aunt. Harry is common, but he's not humble. He wouldn't think the Queen was any too good for him, if he'd a mind to her.'

'Well – It's as well if he has a proper opinion of himself.'

'It depends what you call proper,' said Fanny. 'But he's got his good points –'

'Oh, he's a nice fellow, and I like him, I do like him. Only, as I tell you, he's not good enough for you.'

'I've made up my mind, Aunt,' said Fanny, grimly.

'Yes,' mused the aunt. 'They say all things come to him who waits –'

'More than he's bargained for, eh, Aunt?' laughed Fanny rather bitterly.

The poor aunt, this bitterness grieved her for her niece.

They were interrupted by the ping of the shop-bell, and Harry's call of 'Right!' But as he did not come in at once, Fanny, feeling solicitous for him presumably at the moment, rose and went into the shop. She saw a cart outside, and went to the door.

And the moment she stood in the doorway, she heard a woman's common vituperative voice crying from the darkness of the opposite side of the road:

'Tha'rt theer, are ter? I'll shame thee, Mester. I'll shame thee, see if I dunna.'

Startled, Fanny stared across the darkness, and saw a woman in a black bonnet go under one of the lamps up the side street.

Harry and Bill Heather had dragged the trunk off the little dray, and she retreated before them as they came up the shop step with it.

'Wheer shalt ha'e it?' asked Harry.

'Best take it upstairs,' said Fanny.

She went up first to light the gas.

When Heather had gone, and Harry was sitting down having tea and pork pie, Fanny asked:

'Who was that woman shouting?'

'Nay, I canna tell thee. To somebody, Is'd think,' replied Harry. Fanny looked at him, but asked no more.

He was a fair-haired fellow of thirty-two, with a fair moustache. He was broad in his speech, and looked like a foundry-hand, which he was. But women always liked him. There was something of a mother's lad about him – something warm and playful and really sensitive.

He had his attractions even for Fanny. What she rebelled against so bitterly was that he had no sort of ambition. He was a moulder, but of very commonplace skill. He was thirty-two years old, and hadn't saved twenty pounds. She would have to provide the money for the home. He didn't care. He just didn't care. He had no initiative at all. He had no vices – no obvious ones. But he was just indifferent, spending as he went, and not caring. Yet he did not look happy. She remembered his face in the fire-glow: something haunted, abstracted about it. As he sat there eating his pork pie, bulging his cheek out, she felt he was like a doom to her. And she raged against the doom of him. It wasn't that he was gross. His *way* was common, almost on purpose. But he himself wasn't really common. For instance, his food was not particularly important to him, he was not greedy. He had a charm, too, particularly for women, with his blondeness and his sensitiveness and his way of making a woman feel that she was a higher being. But Fanny knew him, knew the peculiar obstinate limitedness of him, that would nearly send her mad.

He stayed till about half-past nine. She went to the door with him.

'When are you coming up?' he said, jerking his head in the direction, presumably, of his own home.

'I'll come to-morrow afternoon,' she said brightly. Between Fanny and Mrs Goodall, his mother, there was naturally no love lost.

Again she gave him an awkward little kiss, and said good-night.

'You can't wonder, you know, child, if he doesn't seem so very keen,' said her aunt. 'It's your own fault.'

'Oh, Aunt, I couldn't stand him when he was keen. I can do with him a lot better as he is.'

The two women sat and talked far into the night. They understood each other. The aunt, too, had married as Fanny was marrying: a man who was no companion to her, a violent man, brother of Fanny's father. He was dead, Fanny's father was dead.

Poor Aunt Lizzie, she cried woefully over her bright niece, when she had gone to bed.

Fanny paid the promised visit to his people the next afternoon. Mrs Goodall was a large woman with smooth-parted hair, a common, obstinate woman, who had spoiled her four lads and her one vixen of a married daughter. She was one of those old-fashioned powerful natures that couldn't do with looks or education or any form of showing off. She fairly hated the sound of correct English. She *thee'd* and *tha'd* her prospective daughter-in-law, and said:

'I'm none as ormin'[1] as I look, seest ta.'

Fanny did not think her prospective mother-in-law looked at all orming, so the speech was unnecessary.

'I towd him mysen,' said Mrs Goodall. ''Er's held back all this long, let 'er stop as 'er is. 'E'd none ha' had thee for *my* tellin' – tha hears. No, 'e's a fool, an' I know it. I says to him, "Tha looks a man, doesn't ter, at thy age, goin' an' openin' to her when ter hears her scrat' at th' gate, after she's done gallivantin' round wherever she'd a mind. That looks rare an' soft." But it's no use o' any talking: he answered that letter o' thine and made his own bad bargain.'

But in spite of the old woman's anger, she was also flattered at Fanny's coming back to Harry. For Mrs Goodall was impressed by Fanny – a woman of her own match. And more than this, everybody knew that Fanny's Aunt Kate had left her two hundred pounds: this apart from the girl's savings.

So there was high tea in Princes Street when Harry came home black from work, and a rather acrid odour of cordiality, the vixen Jinny darting in to say vulgar things. Of course Jinny lived in a house whose garden end joined the paternal garden. They were a clan who stuck together, these Goodalls.

It was arranged that Fanny should come to tea again on the Sunday, and the wedding was discussed. It should take place in a fortnight's time at Morley Chapel. Morley was a hamlet on the edge of the real country, and in its little Congregational Chapel Fanny and Harry had first met.

What a creature of habit he was! He was still in the choir of Morley Chapel – not very regular. He belonged just because he had a tenor voice, and enjoyed singing. Indeed his solos were only spoilt to local fame because when he sang he handled his aitches so hopelessly.

'And I saw 'eaven hopened
And be'old, a wite 'orse –'

This was one of Harry's classics, only surpassed by the fine outburst of his heaving:

'Hangels – hever bright an' fair –'

It was a pity, but it was inalterable. He had a good voice, and he sang with a certain lacerating fire, but his pronunciation made it all funny. And *nothing* could alter him.

So he was never heard save at cheap concerts and in the little, poorer chapels. The others scoffed.

Now the month was September, and Sunday was Harvest Festival at Morley Chapel, and Harry was singing solos. So that Fanny was to go to afternoon service, and come home to a grand spread of Sunday tea with him. Poor Fanny! One of the most wonderful afternoons had been a Sunday afternoon service, with her cousin Luther at her side, Harvest Festival at Morley Chapel. Harry had sung solos then – ten years ago. She remembered his pale blue tie, and the purple asters and the great vegetable marrows in which he was framed, and her cousin Luther at her side, young, clever, come down from London, where he was getting on well, learning his Latin and his French and German so brilliantly.

However, once again it was Harvest Festival at Morley Chapel, and once again, as ten years before, a soft, exquisite September day, with the last roses pink in the cottage gardens, the last dahlias crimson, the last sunflowers yellow. And again the little old chapel was a bower, with its famous sheaves of corn and corn-plaited pillars, its great bunches of grapes, dangling like tassels from the pulpit corners, its marrows and potatoes and pears and apples and damsons, its purple asters and yellow Japanese sunflowers. Just as before, the red dahlias round the pillars were dropping, weak-headed among the oats. The place was crowded and hot, the plates of tomatoes seemed balanced perilous on the gallery front, the Rev. Enderby was weirder than ever to look at, so long and emaciated and hairless.

The Rev. Enderby, probably forewarned, came and shook hands with her and welcomed her, in his broad northern, melancholy singsong before he mounted the pulpit. Fanny was handsome in a gauzy dress and a beautiful lace hat. Being a little late, she sat in a chair in the side-aisle wedged in, right in the front of the chapel. Harry was in the gallery above, and she could only see him from the eyes upwards. She noticed again how his eyebrows met, blonde and not very marked, over his nose. He was attractive too: physically lovable, very. If only – if only her *pride* had not suffered! She felt he dragged her down.

'Come, ye thankful people, come,
Raise the song of harvest-home.
All is safely gathered in
Ere the winter storms begin –'

Even the hymn was a falsehood, as the season had been wet, and half the crops were still out, and in a poor way.

Poor Fanny! She sang little, and looked beautiful through that inappropriate hymn. Above her stood Harry – mercifully in a dark suit and a dark tie, looking almost handsome. And his lacerating, pure tenor sounded well, when the words were drowned in the general commotion. Brilliant she looked, and brilliant she felt, for she was hot and angrily miserable and inflamed with a sort of fatal despair. Because there was about him a physical attraction which she really hated, but which she could not escape from. He was the first man who had ever kissed her. And his kisses, even while she rebelled from them, had lived in her blood and sent roots down into her soul. After all this time she had come back to them. And her soul groaned, for she felt dragged down, dragged down to earth, as a bird which some dog has got down in the dust. She knew her life would be unhappy. She knew that what she was doing was fatal. Yet it was her doom. She had to come back to him.

He had to sing two solos this afternoon: one before the 'address' from the pulpit and one after. Fanny looked at him, and wondered he was not too shy to stand up there in front of all the people. But no, he was not shy. He had even a kind of assurance on his face as he looked down from the choir gallery at her: the assurance of a common man deliberately entrenched in his commonness. Oh, such a rage went through her veins as she saw the air of triumph, laconic, indifferent triumph which sat so obstinately and recklessly on his eyelids as he looked down at her. Ah, she despised him! But there he stood up in that choir gallery like Balaam's ass[2] in front of her, and she could not get beyond him. A certain winsomeness also about him. A certain physical winsomeness, and as if his flesh were new and lovely to touch. The thorn of desire rankled bitterly in her heart.

He, it goes without saying, sang like a canary this particular afternoon, with a certain defiant passion which pleasantly crisped the blood of the congregation. Fanny felt the crisp flames go through her veins as she listened. Even the curious loud-mouthed vernacular had a certain fascination. But, oh, also, it was so repugnant. He would triumph over her, obstinately he would drag her right back into the common people: a doom, a vulgar doom.

The second performance was an anthem, in which Harry sang the solo parts. It was clumsy, but beautiful, with lovely words.

'They that sow in tears shall reap in joy,
He that goeth forth and weepeth, bearing precious seed
Shall doubtless come again with rejoicing, bringing his sheaves with him –'

'Shall doubtless come, Shall doubtless come –' softly intoned the altos – 'Bringing his she-e-eaves with him,' the trebles flourished brightly, and then again began the half-wistful solo:

'They that sow in tears shall reap in joy –'

Yes, it was effective and moving.

But at the moment when Harry's voice sank carelessly down to his close, and the choir, standing behind him, were opening their mouths for the final triumphant outburst, a shouting female voice rose up from the body of the congregation. The organ gave one startled trump, and went silent; the choir stood transfixed.

'You look well standing there, singing in God's holy house,' came the loud, angry female shout. Everybody turned electrified. A stoutish, red-faced woman in a black bonnet was standing up denouncing the soloist. Almost fainting with shock, the congregation realised it. 'You look well, don't you, standing there singing solos in God's holy house, you, Goodall. But I said I'd shame you. You look well, bringing your young woman here with you, don't you? I'll let her know who she's dealing with. A scamp as won't take the consequences of what he's done.' The hard-faced, frenzied woman turned in the direction of Fanny. '*That's* what Harry Goodall is, if you want to know.'

And she sat down again in her seat. Fanny, startled like all the rest, had turned to look. She had gone white, and then a burning red, under the attack. She knew the woman: a Mrs Nixon, a devil of a woman, who beat her pathetic, drunken, red-nosed second husband, Bob, and her two lanky daughters, grown-up as they were. A notorious character. Fanny turned round again, and sat motionless as eternity in her seat.

There was a minute of perfect silence and suspense. The audience was open-mouthed and dumb; the choir stood like Lot's wife;[3] and Harry, with his music-sheet, stood there uplifted, looking down with a dumb sort of indifference on Mrs Nixon, his face naïve and faintly mocking. Mrs Nixon sat defiant in her seat, braving them all.

Then a rustle, like a wood when the wind suddenly catches the leaves. And then the tall, weird minister got to his feet, and in his strong, bell-like, beautiful voice – the only beautiful thing about him – he said with infinite mournful pathos:

'Let us unite in singing the last hymn on the hymn-sheet; the last hymn on the hymn-sheet, number eleven.

"Fair waved the golden corn,
In Canaan's pleasant land."'

The organ tuned up promptly. During the hymn the offertory was taken. And after the hymn, the prayer.

Mr Enderby came from Northumberland. Like Harry, he had never been able to conquer his accent, which was very broad. He was a little simple, one of God's fools, perhaps, an odd bachelor soul, emotional, ugly, but very gentle.

'And if, O our dear Lord, beloved Jesus, there should fall a shadow of sin upon our harvest, we leave it to Thee to judge, for Thou art judge. We lift our spirits and our sorrow, Jesus, to Thee, and our mouths are dumb. O, Lord, keep us from froward speech, restrain us from foolish words and thoughts, we pray Thee, Lord Jesus, who knowest all and judgest all.'

Thus the minister said in his sad, resonant voice, washed his hands before the Lord. Fanny bent forward open-eyed during the prayer. She could see the roundish head of Harry, also bent forward. His face was inscrutable and expressionless. The shock left her bewildered. Anger perhaps was her dominating emotion.

The audience began to rustle to its feet, to ooze slowly and excitedly out of the chapel, looking with wildly-interested eyes at Fanny, at Mrs Nixon, and at Harry. Mrs Nixon, shortish, stood defiant in her pew, facing the aisle, as if announcing that, without rolling her sleeves up, she was ready for anybody. Fanny sat quite still. Luckily the people did not have to pass her. And Harry, with red ears, was making his way sheepishly out of the gallery. The loud noise of the organ covered all the downstairs commotion of exit.

The minister sat silent and inscrutable in his pulpit, rather like a death's-head, while the congregation filed out. When the last lingerers had unwillingly departed, craning their necks to stare at the still seated Fanny, he rose, stalked in his hooked fashion down the little country chapel and fastened the door. Then he returned and sat down by the silent young woman.

'This is most unfortunate, most unfortunate!' he moaned. 'I am so sorry, I am so sorry, indeed, indeed, ah, indeed!' he sighed himself to a close.

'It's a sudden surprise, that's one thing,' said Fanny brightly.

'Yes – yes – indeed. Yes, a surprise, yes. I don't know the woman, I don't know her.'

'I know her,' said Fanny. 'She's a bad one.'

'Well! Well!' said the minister. 'I don't know her. I don't understand. I don't understand at all. But it is to be regretted, it is very much to be regretted. I am very sorry.'

Fanny was watching the vestry door. The gallery stairs communicated with the vestry, not with the body of the chapel. She knew the choir members had been peeping for information.

At last Harry came – rather sheepishly – with his hat in his hand.

'Well!' said Fanny, rising to her feet.

'We've had a bit of an extra,' said Harry.

'I should think so,' said Fanny.

'A most unfortunate circumstance – a most *unfortunate* circumstance. Do you understand it, Harry? I don't understand it at all.'

'Ay, I understand it. The daughter's goin' to have a childt, an' 'er lays it on to me.'

'And has she no occasion to?' asked Fanny, rather censorious.

'It's no more mine than it is some other chap's,' said Harry, looking aside.

There was a moment of pause.

'Which girl is it?' asked Fanny.

'Annie – the young one –'

There followed another silence.

'I don't think I know them, do I?' asked the minister.

'I shouldn't think so. Their name's Nixon – mother married old Bob for her second husband. She's a tanger – 's driven the gel to what she is. They live in Manners Road.'

'Why, what's amiss with the girl?' asked Fanny sharply. 'She was all right when I knew her.'

'Ay – she's all right. But she's always in an' out o' th' pubs, wi' th' fellows,' said Harry.

'A nice thing!' said Fanny.

Harry glanced towards the door. He wanted to get out.

'Most distressing, indeed!' The minister slowly shook his head.

'What about to-night, Mr Enderby?' asked Harry, in rather a small voice. 'Shall you want me?'

Mr Enderby looked up painedly, and put his hand to his brow. He studied Harry for some time, vacantly. There was the faintest sort of a resemblance between the two men.

'Yes,' he said. 'Yes, I think. I think we must take no notice, and cause as little remark as possible.'

Fanny hesitated. Then she said to Harry.

'But *will* you come?'

He looked at her.

'Ay, I s'll come,' he said.

Then he turned to Mr Enderby.

'Well, good-afternoon, Mr Enderby,' he said.

'Good-afternoon, Harry, good-afternoon,' replied the mournful minister. Fanny followed Harry to the door, and for some time they walked in silence through the late afternoon.

'And it's yours as much as anybody else's?' she said.

'Ay,' he answered shortly.

And they went without another word, for the long mile or so, till they came to the corner of the street where Harry lived. Fanny hesitated. Should she go on to her aunt's? Should she? It would mean leaving all this, for ever. Harry stood silent.

Some obstinacy made her turn with him along the road to his own home. When they entered the house-place, the whole family was there, mother and father and Jinny, with Jinny's husband and children and Harry's two brothers.

'You've been having your ears warmed, they tell me,' said Mrs Goodall grimly.

'Who telled thee?' asked Harry shortly.

'Maggie and Luke's both been in.'

'You look well, don't you!' said interfering Jinny.

Harry went and hung his hat up, without replying.

'Come upstairs and take your hat off,' said Mrs Goodall to Fanny, almost kindly. It would have annoyed her very much if Fanny had dropped her son at this moment.

'What's 'er say, then?' asked the father secretly of Harry, jerking his head in the direction of the stairs whence Fanny had disappeared.

'Nowt yet,' said Harry.

'Serve you right if she chucks you now,' said Jinny. 'I'll bet it's right about Annie Nixon an' you.'

'Tha bets so much,' said Harry.

'Yi – but you can't deny it,' said Jinny.

'I can if I've a mind.'

His father looked at him enquiringly.

'It's no more mine than it is Bill Bower's, or Ted Slaney's, or six or seven on 'em,' said Harry to his father.

And the father nodded silently.

'That'll not get you out of it, in court,' said Jinny.

Upstairs Fanny evaded all the thrusts made by his mother, and did not declare her hand. She tidied her hair, washed her hands, and put the tiniest bit of powder on her face, for coolness, there in front of Mrs Goodall's indignant gaze. It was like a declaration of independence. But the old woman said nothing.

They came down to Sunday tea, with sardines and tinned salmon and tinned peaches, besides tarts and cakes. The chatter was general. It concerned the Nixon family and the scandal.

'Oh, she's a foul-mouthed woman,' said Jinny of Mrs Nixon. 'She may well talk about God's holy house, *she* had. It's first time she's set foot in it, ever since she dropped off from being converted. She's a devil and she always was one. Can't you remember how she treated Bob's children, mother, when we lived down in the Buildings? I can remember when I was a little girl she used to bathe them in the yard, in the cold, so that they shouldn't splash the house. She'd half kill them if they made a mark on the floor, and the language she'd use! And one Saturday I can remember Garry, that was Bob's own girl, she ran off when her stepmother was going to bathe her – ran off without a rag of clothes on – can you remember, mother? And she hid in Smedley's closes – it was the time of mowing-grass – and nobody could find her. She hid out there all night, didn't she, mother? Nobody could find her. My word, there was a talk. They found her on Sunday morning –'

'Fred Coutts threatened to break every bone in the woman's body, if she touched the children again,' put in the father.

'Anyhow, they frightened her,' said Jinny. 'But she was nearly as bad with her own two. And anybody can see that she's driven old Bob till he's gone soft.'

'Ah, soft as mush,' said Jack Goodall. ''E'd never addle a week's wage, nor yet a day's, if th' chaps didn't make it up to him.'

'My word, if he didn't bring her a week's wage, she'd pull his head off,' said Jinny.

'But a clean woman, and respectable, except for her foul mouth,' said Mrs Goodall. 'Keeps to herself like a bull-dog. Never lets anybody come near the house, and neighbours with nobody.'

'Wanted it thrashed out of her,' said Mr Goodall, a silent, evasive sort of man.

'Where Bob gets the money for his drink from is a mystery,' said Jinny.

'Chaps treats him,' said Harry.

'Well, he's got the pair of frightenedest rabbit-eyes you'd wish to see,' said Jinny.

'Ay, with a drunken man's murder in them, *I* think,' said Mrs Goodall.

So the talk went on after tea, till it was practically time to start off to chapel again.

'You'll have to be getting ready, Fanny,' said Mrs Goodall.

'I'm not going to-night,' said Fanny abruptly. And there was a sudden halt in the family. 'I'll stop with *you* to-night, Mother,' she added.

'Best you had, my gel,' said Mrs Goodall, flattered and assured.

You Touched Me

THE Pottery House was a square, ugly, brick house girt in by the wall that enclosed the whole grounds of the pottery itself. To be sure, a privet hedge partly masked the house and its ground from the pottery-yard and works: but only partly. Through the hedge could be seen the desolate yard, and the many-windowed, factory-like pottery, over the hedge could be seen the chimneys and the outhouses. But inside the hedge, a pleasant garden and lawn sloped down to a willow pool, which had once supplied the works.

The Pottery itself was now closed, the great doors of the yard permanently shut. No more the great crates with yellow straw showing through, stood in stacks by the packing shed. No more the drays drawn by great horses rolled down the hill with a high load. No more the pottery-lasses in their clay-coloured overalls, their faces and hair splashed with grey fine mud, shrieked and larked with the men. All that was over.

'We like it much better – oh, much better – quieter,' said Matilda Rockley.

'Oh, yes,' assented Emmie Rockley, her sister.

'I'm sure you do,' agreed the visitor.

But whether the two Rockley girls really liked it better, or whether they only imagined they did, is a question. Certainly their lives were much more grey and dreary now that the grey clay had ceased to spatter its mud and silt its dust over the premises. They did not quite realise how they missed the shrieking, shouting lasses, whom they had known all their lives and disliked so much.

Matilda and Emmie were already old maids. In a thorough industrial district, it is not easy for the girls who have expectations above the common to find husbands. The ugly industrial town was full of men, young men who were ready to marry. But they were all colliers or pottery-hands, mere workmen. The Rockley girls would have about ten thousand pounds each when their father died: ten thousand pounds' worth of profitable house-property. It was not to be sneezed at: they felt so themselves, and refrained from sneezing away such a fortune on any mere member of the proletariat. Consequently, bank-clerks or nonconformist clergymen or even school-teachers having failed to come forward, Matilda had begun to give up all idea of ever leaving the Pottery House.

Matilda was a tall, thin, graceful fair girl, with a rather large nose. She was the Mary to Emmie's Martha:[1] that is, Matilda loved painting and music, and read a good many novels, whilst Emmie looked after the house-keeping. Emmie was shorter, plumper than her sister, and she had no accomplishments. She looked up to Matilda, whose mind was naturally refined and sensible.

In their quiet, melancholy way, the two girls were happy. Their mother was dead. Their father was ill also. He was an intelligent man who had had some education, but preferred to remain as if he were one with the rest of the working people. He had a passion for music and played the violin pretty well. But now he was getting old, he was very ill, dying of a kidney disease. He had been rather a heavy whiskey-drinker.

This quiet household, with one servant-maid, lived on year after year in the Pottery House. Friends came in, the girls went out, the father drank himself more and more ill. Outside in the street there was a continual racket of the colliers and their dogs and children. But inside the pottery wall was a deserted quiet.

In all this ointment there was one little fly. Ted Rockley, the father of the girls, had had four daughters, and no son. As his girls grew, he felt angry at finding himself always in a household of women. He went off to London and adopted a boy out of a Charity Institution. Emmie was fourteen years old, and Matilda sixteen, when their father arrived home with his prodigy, the boy of six, Hadrian.

Hadrian was just an ordinary boy from a Charity Home, with ordinary brownish hair and ordinary bluish eyes and of ordinary rather cockney speech. The Rockley girls – there were three at home at the time of his arrival – had resented his being sprung on them. He, with his watchful, charity-institution instinct, knew this at once. Though he was only six years old, Hadrian had a subtle, jeering look on his face when he regarded the three young women. They insisted he should address them as Cousin: Cousin Flora, Cousin Matilda, Cousin Emmie. He complied, but there seemed a mockery in his tone.

The girls, however, were kind-hearted by nature. Flora married and left home. Hadrian did very much as he pleased with Matilda and Emmie, though they had certain strictnesses. He grew up in the Pottery House and about the Pottery premises, went to an elementary school, and was invariably called Hadrian Rockley. He regarded Cousin Matilda and Cousin Emmie with a certain laconic indifference, was quiet and reticent in his ways. The girls called him sly, but that was unjust. He was merely cautious, and without frankness. His Uncle, Ted Rockley, understood him tacitly, their natures were somewhat akin. Hadrian and the elderly man had a real but unemotional regard for one another.

When he was thirteen years old the boy was sent to a High School in the County town. He did not like it. His Cousin Matilda had longed to make a little gentleman of him, but he refused to be made. He would give a little contemptuous curve to his lip, and take on a shy, charity-boy grin, when refinement was thrust upon him. He played truant from the High School, sold his books, his cap with its badge, even his very scarf and pocket-handkerchief, to his school-fellows, and went raking off heaven knows where with the money. So he spent two very unsatisfactory years.

When he was fifteen he announced that he wanted to leave England to go to the Colonies. He had kept touch with the Home. The Rockleys knew that, when Hadrian made a declaration, in his quiet, half-jeering manner, it was worse than useless to oppose him. So at last the boy departed, going to Canada under the protection of the Institution to which he had belonged. He said good-bye to the Rockleys without a word of thanks, and parted, it seemed without a pang. Matilda and Emmie wept often to think of how he left them: even on their father's face a queer look came. But Hadrian wrote fairly regularly from Canada. He had entered some electricity works near Montreal, and was doing well.

At last, however, the war came. In his turn, Hadrian joined up and came to Europe. The Rockleys saw nothing of him. They lived on, just the same, in the Pottery House. Ted Rockley was dying of a sort of dropsy, and in his heart he wanted to see the boy. When the armistice was signed, Hadrian had a long leave, and wrote that he was coming home to the Pottery House.

The girls were terribly fluttered. To tell the truth, they were a little afraid of Hadrian. Matilda, tall and thin, was frail in her health, both girls were worn with nursing their father. To have Hadrian, a young man of twenty-one, in the house with them, after he had left them so coldly five years before, was a trying circumstance.

They were in a flutter. Emmie persuaded her father to have his bed made finally in the morning-room downstairs, whilst his room upstairs was prepared for Hadrian. This was done, and preparations were going on for the arrival, when, at ten o'clock in the morning the young man suddenly turned up, quite unexpectedly. Cousin

Emmie, with her hair bobbed up in absurd little bobs round her forehead, was busily polishing the stair-rods, while Cousin Matilda was in the kitchen washing the drawing-room ornaments in a lather, her sleeves rolled back on her thin arms, and her head tied up oddly and coquettishly in a duster.

Cousin Matilda blushed deep with mortification when the self-possessed young man walked in with his kit-bag, and put his cap on the sewing machine. He was little and self-confident, with a curious neatness about him that still suggested the Charity Institution. His face was brown, he had a small moustache, he was vigorous enough in his smallness.

'*Well*, is it Hadrian!' exclaimed Cousin Matilda, wringing the lather off her hand. 'We didn't expect you till to-morrow.'

'I got off Monday night,' said Hadrian, glancing round the room.

'Fancy!' said Cousin Matilda. Then, having dried her hands, she went forward, held out her hand, and said:

'How are you?'

'Quite well, thank you,' said Hadrian.

'You're quite a man,' said Cousin Matilda.

Hadrian glanced at her. She did not look her best: so thin, so large-nosed, with that pink-and-white checked duster tied round her head. She felt her disadvantage. But she had had a good deal of suffering and sorrow, she did not mind any more.

The servant entered – one that did not know Hadrian.

'Come and see my father,' said Cousin Matilda.

In the hall they roused Cousin Emmie like a partridge from cover. She was on the stairs pushing the bright stair-rods into place. Instinctively her hand went to the little knobs, her front hair bobbed on her forehead.

'Why!' she exclaimed crossly. 'What have you come to-day for?'

'I got off a day earlier,' said Hadrian, and his man's voice so deep and unexpected was like a blow to Cousin Emmie.

'Well, you've caught us in the midst of it,' she said, with resentment. Then all three went into the middle room.

Mr Rockley was dressed – that is, he had on his trousers and socks – but he was resting on the bed, propped up just under the window, from whence he could see his beloved and resplendent garden, where tulips and apple-trees were ablaze. He did not look as ill as he was, for the water puffed him up, and his face kept its colour. His stomach was much swollen. He glanced round swiftly, turning his eyes without turning his head. He was the wreck of a handsome, well-built man.

Seeing Hadrian, a queer, unwilling smile went over his face. The young man greeted him sheepishly.

'You wouldn't make a life-guardsman,' he said. 'Do you want something to eat?'

Hadrian looked round – as if for the meal.

'I don't mind,' he said.

'What shall you have – egg and bacon?' asked Emmie shortly.

'Yes, I don't mind,' said Hadrian.

The sisters went down to the kitchen, and sent the servant to finish the stairs.

'Isn't he *altered*?' said Matilda, *sotto voce*.[2]

'Isn't he!' said Cousin Emmie. '*What* a little man!'

They both made a grimace, and laughed nervously.

'Get the frying-pan,' said Emmie to Matilda.

'But he's as cocky as ever,' said Matilda, narrowing her eyes and shaking her head knowingly, as she handed the frying-pan.

'Mannie!' said Emmie sarcastically. Hadrian's new-fledged, cock-sure manliness evidently found no favour in her eyes.

'Oh, he's not bad,' said Matilda. 'You don't want to be prejudiced against him.'

'I'm not prejudiced against him, I think he's all right for looks,' said Emmie, 'but there's too much of the little mannie about him.'

'Fancy catching us like this,' said Matilda.

'They've no thought for anything,' said Emmie with contempt. 'You go up and get dressed, our Matilda. I don't care about him. I can see to things, and you can talk to him. I shan't.'

'He'll talk to my father,' said Matilda, meaningful.

'*Sly –!*' exclaimed Emmie, with a grimace.

The sisters believed that Hadrian had come hoping to get something out of their father – hoping for a legacy. And they were not at all sure he would not get it.

Matilda went upstairs to change. She had thought it all out how she would receive Hadrian, and impress him. And he had caught her with her head tied up in a duster, and her thin arms in a basin of lather. But she did not care. She now dressed herself most scrupulously, carefully folded her long, beautiful, blonde hair, touched her pallor with a little rouge, and put her long string of exquisite crystal beads over her soft green dress. Now she looked elegant, like a heroine in a magazine illustration, and almost as unreal.

She found Hadrian and her father talking away. The young man was short of speech as a rule, but he could find his tongue with his 'uncle'. They were both sipping a glass of brandy, and smoking, and chatting like a pair of old cronies. Hadrian was telling about Canada. He was going back there when his leave was up.

'You wouldn't like to stop in England, then?' said Mr Rockley.

'No, I wouldn't stop in England,' said Hadrian.

'How's that? There's plenty of electricians here,' said Mr Rockley.

'Yes. But there's too much difference between the men and the employers over here – too much of that for me,' said Hadrian.

The sick man looked at him narrowly, with oddly smiling eyes.

'That's it, is it?' he replied.

Matilda heard and understood. 'So that's your big idea, is it, my little man,' she said to herself. She had always said of Hadrian that he had no proper *respect* for anybody or anything, that he was sly and *common*. She went down to the kitchen for a *sotto voce* confab with Emmie.

'He thinks a rare lot of himself!' she whispered.

'He's somebody, he is!' said Emmie with contempt.

'He thinks there's too much difference between masters and men, over here,' said Matilda.

'Is it any different in Canada?' asked Emmie.

'Oh, yes – democratic,' replied Matilda. 'He thinks they're all on a level over there.'

'Ay, well he's over here now,' said Emmie drily, 'so he can keep his place.'

As they talked they saw the young man sauntering down the garden, looking casually at the flowers. He had his hands in his pockets, and his soldier's cap neatly on his head. He looked quite at his ease, as if in possession. The two women, flustered, watched him through the window.

'We know what he's come for,' said Emmie, churlishly. Matilda looked a long time at the neat khaki figure. It had something of the charity-boy about it still; but now it was a man's figure, laconic, charged with plebeian energy. She thought of the derisive passion in his voice as he had declaimed against the propertied classes, to her father.

'You don't know, Emmie. Perhaps he's not come for that,' she rebuked her sister. They were both thinking of the money.

They were still watching the young soldier. He stood away at the bottom of the garden, with his back to them, his hands in his pockets, looking into the water of the willow pond. Matilda's dark-blue eyes had a strange, full look in them, the lids, with the faint blue veins showing, dropped rather low. She carried her head light and high, but she had a look of pain. The young man at the bottom of the garden turned and looked up the path. Perhaps he saw them through the window. Matilda moved into shadow.

That afternoon their father seemed weak and ill. He was easily exhausted. The doctor came, and told Matilda that the sick man might die suddenly at any moment – but then he might not. They must be prepared.

So the day passed, and the next. Hadrian made himself at home. He went about in the morning in his brownish jersey and his khaki trousers, collarless, his bare neck showing. He explored the pottery premises, as if he had some secret purpose in so doing, he talked with Mr Rockley, when the sick man had strength. The two girls were always angry when the two men sat talking together like cronies. Yet it was chiefly a kind of politics they talked.

On the second day after Hadrian's arrival, Matilda sat with her father in the evening. She was drawing a picture which she wanted to copy. It was very still, Hadrian was gone out somewhere, no one knew where, and Emmie was busy. Mr Rockley reclined on his bed, looking out in silence over his evening-sunny garden.

'If anything happens to me, Matilda,' he said, 'you won't sell this house – you'll stop here –'

Matilda's eyes took their slightly haggard look as she stared at her father.

'Well, we couldn't do anything else,' she said.

'You don't know what you might do,' he said. 'Everything is left to you and Emmie, equally. You do as you like with it – only don't sell this house, don't part with it.'

'No,' she said.

'And give Hadrian my watch and chain, and a hundred pounds out of what's in the bank – and help him if he ever wants helping. I haven't put his name in the will.'

'Your watch and chain, and a hundred pounds – yes. But you'll be here when he goes back to Canada, father.'

'You never know what'll happen,' said her father.

Matilda sat and watched him, with her full, haggard eyes, for a long time, as if tranced. She saw that he knew he must go soon – she saw like a clairvoyant.

Later on she told Emmie what her father had said about the watch and chain and the money.

'What right has *he*' – *he* – meaning Hadrian – 'to my father's watch and chain – what has it to do with him? Let him have the money, and get off,' said Emmie. She loved her father.

That night Matilda sat late in her room. Her heart was anxious and breaking, her mind seemed entranced. She was too much entranced even to weep, and all the time she thought of her father, only her father. At last she felt she must go to him.

It was near midnight. She went along the passage and to his room. There was a faint light from the moon outside. She listened at his door. Then she softly opened and entered. The room was faintly dark. She heard a movement on the bed.

'Are you asleep?' she said softly, advancing to the side of the bed.

'Are you asleep?' she repeated gently, as she stood at the side of the bed. And she reached her hand in the darkness to touch his forehead. Delicately, her fingers met the nose and the eyebrows, she laid her fine, delicate hand on his brow. It seemed fresh and smooth – very fresh and smooth. A sort of surprise stirred her, in her entranced state. But it could not waken her. Gently, she leaned over the bed and stirred her fingers over the low-growing hair on his brow.

'Can't you sleep to-night?' she said.

There was a quick stirring in the bed. 'Yes, I can,' a voice answered. It was Hadrian's voice. She started away. Instantly, she was awakened from her late-at-night trance. She remembered that her father was downstairs, that Hadrian had his room. She stood in the darkness as if stung.

'Is it you, Hadrian?' she said. 'I thought it was my father.' She was so startled, so shocked, that she could not move. The young man gave an uncomfortable laugh, and turned in his bed.

At last she got out of the room. When she was back in her own room, in the light, and her door was closed, she stood holding up her hand that had touched him, as if it were hurt. She was almost too shocked, she could not endure.

'Well,' said her calm and weary mind, 'it was only a mistake, why take any notice of it.'

But she could not reason her feelings so easily. She suffered, feeling herself in a false position. Her right hand, which she had laid so gently on his face, on his fresh skin, ached now, as if it were really injured. She could not forgive Hadrian for the mistake: it made her dislike him deeply.

Hadrian too slept badly. He had been awakened by the opening of the door, and had not realised what the question meant. But the soft, straying tenderness of her hand on his face startled something out of his soul. He was a charity boy, aloof and more or less at bay. The fragile exquisiteness of her caress startled him most, revealed unknown things to him.

In the morning she could feel the consciousness in his eyes, when she came downstairs. She tried to bear herself as if nothing at all had happened, and she succeeded. She had the calm self-control, self-indifference, of one who has suffered and borne her suffering. She looked at him from her darkish, almost drugged blue eyes, she met the spark of consciousness in his eyes, and quenched it. And with her long, fine hand she put the sugar in his coffee.

But she could not control him as she thought she could. He had a keen memory stinging his mind, a new set of sensations working in his consciousness. Something new was alert in him. At the back of his reticent, guarded mind he kept his secret alive and vivid. She was at his mercy, for he was unscrupulous, his standard was not her standard.

He looked at her curiously. She was not beautiful, her nose was too large, her chin was too small, her neck was too thin. But her skin was clear and fine, she had a high-bred sensitiveness. This queer, brave, high-bred quality she shared with her father. The charity boy could see it in her tapering fingers, which were white and ringed. The same glamour that he knew in the elderly man he now saw in the woman. And he wanted to possess himself of it, he wanted to make himself master of it. As he went about through the old pottery-yard, his secretive mind schemed and worked. To be master of that strange soft delicacy such as he had felt in her hand upon his face, – this was what he set himself towards. He was secretly plotting.

He watched Matilda as she went about, and she became aware of his attention, as of some shadow following her. But her pride made her ignore it. When he sauntered near her, his hands in his pockets, she received him with that same commonplace kindliness which mastered him more than any contempt. Her superior breeding seemed to control him. She made herself feel towards him exactly as she had always felt: he was a young boy who lived in the house with them, but was a stranger. Only, she dared not remember his face under her hand. When she remembered that, she was bewildered. Her hand had offended her, she wanted to cut it off. And she wanted, fiercely, to cut off the memory in him. She assumed she had done so.

One day, when he sat talking with his 'uncle', he looked straight into the eyes of the sick man, and said:

'But I shouldn't like to live and die here in Rawsley.'

'No – well – you needn't,' said the sick man.

'Do you think Cousin Matilda likes it?'

'I should think so.'

'I don't call it much of a life,' said the youth. 'How much older is she than me, Uncle?'

The sick man looked at the young soldier.

'A good bit,' he said.

'Over thirty?' said Hadrian.

'Well, not so much. She's thirty-two.'

Hadrian considered a while.

'She doesn't look it,' he said.

Again the sick father looked at him.

'Do you think she'd like to leave here?' said Hadrian.

'Nay, I don't know,' replied the father, restive.

Hadrian sat still, having his own thoughts. Then in a small, quiet voice, as if he were speaking from inside himself, he said:

'I'd marry her if you wanted me to.'

The sick man raised his eyes suddenly, and stared. He stared for a long time. The youth looked inscrutably out of the window.

'*You!*' said the sick man, mocking, with some contempt. Hadrian turned and met his eyes. The two men had an inexplicable understanding.

'If you wasn't against it,' said Hadrian.

'Nay,' said the father, turning aside, 'I don't think I'm against it. I've never thought of it. But – But Emmie's the youngest.'

He had flushed, and looked suddenly more alive. Secretly he loved the boy.

'You might ask her,' said Hadrian.

The elder man considered.

'Hadn't you better ask her yourself?' he said.

'She'd take more notice of you,' said Hadrian.

They were both silent. Then Emmie came in.

For two days Mr Rockley was excited and thoughtful. Hadrian went about quietly, secretly, unquestioning. At last the father and daughter were alone together. It was very early morning, the father had been in much pain. As the pain abated, he lay still, thinking.

'Matilda!' he said suddenly, looking at his daughter.

'Yes, I'm here,' she said.

'Ay! I want you to do something –'

She rose in anticipation.

'Nay, sit still. I want you to marry Hadrian –'

She thought he was raving. She rose, bewildered and frightened.

'Nay, sit you still, sit you still. You hear what I tell you.'

'But you don't know what you're saying, father.'

'Ay, I know well enough. I want you to marry Hadrian, I tell you.'

She was dumbfounded. He was a man of few words.

'You'll do what I tell you,' he said.

She looked at him slowly.

'What put such an idea in your mind?' she said proudly.

'He did.'

Matilda almost looked her father down, her pride was so offended.

'Why, it's disgraceful,' she said.

'Why?'

She watched him slowly.

'What do you ask me for?' she said. 'It's disgusting.'

'The lad's sound enough,' he replied, testily.

'You'd better tell him to clear out,' she said, coldly.

He turned and looked out of the window. She sat flushed and erect for a long time. At length her father turned to her, looking really malevolent.

'If you won't,' he said, 'you're a fool, and I'll make you pay for your foolishness, do you see?'

Suddenly a cold fear gripped her. She could not believe her senses. She was terrified and bewildered. She stared at her father, believing him to be delirious, or mad, or drunk. What could she do?

'I tell you,' he said. 'I'll send for Whittle tomorrow if you don't. You shall neither of you have anything of mine.'

Whittle was the solicitor. She understood her father well enough: he would send for his solicitor, and make a will leaving all his property to Hadrian: neither she nor Emmie should have anything. It was too much. She rose and went out of the room, up to her own room, where she locked herself in.

She did not come out for some hours. At last, late at night, she confided in Emmie.

'The sliving demon, he wants the money,' said Emmie. 'My father's out of his mind.'

The thought that Hadrian merely wanted the money was another blow to Matilda. She did not love the impossible youth – but she had not yet learned to think of him as a thing of evil. He now became hideous to her mind.

Emmie had a little scene with her father next day.

'You don't mean what you said to our Matilda yesterday, do you, father?' she asked aggressively.

'Yes,' he replied.

'What, that you'll alter your will?'

'Yes.'

'You won't,' said his angry daughter.

But he looked at her with a malevolent little smile.

'Annie!' he shouted. 'Annie!'

He had still power to make his voice carry. The servant maid came in from the kitchen.

'Put your things on, and go down to Whittle's office, and say I want to see Mr Whittle as soon as he can, and will he bring a will-form.'

The sick man lay back a little – he could not lie down. His daughter sat as if she had been struck. Then she left the room.

Hadrian was pottering about in the garden. She went straight down to him.

'Here,' she said. 'You'd better get off. You'd better take your things and go from here, quick.'

Hadrian looked slowly at the infuriated girl.

'Who says so?' he asked.

'*We* say so – get off, you've done enough mischief and damage.'

'Does Uncle say so?'

'Yes, he does.'

'I'll go and ask him.'

But like a fury Emmie barred his way.

'No, you needn't. You needn't ask him nothing at all. We don't want you, so you can go.'

'Uncle's boss here.'

'A man that's dying, and you crawling round and working on him for his money! – you're not fit to live.'

'Oh!' he said. 'Who says I'm working for his money?'

'I say. But my father told our Matilda, and *she* knows what you are. *She* knows what you're after. So you might as well clear out, for all you'll get – guttersnipe!'

He turned his back on her, to think. It had not occurred to him that they would think he was after the money. He *did* want the money – badly. He badly wanted to be an employer himself, not one of the employed. But he knew, in his subtle, calculating way, that it was not for money he wanted Matilda. He wanted both the money and Matilda. But he told himself the two desires were separate, not one.

He could not do with Matilda, *without* the money. But he did not want her *for* the money.

When he got this clear in his mind, he sought for an opportunity to tell it her, lurking and watching. But she avoided him. In the evening the lawyer came. Mr Rockley seemed to have a new access of strength – a will was drawn up, making the previous arrangements wholly conditional. The old will held good, if Matilda would consent to marry Hadrian. If she refused then at the end of six months the whole property passed to Hadrian.

Mr Rockley told this to the young man, with malevolent satisfaction. He seemed to have a strange desire, quite unreasonable, for revenge upon the women who had surrounded him for so long, and served him so carefully.

'Tell her in front of me,' said Hadrian.

So Mr Rockley sent for his daughters.

At last they came, pale, mute, stubborn. Matilda seemed to have retired far off, Emmie seemed like a fighter ready to fight to the death. The sick man reclined on the bed, his eyes bright, his puffed hand trembling. But his face had again some of its old, bright handsomeness. Hadrian sat quiet, a little aside: the indomitable, dangerous charity boy.

'There's the will,' said their father, pointing them to the paper.

The two women sat mute and immovable, they took no notice.

'Either you marry Hadrian, or he has everything,' said the father with satisfaction.

'Then let him have everything,' said Matilda coldly.

'He's not! He's not!' cried Emmie fiercely. 'He's not going to have it. The guttersnipe!'

An amused look came on her father's face.

'You hear that, Hadrian,' he said.

'I didn't offer to marry Cousin Matilda for the money,' said Hadrian, flushing and moving on his seat.

Matilda looked at him slowly, with her dark-blue, drugged eyes. He seemed a strange little monster to her.

'Why, you liar, you know you did,' cried Emmie.

The sick man laughed. Matilda continued to gaze strangely at the young man.

'She knows I didn't,' said Hadrian.

He too had his courage, as a rat has indomitable courage in the end. Hadrian had some of the neatness, the reserve, the underground quality of the rat. But he had perhaps the ultimate courage, the most unquenchable courage of all.

Emmie looked at her sister.

'Oh, well,' she said. 'Matilda – don't you bother. Let him have everything, we can look after ourselves.'

'I know he'll take everything,' said Matilda, abstractedly.

Hadrian did not answer. He knew in fact that if Matilda refused him he would take everything, and go off with it.

'A clever little mannie –!' said Emmie, with a jeering grimace.

The father laughed noiselessly to himself. But he was tired . . .

'Go on, then,' he said. 'Go on, let me be quiet.'

Emmie turned and looked at him.

'You deserve what you've got,' she said to her father bluntly.

'Go on,' he answered mildly. 'Go on.'

Another night passed – a night nurse sat up with Mr Rockley. Another day came. Hadrian was there as ever, in his woollen jersey and coarse khaki trousers and bare neck. Matilda went about, frail and distant, Emmie black-browed in spite of her blondeness. They were all quiet, for they did not intend the mystified servant to learn anything.

Mr Rockley had very bad attacks of pain, he could not breathe. The end seemed near. They all went about quiet and stoical, all unyielding. Hadrian pondered within himself. If he did not marry Matilda he would go to Canada with twenty thousand pounds. This was itself a very satisfactory prospect. If Matilda consented he would have nothing – she would have her own money.

Emmie was the one to act. She went off in search of the solicitor and brought him home with her. There was an interview, and Whittle tried to frighten the youth into withdrawal – but without avail. The clergyman and relatives were summoned – but Hadrian stared at them and took no notice. It made him angry, however.

He wanted to catch Matilda alone. Many days went by, and he was not successful: she avoided him. At last, lurking, he surprised her one day as she came to pick gooseberries, and he cut off her retreat. He came to the point at once.

'You don't want me, then?' he said, in his subtle, insinuating voice.

'I don't want to speak to you,' she said, averting her face.

'You put your hand on me, though,' he said. 'You shouldn't have done that, and then I should never have thought of it. You shouldn't have touched me.'

'If you were anything decent, you'd know that was a mistake, and forget it,' she said.

'I know it was a mistake – but I shan't forget it. If you wake a man up, he can't go to sleep again because he's told to.'

'If you had any decent feeling in you, you'd have gone away,' she replied.

'I didn't want to,' he replied.

She looked away into the distance. At last she asked:

'What do you persecute me for, if it isn't for the money. I'm old enough to be your mother. In a way I've been your mother.'

'Doesn't matter,' he said. 'You've been no mother to me. Let us marry and go out to Canada – you might as well – you've touched me.'

She was white and trembling. Suddenly she flushed with anger.

'It's so *indecent*,' she said.

'How?' he retorted. 'You touched me.'

But she walked away from him. She felt as if he had trapped her. He was angry and depressed, he felt again despised.

That same evening she went into her father's room.

'Yes,' she said suddenly. 'I'll marry him.'

Her father looked up at her. He was in pain, and very ill.

'You like him now, do you?' he said, with a faint smile.

She looked down into his face, and saw death not far off. She turned and went coldly out of the room.

The solicitor was sent for, preparations were hastily made. In all the interval Matilda did not speak to Hadrian, never answered him if he addressed her. He approached her in the morning.

'You've come round to it, then?' he said, giving her a pleasant look from his twinkling, almost kindly eyes. She looked down at him and turned aside. She looked down on him both literally and figuratively. Still he persisted, and triumphed.

Emmie raved and wept, the secret flew abroad. But Matilda was silent and unmoved. Hadrian was quiet and satisfied, and nipped with fear also. But he held out against his fear. Mr Rockley was very ill, but unchanged.

On the third day the marriage took place. Matilda and Hadrian drove straight home from the registrar, and went straight into the room of the dying man. His face lit up with a clear twinkling smile.

'Hadrian, – you've got her?' he said, a little hoarsely.

'Yes,' said Hadrian, who was pale round the gills.

'Ay, my lad, I'm glad you're mine,' replied the dying man. Then he turned his eyes closely on Matilda.

'Let's look at you, Matilda,' he said. Then his voice went strange and unrecognisable. 'Kiss me,' he said.

She stooped and kissed him. She had never kissed him before, not since she was a tiny child. But she was quiet, very still.

'Kiss him,' the dying man said.

Obediently, Matilda put forward her mouth and kissed the young husband.

'That's right! That's right!' murmured the dying man.

Jimmy and the Desperate Woman

'HE is very fine and strong somewhere, but he does need a level-headed woman to look after him.'

That was the *friendly* feminine verdict upon him. It flattered him, it pleased him, it galled him.

Having divorced a very charming and clever wife, who had held this opinion for ten years, and at last had got tired of the level-headed protective game, his gall was uppermost.

'I want to throw Jimmy out on the world, but I know the poor little man will go and fall on some woman's bosom. That's the worst of him. If he could only stand alone for ten minutes. But he can't. At the same time, there *is* something fine about him, something rare.'

This had been Clarissa's summing-up as she floated away in the arms of the rich young American. The rich young American got rather angry when Jimmy's name was mentioned. Clarissa was now *his* wife. But she did sometimes talk as if she were still married to Jimmy.

Not in Jimmy's estimation, however. That worm had turned.[1] Gall was uppermost. Gall and wormwood.[2] He knew exactly what Clarissa thought – and said – about him. And the 'something fine, something rare, something strong' which he was supposed to have 'about him' was utterly outbalanced, in his feelings at least, by the 'poor little man' nestled upon 'some woman's bosom', which he was supposed to *be*.

'I am *not*,' he said to himself, 'a poor little man nestled upon some woman's bosom. If I could only find the right sort of woman, she should nestle on mine.'

Jimmy was now thirty-five, and this point, to nestle or to be nestled, was the emotional crux and turning-point.

He imagined to himself some really *womanly* woman, to whom he should be *only* 'fine and strong', and not for one moment 'the poor little man'. Why not some simple uneducated girl, some Tess of the D'Urbervilles, some wistful Gretchen, some humble Ruth[3] gleaning an aftermath? Why not? Surely the world was full of such!

The trouble was he never met them. He only met sophisticated women. He really never had a chance of meeting 'real' people. So few of us ever do. Only the people we *don't* meet are the 'real' people, the simple, genuine, direct spontaneous, unspoilt souls. Ah, the simple, genuine, unspoilt people we *don't* meet! What a tragedy it is!

Because, of course, they must be there! Somewhere! Only we never come across them.

Jimmy was terribly handicapped by his position. It brought him into contact with so many people. Only never the right sort. Never the 'real' people: the simple, genuine, unspoilt, etc., etc.

He was editor of a high-class, rather high-brow, rather successful magazine, and his rather personal, very candid editorials brought him shoals, swarms, hosts of admiring acquaintances. Realise that he was handsome, and could be extraordinarily 'nice', when he liked, and was really very clever, in his own critical way, and you see how many chances he had of being adored and protected.

In the first place his good looks: the fine, clean lines of his face, like the face of the laughing faun in one of the faun's unlaughing, moody moments. The long, clean lines of the cheeks, the strong chin and the slightly arched, full nose, the beautiful dark-grey eyes with long lashes, and the thick black brows. In his mocking moments, when he seemed most himself, it was a pure Pan face, with thick black eyebrows cocked up, and grey eyes with a sardonic goaty gleam, and nose and mouth curling with satire. A good-looking, smooth-skinned satyr.[4] That was Jimmy at his best. In the opinion of his men friends.

In his own opinion, he was a sort of Martyred Saint Sebastian,[5] at whom the wicked world shot arrow after arrow – Mater Dolorosa[6] nothing to him – and he counted the drops of blood as they fell: when he could keep count. Sometimes – as for instance when Clarissa said she was really departing with the rich young American, and should she divorce Jimmy, or was Jimmy going to divorce her? – then the arrows assailed him like a flight of starlings flying straight at him, jabbing at him, and the drops of martyred blood simply spattered down, he couldn't keep count.

So, naturally, he divorced Clarissa.

In the opinion of his men friends, he was, or should be, a consistently grinning faun, satyr, or Pan-person. In his own opinion, he was a Martyred Saint Sebastian with the mind of Plato. In the opinion of his woman friends, he was a fascinating little man with a profound understanding of life and the capacity really to understand a woman and to make a woman feel a queen; which of course was to make a woman feel her *real* self . . .

He might, naturally, have made rich and resounding marriages, especially after the divorce. He didn't. The reason was, secretly, his resolve never to make any woman feel a queen any more. It was the turn of the women to make him feel a king.

Some unspoilt, unsophisticated, wild-blooded woman, to whom he would be a sort of Solomon of wisdom, beauty, and wealth. She would need to be in reduced circumstances to appreciate his wealth, which amounted to the noble sum of three thousand pounds and a little week-ending cottage in Hampshire. And to be unsophisticated she would have to be a woman of the people. Absolutely.

At the same time, not just the 'obscure vulgar simplican'.

He received many letters, many, many, many, enclosing poems, stories, articles, or more personal unbosomings. He read them all: like a solemn rook pecking and scratching among the litter.

And one – not one letter, but one correspondent – might be *the* one – Mrs Emilia Pinnegar, who wrote from a mining village in Yorkshire. She was, of course, unhappily married.

Now Jimmy had always had a mysterious feeling about these dark and rather dreadful mining villages in the north. He himself had scarcely set foot north of Oxford. He felt that these miners up there must be the real stuff. And Pinnegar was a name, surely! And Emilia!

She wrote a poem, with a brief little note, that, if the editor of the *Commentator* thought the verses of no value, would he simply destroy them. Jimmy, as editor of the *Commentator*, thought the verses quite good and admired the brevity of the note. But he wasn't sure about printing the poem. He wrote back, Had Mrs Pinnegar nothing else to submit?

Then followed a correspondence. And at length, upon request, this from Mrs Pinnegar:

'You ask me about myself, but what shall I say? I am a woman of thirty-one, with one child, a girl of eight, and I am married to a man who lives in the same house with me, but goes to another woman. I try to write poetry, if it is poetry, because I have no other way of expressing myself at all, and even if it doesn't matter to anybody besides myself, I feel I must and will express myself, if only to save myself from developing cancer or some disease that women have. I was a school-teacher before I was married, and I got my certificates at Rotherham College. If I could, I would teach again, and live alone. But married teachers can't get jobs any more, they aren't allowed –'

THE COAL MINER

By His Wife

The donkey-engine's beating noise
And the rattle, rattle of the sorting screens
Come down on me like the beat of his heart,
And mean the same as his breathing means.

The burning big pit-hill with fumes
Fills the air like the presence of that fair-haired man.
And the burning fire burning deeper and deeper
Is his will insisting since time began.

As he breathes the chair goes up and down
In the pit-shaft; he lusts as the wheel-fans spin
The sucking air: he lives in the coal
Underground: and his soul is a strange engine.

That is the manner of man he is.
I married him and I should know.
The mother earth from bowels of coal
Brought him forth for the overhead woe.

This was the poem that the editor of the *Commentator* hesitated about. He reflected, also, that Mrs Pinnegar didn't sound like one of the nestling, unsophisticated rustic type. It was something else that still attracted him: something desperate in a woman, something tragic.

THE NEXT EVENT

If at evening, when the twilight comes,
  You ask me what the day has been,
I shall not know. The distant drums
  Of some new-comer intervene

Between me and the day that's been.
  Some strange man leading long columns
Of unseen soldiers through the green
  Sad twilight of these smoky slums.

And as the darkness slowly numbs
  My senses, everything I've seen
Or heard the daylight through, becomes
  Rubbish behind an opaque screen.

Instead, the sound of muffled drums
  Inside myself: I have to lean
And listen as my strength succumbs,
  To hear what these oncomings mean.

Perhaps the Death-God striking his thumbs
On the drums in a deadly rat-ta-ta-plan.
Or a strange man marching slow as he strums
The tune of a new weird hope in Man.

What does it matter! The day that began
In coal-dust is ending the same, in crumbs
Of darkness like coal. I live if I can;
If I can't, then I welcome whatever comes.

This poem sounded so splendidly desperate, the editor of the *Commentator* decided to print it, and, moreover, to see the authoress. He wrote, Would she care to see him, if he happened to be in her neighbourhood? He was going to lecture in Sheffield. She replied, Certainly.

He gave his afternoon lecture, on *Men in Books and Men in Life*. Naturally, men in books came first. Then he caught a train to reach the mining village where the Pinnegars lived.

It was February, with gruesome patches of snow. It was dark when he arrived at Mill Valley, a sort of thick, turgid darkness full of menace, where men speaking in a weird accent went past like ghosts, dragging their heavy feet and emitting the weird scent of the coal-mine underworld. Weird and a bit gruesome it was.

He knew he had to walk uphill to the little market-place. As he went, he looked back and saw the black valleys with bunches of light, like camps of demons it seemed to him. And the demonish smell of sulphur and coal in the air, in the heavy, pregnant, clammy darkness.

They directed him to New London Lane, and down he went down another hill. His skin crept a little. The place felt uncanny and hostile, hard, as if iron and minerals breathed into the black air. Thank goodness he couldn't see much, or be seen. When he had to ask his way the people treated him in a 'heave-half-a-brick-at-him' fashion.

After much weary walking and asking, he entered a lane between trees, in the cold slushy mud of the unfrozen February. The mines, apparently, were on the outskirts of the town, in some mud-sunk country. He could see the red, sore fires of the burning pit-hill through the trees, and he smelt the sulphur. He felt like some modern Ulysses wandering in the realms of Hecate. How much more dismal and horrible, a modern Odyssey among mines and factories, than any Sirens, Scyllas or Charybdises.[7]

So he mused to himself as he waded through icy black mud, in a black lane, under black trees that moaned an accompaniment to the sound of the coal-mine's occasional hissing and chuffing, under a black sky that quenched even the electric sparkle of the colliery. And the place seemed unhabitated like a cold black jungle.

At last he came in sight of a glimmer. Apparently, there were dwellings. Yes, a new little street, with one street-lamp, and the houses all apparently dark. He paused. Absolute desertion. Then three children.

They told him the house, and he stumbled up a dark passage. There was light on the little backyard. He knocked, in some trepidation. A rather tall woman, looking down at him with a 'Who are you?' look, from the step above.

'Mrs Pinnegar?'

'Oh, is it you, Mr Frith? Come in.'

He stumbled up the step into the glaring light of the kitchen. There stood Mrs Pinnegar, a tall woman with a face like a mask of passive anger, looking at him coldly. Immediately he felt his own shabbiness and smallness. In utter confusion, he stuck out his hand.

'I had an awful time getting here,' he said. 'I'm afraid I shall make a frightful mess of your house.' He looked down at his boots.

'That's all right,' she said. 'Have you had your tea?'

'No – but don't you bother about me.'

There was a little girl with fair hair in a fringe over her forehead, troubled blue eyes under the fringe, and two dolls. He felt easier.

'Is this your little girl?' he asked. 'She's awfully nice. What is her name?'

'Jane.'

'How are you, Jane?' he said. But the child only stared at him with the baffled, bewildered, pained eyes of a child who lives with hostile parents.

Mrs Pinnegar set his tea, bread and butter, jam, and buns. Then she sat opposite him. She was handsome, dark straight brows and grey eyes with yellow grains in them, and a way of looking straight at you as if she were used to holding her own. Her eyes were the nicest part of her. They had a certain kindliness, mingled, like the yellow grains among the grey, with a relentless, unyielding feminine will. Her nose and mouth were straight, like a Greek mask, and the expression was fixed. She gave him at once the impression of a woman who has made a mistake, who knows it, but who will not change: who cannot now change.

He felt very uneasy. Being a rather small, shambling man, she made him aware of his physical inconspicuousness. And she said not a word, only looked down on him, as he drank his tea, with that changeless look of a woman who is holding her own against Man and Fate. While, from the corner across the kitchen, the little girl with her fair hair and her dolls, watched him also in absolute silence, from her hot blue eyes.

'This seems a pretty awful place,' he said to her.

'It is. It's absolutely awful,' the woman said.

'You ought to get away from it,' he said.

But she received this in dead silence.

It was exceedingly difficult to make any headway. He asked about Mr Pinnegar. She glanced at the clock.

'He comes up at nine,' she said.

'Is he down the mine?'

'Yes. He's on the afternoon shift.'

There was never a sound from the little girl.

'Doesn't Jane ever talk?' he asked.

'Not much,' said her mother, glancing round.

He talked a little about his lectures, about Sheffield, about London. But she was not really interested. She sat there rather distant, very laconic, looking at him with those curious unyielding eyes. She looked to him like a woman who has had her revenge, and is left stranded on the reefs where she wrecked her opponent. Still unrelenting, unregretting, unyielding, she seemed rather undecided as to what her revenge had been, and what it had all been about.

'You ought to get away from here,' he said to her.

'Where to?' she asked.

'Oh' – he made a vague gesture – 'anywhere, so long as it is *quite* away.'

She seemed to ponder this, under her portentous brow.

'I don't see what difference it would make,' she said. Then glancing round at her child: 'I don't see what difference anything would make, except getting out of the world altogether. But there's *her* to consider.' And she jerked her head in the direction of the child.

Jimmy felt definitely frightened. He wasn't used to this sort of grimness. At the same time he was excited. This handsome, laconic woman, with her soft brown hair and her unflinching eyes with their gold flecks, seemed to be challenging him to something. There was a touch of challenge in her remaining gold-flecked kindness. Somewhere, she had a heart. But what had happened to it? And why?

What had gone wrong with her? In some way, she must have gone against herself.

'Why don't you come and live with me?' he said, like the little gambler he was.

The queer, conflicting smile was on his face. He had taken up her challenge, like a gambler. The very sense of a gamble, in which he could not lose desperately, excited him. At the same time, he was scared of her, and determined to get beyond his scare.

She sat and watched him, with the faintest touch of a grim smile on her handsome mouth.

'How do you mean, live with you?' she said.

'Oh – I mean what it usually means,' he said, with a little puff of self-conscious laughter.

'You're evidently not happy here. You're evidently in the wrong circumstances altogether. You're obviously *not* just an ordinary woman. Well, then, break away. When I say, Come and live with me, I mean just what I say. Come to London and live with me, as my wife, if you like, and then if we want to marry, when you get a divorce, why, we can do it.'

Jimmy made this speech more to himself than to the woman. That was how he was. He worked out all his things inside himself, as if it were all merely an interior problem of his own. And while he did so, he had an odd way of squinting his left eye and wagging his head loosely, like a man talking absolutely to himself, and turning his eyes inwards.

The woman watched him in a sort of wonder. This was something she was *not* used to. His extraordinary manner, and his extraordinary bald proposition, roused her from her own tense apathy.

'Well!' she said. 'That's got to be thought about. What about *her*?' – and again she jerked her head towards the round-eyed child in the corner. Jane sat with a completely expressionless face, her little red mouth fallen a little open. She seemed in a sort of trance: as if she understood like a grown-up person, but, as a child, sat in a trance, unconscious.

The mother wheeled round in her chair and stared at her child. The little girl stared back at her mother, with hot, troubled, almost guilty blue eyes. And neither said a word. Yet they seemed to exchange worlds of meaning.

'Why, of course,' said Jimmy, twisting his head again; 'she'd come, too.'

The woman gave a last look at her child, then turned to him, and started watching *him* with that slow, straight stare.

'It's not' – he began, stuttering – 'it's not anything *sudden* and unconsidered on my part. I've been considering it for quite a long time – ever since I had the first poem, and your letter.'

He spoke still with his eyes turned inwards, talking to himself. And the woman watched him unflinchingly.

'Before you ever saw me?' she asked, with a queer irony.

'Oh, of course. Of course before I ever saw you. Or else I never *should* have seen you. From the very first, I had a definite feeling –'

He made odd, sharp gestures, like a drunken man, and he spoke like a drunken man, his eyes turned inward, talking to himself. The woman was no more than a ghost moving inside his own consciousness, and he was addressing her there.

The actual woman sat outside looking on in a sort of wonder. This was really something new to her.

'And now you see me, do you want me, really, to come to London?'

She spoke in a dull tone of incredulity. The thing was just a little preposterous to her. But why not? It would have to be something a little preposterous, to get her out of the tomb she was in.

'Of course I do!' he cried, with another scoop of his head and scoop of his hand. '*Now* I do *actually* want you, now I actually see you.' He never looked at her. His eyes were still turned in. He was still talking to himself, in a sort of drunkenness with himself.

To her, it was something extraordinary. But it roused her from apathy.

He became aware of the hot blue eyes of the hot-cheeked little girl fixed upon him from the distant corner. And he gave a queer little giggle.

'Why, it's more than I could ever have hoped for,' he said, 'to have you and Jane to live with me! Why, it will mean *life* to me.' He spoke in an odd, strained voice, slightly delirious. And for the first time he looked up at the woman and, apparently, *straight* at her. But, even as he seemed to look straight at her, the curious cast was in his eye, and he was only looking at himself, inside himself, at the shadows inside his own consciousness.

'And when would you like me to come?' she asked, rather coldly.

'Why, as soon as possible. Come back with me to-morrow, if you will. I've got a little house in St John's Wood, *waiting* for you. Come with me to-morrow. That's the simplest.'

She watched him for some time, as he sat with ducked head. He looked like a man who is drunk – drunk with himself. He was going bald at the crown, his rather curly black hair was thin.

'I couldn't come to-morrow, I should need a few days,' she said.

She wanted to see his face again. It was as if she could not remember what his face was like, this strange man who had appeared out of nowhere, with such a strange proposition.

He lifted his face, his eyes still cast in that inturned, blind look. He looked now like a Mephistopheles[8] who has gone blind. With his black brows cocked up, Mephistopheles, Mephistopheles blind and begging in the street.

'Why, of course it's wonderful that it's happened like this for me,' he said, with odd pouting emphasis, pushing out his lips. 'I was finished, absolutely finished. I was finished while Clarissa was with me. But after she'd gone, I was *absolutely* finished. And I thought there was no chance for me in the world again. It seems to me perfectly marvellous that this has happened – that I've come across you –' he lifted his face sightlessly – 'and Jane – Jane – why she's *really* too good to be true.' He gave a slight hysterical laugh. 'She really is.'

The woman, and Jane, watched him with some embarrassment.

'I shall have to settle up here, with Mr Pinnegar,' she said, rather coldly musing. 'Do you want to see him?'

'Oh, I –' he said, with a deprecating gesture, 'I don't *care*. But if you think I'd better – why, certainly –'

'I do think you'd better,' she said.

'Very well, then, I *will*. I'll see him whenever you like.'

'He comes in soon after nine,' she said.

'All right, I'll see him then. Much better. But I suppose I'd better see about finding a place to sleep first. Better not leave it too late.'

'I'll come with you and ask for you.'

'Oh, you'd better not, really. If you tell me where to go –'

He had taken on a protective tone: he was protecting her against herself and against scandal. It was his manner, his rather Oxfordy manner, more than anything else, that went beyond her. She wasn't used to it.

Jimmy plunged out into the gulfing blackness of the Northern night, feeling how horrible it was, but pressing his hat on his brow in a sense of strong adventure. He was going through with it.

At the baker's shop, where she had suggested he should ask for a bed, they would have none of him. Absolutely they didn't like the looks of him. At the Pub, too, they shook their heads: didn't want to have anything to do with him. But, in a voice more expostulatingly Oxford than ever, he said:

'But look here – you can't ask a man to sleep under one of these hedges. Can't I see the landlady?'

He persuaded the landlady to promise to let him sleep on the big, soft settee in the parlour, where the fire was burning brightly. Then, saying he would be back about ten, he returned through mud and drizzle up New London Lane.

The child was in bed, a saucepan was boiling by the fire. Already the lines had softened a little in the woman's face.

She spread a cloth on the table. Jimmy sat in silence, feeling that she was hardly aware of his presence. She was absorbed, no doubt, in the coming of her husband. The stranger merely sat on the sofa, and waited. He felt himself wound up tight. And once he was really wound up, he could go through with anything.

They heard the nine-o'clock whistle at the mine. The woman then took the saucepan from the fire and went into the scullery. Jimmy could smell the smell of potatoes being strained. He sat quite still. There was nothing for him to do or to say. He was wearing his big black-rimmed spectacles, and his face, blank and expressionless in the suspense of waiting, looked like the death-mask of some sceptical philosopher, who could wait through the ages, and who could hardly distinguish life from death at any time.

Came the heavy-shod tread up the house entry, and the man entered, rather like a blast of wind. The fair moustache stuck out from the blackish, mottled face, and the fierce blue eyes rolled their whites in the coal-blackened sockets.

'This gentleman is Mr Frith,' said Emily Pinnegar.

Jimmy got up, with a bit of an Oxford wriggle, and held out his hand, saying: 'How do you do?'

His grey eyes, behind the spectacles, had an uncanny whitish gleam.

'My hand's not fit to shake hands,' said the miner. 'Take a seat.'

'Oh, nobody minds coal-dust,' said Jimmy, subsiding on to the sofa. 'It's clean dirt.'

'They say so,' said Pinnegar.

He was a man of medium height, thin, but energetic in build.

Mrs Pinnegar was running hot water into a pail from the bright brass tap of the stove, which had a boiler to balance the oven. Pinnegar dropped heavily into a wooden armchair, and stooped to pull off his ponderous grey pit-boots. He smelled of the strange, stale underground. In silence he pulled on his slippers, then rose, taking his boots into the scullery. His wife followed with the pail of hot water. She returned and spread a coarse roller-towel on the steel fender. The man could be heard washing in the scullery, in the semi-dark. Nobody said anything. Mrs Pinnegar attended to her husband's dinner.

After a while, Pinnegar came running in, naked to the waist, and squatted plumb in front of the big red fire, on his heels. His head and face and the front part of his body were all wet. His back was grey and unwashed. He seized the towel from the fender and began to rub his face and head with a sort of brutal vigour, while his wife brought a bowl, and with a soapy flannel silently washed his back, right down to the loins, where the trousers were rolled back. The man was entirely oblivious of the stranger – this washing was part of the collier's ritual, and nobody existed for the moment. The woman, washing her husband's back, stooping there as he kneeled with knees wide apart, squatting on his heels on the rag hearthrug, had a peculiar look on her strong, handsome face, a look sinister and derisive. She was deriding something or somebody; but Jimmy could not make out whom or what.

It was a new experience for him to sit completely and brutally excluded, from a personal ritual. The collier vigorously rubbed his own fair short hair, till it all stood on end, then he stared into the red-hot fire, oblivious, while the red colour burned in his cheeks. Then again he rubbed his breast and his body with the rough towel, brutally, as if his body were some machine he was cleaning, while his wife, with a peculiar slow movement, dried his back with another towel.

She took away the towel and bowl. The man was dry. He still squatted with his hands on his knees, gazing abstractedly, blankly into the fire. That, too, seemed part of his daily ritual. The colour flushed in his cheeks, his fair moustache was rubbed on end. But his hot blue eyes stared hot and vague into the red coals, while the red glare of the coal fell on his breast and naked body.

He was a man of about thirty-five, in his prime, with a pure smooth skin and no fat on his body. His muscles were not large, but quick, alive with energy. And as he squatted bathing abstractedly in the glow of the fire, he seemed like some pure-moulded engine that sleeps between its motions, with incomprehensible eyes of dark iron-blue.

He looked round, always averting his face from the stranger on the sofa, shutting him out of consciousness. The wife took out a bundle from the dresser-cupboard, and handed it to the out-stretched, work-scarred hand of the man on the hearth. Curious, that big, horny, work-battered clean hand, at the end of the suave, thin naked arm.

Pinnegar unrolled his shirt and undervest in front of the fire, warmed them for a moment in the glow, vaguely, sleepily, then pulled them over his head. And then at last he rose, with his shirt hanging over his trousers, and in the same abstract, sleepy way, shutting the world out of his consciousness, he went out again to the scullery, pausing at the same dresser-cupboard to take out his rolled-up day trousers.

Mrs Pinnegar took away the towels and set the dinner on the table – rich, oniony stew out of a hissing brown stew-jar, boiled potatoes, and a cup of tea. The man returned from the scullery, in his clean flannelette shirt and black trousers, his fair hair neatly brushed. He planked his wooden armchair beside the table, and sat heavily down, to eat.

Then he looked at Jimmy, as one wary, probably hostile man looks at another.

'You're a stranger in these parts, I gather?' he said. There was something slightly formal, even a bit pompous, in his speech.

'An absolute stranger,' replied Jimmy, with a slight aside grin.

The man dabbed some mustard on his plate, and glanced at his food to see if he would like it.

'Come from a distance, do you?' he asked, as he began to eat. As he ate, he seemed to become oblivious again of Jimmy, bent his head over his plate, and ate. But probably he was ruminating something all the time, with barbaric wariness.

'From London,' said Jimmy, warily.

'London!' said Pinnegar, without looking from his plate.

Mrs Pinnegar came and sat, in ritualistic silence, in her tall-backed rocking-chair under the light.

'What brings you this way, then?' asked Pinnegar, stirring his tea.

'Oh!' Jimmy writhed a little on the sofa. 'I came to see Mrs Pinnegar.'

The miner took a hasty gulp of tea.

'You're acquainted then, are you?' he said, still without looking round. He sat with his side-face to Jimmy.

'Yes, we are *now*,' explained Jimmy. 'I didn't know Mrs Pinnegar till this evening. As a matter of fact, she sent me some poems for the *Commentator* – I'm the editor – and I thought they were good, so I wrote and told her so. Then I felt I wanted to come and see her, and she was willing, so I came.'

The man reached out, cut himself a piece of bread, and swallowed a large mouthful.

'You thought her poetry was good?' he said, turning at last to Jimmy and looking straight at him, with a stare something like the child's, but aggressive. 'Are you going to put it in your magazine?'

'Yes, I think I am,' said Jimmy.

'I never read but one of her poems – something about a collier she knew all about, because she'd married him,' he said, in his peculiar harsh voice, that had a certain jeering clang in it, and a certain indomitableness.

Jimmy was silent. The other man's harsh fighting-voice made him shrink.

'I could never get on with the *Commentator* myself,' said Pinnegar, looking round for his pudding, pushing his meat-plate aside. 'Seems to me to go a long way round to get nowhere.'

'Well, probably it *does*,' said Jimmy, squirming a little. 'But so long as the *way* is interesting! I don't see that anything gets anywhere at present – certainly no periodical.'

'I don't know,' said Pinnegar. 'There's some facts in the *Liberator* – and there's some ideas in the *Janus*. I can't see the use myself, of all these feelings folk say they have. They get you nowhere.'

'But,' said Jimmy, with a slight pouf of laughter, 'where do you *want* to get? It's all very well talking about getting somewhere, but where, where in the world to-day do you *want* to get? In general, I mean. If you want a better job in the mine – all right, go ahead and get it. But when you begin to talk about getting somewhere in *life* – why, you've got to know what you're talking about.'

'I'm a man, aren't I?' said the miner, going very still and hard.

'But what do you *mean*, when you say you're a man?' snarled Jimmy, really exasperated. 'What do you mean? Yes, you *are* a man. But what about it?'

'Haven't I the right to say I won't be made use of?' said the collier, slow, harsh, and heavy.

'You've got a right to *say* it,' retorted Jimmy, with a pouf of laughter. 'But it doesn't *mean* anything. We're all made use of, from King George downwards. We have to be. When you eat your pudding you're making use of hundreds of people – including your wife.'

'I know it. I know it. It makes no difference, though. I'm not going to be made use of.'

Jimmy shrugged his shoulders.

'Oh, all right!' he said. 'That's just a phrase, like any other.'

The miner sat very still in his chair, his face going hard and remote. He was evidently thinking over something that was stuck like a barb in his consciousness, something he was trying to harden over, as the skin sometimes hardens over a steel splinter in the flesh.

'I'm nothing but made use of,' he said, now talking hard and final, to himself, and staring out into space. 'Down the pit, I'm made use of, and they give me a wage, such as it is. At the house, I'm made use of, and my wife sets the dinner on the table as if I was a customer in a shop.'

'But what do you *expect*?' cried Jimmy, writhing in his chair.

'Me? What do I expect? I expect nothing. But I tell you what –' he turned, and looked straight and hard into Jimmy's eyes – 'I'm not going to put up with anything, either.'

Jimmy saw the hard finality in the other man's eyes, and squirmed away from it.

'If you *know* what you're not going to put up with –' he said.

'I don't want my wife writing poetry! And sending it to a parcel of men she's never seen. *I* don't want my wife sitting like Queen Boadicea,[9] when I come home, and a face like a stone wall with holes in it. I don't know what's wrong with her. She doesn't know herself. But she does as she likes. Only, mark you, I do the same.'

'Of course!' cried Jimmy, though there was no of course about it.

'She's told you I've got another woman?'

'Yes.'

'And I'll tell you for why. If I give in to the coal face, and go down the mine every day to eight hours' slavery, more or less, somebody's got to give in to me.'

'Then,' said Jimmy, after a pause, 'if you mean you want your wife to submit to you – well, that's the problem. You have to marry the woman who *will* submit.'

It was amazing, this from Jimmy. He sat there and lectured the collier like a Puritan Father,[10] completely forgetting the disintegrating flutter of Clarissa, in his own background.

'I want a wife who'll please me, who'll want to please me,' said the collier.

'Why should *you* be pleased, any more than anybody else?' asked the wife coldly.

'My child, my little girl wants to please me – if her mother would let her. But the women hang together. I tell you' – and here he turned to Jimmy, with a blaze in his dark blue eyes – 'I want a woman to please me, a woman who's anxious to please me. And if I can't find her in my own home, I'll find her out of it.'

'I hope she pleases you,' said the wife, rocking slightly.

'Well,' said the man, 'she does.'

'Then why don't you go and live with her altogether?' she said.

He turned and looked at her.

'Why don't I?' he said. 'Because I've got my home. I've got my house, I've got my wife, let her be what she may, as a woman to live with. And I've got my child. Why should I break it all up?'

'And what about me?' she asked, coldly and fiercely.

'You? You've got a home. You've got a child. You've got a man who works for you. You've got what you want. You do as you like –'

'Do I?' she asked, with intolerable sarcasm.

'Yes. Apart from the bit of work in the house, you do as you like. If you want to go, you can go. But while you live in my house, you must respect it. You bring no men here, you see.'

'Do *you* respect your home?' she said.

'Yes! I do! If I get another woman – who pleases me – I deprive you of nothing. All I ask of you is to do your duty as a housewife.'

'Down to washing your back!' she said, heavily sarcastic; and, Jimmy thought, a trifle vulgar.

'Down to washing my back, since it's got to be washed,' he said.

'What about the other woman? Let her do it.'

'This is my home.'

The wife gave a strange movement, like a mad woman.

Jimmy sat rather pale and frightened. Behind the collier's quietness he felt the concentration of almost cold anger and an unchanging will. In the man's lean face he could see the bones, the fixity of the male bones, and it was as if the human soul, or spirit, had gone into the living skull and skeleton, almost invulnerable.

Jimmy, for some strange reason, felt a wild anger against this bony and logical man. It was the hard-driven coldness, fixity, that he could not bear.

'Look here!' he cried, in a resonant Oxford voice, his eyes glaring and casting inwards behind his spectacles. 'You say Mrs Pinnegar is *free* – free to do as she pleases. In that case, you have no objection if she comes with me right away from here.'

The collier looked at the pale, strange face of the editor in wonder. Jimmy kept his face slightly averted, and sightless, seeing nobody. There was a Mephistophelian tilt about the eyebrows, and a Martyred Sebastian straightness about the mouth.

'Does she *want* to?' asked Pinnegar, with devastating incredulity. The wife smiled faintly, grimly. She could see the vanity of her husband in his utter inability to believe that she could prefer the other man to him.

'That,' said Jimmy, 'you must ask her yourself. But it's what I came here for: to ask her to come and live with me, and bring the child.'

'You came without having seen her, to ask her that?' said the husband, in growing wonder.

'Yes,' said Jimmy, vehemently, nodding his head with drunken emphasis. 'Yes! Without ever having seen her!'

'You've caught a funny fish this time, with your poetry,' he said, turning with curious husband-familiarity to his wife. She hated this off-hand husband-familiarity.

'What sort of fish have *you* caught?' she retorted. 'And what did you catch *her* with?'

'Bird-lime!' he said, with a faint, quick grin.

Jimmy was sitting in suspense. They all three sat in suspense, for some time.

'And what are you saying to him?' said the collier at length.

Jimmy looked up, and the malevolent half-smile on his face made him look rather handsome again, a mixture of faun and Mephisto. He glanced curiously, invitingly, at the woman who was watching him from afar.

'I say yes!' she replied, in a cool voice.

The husband became very still, sitting erect in his wooden armchair and staring into space. It was as if he were fixedly watching something fly away from him, out of his own soul. But he was not going to yield at all, to any emotion.

He could not now believe that this woman should *want* to leave him. Yet she did.

'I'm sure it's all for the best,' said Jimmy, in his Puritan-Father voice. 'You don't mind, really' – he drawled uneasily – 'if she brings the child. I give you my word I'll do my very best for it.'

The collier looked at him as if he were very far away. Jimmy quailed under the look. He could see that the other man was relentlessly killing the emotion in himself, stripping himself, as it were, of his own flesh, stripping himself to the hard unemotional bone of the human male.

'I give her a blank cheque,' said Pinnegar, with numb lips. 'She does as she pleases.'

'So much for fatherly love, compared with selfishness,' she said.

He turned and looked at her with that curious power of remote anger. And immediately she became still, quenched.

'I give you a blank cheque, as far as I'm concerned,' he repeated abstractedly.

'It *is* blank indeed!' she said, with her first touch of bitterness.

Jimmy looked at the clock. It was growing late: he might be shut out of the public-house. He rose to go, saying he would return in the morning. He was leaving the next day, at noon, for London.

He plunged into the darkness and mud of that black, night-ridden country. There was a curious elation in his spirits, mingled with fear. But then he always needed an element of fear, really, to elate him. He thought with terror of those two human beings left in that house together. The frightening state of tension! He himself could never bear an extreme tension. He always had to compromise, to become apologetic and pathetic. He would be able to manage Mrs Pinnegar that way. Emily! He must get used to saying it. Emily! The Emilia was absurd. He had never known an Emily.

He felt really scared, and really elated. He was doing something big. It was not that he was in *love* with the woman. But, my God, he wanted to take her away from that man. And he wanted the adventure of her. Absolutely the adventure of her. He felt really elated, really himself, really manly.

But in the morning he returned rather sheepishly to the collier's house. It was another dark, drizzling day, with black trees, black road, black hedges, blackish brick houses, and the smell and the sound of collieries under a skyless day. Like living in some weird underground.

Unwillingly he went up that passage-entry again, and knocked at the back door, glancing at the miserable little back garden with its cabbage-stalks and its ugly sanitary arrangements.

The child opened the door to him: with her fair hair, flushed cheeks, and hot, dark-blue eyes.

'Hello, Jane!' he said.

The mother stood tall and square, by the table, watching him with portentous eyes, as he entered. She was handsome, but her skin was not very good: as if the battle had been too much for her health. Jimmy glanced up at her smiling his slow, ingratiating smile, that always brought a glow of success into a woman's spirit. And as he saw her gold-flecked eyes searching in his eyes, without a bit of kindliness, he thought to himself: 'My God, however am I going to sleep with that woman!' His will was ready, however, and he would manage it somehow.

And when he glanced at the motionless, bony head and lean figure of the collier seated in the wooden armchair by the fire, he was the more ready. He must triumph over that man.

'What train are you going by?' asked Mrs Pinnegar.

'By the twelve thirty.' He looked up at her as he spoke, with the wide, shining, childlike, almost coy eyes that were his peculiar asset. She looked down at him in a sort of interested wonder. She seemed almost fascinated by his childlike, shining, inviting dark-grey eyes, with their long lashes: such an absolute change from that resentful unyielding that looked out always from the back of her husband's blue eyes. Her husband always seemed like a menace to her, in his thinness, his concentration, his eternal unyielding. And this man looked at one with the wide, shining, fascinating eyes of a young Persian kitten, something at once bold and shy and coy and strangely inviting. She fell at once under their spell.

'You'll have dinner before you go,' she said.

'No!' he cried in panic, unwilling indeed to eat before that other man. 'No, I ate a fabulous breakfast. I will get a sandwich when I change in Sheffield: *really*!'

She had to go out shopping. She said she would go out to the station with him when she got back. It was just after eleven.

'But look here,' he said, addressing also the thin abstracted man who sat unnoticing, with a newspaper, 'we've got to get this thing settled. I *want* Mrs Pinnegar to come and live with me, her and the child. And she's coming! So don't you think, now, it would be better if she came right along with me to-day! Just put a few things in a bag and come along. Why drag the thing out?'

'I tell you,' replied the husband, 'she has a blank cheque from me to do as she likes.'

'All right, then! Won't you do that? Won't you come along with me now?' said Jimmy, looking up at her exposedly, but casting his eyes a bit inwards. Throwing himself with deliberate impulsiveness on her mercy.

'I can't!' she said decisively. 'I can't come to-day.'

'But why not – really? Why not, while I'm here? You have that blank cheque, you can do as you please –'

'The blank cheque won't get me far,' she said rudely; 'I can't come to-day, anyhow.'

'When can you come, then?' he said, with that queer, petulant pleading. 'The sooner the better, surely.'

'I can come on Monday,' she said abruptly.

'Monday!' He gazed up at her in a kind of panic, through his spectacles. Then he set his teeth again, and nodded his head up and down. 'All right, then! To-day is Saturday. Then Monday!'

'If you'll excuse me,' she said, 'I've got to go out for a few things. I'll walk to the station with you when I get back.'

She bundled Jane into a little sky-blue coat and bonnet, put on a heavy black coat and black hat herself, and went out.

Jimmy sat very uneasily opposite the collier, who also wore spectacles to read. Pinnegar put down the newspaper and pulled the spectacles off his nose, saying something about a Labour Government.

'Yes,' said Jimmy. 'After all, best be logical. If you *are* democratic, the only logical thing is a Labour Government. Though, personally, one Government is as good as another, to me.'

'Maybe so!' said the collier. 'But *something's* got to come to an end, sooner or later.'

'Oh, a great deal!' said Jimmy, and they lapsed into silence.

'Have you been married before?' asked Pinnegar, at length.

'Yes. My wife and I are divorced.'

'I suppose you want me to divorce *my* wife?' said the collier.

'Why – yes! – that would be best –'

'It's the same to me,' said Pinnegar; 'divorce or no divorce. I'll *live* with another woman, but I'll never *marry* another. Enough is as good as a feast. But if she wants a divorce, she can have it.'

'It would certainly be best,' said Jimmy.

There was a long pause. Jimmy wished the woman would come back.

'I look on you as an instrument,' said the miner. 'Something had to break. You are the instrument that breaks it.'

It was strange to sit in the room with this thin, remote, wilful man. Jimmy was a bit fascinated by him. But, at the same time, he hated him because he could not be in the same room with him without being under his spell. He felt himself dominated. And he hated it.

'My wife,' said Pinnegar, looking up at Jimmy with a peculiar, almost humorous, teasing grin, 'expects to see me go to the dogs when she leaves me. It is her last hope.'

Jimmy ducked his head and was silent, not knowing what to say. The other man sat still in his chair, like a sort of infinitely patient prisoner, looking away out of the window and waiting.

'She thinks,' he said again, 'that she has some wonderful future awaiting her somewhere, and you're going to open the door.'

And again the same amused grin was in his eyes.

And again Jimmy was fascinated by the man. And again he hated the spell of this fascination. For Jimmy wanted to be, in his own mind, the strongest man among men, but particularly among women. And this thin, peculiar man could dominate him. He knew it. The very silent unconsciousness of Pinnegar dominated the room, wherever he was.

Jimmy hated this.

At last Mrs Pinnegar came back, and Jimmy set off with her. He shook hands with the collier.

'Good-bye!' he said.

'Good-bye!' said Pinnegar, looking down at him with those amused blue eyes, which Jimmy knew he would never be able to get beyond.

And the walk to the station was almost a walk of conspiracy against the man left behind, between the man in spectacles and the tall woman. They arranged the details for Monday. Emily was to come by the nine o'clock train: Jimmy would meet her at Marylebone, and instal her in his house in St John's Wood. Then, with the child, they would begin a new life. Pinnegar would divorce his wife, or she would divorce him: and then, another marriage.

Jimmy got a tremendous kick out of it all on the journey home. He felt he had really done something desperate and adventurous. But he was in too wild a flutter to analyse any results. Only, as he drew near London, a sinking feeling came over him. He was desperately tired after it all, almost too tired to keep up.

Nevertheless, he went after dinner and sprang it all on Severn.

'You damn fool!' said Severn, in consternation. 'What did you do it for?'

'Well,' said Jimmy, writhing. 'Because *I wanted* to.'

'Good God! The woman sounds like the head of Medusa.[11] You're a hero of some stomach, I must say! Remember Clarissa?'

'Oh,' writhed Jimmy. 'But this is different.'

'Ay, her name's Emma, or something of that sort, isn't it?'

'Emily!' said Jimmy briefly.

'Well, you're a fool, anyway, so you may as well keep on acting in character. I've no doubt, by playing weeping-willow, you'll outlive all the female storms you ever prepare for yourself. I never yet did see a weeping-willow uprooted by a gale, so keep on hanging your harp on it,[12] and you'll be all right. Here's luck! But for a man who was looking for a little Gretchen to adore him, you're a corker!'

Which was all that Severn had to say. But Jimmy went home with his knees shaking. On Sunday morning he wrote an anxious letter. He didn't know how to begin it: *Dear Mrs Pinnegar* and *Dear Emily* seemed either too late in the day or too early. So he just plunged in, without dear anything.

'I want you to have this before you come. Perhaps we have been precipitate. I only beg you to decide *finally*, for yourself, before you come. Don't come, please, unless you are absolutely sure of yourself. If you are *in the least* unsure, wait a while, wait till you are quite certain, one way or the other.

'For myself, if you don't come I shall understand. But please send me a telegram. If you do come, I shall welcome both you and the child. Yours ever – J.F.'

He paid a man his return fare, and three pounds extra, to go on the Sunday and deliver this letter.

The man came back in the evening. He had delivered the letter. There was no answer.

Awful Sunday night: tense Monday morning!

A telegram: '*Arrive Marylebone 12.50 with Jane. Yours ever. Emily.*'

Jimmy set his teeth and went to the station. But when he felt her looking at him, and so met her eyes: and after that saw her coming slowly down the platform, holding the child by the hand, her slow cat's eyes smouldering under her straight brows, smouldering at him: he almost swooned. A sickly grin came over him as he held out his hand. Nevertheless he said:

'I'm *awfully* glad you came.'

And as he sat in the taxi, a perverse but intense desire for her came over him, making him almost helpless. He could feel, so strongly, the presence of that other man about her, and this went to his head like neat spirits. That other man! In some subtle, inexplicable way, he was actually bodily present, the husband. The woman moved in his aura. She was hopelessly married to him.

And this went to Jimmy's head like neat whisky. Which of the two would fall before him with a greater fall – the woman, or the man, her husband?

The Border Line

KATHERINE FARQUHAR was a handsome woman of forty, no longer slim, but attractive in her soft, full, feminine way. The French porters ran round her, getting a voluptuous pleasure from merely carrying her bags. And she gave them ridiculously high tips, because, in the first place, she had never really known the value of money, and secondly, she had a morbid fear of underpaying anyone, but particularly a man who was eager to serve her.

It was really a joke to her, how eagerly these Frenchmen – all sorts of Frenchmen – ran round her and *Madamed* her. Their voluptuous obsequiousness. Because, after all, she was Boche.[1] Fifteen years of marriage to an Englishman – or rather to two Englishmen – had not altered her racially. Daughter of a German Baron she was, and remained, in her own mind and body, although England had become her life-home. And surely she looked German, with her fresh complexion and her strong, full figure. But like most people in the world, she was a mixture, with Russian blood and French blood also in her veins. And she had lived in one country and another, till she was somewhat indifferent to her surroundings. So that perhaps the Parisian men might be excused for running round her so eagerly, and getting a voluptuous pleasure from calling a taxi for her, or giving up a place in the omnibus to her, or carrying her bags, or holding the menu card before her. Nevertheless, it amused her. And she had to confess she liked them, these Parisians. They had their own kind of manliness, even if it wasn't an English sort; and if a woman looked pleasant and soft-fleshed, and a wee bit helpless, they were ardent and generous. Katherine understood so well that Frenchmen were rude to the dry, hard-seeming, competent Englishwoman or American. She sympathized with the Frenchman's point of view: too much obvious capacity to help herself is a disagreeable trait in a woman.

At the Gare de l'Est, of course, everybody was expected to be Boche, and it was almost a convention, with the porters, to assume a certain small-boyish superciliousness. Nevertheless, there was the same voluptuous scramble to escort Katherine Farquhar to her seat in the first-class carriage. *Madame* was travelling alone.

She was going to Germany via Strasburg, meeting her sister in

Baden-Baden. Philip, her husband, was in Germany collecting some sort of evidence for his newspaper. Katherine felt a little weary of newspapers, and of the sort of 'evidence' that is extracted out of nowhere to feed them. However, Philip was quite clever, he was a little somebody in the world.

Her world, she had realized, consisted almost entirely of little somebodies. She was outside the sphere of the nobodies, always had been. And the Somebodies with a capital S, were all safely dead. She knew enough of the world to-day to know that it is not going to put up with any great Somebody: but many little nobodies and a sufficient number of little somebodies. Which, after all, is as it should be, she felt.

Sometimes she had vague misgivings.

Paris, for example, with its Louvre and its Luxembourg and its cathedral, seemed intended for Somebody. In a ghostly way it called for some supreme Somebody. But all its little men, nobodies and somebodies, were as sparrows twittering for crumbs, and dropping their little droppings on the palace cornices.

To Katherine, Paris brought back again her first husband, Alan Anstruther, that red-haired fighting Celt, father of her two grown-up children. Alan had had a weird innate conviction that he was beyond ordinary judgment. Katherine could never quite see where it came in. Son of a Scottish baronet, and captain in a Highland regiment did not seem to her stupendous. As for Alan himself, he was handsome in uniform, with his kilt swinging and his blue eye glaring. Even stark naked and without any trimmings, he had a bony, dauntless, overbearing manliness of his own. The one thing Katherine could *not quite* appreciate was his silent, indomitable assumption that he was actually first-born, a born lord. He was a clever man too, ready to assume that General This or Colonel That might really be his superior. Until he actually came into contact with General This or Colonel That. Whereupon his overweening blue eye arched in his bony face, and a faint tinge of contempt infused itself into his homage.

Lordly or not, he wasn't much of a success in the worldly sense. Katherine had loved him, and he had loved her: that was indisputable. But when it came to innate conviction of lordliness, it was a question which of them was worse. For she, in her amiable, queen-bee self thought that ultimately hers was the right to the last homage.

Alan had been too unyielding and haughty to say much. But sometimes he would stand and look at her in silent rage, wonder, and indignation. The wondering indignation had been *almost* too much for her. What did the man think he was?

He was one of the hard, clever Scotsmen, with a philosophic tendency, but without sentimentality. His contempt of Nietzsche, whom she adored, was intolerable. Alan just asserted himself like a pillar of rock,[2] and expected the tides of the modern world to recede around him. They didn't.

So he concerned himself with astronomy, gazing through a telescope and watching the worlds beyond worlds. Which seemed to give him relief.

After ten years, they had ceased to live together, passionate as they both were. They were too proud and unforgiving to yield to one another, and much too haughty to yield to any outsider.

Alan had a friend, Philip, also a Scotsman, and a university friend. Philip, trained for the bar, had gone into journalism, and had made himself a name. He was a little black Highlander, of the insidious sort, clever, and *knowing*. This look of knowing in his dark eyes, and the feeling of secrecy that went with his dark little body, made him interesting to women. Another thing he could do was to give off a great sense of warmth and offering, like a dog when it loves you. He seemed to be able to do this at will. And Katherine, after feeling cool about him and rather despising him for years, at last fell under the spell of the dark, insidious fellow.

'You!' she said to Alan, whose overweening masterfulness drove her wild. 'You don't even know that a woman exists. And that's where Philip Farquhar is more than you are. He *does* know something of what a woman *is*.'

'Bah! the little —' said Alan, using an obscene word of contempt.

Nevertheless, the friendship endured, kept up by Philip, who had an almost uncanny love for Alan. Alan was mostly indifferent. But he was used to Philip, and habit meant a great deal to him.

'Alan really is an amazing man!' Philip would say to Katherine. 'He is the only real man, what I call a real man, that I have ever met.'

'But why is he the only real man?' she asked. 'Don't you call *yourself* a real man?'

'Oh, *I* – I'm different! My strength lies in giving in – and then recovering myself. I do let myself be swept away. But so far, I've always managed to get myself back again. Alan –' and Philip even had a half-reverential, half-envious way of uttering the word – 'Alan *never* lets himself be swept away. And he's the only man I know who doesn't.'

'Yah!' she said. 'He is fooled by plenty of things. You can fool him through his vanity.'

'No,' said Philip. 'Never altogether. You *can't* deceive him right through. When a thing really touches Alan, it is tested once and for all. You know if it's false or not. He's the only man I ever met who *can't help* being real.'

'Ha! You overrate his reality,' said Katherine, rather scornfully.

And later, when Alan shrugged his shoulders with that mere indifferent tolerance, at the mention of Philip, she got angry.

'You are a poor friend,' she said.

'Friend!' he answered. 'I never was Farquhar's friend! If he asserts that he's mine, that's his side of the question. I never positively cared for the man. He's too much over the wrong side of the border for me.'

'Then,' she answered, 'you've no business to let him *consider* he is your friend. You've no right to let him think so much of you. You should tell him you don't like him.'

'I've told him a dozen times. He seems to enjoy it. It seems part of his game.'

And he went away to his astronomy.

Came the war, and the departure of Alan's regiment for France.

'There!' he said. 'Now you have to pay the penalty of having married a soldier. You find him fighting your own people. So it is.'

She was too much struck by this blow even to weep.

'Good-bye!' he said, kissing her gently, lingeringly. After all, he had been a husband to her.

And as he looked back at her, with the gentle, protective husband-knowledge in his blue eyes, and at the same time that other quiet realization of destiny, her consciousness fluttered into incoherence. She only wanted to alter everything, to alter the past, to alter all the flow of history – the terrible flow of history. Secretly somewhere inside herself she felt that with her queen-bee love, and queen-bee will, she *could* divert the whole flow of history – nay, even reverse it.

But in the remote, realizing look that lay at the back of his eyes, back of all his changeless husband-care, she saw that it could never be so. That the whole of her womanly, motherly concentration could never put back the great flow of human destiny. That, as he said, only the cold strength of a man, accepting the destiny of destruction, could see the human flow through the chaos and beyond to a new outlet. But the chaos first, and the long rage of destruction.

For an instant her will broke. Almost her soul seemed broken. And then he was gone. And as soon as he was gone she recovered the core of her assurance.

Philip was a great consolation to her. He asserted that the war was monstrous, that it should never have been, and that men should refuse to consider it as anything but a colossal, disgraceful accident.

She, in her German soul, knew that it was no accident. It was inevitable, and even necessary. But Philip's attitude soothed her enormously, restored her to herself.

Alan never came back. In the spring of 1915 he was missing. She had never mourned for him. She had never really considered him dead. In a certain sense she had triumphed. The queen-bee had recovered her sway, as queen of the earth; the woman, the mother, the female with the ear of corn in her hand, as against the man with the sword.

Philip had gone through the war as a journalist, always throwing his weight on the side of humanity, and human truth and peace. He had been an inexpressible consolation. And in 1921 she had married him.

The thread of fate might be spun, it might even be measured out, but the hand of Lachesis[3] had been stayed from cutting it through.

At first it was wonderfully pleasant and restful and voluptuous, especially for a woman of thirty-eight, to be married to Philip. Katherine felt he caressed her senses, and soothed her, and gave her what she wanted.

Then, gradually, a curious sense of degradation started in her spirit. She felt unsure, uncertain. It was almost like having a disease. Life became dull and unreal to her, as it had never been before. She did not even struggle and suffer. In the numbness of her flesh she could feel no reactions. Everything was turning into mud.

Then again, she would recover, and *enjoy* herself wonderfully. And after a while, the suffocating sense of nullity and degradation once more. Why, why, why did she feel degraded, in her secret soul? *Never*, of course, outwardly.

The memory of Alan came back into her. She still thought of him and his relentlessness with an arrested heart, but without the angry hostility she used to feel. A little awe of him, of his memory, stole back into her spirit. She resisted it. She was not used to feeling awe.

She realized, however, the difference between being married to a soldier, a ceaseless born fighter, a sword not to be sheathed, and this other man, this cunning civilian, this subtle equivocator, this adjuster of the scales of truth.

Philip was cleverer than she was. He set her up, the queen-bee, the mother, the woman, the female judgment, and he served her with subtle, cunning homage. He put the scales, the balance in her hand. But also, cunningly, he blindfolded her, and manipulated the scales when she was sightless.

Dimly she realized all this. But only dimly, confusedly, because she was blindfolded. Philip had the subtle, fawning power that could keep her always blindfolded.

Sometimes she gasped and gasped from her oppressed lungs. And sometimes the bony, hard, masterful, but honest face of Alan would come back, and suddenly it would seem to her that she was all right again, that the strange, voluptuous suffocation, which left her soul in mud, was gone, and she could breathe air of the open heavens once more. Even fighting air.

It came to her on the boat crossing the Channel. Suddenly she seemed to feel Alan at her side again, as if Philip had never existed. As if Philip had never meant anything more to her than the shop-assistant measuring off her orders. And, escaping, as it were, by herself across the cold, wintry Channel, she suddenly deluded herself into feeling as if Philip had never existed, only Alan had ever been her husband. He was her husband still. And she was going to meet him.

This gave her her blitheness in Paris, and made the Frenchman so nice to her. For the Latins love to feel a woman is really enveloped in the spell of some man. Beyond all race is the problem of man and woman.

Katherine now sat dimly, vaguely excited and almost happy in the railway-carriage on the Est railroad. It was like the old days when she was going home to Germany. Or even more like the old days when she was coming back to Alan. Because, in the past, when he was her husband, feel as she might towards him, she could never get over the sensation that the wheels of the railway-carriage had wings, when they were taking her back to him. Even when she knew that he was going to be awful to her, hard and relentless and destructive, still the motion went on wings.

Whereas towards Philip she moved with a strange, disintegrating reluctance. She decided not to think of him.

As she looked unseeing out of the carriage window, suddenly, with a jolt, the wintry landscape realized itself in her consciousness. The flat, grey, wintry landscape, ploughed fields of greyish earth that looked as if they were compound of the clay of dead men. Pallid, stark, thin trees stood like wire beside straight, abstract roads. A ruined farm between a few more wire trees. And a dismal village filed past, with smashed houses like rotten teeth between the straight rows of the village street.

With sudden horror she realized that she must be in the Marne country,[4] the ghastly Marne country, century after century digging the corpses of frustrated men into its soil. The border country, where the Latin races and the Germanic neutralize one another into horrid ash.

Perhaps even the corpse of her own man among that grey clay.

It was too much for her. She sat ashy herself with horror, wanting to escape.

'If I had only known,' she said. 'If only I had known, I would have gone by Bâsle.'

The train drew up at Soissons; name ghastly to her. She simply tried to make herself unreceptive to everything. And mercifully luncheon was served, she went down to the restaurant car, and sat opposite to a little French officer in horizon-blue uniform, who suggested anything but war. He looked so naïve, rather childlike and nice, with the certain innocence that so many French people preserve under their so-called wickedness, that she felt really relieved. He bowed to her with an odd, shy little bow when she returned him his half-bottle of red wine, which had slowly jigged its way the length of the table, owing to the motion of the train. How nice he was! And how he would give himself to a woman, if she would only find real pleasure in the male that he was.

Nevertheless, she herself felt very remote from this business of male and female, and giving and taking.

After luncheon, in the heat of the train and the flush of her half-bottle of white wine, she went to sleep again, her feet grilling uncomfortably on the iron plate of the carriage floor. And as she slept, life, as she had known it, seemed all to turn artificial to her, the sunshine of the world an artificial light, with smoke above, like the light of torches, and things artificially growing, in a night that was lit up artificially with such intensity that it gave the illusion of day. It had been an illusion, her life-day, as a ballroom evening is an illusion. Her love and her emotions, her very panic of love, had been an illusion. She realized how love had become panic-stricken inside her, during the war.

And now even this panic of love was an illusion. She had run to Philip to be saved. And now, both her panic-love and Philip's salvation were an illusion.

What remained then? Even panic-stricken love, the intensest thing, perhaps, she had ever felt, was only an illusion. What was left? The grey shadows of death?

When she looked out again it was growing dark, and they were at Nancy. She used to know this country as a girl. At half-past seven she was in Strasburg, where she must stay the night as there was no train over the Rhine till morning.

The porter, a blond, hefty fellow, addressed her at once in Alsatian

German.[5] He insisted on escorting her safely to her hotel – a German hotel – keeping guard over her like an appointed sentinel, very faithful and competent, so different from Frenchmen.

It was a cold, wintry night, but she wanted to go out after dinner to see the minster. She remembered it all so well, in that other life.

The wind blew icily in the street. The town seemed empty, as if its spirit had left it. The few squat, hefty foot-passengers were all talking the harsh Alsatian German. Shop-signs were in French, often with a little concession to German underneath. And the shops were full of goods, glutted with goods from the once-German factories of Mulhausen and other cities.

She crossed the night-dark river, where the washhouses of the washerwomen were anchored along the stream, a few odd women still kneeling over the water's edge, in the dim electric light, rinsing their clothes in the grim, cold water. In the big square the icy wind was blowing, and the place seemed a desert. A city once more conquered.

After all she could not remember her way to the cathedral. She saw a French policeman in his blue cape and peaked cap, looking a lonely, vulnerable, silky specimen in this harsh Alsatian city. Crossing over to him she asked him in French where was the cathedral.

He pointed out to her, the first turning on the left. He did not seem hostile: nobody seemed really hostile. Only the great frozen weariness of winter in a conquered city, on a weary everlasting border-line.

And the Frenchmen seemed far more weary, and also, more sensitive than the crude Alsatians.

She remembered the little street, the old, overhanging houses with black timbers and high gables. And like a great ghost, a reddish flush in its darkness, the uncanny cathedral breasting the oncomer, standing gigantic, looking down in darkness out of darkness, on the pigmy humanness of the city. It was built of reddish stone, that had a flush in the night, like dark flesh. And vast, an incomprehensibly tall, strange thing, it looked down out of the night. The great rose window, poised high, seemed like the breast of the vast Thing, and prisms and needles of stone shot up, as if it were plumage, dimly, half-visible in heaven.

There it was, in the upper darkness of the ponderous winter night, like a menace. She remembered, her spirit used in the past to soar aloft with it. But now, looming with a faint rust of blood out of the upper black heavens, the Thing stood suspended, looking down with vast, demonish menace, calm and implacable.

Mystery and dim, ancient fear came over the woman's soul. The cathedral looked so strange and demonish-heathen. And an ancient, indomitable blood seemed to stir in it. It stood there like some vast silent beast with teeth of stone, waiting, and wondering when to stoop against this pallid humanity.

And dimly she realized that behind all the ashy pallor and sulphur of our civilization, lurks the great blood-creature waiting, implacable and eternal, ready at last to crush our white brittleness and let the shadowy blood move erect once more, in a new implacable pride and strength. Even out of the lower heavens looms the great blood-dusky Thing, blotting out the Cross it was supposed to exalt.

The scroll of the night sky seemed to roll back, showing a huge, blood-dusky presence looming enormous, stooping, looking down, awaiting its moment.

As she turned to go away, to move away from the closed wings of the minster, she noticed a man standing on the pavement, in the direction of the post-office, which functions obscurely in the Cathedral Square. Immediately, she knew that that man, standing dark and motionless, was Alan. He was alone, motionless, remote.

He did not move towards her. She hesitated, then went in his direction, as if going to the post-office. He stood perfectly motionless, and her heart died as she drew near. Then, as she passed, he turned suddenly, looking down on her.

It was he, though she could hardly see his face, it was so dark, with a dusky glow in the shadow.

'Alan!' she said.

He did not speak, but laid his hand detainingly on her arm, as he used in the early days, with strange silent authority. And turning her with a faint pressure on her arm, he went along with her, leisurely, through the main street of the city, under the arcade where the shops were still lighted up.

She glanced at his face: it seemed much more dusky, and duskily ruddy, than she had known him. He was a stranger: and yet it was he, no other. He said nothing at all. But that was also in keeping. His mouth was closed, his watchful eyes seemed changeless, and there was a shadow of silence around him, impenetrable, but not cold. Rather aloof and gentle, like the silence that surrounds a wild animal.

She knew that she was walking with his spirit. But that even did not trouble her. It seemed natural. And there came over her again the feeling she had forgotten, the restful, thoughtless pleasure of a woman who moves in the aura of the man to whom she belongs. As a young woman she had had this unremarkable, yet very precious feeling, when she was with her husband. It had been a full contentment; and perhaps the fullness of it had made her unconscious of it. Later, it seemed to her she had almost wilfully destroyed it, this soft flow of contentment which she, a woman, had from him as a man.

Now, afterwards, she realized it. And as she walked at his side through the conquered city, she realized that it was the one enduring thing a woman can have, the intangible soft flood of contentment that carries her along at the side of the man she is married to. It is her perfection and her highest attainment.

Now, in the afterwards, she knew it. Now the strife was gone. And dimly she wondered why, why, why she had ever fought against it. No matter what the man does or is, as a person, if a woman can move at his side in this dim, full flood of contentment, she has the highest of him, and her scratching efforts at getting more than this, are her ignominious efforts at self-nullity.

Now, she knew it, and she submitted. Now that she was walking with a man who came from the halls of death, to her, for her relief. The strong, silent kindliness of him towards her, even now, was able to wipe out the ashy, nervous horror of the world from her body. She went at his side still and released, like one newly unbound, walking in the dimness of her own contentment.

At the bridge-head he came to a standstill, and drew his hand from her arm. She knew he was going to leave her. But he looked at her from under his peaked cap, darkly but kindly, and he waved his hand with a slight, kindly gesture of farewell and of promise, as if in the farewell he promised never to leave her, never to let the kindliness go out in his heart, to let it stay hers always.

She hurried over the bridge with tears running down her cheeks, and on to her hotel. Hastily she climbed to her room. And as she undressed, she avoided the sight of her own face in the mirror. She must not rupture the spell of his presence.

Now, in the afterwards she realized *how* careful she must be, not to break the mystery that enveloped her. Now that she knew he had come back to her from the dead, she was aware how precious and how fragile the coming was. He had come back with his heart dark and kind, wanting her even in the afterwards. And not in any sense must she go against him. The warm, powerful, silent ghost had come back to her. It was he. She must not even try to think about him definitely, not to realize him or to understand. Only in her own woman's soul could she silently ponder him, darkly, and know him present in her, without ever staring at him or trying to find him out. Once she tried to lay hands on him, to *have* him, to *realize* him, he would be gone for ever, and gone for ever this last precious flood of her woman's peace.

'Ah, no!' she said to herself. 'If he leaves his peace with me, I must ask no questions whatsoever.'

And she repented, silently, of the way she had questioned and demanded answers, in the past. What were the answers, when she had got them? Terrible ash in the mouth.

She now knew the supreme modern terror, of a world all ashy and nerve-dead. If a man could come back out of death to save her from this, she would not ask questions of him, but be humble, and beyond tears grateful.

In the morning, she went out into the icy wind, under the grey sky, to see if he would be there again. Not that she *needed* him: his presence was still about her. But he might be waiting.

The town was stony and cold. The people looked pale, chilled through, and doomed in some way. Very far from her they were. She felt a sort of pity for them, but knew she could do nothing, nothing in time or eternity. And they looked at her, and looked quickly away again, as if they were uneasy in themselves.

The cathedral reared its great reddish-grey façade in the stark light; but it did not loom as in the night. The cathedral square was hard and cold. Inside, the church was cold and repellent, in spite of the glow of stained glass. And he was nowhere to be found.

So she hastened away to her hotel and to the station, to catch the 10.30 train into Germany.

It was a lonely, dismal train, with a few forlorn souls waiting to cross the Rhine. Her Alsatian porter looked after her with the same dogged care as before. She got into the first-class carriage that was going through to Prague – she was the only passenger travelling first. A real French porter, in blouse and moustache, and swagger, tried to say something a bit jeering to her, in his few words of German. But she only looked at him, and he subsided. He didn't really want to be rude. There was a certain hopelessness even about that.

The train crept slowly, disheartened, out of town. She saw the weird humped-up creature of the cathedral in the distance, pointing its one finger above the city. Why, oh, why, had the old Germanic races put it there, like that!

Slowly the country disintegrated into the Rhine flats and marshes, the canals, the willow trees, the overflow streams, the wet places frozen but not flooded. Weary the place all seemed. And old Father Rhine flowing in greenish volume, implacable, separating the races now weary of race struggle, but locked in the toils as in the coils of a great snake, unable to escape. Cold, full, green, and utterly disheartening the river came along under the wintry sky, passing beneath the bridge of iron.

There was a long wait in Kehl, where the German officials and the French observed a numb, dreary kind of neutrality. Passport and customs examination was soon over. But the train waited and waited, as if unable to get away from that one point of pure negation, where the two races neutralized one another, and no polarity was felt, no life – no principle dominated.

Katherine Farquhar just sat still, in the suspended silence of her husband's return. She heeded neither French nor German, spoke one language or the other at need, hardly knowing. She waited, while the hot train steamed and hissed, arrested at the perfect neutral point of the new border line, just across the Rhine.

And at last a little sun came out, and the train silently drew away, nervously, from the neutrality.

In the great flat field, of the Rhine plain, the shallow flood water was frozen, the furrows ran straight towards nowhere, the air seemed frozen too, but the earth felt strong and barbaric, it seemed to vibrate, with its straight furrows, in a deep, savage undertone. There was the frozen, savage thrill in the air also, something wild and unsubdued, pre-Roman.

This part of the Rhine valley, even on the right bank in Germany, was occupied by the French; hence the curious vacancy, the suspense, as if no men lived there, but some spirit was watching, watching over the vast, empty, straight-furrowed fields and the water-meadows. Stillness, emptiness, suspense, and a sense of something still impending.

A long wait in the station of Appenweier, on the main line of the Right-bank Railway. The station was empty. Katherine remembered its excited, thrilling bustle in pre-war days.

'Yes,' said the German guard to the station-master. 'What do they hurry us out of Strasburg for, if they are only going to keep us so long here?'

The heavy Badisch[6] German! The sense of resentful impotence in the Germans! Katherine smiled to herself. She realized that here the train left the occupied territory.

At last they set off, northwards, free for the moment, in Germany. It was the land beyond the Rhine, Germany of the pine forests. The very earth seemed strong and unsubdued, bristling with a few reeds and bushes, like savage hair. There was the same silence, and waiting, and the old barbaric undertone of the white-skinned north, under the waning civilization. The audible over-tone of our civilization seemed to be wearing thin, the old, low, pine-forest hum and roar of the ancient north seemed to be sounding through. At least, in Katherine's inner ear.

And there were the ponderous hills of the Black Forest, heaped and waiting sullenly, as if guarding the inner Germany. Black round hills, black with forest, save where white snow-patches of field had been cut out. Black and white, waiting there in the near distance, in sullen guard.

She knew the country so well. But not in this present mood, the emptiness, the sullenness, the heavy, recoiled waiting.

Steinbach! Then she was nearly there! She would have to change in Oos, for Baden-Baden, her destination. Probably Philip would be there to meet her in Oos; he would have come down from Heidelberg.

Yes, there he was! And at once she thought he looked ill, yellowish. His figure hollow and defeated.

'Aren't you well?' she asked, as she stepped out of the train on to the empty station.

'I'm so frightfully cold,' he said. 'I can't get warm.'

'And the train was so hot,' she said.

At last a porter came to carry her bags across to the little connecting train.

'How are you?' he said, looking at her with a certain pinched look in his face, and fear in his eyes.

'All right! It all feels very queer,' she said.

'I don't know how it is,' he said, 'but Germany freezes my inside, and does something to my chest.'

'We needn't stay long,' she said easily.

He was watching the bright look in her face. And she was thinking how queer and *chétif*[7] he looked! Extraordinary! As she looked at him she felt for the first time, with curious clarity, that it was humiliating to be married to him, even in name. She was humiliated even by the fact that her name was Katherine Farquhar. Yet she used to think it a nice name!

'Just think of me married to that little man!' she thought to herself. 'Think of my having his name!'

It didn't fit. She thought of her own name: Katherine von Todtnau; or of her married name: Katherine Anstruther. The first seemed most fitting. But the second was her second nature. The third, Katherine Farquhar, wasn't her at all.

'Have you seen Marianne?' she asked.

'Oh, yes!'

He was very brief. What was the matter with him?

'You'll have to be careful, with your cold,' she said politely.

'I *am* careful!' he cried petulantly.

Marianne, her sister, was at the station, and in two minutes they were rattling away in German and laughing and crying and exploding with laughter again, Philip quite ignored. In these days of frozen economy, there was no taxi. A porter would wheel up the luggage on a trolley, the new arrivals walked to their little hotel, through the half-deserted town.

'But the little one is quite nice!' said Marianne deprecatingly.

'Isn't he!' cried Katherine in the same tone.

And both sisters stood still and laughed in the middle of the street. 'The little one' was Philip.

'The other was more a man,' said Marianne. 'But I'm sure this one is easier. *The little one!* Yes, he *should* be easier,' and she laughed in her mocking way.

'The stand-up-mannikin!' said Katherine, referring to those little toy men weighted at the base with lead, that always stand up again.

'Yes! Yes!' cried Marianne. 'I'm sure he *always* comes up again! Prumm!' She made a gesture of knocking him over. 'And there he rises once more!' She slowly raised her hand, as if the mannikin were elevating himself.

The two sisters stood in the street laughing consumedly.

Marianne also had lost her husband in the war. But she seemed only more reckless and ruthless.

'Ah, Katy!' she said, after dinner. 'You are always such a good child! But you are different. Harder! No, you are not the same good Katy, the same kind Katy. You are no longer kind.'

'And you?' said Katy.

'Ah, me! I don't matter. I watch what the end will be.'

Marianne was six years older than Katherine, and she had now ceased to struggle for anything at all. She was a woman who had lived her life. So at last, life seemed endlessly quaint and amusing to her. She accepted everything, wondering over the powerful primitiveness of it all, at the root-pulse.

'I don't care any more at all what people do or don't do,' she said. 'Life is a great big tree, and the dead leaves fall. But very wonderful is the pulse in the roots! So strong, and so pitiless.'

It was as if she found a final relief in the radical pitilessness of the Tree of Life.[8]

Philip was very unhappy in this atmosphere. At the core of him a Scotch sentimentalist, he had calculated, very cannily, that the emotional, sentimental values would hold good as long as he lived, which was long enough for him. The old male pride and power were doomed. They had finally fallen in the war. Alan with them. But the emotional, sentimental values still held good.

Only not here in Germany. Here the very emotions had become exhausted. 'Give us pitilessness. Give us the Tree of Life in winter, dehumanized and ruthless.' So everything seemed to say. And it was too much for him.

He wanted to be soft and sweet and loving, at evening, to Katherine. But there came Marianne's hollow, reckless laugh at the door; he was frustrated. And –

'Ach! Is it possible that anybody forty years old should still be in love? Ach! I had thought it impossible any more; after the war! Even a little indecent, shall I say!' laughed Marianne, seeing the frustrated languishing look on his face.

'If *love* isn't left, what is?' he said petulantly.

'Ach! I don't know! Really I don't. Can't you tell me?' she asked with a weird naïveté of the *afterwards*.

He gathered himself together, the little stand-up-mannikin, waiting till Marianne was gone and he could be softly alone with Katherine.

When the two were alone he said:

'I'm most frightfully glad you've come, Kathy. I could hardly have held out another day without you. I feel you're the only thing on earth that remains real.'

'You don't seem very real to me,' she said.

'I'm not real! I'm *not*! – not when I'm alone. But when I am with you I am the most real man alive. I know it!'

He asserted this with vehemence and a weird, personal sort of passion that used to thrill her, but now repelled her.

'Why should you need me?' she said. 'I am real without you.'

She was thinking of Alan.

This was a blow to Philip. He considered for a moment. Then he said:

'Yes. You are! You are always real. But that's because you are a woman. A man without a woman *can't* be real.'

He twisted his face and shook his hand with a sort of false vehemence.

She looked at him, was repelled. After all, Alan could wander alone in the lonely places of the dead, and still be the ultimate real thing, to her.

She had given her allegiance elsewhere. Strange, how unspeakably cold she felt towards this little equivocal civilian.

'Don't let us talk to-night,' she said. 'I am *so* sleepy. I want to go to sleep this very minute. You don't mind, do you? Good-night!'

She went to her room, with the green glazed stove. Outside she could see the trees of Seufzer Allee, and the intense winter night. Curiously dark and wolfish the nights came on, with the little town obscurely lighted, for economy's sake, and no tramcars running, for economy's sake, and the whole place, strangely, slipping back from our civilization, people moving in the dark like in a barbarian village, with the thrill of fear and menace in the wolfish air.

She slept soundly, none the less. But the raw air scraped her chest.

In the morning Philip was looking yellower, and coughing a good deal. She urged him to stay in bed. She wanted, really, to be free of him. And she also wanted him to be safe, too. He insisted, however, on staying about.

She could tell he had something on his mind. At last it came out.

'Do you dream much here?' he said.

'I think I did dream,' she said. 'But I can't remember what about.'

'I dream terribly,' he said.

'What sort of dreams?'

'All sorts!' He gave a rueful laugh. 'But nearly always about Alan.' He glanced at her quickly to see how she took it. She gave no sign.

'And what about him?' she said calmly.

'Oh! –' he gave a desperate little gesture. 'Why last night I dreamed that I woke up, and someone was lying on my bed, *outside* the bed-clothes. I thought at first it was you, so I wanted to speak to you. But I couldn't. Then I knew it was Alan, lying there in the cold. And he was terribly heavy. He was so heavy I couldn't move, because the bed-clothes – you know I don't have that bolster thing – they were so tight on me, I could hardly breathe, they were like tight lead round me. It was so awful, they were like a lead coffin-shell. And he was lying outside with that terrible weight. When I woke at last, I thought I *was* dead.'

'It's because you've got a cold on your chest,' she said. 'Why won't you stay in bed and see a doctor?'

'I don't *want* a doctor,' he said.

'You're so obstinate! At least you should drink the waters here. They'd be good for you.'

During the day she walked in the woods with Marianne. It was sunny, and there was thin snow. But the cold in the air was heavy, stormy, unbreakable, and the woods seemed black, black. In a hollow open space, like a bowl, were little tortured bare vines. Never had she seen the pale vine-stocks look so tortured. And the black trees seemed to grow out of unutterably cold depths, and they seemed to be drinking away what warmth of life there was, while the vines in the clearing writhed with cold as leaves writhe in a fire.

After sunset, before dinner-time, she wanted to go to drink the hot waters from the spring at the big bath-hall under the New Castle. Philip insisted on going with her, though she urged him to stay indoors. They went down the dark hill and between the dark buildings of reddish stone, like the stone of Strasburg Cathedral.

At the obscure fountain in the alcove of the courtyard a little group of people were waiting, dark and silent, like dark spirits round a source of steam. Some had come to drink. Some had come for a pail of hot water. Some had come merely to warm their fingers and get something hot inside them. Some had come furtively, with hot-water bottles, to warm their icy beds a little. Everybody was bed-rock poor and silent, but well-clad, respectable, unbeaten.

Katherine and Philip waited a while. Then, in a far corner of the dark rocky grotto, where the fountain of hot water came out of the wall, Katherine saw Alan standing. He was standing as if waiting his turn to drink, behind the other people. Philip apparently did not see him.

She pressed forward in the silent sombre group of people, and held her glass under the tap, above the pail which a man was filling. The hot water ran over her fingers gratefully. She rinsed her glass down the fountain bowl.

'Na!' said the man of the pail, in his rough, but reckless, good-humoured Badisch: 'Throw it in the bucket. It's only wash-water.'

She laughed, and lifted her pocket-glass to drink. It was something of an ordeal among the group of silent people there in the almost dark. There was a feeble lamp outside in the courtyard; inside the grotto was deep shadow.

Nevertheless, Alan was watching her, and she drank to him, in the hot, queer, hellish-tasting water. She drank a second small glassful. Then she filled the glass again, in front of all the waiting people and handed it to Philip.

She did not look at Alan, but away in the courtyard, where more people were approaching, and where the steam of the springs rose from the grating in the ground, ghostly on the night air.

Philip drew back a little to drink. But at the first mouthful he choked, and began to cough. He coughed and coughed, in a convulsed spasm as if choking. She went to him anxiously. And then she saw that Alan also had come forward, and stood beside her, behind the coughing little Philip.

'What is it?' she said to the coughing man. 'Did some of the water go the wrong way?'

He shook his head, but could not answer. At length, exhausted, but quiet, he handed her the glass, and they moved away from the silent group of watchful dark people.

And Alan was walking on her other side holding her hand.

When they came into the hall of the hotel she saw with horror that there was a red smear of blood on Philip's chin, and red blotches on his overcoat.

'What have you done?' she cried.

He looked down at his breast, then up at her with haunted eyes. Fear, an agony and a horror of fear in his face. He went ghastly pale. Thinking he would swoon, she put her arm round him. But she felt someone silently but firmly, and with strange, cold power, pulling her arm away. She knew it was Alan.

The hotel porter helped Philip up to his room, and she assisted her husband to undress and get to bed. But each time her hand touched the sick man's body, to sustain him, she felt it drawn silently, coldly, powerfully away, with complete relentlessness.

The doctor came and made his examination. He said it was not serious: only the rupture of a superficial blood-vessel. The patient must lie quite still and warm, and take light food. Avoid all excitement or agitation.

Philip's face had a haunted, martyred, guilty look. She soothed him as much as possible, but dared hardly touch him.

'Won't you sleep with me to-night, in case I dream?' he said to her, with big, excruciating eyes full of fear.

'You'll be better alone,' she said softly. 'You'll be better alone. I'll tuck you up warm, and sit with you a while. Keep yourself all covered up!'

She tucked him close, and sat by the bed. On the other side of the bed sat Alan, bare-headed, with his silent, expressionless, reddish face. The closed line of his lips, under the small reddish moustache, never changed, and he kept his eyelids half lowered. But there was a wonderful changeless dignity in his pose, as if he could sit thus, silent, and waiting, through the centuries. And through the warm air of the room he radiated this strange, stony coldness, that seemed heavy as the hand of death. It did not hurt Katherine. But Philip's face seemed chilled and bluish.

Katherine went to her room, when the sick man slept. Alan did not follow her. And she did not question. It was for the two men to work out destiny between them.

In the night, towards morning she heard a hoarse, horrible cry. She ran to Philip's room. He was sitting up in bed, blood running down his chin, his face livid, and his eyes rolling delirious.

'What is it?' she said in panic.

'He lay on top of me!' cried Philip, rolling his eyes inwards in horror. 'He lay on top of me, and turned my heart cold and burst my blood-vessel in my chest.'

Katherine stood petrified. There was blood all over the sheets. She rang the bell violently. Across the bed stood Alan, looking at her with his unmoving blue eyes, just watching her. She could feel the strange stone-coldness of his presence touching even her heart. And she looked back at him humbly, she knew he had power over her too. That strange, cold, stony touch on her heart.

The servants came, and the doctor. And Alan went away. Philip was washed and changed, and went peacefully to sleep, looking like a corpse.

The day passed slowly. Alan did not appear. Even now, Katherine wanted him to come. Awful though he was, she wanted him to be there, to give her her surety, even though it was only the surety of dread; and her contentment, though it were the contentment of death.

At night she had a sofa-bed brought for her into Philip's room. He seemed quieter, better. She had not left him all day. And Alan had not appeared. At half-past nine, Philip sleeping quietly, she too lay down to sleep.

She woke in the night feeling the same stone-coldness in the air. Had the stove gone out? Then she heard Philip's whispering call of terror: '*Katherine! Katherine!*' She went over quickly, and slipped into his bed, putting her arms round him. He was shuddering, and stony cold. She drew him to her.

But immediately two hands cold and strong as iron seized her arms and pulled them away. She was pushed out of the bed, and pushed on to the floor of the bedroom. For an instant, the rage came into her heart, she wanted to get up and fight for the dying man. But a greater power, the knowledge of the uselessness and the fatal dishonourableness of her womanly interference made her desist. She lay for a time helpless and powerless on the floor, in her nightdress.

Then she felt herself lifted. In the dimness of coming dawn, she knew it was Alan. She could see the breast of his uniform – the old uniform she had known long before the war. And his face bending over her, cool and fresh.

He was still cold. But the stoniness had gone out of him, she did not mind his coldness. He pressed her firm hand hard to his own hard body. He was hard and cold like a tree, and alive. And the prickling of his moustache was the cold prickling of fir-needles.

He held her fast and hard, and seemed to possess her through every pore of her body. Not now the old, procreative way of possession. He held her fast, and possessed her through every pore in her body. Then he laid her in her own bed, to sleep.

When she awoke, the sun was shining, and Philip lay dead in a pool of blood.

Somehow she did not mind. She was only thinking of Alan. After all, she belonged to the man who could keep her. To the only man who knew how to keep her, and could only possess her through all the pores of her body, so that there was no recoil from him. Not just through one act, one function holding her. But as a cloud holds a shower.

The men that were just functional men: let them pass and perish. She wanted her contentment like life itself, through every pore, through every bit of her. The man who could hold her as the wind held her, as the air held her, all surrounded. The man whose aura permeated into every vein, through all her pores, as the scent of a pine-tree when one stands beneath it. A man, not like a faun or a satyr or an angel or a demon, but like the Tree of Life itself, implacable and unquestionable and permeating, voiceless, abiding.

In the afternoon she went to walk by herself. She climbed uphill, steep, past the New Castle, and up through the pine-woods, climbing upwards to the Old Castle. There it stood, among dense trees, its old, rose-red stone walls broken and silent. Two men, queer, wild ruffians with bundles on their backs, stood in the broken, roofless hall, looking round.

'Yes,' the elder one, with the round beard, was saying, 'There are no more Dukes of Baden, and counts and barons and peers of the realm are as much in ruin as this place. Soon we shall be all alike, *Lumpen*,[9] tramps.'

'Also no more ladies,' said the younger one, in a lower voice. 'Every tramp can have his lady.'

Katherine heard him, with a pang of fear. Knowing the castle, she climbed the stairs and round the balustrade above the great hall, looking out far over the country. The sun was sinking. The Rhine was a dim magnesium ribbon, away on the plain. Across was the Russian Chapel; below, on the left, the town, and the Lichtenthal.[10] No more gamblers, no more cosmopolitan play. Evening and the dark round hills going lonely, snow on the Merkur hill.

Mercury! Hermes![11] The messenger! Even as she thought it, standing there on the wall, Alan came along and stood beside her, and she felt at ease. The two men down below were looking up at her. They watched in silence, not knowing the way up. They were in the cold shadow of the hall below. A little, lingering sun, reddish, caught her where she was, above.

Again, for the last time, she looked over the land: the sun sinking below the Rhine, the hills of Germany this side, and the frozen stillness of the winter afternoon. 'Yes, let us go,' she heard the elder man's voice. 'We are hardly men or women any more. We are more like the men and women who have drunk in this hall, living after our day.'

'Only we eat and smile still, and the men want the women still.'

'No! No! A man forgets his trouser-lining when he sees the ghost and the woman together.'

The two tramps turned and departed, heavy-shod, up the hill.

Katherine felt Alan's touch on her arm, and she climbed down from the old, broken castle. He led her through the woods, past the red rocks. The sun had sunk, the trees were blue. He lingered again under a great pine-tree, in the shadow. And again, as he pressed her fast, and pressed his cold face against her, it was as if the wood of the tree itself were growing round her, the hard, live wood compressing and almost devouring her, the sharp needles brushing her face, the limbs of the living tree enveloping her, crushing her in the last, final ecstasy of submission, squeezing from her the last drop of her passion, like the cold, white berries of the mistletoe on the Tree of Life.

The Woman Who Rode Away

I

SHE had thought that this marriage, of all marriages, would be an adventure. Not that the man himself was exactly magical to her. A little, wiry, twisted fellow, twenty years older than herself, with brown eyes and greying hair, who had come to America a scrap of a wastrel, from Holland, years ago, as a tiny boy, and from the gold-mines of the west had been kicked south into Mexico, and now was more or less rich, owning silver-mines in the wilds of the Sierra Madre: it was obvious that the adventure lay in his circumstances, rather than his person. But he was still a little dynamo of energy, in spite of accidents survived, and what he had accomplished he had accomplished alone. One of those human oddments there is no accounting for.

When she actually *saw* what he had accomplished, her heart quailed. Great green-covered, unbroken mountain-hills, and in the midst of the lifeless isolation, the sharp pinkish mounds of the dried mud from the silver-works. Under the nakedness of the works, the walled-in, one-storey adobe house, with its garden inside, and its deep inner verandah with tropical climbers on the sides. And when you looked up from this shut-in flowered patio, you saw the huge pink cone of the silver-mud refuse, and the machinery of the extracting plant against heaven above. No more.

To be sure, the great wooden doors were often open. And then she could stand outside, in the vast open world. And see great, void, tree-clad hills piling behind one another, from nowhere into nowhere. They were green in autumn time. For the rest, pinkish, stark dry, and abstract.

And in his battered Ford car her husband would take her into the dead, thrice-dead little Spanish town forgotten among the mountains. The great, sundried dead church, the dead portales, the hopeless covered market-place, where, the first time she went, she saw a dead dog lying between the meat stalls and the vegetable array, stretched out as if for ever, nobody troubling to throw it away. Deadness within deadness.

Everybody feebly talking silver, and showing bits of ore. But silver was at a standstill. The great war came and went. Silver was a dead market. Her husband's mines were closed down. But she and he lived on in the adobe house under the works, among the flowers that were never very flowery to her.

She had two children, a boy and a girl. And her eldest, the boy, was nearly ten years old before she aroused from her stupor of subjected amazement. She was now thirty-three, a large, blue-eyed, dazed woman, beginning to grow stout. Her little, wiry, tough, twisted, brown-eyed husband was fifty-three, a man as tough as wire, tenacious as wire, still full of energy, but dimmed by the lapse of silver from the market, and by some curious inaccessibility on his wife's part.

He was a man of principles, and a good husband. In a way, he doted on her. He never quite got over his dazzled admiration of her. But essentially, he was still a bachelor. He had been thrown out on the world, a little bachelor, at the age of ten. When he married he was over forty, and had enough money to marry on. But his capital was all a bachelor's. He was boss of his own works, and marriage was the last and most intimate bit of his own works.

He admired his wife to extinction, he admired her body, all her points. And she was to him always the rather dazzling Californian girl from Berkeley, whom he had first known. Like any sheik, he kept her guarded among those mountains of Chihuahua. He was jealous of her as he was of his silver-mine: and that is saying a lot.

At thirty-three she really was still the girl from Berkeley, in all but physique. Her conscious development had stopped mysteriously with her marriage, completely arrested. Her husband had never become real to her, neither mentally nor physically. In spite of his late sort of passion for her, he never meant anything to her, physically. Only morally he swayed her, downed her, kept her in an invincible slavery.

So the years went by, in the adobe house strung round the sunny patio, with the silver-works overhead. Her husband was never still. When the silver went dead, he ran a ranch lower down, some twenty miles away, and raised pure-bred hogs, splendid creatures. At the same time, he hated pigs. He was a squeamish waif of an idealist, and really hated the physical side of life. He loved work, work, work, and making things. His marriage, his children, were something he was making, part of his business, but with a sentimental income this time.

Gradually her nerves began to go wrong: she must get out. She must get out. So he took her to El Paso for three months. And at least it was the United States.

But he kept his spell over her. The three months ended: back she was, just the same, in her adobe house among those eternal green or pinky-brown hills, void as only the undiscovered is void. She taught her children, she supervised the Mexican boys who were her servants. And sometimes her husband brought visitors, Spaniards or Mexicans or occasionally white men.

He really loved to have white men staying on the place. Yet he had not a moment's peace when they were there. It was as if his wife were some peculiar secret vein of ore in his mines, which no one must be aware of except himself. And she was fascinated by the young gentlemen, mining engineers, who were his guests at times. He, too, was fascinated by a real gentleman. But he was an old-timer miner with a wife, and if a gentleman looked at his wife, he felt as if his mine were being looted, the secrets of it pryed out.

It was one of these young gentlemen who put the idea into her mind. They were all standing outside the great wooden doors of the patio, looking at the outer world. The eternal, motionless hills were all green, it was September, after the rains. There was no sign of anything, save the deserted mine, the deserted works, and a bunch of half-deserted miner's dwellings.

'I wonder,' said the young man, 'what there is behind those great blank hills.'

'More hills,' said Lederman. 'If you go that way, Sonora and the coast. This way is the desert – you came from there – And the other way, hills and mountains.'

'Yes, but what *lives* in the hills and mountains? *Surely* there is something wonderful? It looks *so* like nowhere on earth: like being on the moon.'

'There's plenty of game, if you want to shoot. And Indians, if you call *them* wonderful.'

'Wild ones?'

'Wild enough.'

'But friendly?'

'It depends. Some of them are quite wild, and they don't let anybody near. They kill a missionary at sight. And where a missionary can't get, nobody can.'

'But what does the government say?'

'They're so far from everywhere, the government leaves 'em alone. And they're wily; if they think there'll be trouble, they send a delegation to Chihuahua and make a formal submission. The government is glad to leave it at that.'

'And do they live quite wild, with their own savage customs and religion?'

'Oh, yes. They use nothing but bows and arrows. I've seen them in town, in the Plaza, with funny sort of hats with flowers round them, and a bow in one hand, quite naked except for a sort of shirt, even in cold weather – striding round with their savage's bare legs.'

'But don't you suppose it's wonderful, up there in their secret villages?'

'No. What would there be wonderful about it? Savages are savages, and all savages behave more or less alike: rather low-down and dirty, unsanitary, with a few cunning tricks, and struggling to get enough to eat.'

'But surely they have old, old religions and mysteries – it *must* be wonderful, surely it must.'

'I don't know about mysteries – howling and heathen practices, more or less indecent. No, I see nothing wonderful in that kind of stuff. And I wonder that you should, when you have lived in London or Paris or New York –'

'Ah, *everybody* lives in London or Paris or New York' – said the young man, as if this were an argument.

And his peculiar vague enthusiasm for unknown Indians found a full echo in the woman's heart. She was overcome by a foolish romanticism more unreal than a girl's. She felt it was her destiny to wander into the secret haunts of these timeless, mysterious, marvellous Indians of the mountains.

She kept her secret. The young man was departing, her husband was going with him down to Torreon, on business: – would be away for some days. But before the departure, she made her husband talk about the Indians: about the wandering tribes, resembling the Navajo, who were still wandering free; and the Yaquis of Sonora: and the different groups in the different valleys of Chihuahua State.

There was supposed to be one tribe, the Chilchuis, living in a high valley to the south, who were the sacred tribe of all the Indians. The descendants of Montezuma and of the old Aztec or Totonac kings[1] still lived among them, and the old priests still kept up the ancient religion, and offered human sacrifices – so it was said. Some scientists had been to the Chilchui country, and had come back gaunt and exhausted with hunger and bitter privation, bringing various curious, barbaric objects of worship, but having seen nothing extraordinary in the hungry, stark village of savages.

Though Lederman talked in this off-hand way, it was obvious he felt some of the vulgar excitement at the idea of ancient and mysterious savages.

'How far away are they?' she asked.

'Oh – three days on horseback – past Cuchitee and a little lake there is up there.'

Her husband and the young man departed. The woman made her crazy plans. Of late, to break the monotony of her life, she had harassed her husband into letting her go riding with him, occasionally, on horseback. She was never allowed to go out alone. The country truly was not safe, lawless and crude.

But she had her own horse, and she dreamed of being free as she had been as a girl, among the hills of California.

Her daughter, nine years old, was now in a tiny convent in the little half-deserted Spanish mining-town five miles away.

'Manuel,' said the woman to her house-servant, 'I'm going to ride to the convent to see Margarita, and take her a few things. Perhaps I shall stay the night in the convent. You look after Freddy and see everything is all right till I come back.'

'Shall I ride with you on the master's horse, or shall Juan?' asked the servant.

'Neither of you. I shall go alone.'

The young man looked her in the eyes, in protest. Absolutely impossible that the woman should ride alone!

'I shall go alone,' repeated the large, placid-seeming, fair-complexioned woman, with peculiar overbearing emphasis. And the man silently, unhappily yielded.

'Why are you going alone, mother?' asked her son, as she made up parcels of food.

'Am I *never* to be let alone? Not one moment of my life?' she cried, with sudden explosion of energy. And the child, like the servant, shrank into silence.

She set off without a qualm, riding astride on her strong roan horse, and wearing a riding suit of coarse linen, a riding skirt over her linen breeches, a scarlet neck-tie over her white blouse, and a black felt hat on her head. She had food in her saddle-bags, an army canteen with water, and a large, native blanket tied on behind the saddle. Peering into the distance, she set off from her home. Manuel and the little boy stood in the gateway to watch her go. She did not even turn to wave them farewell.

But when she had ridden about a mile, she left the wild road and took a small trail to the right, that led into another valley, over steep places and past great trees, and through another deserted mining-settlement. It was September, the water was running freely in the little stream that had fed the now-abandoned mine. She got down to drink, and let the horse drink too.

She saw natives coming through the trees, away up the slope. They had seen her, and were watching her closely. She watched in turn. The three people, two women and a youth, were making a wide détour, so as not to come too close to her. She did not care. Mounting, she trotted ahead up the silent valley, beyond the silver-works, beyond any trace of mining. There was still a rough trail, that led over rocks and loose stones into the valley beyond. This trail she had already ridden, with her husband. Beyond that she knew she must go south.

Curiously she was not afraid, although it was a frightening country, the silent, fatal-seeming mountain-slopes, the occasional distant, suspicious, elusive natives among the trees, the great carrion birds occasionally hovering, like great flies, in the distance, over some carrion or some ranch house or some group of huts.

As she climbed, the trees shrank and the trail ran through a thorny scrub, that was trailed over with blue convolvulus and an occasional pink creeper. Then these flowers lapsed. She was nearing the pine-trees.

She was over the crest, and before her another silent, void, green-clad valley. It was past midday. Her horse turned to a little runlet of water, so she got down to eat her midday meal. She sat in silence looking at the motionless unliving valley, and at the sharp-peaked hills, rising higher to rock and pine-trees, southwards. She rested two hours in the heat of the day, while the horse cropped around her.

Curious that she was neither afraid nor lonely. Indeed, the loneliness was like a drink of cold water to one who is very thirsty. And a strange elation sustained her from within.

She travelled on, and camped at night in a valley beside a stream, deep among the bushes. She had seen cattle and had crossed several trails. There must be a ranch not far off. She heard the strange wailing shriek of a mountain-lion, and the answer of dogs. But she sat by her small camp fire in a secret hollow place and was not really afraid. She was buoyed up always by the curious, bubbling elation within her.

It was very cold before dawn. She lay wrapped in her blanket looking at the stars, listening to her horse shivering, and feeling like a woman who has died and passed beyond. She was not sure that she had not heard, during the night, a great crash at the centre of herself, which was the crash of her own death. Or else it was a crash at the centre of the earth, and meant something big and mysterious.

With the first peep of light she got up, numb with cold, and made a fire. She ate hastily, gave her horse some pieces of oil-seed cake, and set off again. She avoided any meeting – and since she met nobody, it was evident that she in turn was avoided. She came at last in sight of the village of Cuchitee, with its black houses with their reddish roofs, a sombre, dreary little cluster below another silent, long-abandoned mine. And beyond, a long, great mountain-side, rising up green and light to the darker, shaggier green of pine trees. And beyond the pine trees stretches of naked rock against the sky, rock slashed already and brindled with white stripes of snow. High up, the new snow had already begun to fall.

And now, as she neared, more or less, her destination, she began to go vague and disheartened. She had passed the little lake among yellowing aspen trees whose white trunks were round and suave like the white round arms of some woman. What a lovely place! In California she would have raved about it. But here she looked and saw that it was lovely, but she didn't care. She was weary and spent with her two nights in the open, and afraid of the coming night. She didn't know where she was going, or what she was going for. Her horse plodded dejectedly on, towards that immense and forbidding mountain-slope, following a stony little trail. And if she had had any will of her own left, she would have turned back, to the village, to be protected and sent home to her husband.

But she had no will of her own. Her horse splashed through a brook, and turned up a valley, under immense yellowing cotton-wood trees. She must have been near nine thousand feet above sea-level, and her head was light with the altitude and with weariness. Beyond the cotton-wood trees she could see, on each side, the steep sides of mountain-slopes hemming her in, sharp-plumaged with overlapping aspen, and, higher up, with sprouting, pointed spruce and pine tree. Her horse went on automatically. In this tight valley, on this slight trail, there was nowhere to go but ahead, climbing.

Suddenly her horse jumped, and three men in dark blankets were on the trail before her.

'Adios!' came the greeting, in the full, restrained Indian voice.

'Adios!' she replied, in her assured, American woman's voice.

'Where are you going?' came the quiet question, in Spanish.

The men in the dark sarapes had come closer, and were looking up at her.

'On ahead,' she replied coolly, in her hard, Saxon Spanish.

These were just natives to her: dark-faced, strongly-built men in dark sarapes and straw hats. They would have been the same as the men who worked for her husband, except, strangely, for the long black hair that fell over their shoulders. She noted this long black hair with a certain distaste. These must be the wild Indians she had come to see.

'Where do you come from?' the same man asked. It was always the one man who spoke. He was young, with quick, large, bright black eyes that glanced sideways at her. He had a soft black moustache on his dark face, and a sparse tuft of beard, loose hairs on his chin. His long black hair, full of life, hung unrestrained on his shoulders. Dark as he was, he did not look as if he had washed lately.

His two companions were the same, but older men, powerful and silent. One had a thin black line of moustache, but was beardless. The other had the smooth cheeks and the sparse dark hairs marking the lines of his chin with the beard characteristic of the Indians.

'I come from far away,' she replied, with half-jocular evasion.

This was received in silence.

'But where do you live?' asked the young man, with that same quiet insistence.

'In the north,' she replied airily.

Again there was a moment's silence. The young man conversed quietly, in Indian, with his two companions.

'Where do you want to go, up this way?' he asked suddenly, with challenge and authority, pointing briefly up the trail.

'To the Chilchui Indians,' answered the woman laconically.

The young man looked at her. His eyes were quick and black, and inhuman. He saw, in the full evening light, the faint sub-smile of assurance on her rather large, calm, fresh-complexioned face; the weary, bluish lines under her large blue eyes; and in her eyes, as she looked down at him, a half-childish, half-arrogant confidence in her own female power. But in her eyes also, a curious look of trance.

'*Usted es Señora?* You are a lady?' the Indian asked her.

'Yes, I am a lady,' she replied complacently.

'With a family?'

'With a husband and two children, boy and girl,' she said.

The Indian turned to his companions and translated, in the low, gurgling speech, like hidden water running. They were evidently at a loss.

'Where is your husband?' asked the young man.

'Who knows?' she replied airily. 'He has gone away on business for a week.'

The black eyes watched her shrewdly. She, for all her weariness, smiled faintly in the pride of her own adventure and the assurance of her own womanhood, and the spell of the madness that was on her.

'And what do *you* want to do?' the Indian asked her.

'I want to visit the Chilchui Indians – to see their houses and to know their gods,' she replied.

The young man turned and translated quickly, and there was a silence almost of consternation. The grave elder men were glancing at her sideways, with strange looks, from under their decorated hats. And they said something to the young man, in deep chest voices.

The latter still hesitated. Then he turned to the woman.

'Good!' he said. 'Let us go. But we cannot arrive until to-morrow. We shall have to make a camp to-night.'

'Good!' she said. 'I can make a camp.'

Without more ado, they set off at a good speed up the stony trail. The young Indian ran alongside her horse's head, the other two ran behind. One of them had taken a thick stick, and occasionally he struck her horse a resounding blow on the haunch, to urge him forward. This made the horse jump, and threw her back in the saddle, which, tired as she was, made her angry.

'Don't do that!' she cried, looking round angrily at the fellow. She met his black, large, bright eyes, and for the first time her spirit really quailed. The man's eyes were not human to her, and they did not see her as a beautiful white woman. He looked at her with a black, bright inhuman look, and saw no woman in her at all. As if she were some strange, unaccountable *thing*, incomprehensible to him, but inimical. She sat in her saddle in wonder, feeling once more as if she had died. And again he struck her horse, and jerked her badly in the saddle.

All the passionate anger of the spoilt white woman rose in her. She pulled her horse to a standstill, and turned with blazing eyes to the man at her bridle.

'Tell that fellow not to touch my horse again,' she cried.

She met the eyes of the young man, and in their bright black inscrutability she saw a fine spark, as in a snake's eye, of derision. He spoke to his companion in the rear, in the low tones of the Indian. The man with the stick listened without looking. Then, giving a strange low cry to the horse, he struck it again on the rear, so that it leaped forward spasmodically up the stony trail, scattering the stones, pitching the weary woman in her seat.

The anger flew like a madness into her eyes, she went white at the gills. Fiercely she reined in her horse. But before she could turn, the young Indian had caught the reins under the horse's throat, jerked them forward, and was trotting ahead rapidly, leading the horse.

The woman was powerless. And along with her supreme anger there came a slight thrill of exultation. She knew she was dead.

The sun was setting, a great yellow light flooded the last of the aspens, flared on the trunks of the pine-trees, the pine-needles bristled and stood out with dark lustre, the rocks glowed with unearthly glamour. And through this effulgence the Indian at her horse's head trotted unweariedly on, his dark blanket swinging, his bare legs glowing with a strange transfigured ruddiness in the powerful light, and his straw hat with its half-absurd decorations of flowers and feathers shining showily above his river of long black hair. At times he would utter a low call to the horse, and then the other Indian, behind, would fetch the beast a whack with the stick.

The wonder-light faded off the mountains, the world began to grow dark, a cold air breathed down. In the sky, half a moon was struggling against the glow in the west. Huge shadows came down from steep rocky slopes. Water was rushing. The woman was conscious only of her fatigue, her unspeakable fatigue, and the cold wind from the heights. She was not aware how moonlight replaced daylight. It happened while she travelled unconscious with weariness.

For some hours they travelled by moonlight. Then suddenly they came to a standstill. The men conversed in low tones for a moment.

'We camp here,' said the young man.

She waited for him to help her down. He merely stood holding the horse's bridle. She almost fell from the saddle, so fatigued.

They had chosen a place at the foot of rocks that still gave off a little warmth of the sun. One man cut pine-boughs, another erected little screens of pine-boughs against the rock for shelter, and put boughs of balsam pine for beds. The third made a small fire, to heat tortillas. They worked in silence.

The woman drank water. She did not want to eat – only to lie down.

'Where do I sleep?' she asked.

The young man pointed to one of the shelters. She crept in and lay inert. She did not care what happened to her, she was so weary, and so beyond everything. Through the twigs of spruce she could see the three men squatting round the fire on their hams, chewing the tortillas they picked from the ashes with their dark fingers, and drinking water from a gourd. They talked in low, muttering tones, with long intervals of silence. Her saddle and saddle-bags lay not far from the fire, unopened, untouched. The men were not interested in her nor her belongings. There they squatted with their hats on their heads, eating, eating mechanically, like animals, the dark sarape with its fringe falling to the ground before and behind, the powerful dark legs naked and squatting like an animal's, showing the dirty white shirt and the sort of loin-cloth which was the only other garment, underneath. And they showed no more sign of interest in her than if she had been a piece of venison they were bringing home from the hunt, and had hung inside a shelter.

After a while they carefully extinguished the fire, and went inside their own shelter. Watching through the screen of boughs, she had a moment's thrill of fear and anxiety, seeing the dark forms cross and pass silently in the moonlight. Would they attack her now?

But no! They were as if oblivious of her. Her horse was hobbled; she could hear it hopping wearily. All was silent, mountain-silent, cold, deathly. She slept and woke and slept in a semi-conscious numbness of cold and fatigue. A long, long night, icy and eternal, and she aware that she had died.

II

Yet when there was a stirring, and a clink of flint and steel, and the form of a man crouching like a dog over a bone, at a red splutter of fire, and she knew it was morning coming, it seemed to her the night had passed too soon.

When the fire was going, she came out of her shelter with one real desire left: for coffee. The men were warming more tortillas.

'Can we make coffee?' she asked.

The young man looked at her, and she imagined the same faint spark of derision in his eyes. He shook his head.

'We don't take it,' he said. 'There is no time.'

And the elder men, squatting on their haunches, looked up at her in the terrible paling dawn, and there was not even derision in their eyes. Only that intense, yet remote, inhuman glitter which was terrible to her. They were inaccessible. They could not see her as a woman at all. As if she *were* not a woman. As if, perhaps, her whiteness took away all her womanhood, and left her as some giant, female white ant. That was all they could see in her.

Before the sun was up, she was in the saddle again, and they were climbing steeply, in the icy air. The sun came, and soon she was very hot, exposed to the glare in the bare places. It seemed to her they were climbing to the roof of the world. Beyond against heaven were slashes of snow.

During the course of the morning, they came to a place where the horse could not go farther. They rested for a time with a great slant of living rock in front of them, like the glossy breast of some earth-beast. Across this rock, along a wavering crack, they had to go. It seemed to her that for hours she went in torment, on her hands and knees, from crack to crevice, along the slanting face of this pure rock-mountain. An Indian in front and an Indian behind walked slowly erect, shod with sandals of braided leather. But she in her riding-boots dared not stand erect.

Yet what she wondered, all the time, was why she persisted in clinging and crawling along these mile-long sheets of rock. Why she did not hurl herself down, and have done! The world was below her.

When they emerged at last on a stony slope, she looked back, and saw the third Indian coming carrying her saddle and saddle-bags on his back, the whole hung from a band across his forehead. And he had his hat in his hand, as he stepped slowly, with the slow, soft, heavy tread of the Indian, unwavering in the chinks of rock, as if along a scratch in the mountain's iron shield.

The stony slope led downwards. The Indians seemed to grow excited. One ran ahead at a slow trot, disappearing round the curve of stones. And the track curved round and down, till at last in the full blaze of the mid-morning sun, they could see a valley below them, between walls of rock, as in a great wide chasm let in the mountains. A green valley, with a river, and trees, and clusters of low flat sparkling houses. It was all tiny and perfect, three thousand feet below. Even the flat bridge over the stream, and the square with the houses around it, the bigger buildings piled up at opposite ends of the square, the tall cotton-wood trees, the pastures and stretches of yellow-sere maize, the patches of brown sheep or goats in the distance, on the slopes, the railed enclosures by the stream-side. There it was, all small and perfect, looking magical, as any place will look magical, seen from the mountains above. The unusual thing was that the low houses glittered white, whitewashed, looking like crystals of salt, or silver. This frightened her.

They began the long, winding descent at the head of the barranca,[2] following the stream that rushed and fell. At first it was all rocks: then the pine-trees began, and soon, the silver-limbed aspens. The flowers of autumn, big pink daisy-like flowers, and white ones, and many yellow flowers, were in profusion. But she had to sit down and rest, she was so weary. And she saw the bright flowers shadowily, as pale shadows hovering, as one who is dead must see them.

At length came grass and pasture-slopes between mingled aspen and pine-trees. A shepherd, naked in the sun save for his hat and his cotton loin-cloth, was driving his brown sheep away. In a grove of trees they sat and waited, she and the young Indian. The one with the saddle had also gone forward.

They heard a sound of someone coming. It was three men, in fine sarapes of red and orange and yellow and black, and with brilliant feather head-dresses. The oldest had his grey hair braided with fur, and his red and orange-yellow sarape was covered with curious black markings, like a leopard-skin. The other two were not grey-haired, but they were elders too. Their blankets were in stripes, and their head-dresses not so elaborate.

The young Indian addressed the elders in a few quiet words. They listened without answering or looking at him or at the woman, keeping their faces averted and their eyes turned to the ground, only listening. And at length they turned and looked at the woman.

The old chief, or medicine-man, whatever he was, had a deeply wrinkled and lined face of dark bronze, with a few sparse grey hairs round the mouth. Two long braids of grey hair, braided with fur and coloured feathers, hung on his shoulders. And yet, it was only his eyes that mattered. They were black and of extraordinary piercing strength, without a qualm of misgiving in their demonish, dauntless power. He looked into the eyes of the white woman with a long, piercing look, seeking she knew not what. She summoned all her strength to meet his eyes and keep up her guard. But it was no good. He was not looking at her as one human being looks at another. He never even perceived her resistance or her challenge, but looked past them both, into she knew not what.

She could see it was hopeless to expect any human communication with this old being.

He turned and said a few words to the young Indian.

'He asks what do you seek here?' said the young man in Spanish.

'I? Nothing! I only came to see what it was like.'

This was again translated, and the old man turned his eyes on her once more. Then he spoke again, in his low muttering tone, to the young Indian.

'He says, why does she leave her house with the white men? Does she want to bring the white man's God to the Chilchui?'

'No,' she replied, foolhardy. 'I came away from the white man's God myself. I came to look for the God of Chilchui.'

Profound silence followed, when this was translated. Then the old man spoke again, in a small voice almost of weariness.

'Does the white woman seek the gods of the Chilchui because she is weary of her own God?' came the question.

'Yes, she does. She is tired of the white man's God,' she replied, thinking that was what they wanted her to say. She would like to serve the gods of the Chilchui.

She was aware of an extraordinary thrill of triumph and exultance passing through the Indians, in the tense silence that followed when this was translated. Then they all looked at her with piercing black eyes, in which a steely covetous intent glittered incomprehensible. She was the more puzzled, as there was nothing sensual or sexual in the look. It had a terrible glittering purity that was beyond her. She was afraid, she would have been paralysed with fear, had not something died within her, leaving her with a cold, watchful wonder only.

The elders talked a little while, then the two went away, leaving her with the young man and the oldest chief. The old man now looked at her with a certain solicitude.

'He says are you tired?' asked the young man.

'Very tired,' she said.

'The men will bring you a carriage,' said the young Indian.

The carriage, when it came, proved to be a litter consisting of a sort of hammock of dark woollen frieze, slung on to a pole which was borne on the shoulders of two long-haired Indians. The woollen hammock was spread on the ground, she sat down on it, and the two men raised the pole to their shoulders. Swinging rather as if she were in a sack, she was carried out of the grove of trees, following the old chief, whose leopard-spotted blanket moved curiously in the sunlight.

They had emerged in the valley-head. Just in front were the maize fields, with ripe ears of maize. The corn was not very tall, in this high altitude. The well-worn path went between it, and all she could see was the erect form of the old chief, in the flame and black sarape, stepping soft and heavy and swift, his head forward, looking to neither to right nor left. Her bearers followed, stepping rhythmically, the long blue-black hair glistening like a river down the naked shoulders of the man in front.

They passed the maize, and came to a big wall or earthwork

made of earth and adobe bricks. The wooden doors were open. Passing on, they were in a network of small gardens, full of flowers and herbs and fruit trees, each garden watered by a tiny ditch of running water. Among each cluster of trees and flowers was a small, glittering white house, windowless, and with closed door. The place was a network of little paths, small streams, and little bridges among square, flowering gardens.

Following the broadest path – a soft narrow track between leaves and grass, a path worn smooth by centuries of human feet, no hoof of horse nor any wheel to disfigure it – they came to the little river of swift bright water, and crossed on a log bridge. Everything was silent – there was no human being anywhere. The road went on under magnificent cotton-wood trees. It emerged suddenly outside the central plaza or square of the village.

This was a long oblong of low white houses with flat roofs, and two bigger buildings, having as it were little square huts piled on top of bigger long huts, stood at either end of the oblong, facing each other rather askew. Every little house was a dazzling white, save for the great round beam-ends which projected under the flat eaves, and for the flat roofs. Round each of the bigger buildings, on the outside of the square, was a stockyard fence, inside which was garden with trees and flowers, and various small houses.

Not a soul was in sight. They passed silently between the houses into the central square. This was quite bare and arid, the earth trodden smooth by endless generations of passing feet, passing across from door to door. All the doors of the windowless houses gave on to this blank square, but all the doors were closed. The firewood lay near the threshold, a clay oven was still smoking, but there was no sign of moving life.

The old man walked straight across the square to the big house at the end, where the two upper storeys, as in a house of toy bricks, stood each one smaller than the lower one. A stone staircase, outside, led up to the roof of the first storey.

At the foot of this staircase the litter-bearers stood still, and lowered the woman to the ground.

'You will come up,' said the young Indian who spoke Spanish.

She mounted the stone stairs to the earthen roof of the first house, which formed a platform round the wall of the second storey. She followed around this platform to the back of the big house. There they descended again, into the garden at the rear.

So far they had seen no one. But now two men appeared, bareheaded, with long braided hair, and wearing a sort of white shirt gathered into a loin-cloth. These went along with the three newcomers, across the garden where red flowers and yellow flowers were blooming, to a long, low white house. There they entered without knocking.

It was dark inside. There was a low murmur of men's voices. Several men were present, their white shirts showing in the gloom, their dark faces invisible. They were sitting on a great log of smooth old wood, that lay along the far wall. And save for this log, the room seemed empty. But no, in the dark at one end was a couch, a sort of bed, and someone lying there, covered with furs.

The old Indian in the spotted sarape, who had accompanied the woman, now took off his hat and his blanket and his sandals. Laying them aside, he approached the couch, and spoke in a low voice. For some moments there was no answer. Then an old man with the snow-white hair hanging round his darkly-visible face, roused himself like a vision, and leaned on one elbow, looking vaguely at the company, in tense silence.

The grey-haired Indian spoke again, and then the young Indian, taking the woman's hand, led her forward. In her linen riding habit, and black boots and hat, and her pathetic bit of a red tie, she stood there beside the fur-covered bed of the old, old man, who sat reared up, leaning on one elbow, remote as a ghost, his white hair streaming in disorder, his face almost black, yet with a far-off intentness, not of this world, leaning forward to look at her.

His face was so old, it was like dark glass, and the few curling hairs that sprang white from his lips and chin were quite incredible. The long white locks fell unbraided and disorderly on either side of the glassy dark face. And under a faint powder of white eyebrows, the black eyes of the old chief looked at her as if from the far, far dead, seeing something that was never to be seen.

At last he spoke a few deep, hollow words, as if to the dark air.

'He says, do you bring your heart to the god of the Chilchui?' translated the young Indian.

'Tell him yes,' she said, automatically.

There was a pause. The old Indian spoke again, as if to the air. One of the men present went out. There was a silence as if of eternity, in the dim room that was lighted only through the open door.

The woman looked round. Four old men with grey hair sat on the log by the wall facing the door. Two other men, powerful and impassive, stood near the door. They all had long hair, and wore white shirts gathered into a loin-cloth. Their powerful legs were naked and dark. There was a silence like eternity.

At length the man returned, with white and dark clothing on his arm. The young Indian took them, and holding them in front of the woman, said:

'You must take off your clothes, and put these on.'

'If all you men will go out,' she said.

'No one will hurt you,' he said quietly.

'Not while you men are here,' she said.

He looked at the two men by the door. They came quickly forward, and suddenly gripped her arms as she stood, without hurting her, but with great power. Then two of the old men came, and with curious skill slit her boots down with keen knives, and drew them off, and slit her clothing so that it came away from her. In a few moments she stood there white and uncovered. The old man on the bed spoke, and they turned her round for him to see. He spoke again, and the young Indian deftly took the pins and comb from her fair hair, so that it fell over her shoulders in a bunchy tangle.

Then the old man spoke again. The Indian led her to the bedside. The white-haired, glassy-dark old man moistened his finger-tips at his mouth, and most delicately touched her on the breasts and on the body, then on the back. And she winced strangely each time, as the fingertips drew along her skin, as if Death itself were touching her.

And she wondered, almost sadly, why she did not feel shamed in her nakedness. She only felt sad and lost. Because nobody felt ashamed. The elder men were all dark and tense with some other deep, gloomy, incomprehensible emotion, which suspended all her agitation, while the young Indian had a strange look of ecstasy on his face. And she, she was only utterly strange and beyond herself, as if her body were not her own.

They gave her the new clothing: a long white cotton shift, that came to her knees: then a tunic of thick blue woollen stuff, embroidered with scarlet and green flowers. It was fastened over one shoulder only, and belted with a braid sash of scarlet and black wool.

When she was thus dressed, they took her away, barefoot, to a little house in the stockaded garden. The young Indian told her she might have what she wanted. She asked for water to wash herself. He brought it in a jar, together with a long wooden bowl. Then he fastened the gate-door of her house, and left her a prisoner. She could see through the bars of the gate-door of her house, the red flowers of the garden, and a humming bird. Then from the roof of the big house she heard the long, heavy sound of a drum, unearthly to her in its summons, and an uplifted voice calling from the house-top in a strange language, with a far-away emotionless intonation, delivering some speech or message. And she listened as if from the dead.

But she was very tired. She lay down on a couch of skins, pulling over her the blanket of dark wool, and she slept, giving up everything.

When she woke it was late afternoon, and the young Indian was entering with a basket-tray containing food, tortillas and corn-mush with bits of meat, probably mutton, and a drink made of honey, and some fresh plums. He brought her also a long garland of red and yellow flowers with knots of blue buds at the end. He sprinkled the garland with water from a jar, then offered it to her, with a smile. He seemed very gentle and thoughtful, and on his face and in his dark eyes was a curious look of triumph and ecstasy, that frightened her a little. The glitter had gone from the black eyes, with their curving dark lashes, and he would look at her with this strange soft glow of ecstasy that was not quite human, and terribly impersonal, and which made her uneasy.

'Is there anything you want?' he said, in his low, slow, melodious voice, that always seemed withheld, as if he were speaking aside to somebody else, or as if he did not want to let the sound come out to her.

'Am I going to be kept a prisoner here?' she asked.

'No, you can walk in the garden to-morrow,' he said softly. Always this curious solicitude.

'Do you like that drink?' he said, offering her a little earthenware cup. 'It is very refreshing.'

She sipped the liquor curiously. It was made with herbs and sweetened with honey, and had a strange, lingering flavour. The young man watched her with gratification.

'It has a peculiar taste,' she said.

'It is very refreshing,' he replied, his black eyes resting on her always with that look of gratified ecstasy. Then he went away. And presently she began to be sick, and to vomit violently, as if she had no control over herself.

Afterwards she felt a great soothing languor steal over her, her limbs felt strong and loose and full of languor, and she lay on her couch listening to the sounds of the village, watching the yellowing sky, smelling the scent of burning cedar-wood, or pine-wood. So distinctly she heard the yapping of tiny dogs, the shuffle of far-off feet, the murmur of voices, so keenly she detected the smell of smoke, and flowers, and evening falling, so vividly she saw the one bright star infinitely remote, stirring above the sunset, that she felt as if all her senses were diffused on the air, that she could distinguish the sound of evening flowers unfolding, and the actual crystal sound of the heavens, as the vast belts of the world-atmosphere slid past one another, and as if the moisture ascending and the moisture descending in the air resounded like some harp in the cosmos.

She was a prisoner in her house and in the stockaded garden, but she scarcely minded. And it was days before she realised that she never saw another woman. Only the men, the elderly men of the big house, that she imagined must be some sort of temple, and the men priests of some sort. For they always had the same colours, red, orange, yellow, and black, and the same grave, abstracted demeanour.

Sometimes an old man would come and sit in her room with her, in absolute silence. None spoke any language but Indian, save the one younger man. The older men would smile at her, and sit with her for an hour at a time, sometimes smiling at her when she spoke in Spanish, but never answering save with this slow, benevolent-seeming smile. And they gave off a feeling of almost fatherly solicitude. Yet their dark eyes, brooding over her, had something away in their depths that was awesomely ferocious and relentless. They would cover it with a smile, at once, if they felt her looking. But she had seen it.

Always they treated her with this curious impersonal solicitude, this utterly impersonal gentleness, as an old man treats a child. But underneath it she felt there was something else, something terrible. When her old visitor had gone away, in his silent, insidious, fatherly fashion, a shock of fear would come over her; though of what she knew not.

The young Indian would sit and talk with her freely, as if with great candour. But with him, too, she felt that everything real was unsaid. Perhaps it was unspeakable. His big dark eyes would rest on her almost cherishingly, touched with ecstasy, and his beautiful, slow, languorous voice would trail out its simple, ungrammatical Spanish. He told her he was the grandson of the old, old man, son of the man in the spotted sarape: and they were caciques, kings from the old, old days, before even the Spaniards came. But he himself had been in Mexico City, and also in the United States. He had worked as a labourer, building the roads in Los Angeles. He had travelled as far as Chicago.

'Don't you speak English, then?' she asked.

His eyes rested on her with a curious look of duplicity and conflict, and he mutely shook his head.

'What did you do with your long hair, when you were in the United States?' she asked. 'Did you cut it off?'

Again, with the look of torment in his eyes, he shook his head.

'No,' he said, in a low, subdued voice, 'I wore a hat, and a handkerchief tied round my head.'

And he relapsed into silence, as if of tormented memories.

'Are you the only man of your people who has been to the United States?' she asked him.

'Yes. I am the only one who has been away from here for a long time. The others come back soon, in one week. They don't stay away. The old men don't let them.'

'And why did you go?'

'The old men want me to go – because I shall be the Cacique –'

He talked always with the same naiveté, an almost childish candour. But she felt that this was perhaps just the effect of his Spanish. Or perhaps speech altogether was unreal to him. Anyhow, she felt that all the real things were kept back.

He came and sat with her a good deal – sometimes more than she wished – as if he wanted to be near her. She asked him if he was married. He said he was – with two children.

'I should like to see your children,' she said.

But he answered only with that smile, a sweet, almost ecstatic smile, above which the dark eyes hardly changed from their enigmatic abstraction.

It was curious, he would sit with her by the hour, without ever making her self-conscious, or sex-conscious. He seemed to have no sex, as he sat there so still and gentle and apparently submissive, with his head bent a little forward, and the river of glistening black hair streaming maidenly over his shoulders.

Yet when she looked again, she saw his shoulders broad and powerful, his eyebrows black and level, the short, curved, obstinate black lashes over his lowered eyes, the small, fur-like line of moustache above his blackish, heavy lips, and the strong chin, and she knew that in some other mysterious way he was darkly and powerfully male. And he, feeling her watching him, would glance up at her swiftly with a dark, lurking look in his eyes, which immediately he veiled with that half-sad smile.

The days and the weeks went by, in a vague kind of contentment. She was uneasy sometimes, feeling she had lost the power over herself. She was not in her own power, she was under the spell of some other control. And at times she had moments of terror and horror. But then these Indians would come and sit with her, casting their insidious spell over her by their very silent presence, their silent, sexless, powerful physical presence. As they sat they seemed to take her will away, leaving her will-less and victim to her own indifference. And the young man would bring her sweetened drink, often the same emetic drink, but sometimes other kinds. And after drinking, the languor filled her heavy limbs, her senses seemed to float in the air, listening, hearing. They had brought her a little female dog, which she called Flora. And once, in the trance of her senses, she felt she *heard* the little dog conceive, in her tiny womb, and begin to be complex, with young. And another day she could hear the vast sound of the earth going round, like some immense arrow-string booming.

But as the days grew shorter and colder, when she was cold, she would get a sudden revival of her will, and a desire to go out, to go away. And she insisted to the young man, she wanted to go out.

So one day, they let her climb to the topmost roof of the big house where she was, and look down the square. It was the day of the big dance, but not everybody was dancing. Women with babies in their arms stood in their doorways, watching. Opposite, at the other end of the square, there was a throng before the other big house, and a small, brilliant group on the terrace-roof of the first storey, in front of wide open doors of the upper storey. Through these wide open doors she could see fire glinting in darkness and priests in headdresses of black and yellow and scarlet feathers, wearing robe-like blankets of black and red and yellow, with long green fringes, were moving about. A big drum was beating slowly and regularly, in the dense, Indian silence. The crowd below waited –

Then a drum started on a high beat, and there came the deep, powerful burst of men singing a heavy, savage music, like a wind roaring in some timeless forest, many mature men singing in one breath, like the wind; and long lines of dancers walked out from under the big house. Men with naked, golden-bronze bodies and streaming black hair, tufts of red and yellow feathers on their arms, and kilts of white frieze with a bar of heavy red and black and green embroidery round their waists, bending slightly forward and stamping the earth in their absorbed, monotonous stamp of the dance, a fox-fur, hung by the nose from their belt behind, swaying with the sumptuous swaying of a beautiful fox-fur, the tip of the tail writhing above the dancer's heels. And after each man, a woman with a strange elaborate headdress of feathers and seashells, and wearing a short black tunic, moving erect, holding up tufts of feathers in each hand, swaying her wrists rhythmically and subtly beating the earth with her bare feet.

So, the long line of the dance unfurling from the big house opposite. And from the big house beneath her, strange scent of incense, strange tense silence, then the answering burst of inhuman male singing, and the long line of the dance unfurling.

It went on all day, the insistence of the drum, the cavernous, roaring, storm-like sound of male singing, the incessant swinging of the fox-skins behind the powerful, gold-bronze, stamping legs of the men, the autumn sun from a perfect blue heaven pouring on the rivers of black hair, men's and women's, the valley all still, the walls of rock beyond, the awful huge bulking of the mountain against the pure sky, its snow seething with sheer whiteness.

For hours and hours she watched, spell-bound, and as if drugged. And in all the terrible persistence of the drumming and the primeval, rushing deep singing, and the endless stamping of the dance of fox-tailed men, the tread of heavy, bird-erect women in their black tunics, she seemed at last to feel her own death; her own obliteration. As if she were to be obliterated from the field of life again. In the strange towering symbols on the heads of the changeless, absorbed women she seemed to read once more the *Mene Mene Tekel Upharsin.*[3] Her kind of womanhood, intensely personal and individual, was to be obliterated again, and the great primeval symbols were to tower once more over the fallen individual independence of woman. The sharpness and the quivering nervous consciousness of the highly-bred white woman was to be destroyed again, womanhood was to be cast once more into the great stream of impersonal sex and impersonal passion. Strangely, as if clairvoyant, she saw the immense sacrifice prepared. And she went back to her little house in a trance of agony.

After this, there was always a certain agony when she heard the drums at evening, and the strange uplifted savage sound of men singing round the drum, like wild creatures howling to the invisible gods of the moon and the vanished sun. Something of the chuckling, sobbing cry of the coyote, something of the exultant bark of the fox, the far-off wild melancholy exultance of the howling wolf, the torment of the puma's scream, and the insistence of the ancient fierce human male, with his lapses of tenderness and his abiding ferocity.

Sometimes she would climb the high roof after nightfall, and listen to the dim cluster of young men round the drum on the bridge just beyond the square, singing by the hour. Sometimes there would be a fire, and in the fire-glow, men in their white shirts or naked save for a loin-cloth, would be dancing and stamping like spectres, hour after hour in the dark cold air, within the fire-glow, forever dancing and stamping like turkeys, or dropping squatting by the fire to rest, throwing their blankets round them.

'Why do you all have the same colours?' she asked the young Indian. 'Why do you all have red and yellow and black, over your white shirts? And the women have black tunics?'

He looked into her eyes, curiously, and the faint, evasive smile came on to his face. Behind the smile lay a soft, strange malignancy.

'Because our men are the fire and the daytime, and our women are the spaces between the stars at night,' he said.

'Aren't the women even stars?' she said.

'No. We say they are the spaces between the stars, that keep the stars apart.'

He looked at her oddly, and again the touch of derision came into his eyes.

'White people,' he said, 'they know nothing. They are like children, always with toys. We know the sun, and we know the moon. And we say, when a white woman sacrifice herself to our gods, then our gods will begin to make the world again, and the white man's gods will fall to pieces.'

'How sacrifice herself?' she asked quickly.

And he, as quickly covered, covered himself with a subtle smile.

'She sacrifice her own gods and come to our gods, I mean that,' he said, soothingly.

But she was not reassured. An icy pang of fear and certainty was at her heart.

'The sun he is alive at one end of the sky,' he continued, 'and the moon lives at the other end. And the man all the time have to keep the sun happy in his side of the sky, and the woman have to keep the moon quiet at her side of the sky. All the time she have to work at this. And the sun can't ever go into the house of the moon, and the moon can't ever go into the house of the sun, in the sky. So the woman, she asks the moon to come into her cave, inside her. And the man, he draws the sun down till he has the power of the sun. All the time he do this. Then when the man gets a woman, the sun goes into the cave of the moon, and that is how everything in the world starts.'

She listened, watching him closely, as one enemy watches another who is speaking with double meaning.

'Then,' she said, 'why aren't you Indians masters of the white men?'

'Because,' he said, 'the Indian got weak, and lost his power with the sun, so the white men stole the sun. But they can't keep him – they don't know how. They got him, but they don't know what to do with him, like a boy who catch a big grizzly bear, and can't kill him, and can't run away from him. The grizzly bear eats the boy that catch him, when he want to run away from him. White men don't know what they are doing with the sun, and white women don't know what they do with the moon. The moon she got angry with white women, like a puma when someone kills her little ones. The moon, she bites white women – here inside,' and he pressed his side. 'The moon, she is angry in a white woman's cave. The Indian can see it – And soon,' he added, 'the Indian women get the moon back and keep her quiet in their house. And the Indian men get the sun, and the power over all the world. White men don't know what the sun is. They never know.'

He subsided into a curious exultant silence.

'But,' she faltered, 'why do you hate us so? Why do you hate me?'

He looked up suddenly with a light on his face, and a startling flame of a smile.

'No, we don't hate,' he said softly, looking with a curious glitter into her face.

'You do,' she said, forlorn and hopeless.

And after a moment's silence, he rose and went away.

III

Winter had now come, in the high valley, with snow that melted in the day's sun, and nights that were bitter cold. She lived on, in a kind of daze, feeling her power ebbing more and more away from her, as if her will were leaving her. She felt always in the same relaxed, confused, victimised state, unless the sweetened herb drink would numb her mind altogether, and release her senses into a sort of heightened, mystic acuteness and a feeling as if she were diffusing out deliciously into the harmony of things. This at length became the only state of consciousness she really recognised: this exquisite sense of bleeding out into the higher beauty and harmony of things. Then she could actually hear the great stars in heaven, which she saw through her door, speaking from their motion and brightness, saying things perfectly to the cosmos, as they trod in perfect ripples, like bells on the floor of heaven, passing one another and grouping in the timeless dance, with the spaces of dark between. And she could hear the snow on a cold, cloudy day twittering and faintly whistling in the sky, like birds that flock and fly away in autumn, suddenly calling farewell to the invisible moon, and slipping out of the plains of the air, releasing peaceful warmth. She herself would call to the arrested snow to fall from the upper air. She would call to the unseen moon to cease to be angry, to make peace again with the unseen sun like a woman who ceases to be angry in her house. And she would smell the sweetness of the moon relaxing to the sun in the wintry heaven, when the snow fell in a faint, cold-perfumed relaxation, as the peace of the sun mingled again in a sort of unison with the peace of the moon.

She was aware too of the sort of shadow that was on the Indians of the valley, a deep, stoical disconsolation, almost religious in its depth.

'We have lost our power over the sun, and we are trying to get him back. But he is wild with us, and shy like a horse that has got away. We have to go through a lot.' So the young Indian said to her, looking into her eyes with a strained meaning. And she, as if bewitched, replied:

'I hope you will get him back.'

The smile of triumph flew over his face.

'Do you hope it?' he said.

'I do,' she answered fatally.

'Then all right,' he said. 'We shall get him.'

And he went away in exultance.

She felt she was drifting on some consummation, which she had no will to avoid, yet which seemed heavy and finally terrible to her.

It must have been almost December, for the days were short, when she was taken again before the aged man, and stripped of her clothing, and touched with the old finger-tips.

The aged cacique looked her in the eyes, with his eyes of lonely, far-off, black intentness, and murmured something to her.

'He wants you to make the sign of peace,' the young man translated, showing her the gesture. 'Peace and farewell to him.'

She was fascinated by the black, glass-like, intent eyes of the old cacique, that watched her without blinking, like a basilisk's, overpowering her. In their depths also she saw a certain fatherly compassion, and pleading. She put her hand before her face, in the required manner, making the sign of peace and farewell. He made the sign of peace back again to her, then sank among his furs. She thought he was going to die, and that he knew it.

There followed a day of ceremonial, when she was brought out before all the people, in a blue blanket with white fringe, and holding blue feathers in her hands. Before an altar of one house, she was perfumed with incense and sprinkled with ash. Before the altar of the opposite house she was fumigated again with incense by the gorgeous, terrifying priests in yellow and scarlet and black, their faces painted with scarlet paint. And then they threw water on her. Meanwhile she was faintly aware of the fire on the altar, the heavy, heavy sound of a drum, the heavy sound of men beginning powerfully, deeply, savagely to sing, the swaying of the crowd of faces in the plaza below, and the formation for a sacred dance.

But at this time her commonplace consciousness was numb, she was aware of her immediate surroundings as shadows, almost immaterial. With refined and heightened senses she could hear the sound of the earth winging on its journey, like a shot arrow, the ripple-rustling of the air, and the boom of the great arrow-string. And it seemed to her there were two great influences in the upper air, one golden towards the sun, and one invisible silver; the first travelling like rain ascending to the gold presence sunwards, the second like rain silverily descending the ladders of space towards the hovering, lurking clouds over the snowy mountain-top. Then between them, another presence, waiting to shake himself free of moisture, of heavy white snow that had mysteriously collected about him. And in summer, like a scorched eagle, he would wait to shake himself clear of the weight of heavy sunbeams. And he was coloured like fire. And he was always shaking himself clear, of snow or of heavy heat, like an eagle rustling.

Then there was a still stranger presence, standing watching from the blue distance, always watching. Sometimes running in upon the wind, or shimmering in the heat-waves. The blue wind itself, rushing as it were out of the holes in the earth into the sky, rushing out of the sky down upon the earth. The blue wind, the go-between, the invisible ghost that belonged to two worlds, that played upon the ascending and the descending chords of the rains.

More and more her ordinary personal consciousness had left her, she had gone into that other state of passional cosmic consciousness, like one who is drugged. The Indians, with their heavily religious natures, had made her succumb to their vision.

Only one personal question, she asked the young Indian:

'Why am I the only one that wears blue?'

'It is the colour of the wind. It is the colour of what goes away and is never coming back, but which is always here, waiting like death among us. It is the colour of the dead. And it is the colour that stands away off, looking at us from the distance, that cannot come near to us. When we go near, it goes farther. It can't be near. We are all brown and yellow and black hair, and white teeth and red blood. We are the ones that are here. You with blue eyes, you are the messengers from the far-away, you cannot stay, and now it is time for you to go back.'

'Where to?' she asked.

'To the way-off things like the sun and the blue mother of rain, and tell them that we are the people on the world again, and we can bring the sun to the moon again, like a red horse to a blue mare; we are the people. The white women have driven back the moon in the sky, won't let her come to the sun. So the sun is angry. And the Indian must give the moon to the sun.'

'How?' she said.

'The white woman got to die and go like a wind to the sun, tell him the Indians will open the gate to him. And the Indian women will open the gate to the moon. The white women don't let the moon come down out of the blue coral. The moon used to come down among the Indian women, like a white goat among the flowers. And the sun want to come down to the Indian men, like an eagle to the pine-trees. The sun, he is shut out behind the white man, and the moon she is shut out behind the white woman, and they can't get away. They are angry, everything in the world gets angrier. The Indian says, he will give the white woman to the sun, so the sun will leap over the white man and come to the Indian again. And the moon will be surprised, she will see the gate open, and she not know which way to go. But the Indian woman will call to the moon, *Come! Come! Come back into my grasslands. The wicked white woman can't harm you any more*. Then the sun will look over the heads of the white men, and see the moon in the pastures of our women, with the Red Men standing around like pine trees. Then he will leap over the heads of the white men, and come running past to the Indians through the spruce trees. And we, who are red and black and yellow, we who stay, we shall have the sun on our right hand and the moon on our left. So we can bring the rain down out of the blue meadows, and up out of the black; and we can call the wind that tells the corn to grow, when we ask him, and we shall make the clouds to break, and the sheep to have twin lambs. And we shall be full of power, like a spring day. But the white people will be a hard winter, without snow –'

'But,' said the white woman, 'I don't shut out the moon – how can I?'

'Yes,' he said, 'you shut the gate, and then laugh, think you have it all your own way.'

She could never quite understand the way he looked at her. He was always so curiously gentle, and his smile was so soft. Yet there was such glitter in his eyes, and an unrelenting sort of hate came out of his words, a strange, profound, impersonal hate. Personally he liked her, she was sure. He was gentle with her, attracted by her in some strange, soft, passionless way. But impersonally he hated her with a mystic hatred. He would smile at her, winningly. Yet if, the next moment, she glanced round at him unawares, she would catch that gleam of pure after-hate in his eyes.

'Have I got to die and be given to the sun?' she asked.

'Sometime,' he said, laughing evasively. 'Sometime we all die.'

They were gentle with her, and very considerate with her. Strange men, the old priests and the young cacique alike, they watched over her and cared for her like women. In their soft, insidious understanding, there was something womanly. Yet their eyes, with that strange glitter, and their dark, shut mouths that would open to the broad jaw, the small, strong, white teeth, had something very primitively male and cruel.

One wintry day, when snow was falling, they took her to a great dark chamber in the big house. The fire was burning in a corner on a high raised dais under a sort of hood or canopy of adobe-work. She saw in the fire-glow, the glowing bodies of the almost naked priests, and strange symbols on the roof and walls of the chamber. There was no door or window in the chamber, they had descended by a ladder from the roof. And the fire of pinewood danced continually, showing walls painted with strange devices, which she could not understand, and a ceiling of poles making a curious pattern of black and red and yellow, and alcoves or niches in which were curious objects she could not discern.

The older priests were going through some ceremony near the fire, in silence, intense Indian silence. She was seated on a low projection of the wall, opposite the fire, two men seated beside her. Presently they gave her a drink from a cup, which she took gladly, because of the semi-trance it would induce.

In the darkness and in the silence she was accurately aware of everything that happened to her: how they took off her clothes, and, standing her before a great, weird device on the wall, coloured blue and white and black, washed her all over with water and the amole[4] infusion; washed even her hair, softly, carefully, and dried it on white cloths, till it was soft and glistening. Then they laid her on a couch under another great indecipherable image of red and black and yellow, and now rubbed all her body with sweet-scented oil, and massaged all her limbs, and her back, and her sides, with a long, strange, hypnotic massage. Their dark hands were incredibly powerful, yet soft with a watery softness she could not understand. And the dark faces, leaning near her white body, she saw were darkened with red pigment, with lines of yellow round the cheeks. And the dark eyes glittered absorbed, as the hands worked upon the soft white body of the woman.

They were so impersonal, absorbed in something that was beyond her. They never saw her as a personal woman: she could tell that. She was some mystic object to them, some vehicle of passions too remote for her to grasp. Herself in a state of trance, she watched their faces bending over her, dark, strangely glistening with the transparent red paint, and lined with bars of yellow. And in this weird, luminous-dark mask of living face, the eyes were fixed with an unchanging steadfast gleam, and the purplish-pigmented lips were closed in a full, sinister, sad grimness. The immense fundamental sadness, the grimness of ultimate decision, the fixity of revenge, and the nascent exultance of those that are going to triumph – these things she could read in their faces, as she lay and was rubbed into a misty glow, by their uncanny dark hands. Her limbs, her flesh, her very bones at last seemed to be diffusing into a roseate sort of mist, in which her consciousness hovered like some sun-gleam in a flushed cloud.

She knew the gleam would fade, the cloud would go grey. But at present she did not believe it. She knew she was a victim; that all this elaborate work upon her was the work of victimising her. But she did not mind. She wanted it.

Later, they put a short blue tunic on her and took her to the upper terrace, and presented her to the people. She saw the plaza below her full of dark faces and of glittering eyes. There was no pity: only the curious hard exultance. The people gave a subdued cry when they saw her, and she shuddered. But she hardly cared.

Next day was the last. She slept in a chamber of the big house. At dawn they put on her a big blue blanket with a fringe, and led her out into the plaza, among the throng of silent, dark-blanketed people. There was pure white snow on the ground, and the dark people in their dark-brown blankets looked like inhabitants of another world.

A large drum was slowly pounding, and an old priest was declaring from a housetop. But it was not till noon that a litter came forth, and the people gave that low, animal cry which was so moving. In the sack-like litter sat the old, old cacique, his white hair braided with black braid and large turquoise stones. His face was like a piece of obsidian. He lifted his hand in token, and the litter stopped in front of her. Fixing her with his old eyes, he spoke to her for a few moments, in his hollow voice. No one translated.

Another litter came, and she was placed in it. Four priests moved ahead, in their scarlet and yellow and black, with plumed head-dresses. Then came the litter of the old cacique. Then the light drums began, and two groups of singers burst simultaneously into song, male and wild. And the golden-red, almost naked men, adorned with ceremonial feathers and kilts, the rivers of black hair down their backs, formed into two files and began to tread the dance. So they threaded out of the snowy plaza, in two long, sumptuous lines of dark red-gold and black and fur, swaying with a faint tinkle of bits of shell and flint, winding over the snow between the two bee-clusters of men who sang around the drum.

Slowly they moved out, and her litter, with its attendance of feathered, lurid, dancing priests, moved after. Everybody danced the tread of the dance-step, even, subtly, the litter-bearers. And out of the plaza they went, past smoking ovens, on the trail to the great cotton-wood trees, that stood like grey-silver lace against the blue sky, bare and exquisite above the snow. The river, diminished, rushed among fangs of ice. The chequer-squares of gardens within fences were all snowy, and the white houses now looked yellowish.

The whole valley glittered intolerably with pure snow, away to the walls of the standing rock. And across the flat cradle of snow-bed wound the long thread of the dance, shaking slowly and sumptuously in its orange and black motion. The high drums thudded quickly, and on the crystalline frozen air the swell and roar of the chant of savages was like an obsession.

She sat looking out of her litter with big, transfixed blue eyes, under which were the wan markings of her drugged weariness. She knew she was going to die, among the glisten of this snow, at the hands of this savage, sumptuous people. And as she stared at the blaze of blue sky above the slashed and ponderous mountain, she thought: 'I am dead already. What difference does it make, the transition from the dead I am to the dead I shall be, very soon!' Yet her soul sickened and felt wan.

The strange procession trailed on, in perpetual dance, slowly across the plain of snow, and then entered the slopes between the pine-trees. She saw the copper-dark men dancing the dance-tread, onwards, between the copper-pale tree trunks. And at last she, too, in her swaying litter, entered the pine-trees.

They were travelling on and on, upwards, across the snow under the trees, past the superb shafts of pale, flaked copper, the rustle and shake and tread of the threading dance, penetrating into the forest, into the mountain. They were following a stream-bed: but the stream was dry, like summer, dried up by the frozenness of the head-waters. There were dark, red-bronze willow bushes with wattles like wild hair, and pallid aspen trees looking like cold flesh against the snow. Then jutting dark rocks.

At last she could tell that the dancers were moving forward no more. Nearer and nearer she came upon the drums, as to a lair of mysterious animals. Then through the bushes she emerged into a strange amphitheatre. Facing was a great wall of hollow rock, down the front of which hung a great, dripping, fang-like spoke of ice. The ice came pouring over the rock from the precipice above, and then stood arrested, dripping out of high heaven, almost down to the hollow stones where the stream-pool should be below. But the pool was dry.

On either side the dry pool, the lines of dancers had formed, and the dance was continuing without intermission, against a background of bushes.

But what she felt was that fanged inverted pinnacle of ice, hanging from the lip of the dark precipice above. And behind the great rope of ice, she saw the leopard-like figures of priests climbing the hollow cliff face, to the cave that, like a dark socket, bored a cavity, an orifice, half way up the crag.

Before she could realise, her litter-bearers were staggering in the footholds, climbing the rock. She, too, was behind the ice. There it hung, like a curtain that is not spread, but hangs like a great fang. And near above her was the orifice of the cave sinking dark into the rock. She watched it as she swayed upwards.

On the platform of the cave stood the priests, waiting in all their gorgeousness of feathers and fringed robes, watching her ascent. Two of them stooped to help her litter-bearer. And at length she was on the platform of the cave, far in behind the shaft of ice, above the hollow amphitheatre among the bushes below, where men were dancing, and the whole populace of the village was clustered in silence.

The sun was sloping down the afternoon sky, on the left. She knew that this was the shortest day of the year, and the last day of her life. They stood her facing the iridescent column of ice, which fell down marvellously arrested, away in front of her.

Some signal was given, and the dance below stopped. There was now absolute silence. She was given a little to drink, then two priests took off her mantle and her tunic, and in her strange pallor she stood there, between the lurid robes of the priests, beyond the pillar of ice, beyond and above the dark-faced people. The throng below gave the low, wild cry. Then the priests turned her round, so she stood with her back to the open world, her long blond hair to the people below. And they cried again.

She was facing the cave, inwards. A fire was burning and flickering in the depths. Four priests had taken off their robes, and were almost as naked as she was. They were powerful men in the prime of life, and they kept their dark, painted faces lowered.

From the fire came the old, old priest, with an incense-pan. He was naked and in a state of barbaric ecstasy. He fumigated his victim, reciting at the same time in a hollow voice. Behind him came another robeless priest, with two flint knives.

When she was fumigated, they laid her on a large flat stone, the four powerful men holding her by the outstretched arms and legs. Behind stood the aged man, like a skeleton covered with dark glass, holding a knife and transfixedly watching the sun; and behind him again was another naked priest, with a knife.

She felt little sensation, though she knew all that was happening. Turning to the sky, she looked at the yellow sun. It was sinking. The shaft of ice was like a shadow between her and it. And she realised that the yellow rays were filling half the cave, though they had not reached the altar where the fire was, at the far end of the funnel-shaped cavity.

Yes, the rays were creeping round slowly. As they grew ruddier, they penetrated farther. When the red sun was about to sink, he would shine full through the shaft of ice deep into the hollow of the cave, to the innermost.

She understood now that this was what the men were waiting for. Even those that held her down were bent and twisted round, their black eyes watching the sun with a glittering eagerness, and awe, and craving. The black eyes of the aged cacique were fixed like black mirrors on the sun, as if sightless, yet containing some terrible answer to the reddening winter planet. And all the eyes of the priests were fixed and glittering on the sinking orb, in the reddening, icy silence of the winter afternoon.

They were anxious, terribly anxious, and fierce. Their ferocity wanted something, and they were waiting the moment. And their ferocity was ready to leap out into a mystic exultance, of triumph. But still they were anxious.

Only the eyes of that oldest man were not anxious. Black, and fixed, and as if sightless, they watched the sun, seeing beyond the sun. And in their black, empty concentration there was power, power intensely abstract and remote, but deep, deep to the heart of the earth, and the heart of the sun. In absolute motionlessness he watched till the red sun should send his ray through the column of ice. Then the old man would strike, and strike home, accomplish the sacrifice and achieve the power.

The mastery that man must hold, and that passes from race to race.

Sun

'TAKE her away, into the sun,' the doctor said. She herself was sceptical of the sun, but she permitted herself to be carried away, with her child, and a nurse, and her mother, over the sea.

The ship sailed at midnight. And for two hours her husband stayed with her, while the child was put to bed, and the passengers came on board. It was a black night, the Hudson swayed with heaving blackness, shaken over with spilled dribbles of light. She leaned over the rail, and looking down thought: this is the sea; it is deeper than one imagines, and fuller of memories. At that moment the sea seemed to heave like the serpent of chaos[1] that has lived for ever.

'These partings are no good, you know,' her husband was saying, at her side. 'They're no good. I don't like them.'

His tone was full of apprehension, misgiving, and there was a certain clinging to the last straw of hope.

'No, neither do I,' she responded in a flat voice. She remembered how bitterly they wanted to get away from one another, he and she. The emotion of parting gave a slight tug at her emotions, but only caused the iron that had gone into her soul to gore deeper.

So, they looked at their sleeping son, and the father's eyes were wet. But it is not the wetting of the eyes that counts, it is the deep iron rhythm of habit, the year-long, life-habits; the deep-set stroke of power.

And in their two lives, the stroke of power was hostile, his and hers. Like two engines running at variance, they shattered one another.

'All ashore! All ashore!'

'Maurice, you must go.'

And she thought to herself: For him it is All Ashore! For me it is Out to Sea!

Well, he waved his hanky on the midnight dreariness of the pier, as the boat inched away; one among a crowd. One among a crowd! C'est ça![2]

The ferry-boats, like great dishes piled with rows of lights, were still slanting across the Hudson. That black mouth must be the Lackawanna Station.[3]

The ship ebbed on between the lights, the Hudson seemed interminable. But at last they were round the bend, and there was the poor harvest of lights at the Battery.[4] Liberty flung up her torch in a tantrum. There was the wash of the sea.

And though the Atlantic was grey as lava, they did come at last into the sun. Even she had a house above the bluest of seas, with a vast garden, or vineyard, all vines and olives, dropping steeply in terrace after terrace, to the strip of coast plain; and the garden full of secret places, deep groves of lemon far down in the cleft of earth, and hidden, pure green reservoirs of water; then a spring issuing out of a little cavern, where the old Sicules[5] had drunk before the Greeks came; and a grey goat bleating, stabled in an ancient tomb with the niches empty. There was the scent of mimosa, and beyond, the snow of the volcano.

She saw it all, and in a measure it was soothing. But it was all external. She didn't really care about it. She was herself just the same, with all her anger and frustration inside her, and her incapacity to feel anything real. The child imitated her, and preyed on her peace of mind. She felt so horribly, ghastly responsible for him: as if she must be responsible for every breath he drew. And that was torture to her, to the child, and to everybody else concerned.

'You know, Juliet, the doctor told you to lie in the sun, without your clothes. Why don't you?' said her mother.

'When I am fit to do so, I will. Do you want to kill me?' Juliet flew at her.

'To kill you, no! Only to do you good.'

'For God's sake, leave off wanting to do me good.'

The mother at last was so hurt and incensed, she departed.

The sea went white, and then invisible. Pouring rain fell. It was cold, in the house built for the sun.

Again a morning when the sun lifted himself molten and sparkling, naked over the sea's rim. The house faced south-east, Juliet lay in her bed and watched him rise. It was as if she had never seen the sun rise before. She had never seen the naked sun stand up pure upon the sea-line, shaking the night off himself, like wetness. And he was full and naked. And she wanted to come to him.

So the desire sprang secretly in her, to be naked to the sun. She cherished her desire like a secret. She wanted to come together with the sun.

But she would have to go away from the house – away from people. And it is not easy, in a country where every olive tree has eyes, and every slope is seen from afar, to go hidden, and have intercourse with the sun.

But she found a place: a rocky bluff shoved out to the sea and sun, and overgrown with the large cactus called prickly pear. Out of this thicket of cactus rose one cypress tree, with a pallid, thick trunk, and a tip that leaned over, flexible, in the blue. It stood like a guardian looking to sea; or a candle whose huge flame was darkness against light: the long tongue of darkness licking up at the sky.

Juliet sat down by the cypress tree, and took off her clothes. The contorted cactus made a forest, hideous yet fascinating, about her. She sat and offered her bosom to the sun, sighing, even now, with a certain hard pain, against the cruelty of having to give herself: but exulting that at last it was no human lover.

But the sun marched in blue heaven and sent down his rays as he went. She felt the soft air of the sea on her breasts, that seemed as if they would never ripen. But she hardly felt the sun. Fruits that would wither and not mature, her breasts.

Soon, however, she felt the sun inside them, warmer than ever love had been, warmer than milk or the hands of her baby. At last, her breasts were like long white grapes in the hot sun.

She slid off all her clothes, and lay naked in the sun, and as she lay she looked up through her fingers at the central sun, his blue pulsing roundness, whose outer edges streamed brilliance. Pulsing with marvellous blue, and alive, and streaming white fire from his edges, the Sun! He faced down to her with blue body of fire, and enveloped her breasts and her face, her throat, her tired belly, her knees, her thighs and her feet.

She lay with shut eyes, the colour of rosy flame through her lids. It was too much. She reached and put leaves over her eyes. Then she lay again, like a long gourd in the sun, green that must ripen to gold.

She could feel the sun penetrating into her bones; nay, further, even into her emotions and thoughts. The dark tensions of her emotion began to give way, the cold dark clots of her thoughts began to dissolve. She was beginning to be warm right through. Turning over, she let her shoulders lie in the sun, her loins, the backs of her thighs, even her heels. And she lay half stunned with the strangeness of the thing that was happening to her. Her weary, chilled heart was melting, and in melting, evaporating. Only her womb remained tense and resistant, the eternal resistance. It would resist even the sun.

When she was dressed again she lay once more and looked up at the cypress tree, whose crest, a filament, fell this way and that in the breeze. Meanwhile, she was conscious of the great sun roaming in heaven, and of her own resistance.

So, dazed, she went home, only half-seeing, sun-blinded and sun-dazed. And her blindness was like a richness to her, and her dim, warm, heavy half-consciousness was like wealth.

'Mummy! Mummy!' her child came running towards her, calling in that peculiar bird-like little anguish of want, always wanting her. She was surprised that her drowsed heart for once felt none of the anxious love-tension in return. She caught the child up in her arms, but she thought: He should not be such a lump! If he had any sun in him, he would spring up. – And she felt again the unyielding resistance of her womb, against him and everything.

She resented, rather, his little hands clutching at her, especially her neck. She pulled her throat away. She did not want him getting hold of it. She put the child down.

'Run!' she said. 'Run in the sun!'

And there and then she took off his clothes and set him naked on the warm terrace.

'Play in the sun!' she said.

He was frightened and wanted to cry. But she, in the warm indolence of her body, and the complete indifference of her heart, and the resistance of her womb, rolled him an orange across the red tiles, and with his soft, unformed little body he toddled after it. Then, immediately he had it, he dropped it because it felt strange against his flesh. And he looked back at her, wrinkling his face to cry, frightened because he was stark.

'Bring me the orange,' she said, amazed at her own deep indifference to his trepidation. 'Bring Mummy the orange.'

'He shall not grow up like his father,' she said to herself. 'Like a worm that the sun has never seen.'

II

She had had the child so much on her mind, in a torment of responsibility, as if, having borne him, she had to answer for his whole existence. Even if his nose were running, it had been repulsive and a goad in her vitals, as if she must say to herself: Look at the thing you brought forth!

Now a change took place. She was no longer vitally consumed about the child, she took the strain of her anxiety and her will from off him. And he thrived all the more for it.

She was thinking inside herself, of the sun in his splendour, and his entering into her. Her life was now a secret ritual. She always lay awake, before dawn, watching for the grey to colour to pale gold, to know if clouds lay on the sea's edge. Her joy was when he rose all molten in his nakedness, and threw off blue-white fire, into the tender heaven.

But sometimes he came ruddy, like a big, shy creature. And sometimes slow and crimson red, with a look of anger, slowly pushing and shouldering. Sometimes again she could not see him, only the level cloud threw down gold and scarlet from above, as he moved behind the wall.

She was fortunate. Weeks went by, and though the dawn was sometimes clouded, and afternoon was sometimes grey, never a day passed sunless, and most days, winter though it was, streamed radiant. The thin little wild crocuses came up mauve and striped, the wild narcissus hung their winter stars.

Every day, she went down to the cypress tree, among the cactus grove on the knoll with yellowish cliffs at the foot. She was wiser and subtler now, wearing only a dove-grey wrapper, and sandals. So that in an instant, in any hidden niche, she was naked to the sun. And the moment she was covered again she was grey and invisible.

Every day, in the morning towards noon, she lay at the foot of the powerful, silver-pawed cypress tree, while the sun strode jovial in heaven. By now she knew the sun in every thread of her body. Her heart of anxiety, that anxious, straining heart, had disappeared altogether, like a flower that falls in the sun, and leaves only a little ripening fruit. And her tense womb, though still closed, was slowly unfolding, slowly, slowly, like a lily bud under water, as the sun mysteriously touched it. Like a lily bud under water it was slowly rising to the sun, to expand at last, to the sun, only to the sun.

She knew the sun in all her body, the blue-molten with his white fire edges, throwing off fire. And, though he shone on all the world, when she lay unclothed he focussed on her. It was one of the wonders of the sun, he could shine on a million people, and still be the radiant, splendid, unique sun, focussed on her alone.

With her knowledge of the sun, and her conviction that the sun was gradually penetrating her to know her, in the cosmic carnal sense of the word, came over her a feeling of a detachment from people, and a certain contemptuous tolerance for human beings altogether. They were so un-elemental, so un-sunned. They were so like graveyard worms.

Even the peasants passing up the rocky, ancient little road with their donkeys, sun-blackened as they were, were not sunned right through. There was a little soft white core of fear, like a snail in a shell, where the soul of the man cowered in fear of the natural blaze of life. He dared not quite see the sun: always innerly cowed. All men were like that.

Why admit men!

With her indifference to people, to men, she was not now so cautious about being seen. She had told Marinina, who went shopping for her in the village, that the doctor had ordered sun-baths. Let that suffice.

Marinina was a woman of sixty or more, tall, thin, erect, with curling dark-grey hair, and dark-grey eyes that had the shrewdness of thousands of years in them, with the laugh, half mockery, that underlies all long experience. Tragedy is lack of experience.

'It must be beautiful to go naked in the sun,' said Marinina, with a shrewd laugh in her eyes as she looked keenly at the other woman. Juliet's fair, bobbed hair curled in a little cloud at her temples. Marinina was a woman of Magna Graecia,[6] and had far memories. She looked again at Juliet.

'But when a woman is beautiful, she can show herself to the sun? eh? isn't it true?' she added, with that queer, breathless little laugh of the women of the past.

'Who knows if I am beautiful!' said Juliet.

But beautiful or not, she felt that by the sun she was appreciated. Which is the same.

When, out of the sun at noon, sometimes she stole down over the rocks and past the cliff-edge, down to the deep gully where the lemons hung in cool eternal shadow; and in the silence slipped off her wrapper to wash herself quickly at one of the deep, clear green basins, she would notice, in the bare green twilight under the lemon leaves, that all her body was rosy, rosy, and turning to gold. She was like another person. She was another person.

So she remembered that the Greeks had said a white unsunned body was unhealthy, and fishy.

And she would rub a little olive oil into her skin, and wander a moment in the dark underworld of the lemons, balancing a lemon-flower in her navel, laughing to herself. There was just a chance some peasant might see her. But if he did, he would be more afraid of her than she of him. She knew of the white core of fear in the clothed bodies of men.

She knew it even in her little son. How he mistrusted her, now that she laughed at him, with the sun in her face! She insisted on his toddling naked in the sunshine, every day. And now his little body was pink too, his blond hair was pushed thick from his brow, his cheeks had a pomegranate scarlet, in the delicate gold of the sunny skin. He was bonny and healthy, and the servants, loving his gold and red and blue, called him an angel from heaven.

But he mistrusted his mother: she laughed at him. And she saw, in his wide blue eyes, under the little frown, that centre of fear, misgiving, which she believed was at the centre of all male eyes, now. She called it fear of the sun. And her womb stayed shut against all men, sun-fearers.

'He fears the sun,' she would say to herself, looking down into the eyes of the child.

And as she watched him toddling, swaying, tumbling in the sunshine, making his little bird-like noises, she saw that he held himself tight and hidden from the sun, inside himself, and his balance was clumsy, his movements a little gross. His spirit was like a snail in a shell, in a damp, cold crevice inside himself. It made her think of his father. And she wished she could make him come forth, break out in a gesture of recklessness, a salutation to the sun.

She determined to take him with her, down to the cypress tree among the cactus. She would have to watch him, because of the thorns. But surely in that place he would come forth from the little shell, deep inside him. That little civilised tension would disappear off his brow.

She spread a rug for him and sat down. Then she slid off her wrapper and lay down herself, watching a hawk high in the blue, and the tip of the cypress hanging over.

The boy played with stones on the rug. When he got up to toddle away, she got up too. He turned and looked at her. Almost, from his blue eyes, it was the challenging, warm look of the true male. And he was handsome, with the scarlet in the golden blond of his skin. He was not really white. His skin was gold-dusky.

'Mind the thorns, darling,' she said.

'Thorns!' re-echoed the child, in a birdy chirp, still looking at her over his shoulder, like some naked *putto*[7] in a picture, doubtful.

'Nasty prickly thorns.'

'Ickly thorns!'

He staggered in his little sandals over the stones, pulling at the dry mint. She was quick as a serpent, leaping to him, when he was going to fall against the prickles. It surprised even herself. 'What a wild cat I am, really!' she said to herself.

She brought him every day, when the sun shone, to the cypress tree.

'Come!' she said, 'Let us go to the cypress tree.'

And if there was a cloudy day, with the tramontana[8] blowing, so that she could not go down, the child would chirp incessantly: 'Cypress tree! Cypress tree!'

He missed it as much as she did.

It was not just taking sun-baths. It was much more than that. Something deep inside her unfolded and relaxed, and she was given to a cosmic influence. By some mysterious will inside her, deeper than her known consciousness and her known will, she was put into connection with the sun, and the stream of the sun flowed through her, round her womb. She herself, her conscious self, was secondary, a secondary person, almost an onlooker. The true Juliet lived in the dark flow of the sun within her deep body, like a river of dark rays circling, circling dark and violet round the sweet, shut bud of her womb.

She had always been mistress of herself, aware of what she was doing, and held tense in her own command. Now she felt inside her quite another sort of power, something greater than herself, darker and more savage, the element flowing upon her. Now she was vague, in the spell of a power beyond herself.

III

The end of February was suddenly very hot. Almond blossom was falling like pink snow, in the touch of the smallest breeze. The mauve, silky little anemones were out, the asphodels tall in bud, and the sea was corn-flower blue.

Juliet had ceased to care about anything. Now, most of the day, she and the child were naked in the sun, and it was all she wanted. Sometimes she went down to the sea to bathe: often she wandered in the gullies where the sun shone in, and she was out of sight. Sometimes she saw a peasant with an ass, and he saw her. But she went so simply and quietly with her child; and the fame of the sun's healing power, for the soul as well as for the body, had already spread among the people; so that there was no excitement.

The child and she were now both tanned with a rosy-golden tan, all over. 'I am another being,' she said to herself, as she looked at her red-gold breasts and thighs.

The child, too, was another creature, with a peculiar, quiet, sun-darkened absorption. Now he played by himself in silence, and she need hardly notice him. He seemed no longer to notice when he was alone.

There was not a breeze, and the sea was ultramarine. She sat by the great silver paw of the cypress tree, drowsed in the sun, but her breasts alert, full of sap. She was becoming aware of an activity rousing in her, an activity which would bring another self awake in her. She still did not want to be aware. The new rousing would mean a new contact, and this she did not want. She knew well enough the vast cold apparatus of civilisation, and what contact with it meant; and how difficult it was to evade.

The child had gone a few yards down the rocky path, round the great sprawling of a cactus. She had seen him, a real gold-brown infant of the winds, with burnt gold hair and red cheeks, collecting the speckled pitcher-flowers and laying them in rows. He could balance now, and was quick for his own emergencies, like an absorbed young animal playing.

Suddenly she heard him speaking: *Look, Mummy! Mummy look!* A note in his bird-like voice made her lean forward sharply.

Her heart stood still. He was looking over his naked little shoulder at her, and pointing with a loose little hand at a snake which had reared itself up a yard away from him, and was opening its mouth so that its forked, soft tongue flickered black like a shadow, uttering a short hiss.

'Look! Mummy!'

'Yes, darling, it's a snake!' came the slow deep voice. He looked at her, his wide blue eyes uncertain whether to be afraid or not. Some stillness of the sun in her reassured him.

'Snake!' he chirped.

'Yes, darling! Don't touch it, it can bite.'

The snake had sunk down, and was reaching away from the coils in which it had been basking asleep, and slowly easing its long, gold-brown body into the rocks, with slow curves. The boy turned and watched it in silence. Then he said:

'Snake going!'

'Yes! Let it go. It likes to be alone.'

He still watched the slow, easing length as the creature drew itself apathetic out of sight.

'Snake gone back,' he said.

'Yes, it is gone back. Come to Mummy a moment.'

He came and sat with his plump, naked little body on her naked lap, and she smoothed his burnt, bright hair. She said nothing, feeling that everything was past. The curious careless power of the sun filled her, filled the whole place like a charm, and the snake was part of the place, along with her and the child.

Another day, in the dry stone wall of one of the olive terraces, she saw a black snake horizontally creeping.

'Marinina,' she said, 'I saw a black snake. Are they harmful?'

'Ah, the black snakes, no! But the yellow ones, yes! If the yellow ones bite you, you die. But they frighten me, they frighten me, even the black ones, when I see one.'

Juliet still went to the cypress tree with the child. But she always looked carefully round, before she sat down, examining everywhere the child might go. Then she would lie and turn to the sun again, her tanned, pear-shaped breasts pointing up. She would take no thought for the morrow. She refused to think outside the garden, and she could not write letters. She would tell the nurse to write. So she lay in the sun, but not for long, for it was getting strong, fierce. And in spite of herself, the bud that had been tight and deep immersed in the innermost gloom of her, was rearing, rearing and straightening its curved stem, to open its dark tips and show a gleam of rose. Her womb was coming open wide with rosy ecstasy, like a lotus flower.[9]

IV

Spring was becoming summer, in the south of the sun, and the rays were very powerful. In the hot hours she would lie in the shade of trees, or she would even go down to the depths of the cool lemon grove. Or sometimes she went in the shadowy deeps of the gullies, at the bottom of the little ravine, towards home. The child fluttered around in silence, like a young animal absorbed in life.

Going slowly home in her nakedness down among the bushes of the dark ravine, one noon, she came round a rock suddenly upon the peasant of the next *podere*,[10] who was stooping binding up a bundle of brush-wood he had cut, his ass standing near. He was wearing summer cotton trousers, and stooping his buttocks towards her. It was utterly still and private down in the dark bed of the little ravine. A weakness came over her, for a moment she could not move. The man lifted the bundle of wood with powerful shoulders, and turned to the ass. He started and stood transfixed as he saw her, as if it were a vision. Then his eyes met hers, and she felt the blue fire running through her limbs to her womb, which was spreading in the helpless ecstasy. Still they looked into each other's eyes, and the fire flowed between them, like the blue, streaming fire from the heart of the sun. And she saw the phallus rise under his clothing, and knew he would come towards her.

'Mummy, a man! Mummy!' The child had put a hand against her thigh. 'Mummy, a man!'

She heard the note of fear and swung round.

'It's all right, boy!' she said, and taking him by the hand, she led him back round the rock again, while the peasant watched her naked, retreating buttocks lift and fall.

She put on her wrap, and taking the boy in her arms, began to stagger up a steep goat-track through the yellow-flowering tangle of shrubs, up to the level of day, and the olive trees below the house. There she sat down to collect herself.

The sea was blue, very blue and soft and still-looking, and her womb inside her was wide open, wide open like a lotus flower, or a cactus flower, in a radiant sort of eagerness. She could feel it, and it dominated her consciousness. And a biting chagrin burned in her breast, against the child, against the complication of frustration.

She knew the peasant by sight: a man something over thirty, broad and very powerfully set. She had many times watched him from the terrace of her house: watched him come with his ass, watched him trimming the olive trees, working alone, always alone and physically powerful, with a broad red face and a quiet self-possession. She had spoken to him once or twice, and met his big blue eyes, dark and southern hot. And she knew his sudden gestures, a little violent and over-generous. But she had never thought of him. Save she had noticed that he was always very clean and well-cared for: and then she had seen his wife one day, when the latter had brought the man's meal, and they sat in the shade of a carob tree, on either side the spread white cloth. And then Juliet had seen that the man's wife was older than he, a dark, proud, gloomy woman. And then a young woman had come with a child, and the man had danced with the child, so young and passionate. But it was not his own child: he had no children. It was when he danced with the child, in such a sprightly way, as if full of suppressed passion, that Juliet had first really noticed him. But even then, she had never thought of him. Such a broad red face, such a great chest, and rather short legs. Too much a crude beast for her to think of, a peasant.

But now the strange challenge of his eyes had held her, blue and overwhelming like the blue sun's heart. And she had seen the fierce stirring of the phallus under his thin trousers: for her. And with his red face, and with his broad body, he was like the sun to her, the sun in its broad heat.

She felt him so powerfully, that she could not go further from him.

She continued to sit there under the tree. Then she heard nurse tinkling a bell at the house and calling. And the child called back. She had to rise and go home.

In the afternoon she sat on the terrace of her house, that looked over the olive slopes to the sea. The man came and went, came and went to the little hut on his *podere*, on the edge of the cactus grove. And he glanced again at her house, at her sitting on the terrace. And her womb was open to him.

Yet she had not the courage to go down to him. She was paralysed. She had tea, and still sat there on the terrace. And the man came and went, and glanced, and glanced again. Till the evening bell had jangled from the capuchin church at the village gate, and the darkness came on. And still she sat on the terrace. Till at last in the moonlight she saw him load his ass and drive it sadly along the path to the little road. She heard him pass on the stones of the road behind her house. He was gone – gone home to the village, to sleep, to sleep with his wife, who would want to know why he was so late. He was gone in dejection.

Juliet sat late on into the night, watching the moon on the sea. The sun had opened her womb, and she was no longer free. The trouble of the open lotus blossom had come upon her, and now it was she who had not the courage to take the steps across the gully.

But at last she slept. And in the morning she felt better. Her womb seemed to have closed again: the lotus flower seemed back in bud again. She wanted so much that it should be so. Only the immersed bud, and the sun! She would never think of that man.

She bathed in one of the great tanks away down in the lemon-grove, down in the far ravine, far as possible from the other wild gully, and cool. Below, under the lemons, the child was wading among the yellow oxalis flowers of the shadow, gathering fallen lemons, passing with his tanned little body into flecks of light, moving all dappled. She sat in the sun on the steep bank in the gully, feeling almost free again, the flower drooping in shadowy bud, safe inside her.

Suddenly, high over the land's edge, against the full-lit pale blue sky, Marinina appeared, a black cloth tied round her head, calling quietly: *Signora! Signora Giulietta!*

Juliet faced round, standing up. Marinina paused a moment, seeing the naked woman standing alert, her sun-faded hair in a little cloud. Then the swift old woman came down the slant of the steep, sun-blazed track.

She stood a few steps, erect, in front of the sun-coloured woman, and eyed her shrewdly.

'But how beautiful you are, you!' she said coolly, almost cynically. 'Your husband has come.'

'What husband?' cried Juliet.

The old woman gave a shrewd bark of a little laugh, the mockery of the woman of the past.

'Haven't you got one, a husband, you?' she said, taunting.

'How? Where? In America,' said Juliet.

The old woman glanced over her shoulder, with another noiseless laugh.

'No America at all. He was following me here. He will have missed the path.' And she threw back her head in the noiseless laugh of women.

The paths were all grown high with grass and flowers and nepitella, till they were like bird-tracks in an eternally wild place. Strange, the vivid wildness of the old classic places, that have known men so long.

Juliet looked at the Sicilian woman with meditating eyes.

'Oh very well,' she said at last. 'Let him come.'

And a little flame leaped in her. It was the opening flower. At least he was a man.

'Bring him here? Now?' asked Marinina, her mocking, smoke-grey eyes looking with laughter into Juliet's eyes. Then she gave a little jerk of her shoulders.

'All right! As you wish! But for him it is a rare one!' She opened her mouth with a noiseless laugh of amusement then she pointed down to the child, who was heaping lemons against his little chest. 'Look how beautiful the child is! An angel from heaven! That certainly will please him, poor thing. Then I shall bring him?'

'Bring him,' said Juliet.

The old woman scrambled rapidly up the track again, and found Maurice at a loss among the vine terraces, standing there in his grey felt hat and dark-grey city suit. He looked pathetically out of place, in that resplendent sunshine and the grace of the old Greek world; like a blot of ink on the pale, sun-glowing slope.

'Come!' said Marinina to him. 'She is down here.'

And swiftly she led the way, striding with a long stride, marking the way through the grasses. Suddenly she stopped on the brow of the slope. The tops of the lemon trees were dark, away below.

'You, you go down here,' she said to him, and he thanked her, glancing up at her swiftly.

He was a man of forty, clean-shaven, grey-faced, very quiet and really shy. He managed his own business carefully without startling success, but efficiently. And he confided in nobody. The old woman of Magna Graecia saw him at a glance: he is good, she said to herself, but not a man, poor thing.

'Down there is the Signora,' said Marinina, pointing like one of the Fates.[11]

And again he said, 'Thank you! Thank you!' without a twinkle, and stepped carefully into the track. Marinina lifted her chin with a joyful wickedness. Then she strode off towards the house.

Maurice was watching his step, through the tangle of Mediterranean herbage, so he did not catch sight of his wife till he came round a little bend, quite near her. She was standing erect and nude by the jutting rock, glistening with the sun and with warm life. Her breasts seemed to be lifting up, alert, to listen, her thighs looked brown and fleet. Inside her, the lotus of her womb was wide open, spread almost gaping in the violet rays of the sun, like a great lotus flower. And she thrilled helplessly: a man was coming. Her glance on him, as he came gingerly, like ink on blotting-paper, was swift and nervous.

Maurice, poor fellow, hesitated and glanced away from her, turning his face aside.

'Hello, Julie!' he said, with a little nervous cough. 'Splendid! Splendid!'

He advanced with his face averted, shooting further glances at her, furtively, as she stood with the peculiar satiny gleam of the sun on her tanned skin. Somehow she did not seem so terribly naked. It was the golden-rose of the sun that clothed her.

'Hello Maurice!' she said, hanging back from him, and a cold shadow falling on the open flower of her womb. 'I wasn't expecting you so soon.'

'No,' he said. 'No! I managed to slip away a little earlier.'

And again he coughed unawares. Furtively, purposely he had taken her by surprise. They stood several yards away from one another, and there was silence. But this was a new Julie to him, with the sun-tanned, wind-stroked thighs: not that nervous New York woman.

'Well!' he said, 'er – this is splendid – splendid! You are – er – splendid! – Where is the boy?'

He felt, in his far-off depths, the desire stirring in him for the limbs and sun-wrapped flesh of the woman: the woman of flesh. It was a new desire in his life, and it hurt him. He wanted to side-track.

'There he is,' she said, pointing down to where a naked urchin in the deep shade was piling fallen lemons together.

The father gave an odd little laugh, almost neighing.

'Ah! yes! There he is! So there's the little man! Fine!' His nervous, suppressed soul was thrilling with violent thrills, he clung to the straw of his upper consciousness. 'Hello, Johnny!' he called, and it sounded rather feeble. 'Hello Johnny!'

The child looked up, spilling lemons from his chubby arms, but did not respond.

'I guess we'll go down to him,' said Juliet, as she turned and went striding down the path. In spite of herself, the cold shadow was lifting off the open flower of her womb, and every petal was thrilling again. Her husband followed, watching the rosy, fleet-looking lifting and sinking of her quick hips, as she swayed a little in the socket of her waist. He was dazed with admiration, but also at a deadly loss. He was used to her as a person. And this was no longer a person, but a fleet sun-strong body, soulless and alluring as a nymph, twinkling its haunches. What would he do with himself? He was utterly out of the picture, in his dark grey suit and pale grey hat, and his grey, monastic face of a shy business man, and his grey mercantile mentality. Strange thrills shot through his loins and his legs. He was terrified, and he felt he might give a wild whoop of triumph, and jump towards that woman of tanned flesh.

'He looks all right, doesn't he,' said Juliet, as they came through the deep sea of yellow-flowering oxalis, under the lemon-trees.

'Ah! – yes! yes! Splendid! Splendid! – Hello Johnny! Do you know Daddy? Do you know Daddy, Johnny?'

He squatted down, forgetting his trouser-crease, and held out his hands.

'Lemons!' said the child, birdily chirping. 'Two lemons!'

'Two lemons!' replied the father. 'Lots of lemons!'

The infant came and put a lemon in each of his father's open hands. Then he stood back to look.

'Two lemons!' repeated the father. 'Come, Johnny! Come and say Hello! to Daddy.'

'Daddy going back?' said the child.

'Going back? Well – well – not today.'

And he took his son in his arms.

'Take a coat off! Daddy take a coat off!' said the boy, squirming debonair away from the cloth.

'All right, son! Daddy take a coat off.'

He took off his coat and laid it carefully aside, then looked at the creases in his trousers, hitched them a little, and crouched down and took his son in his arms. The child's warm naked body against him made him feel faint. The naked woman looked down at the rosy infant in the arms of the man in his shirt-sleeves. The boy had pulled off his father's hat, and Juliet looked at the sleek black-and-grey hair of her husband, not a hair out of place. And utterly, utterly sunless! The cold shadow was over the flower of her womb again. She was silent for a long time, while the father talked to the child, who had been fond of his Daddy.

'What are you going to do about it, Maurice?' she said suddenly. He looked at her swiftly, sideways, hearing her abrupt American voice. He had forgotten her.

'Er – about what, Julie?'

'Oh, everything! About this! I can't go back into East Forty-Seventh.'

'Er –' he hesitated, 'no, I suppose not – Not just now, at least.'

'Never!' she said abruptly, and there was a silence.

'Well – er – I don't know,' he said.

'Do you think you can come out here?' she said savagely.

'Yes! – I can stay for a month. I think I can manage a month,' he hesitated. Then he ventured a complicated, shy peep at her, and turned away his face again.

She looked down at him, her alert breasts lifted with a sigh, as if she would impatiently shake the cold shadow of sunlessness off her.

'I can't go back,' she said slowly, 'I can't go back on this sun. If you can't come here –'

She ended on an open note. But the voice of the abrupt, personal American woman had died out, and he heard the voice of the woman of flesh, the sun-ripe body. He glanced at her again and again, with growing desire and lessening fear.

'No!' he said. 'This kind of thing suits you. You are splendid. – No, I don't think you can go back.'

And at the caressive sound of his voice, in spite of her, her womb-flower began to open and thrill its petals.

He was thinking visionarily of her in the New York flat, pale, silent, oppressing him terribly. He was the soul of gentle timidity in his human relations, and her silent, awful hostility after the baby was born had frightened him deeply. Because he had realized that she could not help it. Women were like that. Their feelings took a reverse direction, even against their own selves, and it was awful – devastating. Awful, awful to live in the house with a woman like that, whose feelings were reversed even against herself. He had felt himself borne down under the stream of her heavy hostility. She had ground even herself down to the quick, and the child as well. No, anything rather than that. Thank God, that menacing ghost-woman seemed to be sunned out of her now.

'But what about you?' she asked.

'I? Oh, I! – I can carry on in the business, and – er come over here for long holidays – so long as you like to stay here. You stay as long as you wish –' He looked down a long time at the earth. He was so frightened of rousing that menacing, avenging spirit of womanhood in her, he did so hope she might stay as he had seen her now, like a naked, ripening strawberry, a female like a fruit. He glanced up at her with a touch of supplication in his uneasy eyes.

'Even for ever?' she said.

'Well – er – yes, if you like. For ever is a long time. One can't set a date.'

'And can I do anything I like?' She looked him straight in the eyes, challenging. And he was powerless against her rosy, wind-hardened nakedness, in his fear of arousing that other woman in her, the personal American woman, spectral and vengeful.

'Er – yes! – I suppose so! So long as you don't make yourself unhappy – or the boy.'

Again he looked up at her with a complicated, uneasy appeal – thinking of the child, but hoping for himself.

'I won't,' she said quickly.

'No!' he said, 'No! I don't think you will.'

There was a pause. The bells of the village were hastily clanging mid-day. That meant lunch.

She slipped into her grey crêpe kimono, and fastened a broad green sash around her waist. Then she slipped a little blue shirt over the boy's head, and they went up to the house.

At table she watched her husband, his grey city face, his glued, grey-black hair, his very precise table manners, and his extreme moderation in eating and drinking. Sometimes he glanced at her furtively, from under his black lashes. He had the uneasy, gold-grey eyes of a creature that has been caught young, and reared entirely in captivity, strange and cold, knowing no warm hopes. Only his black eye-brows and eye-lashes were nice. She did not take him in. She did not realize him. Being so sunned, she could not see him, his sunlessness was like nonentity.

They went on to the balcony for coffee, under the rosy mass of the bougainvillea. Below, beyond, on the next *podere*, the peasant and his wife were sitting under the carob tree, near the tall green wheat, sitting facing one another across a little white cloth spread on the ground. There was still a huge piece of bread – but they had finished eating and sat with dark wine in their glasses.

The peasant looked up at the terrace, as soon as the American emerged. Juliet put her husband with his back to the scene. Then she sat down, and looked back at the peasant. Until she saw his dark-visaged wife turn to look too.

V

The man was hopelessly in love with her. She saw his broad, rather short red face gazing up at her fixedly: till his wife turned too to look, then he picked up his glass and tossed the wine down his throat. The wife stared long at the figures on the balcony. She was handsome and rather gloomy, and surely older than he, with that great difference that lies between a rather overwhelming, superior woman over forty, and her more irresponsible husband of thirty-five or so. It seemed like the difference of a whole generation. 'He is my generation,' thought Juliet, 'and she is Maurice's generation.' Juliet was not yet thirty.

The peasant in his white cotton trousers and pale pink shirt, and battered old straw hat, was attractive, so clean, and full of the cleanliness of health. He was stout and broad, and seemed shortish, but his flesh was full of vitality, as if he were always about to spring up into movement, to work, even, as she had seen him with the child, to play. He was the type of Italian peasant that wants to make an offering of himself, passionately wants to make an offering of himself, of his powerful flesh and thudding blood-stroke. But he was also completely a peasant, in that he would wait for the woman to make the move. He would hang round in a long, consuming passivity of desire, hoping, hoping for the woman to come for him. But he would never try to advance to her: never. She would have to make the advance. Only he would hang round, within reach.

Feeling her look at him, he flung off his old straw hat, showing his round, close-cropped brown head, and reached out with a large brown-red hand for the great loaf, from which he broke a piece and started chewing with bulging cheek. He knew she was looking at him. And she had such power over him, the hot inarticulate animal, with such a hot, massive blood-stream down his great veins! He was hot through with countless suns, and mindless as noon. And shy with a violent, farouche shyness, that would wait for her with consuming wanting, but would never, never move towards her.

With him, it would be like bathing in another kind of sunshine, heavy and big and perspiring: and afterwards one would forget. Personally, he would not exist. It would be just a bath of warm, powerful life – then separating and forgetting. Then again, the procreative bath, like sun.

But would that not be good! She was so tired of personal contacts, and having to talk with the man afterwards. With that healthy creature, one would just go satisfied away, afterwards. As she sat there, she felt the life streaming from him to her, and her to him. She knew by his movements he felt her even more than she felt him. It was almost a definite pain of consciousness in the body of each of them, and each sat as if distracted, watched by a keen-eyed spouse, possessor.

And Juliet thought: Why shouldn't I go to him! Why shouldn't I bear his child? It would be like bearing a child to the unconscious sun and the unconscious earth, a child like a fruit. – And the flower of her womb radiated. It did not care about sentiment or possession. It wanted man-dew only, utterly improvident. But her heart was clouded with fear. She dare not! She dare not! If only the man would find some way! But he would not. He would only hover and wait, hover in endless desire, waiting for her to cross the gully. And she dare not, she dare not. And he would hang round.

'You are not afraid of people seeing you when you take your sun-baths?' said her husband, turning round and looking across at the peasants. The saturnine wife over the gully, turned also to stare at the Villa. It was a kind of battle.

'No! One needn't be seen. Will you do it too? Will you take the sun-baths?' said Juliet to him.

'Why – er – yes! I think I should like to, while I am here.'

There was a gleam in his eyes, a desperate kind of courage of desire to taste this new fruit, this woman with rosy, sun-ripening breasts tilting within her wrapper. And she thought of him with his blanched, etiolated little city figure, walking in the sun in the desperation of a husband's rights. And her mind swooned again. The strange, branded little fellow, the good citizen, branded like a criminal in the naked eye of the sun. How he would hate exposing himself!

And the flower of her womb went dizzy, dizzy. She knew she would take him. She knew she would bear his child. She knew it was for him, the branded little city man, that her womb was open radiating like a lotus, like the purple spread of a daisy anemone, dark at the core. She knew she would not go across to the peasant; she had not enough courage, she was not free enough. And she knew the peasant would never come for her, he had the dogged passivity of the earth, and would wait, wait, only putting himself in her sight, again and again, lingering across her vision, with the persistency of animal yearning.

She had seen the flushed blood in the peasant's burnt face, and felt the jetting, sudden blue heat pouring over her from his kindled eyes, and the rousing of his big penis against his body – for her, surging for her. Yet she would never come to him – she daren't, she daren't, so much was against her. And the little etiolated body of her husband, city-branded, would possess her, and his little, frantic penis would beget another child in her. She could not help it. She was bound to the vast, fixed wheel of circumstance, and there was no Perseus[12] in the universe to cut the bonds.

The Rocking-Horse Winner

THERE was a woman who was beautiful, who started with all the advantages, yet she had no luck. She married for love, and the love turned to dust. She had bonny children, yet she felt they had been thrust upon her, and she could not love them. They looked at her coldly, as if they were finding fault with her. And hurriedly she felt she must cover up some fault in herself. Yet what it was that she must cover up she never knew. Nevertheless, when her children were present, she always felt the centre of her heart go hard. This troubled her, and in her manner she was all the more gentle and anxious for her children, as if she loved them very much. Only she herself knew that at the centre of her heart was a hard little place that could not feel love, no, not for anybody. Everybody else said of her: 'She is such a good mother. She adores her children.' Only she herself, and her children themselves, knew it was not so. They read it in each other's eyes.

There were a boy and two little girls. They lived in a pleasant house, with a garden, and they had discreet servants, and felt themselves superior to anyone in the neighbourhood.

Although they lived in style, they felt always an anxiety in the house. There was never enough money. The mother had a small income, and the father had a small income, but not nearly enough for the social position which they had to keep up. The father went in to town to some office. But though he had good prospects, these prospects never materialised. There was always the grinding sense of the shortage of money, though the style was always kept up.

At last the mother said, 'I will see if *I* can't make something.' But she did not know where to begin. She racked her brains, and tried this thing and the other, but could not find anything successful. The failure made deep lines come into her face. Her children were growing up, they would have to go to school. There must be more money, there must be more money. The father, who was always very handsome and expensive in his tastes, seemed as if he never *would* be able to do anything worth doing. And the mother, who had a great belief in herself, did not succeed any better, and her tastes were just as expensive.

And so the house came to be haunted by the unspoken phrase: *There must be more money! There must be more money!* The children could hear it all the time, though nobody said it aloud. They heard it at Christmas, when the expensive and splendid toys filled the nursery. Behind the shining modern rocking-horse, behind the smart doll's-house, a voice would start whispering: 'There *must* be more money! There *must* be more money!' And the children would stop playing, to listen for a moment. They would look into each other's eyes, to see if they had all heard. And each one saw in the eyes of the other two that they too had heard. 'There *must* be more money! There *must* be more money!'

It came whispering from the springs of the still-swaying rocking-horse, and even the horse, bending his wooden, champing head, heard it. The big doll, sitting so pink and smirking in her new pram, could hear it quite plainly, and seemed to be smirking all the more self-consciously because of it. The foolish puppy, too, that took the place of the teddy-bear, he was looking so extraordinarily foolish for no other reason but that he heard the secret whisper all over the house: 'There *must* be more money.'

Yet nobody ever said it aloud. The whisper was everywhere, and therefore no one spoke it. Just as no one ever says: 'We are breathing!' in spite of the fact that breath is coming and going all the time.

'Mother!' said the boy Paul one day. 'Why don't we keep a car of our own? Why do we always use uncle's, or else a taxi?'

'Because we're the poor members of the family,' said the mother.

'But why *are* we, mother?'

'Well – I suppose,' she said slowly and bitterly, 'it's because your father has no luck.'

The boy was silent for some time.

'Is luck money, mother?' he asked, rather timidly.

'No, Paul! Not quite. It's what causes you to have money.'

'Oh!' said Paul vaguely. 'I thought when Uncle Oscar said *filthy lucker*, it meant money.'

'*Filthy lucre* does mean money,' said the mother. 'But it's lucre, not luck.'

'Oh!' said the boy. 'Then what *is* luck, mother?'

'It's what causes you to have money. If you're lucky you have money. That's why it's better to be born lucky than rich. If you're rich, you may lose your money. But if you're lucky, you will always get more money.'

'Oh! Will you! And is father not lucky?'

'Very unlucky, I should say,' she said bitterly.

The boy watched her with unsure eyes.

'Why?' he asked.

'I don't know. Nobody ever knows why one person is lucky and another unlucky.'

'Don't they? Nobody at all? Does *nobody* know?'

'Perhaps God! But He never tells.'

'He ought to, then. And aren't you lucky either, mother?'

'I can't be, if I married an unlucky husband.'

'But by yourself, aren't you?'

'I used to think I was, before I married. Now I think I am very unlucky indeed.'

'Why?'

'Well – never mind! Perhaps I'm not really,' she said.

The child looked at her, to see if she meant it. But he saw, by the lines of her mouth, that she was only trying to hide something from him.

'Well, anyhow,' he said stoutly, 'I'm a lucky person.'

'Why?' said his mother, with a sudden laugh.

He stared at her. He didn't even know why he had said it.

'God told me,' he asserted, brazening it out.

'I hope He did, dear!' she said, again with a laugh, but rather bitter.

'He did, mother!'

'Excellent!' said the mother, using one of her husband's exclamations.

The boy saw she did not believe him; or rather, that she paid no attention to his assertion. This angered him somewhere, and made him want to compel her attention.

He went off by himself, vaguely, in a childish way, seeking for the clue to 'luck'. Absorbed, taking no heed of other people, he went about with a sort of stealth, seeking inwardly for luck. He wanted luck, he wanted it, he wanted it. When the two girls were playing dolls, in the nursery, he would sit on his big rocking-horse, charging madly into space, with a frenzy that made the little girls peer at him uneasily. Wildly the horse careered, the waving dark hair of the boy tossed, his eyes had a strange glare in them. The little girls dared not speak to him.

When he had ridden to the end of his mad little journey, he climbed down and stood in front of his rocking-horse, staring fixedly into its lowered face. Its red mouth was slightly open, its big eye was wide and glassy bright.

'Now!' he would silently command the snorting steed. 'Now take me to where there is luck! Now take me!'

And he would slash the horse on the neck with the little whip he had asked Uncle Oscar for. He *knew* the horse could take him to where there was luck, if only he forced it. So he would mount again, and start on his furious ride, hoping at last to get there. He knew he could get there.

'You'll break your horse, Paul!' said the nurse.

'He's always riding like that! I wish he'd leave off!' said his elder sister Joan.

But he only glared down on them in silence. Nurse gave him up. She could make nothing of him. Anyhow he was growing beyond her.

One day his mother and his Uncle Oscar came in when he was on one of his furious rides. He did not speak to them.

'Hallo! you young jockey! Riding a winner?' said his uncle.

'Aren't you growing too big for a rocking-horse? You're not a very little boy any longer, you know,' said his mother.

But Paul only gave a blue glare from his big, rather close-set eyes. He would speak to nobody when he was in full tilt. His mother watched him with an anxious expression on her face.

At last he suddenly stopped forcing his horse into the mechanical gallop, and slid down.

'Well, I got there!' he announced fiercely, his blue eyes still flaring, and his sturdy long legs straddling apart.

'Where did you get to?' asked his mother.

'Where I wanted to go to,' he flared back at her.

'That's right, son!' said Uncle Oscar. 'Don't you stop till you get there. What's the horse's name?'

'He doesn't have a name,' said the boy.

'Gets on without all right?' asked the uncle.

'Well, he has different names. He was called Sansovino last week.'

'Sansovino, eh? Won the Ascot. How did you know his name?'

'He always talks about horse-races with Bassett,' said Joan.

The uncle was delighted to find that his small nephew was posted with all the racing news. Bassett, the young gardener who had been wounded in the left foot in the war, and had got his present job through Oscar Cresswell, whose batman he had been, was a perfect blade of the 'turf'. He lived in the racing events, and the small boy lived with him.

Oscar Cresswell got it all from Bassett.

'Master Paul comes and asks me, so I can't do more than tell him, sir,' said Bassett, his face terribly serious, as if he were speaking of religious matters.

'And does he ever put anything on a horse he fancies?'

'Well – I don't want to give him away – he's a young sport, a fine sport, sir. Would you mind asking him himself? He sort of takes a pleasure in it, and perhaps he'd feel I was giving him away, sir, if you don't mind.'

Bassett was serious as a church.

The uncle went back to his nephew, and took him off for a ride in the car.

'Say, Paul, old man, do you ever put anything on a horse?' the uncle asked.

The boy watched the handsome man closely.

'Why, do you think I oughtn't to?' he parried.

'Not a bit of it! I thought perhaps you might give me a tip for the Lincoln.'

The car sped on into the country, going down to Uncle Oscar's place in Hampshire.

'Honour bright?' said the nephew.

'Honour bright, son!' said the uncle.

'Well, then, Daffodil.'

'Daffodil! I doubt it, sonny. What about Mirza?'

'I only know the winner,' said the boy. 'That's Daffodil!'

'Daffodil, eh?'

There was a pause. Daffodil was an obscure horse comparatively.

'Uncle!'

'Yes, son?'

'You won't let it go any further, will you? I promised Bassett.'

'Bassett be damned, old man! What's he got to do with it?'

'We're partners! We've been partners from the first! Uncle, he lent me my first five shillings, which I lost. I promised him, honour bright, it was only between me and him: only you gave me that ten-shilling note I started winning with, so I thought you were lucky. You won't let it go any further, will you?'

The boy gazed at his uncle from those big, hot, blue eyes, set rather close together. The uncle stirred and laughed uneasily.

'Right you are, son! I'll keep your tip private. Daffodil, eh! How much are you putting on him?'

'All except twenty pounds,' said the boy. 'I keep that in reserve.'

The uncle thought it a good joke.

'You keep twenty pounds in reserve, do you, you young romancer? What are you betting, then?'

'I'm betting three hundred,' said the boy gravely. 'But it's between you and me, Uncle Oscar! Honour bright?'

The uncle burst into a roar of laughter.

'It's between you and me all right, you young Nat Gould,'[1] he said, laughing. 'But where's your three hundred?'

'Bassett keeps it for me. We're partners.'

'You are, are you! And what is Bassett putting on Daffodil?'

'He won't go quite as high as I do, I expect. Perhaps he'll go a hundred and fifty.'

'What, pennies?' laughed the uncle.

'Pounds,' said the child, with a surprised look at his uncle. 'Bassett keeps a bigger reserve than I do.'

Between wonder and amusement, Uncle Oscar was silent. He pursued the matter no further, but he determined to take his nephew with him to the Lincoln races.

'Now, son,' he said, 'I'm putting twenty on Mirza, and I'll put five for you on any horse you fancy. What's your pick?'

'Daffodil, uncle!'

'No, not the fiver on Daffodil!'

'I should if it was my own fiver,' said the child.

'Good! Good! Right you are! A fiver for me and a fiver for you on Daffodil.'

The child had never been to a race-meeting before, and his eyes were blue fire. He pursed his mouth tight, and watched. A Frenchman just in front had put his money on Lancelot. Wild with excitement, he flayed his arms up and down, yelling '*Lancelot! Lancelot!*' in his French accent.

Daffodil came in first, Lancelot second, Mirza third. The child, flushed and with eyes blazing, was curiously serene. His uncle brought him five five-pound notes: four to one.

'What am I to do with these?' he cried, waving them before the boy's eyes.

'I suppose we'll talk to Bassett,' said the boy. 'I expect I have fifteen hundred now: and twenty in reserve: and this twenty.'

His uncle studied him for some moments.

'Look here, son!' he said. 'You're not serious about Bassett and that fifteen hundred, are you?'

'Yes, I am. But it's between you and me, uncle! Honour bright!'

'Honour bright all right, son! But I must talk to Bassett.'

'If you'd like to be a partner, uncle, with Bassett and me, we could all be partners. Only you'd have to promise, honour bright, uncle, not to let it go beyond us three. Bassett and I are lucky, and you must be lucky, because it was your ten shillings I started winning with . . .'

Uncle Oscar took both Bassett and Paul into Richmond Park for an afternoon, and there they talked.

'It's like this, you see, sir,' Bassett said. 'Master Paul would get me talking about racing events, spinning yarns, you know, sir. And he was always keen on knowing if I'd made or if I'd lost. It's about a year since, now, that I put five shillings on Blush of Dawn for him: and we lost. Then the luck turned, with that ten shillings he had from you: that we put on Singhalese. And since that time, it's been pretty steady, all things considering. What do you say, Master Paul?'

'We're all right when we're *sure*,' said Paul. 'It's when we're not quite sure that we go down.'

'Oh, but we're careful then,' said Bassett.

'But when are you *sure*?' smiled Uncle Oscar.

'It's Master Paul, sir,' said Bassett, in a secret, religious voice. 'It's as if he had it from heaven. Like Daffodil now, for the Lincoln. That was as sure as eggs.'

'Did you put anything on Daffodil?' asked Oscar Cresswell.

'Yes, sir. I made my bit.'

'And my nephew?'

Bassett was obstinately silent, looking at Paul.

'I made twelve hundred, didn't I, Bassett? I told uncle I was putting three hundred on Daffodil.'

'That's right,' said Bassett, nodding.

'But where's the money?' asked the uncle.

'I keep it safe locked up, sir. Master Paul, he can have it any minute he likes to ask for it.'

'What, fifteen hundred pounds?'

'And twenty! And *forty*, that is, with the twenty he made on the course.'

'It's amazing!' said the uncle.

'If Master Paul offers you to be partners, sir, I would, if I were you: if you'll excuse me,' said Bassett.

Oscar Cresswell thought about it.

'I'll see the money,' he said.

They drove home again, and sure enough, Bassett came round to the garden-house with fifteen hundred pounds in notes. The twenty pounds reserve was left with Joe Glee, in the Turf Commission[2] deposit.

'You see, it's all right, uncle, when I'm *sure*! Then we go strong, for all we're worth. Don't we, Bassett?'

'We do that, Master Paul.'

'And when are you sure?' said the uncle, laughing.

'Oh, well, sometimes I'm *absolutely* sure, like about Daffodil,' said the boy; 'and sometimes I have an idea; and sometimes I haven't even an idea, have I, Bassett? Then we're careful, because we mostly go down.'

'You do, do you! And when you're sure, like about Daffodil, what makes you sure, sonny?'

'Oh, well, I don't know,' said the boy uneasily. 'I'm sure, you know, uncle; that's all.'

'It's as if he had it from heaven, sir,' Bassett reiterated.

'I should say so!' said the uncle.

But he became a partner. And when the Leger was coming on, Paul was 'sure' about Lively Spark, which was a quite inconsiderable horse. The boy insisted on putting a thousand on the horse, Bassett went for five hundred, and Oscar Cresswell two hundred. Lively Spark came in first, and the betting had been ten to one against him. Paul had made ten thousand.

'You see,' he said, 'I was absolutely sure of him.'

Even Oscar Cresswell had cleared two thousand.

'Look here, son,' he said, 'this sort of thing makes me nervous.'

'It needn't, uncle! Perhaps I shan't be sure again for a long time.'

'But what are you going to do with your money?' asked the uncle.

'Of course,' said the boy, 'I started it for mother. She said she had no luck, because father is unlucky, so I thought if *I* was lucky, it might stop whispering.'

'What might stop whispering?'

'Our house! I *hate* our house for whispering.'

'What does it whisper?'

'Why – why' – the boy fidgeted – 'why, I don't know! But it's always short of money, you know, uncle.'

'I know it, son, I know it.'

'You know people send mother writs, don't you, uncle?'

'I'm afraid I do,' said the uncle.

'And then the house whispers like people laughing at you behind your back. It's awful, that is! I thought if I was lucky –'

'You might stop it,' added the uncle.

The boy watched him with big blue eyes, that had an uncanny cold fire in them, and he said never a word.

'Well then!' said the uncle. 'What are we doing?'

'I shouldn't like mother to know I was lucky,' said the boy.

'Why not, son?'

'She'd stop me.'

'I don't think she would.'

'Oh!' – and the boy writhed in an odd way – 'I *don't* want her to know, uncle.'

'All right, son! We'll manage it without her knowing.'

They managed it very easily. Paul, at the other's suggestion, handed over five thousand pounds to his uncle, who deposited it with the family lawyer, who was then to inform Paul's mother that a relative had put five thousand pounds into his hands, which sum was to be paid out a thousand pounds at a time, on the mother's birthday, for the next five years.

'So she'll have a birthday present of a thousand pounds for five successive years,' said Uncle Oscar. 'I hope it won't make it all the harder for her later.'

Paul's mother had her birthday in November. The house had been 'whispering' worse than ever lately, and even in spite of his luck, Paul could not bear up against it. He was very anxious to see the effect of the birthday letter, telling his mother about the thousand pounds.

When there were no visitors, Paul now took his meals with his parents, as he was beyond the nursery control. His mother went into town nearly every day. She had discovered that she had an odd knack of sketching furs and dress materials, so she worked secretly in the studio of a friend who was the chief 'artist' for the leading drapers. She drew the figures of ladies in furs and ladies in silk and sequins for the newspaper advertisements. This young woman artist earned several thousand pounds a year, but Paul's mother only made several hundreds, and she was again dissatisfied. She so wanted to be first in something, and she did not succeed, even in making sketches for drapery advertisements.

She was down to breakfast on the morning of her birthday. Paul watched her face as she read her letters. He knew the lawyer's letter. As his mother read it, her face hardened and became more expressionless. Then a cold, determined look came on her mouth. She hid the letter under the pile of others, and said not a word about it.

'Didn't you have anything nice in the post for your birthday, mother?' said Paul.

'Quite moderately nice,' she said, her voice cold and absent.

She went away to town without saying more.

But in the afternoon Uncle Oscar appeared. He said Paul's mother had had a long interview with the lawyer, asking if the whole five thousand could not be advanced at once, as she was in debt.

'What do you think, uncle?' said the boy.

'I leave it to you, son.'

'Oh, let her have it, then! We can get some more with the other,' said the boy.

'A bird in the hand is worth two in the bush, laddie!' said Uncle Oscar.

'But I'm sure to *know* for the Grand National; or the Lincolnshire; or else the Derby. I'm sure to know for *one* of them,' said Paul.

So Uncle Oscar signed the agreement, and Paul's mother touched the whole five thousand. Then something very curious happened. The voices in the house suddenly went mad, like a chorus of frogs on a spring evening. There were certain new furnishings, and Paul had a tutor. He was *really* going to Eton, his father's school, in the following autumn. There were flowers in the winter, and a blossoming of the luxury Paul's mother had been used to. And yet the voices in the house, behind the sprays of mimosa and almond-blossom, and from under the piles of iridescent cushions, simply trilled and screamed in a sort of ecstasy: 'There *must* be more money! Oh-h-h! There *must* be more money! Oh, now, now-w! now-w-w – there *must* be more money! – more than ever! More than ever!'

It frightened Paul terribly. He studied away at his Latin and Greek with his tutors. But his intense hours were spent with Bassett. The Grand National had gone by: he had not 'known', and had lost a hundred pounds. Summer was at hand. He was in agony for the Lincoln. But even for the Lincoln he didn't 'know', and he lost fifty pounds. He became wild-eyed and strange, as if something were going to explode in him.

'Let it alone, son! Don't you bother about it!' urged Uncle Oscar. But it was as if the boy couldn't really hear what his uncle was saying.

'I've got to know for the Derby! I've *got* to know for the Derby!' the child reiterated, his big blue eyes blazing with a sort of madness.

His mother noticed how overwrought he was.

'You'd better go to the seaside. Wouldn't you like to go now to the seaside, instead of waiting? I think you'd better,' she said, looking down at him anxiously, her heart curiously heavy because of him.

But the child lifted his uncanny blue eyes.

'I couldn't possibly go before the Derby, mother!' he said. 'I couldn't possibly!'

'Why not?' she said, her voice becoming heavy when she was opposed. 'Why not? You can still go from the seaside to see the Derby with your Uncle Oscar, if that's what you wish. No need for you to wait here. Besides, I think you care too much about these races. It's a bad sign. My family has been a gambling family, and you won't know till you grow up how much damage it has done. But it has done damage. I shall have to send Bassett away, and ask Uncle Oscar not to talk racing to you, unless you promise to be reasonable about it: go away to the seaside and forget it. You're all nerves!'

'I'll do what you like, mother, so long as you don't send me away till after the Derby,' the boy said.

'Send you away from where? Just from this house?'

'Yes,' he said, gazing at her.

'Why, you curious child, what makes you care about this house so much, suddenly? I never knew you loved it!'

He gazed at her without speaking. He had a secret within a secret, something he had not divulged, even to Bassett or to his Uncle Oscar.

But his mother, after standing undecided and a little bit sullen for some moments, said:

'Very well, then! Don't go to the seaside till after the Derby, if you don't wish it. But promise me you won't let your nerves go to pieces! Promise you won't think so much about horse-racing and *events*, as you call them!'

'Oh no!' said the boy, casually. 'I won't think much about them, mother. You needn't worry. I wouldn't worry, mother, if I were you.'

'If you were me and I were you,' said his mother, 'I wonder what we *should* do!'

'But you know you needn't worry, mother, don't you?' the boy repeated.

'I should be awfully glad to know it,' she said wearily.

'Oh, well, you *can*, you know. I mean you *ought* to know you needn't worry!' he insisted.

'Ought I? Then I'll see about it,' she said.

Paul's secret of secrets was his wooden horse, that which had no name. Since he was emancipated from a nurse and a nursery governess, he had had his rocking-horse removed to his own bedroom at the top of the house.

'Surely you're too big for a rocking-horse!' his mother had remonstrated.

'Well, you see, mother, till I can have a *real* horse, I like to have *some* sort of animal about,' had been his quaint answer.

'Do you feel he keeps you company?' she laughed.

'Oh yes! He's very good, he always keeps me company, when I'm there,' said Paul.

So the horse, rather shabby, stood in an arrested prance in the boy's bedroom.

The Derby was drawing near, and the boy grew more and more tense. He hardly heard what was spoken to him, he was very frail, and his eyes were really uncanny. His mother had sudden strange seizures of uneasiness about him. Sometimes, for half an hour, she would feel a sudden anxiety about him that was almost anguish. She wanted to rush to him at once, and know he was safe.

Two nights before the Derby, she was at a big party in town, when one of her rushes of anxiety about her boy, her first-born, gripped her heart till she could hardly speak. She fought with the feeling, might and main, for she believed in common-sense. But it was too strong. She had to leave the dance and go downstairs to telephone to the country. The children's nursery governess was terribly surprised and startled at being rung up in the night.

'Are the children all right, Miss Wilmot?'

'Oh yes, they are quite all right.'

'Master Paul? Is he all right?'

'He went to bed as right as a trivet.[3] Shall I run up and look at him?'

'No!' said Paul's mother reluctantly. 'No! Don't trouble. It's all right. Don't sit up. We shall be home fairly soon.' She did not want her son's privacy intruded upon.

'Very good,' said the governess.

It was about one o'clock when Paul's mother and father drove up to their house. All was still. Paul's mother went to her room and slipped off her white fur cloak. She had told her maid not to wait up for her. She heard her husband downstairs, mixing a whisky-and-soda.

And then, because of the strange anxiety at her heart, she stole upstairs to her son's room. Noiselessly she went along the upper corridor. Was there a faint noise? What was it?

She stood, with arrested muscles, outside his door, listening. There was a strange, heavy, and yet not loud noise. Her heart stood still. It was a soundless noise, yet rushing and powerful. Something huge, in violent, hushed motion. What was it? What in God's Name was it? She ought to know. She felt that she *knew* the noise. She knew what it was.

Yet she could not place it. She couldn't say what it was. And on and on it went, like a madness.

Softly, frozen with anxiety and fear, she turned the door-handle.

The room was dark. Yet in the space near the window, she heard and saw something plunging to and fro. She gazed in fear and amazement.

Then suddenly she switched on the light, and saw her son, in his green pyjamas, madly surging on his rocking-horse. The blaze of light suddenly lit him up, as he urged the wooden horse, and lit her up, as she stood, blonde, in her dress of pale green and crystal, in the doorway.

'Paul!' she cried. 'Whatever are you doing?'

'It's Malabar!' he screamed, in a powerful, strange voice. 'It's Malabar!'

His eyes blazed at her for one strange and senseless second, as he ceased urging his wooden horse. Then he fell with a crash to the ground, and she, all her tormented motherhood flooding upon her, rushed to gather him up.

But he was unconscious, and unconscious he remained, with some brain-fever. He talked and tossed, and his mother sat stonily by his side.

'Malabar! It's Malabar! Bassett, Bassett, I *know*: it's Malabar!'

So the child cried, trying to get up and urge the rocking-horse that gave him his inspiration.

'What does he mean by Malabar?' asked the heart-frozen mother.

'I don't know,' said the father, stonily.

'What does he mean by Malabar?' she asked her brother Oscar.

'It's one of the horses running for the Derby,' was the answer.

And, in spite of himself, Oscar Cresswell spoke to Bassett, and himself put a thousand on Malabar: at fourteen to one.

The third day of the illness was critical: they were watching for a change. The boy, with his rather long, curly hair, was tossing ceaselessly on the pillow. He neither slept nor regained consciousness, and his eyes were like blue stones. His mother sat, feeling her heart had gone, turned actually into a stone.

In the evening, Oscar Cresswell did not come, but Bassett sent a message, saying could he come up for one moment, just one moment? Paul's mother was very angry at the intrusion, but on second thoughts she agreed. The boy was the same. Perhaps Bassett might bring him to consciousness.

The gardener, a shortish fellow with a little brown moustache and sharp little brown eyes, tiptoed into the room, touched his imaginary cap to Paul's mother, and stole to the bedside, staring with glittering, smallish eyes at the tossing, dying child.

'Master Paul!' he whispered. 'Master Paul! Malabar came in first all right, a clean win. I did as you told me. You've made over seventy thousand pounds, you have; you've got over eighty thousand. Malabar came in all right, Master Paul.'

'Malabar! Malabar! Did I say Malabar, mother? Did I say Malabar? Do you think I'm lucky, mother? I knew Malabar, didn't I? Over eighty thousand pounds! I call that lucky, don't you, mother? Over eighty thousand pounds! I knew, didn't I know I knew? Malabar came in all right. If I ride my horse till I'm sure, then I tell you, Bassett, you can go as high as you like. Did you go for all you were worth, Bassett?'

'I went a thousand on it, Master Paul.'

'I never told you, mother, that if I can ride my horse, and *get there*, then I'm absolutely sure – oh, absolutely! Mother, did I ever tell you? I *am* lucky!'

'No, you never did,' said the mother.

But the boy died in the night.

And even as he lay dead, his mother heard her brother's voice saying to her: 'My God, Hester, you're eighty-odd thousand to the good, and a poor devil of a son to the bad. But, poor devil, poor devil, he's best gone out of a life where he rides his rocking-horse to find a winner.'

The Man Who Loved Islands

FIRST ISLAND

THERE was a man who loved islands. He was born on one, but it didn't suit him, as there were too many other people on it, besides himself. He wanted an island all of his own: not necessarily to be alone on it, but to make it a world of his own.

An island, if it is big enough, is no better than a continent. It has to be really quite small, before it *feels like* an island; and this story will show how tiny it has to be, before you can presume to fill it with your own personality.

Now circumstances so worked out, that this lover of islands, by the time he was thirty-five, actually acquired an island of his own. He didn't own it as freehold property, but he had a ninety-nine years' lease of it, which, as far as a man and an island are concerned, is as good as everlasting. Since, if you are like Abraham, and want your offspring to be numberless as the sands of the sea-shore,[1] you don't choose an island to start breeding on. Too soon there would be overpopulation, overcrowding, and slum conditions. Which is a horrid thought, for one who loves an island for its insulation. No, an island is a nest which holds one egg, and one only. This egg is the islander himself.

The island acquired by our potential islander was not in the remote oceans. It was quite near at home, no palm-trees nor boom of surf on the reef, nor any of that kind of thing; but a good solid dwelling-house, rather gloomy, above the landing-place, and beyond, a small farm-house with sheds, and a few outlying fields. Down on the little landing bay were three cottages in a row, like coastguards' cottages, all neat and white-washed.

What could be more cozy and home-like? It was four miles if you walked all round your island, through the gorse and the blackthorn bushes, above the steep rocks of the sea and down in the little glades where the primroses grew. If you walked straight over the two humps of hills, the length of it, through the rocky fields where the cows lay chewing, and through the rather sparse oats, on into the gorse again, and so to the low cliffs' edge, it took you only twenty minutes. And when you came to the edge, you could see another, bigger island lying beyond. But the sea was between you and it. And as you returned over the turf where the short, downland cowslips nodded you saw to the east still another island, a tiny one this time, like the calf of the cow. This tiny island also belonged to the islander.

Thus it seems that even islands like to keep each other company.

Our islander loved his island very much. In early spring, the little ways and glades were a snow of blackthorn, a vivid white among the celtic stillness of close green and grey rock, blackbirds calling out in the whiteness their first long, triumphant calls. After the blackthorn and the nestling primroses came the blue apparition of hyacinths, like elfin lakes and slipping sheets of blue, among the bushes and under the glade of trees. And many birds with nests you could peep into, on the island all your own. Wonderful what a great world it was!

Followed summer, and the cowslips gone, the wild roses faintly fragrant through the haze. There was a field of hay, the foxgloves stood looking down. In a little cove, the sun was on the pale granite where you bathed, and the shadow was in the rocks. Before the mist came stealing, and you went home through the ripening oats, the glare of the sea fading from the high air as the foghorn started to moo on the other island. And then the sea-fog went, it was autumn, and oat-sheaves lying prone; the great moon, another island, rose golden out of the sea, and, rising higher, the world of the sea was white.

So autumn ended with rain, and winter came, dark skies and dampness and rain, but rarely frost. The island, your island, cowered dark, holding away from you. You could feel, down in the wet, sombre hollows, the resentful spirit coiled upon itself, like a wet dog coiled in gloom, or a snake that is neither asleep nor awake. Then in the night, when the wind left off blowing in great gusts and volleys, as at sea, you felt that your island was a universe, infinite and old as the darkness; not an island at all, but an infinite dark world where all the souls from all the other bygone nights lived on, and the infinite distance was near.

Strangely, from your little island in space, you were gone forth into the dark, great realms of time, where all the souls that never die veer and swoop on their vast, strange errands. The little earthly island has dwindled, like a jumping-off place, into nothingness, for you have jumped off, you know not how, into the dark wide mystery of time, where the past is vastly alive, and the future is not separated off.

This is the danger of becoming an islander. When, in the city, you wear your white spats and dodge the traffic with the fear of death down your spine, then you are quite safe from the terrors of infinite time.

The moment is your little islet in time, it is the spatial universe that careers round you.

But once isolate yourself on a little island in the sea of space, and the moment begins to heave and expand in great circles, the solid earth is gone, and your slippery, naked dark soul finds herself out in the timeless world, where the chariots of the so-called dead dash down the old streets of centuries, and souls crowd on the footways that we, in the moment, call bygone years. The souls of all the dead are alive again, and pulsating actively around you. You are out in the other infinity.

Something of this happened to our islander. Mysterious 'feelings' came upon him, that he wasn't used to; strange awarenesses of old, far-gone men, and other influences; men of Gaul,[2] with big moustaches, who had been on his island, and had vanished from the face of it, but not out of the air of night. They were there still, hurtling their big, violent, unseen bodies through the night. And there were priests, with golden knives and mistletoe; then other priests with a crucifix;[3] then pirates with murder on the sea.

Our islander was uneasy. He didn't believe, in the daytime, in any of this nonsense. But at night it just was so. He had reduced himself to a single point in space, and, a point being that which has neither length nor breadth, he had to step off it into somewhere else. Just as you must step into the sea, if the waters wash your foothold away, so he had, at night, to step off into the otherworld of undying time.

He was uncannily aware, as he lay in the dark, that the blackthorn grove that seemed a bit uncanny even in the realm of space and day, at night was crying with old men of an invisible race, around the altar stone. What was a ruin under the hornbeam trees by day, was a moaning of bloodstained priests with crucifixes, on the ineffable night. What was a cave and hidden beach between coarse rocks, became in the invisible dark the purple-lipped imprecation of pirates.

To escape any more of this sort of awareness, our islander daily concentrated upon his material island. Why should it not be the Happy Isle at last? Why not the last small isle of the Hesperides,[4] the perfect place, all filled with his own gracious, blossom-like spirit? A minute world of pure perfection, made by man, himself.

He began, as we begin all our attempts to regain Paradise, by spending money. The old, semi-feudal dwelling-house he restored, let in more light, put clear lovely carpets on the floor, clear, flower-petal curtains at the sullen windows, and wines in the cellars of rock. He brought over a buxom housekeeper from the world, and a soft-spoken, much-experienced butler. These too were to be islanders.

In the farm-house he put a bailiff, with two farm-hands. There were Jersey cows, tinkling a slow bell, among the gorse. There was a call to meals at midday, and the peaceful smoking of chimneys at evening, when rest descended.

A jaunty sailing-boat with a motor accessory rode in the shelter in the bay, just below the row of three white cottages. There was also a little yawl, and two row-boats drawn up on the sand. A fishing net was drying on its supports, a boat-load of new white planks stood criss-cross, a woman was going to the well with a bucket.

In the end cottage lived the skipper of the yacht, and his wife and son. He was a man from the other, large island, at home on this sea. Every fine day he went out fishing, with his son, every fine day there was fresh fish on the island.

In the middle cottage lived an old man and wife, a very faithful couple. The old man was a carpenter, and man of many jobs. He was always working, always the sound of his plane or his saw: lost in his work, he was another kind of islander.

In the third cottage was the mason, a widower with a son and two daughters. With the help of his boy, this man dug ditches and built fences, raised buttresses and erected a new outbuilding, and hewed stone from the little quarry. His daughters worked at the big house.

It was a quiet, busy little world. When the islander brought you over as his guest, you met first the dark-bearded, thin, smiling skipper, Arnold, then his boy Charles. At the house, the smooth-lipped butler who had lived all over the world valeted you, and created that curious creamy-smooth, disarming sense of luxury around you which only a perfect and rather untrustworthy servant can create. He disarmed you and had you at his mercy. The buxom housekeeper smiled and treated you with the subtly respectful familiarity, that is only dealt out to the true gentry. And the rosy maid threw a glance at you, as if you were very wonderful, coming from the great outer world. Then you met the smiling but watchful bailiff, who came from Cornwall, and the shy farm-hand from Berkshire, with his clean wife and two little children, then the rather sulky farm-hand from Suffolk. The mason, a Kent man, would talk to you by the yard, if you let him. Only the old carpenter was gruff and elsewhere absorbed.

Well then, it was a little world to itself, and everybody feeling very safe, and being very nice to you, as if you were really something special. But it was the islander's world, not yours. He was the Master. The special smile, the special attention was to the Master. They all knew how well off they were. So the islander was no longer Mr So-

and-So. To everyone on the island, even to you yourself, he was 'the Master'.

Well, it was ideal. The Master was no tyrant. Ah no! He was a delicate, sensitive, handsome Master, who wanted everything perfect and everybody happy. Himself, of course, to be the fount of this happiness and perfection.

But in his way, he was a poet. He treated his guests royally, his servants liberally. Yet he was shrewd, and very wise. He never came the boss over his people. Yet he kept his eye on everything, like a shrewd, blue-eyed young Hermes.[5] And it was amazing what a lot of knowledge he had at hand. Amazing what he knew about Jersey cows, and cheese-making, ditching and fencing, flowers and gardening, ships and the sailing of ships. He was a fount of knowledge about everything, and this knowledge he imparted to his people in an odd, half-ironical, half-portentous fashion, as if he really belonged to the quaint, half-real world of the gods.

They listened to him with their hats in their hands. He loved white clothes; or creamy white; and cloaks, and broad hats. So, in fine weather, the bailiff would see the elegant tall figure in creamy-white serge coming like some bird over the fallow, to look at the weeding of the turnips. Then there would be a doffing of hats, and a few minutes of whimsical, shrewd, wise talk, to which the bailiff answered admiringly, and the farm-hands listened in silent wonder, leaning on their hoes. The bailiff was almost tender, to the Master.

Or, on a windy morning, he would stand with his cloak blowing in the sticky sea-wind, on the edge of the ditch that was being dug to drain a little swamp, talking in the teeth of the wind to the man below, who looked up at him with steady and inscrutable eyes.

Or at evening in the rain he would be seen hurrying across the yard, the broad hat turned against the rain. And the farm-wife would hurriedly exclaim: 'The Master! Get up, John, and clear him a place on the sofa.' And then the door opened, and it was a cry of: 'Why of all things, if it isn't the Master! Why, have ye turned out then of a night like this, to come across to the like of we?' And the bailiff took his cloak, and the farm-wife his hat, the two farm-hands drew their chairs to the back, he sat on the sofa and took a child up near him. He was wonderful with children, talked to them simply wonderful, made you think of Our Saviour Himself, said the woman.

Always he was greeted with smiles, and the same peculiar deference, as if he were a higher, but also frailer being. They handled him almost tenderly, and almost with adulation. But when he left, or when they spoke of him, they had often a subtle, mocking smile on their faces. There was no need to be afraid of 'the Master'. Just let him have his own way. Only the old carpenter was sometimes sincerely rude to him; so he didn't care for the old man.

It is doubtful whether any of them really liked him, man to man, or even woman to man. But then it is doubtful if he really liked any of them, as man to man, or man to woman. He wanted them to be happy, and the little world to be perfect. But any one who wants the world to be perfect must be careful not to have real likes and dislikes. A general good-will is all you can afford.

The sad fact is, alas, that general good-will is always felt as something of an insult, by the mere object of it; and so it breeds a quite special brand of malice. Surely general good-will is a form of egoism, that it should have such a result!

Our islander, however, had his own resources. He spent long hours in his library, for he was compiling a book of reference to all the flowers mentioned in the Greek and Latin authors. He was not a great classical scholar: the usual public-school equipment. But there are such excellent translations nowadays. And it was so lovely, tracing flower after flower as it blossomed in the ancient world.

So the first year on the island passed by. A great deal had been done. Now the bills flooded in, and the Master, conscientious in all things, began to study them. The study left him pale and breathless. He was not a rich man. He knew he had been making a hole in his capital, to get the island into running order. When he came to look, however, there was hardly anything left but hole. Thousands and thousands of pounds had the island swallowed into nothingness.

But surely the bulk of the spending was over! Surely the island would now begin to be self-supporting, even if it made no profit! Surely he was safe. He paid a good many of the bills, and took a little heart. But he had had a shock, and the next year, the coming year, there must be economy, frugality. He told his people so, in simple and touching language. And they said: 'Why surely! Surely!'

So, while the wind blew and the rain lashed outside, he would sit in his library with the bailiff over a pipe and a pot of beer, discussing farm projects. He lifted his narrow handsome face, and his blue eye became dreamy. '*What* a wind!' It blew like cannon shots. He thought of his island, lashed with foam, and inaccessible, and he exulted ... No, he must not lose it. He turned back to the farm projects with the zest of genius, and his hands flicked white emphasis, while the bailiff intoned: 'Yes, Sir! Yes, Sir! You're right, Master!'

But the man was hardly listening. He was looking at the Master's blue lawn shirt and curious pink tie with the fiery red stone, at the enamel sleeve-links, and at the ring with the peculiar scarab. The brown searching eyes of the man of the soil glanced repeatedly over the fine, immaculate figure of the Master, with a sort of slow, calculating wonder. But if he happened to catch the Master's bright, exalted glance, his own eye lit up with a careful cordiality and deference, as he bowed his head slightly.

Thus between them they decided what crops should be sown, what fertilizers should be used in different places, which breed of pigs should be imported, and which line of turkeys. That is to say, the bailiff, by continually cautiously agreeing with the Master, kept out of it, and let the young man have his own way.

The Master knew what he was talking about. He was brilliant at grasping the gist of a book, and knowing how to apply his knowledge. On the whole, his ideas were sound. The bailiff even knew it. But in the man of the soil there was no answering enthusiasm. The brown eyes smiled their cordial deference, but the thin lips never changed. The Master pursed his own flexible mouth in a boyish versatility, as he cleverly sketched in his ideas to the other man, and the bailiff made eyes of admiration, but in his heart he was not attending, he was only watching the Master as he would have watched a queer, alien animal, quite without sympathy, not implicated.

So, it was settled, and the Master rang for Elvery, the butler, to bring a sandwich. He, the Master, was pleased. The butler saw it, and came back with anchovy and ham sandwiches, and a newly opened bottle of vermouth. There was always a newly opened bottle of something.

It was the same with the mason. The Master and he discussed the drainage of a bit of land, and more pipes were ordered, more special bricks, more this, more that.

Fine weather came at last, there was a little lull in the hard work on the island. The Master went for a short cruise in his yacht. It was not really a yacht, just a neat little bit of a yawl. They sailed along the coast of the mainland, and put in at the ports. At every port some friend turned up, the butler made elegant little meals in the cabin. Then the Master was invited to villas and hotels, his people disembarked him as if he were a prince.

And oh, how expensive it turned out! He had to telegraph to the bank for money. And he went home again, to economize.

The marsh-marigolds were blazing in the little swamp where the ditches were being dug for drainage. He almost regretted, now, the work in hand. The yellow beauties would not blaze again.

Harvest came, and a bumper crop. There must be a harvest-home supper. The long barn was now completely restored and added to. The carpenter had made long tables. Lanterns hung from the beams of the high-pitched roof. All the people of the island were assembled. The bailiff presided. It was a gay scene.

Towards the end of the supper the Master, in a velvet jacket, appeared with his guests. Then the bailiff rose and proposed: 'The Master! Long life and health to the Master!' All the people drank the health with great enthusiasm and cheering. The Master replied with a little speech: They were on an island in a little world of their own. It depended on them all to make this world a world of true happiness and content. Each must do his part. He hoped he himself did what he could, for his heart was in his island, and with the people of his island.

The butler responded: As long as the island had such a Master, it could not but be a little heaven for all the people on it. – This was seconded with virile warmth by the bailiff and the mason, the skipper was beside himself. Then there was dancing, the old carpenter was fiddler.

But under all this, things were not well. The very next morning came the farm-boy to say that a cow had fallen over the cliff. The Master went to look. He peered over the not very high declivity, and saw her lying dead, on a green ledge under a bit of late-flowering broom. A beautiful, expensive creature, already looking swollen. But what a fool, to fall so unnecessarily!

It was a question of getting several men to haul her up the bank: and then of skinning and burying her. No one would eat the meat. How repulsive it all was!

This was symbolic of the island. As sure as the spirits rose in the human breast, with a movement of joy, an invisible hand struck malevolently out of the silence. There must not be any joy, nor even any quiet peace. A man broke a leg, another was crippled with rheumatic fever. The pigs had some strange disease. A storm drove the yacht on a rock. The mason hated the butler, and refused to let his daughter serve at the house.

Out of the very air came a stony, heavy malevolence. The island itself seemed malicious. It would go on being hurtful and evil for weeks at a time. Then suddenly again one morning it would be fair, lovely as a morning in Paradise, everything beautiful and flowing. And everybody would begin to feel a great relief, and a hope for happiness.

Then as soon as the Master was opened out in spirit like an open flower, some ugly blow would fall. Somebody would send him an anonymous note, accusing some other person on the island. Somebody else would come hinting things against one of his servants.

'Some folks thinks they've got an easy job out here, with all the pickings they make!' the mason's daughter screamed at the suave butler, in the Master's hearing. He pretended not to hear.

'My man says this island is surely one of the lean kine of Egypt,[6] it would swallow a sight of money, and you'd never get anything back out of it,' confided the farm-hand's wife to one of the Master's visitors.

The people were not contented. They were not islanders. 'We feel we're not doing right by the children,' said those who had children. 'We feel we're not doing right by ourselves,' said those who had no children. And the various families fairly came to hate one another.

Yet the island was so lovely. When there was a scent of honey-suckle, and the moon brightly flickering down on the sea, then even the grumblers felt a strange nostalgia for it. It set you yearning, with a wild yearning; perhaps for the past, to be far back in the mysterious past of the island, when the blood had a different throb. Strange floods of passion came over you, strange violent lusts and imaginations of cruelty. The blood and the passion and the lust which the island had known. Uncanny dreams, half-dreams, half-evocated yearnings.

The Master himself began to be a little afraid of his island. He felt here strange violent feelings he had never felt before, and lustful desires that he had been quite free from. He knew quite well now that his people didn't love him at all. He knew that their spirits were secretly against him, malicious, jeering, envious, and lurking to down him. He became just as wary and secretive with regard to them.

But it was too much. At the end of the second year, several departures took place. The housekeeper went. The Master always blamed self-important women most. The mason said he wasn't going to be monkeyed about any more, so he took his departure, with his family. The rheumatic farm-hand left.

And then the year's bills came in, the Master made up his accounts. In spite of good crops, the assets were ridiculous, against the spending. The island had again lost, not hundreds but thousands of pounds. It was incredible. But you simply couldn't believe it! Where had it all gone?

The Master spent gloomy nights and days, going through accounts in the library. He was thorough. It became evident, now the housekeeper had gone, that she had swindled him. Probably everybody was swindling him. But he hated to think it, so he put the thought away.

He emerged, however, pale and hollow-eyed from his balancing of unbalanceable accounts, looking as if something had kicked him in the stomach. It was pitiable. But the money had gone, and there was an end of it. Another great hole in his capital. How could people be so heartless?

It couldn't go on, that was evident. He would soon be bankrupt. He had to give regretful notice to his butler. He was afraid to find out how much his butler had swindled him. Because the man was such a wonderful butler, after all. And the farm-bailiff had to go. The Master had no regrets in that quarter. The losses on the farm had almost embittered him.

The third year was spent in rigid cutting down of expenses. The island was still mysterious and fascinating. But it was also treacherous and cruel, secretly, fathomlessly malevolent. In spite of all its fair show of white blossom and bluebells, and the lovely dignity of foxgloves bending their rose-red bells, it was your implacable enemy.

With reduced staff, reduced wages, reduced splendour, the third year went by. But it was fighting against hope. The farm still lost a good deal. And once more, there was a hole in that remnant of capital. Another hole, in that which was already a mere remnant round the old holes. The island was mysterious in this also: it seemed to pick the very money out of your pocket, as if it were an octopus with invisible arms stealing from you in every direction.

Yet the Master still loved it. But with a touch of rancour now.

He spent, however, the second half of the fourth year intensely working on the mainland, to be rid of it. And it was amazing how difficult he found it to dispose of an island. He had thought that everybody was pining for such an island as his; but not at all. Nobody would pay any price for it. And he wanted now to get rid of it, as a man who wants a divorce at any cost.

It was not till the middle of the fifth year that he transferred it, at a considerable loss to himself, to an hotel company who were willing to speculate in it. They were to turn it into a handy honeymoon-and-golf island!

Then, take that island which didn't know when it was well off! Now be a honeymoon-and-golf island!

SECOND ISLAND

The islander had to move. But he was not going to the mainland. Oh, no! He moved to the smaller island, which still belonged to him. And he took with him the faithful old carpenter and wife, the couple he never really cared for; also a widow and daughter, who had kept house for him the last year; also an orphan lad, to help the old man.

The small island was very small; but, being a hump of rock in the sea, it was bigger than it looked. There was a little track among rocks and bushes, winding and scrambling up and down around the islet, so that it took you twenty minutes to do the circuit. It was more than you would have expected.

Still, it was an island. The islander moved himself, with all his books, into the commonplace six-roomed house up to which you had to scramble from the rocky landing-place. There were also two joined-together cottages. The old carpenter lived in one, with his wife and the lad, the widow and daughter lived in the other.

At last all was in order. The Master's books filled two rooms. It was already autumn, Orion lifting out of the sea. And in the dark nights, the Master could see the lights on his late island, where the hotel company were entertaining guests who would advertise the new resort for honeymoon-golfers.

On his hump of rock, however, the Master was still master. He explored the crannies, the odd handbreadths of grassy level, the steep little cliffs where the last harebells hung, and the seeds of summer were brown above the sea, lonely and untouched. He peered down the old well. He examined the stone pen where the pig had been kept. Himself, he had a goat.

Yes, it was an island. Always, always, underneath among the rocks the celtic sea sucked and washed and smote its feathery greyness. How many different noises of the sea! deep explosions, rumblings, strange long sighs and whistling noises; then voices, real voices of people clamouring as if they were in a market, under the waters; and again, the far-off ringing of a bell, surely an actual bell! then a tremulous trilling noise, very long and alarming, and an undertone of hoarse gasping.

On this island there were no human ghosts, no ghosts of any ancient race. The sea, and the spume and the wind and the weather, had washed them all out, washed them out, so there was only the sound of the sea itself, its own ghost, myriad-voiced, communing and plotting and shouting all winter long. And only the smell of the sea, with a few bristly bushes of gorse and coarse tufts of heather, among the grey, pellucid rocks, in the grey, more pellucid air. The coldness, the greyness, even the soft, creeping fog of the sea! and the islet of rock humped up in it all, like the last point in space.

Green star Sirius stood over the sea's rim. The island was a shadow. Out at sea a ship showed small lights. Below, in the rocky cove, the row-boat and the motor-boat were safe. A light shone in the carpenter's kitchen. That was all.

Save, of course, that the lamp was lit in the house, where the widow was preparing supper, her daughter helping. The islander went in to his meal. Here he was no longer the Master, he was an islander again and he had peace. The old carpenter, the widow and daughter were all faithfulness itself. The old man worked while ever there was light to see, because he had a passion for work. The widow and her quiet, rather delicate daughter of thirty-three worked for the Master, because they loved looking after him, and they were infinitely grateful for the haven he provided them. But they didn't call him 'the Master'. They gave him his name: 'Mr Cathcart, Sir!' softly, and reverently. And he spoke back to them also softly, gently, like people far from the world, afraid to make a noise.

The island was no longer a 'world'. It was a sort of refuge. The islander no longer struggled for anything. He had no need. It was as if he and his few dependents were a small flock of sea-birds alighted on this rock, as they travelled through space, and keeping together without a word. The silent mystery of travelling birds.

He spent most of his day in his study. His book was coming along. The widow's daughter could type out his manuscript for him, she was not uneducated. It was the one strange sound on the island, the typewriter. But soon even its spattering fitted in with the sea's noises, and the wind's.

The months went by. The islander worked away in his study, the people of the island went quietly about their concerns. The goat had a little black kid with yellow eyes. There were mackerel in the sea. The old man went fishing in the row-boat, with the lad. When the weather was calm enough, they went off in the motor-boat to the biggest island, for the post. And they brought supplies, never a penny wasted. And the days went by, and the nights, without desire, without *ennui*.

The strange stillness from all desire was a kind of wonder to the islander. He didn't want anything. His soul at last was still in him, his spirit was like a dim-lit cave under water, where strange sea-foliage expands upon the watery atmosphere, and scarcely sways, and a mute fish shadowily slips in and slips away again. All still and soft and uncrying, yet alive as rooted sea-weed is alive.

The islander said to himself: 'Is this happiness?' He said to himself: 'I am turned into a dream. I feel nothing, or I don't know what I feel. Yet it seems to me I am happy.'

Only he had to have something upon which his mental activity could work. So he spent long, silent hours in his study, working not very fast, nor very importantly, letting the writing spin softly from him as if it were drowsy gossamer. He no longer fretted whether it were good or not, what he produced. He slowly, softly spun it like gossamer, and, if it were to melt away as gossamer in autumn melts, he would not mind. It was only the soft evanescence of gossamery things which now seemed to him permanent. The very mist of eternity was in them. Whereas stone buildings, cathedrals for example, seemed to him to howl with temporary resistance, knowing they must fall at last; the tension of their long endurance seemed to howl forth from them all the time.

Sometimes he went to the mainland and to the city. Then he went elegantly, dressed in the latest style, to his club. He sat in a stall at the theatre, he shopped in Bond Street. He discussed terms for publishing his book. But over his face was that gossamery look of having dropped out of the race of progress, which made the vulgar city people feel they had won it over him, and made him glad to go back to his island.

He didn't mind if he never published his book. The years were blending into a soft mist, from which nothing obtruded. Spring came. There was never a primrose on his island, but he found a winter-aconite. There were two little sprayed bushes of blackthorn, and some wind-flowers. He began to make a list of the flowers on his islet, and that was absorbing. He noted a wild currant bush, and watched for the elder flowers on a stunted little tree, then for the first yellow rags of the broom, and wild roses. Bladder campion, orchids, stitchwort, celandine, he was prouder of them than if they had been people on his island. When he came across the golden saxifrage, so inconspicuous in a damp corner, he crouched over it in a trance, he knew not for how long, looking at it. Yet it was nothing to look at. As the widow's daughter found, when he showed it her.

He had said to her, in real triumph:

'I found the golden saxifrage this morning.'

The name sounded splendid. She looked at him with fascinated brown eyes, in which was a hollow ache that frightened him a little.

'Did you, Sir? Is it a nice flower?'

He pursed his lips and tilted his brows.

'Well – not showy exactly. I'll show it you if you like.'

'I should like to see it.'

She was so quiet, so wistful. But he sensed in her a persistency which made him uneasy. She said she was so happy: really happy. She followed him quietly, like a shadow, on the rocky track where there was never room for two people to walk side by side. He went first, and could feel her there, immediately behind him, following so submissively, gloating on him from behind.

It was a kind of pity for her which made him become her lover: though he never realized the extent of the power she had gained over him, and how *she* willed it. But the moment he had fallen, a jangling feeling came upon him, that it was all wrong. He felt a nervous dislike of her. He had not wanted it. And it seemed to him, as far as her physical self went, she had not wanted it either. It was just her will. He went away, and climbed at the risk of his neck down to a ledge near the sea. There he sat for hours, gazing all jangled at the sea, and saying miserably to himself: 'We didn't want it. We didn't really want it.'

It was the automatism of sex that had caught him again. Not that he hated sex. He deemed it, as the Chinese do, one of the great life-mysteries. But it had become mechanical, automatic, and he wanted to escape that. Automatic sex shattered him, and filled him with a sort of death. He thought he had come through, to a new stillness of desirelessness. Perhaps beyond that, there was a new fresh delicacy of desire, an unentered frail communion of two people meeting on untrodden ground.

But be that as it might, this was not it. This was nothing new or fresh. It was automatic, and driven from the will. Even she, in her true self, hadn't wanted it. It was automatic in her.

When he came home, very late, and saw her face white with fear and apprehension of his feeling against her, he pitied her, and spoke to her delicately, reassuringly. But he kept himself remote from her.

She gave no sign. She served him with the same silence, the same hidden hunger to serve him, to be near where he was. He felt her love following him with strange, awful persistency. She claimed nothing. Yet now, when he met her bright, brown, curiously vacant eyes, he saw in them the mute question. The question came direct at him, with a force and a power of will he never realized.

So he succumbed, and asked her again.

'Not,' she said, 'if it will make you hate me.'

'Why should it?' he replied, nettled. 'Of course not.'

'You know I would do anything on earth for you.'

It was only afterwards, in his exasperation, he remembered what she had said, and was more exasperated. Why should she pretend to do this *for him*? Why not for herself? But in his exasperation, he drove himself deeper in. In order to achieve some sort of satisfaction, which he never did achieve, he abandoned himself to her. Everybody on the island knew. But he did not care.

Then even what desire he had left him, and he felt only shattered. He felt that only with her will had she wanted him. Now he was shattered and full of self-contempt. His island was smirched and spoiled. He had lost his place in the rare, desireless levels of Time to which he had at last arrived, and he had fallen right back. If only it had been true, delicate desire between them, and a delicate meeting on the third rare place where a man might meet a woman, when they were both true to the frail, sensitive, crocus flame of desire in them. But it had been no such thing: automatic, an act of will, not of true desire, it left him feeling humiliated.

He went away from the islet, in spite of her mute reproach. And he wandered about the continent, vainly seeking a place where he could stay. He was out of key; he did not fit in the world any more.

There came a letter from Flora – her name was Flora – to say she was afraid she was going to have a child. He sat down as if he were shot, and he remained sitting. But he replied to her: 'Why be afraid? If it is so, it is so, and we should rather be pleased than afraid.'

At this very moment, it happened there was an auction of islands. He got the maps, and studied them. And at the auction he bought, for very little money, another island. It was just a few acres of rock away in the north, on the outer fringe of the isles. It was low, it rose out of the great ocean. There was not a building, not even a tree on it. Only northern sea-turf, a pool of rain-water, a bit of sedge, rock, and sea-birds. Nothing else. Under the weeping wet western sky.

He made a trip to visit his new possession. For several days, owing to the seas, he could not approach it. Then, in a light sea-mist, he landed, and saw it hazy, low, stretching apparently a long way. But it was illusion. He walked over the wet, springy turf, and dark-grey sheep tossed away from him, spectral, bleating hoarsely. And he came to the dark pool, with the sedge. Then on in the dampness, to the grey sea sucking angrily among the rocks.

This was indeed an island.

So he went home to Flora. She looked at him with guilty fear, but also with a triumphant brightness in her uncanny eyes. And again he was gentle, he reassured her, even he wanted her again, with that curious desire that was almost like toothache. So he took her to the mainland, and they were married, since she was going to have his child.

They returned to the island. She still brought in his meals, her own along with them. She sat and ate with him. He would have it so. The widowed mother preferred to stay in the kitchen. And Flora slept in the guest-room of his house, mistress of his house.

His desire, whatever it was, died in him with nauseous finality. The child would still be months coming. His island was hateful to him, vulgar, a suburb. He himself had lost all his finer distinction. The weeks passed in a sort of prison, in humiliation. Yet he stuck it out, till the child was born. But he was meditating escape. Flora did not even know.

A nurse appeared, and ate at table with them. The doctor came sometimes, and, if the sea were rough, he too had to stay. He was cheery over his whisky.

They might have been a young couple in Golders Green.

The daughter was born at last. The father looked at the baby, and felt depressed, almost more than he could bear. The millstone was tied round his neck. But he tried not to show what he felt. And Flora did not know. She still smiled with a kind of half-witted triumph in her joy, as she got well again. Then she began again to look at him with those aching, suggestive, somehow impudent eyes. She adored him so.

This he could not stand. He told her that he had to go away for a time. She wept, but she thought she had got him. He told her he had settled the best part of his property on her, and wrote down for her what income it would produce. She hardly listened, only looked at him with those heavy, adoring, impudent eyes. He gave her a cheque-book, with the amount of her credit duly entered. This did arouse her interest. And he told her, if she got tired of the island, she could choose her home wherever she wished.

She followed him with those aching, persistent brown eyes, when he left, and he never even saw her weep.

He went straight north, to prepare his third island.

THE THIRD ISLAND

The third island was soon made habitable. With cement and the big pebbles from the shingle beach, two men built him a hut, and roofed it with corrugated iron. A boat brought over a bed and table, and three chairs, with a good cupboard, and a few books. He laid in a supply of coal and paraffin and food – he wanted so little.

The house stood near the flat shingle bay where he landed, and where he pulled up his light boat. On a sunny day in August the men sailed away and left him. The sea was still and pale blue. On the horizon he saw the small mail-steamer slowly passing northwards, as if she were walking. She served the outer isles twice a week. He could row out to her if need be, in calm weather, and he could signal her from a flagstaff behind his cottage.

Half a dozen sheep still remained on the island, as company; and he had a cat to rub against his legs. While the sweet, sunny days of the northern autumn lasted, he would walk among the rocks, and over the springy turf of his small domain, always coming to the ceaseless, restless sea. He looked at every leaf, that might be different from another, and he watched the endless expansion and contraction of the water-tossed sea-weed. He had never a tree, not even a bit of heather to guard. Only the turf, and tiny turf-plants, and the sedge by the pool, the seaweed in the ocean. He was glad. He didn't want trees or bushes. They stood up like people, too assertive. His bare, low-pitched island in the pale blue sea was all he wanted.

He no longer worked at his book. The interest had gone. He liked to sit on the low elevation of his island, and see the sea; nothing but the pale, quiet sea. And to feel his mind turn soft and hazy, like the hazy ocean. Sometimes, like a mirage, he would see the shadow of land rise hovering to northwards. It was a big island beyond. But quite without substance.

He was soon almost startled when he perceived the steamer on the near horizon, and his heart contracted with fear, lest it were going to pause and molest him. Anxiously he watched it go, and not till it was out of sight did he feel truly relieved, himself again. The tension of waiting for human approach was cruel. He did not want to be approached. He did not want to hear voices. He was shocked by the sound of his own voice, if he inadvertently spoke to his cat. He rebuked himself for having broken the great silence. And he was irritated when his cat would look up at him and mew faintly, plaintively. He frowned at her. And she knew. She was becoming wild, lurking in the rocks, perhaps fishing.

But what he disliked most was when one of the lumps of sheep opened its mouth and baa-ed its hoarse, raucous baa. He watched it, and it looked to him hideous and gross. He came to dislike the sheep very much.

He wanted only to hear the whispering sound of the sea, and the sharp cries of the gulls, cries that came out of another world to him. And best of all, the great silence.

He decided to get rid of the sheep, when the boat came. They were accustomed to him now, and stood and stared at him with yellow or colourless eyes, in an insolence that was almost cold ridicule. There was a suggestion of cold indecency about them. He disliked them very much. And when they jumped with staccato jumps off the rocks, and their hoofs made the dry, sharp hit, and the fleece flopped on their square backs – he found them repulsive, degrading.

The fine weather passed, and it rained all day. He lay a great deal on his bed, listening to the water trickling from his roof into the zinc water-butt, looking through the open door at the rain, the dark rocks, the hidden sea. Many gulls were on the island now: many sea-birds of all sorts. It was another world of life. Many of the birds he had never seen before. His old impulse came over him, to send for a book, to know their names. In a flicker of the old passion, to know the name of everything he saw, he even decided to row out to the steamer. The names of these birds! he must know their names, otherwise he had not got them, they were not quite alive to him.

But the desire left him, and he merely watched the birds as they wheeled or walked around him, watched them vaguely, without discrimination. All interest had left him. Only there was one gull, a big handsome fellow, who would walk back and forth, back and forth in front of the open door of the cabin, as if he had some mission there. He was big, and pearl-grey, and his roundnesses were as smooth and lovely as a pearl. Only the folded wings had shut black pinions, and on the closed black feathers were three very distinct white dots, making a pattern. The islander wondered very much, why this bit of trimming on the bird out of the far, cold seas. And as the gull walked back and forth, back and forth in front of the cabin, strutting on pale-dusky gold feet, holding up his pale yellow beak, that was curved at the tip, with curious alien importance, the man wondered over him. He was portentous, he had a meaning.

Then the bird came no more. The island, which had been full of seabirds, the flash of wings, the sound and cut of wings and sharp eerie cries in the air, began to be deserted again. No longer they sat like living eggs on the rocks and turf, moving their heads, but scarcely rising into flight round his feet. No longer they ran across the turf among the sheep, and lifted themselves upon low wings. The host had gone. But some remained, always.

The days shortened, and the world grew eerie. One day the boat came: as if suddenly, swooping down. The islander found it a violation. It was torture to talk to those two men, in their homely clumsy clothes. The air of familiarity around them was very repugnant to him. Himself, he was neatly dressed, his cabin was neat and tidy. He resented any intrusion, the clumsy homeliness, the heavy-footedness of the two fishermen was really repulsive to him.

The letters they had brought, he left lying unopened in a little box. In one of them was his money. But he could not bear to open even that one. Any kind of contact was repulsive to him. Even to read his name on an envelope. He hid the letters away.

And the hustle and horror of getting the sheep caught and tied and put in the ship made him loathe with profound repulsion the whole of the animal creation. What repulsive god invented animals, and evil-smelling men? To his nostrils, the fishermen and the sheep alike smelled foul; an uncleanness on the fresh earth.

He was still nerve-wracked and tortured when the ship at last lifted sail and was drawing away, over the still sea. And sometimes days after, he would start with repulsion, thinking he heard the munching of sheep.

The dark days of winter drew on. Sometimes there was no real day at all. He felt ill, as if he were dissolving, as if dissolution had already set in inside him. Everything was twilight, outside, and in his mind and soul. Once, when he went to the door, he saw black heads of men swimming in his bay. For some moments he swooned unconscious. It was the shock, the horror of unexpected human approach. The horror in the twilight! And not till the shock had undermined him and left him disembodied, did he realize that the black heads were the heads of seals swimming in. A sick relief came over him. But he was barely conscious, after the shock. Later on, he sat and wept with gratitude, because they were not men. But he never realized that he wept. He was too dim. Like some strange, ethereal animal, he no longer realized what he was doing.

Only he still derived his single satisfaction from being alone, absolutely alone, with the space soaking into him. The grey sea alone, and the footing of his sea-washed island. No other contact. Nothing human to bring its horror into contact with him. Only space, damp, twilit, sea-washed space! This was the bread of his soul.

For this reason, he was most glad when there was a storm, or when the sea was high. Then nothing could get at him. Nothing could come through to him from the outer world. True, the terrific violence of the wind made him suffer badly. At the same time, it swept the world utterly out of existence for him. He always liked the sea to be heavily rolling and tearing. Then no boat could get at him. It was like eternal ramparts round his island.

He kept no track of time, and no longer thought of opening a book. The print, the printed letters, so like the depravity of speech, looked obscene. He tore the brass label from his paraffin stove. He obliterated any bit of lettering in his cabin.

His cat had disappeared. He was rather glad. He shivered at her thin, obtrusive call. She had lived in the coal shed. And each morning he had put her a dish of porridge, the same as he ate. He washed her saucer with repulsion. He did not like her writhing about. But he fed her scrupulously. Then one day she did not come for her porridge: she always mewed for it. She did not come again.

He prowled about his island in the rain, in a big oil-skin coat, not knowing what he was looking at, nor what he went out to see. Time had ceased to pass. He stood for long spaces, gazing from a white, sharp face, with those keen, far-off blue eyes of his, gazing fiercely and almost cruelly at the dark sea under the dark sky. And if he saw the labouring sail of a fishing boat away on the cold waters, a strange malevolent anger passed over his features.

Sometimes he was ill. He knew he was ill, because he staggered as he walked, and easily fell down. Then he paused to think what it was. And he went to his stores and took out dried milk and malt, and ate that. Then he forgot again. He ceased to register his own feelings.

The days were beginning to lengthen. All winter the weather had been comparatively mild, but with much rain, much rain. He had forgotten the sun. Suddenly, however, the air was very cold, and he began to shiver. A fear came over him. The sky was level and grey, and never a star appeared at night. It was very cold. More birds began to arrive. The island was freezing. With trembling hands he made a fire in his grate. The cold frightened him.

And now it continued, day after day, a dull, deathly cold. Occasional crumblings of snow were in the air. The days were greyly longer, but no change in the cold. Frozen grey daylight. The birds passed away, flying away. Some he saw lying frozen. It was as if all life were drawing away, contracting away from the north, contracting southwards. 'Soon', he said to himself, 'it will all be gone, and in all these regions nothing will be alive.' He felt a cruel satisfaction in the thought.

Then one night there seemed to be a relief: he slept better, did not tremble half awake, and writhe so much, half-conscious. He had become so used to the quaking and writhing of his body, he hardly noticed it. But when for once it slept deep, he noticed that.

He awoke in the morning to a curious whiteness. His window was muffled. It had snowed. He got up and opened his door, and shuddered. Ugh! how cold! All white, with a dark leaden sea, and black rocks curiously speckled with white. The foam was no longer pure. It seemed dirty. And the sea ate at the whiteness of the corpse-like land. Crumbles of snow were silting down the dead air.

On the ground the snow was a foot deep, white and smooth and soft, windless. He took a shovel to clear round his house and shed. The pallor of morning darkened. There was a strange rumbling of far-off thunder, in the frozen air, and through the newly-falling snow, a dim flash of lightning. Snow now fell steadily down, in the motionless obscurity.

He went out for a few minutes. But it was difficult. He stumbled and fell in the snow, which burned his face. Weak, faint, he toiled home. And when he recovered, he took the trouble to make hot milk.

It snowed all the time. In the afternoon again there was a muffled rumbling of thunder, and flashes of lightning blinking reddish through the falling snow. Uneasy, he went to bed and lay staring fixedly at nothing.

Morning seemed never to come. An eternity long he lay and waited for one alleviating pallor on the night. And at last it seemed the air was paler. His house was a cell faintly illuminated with white light. He realized the snow was walled outside his window. He got up, in the dead cold. When he opened his door, the motionless snow stopped him in a wall as high as his breast. Looking over the top of it, he felt the dead wind slowly driving, saw the snow-powder lift and travel like a funeral train. The blackish sea churned and champed, seeming to bite at the snow, impotent. The sky was grey, but luminous.

He began to work in a frenzy, to get at his boat. If he was to be shut in, it must be by his own choice, not by the mechanical power of the elements. He must get to the sea. He must be able to get at his boat.

But he was weak, and at times the snow overcame him. It fell on him, and he lay buried and lifeless. Yet every time, he struggled alive before it was too late, and fell upon the snow with the energy of fever. Exhausted, he would not give in. He crept indoors and made coffee and bacon. Long since he had cooked so much. Then he went at the snow once more. He must conquer the snow, this new, white brute force which had accumulated against him.

He worked in the awful, dead wind, pushing the snow aside, pressing it with his shovel. It was cold, freezing hard in the wind, even when the sun came out for a while, and showed him his white, lifeless surroundings, the black sea rolling sullen, flecked with dull spume, away to the horizons. Yet the sun had power on his face. It was March.

He reached the boat. He pushed the snow away, then sat down under the lee of the boat, looking at the sea, which nearly swirled to his feet, in the high tide. Curiously natural the pebbles looked, in a world gone all uncanny. The sun shone no more. Snow was falling in hard crumbs, that vanished as if by miracle as they touched the hard blackness of the sea. Hoarse waves rang in the shingle, rushing up at the snow. The wet rocks were brutally black. And all the time the myriad swooping crumbs of snow, demonish, touched the dark sea and disappeared.

During the night there was a great storm. It seemed to him he could hear the vast mass of the snow striking all the world with a ceaseless thud; and over it all, the wind roared in strange hollow volleys, in between which came a jump of blindfold lightning, then the low roll of thunder heavier than the wind. When at last the dawn faintly discoloured the dark, the storm had more or less subsided, but a steady wind drove on. The snow was up to the top of his door.

Sullenly, he worked to dig himself out. And he managed, through sheer persistency, to get out. He was in the tail of a great drift, many feet high. When he got through, the frozen snow was not more than two feet deep. But his island was gone. Its shape was all changed, great heaping white hills rose where no hills had been, inaccessible, and they fumed like volcanoes, but with snow powder. He was sickened and overcome.

His boat was in another, smaller drift. But he had not the strength to clear it. He looked at it helplessly. The shovel slipped from his hands, and he sank in the snow, to forget. In the snow itself, the sea resounded.

Something brought him to. He crept to his house. He was almost without feeling. Yet he managed to warm himself, just that part of him which leaned in snow-sleep over the coal fire. Then again, he made hot milk. After which, carefully, he built up the fire.

The wind dropped. Was it night again? In the silence, it seemed he could hear the panther-like dropping of infinite snow. Thunder rumbled nearer, crackled quick after the bleared reddened lightning. He lay in bed in a kind of stupor. The elements! The elements! His mind repeated the word dumbly. You can't win against the elements.

How long it went on, he never knew. Once, like a wraith, he got out, and climbed to the top of a white hill on his unrecognizable island. The sun was hot. 'It is summer', he said to himself, 'and the time of leaves.' He looked stupidly over the whiteness of his foreign island, over the waste of the lifeless sea. He pretended to imagine he saw the wink of a sail. Because he knew too well there would never again be a sail on that stark sea.

As he looked, the sky mysteriously darkened and chilled. From far off came the mutter of the unsatisfied thunder, and he knew it was the signal of the snow rolling over the sea. He turned, and felt its breath on him.

The Lovely Lady

At seventy-two, Pauline Attenborough could still sometimes be mistaken, in the half-light, for thirty. She really was a wonderfully-preserved woman, of perfect *chic*. Of course it helps a great deal to have the right frame. She would be an exquisite skeleton, and her skull would be an exquisite skull, like that of some Etruscan woman with feminine charm still in the swerve of the bone and the pretty, naïve teeth.

Mrs Attenborough's face was of the perfect oval and slightly flat type that wears best. There is no flesh to sag. Her nose rode serenely, in its finely-bridged curve. Only the big grey eyes were a tiny bit prominent, on the surface of her face, and they gave her away most. The bluish lids were heavy, as if they ached sometimes with the strain of keeping the eyes beneath them arch and bright; and at the corners of the eyes were fine little wrinkles which would slacken into haggardness, then be pulled up tense again to that bright, gay look like a Leonardo woman who really could laugh outright.[1]

Her niece Cecilia was perhaps the only person in the world who was aware of the invisible little wire which connected Pauline's eye-wrinkles with Pauline's willpower. Only Cecilia consciously watched the eyes go haggard and old and tired, and remain so, for hours; until Robert came home. Then ping! – the mysterious little wire that worked between Pauline's will and her face went taut, the weary, haggard, prominent eyes suddenly began to gleam, the eyelids arched, the queer, curved eyebrows which floated in such frail arches on Pauline's forehead began to gather a mocking significance, and you had the *real* lovely lady, in all her charm.

She really had the secret of everlasting youth; that is to say, she could don her youth again like an eagle. But she was sparing of it. She was wise enough not to try being young for too many people. Her son Robert, in the evenings, and Sir Wilfrid Knipe sometimes in the afternoon to tea; then occasional visitors on Sunday, when Robert was home – for these she was her lovely and changeless self, that age could not wither, nor custom stale; so bright and kindly and yet subtly mocking, like Mona Lisa, who knew a thing or two. But Pauline knew more, so she needn't be smug at all. She could laugh that lovely, mocking Bacchante laugh of hers, which was at the same time never malicious, always good-naturedly tolerant, both of virtues and vices – the former, of course, taking much more tolerating. So she suggested, roguishly.

Only with her niece Cecilia she did not trouble to keep up the glamour. Ciss was not very observant, anyhow; and, more than that, she was plain; more still, she was in love with Robert; and most of all, she was thirty, and dependent on her aunt Pauline. Oh, Cecilia – why make music for her?

Cecilia, called by her aunt and by her cousin Robert just Ciss, like a cat spitting, was a big, dark-complexioned, pug-faced young woman who very rarely spoke, and when she did couldn't get it out. She was the daughter of a poor Congregational clergyman who had been, while he lived, brother to Ronald, Aunt Pauline's husband. Ronald and the Congregational minister were both well dead, and Aunt Pauline had had charge of Ciss for the last five years.

They lived all together in a quite exquisite though rather small Queen Anne house some twenty-five miles out of town, secluded in a little dale, and surrounded by small but very quaint and pleasant grounds. It was an ideal place and an ideal life for Aunt Pauline, at the age of seventy-two. When the kingfishers flashed up the little stream in her garden, going under the alders, something still flashed in her heart. She was that kind of woman.

Robert, who was two years older than Ciss, went every day to town, to his chambers in one of the Inns. He was a barrister, and, to his secret but very deep mortification, he earned about a hundred pounds a year. He simply *couldn't* get above that figure, though it was rather easy to get below it. Of course, it didn't matter. Pauline had money. But then, what was Pauline's was Pauline's, and though she could give almost lavishly, still, one was always aware of having a *lovely* and *undeserved* present made to one. Presents are so much nicer when they're undeserved, Aunt Pauline would say.

Robert, too, was plain, and almost speechless. He was medium sized, rather broad and stout, though not fat. Only his creamy, clean-shaven face was rather fat, and sometimes suggestive of an Italian priest, in its silence and its secrecy. But he had grey eyes like his mother, but very shy and uneasy, not bold like hers. Perhaps Ciss was the only person who fathomed his awful shyness and *malaise*, his habitual feeling that he was in the wrong place: almost like a soul that has got into a wrong body. But he never did anything about it. He went up to Chambers, and read law. It was, however, all the weird old processes that interested him. He had, unknown to everybody but his mother, a quite extraordinary collection of old Mexican legal documents – reports of processes and trials, pleas, accusations: the weird and awful mixture of ecclesiastical law and common law in seventeenth-century Mexico. He had started a study in this direction through coming across the report of a trial of two English sailors, for murder, in Mexico, in 1620, and he had gone on, when the next document was an accusation against a Don Miguel Estrada for seducing one of the nuns of the Sacred Heart Convent in Oaxaca in 1680.

Pauline and her son Robert had wonderful evenings with these old papers. The lovely lady knew a little Spanish. She even looked a trifle Spanish herself, with a high comb and a marvellous dark-brown shawl embroidered in thick silvery silk embroidery. So she would sit at the perfect old table, soft as velvet in its deep brown surface, a high comb in her hair, ear-rings with dropping pendants in her ears, her arms bare and still beautiful, a few strings of pearls round her throat, a puce velvet dress on and this or another beautiful shawl, and by candlelight she looked, yes, a Spanish high-bred beauty of thirty-two or three. She set the candles to give her face just the chiaroscuro she knew suited her; her high chair that rose behind her face was done in old green brocade, against which her face emerged like a Christmas rose.

They were always three at table, and they always drank a bottle of champagne: Pauline two glasses, Ciss two glasses, Robert the rest. The lovely lady sparkled and was radiant. Ciss, her black hair bobbed, her broad shoulders in a very nice and becoming dress that Aunt Pauline had helped her to make, stared from her aunt to her cousin and back again, with rather confused, mute hazel eyes, and played the part of an audience suitably impressed. She *was* impressed, somewhere, all the time. And even rendered speechless by Pauline's brilliancy, even after five years. But at the bottom of her consciousness was the *data* of as weird a document as Robert ever studied: all the things she knew about her aunt and her cousin.

Robert was always a gentleman, with an old-fashioned, punctilious courtesy that covered his shyness quite completely. He was, and Ciss knew it, more confused than shy. He was worse than she was. Cecilia's own confusion dated from only five years back. Robert's must have started before he was born. In the lovely lady's womb he must have felt *very* confused.

He paid all his attention to his mother, drawn to her as a humble flower to the sun. And yet, priest-like, he was all the time aware, with the tail of his consciousness, that Ciss was there, and that she was a bit shut out of it, and that something wasn't right. He was aware of the third consciousness in the room. Whereas to Pauline, her niece Cecilia was an appropriate part of her own setting, rather than a distinct consciousness.

Robert took coffee with his mother and Ciss in the warm drawing-room, where all the furniture was so lovely, all collectors' pieces – Mrs Attenborough had made her own money, dealing privately in pictures and furniture and rare things from barbaric countries – and the three talked desultorily till about eight or half-past. It was very pleasant, very cosy, very homely even; Pauline made a real home cosiness out of so much elegant material. The chat was simple, and nearly always bright. Pauline was her *real* self, emanating a friendly mockery and an odd, ironic gaiety – till there came a little pause.

At which Ciss always rose and said good-night, and carried out the coffee-tray, to prevent Burnett from intruding any more.

And then! ah, then, the lovely, glowing intimacy of the evening, between mother and son, when they deciphered manuscripts and discussed points, Pauline with that eagerness of a girl for which she was famous. And it was quite genuine. In some mysterious way she had *saved up* her power for being thrilled, in connection with a man. Robert, solid, rather quiet and subdued, seemed like the elder of the two – almost like a priest with a young girl pupil. And that was rather how he felt.

Ciss had a flat for herself just across the courtyard, over the old coach-house and stables. There were no horses. Robert kept his car in the coach-house. Ciss had three very nice rooms up there, stretching along in a row one after the other, and she had got used to the ticking of the stable clock.

But sometimes she did not go to her rooms. In the summer she would sit on the lawn, and from the open window of the drawing-room upstairs she would hear Pauline's wonderful, heart-searching laugh. And in winter the young woman would put on a thick coat and walk slowly to the little balustraded bridge over the stream, and then look back at the three lighted windows of that drawing-room where mother and son were so happy together.

Ciss loved Robert, and she believed that Pauline intended the two of them to marry – when she was dead. But poor Robert, he was so convulsed with shyness already, with man or woman. What would he be when his mother was dead? – in a dozen more years. He would be just a shell, the shell of a man who had never lived.

The strange, unspoken sympathy of the young with one another, when they are overshadowed by the old, was one of the bonds between Robert and Ciss. But another bond, which Ciss did not know how to draw tight, was the bond of passion. Poor Robert was by nature a passionate man. His silence and his agonised, though hidden, shyness were both the result of a secret physical passionateness. And how Pauline could play on this! Ah, Ciss was not blind to the eyes which he fixed on his mother – eyes fascinated yet humiliated, full of shame. He was ashamed that he was not a man. And he did not love his mother. He was fascinated by her. Completely fascinated. And for the rest, paralysed in a life-long confusion.

Ciss stayed in the garden till the lights leapt up in Pauline's bedroom – about ten o'clock. The lovely lady had retired. Robert would now stay another hour or so, alone. Then he, too, would retire. Ciss, in the dark outside, sometimes wished she could creep up to him and say: 'Oh, Robert! It's all wrong!' But Aunt Pauline would hear. And, anyhow, Ciss couldn't do it. She went off to her own rooms, once more, once more, and so for ever.

In the morning coffee was brought up on a tray to each of the rooms of the three relatives. Ciss had to be at Sir Wilfrid Knipe's at nine o'clock, to give two hours' lessons to his little grand-daughter. It was her sole serious occupation, except that she played the piano for the love of it. Robert set off to town about nine. And as a rule, Aunt Pauline appeared to lunch, though sometimes not till tea-time. When she appeared, she looked fresh and young. But she was inclined to fade rather rapidly, like a flower without water, in the daytime. Her hour was the candle hour.

So she always rested in the afternoon. When the sun shone, if possible she took a sun-bath. This was one of her secrets. Her lunch was very light; she could take her sun-and-air-bath before noon or after, as it pleased her. Often it was in the afternoon, when the sun shone very warmly into a queer little yew-walled square just behind the stables. Here Ciss stretched out the lying-chair and rugs, and put the light parasol handy in the silent little enclosure of thick dark yew-hedges beyond the old red walls of the unused stables. And hither came the lovely lady with her book. Ciss then had to be on guard in one of her own rooms, should her aunt, who was very keen-eared, hear a footstep.

One afternoon it occurred to Cecilia that she herself might while away this rather long afternoon hour by taking a sun-bath. She was growing restive. The thought of the flat roof of the stable buildings, to which she could climb from a loft at the end, started her on a new adventure. She often went on to the roof; she had to, to wind up the stable clock, which was a job she had assumed to herself. Now she took a rug, climbed out under the heavens, looked at the sky and the great elm-tops, looked at the sun, then took off her things and lay down perfectly securely, in a corner of the roof under the parapet, full in the sun.

It was rather lovely, to bask all one's length like this in warm sun and air. Yes, it was very lovely! It even seemed to melt some of the hard bitterness of her heart, some of that core of unspoken resentment which never dissolved. Luxuriously, she spread herself, so that the sun should touch her limbs fully, fully. If she had no other lover, she should have the sun! She rolled over voluptuously.

And suddenly her heart stood still in her body, and her hair almost rose on end as a voice said very softly, musingly, in her ear:

'No, Henry dear! It was not my fault you died instead of marrying that Claudia. No, darling. I was quite, quite willing for you to marry her, unsuitable though she was.'

Cecilia sank down on her rug, powerless and perspiring with dread. That awful voice, so soft, so musing, yet so unnatural. Not a human voice at all. Yet there must, there *must* be someone on the roof! Oh, how unspeakably awful!

She lifted her weak head and peeped across the sloping leads. Nobody! The chimneys were too narrow to shelter anybody. There was nobody on the roof. Then it must be someone in the trees, in the elms. Either that, or – terror unspeakable – a bodiless voice! She reared her head a little higher.

And as she did so, came the voice again:

'No, darling! I told you you would tire of her in six months. And you see it was true, dear. It was true, true, true! I wanted to spare you that. So it wasn't I who made you feel weak and disabled, wanting that very silly Claudia – poor thing, she looked so woebegone afterwards! – wanting her and not wanting her. You got yourself into that perplexity, my dear. I only warned you. What else could I do? And you lost your spirit and died without ever knowing me again. It was bitter, bitter –'

The voice faded away. Cecilia subsided weakly on to her rug, after the anguished tension of listening. Oh, it was awful. The sun shone, the sky was blue, all seemed so lovely and afternoony and summery. And yet, oh, horror! – she was going to be forced to believe in the supernatural! And she loathed the supernatural, ghosts and voices and rappings and all the rest.

But that awful, creepy, bodiless voice, with its rusty sort of whispers of an overtone! It had something so fearfully familiar in it, too! And yet was so utterly uncanny. Poor Cecilia could only lie there unclothed, and so all the more agonisingly helpless, inert, collapsed in sheer dread.

And then she heard the thing sigh! – a deep sigh that seemed weirdly familiar, yet was not human. 'Ah well, ah well! the heart must bleed. Better it should bleed than break. It is grief, grief! But it wasn't my fault, dear. And Robert could marry our poor, dull Ciss tomorrow, if he wanted her. But he doesn't care about it, so why force him into anything?' The sounds were very uneven, sometimes only a husky sort of whisper. Listen! Listen!

Cecilia was about to give vent to loud and piercing screams of hysteria, when the last two sentences arrested her. All her caution and her cunning sprang alert. It was Aunt Pauline! It *must* be Aunt Pauline, practising ventriloquism, or something like that. What a devil she was!

Where was she? She must be lying down there, right below where Cecilia herself was lying. And it was either some fiend's trick of ventriloquism, or else thought-transference. The sounds were very uneven; sometimes quite inaudible, sometimes only a brushing sort of noise. Ciss listened intently. No, it could not be ventriloquism. It was worse: some form of thought-transference that conveyed itself like sound. Some horror of that sort! Cecilia still lay weak and inert, too terrified to move; but she was growing calmer with suspicion. It was some diabolic trick of that unnatural woman.

But *what* a devil of a woman! She even knew that she, Cecilia, had mentally accused her of killing her son Henry. Poor Henry was Robert's elder brother, twelve years older than Robert. He had died suddenly when he was twenty-two, after an awful struggle with himself, because he was passionately in love with a young and very good-looking actress, and his mother had humorously despised him for the attachment. So he had caught some sudden ordinary disease, but the poison had gone to his brain and killed him before he ever regained consciousness. Ciss knew the few facts from her own father. And lately she had been thinking that Pauline was going to kill Robert as she had killed Henry. It was clear murder: a mother murdering her sensitive sons, who were fascinated by her: the Circe![2]

'I suppose I may as well get up,' murmured the dim, unbreathing voice. 'Too much sun is as bad as too little. Enough sun, enough love-thrill, enough proper food, and not too much of any of them, and a woman might live for ever. I verily believe, for ever. If she absorbs as much vitality as she expends. Or perhaps a trifle more!'

It was certainly Aunt Pauline! How – how terrible! She, Ciss, was hearing Aunt Pauline's thoughts. Oh, how ghastly! Aunt Pauline was sending out her thoughts in a sort of radio, and she, Ciss, had to *hear* what her aunt was thinking. How ghastly! How insufferable! One of them would surely have to die.

She twisted and lay inert and crumpled, staring vacantly in front of her. Vacantly! Vacantly! And her eyes were staring almost into a hole. She was staring in it unseeing, a hole going down in the corner, from the lead gutter. It meant nothing to her. Only it frightened her a little more.

When suddenly, out of the hole came a sigh and a last whisper: 'Ah well! Pauline! Get up, it's enough for to-day.' Good God! Out of the hole of the rain-pipe! The rain-pipe was acting as a speaking-tube! Impossible! No, quite possible. She had read of it even in some book. And Aunt Pauline, like the old and guilty woman she was, talked aloud to herself. That was it!

A sullen exultance sprang in Ciss's breast. *That* was why she would never have anybody, not even Robert, in her bedroom. That was why she never dozed in a chair, never sat absent-minded anywhere, but went to her room, and kept to her room, except when she roused herself to be alert. When she slackened off she talked to herself! She talked in a soft little crazy voice to herself. But she was not crazy. It was only her thoughts murmuring themselves aloud.

So she had qualms about poor Henry! Well she might have! Ciss believed that Aunt Pauline had loved her big, handsome, brilliant first-born much more than she loved Robert, and that his death had been a terrible blow and a chagrin to her. Poor Robert had been only ten years old when Henry died. Since then he had been the substitute.

Ah, how awful!

But Aunt Pauline was a strange woman. She had left her husband when Henry was a small child, some years even before Robert was born. There was no quarrel. Sometimes she saw her husband again, quite amiably, but a little mockingly. And she even gave him money.

For Pauline earned all her own. Her father had been a Consul in the East and in Naples, and a devoted collector of beautiful exotic things. When he died, soon after his grandson Henry was born, he left his collection of treasures to his daughter. And Pauline, who had really a passion and a genius for loveliness, whether in texture or form or colour, had laid the basis of her fortune on her father's collection. She had gone on collecting, buying where she could, and selling to collectors or to museums. She was one of the first to sell old, weird African figures to the museums, and ivory carvings from New Guinea. She bought Renoir as soon as she saw his pictures. But not Rousseau. And all by herself she made a fortune.

After her husband died she had not married again. She was not even *known* to have had lovers. If she did have lovers, it was not among the men who admired her most and paid her devout and open attendance. To these she was a 'friend'.

Cecilia slipped on her clothes and caught up her rug, hastening carefully down the ladder to the loft. As she descended she heard the ringing, musical call: 'All right, Ciss' – which meant that the lovely lady was finished, and returning to the house. Even her voice was wonderfully young and sonorous, beautifully balanced and self-possessed. So different from the little voice in which she talked to herself. *That* was much more the voice of an old woman.

Ciss hastened round to the yew enclosure, where lay the comfortable *chaise longue* with the various delicate rugs. Everything Pauline had was choice, to the fine straw mat on the floor. The great yew walls were beginning to cast long shadows. Only in the corner where the rugs tumbled their delicate colours was there hot, still sunshine.

The rugs folded up, the chair lifted away, Cecilia stooped to look at the mouth of the rain-pipe. There it was, in the corner, under a little hood of masonry and just projecting from the thick leaves of the creeper on the wall. If Pauline, lying there, turned her face towards the wall, she would speak into the very mouth of the tube. Cecilia was reassured. She had heard her aunt's thoughts indeed, but by no uncanny agency.

That evening, as if aware of something, Pauline was a little quieter than usual, though she looked her own serene, rather mysterious self. And after coffee she said to Robert and Ciss:

'I'm so sleepy. The sun has made me so sleepy. I feel full of sunshine like a bee. I shall go to bed, if you don't mind. You two sit and have a talk.'

Cecilia looked quickly at her cousin.

'Perhaps you'd rather be alone?' she said to him.

'No – no,' he replied. 'Do keep me company for a while, if it doesn't bore you.'

The windows were open, the scent of honeysuckle wafted in, with the sound of an owl. Robert smoked in silence. There was a sort of despair in his motionless, rather squat body. He looked like a caryatid bearing a weight.

'Do you remember Cousin Henry?' Cecilia asked him suddenly.

He looked up in surprise.

'Yes. Very well,' he said.

'What did he look like?' she said, glancing into her cousin's big, secret-troubled eyes, in which there was so much frustration.

'Oh, he was handsome: tall, and fresh-coloured, with mother's soft brown hair.' As a matter of fact, Pauline's hair was grey. 'The ladies admired him very much; and he was at all the dances.'

'And what kind of character had he?'

'Oh, very good-natured and jolly. He liked to be amused. He was rather quick and clever, like mother, and very good company.'

'And did he love your mother?'

'Very much. She loved him too – better than she does me, as a matter of fact. He was so much more nearly her idea of a man.'

'Why was he more her idea of a man?'

'Tall – handsome – attractive, and very good company – and would, I believe, have been very successful at law. I'm afraid I am merely negative in all those respects.'

Ciss looked at him attentively, with her slow-thinking hazel eyes. Under his impassive mask she knew he suffered.

'Do you think you are so much more negative than he?' she said.

He did not lift his face. But after a few moments he replied:

'My life, certainly, is a negative affair.'

She hesitated before she dared ask him:

'And do you mind?'

He did not answer her at all. Her heart sank.

'You see, I'm afraid my life is as negative as yours is,' she said. 'And I'm beginning to mind bitterly. I'm thirty.'

She saw his creamy, well-bred hand tremble.

'I suppose,' he said, without looking at her, 'one will rebel when it is too late.'

That was queer, from him.

'Robert!' she said. 'Do you like me at all?'

She saw his dusky-creamy face, so changeless in its folds, go pale.

'I am very fond of you,' he murmured.

'Won't you kiss me? Nobody ever kisses me,' she said pathetically.

He looked at her, his eyes strange with fear and a certain haughtiness. Then he rose, and came softly over to her, and kissed her gently on the cheek.

'It's an awful shame, Ciss!' he said softly.

She caught his hand and pressed it to her breast.

'And sit with me sometimes in the garden,' she said, murmuring with difficulty. 'Won't you?'

He looked at her anxiously and searchingly.

'What about mother?'

Ciss smiled a funny little smile, and looked into his eyes. He suddenly flushed crimson, turning aside his face. It was a painful sight.

'I know,' he said. 'I am no lover of women.'

He spoke with sarcastic stoicism, against himself, but even she did not know the shame it was to him.

'You never try to be,' she said.

Again his eyes changed uncannily.

'Does one have to try?' he said.

'Why, yes. One never does anything if one doesn't try.'

He went pale again.

'Perhaps you are right,' he said.

In a few minutes she left him, and went to her rooms. At least she had tried to take off the everlasting lid from things.

The weather continued sunny, Pauline continued her sun-baths, and Ciss lay on the roof eavesdropping, in the literal sense of the word. But Pauline was not to be heard. No sound came up the pipe. She must be lying with her face away into the open. Ciss listened with all her might. She could just detect the faintest, faintest murmur away below, but no audible syllable.

And at night, under the stars, Cecilia sat and waited in silence, on the seat which kept in view the drawing-room windows and the side door into the garden. She saw the light go up in her aunt's room. She saw the lights at last go out in the drawing-room. And she waited. But he did not come. She stayed on in the darkness half the night, while the owl hooted. But she stayed alone.

Two days she heard nothing; her aunt's thoughts were not revealed; and at evening nothing happened. Then, the second night, as she sat with heavy, helpless persistence in the garden, suddenly she started. He had come out. She rose and went softly over the grass to him.

'Don't speak!' he murmured.

And in silence, in the dark, they walked down the garden and over the little bridge to the paddock, where the hay, cut very late, was in cock. There they stood disconsolate under the stars.

'You see,' he said, 'how can I ask for love, if I don't feel any love in myself? You know I have a real regard for you –'

'How *can* you feel any love, when you never feel anything?' she said.

'That is true,' he replied.

And she waited for what next.

'And how can I marry?' he said. 'I am a failure even at making money. I can't ask my mother for money.'

She sighed deeply.

'Then don't bother yet about marrying,' she said. 'Only love me a little. Won't you?'

He gave a short laugh.

'It sounds so atrocious, to say it is hard to begin,' he said.

She sighed again. He was so stiff to move.

'Shall we sit down a minute?' she said. And then, as they sat on the hay, she added: 'May I touch you? Do you mind?'

'Yes, I mind. But do as you wish,' he replied, with that mixture of shyness and queer candour which made him a little ridiculous, as he knew quite well. But in his heart there was almost murder.

She touched his black, always tidy, hair, with her fingers.

'I suppose I shall rebel one day,' he said again suddenly.

They sat some time, till it grew chilly. And he held her hand fast, but he never put his arms round her. At last she rose, and went indoors, saying good-night.

The next day, as Cecilia lay stunned and angry on the roof, taking her sun-bath, and becoming hot and fierce with sunshine, suddenly she started. A terror seized her in spite of herself. It was the voice.

'Caro, caro, tu non l'hai visto!'[3] it was murmuring away, in a language Cecilia did not understand. She lay and writhed her limbs in the sun, listening intently to words she could not follow. Softly, whisperingly, with infinite caressiveness and yet with that subtle, insidious arrogance under its velvet, came the voice, murmuring in Italian: 'Bravo, si, molto bravo, poverino, ma uomo come te non sarà mai, mai, mai!'[4] Oh, especially in Italian Cecilia heard the poisonous charm of the voice, so caressive, so soft and flexible, yet so utterly egoistic. She hated it with intensity as it sighed and whispered out of nowhere. Why, why should it be so delicate, so subtle and flexible and beautifully controlled, when she herself was so clumsy? Oh, poor Cecilia, she writhed in the afternoon sun, knowing her own clownish clumsiness and lack of suavity, in comparison.

'No, Robert dear, you will never be the man your father was, though you have some of his looks. He was a marvellous lover, soft as a flower yet piercing as a humming-bird. Cara, cara mia bellissima, ti ho aspettato come l'agonissante aspetta la morte, morte deliziosa, quasi quasi troppo deliziosa per una mera anima humana.[5] He gave himself to a woman as he gave himself to God. Mauro! Mauro! How you loved me! How you loved me!'

The voice ceased in reverie, and Cecilia knew what she had guessed before – that Robert was not the son of her Uncle Ronald, but of some Italian.

'I am disappointed in you, Robert. There is no poignancy in you. Your father was a Jesuit, but he was the most perfect and poignant lover in the world. You are a Jesuit like a fish in a tank. And that Ciss of yours is the cat fishing for you. It is less edifying even than poor Henry.'

Cecilia suddenly bent her mouth down to the tube, and said in a deep voice:

'Leave Robert alone! Don't kill him as well.'

There was dead silence in the hot July afternoon that was lowering for thunder. Cecilia lay prostrate, her heart beating in great thumps. She was listening as if her whole soul were an ear. At last she caught the whisper:

'Did someone speak?'

She leaned again to the mouth of the tube:

'Don't kill Robert as you killed me,' she said, with slow enunciation, and a deep but small voice.

'Ah!' came the sharp little cry. 'Who is that speaking?'

'Henry,' said the deep voice.

There was dead silence. Poor Cecilia lay with all the use gone out of her. And there was dead silence. Till at last came the whisper:

'I didn't kill Henry. No, no! No, no! Henry, surely you can't blame me! I loved you, dearest; I only wanted to help you.'

'You killed me!' came the deep, artificial, accusing voice. 'Now let Robert live. Let him go! Let him marry!'

There was a pause.

'How very, very awful!' mused the whispering voice. 'Is it possible, Henry, you are a spirit, and you condemn me?'

'Yes, I condemn you!'

Cecilia felt all the pent-up rage going down that rain-pipe. At the same time, she almost laughed. It was awful.

She lay and listened and listened. No sound! As if time had ceased, she lay inert in the weakening sun, till she heard a far-off rumble of thunder. She sat up. The sky was yellowing. Quickly she dressed herself, went down, and out to the corner of the stables.

'Aunt Pauline!' she called discreetly. 'Did you hear thunder?'

'Yes. I am going in. Don't wait,' came a feeble voice.

Cecilia retired, and from the loft watched, spying, as the figure of the lovely lady, wrapped in a lovely wrap of old blue silk, went rather totteringly to the house.

The sky gradually darkened. Cecilia hastened in with the rugs. Then the storm broke. Aunt Pauline did not appear to tea. She found the thunder trying. Robert also did not arrive till after tea, in the pouring rain. Cecilia went down the covered passage to her own house, and dressed carefully for dinner, putting some white columbines at her breast.

The drawing-room was lit with a softly-shaded lamp. Robert, dressed, was waiting, listening to the rain. He too seemed strangely crackling and on edge. Cecilia came in, with the white flowers nodding at her dusky breast. Robert was watching her curiously, a new look on his face. Cecilia went to the bookshelves near the door, and was peering for something, listening acutely. She heard a rustle, then the door softly opening. And as it opened, Ciss suddenly switched on the strong electric light by the door.

Her aunt, in a dress of black lace over ivory colour, stood in the doorway. Her face was made up, but haggard with a look of unspeakable irritability, as if years of suppressed exasperation and dislike of her fellow-men had suddenly crumpled her into an old witch.

'Oh, aunt!' cried Cecilia.

'Why, mother, you're a little old lady!' came the astounded voice of Robert – like an astonished boy, as if it were a joke.

'Have you only just found it out?' snapped the old woman venomously.

'Yes! Why, I thought –' his voice tailed out in misgiving.

The haggard, old Pauline, in a frenzy of exasperation, said:

'Aren't we going down?'

She had not even noticed the excess of light, a thing she shunned. And she went downstairs almost tottering.

At table she sat with her face like a crumpled mask of unspeakable irritability. She looked old, very old, and like a witch. Robert and Cecilia fetched furtive glances at her. And Ciss, watching Robert, saw that he was so astonished and repelled by his mother's looks that he was another man.

'What kind of a drive home did you have?' snapped Pauline, with an almost gibbering irritability.

'It rained, of course,' he said.

'How clever of you to have found that out!' said his mother, with the grisly grin of malice that had succeeded her arch smile.

'I don't understand,' he said, with quiet suavity.

'It's apparent,' said his mother, rapidly and sloppily eating her food.

She rushed through the meal like a crazy dog, to the utter consternation of the servant. And the moment it was over she darted in a queer, crab-like way upstairs. Robert and Cecilia followed her, thunderstruck, like two conspirators.

'You pour the coffee. I loathe it! I'm going. Good-night!' said the old woman, in a succession of sharp shots. And she scrambled out of the room.

There was a dead silence. At last he said:

'I'm afraid mother isn't well. I must persuade her to see a doctor.'

'Yes,' said Cecilia.

The evening passed in silence. Robert and Ciss stayed on in the drawing-room, having lit a fire. Outside was cold rain. Each pretended to read. They did not want to separate. The evening passed with ominous mysteriousness, yet quickly.

At about ten o'clock the door suddenly opened, and Pauline appeared, in a blue wrap. She shut the door behind her, and came to the fire. Then she looked at the two young people in hate, real hate.

'You two had better get married quickly,' she said, in an ugly voice. 'It would look more decent; such a passionate pair of lovers!'

Robert looked up at her quietly.

'I thought you believed that cousins should not marry, mother,' he said.

'I do. But you're not cousins. Your father was an Italian priest.' Pauline held her daintily-slippered foot to the fire, in an old coquettish gesture. Her body tried to repeat all the old graceful gestures. But the nerve had snapped, so it was a rather dreadful caricature.

'Is that really true, mother?' he asked.

'True! What do you think? He was a distinguished man, or he wouldn't have been my lover. He was far too distinguished a man to have had you for a son. But that joy fell to me.'

'How unfortunate all round,' he said slowly.

'Unfortunate for you? *You* were lucky. It was *my* misfortune,' she said acidly to him.

She was really a dreadful sight, like a piece of lovely Venetian glass that has been dropped and gathered up again in horrible, sharp-edged fragments.

Suddenly she left the room again.

For a week it went on. She did not recover. It was as if every nerve in her body had suddenly started screaming in an insanity of discordance. The doctor came, and gave her sedatives, for she never slept. Without drugs she never slept at all, only paced back and forth in her room, looking hideous and evil, reeking with malevolence. She could not bear to see either her son or her niece. Only when either of them came she asked, in pure malice:

'Well! When's the wedding? Have you celebrated the nuptials yet?'

At first Cecilia was stunned by what she had done. She realised vaguely that her aunt, once a definite thrust of condemnation had penetrated her beautiful armour, had just collapsed, squirming, inside her shell. It was too terrible. Ciss was almost terrified into repentance. Then she thought: 'This is what she always was. Now let her live the rest of her days in her true colours.'

But Pauline would not live long. She was literally shrivelling away. She kept her room, and saw no one. She had her mirrors taken away.

Robert and Cecilia sat a good deal together. The jeering of the mad Pauline had not driven them apart, as she had hoped. But Cecilia dared not confess to him what she had done.

'Do you think your mother ever loved anybody?' Ciss asked him tentatively, rather wistfully, one evening.

He looked at her fixedly.

'Herself!' he said at last.

'She didn't even *love* herself,' said Ciss. 'It was something else. What was it?' She lifted a troubled, utterly puzzled face to him.

'Power,' he said curtly.

'But what power?' she asked. 'I don't understand.'

'Power to feed on other lives,' he said bitterly. 'She was beautiful, and she fed on life. She has fed on me as she fed on Henry. She put a sucker into one's soul, and sucked up one's essential life.'

'And don't you forgive her?'

'No.'

'Poor Aunt Pauline!'

But even Ciss did not mean it. She was only aghast.

'I *know* I've got a heart,' he said, passionately striking his breast. 'But it's almost sucked dry. I *know* I've got a soul, somewhere. But it's gnawed bare. I *hate* people who want power over others.'

Ciss was silent. What was there to say?

And two days later Pauline was found dead in her bed, having taken too much veronal, for her heart was weakened.

From the grave even she hit back at her son and her niece. She left Robert the noble sum of one thousand pounds, and Ciss one hundred. All the rest, with the nucleus of her valuable antiques, went to form the 'Pauline Attenborough Museum'.

Things

THEY were true idealists, from New England. But that is some time ago: before the War. Several years before the War they met and married; he a tall, keen-eyed young man from Connecticut, she a smallish, demure, Puritan-looking young woman from Massachusetts. They both had a little money. Not much, however. Even added together it didn't make three thousand dollars a year. Still – they were free. Free!

Ah! – freedom! To be free to live one's own life! To be twenty-five and twenty-seven, a pair of true idealists with a mutual love of beauty and an inclination towards 'Indian thought' – meaning, alas! Mrs Besant[1] – and an income a little under three thousand dollars a year! But what is money? All one wishes to do is to live a full and beautiful life. In Europe, of course, right at the fountain-head of tradition. It might possibly be done in America: in New England, for example. But at forfeiture of a certain amount of 'beauty'. True beauty takes a long time to mature. The baroque is only half-beautiful, half-matured. No, the real silver bloom, the real golden-sweet bouquet of beauty, had its roots in the Renaissance, not in any later or shallower period.

Therefore, the two idealists, who were married in New Haven, sailed at once to Paris: Paris of the old days. They had a studio apartment on the Boulevard Montparnasse, and they became real Parisians, in the old, delightful sense, not in the modern, vulgar. It was the shimmer of the pure impressionists, Monet and his followers, the world seen in terms of pure light, light broken and unbroken. How lovely! How lovely! how lovely the nights, the river, the mornings in the old streets and by the flower-stalls and the book-stalls, the afternoons up on Montmartre or in the Tuileries, the evenings on the boulevards!

They both painted, but not desperately. Art had not taken them by the throat, and they did not take Art by the throat. They painted: that's all. They knew people – nice people, if possible, though one had to take them mixed. And they were happy.

Yet it seems as if human beings must set their claws in *something*. To be 'free', to be 'living a full and beautiful life', you must, alas! be attached to something. A 'full and beautiful life' means a tight attachment to *something* – at least, it is so for all idealists – or else a certain boredom supervenes; there is a certain waving of loose ends upon the air, like the waving, yearning tendrils of the vine that spread and rotate, seeking something to clutch, something up which to climb towards the necessary sun. Finding nothing, the vine can only trail, half-fulfilled, upon the ground. Such is freedom – a clutching of the right pole. And human beings are all vines. But especially the idealist. He is a vine, and he needs to clutch and climb. And he despises the man who is a mere *potato*, or turnip, or lump of wood.

Our idealists were frightfully happy, but they were all the time reaching out for something to cotton on to. At first, Paris was enough. They explored Paris *thoroughly*. And they learned French till they almost felt like French people, they could speak it so glibly.

Still, you know, you never talk French with your *soul*. It can't be done. And though it's very thrilling, at first, talking in French to clever Frenchmen – they seem *so* much cleverer than oneself – still, in the long run, it is not satisfying. The endlessly clever *materialism* of the French leaves you cold, in the end, gives a sense of barrenness and incompatibility with true New England depth. So our two idealists felt.

They turned away from France – but ever so gently. France had disappointed them. 'We've loved it, and we've got a great deal out of it. But after a while, a considerable while – several years, in fact – Paris leaves one feeling disappointed. It hasn't quite got what one wants.'

'But Paris isn't France.'

'No, perhaps not. France is quite different from Paris. And France is lovely – quite lovely. But *to us*, though we love it, it doesn't say a great deal.'

So, when the War came, the idealists moved to Italy. And they loved Italy. They found it beautiful, and more poignant than France. It seemed much nearer to the New England conception of beauty: something pure, and full of sympathy, without the *materialism* and the *cynicism* of the French. The two idealists seemed to breathe their own true air in Italy.

And in Italy, much more than in Paris, they felt they could thrill to the teachings of the Buddha. They entered the swelling stream of modern Buddhistic emotion, and they read the books, and they practised meditation, and they deliberately set themselves to eliminate from their own souls greed, pain, and sorrow. They did not realise – yet – that Buddha's very eagerness to free himself from pain and sorrow is in itself a sort of greed. No, they dreamed of a perfect world, from which all greed, and nearly all pain, and a great deal of sorrow, were eliminated.

But America entered the War, so the two idealists had to help. They did hospital work. And though their experience made them realise more than ever that greed, pain, and sorrow *should* be eliminated from the world, nevertheless, the Buddhism, or the theosophy, didn't emerge very triumphant from the long crisis. Somehow, somewhere, in some part of themselves, they felt that greed, pain and sorrow would never be eliminated, because most people don't care about eliminating them, and never will care. Our idealists were far too Western to think of abandoning all the world to damnation while they saved their two selves. They were far too unselfish to sit tight under a bho-tree and reach Nirvana[2] in a mere couple.

It was more than that, though. They simply hadn't enough *Sitzfleisch*[3] to squat under a bho-tree and get to Nirvana by contemplating anything, least of all their own navel. If the whole wide world was not going to be saved, they, personally, were not so very keen on being saved just by themselves. No, it would be so lonesome. They were New Englanders, so it must be all or nothing. Greed, pain and sorrow must either be eliminated *from all the world*, or else what was the use of eliminating them from oneself? No use at all! One was just a victim.

And so – although they still *loved* 'Indian thought', and felt very tender about it: well, to go back to our metaphor, the pole up which the green and anxious vines had clambered so far now proved dry-rotten. It snapped, and the vines came slowly subsiding to earth again. There was no crack and crash. The vines held themselves up by their own foliage, for a while. But they subsided. The beanstalk of 'Indian thought' had given way before Jack had climbed off the tip of it to a further world.

They subsided with a slow rustle back to earth again. But they made no outcry. They were again 'disappointed'. But they never admitted it. 'Indian thought' had let them down. But they never complained. Even to one another they never said a word. But they were disappointed, faintly but deeply disillusioned, and they both knew it. But the knowledge was tacit.

And they still had so much in their lives. They still had Italy – dear Italy. And they still had freedom, the priceless treasure. And they still had so much 'beauty'. About the fullness of their lives they were not quite so sure. They had one little boy, whom they loved as parents should love their children, but whom they wisely refrained from fastening upon, to build their lives on him. No, no, they must live their own lives! They still had strength of mind to know that.

But they were now no longer so very young. Twenty-five and twenty-seven had become thirty-five and thirty-seven. And though they had had a very wonderful time in Europe, and though they still loved Italy – dear Italy! – yet: they were disappointed. They had got a lot out of it: oh, a very great deal indeed! Still, it hadn't given them quite, not *quite*, what they had expected; Europe was lovely, but it was dead. Living in Europe, you were living on the past. And Europeans, with all their superficial charm, were not *really* charming. They were materialistic, they had no real *soul*. They just did not understand the inner urge of the spirit, because the inner urge was dead in them; they were all survivals. There, that was the truth about Europeans: they were survivals, with no more getting ahead in them.

It was another bean-pole, another vine-support crumbled under the green life of the vine. And very bitter it was, this time. For up the old tree-trunk of Europe the green vine had been clambering silently for more than ten years, ten hugely important years, the years of real living. The two idealists had *lived* in Europe, lived on Europe and on European life and European things as vines in an everlasting vineyard.

They had made their home here: a home such as you could never make in America. Their watchword had been 'beauty'. They had rented, the last four years, the second floor of an old Palazzo on the Arno,[4] and here they had all their 'things'. And they derived a profound satisfaction from their apartment: the lofty, silent, ancient rooms with windows on the river, with glistening, dark-red floors, and the beautiful furniture that the idealists had 'picked up'.

Yes, unknown to themselves, the lives of the idealists had been running with a fierce swiftness horizontally, all the time. They had become tense, fierce hunters of 'things' for their home. While their soul was climbing up to the sun of old European culture or old Indian thought, their passions were running horizontally, clutching at 'things'. Of course, they did not buy the things for the things' sakes, but for the sake of 'beauty'. They looked upon their home as a place entirely furnished by loveliness, not by 'things' at all. Valerie had some very lovely curtains at the windows of the long *salotto*,[5] looking on the river: curtains of queer ancient material that looked like finely knitted silk, most beautifully faded down from vermilion and orange and gold and black, to a sheer soft glow. Valerie hardly ever came into the *salotto* without mentally falling on her knees before the curtains. 'Chartres!' she said. 'To me they are Chartres!' And Melville never turned and looked at his sixteenth-century Venetian book-case, with its two or three dozen of choice books, without feeling his marrow stir in his bones. The holy of holies!

The child silently, almost sinisterly, avoided any rude contact with these ancient monuments of furniture, as if they had been nests of sleeping cobras, or that 'thing' most perilous to the touch – the Ark of the Covenant.[6] His childish awe was silent, and cold, but final.

Still, a couple of New England idealists cannot live merely on the by-gone glory of their furniture. At least, one couple could not. They got used to the marvellous Bologna cupboard, they got used to the wonderful Venetian book-case, and the books, and the Siena curtains and bronzes, and the lovely sofas and side-tables and chairs they had 'picked up' in Paris. Oh, they had been picking things up since the first day they landed in Europe. And they were still at it. It is the last interest Europe can offer to an outsider: or to an insider either.

When people came, and were thrilled by the Melville interior, then Valerie and Erasmus felt they had not lived in vain: that they still were living. But in the long mornings, when Erasmus was desultorily working at Renaissance Florentine literature, and Valerie was attending to the apartment; and in the long hours after lunch; and in the long, usually very cold and oppressive evenings in the ancient palazzo: then the halo died from around the furniture, and the things became things; lumps of matter that just stood there or hung there, *ad infinitum*, and said nothing; and Valerie and Erasmus almost hated them. The glow of beauty, like every other glow, dies down unless it is fed. The idealists still dearly loved their things. But they had got them. And the sad fact is, things that glow vividly while you're getting them go almost quite cold after a year or two. Unless, of course, people envy you them very much, and the museums are pining for them. And the Melvilles' 'things', though very good, were not quite as good as that.

So the glow gradually went out of everything, out of Europe, out of Italy – 'the Italians are *dears*' – even out of that marvellous apartment on the Arno. 'Why, if I had this apartment I'd never, never even want to go out of doors! It's too lovely and perfect.' That was something, of course, to hear that.

And yet Valerie and Erasmus went out of doors; they even went out to get away from its ancient, cold-floored, stone-heavy silence and dead dignity. 'We're living on the past, you know, Dick,' said Valerie to her husband. She called him Dick.

They were grimly hanging on. They did not like to give in. They did not like to own up that they were through. For twelve years, now, they had been 'free' people, living a 'full and beautiful life'. And America for twelve years had been their anathema, the Sodom and Gomorrah[7] of industrial materialism.

It wasn't easy to own that you were 'through'. They hated to admit that they wanted to go back. But at last, reluctantly, they decided to go, 'for the boy's sake'. 'We can't *bear* to leave Europe. But Peter is an American, so he had better look at America while he's young.' The Melvilles had an entirely English accent and manner – almost – a little Italian and French here and there.

They left Europe behind, but they took as much of it along with them as possible. Several van-loads, as a matter of fact. All those adorable and irreplaceable 'things'. And all arrived in New York, idealists, child, and the huge bulk of Europe they had lugged along.

Valerie had dreamed of a pleasant apartment, perhaps on Riverside Drive, where it was not so expensive as east of Fifth Avenue, and where all their wonderful things would look marvellous. She and Erasmus house-hunted. But, alas! their income was quite under three thousand dollars a year. They found – well, everybody knows what they found. Two small rooms and a kitchenette, and don't let us unpack a *thing*!

The chunk of Europe which they had bitten off went into a warehouse, at fifty dollars a month. And they sat in two small rooms and a kitchenette, and wondered why they'd done it.

Erasmus, of course, ought to get a job. This was what was written on the wall, and what they both pretended not to see. But it had been the strange, vague threat that the Statue of Liberty had always held over them: 'Thou shalt get a job!' Erasmus had the tickets, as they say. A scholastic career was still possible for him. He had taken his exams, brilliantly at Yale, and had kept up his 'researches' all the time he had been in Europe.

But both he and Valerie shuddered. A scholastic career! The scholastic world! The *American* scholastic world! Shudder upon shudder! Give up their freedom, their full and beautiful life? Never! Never! Erasmus would be forty next birthday.

The 'things' remained in warehouse. Valerie went to look at them. It cost her a dollar an hour, and horrid pangs. The 'things', poor things, looked a bit shabby and wretched in that warehouse.

However, New York was not all America. There was the great clean West. So the Melvilles went West, with Peter, but without the things. They tried living the simple life in the mountains. But doing their own chores became almost a nightmare. 'Things' are all very well to look at, but it's awful handling them, even when they're beautiful.

To be the slave of hideous things, to keep a stove going, cook meals, wash dishes, carry water, and clean floors: pure horror of sordid anti-life!

In the cabin on the mountains Valerie dreamed of Florence, the lost apartment; and her Bologna cupboard and Louis Quinze chairs, above all, her 'Chartres' curtains, stored in New York – and costing fifty dollars a month.

A millionaire friend came to the rescue, offering them a cottage on the Californian coast – California! Where the new soul is to be born in man. With joy the idealists moved a little farther west, catching at new vine-props of hope.

And finding them straws! The millionaire cottage was perfectly equipped. It was perhaps as labour-savingly perfect as is possible: electric heating and cooking, a white-and-pearl-enamelled kitchen, nothing to make dirt except the human being himself. In an hour or so the idealists had got through their chores. They were 'free' – free to hear the great Pacific pounding the coast, and to feel a new soul filling their bodies.

Alas! the Pacific pounded the coast with hideous brutality, brute force itself! And the new soul, instead of sweetly stealing into their bodies, seemed only meanly to gnaw the old soul out of their bodies. To feel you are under the fist of the most blind and crunching brute force: to feel that your cherished idealist's soul is being gnawed out of you, and only irritation left in place of it: well, it isn't good enough.

After about nine months the idealists departed from the Californian west. It had been a great experience; they were glad to have had it. But, in the long run, the West was not the place for them, and they knew it. No, the people who wanted new souls had better get them. They, Valerie and Erasmus Melville, would like to develop the old soul a little further. Anyway, they had not felt any influx of new soul on the Californian coast. On the contrary.

So, with a slight hole in their material capital, they returned to Massachusetts and paid a visit to Valerie's parents, taking the boy along. The grandparents welcomed the child – poor expatriated boy – and were rather cold to Valerie, but really cold to Erasmus. Valerie's mother definitely said to Valerie one day that Erasmus ought to take a job, so that Valerie could live decently. Valerie haughtily reminded her mother of the beautiful apartment on the Arno, and the 'wonderful' things in store in New York, and of the 'marvellous and satisfying life' she and Erasmus had led. Valerie's mother said that she didn't think her daughter's life looked so very marvellous at present: homeless, with a husband idle at the age of forty, a child to educate, and a dwindling capital, looked the reverse of marvellous to *her*. Let Erasmus take some post in one of the universities.

'What post? What university?' interrupted Valerie.

'That could be found, considering your father's connections and Erasmus's qualifications,' replied Valerie's mother. 'And you could get all your valuable things out of store, and have a really lovely home, which everybody in America would be proud to visit. As it is, your furniture is eating up your income, and you are living like rats in a hole, with nowhere to go to.'

This was very true. Valerie was beginning to pine for a home, with her 'things'. Of course, she could have sold her furniture for a substantial sum. But nothing would have induced her to. Whatever else passed away – religions, cultures, continents, and hopes – Valerie would *never* part from the 'things' which she and Erasmus had collected with such passion. To these she was nailed.

But she and Erasmus still would not give up that freedom, that full and beautiful life they had so believed in. Erasmus cursed America. He did not *want* to earn a living. He panted for Europe.

Leaving the boy in charge of Valerie's parents, the two idealists once more set off for Europe. In New York they paid two dollars and looked for a brief, bitter hour at their 'things'. They sailed 'student class' – that is, third. Their income now was less than two thousand dollars, instead of three. And they made straight for Paris – cheap Paris.

They found Europe, this time, a complete failure. 'We have returned like dogs to our vomit,' said Erasmus; 'but the vomit has staled in the meantime.' He found he couldn't stand Europe. It irritated every nerve in his body. He hated America, too. But America at least was a darn sight better than this miserable, dirt-eating continent; which was by no means cheap any more, either.

Valerie, with her heart on her things – she had really burned to get them out of that warehouse, where they had stood now for three years, eating up two thousand dollars – wrote to her mother she thought Erasmus would come back if he could get some suitable work in America. Erasmus, in a state of frustration bordering on rage and insanity, just went round Italy in a poverty-stricken fashion, his coat-cuffs frayed, hating everything with intensity. And when a post was found for him in Cleveland University, to teach French, Italian, and Spanish literature, his eyes grew more beady, and his long, queer face grew sharper and more rat-like with utter baffled fury. He was forty, and the job was upon him.

'I think you'd better accept, dear. You don't care for Europe any longer. As you say, it's dead and finished. They offer us a house on the College lot, and mother says there's room in it for all our things. I think we'd better cable "Accept".'

He glowered at her like a cornered rat. One almost expected to see rat's whiskers twitching at the sides of the sharp nose.

'Shall I send the cablegram?' she asked.

'Send it!' he blurted.

And she went out and sent it.

He was a changed man, quieter, much less irritable. A load was off him. He was inside the cage.

But when he looked at the furnaces of Cleveland, vast and like the greatest of black forests, with red- and white-hot cascades of gushing metal, and tiny gnomes of men, and terrific noises, gigantic, he said to Valerie:

'Say what you like, Valerie, this is the biggest thing the modern world has to show.'

And when they were in their up-to-date little house on the college lot of Cleveland University, and that woe-begone débris of Europe – Bologna cupboard, Venice book-shelves, Ravenna bishop's chair, Louis Quinze side-tables, 'Chartres' curtains, Siena bronze lamps – all were arrayed, and all looked perfectly out of keeping, and therefore very impressive; and when the idealists had had a bunch of gaping people in, and Erasmus had showed off in his best European manner, but still quite cordial and American, and Valerie had been most lady-like, but for all that 'we prefer America'; then Erasmus said, looking at her with the queer sharp eyes of a rat: –

'Europe's the mayonnaise all right, but America supplies the good old lobster – what?'

'Every time!' she said, with satisfaction.

And he peered at her. He was in the cage: but it was safe inside. And she, evidently, was her real self at last. She had got the goods. Yet round his nose was a queer, evil, scholastic look, of pure scepticism. But he liked lobster.

Mother and Daughter

VIRGINIA BODOIN had a good job: she was head of a department in a certain government office, held a responsible position, and earned, to imitate Balzac and be precise about it, seven hundred and fifty pounds a year. That is already something. Rachel Bodoin, her mother, had an income of about six hundred a year, on which she had lived in the capitals of Europe since the effacement of a never very important husband.

Now, after some years of virtual separation and 'freedom', mother and daughter once more thought of settling down. They had become, in course of time, more like a married couple than mother and daughter. They knew one another very well indeed, and each was a little 'nervous' of the other. They had lived together and parted several times. Virginia was now thirty, and she didn't look like marrying. For four years she had been as good as married to Henry Lubbock, a rather spoilt young man who was musical. Then Henry let her down: for two reasons. He couldn't stand her mother. Her mother couldn't stand him. And anybody whom Mrs Bodoin could not stand she managed to sit on, disastrously. So Henry had writhed horribly, feeling his mother-in-law sitting on him tight, and Virginia, after all, in a helpless sort of family loyalty, sitting alongside her mother. Virginia didn't really want to sit on Henry. But when her mother egged her on, she couldn't help it. For ultimately, her mother had power over her; a strange *female* power, nothing to do with parental authority. Virginia had long thrown parental authority to the winds. But her mother had another, much subtler form of domination, female and thrilling, so that when Rachel said: Let's squash him! Virginia had to rush wickedly and gleefully to the sport. And Henry knew quite well when he was being squashed. So that was one of his reasons for going back on Vinny. – He called her Vinny, to the superlative disgust of Mrs Bodoin, who always corrected him: My daughter *Virginia* –

The second reason was, again to be Balzacian, that Virginia hadn't a sou of her own. Henry had a sorry two hundred and fifty. Virginia, at the age of twenty-four, was already earning four hundred and fifty. But she was earning them. Whereas Henry managed to earn about twelve pounds per annum, by his precious music. He had realized that he would find it hard to earn more. So that marrying, except with a wife who could keep him, was rather out of the question. Vinny would inherit her mother's money. But then Mrs Bodoin had the health and muscular equipment of the Sphinx. She would live forever, seeking whom she might devour, and devouring him. Henry lived with Vinny for two years, in the married sense of the words: and Vinny felt they *were* married, minus a mere ceremony. But Vinny had her mother always in the background; often as far back as Paris or Biarritz, but still, within letter reach. And she never realized the funny little grin that came on her own elvish face when her mother, even in a letter, spread her skirts and calmly sat on Henry. She never realized that in spirit she promptly and mischievously sat on him too: she could no more have helped it than the tide can help turning to the moon. And she did not dream that he felt it, and was utterly mortified in his masculine vanity. Women, very often, hypnotize one another, and then, hypnotized, they proceed gently to wring the neck of the man they think they are loving with all their hearts. Then they call it utter perversity on his part, that he doesn't like having his neck wrung. They think he is repudiating a heart-felt love. For they are hypnotized. Women hypnotize one another, without knowing it.

In the end, Henry backed out. He saw himself being simply reduced to nothingness by two women, an old witch with muscles like the Sphinx, and a young, spell-bound witch, lavish, elvish and weak, who utterly spoilt him but who ate his marrow.

Rachel would write from Paris: My dear Virginia, as I had a windfall in the way of an investment, I am sharing it with you. You will find enclosed my cheque for twenty pounds. No doubt you will be needing it to buy Henry a suit of clothes, since the spring is apparently come, and the sunlight may be tempted to show him up for what he is worth. I don't want my daughter going around with what is presumably a street-corner musician, but please pay the tailor's bill yourself, or you may have to do it over again later. – Henry got a suit of clothes, but it was as good as a shirt of Nessus,[1] eating him away with subtle poison.

So he backed out. He didn't jump out, or bolt, or carve his way out at the sword's point. He sort of faded out, distributing his departure over a year or more. He was fond of Vinny, and he could hardly do without her, and he was sorry for her. But at length he couldn't see her apart from her mother. She was a young, weak, spendthrift witch, accomplice of her tough-clawed witch of a mother.

Henry made other alliances, got a good hold on elsewhere, and gradually extricated himself. He saved his life, but he had lost, he felt, a good deal of his youth and marrow. He tended now to go fat, a little puffy, somewhat insignificant. And he had been handsome and striking-looking.

The two witches howled when he was lost to them. Poor Virginia was really half crazy, she didn't know what to do with herself. She had a violent recoil from her mother. Mrs Bodoin was filled with furious contempt for her daughter: that she should let such a hooked fish slip out of her hands! that she should allow such a person to turn her down! – 'I don't quite see my daughter seduced and thrown over by a sponging individual such as Henry Lubbock,' she wrote. 'But if it has happened, I suppose it is somebody's fault –'

There was a mutual recoil, which lasted nearly five years. But the spell was not broken. Mrs Bodoin's mind never left her daughter, and Virginia was ceaselessly aware of her mother, somewhere in the universe. They wrote, and met at intervals, but they kept apart in recoil.

The spell, however, was between them, and gradually it worked. They felt more friendly. Mrs Bodoin came to London. She stayed in the same quiet hotel with her daughter: Virginia had had two rooms in an hotel for the past three years. And, at last, they thought of taking an apartment together.

Virginia was now over thirty. She was still thin and odd and elvish, with a very slight and piquant cast in one of her brown eyes, and she still had her odd, twisted smile, and her slow, rather deep-toned voice, that caressed a man like the stroking of subtle finger-tips. Her hair was still a natural tangle of curls, a bit dishevelled. She still dressed with a natural elegance which tended to go wrong and a tiny bit sluttish. She still might have a hole in her expensive and perfectly new stockings, and still she might have to take off her shoes in the drawing-room, if she came to tea, and sit there in her stockinged-feet. True, she had elegant feet: she was altogether elegantly shaped. But it wasn't that. It was neither coquetry nor vanity. It was simply that, after having gone to a good shoemaker and paid five guineas for a pair of perfectly simple and natural shoes, made to her feet, the said shoes would hurt her excruciatingly, when she had walked half a mile in them, and she would simply have to take them off, even if she sat on the kerb to do it. It was a fatality. There was a touch of the *gamin*[2] in her very feet, a certain sluttishness that wouldn't let them stay properly in nice proper shoes. She practically always wore her mother's old shoes. – Of course I go through life in mother's old shoes. If she died and left me without a supply, I suppose I should have to go in a bathchair, she would say, with her odd twisted little grin. She was so elegant, and yet a slut. It was her charm, really.

Just the opposite of her mother. They could wear each other's shoes and each other's clothes, which seemed remarkable, for Mrs Bodoin seemed so much the bigger of the two. But Virginia's shoulders were broad, if she was thin, she had a strong frame, even when she looked a frail rag.

Mrs Bodoin was one of those women of sixty or so, with a terrible inward energy and a violent sort of vitality. But she managed to hide it. She sat with perfect repose, and folded hands. One thought: What a calm woman! Just as one may look at the snowy summit of a quiescent volcano, in the evening light, and think: What peace!

It was a strange *muscular* energy which possessed Mrs Bodoin, as it possesses, curiously enough, many women over fifty, and is usually distasteful in its manifestations. Perhaps it accounts for the lassitude of the young.

But Mrs Bodoin recognized the bad taste in her energetic coevals, so she cultivated repose. Her very way of pronouncing the word, in two syllables: re-pòse, making the second syllable run on into the twilight, showed how much suppressed energy she had. Faced with the problem of iron-grey hair and black eyebrows, she was too clever to try dyeing herself back into youth. She studied her face, her whole figure, and decided that it was *positive*. There was no denying it. There was no wispiness, no hollowness, no limp frail blossom-on-a-bending-stalk about her. Her figure, though not stout, was full, strong, and *cambré*.[3] Her face had an aristocratic arched nose, aristocratic, who-the-devil-are-you grey eyes, and cheeks rather long but also rather full. Nothing appealing or youthfully skittish here.

Like an independent woman, she used her wits, and decided most emphatically not to be either youthful or skittish or appealing. She would keep her dignity, for she was fond of it. She was positive. She liked to be positive. She was used to her positivity. So she would just *be* positive.

She turned to the positive period; to the eighteenth century, to Voltaire, to Ninon de l'Enclos and the Pompadour, to Madame la Duchesse and Monsieur le Marquis.[4] She decided that she was not much in the line of la Pompadour or la Duchesse, but almost exactly in the line of Monsieur le Marquis. And she was right. With hair silvering to white, brushed back clean from her positive brow and temples, cut short, but sticking out a little behind, with her rather full, pink face and thin black eyebrows plucked to two fine, superficial crescents, her arching nose and her rather full insolent eyes she was perfectly eighteenth-century, the early half. That she was Monsieur le Marquis rather than Madame la Marquise made her really modern.

Her appearance was perfect. She wore delicate combinations of grey and pink, maybe with a darkening iron-grey touch, and her jewels were of soft old coloured paste. Her bearing was a sort of alert repose, very calm, but very assured. There was, to use a vulgarism, no getting past her.

She had a couple of thousand pounds she could lay hands on. Virginia, of course, was always in debt. But, after all, Virginia was not to be sniffed at. She made seven hundred and fifty a year.

Virginia was oddly clever, and not clever. She didn't *really* know anything, because anything and everything was interesting to her for the moment, and she picked it up at once. She picked up languages with extraordinary ease, she was fluent in a fortnight. This helped her enormously with her job. She could prattle away with heads of industry, let them come from where they liked. But she didn't *know* any language, not even her own. She picked things up in her sleep, so to speak, without knowing anything about them.

And this made her popular with men. With all her curious facility, they didn't feel small in front of her, because she was like an instrument. She had to be prompted. Some man had to set her in motion, and then she worked, really cleverly. She could collect the most valuable information. She was very useful. She worked with men, spent most of her time with men, her friends were practically all men. She didn't feel easy with women.

Yet she had no lover, nobody seemed eager to marry her, nobody seemed eager to come close to her at all. Mrs Bodoin said: I'm afraid Virginia is a one-man woman. I am a one-man woman. So was my mother, and so was my grandmother. Virginia's father was the only man in my life, the only one. And I'm afraid Virginia is the same, tenacious. Unfortunately, the man was what he was, and her life is just left there.

Henry had said, in the past, that Mrs Bodoin wasn't a one-man woman, she was a no-man woman, and that if she could have had her way, everything male would have been wiped off the face of the earth, and only the female element left.

However, Mrs Bodoin thought that it was now time to make a move. So she and Virginia took a quite handsome apartment in one of the old Bloomsbury Squares, fitted it up and furnished it with extreme care, and with some quite lovely things, got in a very good man, an

Austrian, to cook, and they set up married life together, mother and daughter.

At first it was rather thrilling. The two reception-rooms, looking down on the dirty old trees of the square garden, were of splendid proportions, and each with three great windows coming down low, almost to the level of the knees. The chimney-piece was late eighteenth-century. Mrs Bodoin furnished the rooms with a gentle suggestion of Louis Seize merged with Empire, without keeping to any particular style. But she had, saved from her own home, a really remarkable Aubusson carpet.[5] It looked almost new, as if it had been woven two years ago, and was startling, yet somehow rather splendid, as it spread its rose-red borders and wonderful florid array of silver-grey and gold-grey roses, lilies and gorgeous swans and trumpeting volutes away over the floor. Very aesthetic people found it rather loud, they preferred the worn, dim yellowish Aubusson in the big bedroom. But Mrs Bodoin loved her drawing-room carpet. It was positive, but it was not vulgar. It had a certain grand air in its floridity. She felt it gave her a proper footing. And it behaved very well with her painted cabinets and grey-and-gold brocade chairs and big Chinese vases, which she liked to fill with big flowers: single Chinese peonies, big roses, great tulips, orange lilies. The dim room of London, with all its atmospheric colour, would stand the big, free, fisticuffing flowers.

Virginia, for the first time in her life, had the pleasure of making a home. She was again entirely under her mother's spell, and swept away, thrilled to her marrow. She had had no idea that her mother had got such treasures as the carpets and painted cabinets and brocade chairs up her sleeve: many of them the débris of the Fitzpatrick home in Ireland, Mrs Bodoin being a Fitzpatrick. Almost like a child, like a bride, Virginia threw herself into the business of fixing up the rooms. 'Of course, Virginia, I consider this is *your* apartment,' said Mrs Bodoin. 'I am nothing but your *dame de compagnie*,[6] and shall carry out your wishes entirely, if you will only express them.'

Of course Virginia expressed a few, but not many. She introduced some wild pictures bought from impecunious artists whom she patronized. Mrs Bodoin thought the pictures positive about the wrong things, but as far as possible, she let them stay: looking on them as the necessary element of modern ugliness. But by that element of modern ugliness, wilfully so, it was easy to see the things that Virginia had introduced into the apartment.

Perhaps nothing goes to the head like setting up house. You can get drunk on it. You feel you are creating something. Nowadays it is no longer the 'home', the domestic nest. It is 'my rooms', or 'my house', the great garment which reveals and clothes 'my personality'. Mrs Bodoin, deliberately scheming for Virginia, kept moderately cool over it, but even she was thrilled to the marrow, and of an intensity and ferocity with the decorators and furnishers, astonishing. But Virginia was just all the time tipsy with it, as if she had touched some magic button on the grey wall of life, and with an Open Sesame![7] her lovely and coloured rooms had begun to assemble out of fairyland. It was far more vivid and wonderful to her than if she had inherited a duchy.

The mother and daughter, the mother in a sort of faded russet crimson and the daughter in silver, began to entertain. They had, of course, mostly men. It filled Mrs Bodoin with a sort of savage impatience to entertain women. Besides, most of Virginia's acquaintances were men. So there were dinners and well-arranged evenings.

It went well, but something was missing. Mrs Bodoin wanted to be gracious, so she held herself rather back. She stayed a little distant, was calm, reposed, eighteenth-century, and determined to be a foil to the clever and slightly-elvish Virginia. It was a pose, and alas, it stopped something. She was very nice with the men, no matter what her contempt of them. But the men were uneasy with her: afraid.

What they all felt, all the men guests, was that *for them*, nothing really happened. Everything that happened was between mother and daughter. All the flow was between mother and daughter. A subtle, hypnotic spell encompassed the two women, and try as they might, the men were shut out. More than one young man, a little dazzled, *began* to fall in love with Virginia. But it was impossible. Not only was he shut out, he was, in some way, annihilated. The spontaneity was killed in his bosom. While the two women sat, brilliant and rather wonderful, in magnetic connection at opposite ends of the table, like two witches, a double Circe[8] turning the men not into swine – the men would have liked that well enough – but into lumps.

It was tragic. Because Mrs Bodoin wanted Virginia to fall in love and marry. She really wanted it, and she attributed Virginia's lack of forthcoming to the delinquent Henry. She never realized the hypnotic spell, which of course encompassed her as well as Virginia, and made men just an impossibility to both women, mother and daughter alike.

At this time, Mrs Bodoin hid her humour. She had a really marvellous faculty of humorous imitation. She could imitate the Irish servants from her old home, or the American women who called on her, or the modern lady-like young men, the asphodels, as she called them:

'Of course you know the asphodel is a kind of onion! Oh yes, just an over-bred onion': who wanted, with their murmuring voices and peeping under their brows, to make her feel very small and very bourgeois. She could imitate them all with a humour that was really touched with genius. But it was devastating. It demolished the objects of her humour so absolutely, smashed them to bits with a ruthless hammer, pounded them to nothing so terribly, that it frightened people, particularly men. It frightened men off.

So she hid it. She hid it. But there it was, up her sleeve, her merciless, hammer-like humour, which just smashed its object on the head and left him brained. She tried to disown it. She tried to pretend, even to Virginia, that she had the gift no more. But in vain; the hammer hidden up her sleeve hovered over the head of every guest, and every guest felt his scalp creep, and Virginia felt her inside creep with a little, mischievous, slightly idiotic grin, as still another fool male was mystically knocked on the head. It was a sort of uncanny sport.

No, the plan was not going to work: the plan of having Virginia fall in love and marry. Of course the men *were* such lumps, such *oeufs farcies*.[9] There was one, at least, that Mrs Bodoin had real hopes of. He was a healthy and normal and very good-looking boy of good family, with no money, alas, but clerking to the House of Lords and very hopeful, and not very clever, but simply in love with Virginia's cleverness. He was just the one Mrs Bodoin would have married for herself. True, he was only twenty-six, to Virginia's thirty-one. But he had rowed in the Oxford eight, and adored horses, talked horses adorably, and was simply infatuated by Virginia's cleverness. To him Virginia had the finest mind on earth. She was as wonderful as Plato, but infinitely more attractive, because she was a woman, and winsome with it. Imagine a winsome Plato with untidy curls and the tiniest little brown-eyed squint and just a hint of woman's pathetic need for a protector, and you may imagine Adrian's feeling for Virginia. He adored her on his knees, but he felt he could protect her.

'Of course he's just a very nice *boy*!' said Mrs Bodoin. 'He's a boy, and that's all you can say. And he always will be a boy. But that's the very nicest kind of man, the only kind you can live with: the eternal boy. Virginia, aren't you attracted to him?'

'Yes, Mother! I think he's an awfully nice *boy*, as you say,' replied Virginia, in her rather slow, musical, whimsical voice. But the mocking little curl in the intonation put the lid on Adrian. Virginia was not marrying a nice *boy*! She could be malicious too, against her mother's taste. And Mrs Bodoin let escape her a faint gesture of impatience.

For she had been planning her own retreat, planning to give Virginia the apartment outright, and half of her own income, if she would marry Adrian. Yes, the mother was already scheming how best she could live with dignity on three hundred a year, once Virginia was happily married to that most attractive if slightly brainless *boy*.

A year later, when Virginia was thirty-two, Adrian, who had married a wealthy American girl and been transferred to a job in the legation at Washington in the meantime, faithfully came to see Virginia as soon as he was in London, faithfully kneeled at her feet, faithfully thought her the most wonderful spiritual being, and faithfully felt that she, Virginia, could have done wonders with him, which wonders would now never be done, for he had married in the meantime.

Virginia was looking haggard and worn. The scheme of a *ménage à deux*[10] with her mother had not succeeded. And now, work was telling on the younger woman. It is true, she was amazingly facile. But facility wouldn't get her all the way. She had to earn her money, and earn it hard. She had to slog, and she had to concentrate. While she could work by quick intuition and without much responsibility, work thrilled her. But as soon as she had to get down to it, as they say, grip and slog and concentrate, in a really responsible position, it wore her out terribly. She had to do it all off her nerves. She hadn't the same sort of fighting power as a man. Where a man can summon his old Adam in him to fight through his work, a woman has to draw on her nerves, and on her nerves alone. For the old Eve in her will have nothing to do with such work. So that mental responsibility, mental concentration, mental slogging wear out a woman terribly, especially if she is head of a department, and not working *for* somebody.

So poor Virginia was worn out. She was thin as a rail. Her nerves were frayed to bits. And she could never forget her beastly work. She would come home at teatime speechless and done for. Her mother, tortured by the sight of her, longed to say: Has anything gone wrong, Virginia? Have you had anything particularly trying at the office today? – But she learned to hold her tongue, and say nothing. The question would be the last straw to Virginia's poor overwrought nerves, and there would be a little scene which, despite Mrs Bodoin's calm and forbearance, offended the elder woman to the quick. She had learned, by bitter experience, to leave her child alone, as one would leave a frail tube of vitriol alone. But of course, she could not keep her *mind* off Virginia. That was impossible. And poor Virginia, under the strain of work and the strain of her mother's awful ceaseless mind, was at the very end of her strength and resources.

Mrs Bodoin had always disliked the fact of Virginia's doing a job. But now she hated it. She hated the whole government office with violent and virulent hate. Not only was it undignified for Virginia to be tied up there, but it was turning her, Mrs Bodoin's daughter, into a thin, nagging, fearsome old maid. Could anything be more utterly English and humiliating to a well-born Irishwoman?

After a long day attending to the apartment, skilfully darning one of the brocade chairs, polishing the Venetian mirrors to her satisfaction, selecting flowers, doing certain shopping and housekeeping, attending perfectly to everything, then receiving callers in the afternoon, with never-ending energy, Mrs Bodoin would go up from the drawing-room after tea and write a few letters, take her bath, dress with great care – she enjoyed attending to her person – and come down to dinner as fresh as a daisy, but far more energetic than that quiet flower. She was ready now for a full evening.

She was conscious, with gnawing anxiety, of Virginia's presence in the house, but she did not see her daughter till dinner was announced. Virginia slipped in, and away to her room unseen, never going into the drawing-room to tea. If Mrs Bodoin heard her daughter's key in the latch, she quickly retired into one of the rooms till Virginia was safely through. It was too much for poor Virginia's nerves even to catch sight of anybody in the house, when she came in from the office. Bad enough to hear the murmur of visitors' voices behind the drawing-room door.

And Mrs Bodoin would wonder: How is she? How is she to-night? I wonder what sort of a day she's had? – And this thought would roam prowling through the house, to where Virginia was lying on her back in her room. But the mother would have to consume her anxiety till dinner-time. And then Virginia would appear, with black lines under her eyes, thin, tense, a young woman out of an office, the stigma upon her: badly dressed, a little acid in humour, with an impaired digestion, not interested in anything, blighted by her work. And Mrs Bodoin, humiliated at the very sight of her, would control herself perfectly, say nothing but the mere smooth nothings of casual speech, and sit in perfect form presiding at a carefully-cooked dinner thought out entirely to please Virginia. Then Virginia hardly noticed what she ate.

Mrs Bodoin was pining for an evening with life in it. But Virginia would lie on the couch and put on the loudspeaker. Or she would put a humorous record on the gramophone, and be amused, and hear it again, and be amused, and hear it again, six times, and six times be amused by a mildly funny record that Mrs Bodoin now knew off by heart. 'Why, Virginia, I could repeat that record over to you, if you wished it, without your troubling to wind up that gramophone.' – And Virginia, after a pause in which she seemed not to have heard what her mother said, would reply, 'I'm sure you could, mother'. And that simple speech would convey such volumes of contempt for all that Rachel Bodoin was or ever could be or ever had been, contempt for her energy, her vitality, her mind, her body, her very existence, that the elder woman would curl. It seemed as if the ghost of Robert Bodoin spoke out of the mouth of the daughter, in deadly venom. – Then Virginia would put on the record for the seventh time.

During the second ghastly year, Mrs Bodoin realized that the game was up. She was a beaten woman, a woman without object or meaning any more. The hammer of her awful female humour, which had knocked so many people on the head, all the people, in fact, that she had come into contact with, had at last flown backwards and hit herself on the head. For her daughter was her other self, her *alter ego*. The secret and the meaning and the power of Mrs Bodoin's whole life lay in the hammer, that hammer of her living humour which knocked everything on the head. That had been her lust and her passion, knocking everybody and everything humorously on the head. She had felt inspired in it: it was a sort of mission. And she had hoped to hand on the hammer to Virginia, her clever, unsolid but still actual daughter, Virginia. Virginia was the continuation of Rachel's own self. Virginia was Rachel's *alter ego*, her other self.

But, alas, it was a half-truth. Virginia had had a father. This fact, which had been utterly ignored by the mother, was gradually brought home to her by the curious recoil of the hammer. Virginia was her father's daughter. Could anything be more unseemly, horrid, more perverse in the natural scheme of things? For Robert Bodoin had been fully and deservedly knocked on the head by Rachel's hammer. Could anything, then, be more disgusting than that he should resurrect again in the person of Mrs Bodoin's own daughter, her own *alter ego* Virginia, and start hitting back with a little spiteful hammer that was David's pebble against Goliath's battle-axe![11]

But the little pebble was mortal. Mrs Bodoin felt it sink into her brow, her temple, and she was finished. The hammer fell nerveless from her hand.

The two women were now mostly alone. Virginia was too tired to have company in the evening. So there was the gramophone or loud-speaker, or else silence. Both women had come to loathe the apartment.

Virginia felt it was the last grand act of bullying on her mother's part, she felt bullied by the assertive Aubusson carpet, by the beastly Venetian mirrors, by the big overcultured flowers. She even felt bullied by the excellent food, and longed again for a Soho restaurant and her two poky shabby rooms in the hotel. She loathed the apartment: she loathed everything. But she had not the energy to move. She had not the energy to do anything. She crawled to her work, and for the rest, she lay flat, gone.

It was Virginia's worn-out inertia that really finished Mrs Bodoin. That was the pebble that broke the bone of her temple: 'To have to attend my daughter's funeral, and accept the sympathy of all her fellow-clerks in her office, no, that is a final humiliation which I must spare myself. No! If Virginia must be a lady-clerk, she must be it henceforth on her own responsibility. I will retire from her existence.'

Mrs Bodoin had tried hard to persuade Virginia to give up her work and come and live with her. She had offered her half her income. In vain. Virginia stuck to her office.

Very well! So be it! – The apartment was a fiasco, Mrs Bodoin was longing, longing to tear it to pieces again. One last and final blow of the hammer! – 'Virginia, don't you think we'd better get rid of this apartment, and live around as we used to? Don't you think we'll do that?' – 'But all the money you've put into it? And the lease for ten years!' cried Virginia, in a kind of inertia. – 'Never mind! We had the pleasure of making it. And we've had as much pleasure out of living in it as we shall ever have. Now we'd better get rid of it – quickly – don't you think?'

Mrs Bodoin's arms were twitching to snatch the pictures off the walls, roll up the Aubusson carpet, take the china out of the ivory-inlaid cabinet there and then, at that very moment.

'Let us wait till Sunday before we decide,' said Virginia.

'Till Sunday! Four days! As long as that? Haven't we already decided in our own minds?' said Mrs Bodoin.

'We'll wait till Sunday, anyhow,' said Virginia.

The next evening, the Armenian came to dinner. Virginia called him Arnold, with the French pronunciation, Arnault. Mrs Bodoin, who barely tolerated him, and could never get his name, which seemed to have a lot of bouyoums in it, called him either the Armenian, or the Rahat Lakoum, after the name of the sweetmeat, or simply The Turkish Delight.

'Arnault is coming to dinner to-night, Mother.'

'Really! The Turkish Delight is coming here to dinner? Shall I provide anything special?' – Her voice sounded as if she would suggest snails in aspic.

'I don't think so.'

Virginia had seen a good deal of the Armenian at the office, when she had to negotiate with him on behalf of the Board of Trade. He was a man of about sixty, a merchant, had been a millionaire, was ruined during the war, but was now coming on again, and represented trade in Bulgaria. He wanted to negotiate with the British Government, and the British Government sensibly negotiated with him: at first through the medium of Virginia. Now things were going satisfactorily between Monsieur Arnault, as Virginia called him, and the Board of Trade, so that a sort of friendship had followed the official relations.

The Turkish Delight was sixty, grey-haired and fat. He had numerous grandchildren growing up in Bulgaria, but he was a widower. He had a grey moustache cut like a brush, and glazed brown eyes over which hung heavy lids with white lashes. His manner was humble, but in his bearing there was a certain dogged conceit. One notices the combination sometimes in Jews. He had been very wealthy and kow-towed to, he had been ruined and humiliated, terribly humiliated, and now, doggedly, he was rising up again, his sons backing him, away in Bulgaria. One felt he was not alone. He had his sons, his family, his tribe behind him, away in the Near East.

He spoke bad English, but fairly fluent guttural French. He did not speak much, but he sat. He sat, with his short, fat thighs, as if for eternity, *there*. There was a strange potency in his fat immobile sitting, as if his posterior were connected with the very centre of the earth. And his brain, spinning away at the one point in question, business, was very agile. Business absorbed him. But not in a nervous, personal way. Somehow the family, the tribe was always felt behind him. It was business for the family, the tribe.

With the English he was humble, for the English like such aliens to be humble, and he had had a long schooling from the Turks. And he was always an outsider. Nobody would ever take any notice of him in society. He would just be an outsider, *sitting*.

'I hope, Virginia, you won't ask that Turkish-carpet gentleman when we have other people. *I* can bear it,' said Mrs Bodoin. 'Some people might mind.'

'Isn't it hard when you can't choose your own company in your own house!' mocked Virginia.

'No! *I* don't care. I can meet anything; and I'm sure, in the way of selling Turkish carpets, your acquaintance is very good. But I don't suppose you look on him as a personal friend –?'

'I do. I like him quite a lot.'

'Well –! as you will. But consider your *other* friends.'

Mrs Bodoin was really mortified this time. She looked on the Armenian as one looks on the fat Levantine in a fez who tries to sell one hideous tapestries at Port Said, or on the sea-front at Nice, as being outside the class of human beings, and in the class of insects. That he had been a millionaire, and might be a millionaire again, only added venom to her feeling of disgust at being forced into contact with such scum. She could not even squash him, or annihilate him. In scum, there is nothing to squash, for scum is only the unpleasant residue of that which was never anything but squashed.

However, she was not quite just. True, he was fat, and he sat, with short thighs, like a toad, as if seated for a toad's eternity. His colour was of a dirty sort of paste, his black eyes were glazed under heavy lids. And he never spoke until spoken to, waiting in his toad's silence, like a slave.

But his thick, fine white hair, which stood up on his head like a soft brush, was curiously virile. And his curious small hands, of the same soft dull paste, had a peculiar, fat, soft masculine breeding of their own. And his dull brown eye could glint with the subtlety of serpents, under the white brush of eyelash. He was tired, but he was not defeated. He had fought, and won, and lost, and was fighting again, always at a disadvantage. He belonged to a defeated race which accepts defeat, but which gets its own back by cunning. He was the father of sons, the head of a family, one of the heads of a defeated but indestructible tribe. He was not alone, and so you could not lay your finger on him. His whole consciousness was patriarchal and tribal. And somehow, he was humble, but he was indestructible.

At dinner he sat half-effaced, humble, yet with the conceit of the humble. His manners were perfectly good, rather French. Virginia chattered to him in French, and he replied with that peculiar nonchalance of the boulevards, which was the only manner he could command when speaking French. Mrs Bodoin understood, but she was what one would call a heavy-footed linguist, so when she said anything, it was intensely in English. And the Turkish Delight replied in his clumsy English, hastily. It was not his fault that French was being spoken. It was Virginia's.

He was very humble, conciliatory, with Mrs Bodoin. But he cast at her sometimes that rapid glint of a reptilian glance as if to say: Yes!

I see you! You are a handsome figure. As an *objet de vertu*[12] you are almost perfect. – Thus his connoisseur's, antique-dealer's eye would appraise her. But then his thick white eyebrows would seem to add: But what, under holy Heaven, are you as a woman? You are neither wife nor mother nor mistress, you have no perfume of sex, you are more dreadful than a Turkish soldier or an English official. No man on earth could embrace you. You are a ghoul, you are a strange genie from the underworld! – And he would secretly invoke the holy names, to shield him.

Yet he was in love with Virginia. He saw, first and foremost, the child in her, as if she were a lost child in the gutter, a waif with a faint, fascinating cast in her brown eyes, waiting till someone would pick her up. A fatherless waif! And he was tribal father, father through all the ages.

Then, on the other hand, he knew her peculiar disinterested cleverness in affairs. That, too, fascinated him: that odd, almost second-sight cleverness about business, and entirely impersonal, entirely in the air. It seemed to him very strange. But it would be an immense help to him in his schemes. He did not really understand the English. He was at sea with them. But with her, he would have a clue to everything. For she was, finally, quite a somebody among these English, these English officials.

He was about sixty. His family was established, in the East, his grandsons were growing up. It was necessary for him to live in London, for some years. This girl would be useful. She had no money, save what she would inherit from her mother. But he would risk that: she would be an investment in his business. And then the apartment. He liked the apartment extremely. He recognized the *cachet*,[13] and the lilies and swans of the Aubusson carpet really did something to him. Virginia said to him: Mother gave me the apartment. – So he looked on that as safe. And finally, Virginia was almost a virgin, probably quite a virgin, and, as far as the paternal oriental male like himself was concerned, entirely virgin. He had a very small idea of the silly puppy-sexuality of the English, so different from the prolonged male voluptuousness of his own pleasures. And last of all, he was physically lonely, getting old, and tired.

Virginia of course did not know why she liked being with Arnault. Her cleverness was amazingly stupid when it came to life, to living. She said he was 'quaint'. She said his nonchalant French of the boulevards was 'amusing'. She found his business cunning 'intriguing', and the glint in his dark glazed eyes, under the white, thick lashes, 'sheiky'. She saw him quite often, had tea with him in his hotel, and motored with him one day down to the sea.

When he took her hand in his own soft still hands, there was something so caressing, so possessive in his touch, so strange and positive in his leaning towards her, that though she trembled with fear, she was helpless. – 'But you are so thin, dear little thin thing, you need repose, repose, for the blossom to open, poor little blossom, to become a little fat!' he said in his French.

She quivered, and was helpless. It certainly was quaint! He was so strange and positive, he seemed to have all the power. The moment he realized that she would succumb into his power, he took full charge of the situation, he lost all his hesitation and his humility. He did not want just to make love to her: he wanted to marry her, for all his multifarious reasons. And he must make himself master of her.

He put her hand to his lips, and seemed to draw her life to his in kissing her thin hand. 'The poor child is tired, she needs repose, she needs to be caressed and cared for,' he said in his French. And he drew nearer to her.

She looked up in dread at his glinting, tired dark eyes under the white lashes. But he used all his will, looking back at her heavily and calculating that she must submit. And he brought his body quite near to her, and put his hand softly on her face, and made her lay her face against his breast, as he soothingly stroked her arm with his other hand. 'Dear little thing! dear little thing! Arnault loves her so dearly! Arnault loves her! Perhaps she will marry her Arnault. Dear little girl, Arnault will put flowers in her life, and make her life perfumed with sweetness and content.'

She leaned against his breast and let him caress her. She gave a fleeting, half poignant, half vindictive thought to her mother. Then she felt in the air the sense of destiny, destiny. Oh so nice, not to have to struggle. To give way to destiny.

'Will she marry her old Arnault? Eh? Will she marry him?' he asked in a soothing, caressing voice, at the same time compulsive.

She lifted her head and looked at him: the thick white brows, the glinting, tired dark eyes. How queer and comic! How comic to be in his power! And he was looking a little baffled.

'Shall I?' she said, with her mischievous twist of a grin.

'Mais oui!' he said, with all the sang froid of his old eyes. 'Mais oui! Je te contenterai, tu le verras.'[14]

'Tu me contenteras!' she said, with a flickering smile of real amusement at his assurance. 'Will you really content me?'

'But surely! I assure it you. And you will marry me?'

'You must tell mother,' she said, and hid wickedly against his waistcoat again, while the male pride triumphed in him.

Mrs Bodoin had no idea that Virginia was intimate with the Turkish Delight: she did not inquire into her daughter's movements. During the famous dinner, she was calm and a little aloof, but entirely self-possessed. When, after coffee, Virginia left her alone with the Turkish Delight, she made no effort at conversation, only glanced at the rather short, stout man in correct dinner-jacket, and thought how his sort of fatness called for a fez and the full muslin breeches of a bazaar merchant in *The Thief of Baghdad*.[15]

'Do you really prefer to smoke a hookah?' she asked him, with a slow drawl.

'What is a hookah, please?'

'One of those water-pipes. Don't you all smoke them, in the East?'

He only looked mystified and humble, and silence resumed. She little knew what was simmering inside his stillness.

'Madame,' he said, 'I want to ask you something.'

'You do? Then why not ask it?' came her slightly melancholy drawl.

'Yes! It is this. I wish I may have the honour to marry your daughter. She is willing.'

There was a moment's blank pause. Then Mrs Bodoin leaned towards him from her distance, with curious portentousness.

'What was that you said?' she asked. 'Repeat it!'

'I wish I may have the honour to marry your daughter. She is willing to take me.'

His dark, glazed eyes looked at her, then glanced away again. Still leaning forward, she gazed fixedly on him, as if spellbound, turned to stone. She was wearing pink topaz ornaments, but he judged they were paste, moderately good.

'Did I hear you say she is willing to take you?' came the slow, melancholy, remote voice.

'Madame, I think so,' he said, with a bow.

'I think we'll wait till she comes,' she said, leaning back.

There was silence. She stared at the ceiling. He looked closely round the room, at the furniture, at the china in the ivory-inlaid cabinet.

'I can settle five thousand pounds on Mademoiselle Virginia, Madame,' came his voice. 'Am I correct to assume that she will bring this apartment and its appointments into the marriage settlement?'

Absolute silence. He might as well have been on the moon. But he was a good sitter. He just sat until Virginia came in.

Mrs Bodoin was still staring at the ceiling. The iron had entered her soul finally and fully. Virginia glanced at her, but said:

'Have a whisky-and-soda, Arnault?'

He rose and came towards the decanters, and stood beside her: a rather squat, stout man with white head, silent with misgiving. There was the fizz of the syphon: then they came to their chairs.

'Arnault has spoken to you, Mother?' said Virginia.

Mrs Bodoin sat up straight, and gazed at Virginia with big, owlish eyes, haggard. Virginia was terrified, yet a little thrilled. Her mother was beaten.

'Is it true, Virginia, that you are *willing* to marry this – oriental gentleman?' asked Mrs Bodoin slowly.

'Yes, Mother, quite true,' said Virginia, in her teasing soft voice.

Mrs Bodoin looked owlish and dazed.

'May I be excused from having any part in it, or from having anything to do with your future *husband* – I mean having any business to transact with him?' she asked dazedly, in her slow, distinct voice.

'Why, of course!' said Virginia, frightened, smiling oddly.

There was a pause. Then Mrs Bodoin, feeling old and haggard, pulled herself together again.

'Am I to understand that your future husband would like to possess this apartment?' came her voice.

Virginia smiled quickly and crookedly. Arnault just sat, planted on his posterior, and heard. She reposed on him.

'Well – perhaps!' said Virginia. 'Perhaps he would like to know that I possessed it.' She looked at him.

Arnault nodded gravely.

'And do you *wish* to possess it?' came Mrs Bodoin's slow voice. 'Is it your intention to *inhabit* it, with your *husband*?' She put eternities into her long, stressed words.

'Yes, I think it is,' said Virginia. 'You know you *said* the apartment was mine, Mother.'

'Very well! It shall be so. I shall send my lawyer to this – oriental gentleman, if you will leave written instructions on my writing-table. May I ask when you think of getting – *married*?'

'When do you think, Arnault?' said Virginia.

'Shall it be, in two weeks?' he said, sitting erect, with his fists on his knees.

'In about a fortnight, Mother,' said Virginia.

'I have heard! In two weeks! Very well! In two weeks everything shall be at your disposal. And now, please excuse me.' She rose, made a slight general bow, and moved calmly and dimly from the room. It was killing her, that she could not shriek aloud and beat that Levantine out of the house. But she couldn't. She had imposed the restraint on herself.

Arnault stood and looked with glistening eyes round the room. It would be his. When his sons came to England, here he would receive them.

He looked at Virginia. She too was white and haggard, now. And she hung away from him, as if in resentment. She resented the defeat of her mother. She was still capable of dismissing him for ever, and going back to her mother.

'Your mother is a wonderful lady,' he said, going to Virginia and taking her hand. 'But she has no husband to shelter her, she is unfortunate. I am sorry she will be alone. I should be happy if she would like to stay here with us.'

The sly old fox knew what he was about.

'I'm afraid there's no hope of that,' said Virginia, with a return to her old irony.

She sat on the couch, and he caressed her softly and paternally, and the very incongruity of it, there in her mother's drawing-room, amused her. And because he saw that the things in the drawing-room were handsome and valuable, and now they were his, his blood flushed and he caressed the thin girl at his side with passion, because she represented these valuable surroundings, and brought them to his possession. And he said: 'And with me you will be very comfortable, very content, oh, I shall make you content, not like Madame your mother. And you will get fatter, and bloom like the rose. I shall make you bloom like the rose. And shall we say next week, hein? Shall it be next week, next Wednesday, that we marry? Wednesday is a good day. Shall it be then?'

'Very well!' said Virginia, caressed again into a luxurious sense of destiny, reposing on fate, having to make no effort, no more effort, all her life.

Mrs Bodoin moved into an hotel next day, and came into the apartment to pack up and extricate herself and her immediate personal belongings only when Virginia was necessarily absent. She and her daughter communicated by letter, as far as was necessary.

And in five days' time Mrs Bodoin was clear. All business that could be settled was settled, all her trunks were removed. She had five trunks, and that was all. Denuded and outcast, she would depart to Paris, to live out the rest of her days.

The last day, she waited in the drawing-room till Virginia should come home. She sat there in her hat and street things, like a stranger.

'I just waited to say good-bye,' she said. 'I leave in the morning for Paris. This is my address. I think everything is settled; if not, let me know and I'll attend to it. Well, good-bye! – and I hope you'll be *very happy*!'

She dragged out the last words sinisterly; which restored Virginia, who was beginning to lose her head.

'Why, I think I may be,' said Virginia, with the twist of a smile.

'I shouldn't wonder,' said Mrs Bodoin pointedly and grimly. 'I think the Armenian grandpapa knows very well what he's about. You're just the harem type, after all.' The words came slowly, dropping, each with a plop! of deep contempt.

'I suppose I am! Rather fun!' said Virginia. 'But I wonder where I got it? Not from you, Mother –' she drawled mischievously.

'I should say *not*.'

'Perhaps daughters go by contraries, like dreams,' mused Virginia wickedly. 'All the harem was left out of you, so perhaps it all had to be put back into me.'

Mrs Bodoin flashed a look at her.

'You have *all* my *pity*!' she said.

'Thank you, dear. You have just a bit of mine.'

Notes

LOVE AMONG THE HAYSTACKS

This story is loosely based on a night that Lawrence spent camping under a haystack with Alan Chambers in July 1908 when he was helping the Chambers family haymaking in the two fields to the south of Greasley church that Alan's father rented. Lawrence might have written an early version soon after the haymaking was done. He had written it up as a 'long short story' by early November 1911. After it was rejected by the *English Review* as 'too steaming', he rewrote it in July 1913. But when he was putting his first collection of stories together in July 1914 he was still dissatisfied with it and left it with his typist to be worked at later. There it lay forgotten until it was unearthed just before Lawrence's death, but too late for him to revise it. So in 1930 it was published posthumously by the Nonesuch Press in the form in which he left it *c.* 1913.

1 (p. 33) *winrows*: Windrows: rows in which hay is laid to dry.

2 (p. 35) '*Ich bin ... allein.*': 'I am small, my heart is pure,/There is no one there except Christ alone.' (German).

3 (p. 36) *scotches*: Blocks placed under the wheels to prevent moving.

4 (p. 39) *had as lief*: Would rather (dial.).

5 (p. 43) *th' loose a'*: The loose-all. The hooter signifying the end of a shift (dial.).

6 (p. 61) *câline*: Caressing, winning (French).

THE WHITE STOCKING

Originally written in late 1907 as an entry for a Christmas competition in the *Nottingham Guardian*, the first version was based on an incident in his mother's youth when she went to a ball at the Castle in Nottingham. Twice revised in January 1910 and April 1911, it was rejected by the *English Review* and further revised in the summer of 1913. This version was published in the *Smart Set* in October 1914. Lawrence rewrote it once more in July 1914 for its inclusion in *The Prussian Officer* volume published in November 1914.

1 (p. 67) *What the Hanover*: What the hell. The expression dates from the unpopularity of the first two Hanoverian monarchs, George I and II, especially among Jacobite sympathizers.

2 (p. 72) *At night ... to roost*: From the proverb: curses, like chickens, come home to roost, i.e. rebound on the head of the curser.

3 (p. 74) *amourette*: Passing love-affair or amorous intrigue (French). Cf. Amoret: female love personified (Spenser *Fairie Queene III*, 6–12).

ODOUR OF CHRYSANTHEMUMS

First written in late 1909, this story was subsequently altered in April 1911 at the request of the editor of the *English Review* where it subsequently appeared in June 1911. It was further revised, probably in July 1914, for inclusion in *The Prussian Officer* (1914). In its externals the story is modelled on Lawrence's Aunt Polly, whose husband (James Lawrence) had been killed in a mining accident, and who lived in a cottage close to the colliery railway crossing at Brinsley near Eastwood. But Lawrence's insight into the relationship between Elizabeth and Walter Bates owes more to his memories of his own mother and father.

1 (p. 92) *ripping*: To cut away: part of the coal-mining process.

2 (p. 96) *Loose-all*: See note 5 to 'Love Among the Haystacks'.

3 (p. 96) *bantle*: A cage-full of men (dial.).

4 (p. 105) *She knew ... shame*: Until he deleted it at the proof stage of *The Prussian Officer*, this somewhat enigmatic ending continued: 'For in death she would have no life, for she had never loved. She had life on earth with her children, that was all.'

DAUGHTERS OF THE VICAR

Written as 'Two Marriages' in July 1911 and revised that autumn for submission to the *Century* magazine which returned it as unsuitable, this story was rewritten in July 1913 as 'Daughters of the Vicar'. After a further rejection it was revised in July 1914 for inclusion in *The Prussian Officer* (1914). The Durants and their cottage are modelled on the outward appearance of his grandparents and their cottage in the quarry hole near Brinsley level-crossing, although Alfred's volunteering to serve with the navy is probably based on Lawrence's eldest brother, George, who joined the King's Own Scottish Borderers in 1895 to the vexation of his mother.

1 (p. 107) *throng*: Busy; pressed for time (dial.).

2 (p. 108) *wideawake*: A soft felt hat with a broad brim and low crown (dial.).

3 (p. 109) *tundish*: Funnel (dial.).

4 (p. 114) *chétif*: Weak, puny, sickly (French).

5 (p. 130) *swaled away*: Consumed or melted away (dial.).

6 (p. 132) *Fabians*: Members of the socialist Fabian Society founded in 1884.

SECOND BEST

First written in 1911, this story was published in the *English Review* in February 1912. Dissatisfied with it as soon as it appeared, Lawrence revised it, probably in July 1914, for inclusion in *The Prussian Officer* (1914).

1 (p. 153) *Ollerton Feast*: Ollerton in Nottinghamshire had two fairs or feast-days, one on May-day, the other on 26 September, for hops.

2 (p. 153) *fret her fat*: Wear away her fat through worry (dial.).

THE SHADES OF SPRING

Lawrence first wrote a story on this theme called 'A Modern Lover' early in 1910 after he had revived his love affair with Jessie Chambers by calling on her at the Haggs Farm over the Christmas holidays. In December 1911 he wrote a second story on the same theme, 'The Soiled Rose', which he further revised in March 1912 for publication in the *Forum* in March 1913. It was also published in the *Blue Review* in May 1913. By then he already thought it 'a bit affected' and further revised it, probably in July 1914, for inclusion in *The Prussian Officer* (1914), first as 'The Dead Rose', then at proof stage under its present title.

1 (p. 165) *What a ballad of dead ladies!*: cf. Shakespeare's Sonnet 106 ('When in the chronicle of wasted time').

2 (p. 167) *Arcady*: Arcadia. A district of the Peloponnese chiefly inhabited by shepherds. Hence an ideal region of rural felicity.

3 (p. 171) *'Qu'il était ... l'espoir'*: 'How blue was the sky and hope high' (French). Line 13 from Paul Verlaine's 'Colloque Sentimental' published in *Fêtes Galantes* (1869).

4 (p. 171) *like Dante ... brain*: Dante Alighieri (1265–1321) wrote the *Vita Nuova* about his youthful concealed love for Beatrice – whose identity and very existence cannot be absolutely proven even today.

5 (p. 172) *the poem ... passed away*: William Morris's 'The Chapel in Lyoness' was first published in 1856 and collected in *The Defence of Guenevere* (1858).

THE PRUSSIAN OFFICER

Written in June 1913 as 'Honour and Arms' (a quotation from Handel's oratorio, *Samson*), this story was revised in October 1913 for publication in the *English Review* in August 1914 where it was cut by Norman Douglas. It was also published in the *Metropolitan* in November 1914. Lawrence restored the cuts and made a few minor alterations at proof stage for its appearance in *The Prussian Officer* (1914) where the title was changed to the present one by Edward Garnett without Lawrence's prior knowledge or approval. The setting for the story is that of the Isar valley and Icking where Lawrence was staying in the summer of 1913.

THE THORN IN THE FLESH

Written in June 1913 as 'Vin Ordinaire', this story is set in Metz where Lawrence, who had eloped with Frieda in May 1913, was hiding out at the Deutscher Hof while Frieda stayed at her parents' old French grange outside the town. Her father, Baron Friedrick von Richthofen, had been a Prussian officer and was by then retired into the local civil administration after being wounded in the right hand, like the Baron in the story. Eventually Lawrence was arrested near Vauban's military fortifications on suspicion of spying and had to be extricated by Frieda's influential father. Published in the *English Review* in June 1914, the story was the last to be rewritten for *The Prussian Officer* (1914) where Lawrence gave it its new title, a quotation from St Paul in 2 Corinthians xii, 7.

1 (p. 202) *a picture of the Sacred Heart*: A French nun, Marguerite Marie Alacoque, had a vision of the Sacred Heart of Jesus. Devotion directed at the Saviour's heart became an official festival in the Roman Catholic calendar in 1856.

2 (p. 202) *a prie-Dieu*: A prayer-stool (French).

3 (p. 203) *Reichshalle*: Official building of the state (German).

4 (p. 205) '*Wenn ich ... seh ...*': 'When I go to my child/I see its mother in its eye' (German).

THE MORTAL COIL

Encouraged by the *English Review*'s acceptance of the previous two 'soldier stories', Laurence drew further on Baron von Richthofen's military past when he wrote the first version of 'The Mortal Coil' (a quotation from *Hamlet* III.vii. 56) in October 1913 while he was living at Lerici in Italy. The Baron, a great gambler in his time, had managed to retain his commission despite an incident in the 1860s in which two young women were found asphyxiated by fumes from the stove in his and another officer's barracks quarters prohibited to women. Lawrence left the manuscript of this story behind in Lerici and only got it back via the local British consul in 1916. He revised the original manuscript in October 1916 and it was published in the *Seven Arts* magazine in July 1917. It was never published in a collection of stories during Lawrence's lifetime because he drastically rewrote it as a novella, 'The Captain's Doll', in late 1921.

1 (p. 213) '*Tant pis que mal*': There is no such phrase in French. Presumably intended to read: 'Tant bien que mal'. 'As well as may be' or 'So-so' (French).

2 (p. 213) *Gretchen*: The heroine of Goethe's *Faust* (1808), subsequently called Margarete, who is seduced by Faust, becomes pregnant and is condemned to death for infanticide.

3 (p. 214) *Lenora-fuhr-ums-Morgenrot*: From the ballad 'Lenore' by G. A. Bürger, published in 1774, which tells of her grief at the death of her lover whose spectre returns to take her on a night-ride at the end of which she dies.

4 (p. 216) *sang froid*: Self-composure (French).

5 (p. 219) *dragées*: Sugared almonds (French).

6 (p. 229) *The sword of Damocles*: Damocles was invited by a Tyrant of

Syracuse to try taking his place (which he envied) at a sumptuous banquet. But a sword suspended over his head by a hair left Damocles too afraid to stir or partake of the feast.

7 (p. 229) *suffisance*: Self-complacency (French).

ENGLAND, MY ENGLAND

During the first half of 1915 Lawrence was lent a cottage by Viola Meynell at Greatham in Sussex. On the same estate Viola's father Wilfred had enlarged a seventeenth-century cottage, Rackham Cottage, for his daughter and son-in-law, Madeline and Percy Lucas. In 1913 the eldest of the Lucases' three daughters, Sylvia, had fallen over a sickle in the grass and become lame. In September 1914 Percy Lucas had volunteered to join the army. In early June 1915 Lawrence drew on these circumstances to write the first version of this story which was published in the *English Review* in October 1915. On 6 July 1916 Percy Lucas died of wounds received at the Battle of the Somme, uncannily fulfilling Lawrence's fictional end to the story. Although upset by the coincidence, Lawrence left the story little altered for its appearance in the American periodical, the *Metropolitan*, in April 1917. However in December 1921, when he was preparing his second collection of stories for publication, he rewrote and lengthened the title-story of the volume, *England, My England*, which was published in October 1922. The title is a quotation from W. E. Henley's patriotic poem, 'Pro Rege Nostro', from *For England's Sake, Verses and Songs in Time of War* (1900).

1 (p. 238) *casus belli*: Ground for war (Latin).

2 (p. 238) *consider the lilies ... spin*: cf. Christ's sermon on the mount. Matthew vi, 28; Luke xii, 27.

3 (p. 241) *Basta!*: Enough! (Spanish, Italian).

4 (p. 242) '*A little child shall lead them* –': cf. Isaiah xi, 6.

5 (p. 242) *turning to salt*: cf. Lot's wife turning to a pillar of salt when she looked back at the destruction of Sodom and Gomorrah. Genesis xix, 26.

6 (p. 244) *Mater Dolorata*: Sorrowing Mother (Latin); i.e. the Virgin Mary weeping over the dead body of her son.

7 (p. 248) *The Mother ... breast*: The Virgin Mary as Our Lady of the Dolours with her breast pierced by seven swords emblematic of her seven sorrows.

8 (p. 251) *Ishmael*: An outcast: 'his hand will be against every man, and every man's hand against him.' Genesis xvi, 12.

9 (p. 252) *Baal and Ashtaroth*: False gods worshipped by the children of Israel. Judges ii, 10–23.

10 (p. 253) *canaille*: Vulgar riff-raff (French).

11 (p. 256) *Whither ... go*: An echo of the words spoken to Christ by a scribe. Matthew viii, 19; Luke ix, 57.

THE HORSE DEALER'S DAUGHTER

Modelled on the family of Lawrence's school friend, Duncan Meakin, who lived at Hill Top House, Eastwood, this story was begun in January 1916 as 'a midwinter story of oblivion' which he left unfinished because he found it 'difficult to break into a new world'. In November 1916 he gave it its optimistic ending and called it 'The Miracle'. In October 1921 he revised the story and gave it its present title. This final version was published in the *English Review* in April 1922 and subsequently appeared in his collection *England, My England* in October 1922.

1 (p. 260) *sang-froid*: See note 4 to 'The Mortal Coil'.
2 (p. 261) *museau*: Muzzle of an animal. Hence colloquial for face: mug (French).

SAMSON AND DELILAH

In February 1916 Lawrence stayed at the Tinner's Arms, the local inn at Zennor in Cornwall. His brief sojourn there suggested the setting for the 'Prodigal Husband', as he first called this story after Christ's parable of the prodigal son. It was written and re-christened with its final Old Testament title by November 1916. This version was published in the *English Review* in March 1917 and in the *Lantern* magazine in June of that year. Lawrence confessed at the time that he didn't 'much care for it' as it stood. In November 1921, when he was preparing his stories for publication in the collection *England, My England* (1922), he revised it.

1 (p. 283) *Laocoon*. A son of Priam, he and his two sons were strangled by serpents for offending Apollo, an event commemorated in a famous group sculpture dating from the second century B.C. located in the Vatican.

TICKETS, PLEASE

Written as 'John Thomas' in November 1918, this version of the story was published under its final title by the *Strand* magazine in April 1919 and as 'The Eleventh Commandment' by the *Metropolitan* magazine in August 1919. It was revised in November 1921 for its appearance in the collection *England, My England* (1922).

1 (p. 289) *county town*: Modelled on Nottingham.
2 (p. 290) *sang-froid*: See note 4 to 'The Mortal Coil'.
3 (p. 290) *Thermopylae*: The pass held by Leonidas and his men in 480 B.C. against the far larger forces of Xerxes.
4 (p. 291) *John Thomas . . . Coddy*: Slang expressions for a penis.
5 (p. 291) *Tartar*: From the Asiatic Tartars who under Jenghis Kahn threatened thirteenth-century Europe. Hence a savage or fierce person.

6 (p. 291) *The Statutes fair*: Held every November at the west end of Eastwood, it has its origins in the annual hiring of farm labour.

7 (p. 294) *qui-vive*: Alert, look-out (French).

THE BLIND MAN

Between 26 and 31 August 1918 Lawrence stayed with Catherine Carswell and her husband at a rented vicarage at Upper Lydbrook, Ross-on-Wye, in the Forest of Dean. There Lawrence first recounted to Catherine Carswell the outline of this story which was partly modelled on her and the house they were renting. Written up in November 1918, it was published in the *English Review* in July 1920, the *Living Age* on 7 August 1920, and collected in *England, My England* (1922).

1 (p. 308) *qui vive*: See note 7 to 'Tickets, Please'.

2 (p. 317) *colossus*: Giant statue (Latin). From the hundred-foot-high colossus of Rhodes, one of the Seven Wonders of the Ancient World.

FANNY AND ANNIE

In November 1918 Lawrence was given the initial idea for this story when he alighted at Butterley station, Ripley, Derbyshire, on a Saturday night and was struck how 'everything was lit up red' from the ironworks nearby. One of the men on the platform made him think of the Assyrian god, Ashurbanipal. 'I could write a story about him,' Lawrence wrote. When he came to write the story in May 1919 his central character, Harry, had acquired more comic attributes. His choir-singing may originate in Lawrence's father's memories of singing in the choir at Newstead Abbey as a boy. After at least one rejection the story was published in *Hutchinson's Magazine* for 21 November 1921. The same month he revised it for its inclusion in *England, My England* (1922). At the same time he asked his publisher to change the title to 'The Last Straw', although this was never done.

1 (p. 323) *ormin'*: Loafing or clumsy (dial.).

2 (p. 325) *Balaam's ass*: The ass saw the angel of the Lord barring the way and thrice refused to move forward despite being beaten by Balaam. Numbers xxii, 21–35.

3 (p. 326) *Lot's wife*: See note 5 to 'England, My England'.

YOU TOUCHED ME

Written in the summer of 1919 and at first simply called 'Hadrian', this story originally appeared under its present title but with a number of cuts in *Land and Water* on 29 April 1920. In November 1921, when he was preparing the story for publication in *England, My England* (1922), Lawrence restored the omitted passages and made a number of minor revisions to his earlier version.

1 (p. 333) *Mary ... Martha*: cf. Luke x, 38–42.
2 (p. 336) *sotto voce*: In a low voice (Italian).

JIMMY AND THE DESPERATE WOMAN

In December 1923 Lawrence reluctantly left America at Frieda's insistence to rejoin her in England where she was seeing much of John Middleton Murry. Lawrence must have been inspired to write this story by Murry's recent abortive visit to the wife of a miner in Mansfield who had sent him poems for possible publication in his magazine, the *Adelphi*. Written in late January or early February 1924, the story was published in the *Criterion* in October of that year, first collected in *The Best British Stories of 1925* and reprinted unaltered in Lawrence's third collection of short stories, *The Woman Who Rode Away* (1928).

1 (p. 348) *That worm had turned*: Proverb signifying that even the most abject of creatures will turn on its persecutors if driven to extremity.

2 (p. 348) *Gall and wormwood*: Affliction and misery. cf. Lamentations iii, 19.

3 (p. 348) *Tess ... Gretchen ... Ruth*: All three heroines were raised up from their low station in life by a man of higher birth whom they served with consequent humility. cf. Thomas Hardy's heroine in *Tess of the D'Urbervilles* (1891); Gretchen, the heroine of Goethe's *Faust* (cf. note 2 to 'The Mortal Coil'); and Ruth i–iv.

4 (p. 349) *faun ... Pan ... satyr*: Pan was an Arcadian deity, partly goat-like, renowned for his lust. The Romans associated him with the woodland deities known as fauns and satyrs.

5 (p. 349) *Martyred Saint Sebastian*: A Christian martyr shot to death with arrows in A.D. 288.

6 (p. 349) *Mater Dolorosa* (Italian). See note 6 to 'England, My England'.

7 (p. 352) *Ulysses ... Charybdises*: In Homer's *Odyssey* Ulysses, on his return from the Trojan War, has to visit Hades, the underworld of Hecate (Book XI), and encounters numerous hazards on his journey, including the sirens who lure ships onto the rocks with their singing, and the twin dangers of Scylla, a monster who lured mariners into her cave to devour them, and Charybdis, a whirlpool (Book XII).

8 (p. 357) *Mephistopheles*: The evil spirit in the Faust legend who tempted Faust to sell his soul to the Devil. A composite word, possibly from three Greek words meaning 'not loving the light'.

9 (p. 362) *Queen Boadicea*: The famous British warrior queen of the first century A.D. who rebelled against the Romans.

10 (p. 362) *Puritan Father*: Presumably a reference to the Pilgrim Fathers, puritan extremists who founded Plymouth, New England in 1620.

11 (p. 368) *the head of Medusa*: The Gorgon with a hideous face and serpents in her hair who turned to stone anyone that met her gaze.

12 (p. 368) *hanging your harp on it*: From the popular song, 'There's a tavern in the town': 'I'll hang my harp on a weeping willow tree / And tell the world I died of love.'

THE BORDER LINE

Prior to Lawrence's return to London in December 1923 Frieda had travelled with John Middleton Murry as far as Frieburg on her way to visit her mother in Baden-Baden. On the journey they had confessed their attraction for one another, but Murry had refused to become her lover at the time. Lawrence must have sensed what had been occurring between them in his absence. His story is a fictionalized rendering of their journey-ending, as Frieda put it, with the victory of Alan's / Lawrence's 'jealousy beyond the grave'. In the first version which Lawrence wrote in Baden-Baden in February 1924 (called 'Crossing the Frontier') Philip is actually called Jack (Murry's forename). On his return to Taos in early April 1924 Lawrence rewrote and lengthened the story. This version with its present title was published in *Hutchinson's Magazine* and the *Smart Set* in September 1924. In January 1928, when Lawrence was checking the proofs of *The Woman Who Rode Away* volume of stories, he discovered that the printer's typescript was missing the end of the story from just after Katherine's arrival in Baden-Baden. Unable to locate either magazine version in Italy he was forced under protest to concoct for *The Woman Who Rode Away* a new, shorter ending which, he complained, lacked the authenticity of the post-war German atmosphere he had observed at first hand. The result was that Lawrence substituted 'the old procreative way of possession' for the thematically more appropriate pine-like embrace of the 1924 version. The text used for this edition is that in *Hutchinson's Magazine* (September 1924).

1 (p. 370) *Gare de l'Est . . . Boche*: This is the station in Paris from which the railway follows the Marne due east to Strasbourg and Germany. 'Boche' is French slang for 'German'; from 'caboche' meaning 'hard-head' (French).

2 (p. 372) *pillar of rock*: See note 5 to 'England, My England'.

3 (p. 374) *Lachesis*: One of the three Fates normally identified as the one who measured the length of a person's life, not the one who cut it short.

4 (p. 375) *Marne country*: The Battle of the Marne was fought in September 1914, but the Marne country was also the scene of later bloodier battles in the First World War.

5 (p. 377) *Alsatian German*: In 1871 Prussia invaded Alsace-Lorraine and annexed it. In 1919 the Treaty of Versailles returned the territory to France.

6 (p. 381) *Badisch*: Adjective: of Baden (German).

7 (p. 382) *chétif*: See note 4 to 'Daughters of the Vicar'.

8 (p. 383) *Tree of Life*: In the Garden of Eden. Genesis ii, 9 and iii, 22–3.

9 (p. 389) *Lumpen*: Ragamuffins (German).

10 (p. 390) *Lichtenthal*: Literally, valley of light (German). The name of the casino in pre-war Baden-Baden.

11 (p. 390) *Mercury! Hermes!*: The Roman and Greek names respectively of the messenger or herald of the gods who also conducted the souls of the dead to Hades.

THE WOMAN WHO RODE AWAY

Written in June 1924, this story draws on the landscape of Mexico and New Mexico, especially on the Swiss' silver mine at Minas Nuevas near Navajoa, Mexico which Lawrence visited in October 1923, and on an ancient ceremonial cave above Arroyo Seco, New Mexico to which he made an expedition in May 1924. First published in the *Dial* in July and August 1925 and the *New Criterion* in July 1925 and January 1926, it was included in *The Best British Stories of 1926* and became the title story of his third collection of short stories, *The Woman Who Rode Away* (1928).

1 (p. 394) *Montezuma . . . old Aztec or Totonac kings*: Montezuma II (d. 1520) was the last Aztec ruler of pre-conquest Mexico. Aztecs and Totonacs were Indian tribes that flourished in the century immediately prior to the conquest of Mexico by Cortes in 1521.

2 (p. 402) *barranca*: Gorge or ravine (Spanish).

3 (p. 412) *Mene Mene Tekel Upharsin*: The writing on the wall of Belshazzar's palace which Daniel interpreted as foretelling the end of his reign. Daniel v, 25–8.

4 (p. 418) *amole*: The Mexican name of several plants used for making soap (Spanish).

SUN

Lawrence first wrote 'Sun', set in the garden of the house he occupied in Sicily between 1920 and 1922, in December 1925 after his return to Italy the previous month. Whether this was the longer 'unexpurgated' version, as he later called it, or – more likely on present evidence – the shorter version, published in the *New Coterie* and separately by E. Archer in September 1926, has been a matter of dispute. The short version was also reprinted in his collection *The Woman Who Rode Away* in May 1928. On 1 April 1928 Lawrence was sent $100 for the manuscript of 'Sun' by Harry Crosby, the American co-owner of the Black Sun Press, Paris. Unable to recover the shorter version from his London agent, Lawrence sent Crosby a bound copy of what he called the 'final MS' of the longer version in late April 1928. 'I wish the story had been printed as it stands there, really complete,' Lawrence wrote. Crosby took him at his word and published this version in a limited de luxe edition of 165 copies in October 1928. This edition reproduces that text.

1 (p. 424) *serpent of chaos*: cf. 'that old serpent, which is the Devil and Satan ... cast ... into the bottomless pit.' Revelation xx, 1–3.

2 (p. 424) *C'est ça!*: That's that (French).

3 (p. 424) *Lackawanna Station*: The Delaware, Lackawanna and Western Railway had its terminal in Hoboken, New Jersey, facing Manhattan across the Hudson River.

4 (p. 425) *the Battery*: At the southern tip of Manhattan.

5 (p. 425) *the old Sicules*: Prior to Greek colonization eastern Sicily was principally occupied by the Sicels after whom the island is named.

6 (p. 429) *Magna Graecia*: A term applied to the Greek cities on the shores of the Gulf of Taranto in southern Italy.

7 (p. 430) *putto*: Child in painting or sculpture (Italian).

8 (p. 431) *tramontana*: Cold wind blowing from beyond the Alps (Italian).

9 (p. 433) *lotus flower*: According to Buddhist belief the open lotus represents Nirvana, the ultimate repose of the soul.

10 (p. 433) *podere*: Small-holding (Italian).

11 (p. 437) *the Fates*: In Latin 'Fata' appears to have been adapted from 'fatum', that which is spoken, the decree of the gods.

12 (p. 443) *Perseus*: Perseus saved Andromeda who had been chained to a rock as a sacrifice in classical mythology.

THE ROCKING-HORSE WINNER

In November 1925 Lady Cynthia Asquith wrote to Lawrence asking him for a contribution to a collection of ghost stories she was compiling. By December Lawrence had written 'Glad Ghosts' in response to her request. But since its heroine is closely modelled on Cynthia Asquith herself and she spends a far-from-ghostly night with the autobiographically-based narrator, it is hardly surprising that in February 1926 Lawrence decided to write another story, 'The Rocking-Horse Winner', for her collection. The mother and child of this story were loosely modelled on Brett's sister, Lady Sylvia Brooke, and her daughter, Leonora, who was in the habit of placing bets on horses through a servant when left at home by her holidaying parents. The story was first published in *Harper's Bazaar* (New York) in July 1926. That September it appeared in *The Ghost Book, 16 New Stories of the Uncanny Compiled by Lady Cynthia Asquith*, published by Hutchinson. It was first published in collected form posthumously in *The Lovely Lady* (1933).

1 (p. 439) *Nat Gould*: Editor of the *Sporting Annual*, London, and author of a number of sporting novels and reminiscences.

2 (p. 450) *Turf Commission*: Lawrence probably meant turf commissioner or accountant, i.e. bookmaker.

3 (p. 455) *as right as a trivet*: Perfectly right (just as a trivet, a stand for a cooking pot, always stays firm on its three feet).

THE MAN WHO LOVED ISLANDS

In August 1920 Compton Mackenzie took out a lease on the two Channel Islands of Herm and Jethou. The following month Lawrence prophetically wrote to him about his recent purchase: 'I shall write a skit on you one day.' In March 1926 Lawrence saw Faith Mackenzie who told him how her husband had been forced by farming losses to abandon Herm (and many of his retainers there) for Jethou in 1923. She also informed him of her husband's purchase of the Shiant Islands in the Outer Hebrides the previous October. Lawrence drew on these facts to write 'The Man Who Loved Islands' by 10 July 1926. The story was duly published the following year in the *Dial* in July and in the *London Mercury* in August. Mackenzie then took umbrage at it and asked Secker, their joint publisher, to omit it from Lawrence's next collection of stories. In self-defence Lawrence wrote to Secker that, 'though the circumstances are some of them his, the man is no more he than I am'. Nevertheless, due to Mackenzie's objection, the story was left out of Secker's, but not Knopf's, edition of *The Woman Who Rode Away* (1928). In England it was first published in collected form posthumously in *The Lovely Lady* (1933), after Mackenzie had withdrawn his veto in 1929.

1 (p. 458) *Abraham ... sea-shore*: After Abraham had showed himself willing to sacrifice his son, the Lord promised him: 'I will multiply thy seed as the sand which is upon the sea-shore.' Genesis xxii, 17.

2 (p. 460) *men of Gaul*: The Roman conquest of Britain reached the Channel Islands but not the Outer Hebrides.

3 (p. 460) *priests ... crucifix*: Pre-Roman Druid priests (who practised human sacrifice and regarded mistletoe with special veneration) and post-Roman Christian evangelists, respectively.

4 (p. 460) *Happy Isle ... Hesperides*: The Hesperides in Greek mythology helped guard the garden in which the golden apples grew in the Isles of the Blest at the western extremity of the earth.

5 (p. 462) *Hermes*: One of Hermes' tasks in Greek mythology was to guard herds and flocks.

6 (p. 466) *lean kine of Egypt*: cf. Pharaoh's dream of seven lean kine that ate up the seven fat-fleshed ones in Genesis xli.

THE LOVELY LADY

In November 1926 Lady Cynthia Asquith approached Lawrence a second time to write a story for a new collection of murder stories that she was compiling. Written in late February and early March 1927, the story turned out 'not very murderous', as Lawrence admitted. After reading it, Cynthia Asquith objected to the device of the rain-pipe and asked him to shorten it. Without abandoning the use of the rain-pipe, he rewrote the story in condensed form in early May. In October 1927 it was published by Hutchinson in *The Black Cap*,

New Stories of Murder and Mystery Compiled by C. Asquith. It was first published in collected form in *The Lovely Lady* (1933).

1 (p. 481) *a Leonardo woman . . . laugh outright*: An allusion to Leonardo da Vinci's portrait of the wife of a Florentine official known as 'Mona Lisa' or 'La Gioconda' (Italian for 'the mirthful woman'). Janet Spence in Aldous Huxley's story 'The Gioconda Smile' published in *Mortal Coils* (1922) shows some resemblances to Lawrence's portrait of Pauline Attenborough.

2 (p. 487) *Circe*: In Greek mythology Circe was a sorceress who lived on the island of Æœa and turned Ulysses and his companions, among others, into swine.

3 (p. 492) *Caro, caro, tu non l'hai visto!*: Dear one, dear one, you didn't see him! (Italian).

4 (p. 492) *Bravo, si . . . mai!*: Good, yes, very good, poor little man, but a man like you he will never, never, never be! (Italian).

5 (p. 493) *Cara, cara . . . humana*: Dear one, my most beautiful dear one, I have waited for you as one dying waits for death, delicious death, almost too delicious for a mere human spirit (Italian).

THINGS

Written by March 1928, 'Things' was first published in the *Bookman* in August 1928. The month after it was published Lawrence wrote to his American friend, Earl Brewster: 'Have a most amusing story of mine in the *American Bookman* – called *Things* – you'll think it's you, but it isn't.' As is normally the case with Lawrence, the truth lies somewhere between his disclaimer and the obvious resemblances that exist between the Melvilles in his story and the Brewsters with their enthusiasm for European art, Buddhism, etc. The story was also published in the *Fortnightly Review* in October 1928 and was first collected in *The Lovely Lady* (1933).

1 (p. 498) *Mrs Besant*: One of the founders of the Theosophical Society in 1875.

2 (p. 500) *a bho-tree . . . Nirvana*: After his victory over the hosts of Mara, the Evil One, the newly reborn Buddha rested for seven days under a Bohdi- or Bo-Tree, at the end of which time he rejected the temptation to keep to himself the path which leads to Nirvana, the release from all pain.

3 (p. 500) *Sitzfleisch*: Literally, seat-flesh. Hence, steadiness, perseverence (German).

4 (p. 501) *Palazzo on the Arno*: Palace (Italian) overlooking the River Arno in Florence.

5 (p. 501) *salotto*: Sitting-room (Italian).

6 (p. 502) *the Ark of the Covenant*: The holy of holies of the Israelites that caused destruction to the Philistines when they captured and opened it. 1 Samuel iv–vi.

7 (p. 503) *Sodom and Gomorrah*: See note 5 to 'England, My England'.

MOTHER AND DAUGHTER

Written in May 1928, this story was first published in the *New Criterion* in April 1929 and first appeared in collected form in *The Lovely Lady* (1933).

1 (p. 508) *shirt of Nessus*: To win back Heracles' love his misinformed wife sent him a shirt which was smeared with the poisoned blood of the Centaur, Nessus. This clung to Heracles' flesh and caused him such suffering that he immolated himself on a pyre.

2 (p. 509) *gamin*: Urchin, street-arab (French).

3 (p. 510) *cambré*: Arched (French).

4 (p. 510) *Ninon de l'Enclos and the Pompadour ... Madame la Duchesse and Monsieur le Marquis*: Anne de Lenclos, known as Ninon de Lenclos (1620–1705), a French wit and writer famous for her liaison with Saint-Evrémond. Antoinette Poissons, Marquise de Pompadour (1721–64), patroness of the arts and mistress of Louis XV. The aristocratic titles of Duchess and Marquis were much used in eighteenth-century France, an era which Lawrence despised (cf. his essays, 'The Duc de Lauzun' and 'The Good Man' in *Phoenix*, Heinemann, 1936).

5 (p. 512) *Aubusson carpet*: The Aubusson factories in France were mainly famous for their tapestry-woven carpets of the eighteenth and nineteenth centuries.

6 (p. 512) *dame de compagnie*: Lady's companion (French).

7 (p. 513) *Open Sesame!*: The password at which the door of the robbers' cave flew open in the tale of 'The Forty Thieves' in *The Arabian Nights Entertainments*.

8 (p. 513) *Circe*: See note 2 to 'The Lovely Lady'.

9 (p. 514) *oeufs farcies*: Stuffed eggs (French).

10 (p. 515) *ménage à deux*: Household of two people (French).

11 (p. 517) *David's pebble ... Goliath's battle-axe*: cf. 1 Samuel xvii.

12 (p. 521) *objet de vertu*: Article of quality (French).

13 (p. 521) *cachet*: Stamp, seal, hallmark (French).

14 (p. 522) *Mais oui! Je te contenterai, tu le verras*: But yes! I will make you satisfied, you will see (French).

15 (p. 523) *The Thief of Baghdad*: A tale from *The Arabian Nights Entertainments* turned into a film starring Douglas Fairbanks in 1924.

Select Bibliography

The following books, which are either wholly or partially devoted to a consideration of Lawrence's short fiction, are recommended as especially helpful to the reader or student of his stories:

F. R. Leavis, *D. H. Lawrence, Novelist* (Chatto & Windus, 1955)
Kingsley Widmer, *The Art of Perversity, D. H. Lawrence's Shorter Fiction* (University of Washington Press, 1962)
Julian Moynahan, *The Deed of Life, The Novels and Tales of D. H. Lawrence* (Princeton University Press, 1963)
George H. Ford, *Double Measure, A Study of the Novels and Stories of D. H. Lawrence* (Holt, Rinehart & Winston, 1965)
Keith Cushman, *D. H. Lawrence at Work: The Emergence of the 'Prussian Officer' Stories* (University Press of Virginia, 1978)

Much of the best criticism of the short stories is to be found in articles in various periodicals which are listed yearly in *The D. H. Lawrence Review* (University of Arkansas, Fayetteville, 1968–).

aplomb.